The Year's Best
Fantasy and
Horror

The Year's Best
Fantasy and
Horror

SEVENTH ANNUAL COLLECTION

Edited by Ellen Datlow
and Terri Windling

ST. MARTIN'S PRESS   NEW YORK

For Arnold R. Deutsch, who taught by example that
excellence is its own reward.

—J. F.

Hardcover ISBN 0-312-11103-7

First Edition: September 1994

A Blue Cows–Mad City production.

CONTENTS

x   Contents

Acknowledgments

I would like to thank Bill Congreve, Linda Marotta, Gardner Dozois, Robert Killheffer, Robert Stauffer, Merrilee Heifetz, Liza Landsman, Keith Ferrell, Edward Bryant, Matthew Rettenmund, William Meikle, Rachel Holman, Stephen Pagel, Steve Jones, K. W. Jeter, and Jonathan Lethem for their encouragement, help, and suggestions. I would also like to specially thank Jim Frenkel, Nevenah Smith, and Gordon Van Gelder for their continuing support. And finally, I'd like to thank my partner in crime, Terri Windling, and Tom Canty, the man who does the gorgeous covers.

(Please note: It's difficult to cover all nongenre sources of short horror, so should readers see a story or poem from such a source, I'd appreciate it being brought to my attention. Drop me a line c/o OMNI Magazine, 1965 Broadway, New York, NY 10023.)

I'd like to acknowledge Andrew I. Porter's *Science Fiction Chronicle* (S.F.C., P.O. Box 022730, Brooklyn, NY 11202-0056; $36 for a one-year first class subscription [12 issues], $30 second class) as an invaluable reference source throughout the Summation; and Charles N. Brown's *Locus Magazine* (Locus Publications, P.O. Box 13305, Oakland, CA 94661; $38 for a one-year subscription [12 issues] credit card orders (510)339-9198), also an invaluable resource throughout.

—Ellen Datlow

I am grateful to the publishers, editors, writers, artists, booksellers, librarians and readers who sent material and recommended favorite titles for this volume; and to *Locus*, *SF Chronicle*, *Library Journal*, *Publishers Weekly*, and *Folk Roots* magazines, which are invaluable reference resources.

Many thanks to the Tucson public library staff, Coyote's Voice and Antigone bookstores in Tucson, Peter Crowther, Charles de Lint, Beth Meacham & Tappan King, Greg Ketter, Bill Murphy, Jack Rems and Jay Scheckley, Munro Sickafoose, Valerie Smith, Ellen Steiber, Jane Yolen, Patrick Nielsen Hayden, Donald G. Keller, and the supportive crew over in Chagford, England. Special thanks to series creator/packager Jim Frenkel and his assistant Nevenah Smith; to our St. Martin's editor Gordon Van Gelder; cover artist (and editorial hand-holder) Thomas Canty; and especially my hard-working co-editor and friend Ellen Datlow.

—Terri Windling

This book is truly a collaborative effort, and could not be as rich and full without the tireless work of the editors, our contributors, our SMP editor, the indomitable Gordon Van Gelder, and columnists Ed Bryant, Emma Bull, and Will Shetterly. In Madison, Wisconsin, Nevenah Smith and I work to put all the elements of this book into final form, aided by interns Jim Feken, Craig Gurrie, John Klima, Jim Minz, Andy Scott, and Sten Westgard.

—James Frenkel

Summation 1993
Fantasy

Fantasy fiction, as we've defined it for this anthology, is an inclusive rather than narrow term, embracing all forms of magical, surrealist, myth- and fairy tale-based stories, novels and poems. You need never have read the works of J. R. R. Tolkien or his many imitators to have read fantasy fiction, for as a form of storytelling it is broad and diverse, encompassing such dissimilar works as the Magic Realism of Gabriel García Márquez, Joyce Carol Oates, and John Crowley at one end of the spectrum and the sword-and-loincloth adventure tales beloved by adolescent boys at the other. What such books have in common are narrative roots in forms of storytelling much older than the twentieth-century novel of social realism; the "reality" they describe or create is a subjective one, filtered through the colored lens of myth and mystery, memory, and dream.

Modern fantasy fiction grew into an enormous field in the 1980s; and despite publisher cutbacks in all areas of fiction, a bewildering number of magical stories continue to be published in the 1990s—not only in the segregated genre labelled "fantasy" by publishing marketers, but in mainstream fiction as well. Some of these books are excellent, some negligible, and some a disgrace to the trees who died for them. Cover art, blurbs, and bookstore category being notoriously bad ways to judge the quality of a book (these things are tailored to the needs of the book distributor, not the reader), one is advised to enter this forest of titles armed with recommendations or reviews (and not the untrustworthy distinction of popularity. Some of the best-selling titles can be the most tedious of all).

It is the purpose of this anthology to search for and sift through the fantasy fiction published each year by hundreds of English-language publishers in this country and abroad, and to help make the best of it accessible to aficionados of magical literature. Because fantasy is such a broad field, our search for the best of the year begins with the fantasy genre publications and then wanders far beyond them, into mainstream novels and anthologies, newsstand magazines, literary quarterlies, small press publications, compilations of foreign works in translation, poetry volumes, and children's collections.

The stories we choose each year range from the dark psychological landscapes of horror fiction to the bright Jungian poetics of fairy tales, *the blue and the dim and the dark cloths, of night and light and the half-light* (to borrow a description from W. B. Yeats, who was no slouch as a fantasist himself). With this deliberate diversity of tales in mind, we cannot promise that every selection in this volume will appeal to every reader's taste. But taken collectively, the poems and stories of *The Year's Best: Seventh Annual* demonstrate the fantasy field's greatest strength: that the ways a writer can use the fantasy form are as varied and as complex as the writers themselves.

In these annual Summaries my co-editor and I attempt to identify the changes evident in the fantasy/horror field in the year that has passed. And yet in most years (without the publication of some revolutionary new book) such changes are slow, gradual, cumulative; indeed, we will have to wait until the decade has passed before we can see with true clarity what changes the nineties have wrought. In the meantime, as we talk to writers about their work and keep a close eye on the books that appear and disappear from the bookstore shelves, certain trends emerge, certain themes recur, particularly within the confines of the genre—for one of the most interesting things about genre fantasy (or horror, or mystery, or science fiction) is the degree to which the writers in the field know and communicate with one another: via conventions and conferences, telecommunications, writers' groups, small presses, and kitchen table 'zines. The traditional image of the fiction writer working in self-imposed solitude is one rarely upheld in our young field. (I say "young" because the genre itself is still young, dating back—as a distinct genre in American publishing— only to the mid-seventies, with the republication of Tolkien's works and Lin Carter's Sign of the Unicorn list. As a form of storytelling, of course, fantasy is as old as the hills.)

This lively exchange of ideas between writers passionately committed to their field is at the core of why genre fantasy has become more than just a publisher's gimmick to categorize and package books. As we look at this ongoing discourse among writers, as well as the books they have published, the most distinct trend to be found in recent years is the degree to which Latin American Magic Realism has entered into the genre. It has made a strong mark on the field both by influencing works published in the genre and by popularizing magical narratives outside of it. Where ten years ago the dominant strains in the genre were still Tolkienesque "Imaginary World" epics and Howardian "swords-and-sorcery" adventures, there is now a whole branch of the field with a distinct literary Márquezian flavor, works where contemporary stories are told through the metaphorical use of myth, magic, miracles, and dreams.

The influence of Gabriel García Márquez, Jorge Amado, Isabel Allende and their kind goes far beyond the genre, of course. A young generation of writers as far away as China, Japan, Czechoslovakia, and Russia cite Márquez's work as a formative influence; and the degree to which contemporary American fiction with magical overtones continues to gain critical acceptance in the literary mainstream is largely due to the groundbreaking work of the Latin American writers. (A mid-1980s writers' joke: *Fantasy writer to his/her editor:* "How can I get my book reviewed in the *Times*?" *Editor to writer:* "Move to Brazil and change your name.") There is now a strong, growing body of work that forms a distinctly North American branch of Magic Realism, including books published in both the mainstream and the fantasy genres—books like John Crowley's *Little, Big*, Leslie Marmon Silko's *The Almanac of the Dead*, Karen Joy Fowler's *Sarah Canary*, Thomas King's *Green Grass Running Water*, Megan Lindholm's *Cloven Hooves*, Charlotte Watson Sherman's *Killing Color*, to name but a few.

Magic Realism has now even entered the popular culture mainstream with the popularity of the Mexican cult film *Like Water for Chocolate*, and the charming novel by Laura Esquivel on which it is based, a *New York Times* best-seller. Yet our culture's taste for magic in everyday life becomes much more pronounced, and more commercial, when we look at books of dark magic—at the dark fantasy and horror tales that have become such a staple of popular fiction and entertainment. In a society that finds it diffcult to believe in saints, miracles, and angels (although some would dispute the latter), the darker figures of folklore populate our mythic landscape: vampires, werewolves, supernatural serial killers, demon-possessed children and demonic lovers . . . these are the dreams easily fleshed into life in a country where escalating violence shouts from the daily newspaper headlines.

It is not surprising that often the most simplistic, violence-as-entertainment fantasies reach a wider audience. In this day and age, it is not easy to portray the miraculous convincingly, and to make it as compelling as the dark. It is a harder job, asking more of a writer than Hollywood-style romanticized violence and the easy shock value of gore and guts. Those gifted writers who can look unflinchingly at the dark and still find transcendence in the light (including writers, like Peter Straub, in the horror field itself) are a rare breed indeed. They display a maturity of vision and art too often at odds with the troubled adolescence of our culture.

"Beauty is the forbidden word of our age," Shirley Hazzard wrote in her novel *Transit of Venus*, "as sex was to the Victorians. But without the same power to reassert itself." She was speaking of the post-World War II generation, but she might as well have been addressing a generation of fiction writers today. The pose of cynicism, meant to convey a wealth of jaded experience, is as easily donned as a carefully ripped leather jacket; while finding meaning, value, even beauty in this world (a beauty that is not simply surface gloss, naiveté or blind optimism) takes a Márquez, a Le Guin, a Crowley, a Calvino: experience combined with clarity, heart, and that singular talent we call "vision." It also takes storytellers willing to accept responsibility for the stories, the myths, that they conjure or create and then put out into the world we share.

While I do not advocate government-imposed censorship, I'd like to suggest respectfully that we remember this uncomfortable word: responsibility. In this field, we are not journalists, we are not realist writers, we are not reporting, we are *creating*. We are all responsible for the worlds we create, on the page and then again outside the front door—and accountable, too, to the generations that follow. This responsibility does not stop with the writer or publisher (or musician or painter or Hollywood filmmaker) but includes the reader and the audience as well. When you put down your money you are casting your vote—for the quality of the art and entertainment that fills our lives, for the myths we create, the dreams we nurture or destroy.

Nigerian writer Ben Okri tells us (in his new novel *Songs of Enchantment*), "Stories can conquer fear, you know. They make the heart bigger." Children's book author Katherine Paterson, in her essay collection *Gates of Excellence* (which I highly recommend to all aspiring writers) speaks eloquently of those difficult, necessary works of fiction that build a bridge of hope over the valley of despair. Despite the troubled society we live in, we are fortunate indeed to live in a time when writers like Ben Okri, Katherine Paterson and Nobel Prize-winner Gabriel García Márquez are out there building such magical bridges. They remind us that stories *have power*. Stories have lives of their own, ranging far beyond the artist who brings them into the world.

Overall, 1993 was a good year for fantasy dark and light and all shades in between. The best of the genre storytellers (with a few highly laudable exceptions) largely eschewed the area of Imaginary World fantasy, filled as it can be with simplistic, naive tales of cardboard cutout Good and Evil. Some fantasists (such as Delia Sherman and Jonathan Carroll) are heading into mainstream fiction; some (like Charles de Lint and Will Shetterly) are doing their best work in the area of contemporary urban fantasy; while others (like Melanie Tem and Nina Kiriki Hoffman) are working in the shadow realm between fantasy and horror. Yet there are still a few stalwart souls proving that good Imaginary World fantasy, like myth or fine poetry, is a storytelling form that speaks directly to the heart: Peter S. Beagle, Patricia A. McKillip, Paul Hazel, and others have produced fine novels in 1993 to reawaken a sense of wonder put to sleep by the works of less inspired storytellers. (See below for specific recommendations.)

Works of dark romantic fantasy (the vampire novels of Anne Rice, the last works of Angela Carter, the macabre tales of Steven Millhauser, Brian Stableford, Tanith Lee, and others) continue to grace the fantasy field with imagination, delicious prose and style. Cynicism and romanticism dance a sensual tango in the best of these works: the ones that stay poised on the knife edge between the dark and light, instead of opting for the easy shock value of violent overkill. Intriguing additions to the field of "adult fairy tales" make deft use of this weaving of dark and light threads, such as the contributions to the anthology *Snow White, Blood Red*, or Robin McKinley's *Deerskin*, a hard-hitting reworking of a disturbing Perrault tale.

Swords-and-sorcery adventure, on the other hand, is currently an area of the fantasy field overfilled with cookie cutter books virtually indistinguishable from one another: young man/woman with sword/magic implement/versifying elf overthrows the evil _____ (fill in the blank). I suppose that as long as there are new generations of young men and women growing up to discover role-playing games and fantasy adventures there will continue to be a readership for even the worst of these stories; I don't expect to see them disappear from the newsstands or best-seller lists any time soon. Nor should they all, for among the embarrassingly bad series that give the fantasy genre its dubious reputation are the worthwhile novels of some seriously talented storytellers, like Barbara Hambly, R. A. MacAvoy, Steven Brust, and Midori Snyder. And it's a delight to see Tad Williams hit the best-seller lists; he's an intelligent writer, and a sincere one, with a palpable love for stories and characters instead of for royalty checks.

The overall large number of fantasy books published did not diminish in 1993. For every genre list cutback by a large publishing house, there were two mainstream and small press offerings jumping in to pick up the slack. There is no dearth of good fantasy fiction to read for those willing to go beyond the selections of the chain stores to track down the best of it. It's going to be a particularly tough year for the judges of the World Fantasy Award; Robin McKinley, Peter S. Beagle, Delia Sherman, Michael Swanwick and others have written books that all deserve to be contenders at the October ceremony in New Orleans.

I can't claim to have achieved the Herculean task of reading *every* magical work published here and abroad—but I hope that through my readings for this volume and my experiences as a fantasy editor working with writers and artists across this country and England, I can lead you to some books you might have overlooked or some new authors whom you might enjoy. The following list, in particular, consists of novels no fantasy reader's shelves should be without. Well written and entertaining, they exemplify collectively the sheer diversity of approaches to magical storytelling:

In alphabetical order . . .

The War of the Saints, Jorge Amado (Bantam). Amado, the author of *Doña Flor and Her Two Husbands* and other works, is one of the most popular and prolific writers in Latin America. Born in Brazil, he now lives and writes in Bahía and Paris. His latest novel, *The War of the Saints*, is a sensual, colorful, satiric evocation of South American life, set in a city where the unexpected arrival of a statue of Saint Barbara takes an unexpected turn when the statue comes to life. Highly recommended.

The Innkeeper's Song, Peter S. Beagle (Roc). Peter Beagle is the author of the fantasy classics *The Last Unicorn* and *A Fine and Private Place*. First published in 1968, *The Last Unicorn* shaped the field as we know it today. With this new novel, Beagle has returned to his own distinctive brand of Imaginary World fantasy: whimsical, wonderful and wise, full of descriptive passages that sing. If you were vaguely disappointed with Beagle's last book, don't worry. *This* is the one we've been waiting for.

Ecstasia, Francesca Lia Block (Roc). The first adult fantasy novel from the author of several wild urban fantasy books for teenagers, *Ecstasia* is the story of a brother and sister and their rock-and-roll band in a highly inventive magical landscape, inspired by the Orpheus myth. This is a terrific, quirky, almost indescribable book: musical, poetic, hip without being trendy, unabashedly romantic without being naive. I hope we see much more from this unusual writer.

Agyar, Steven Brust (Tor). Steven Brust's work, although enormously popular with genre readers, is still somewhat underrated, for Brust generally writes in the "adventure fantasy" field that is often critically dismissed as a whole. Yet he is one of the finest storytellers around with his rousing good tales reminiscent of Dumas and Sabatini, filtered through an intelligent, witty, and thoroughly idiosyncratic world view. Occasionally Brust strays from the adventure form and tries something more experimental. His latest story is a character study, a dark fantasy set in a midwestern college town. *Agyar* is a vampire novel—not the kind of vampires who lurk in gothic castles, but the kind who prey on us in everyday life. He sets up a thoroughly reprehensible protagonist, and then makes us care about what happens to him. That's no mean feat, and this is no mean book. One reviewer called it Brust's best since *The Sun, the Moon and the Stars,* and I agree.

Elephantasm, Tanith Lee (Headline, U.K.). British writer Tanith Lee works in many genres, but is particularly skilled working in the shadow realm that lies midway between fantasy and gothic horror. At its best, Lee's work is reminiscent of the lush prose and sensual imagery of Angela Carter. This nineteenth-century fantasy story, with dark fairy tale overtones and oriental embellishments, allows Lee to draw upon all her storytelling strengths.

The Hollowing, Robert Holdstock (Gollancz, U.K.). British author Robert Holdstock has created one of the most mysterious, compelling, and haunting landscapes in modern fiction in the novels (and one novella) set set in Ryhope Wood, a small patch of primeval forest in contemporary England. Holdstock continues this Campbellian exploration into the heart of myth in his latest Ryhope novel—although this time it's the story of a father who has lost a son, instead of the other way around. Holdstock's Wood keeps getting richer, denser, stranger with every book. If you haven't read the other books, don't start with this one. (*Mythago Wood* is the first published book in the sequence, though many find *Lavondyss*—the best of the sequence so far—to be an easier entry point.) Holdstock is doing important work in these books; they are not quick reads, but enormously rewarding ones, with images that stick with you long, long after they are done.

The Crown of Dalemark, Diana Wynne Jones (Mandarin, U.K.). Although published as Young Adult fiction, British writer Diana Wynne Jones's work (like that of Ursula K. Le Guin, Susan Cooper, Jane Yolen, and other important fantasists) is ageless and has a strong following among adult readers as well. Her best Imaginary World work is in the "Dalemark" books: *Cart & Cwidder, Drowned Ammet,* and *The Spellcoats.* Now, after almost a decade, Wynne Jones has returned to Dalemark. This is a lovely book, full of magic and grace. Share it with a child if you have one around; keep it for yourself if you don't.

The Wealdwife's Tale, Paul Hazel (AvoNova). Paul Hazel's lovely, powerfully mythic novel is set in a quasi-Medieval England that is deliberately anachronistic; discordant modern touches in an otherwise ancient, almost Jungian landscape make for a storytelling atmosphere both compelling and disturbing. Hazel deftly weaves myth, folklore, Christmas carols, and the archetypal mystery of the Weald (the forest) into a dark and thoroughly adult fairy tale that is this author's best book to date.

Green Grass Running Water, Thomas King (HarperCollins). This is my personal favorite of the year (with thanks to Charles de Lint for recommending it): a brilliant, idiosyncratic contemporary story about five Canadian Blackfoot Indians, interspersed with the hilarious tales of four old Indians who have escaped from a mental institution and drift in and out of time. Native Canadian author Thomas King mixes Indian tradition, western myhtology, and the mischief of Coyote into a beautifully crafted and highly entertaining tale of North American Magic Realism.

The Cygnet and the Firebird, Patricia A. McKillip (Ace). Like Peter S. Beagle, Patricia A. McKillip's early work, published in the mid-seventies (*The Forgotten Beasts of Eld,* etc.), strongly influenced a whole generation of fantasy writers, and she is still one of the very best prose stylists writing in any field today. Her stories are lyrical, rich with the resonances of myth and folklore, and anchored with mature, complex characterization. Her storytelling voice is gentle and subtle; her prose is so lovely you could weep. This new book is an adult Imaginary World fantasy, the satisfying sequel to *The Sorceress and the Cygnet.*

Deerskin, Robin McKinley (Ace). Newbery Award-winner Robin McKinley is another writer like McKillip whose virtuosity as a prose stylist is often held up as an example to younger writers and has put her at the top of both the fantasy and children's book fields. While McKillip's forte is poetic lyricism, McKinley's is a spare elegance of language that makes her fairy tale and Kipling-flavored stories read like timeless classics from another age. In *Deerskin*, her first novel written expressly for adult readers, the inspiration comes from Perrault's French fairy tale "Donkey Skin" (and the Brothers Grimm story "Allerleirauh"), a dark and chilling presentation of an incestuous father/daughter relationship. Fans of McKinley's fairy tale work will be pleased to see her working with the form again—and doing so with consummate skill. This is a "must read" book, and deserves World Fantasy Award recognition.

Songs of Enchantment, Ben Okri (Doubleday). This amazing novel is a follow-up volume to *The Famished Road*, for which Nigerian writer Ben Okri won England's Booker Prize. Once again, Okri has created a witty, weird, and wild tale of a magical modern Africa, as viewed through the eyes of a spirit-child and his family. This volume has all the sparkling charm of the first book without feeling like a simple replay. The story is exotic, entertaining, and very moving. I recommend it highly, as well as the novel that preceded it.

Damascus Nights, Rafik Schami (Farrar, Straus & Giroux). Schami is a Syrian storyteller and children's book writer now living in Germany. His new novel for adults consists of stories within stories within stories (not unlike the King book above), spanning just seven nights in the city of Damascus. It is a contemporary story *about* stories and storytellers (set in the 1950s)—a mix of the magical, mundane and political, leavened with sly good humor. Originally published in German, it has been translated by Phillip Boehm. (One story from the book has been excerpted for this volume of *The Year's Best Fantasy and Horror.*)

The Porcelain Dove, Delia Sherman (Dutton). Delia Sherman's first novel, *Through a Brazen Mirror*, was published as a genre title; this, her second novel, though equally magical in content, can be found on the mainstream shelves. *The Porcelain Dove* is an intricate and intelligently rendered historical novel (as well as a dark French fairy tale) about a chambermaid employed by an aristocratic family during the French Revolution. The intersting gay love affair between the maid and her mistress permeates the book and contributes to its fascination, yet is so understated it goes right by some readers. Sherman's writing skillfully evokes another age, deliciously flavored with Gallic magic and Sadean horror.

Glimpses, Lewis Shiner (Morrow). This fantasy novel opens with the line: *Once upon a time there was going to be a Beatles album called* Get Back. . . . Shiner goes on from there to create a contemporary fairy tale about a man who finds he can reach into the past (in this case, the music scene of the 1960s) and actually *change* what happened. Shiner is a gifted writer who avoids all the obvious pitfalls of such a premise and emerges with a book that goes beyond sixties nostalgia to explore the realities of that time, and in the process tells us much about the world as we know it today. A fascinating work.

The Iron Dragon's Daughter, Michael Swanwick (AvoNova). Swanwick's stunningly good new fantasy is a "must read" book for those interested in seeing the cutting edge of the fantasy field. *The Iron Dragon's Daughter* evokes comparisons to Dickens and to Mervyn Peake's *Gormenghast*, but it is also utterly contemporary and new—a high-tech vision of faery and folklore at once violent and funny, nasty and moving. The heroine of the title is a changeling, stolen from her human home to work with other children in the abusive Dragon Factory. This is not a children's book, however; it's a complex and savage dystopian novel, and one of the best fantasy books written in this decade. My hat's off to you, Mr. Swanwick.

Wilding, Melanie Tem (Dell/Abyss). Melanie Tem's new novel is a dark fantasy gem: a multigenerational family saga about a matriarchal clan of werewolves set in the city of Denver and the Colorado mountains. Tem's fascinating tale is not only a chilling page-turner but also an exploration of the relationships between women and the world, women and other women, and the intricate structures that make up a family. A beautifully told story, published in the Abyss horror line but recommended to fantasy readers as well. This is Tem's third novel; she is definitely a writer to watch.

Sister Water, Nancy Willard (Knopf). This extraordinary mainstream novelist, poet, and children's book writer often ventures into the fantasy realm, as with her recent "Angel" poems (to be published as part of a collaboration with Jane Yolen), her picture book *Pish, Posh, Said Hieronymus Bosch* (with Leo and Diane Dillon), and hauntingly magical stories such as "Dogstar Man" (reprinted in our Fifth Annual *Year's Best*). Willard's new novel is an excellent contemporary literary fantasy novel about a woman, her family, the angel of death, and the subtle magic that surrounds us all. Highly recommended.

First Novels:
   La Maravilla, by Alfredo Veaq Jr. (Dutton), has my vote for the best first novel of 1993. Set in the American Southwest in the 1950s, this is a lovely Magic Realist story of a young boy's life interwoven with both Hispanic and Native American mythology.
   Voodoo Dreams, by Jewell Parker Rhodes (St. Martin's), is an historical fantasy set in 19th century New Orleans, a fictional biography of legendary "voodoo queen" Marie Laveau. The prose tends toward the purple at times, but the story, the setting, and the race/gender politics of the time and place make for fascinating reading.
   The Winter Prince, by Elizabeth E. Wein (Atheneum), was published as a Young Adult novel, but this grim and intense Arthurian story is well suited to older readers. Wein recasts the familiar legend, telling her tale from the point of view of Arthur's children (in this version he has three). The book is written in the form of a letter from Medraut (Mordred) to his mother (Morgana). This is a writer to watch.

Oddities:
   The "Best Peculiar Book" distinction goes to Scottish author Alasdair Gray for *Poor Things* (Bloomsbury, U.K.). Winner of the Whitbread Award, this bizarre and wonderful novel combines Shelley's *Frankenstein*, Shaw's *Pygmalion*, and other stories (primarily 19th century) into a book that defies genre—or indeed literary—classification. The runner-up is *Felidae*, by Akif Pirincci (Villard), a mystery thriller about a housecat investigating the murder (by decapitation) of cats in his neighborhood. (Originally published in Germany in 1989; translated by Ralph Noble.)

Other recommended fantasy novels published in 1993:

Imaginary-World Fantasy:

Dog Wizard, Barbara Hambly (Del Rey). Hambly is one of those writers who makes open-minded critics unable to simply dismiss the series fantasy form as a whole. *Dog Wizard*, book number three in her ongoing "Windrose Chronicles," is intelligent, subversive, eccentric, complex, and thoroughly entertaining. This is terrific storytelling.

Winter of the Wolf, R. A. MacAvoy (Headline, U.K.). MacAvoy is another excellent writer who prefers the expansiveness of the series form. Her latest is the third and best of the magical sequence that began with *The Lens of the World*.

The Far Kingdoms, Chris Bunch and Alan Cole (Del Rey). This is an extremely well-told adventure story, a quest fantasy (in this case the quest involves the discovery of magical lands rather than the tired old quest-to-end-great-evil formula). Cole and Bunch have created an exotic far-flung epic tale that is very much a "man's" book, and a thoughtful one at that.

To Green Angel Tower, Tad Williams (DAW). This fat *New York Times* best-seller ends the "Memory, Sorrow, Thorn" trilogy, an epic-length fantasy that is intelligently written, entertaining, and full of engaging, three-dimensional characters.

Athyra, Steven Brust (Ace). Brust's latest addition to the witty and stylish "Vlad Taltos" series is the first not to be told from Vlad's point of view. A country boy watches a strange Easterner come to town with two winged zheregs perched upon his shoulder. . . . This engaging book could be called the *Shane* of fantasy.

Faery in Shadow, C. J. Cherryh (Legend, U.K.). Literate, beautifully written, and rather grim fantasy inspired by the faery world depicted in the darker legends of folklore. Recommended, but not for those looking for a lightweight read.

The Shining One, David Eddings (Del Rey). The second book of the "Tamuli" series from one of the best epic storytellers around. Eddings works in the tradition of Tolkien without being merely imitative.

Traitors, Kristine Kathryn Rusch (Millennium). An intelligently magical and thoughtful work set in a fantasy world of island nations; the intriguing story is about a kingdom ruled by artists.

Shroud of Shadow, Gael Baudino (Roc). We're still awaiting the novel that will fulfill the promise evidenced in Baudino's musical fantasy *The Gossamer Axe*. This new novel isn't quite it, this is fairly standard fantasy fare, but Baudino's spirited inventiveness puts it a cut above the rest.

Child of Thunder, Mickey Zucker Reichert (DAW). The third book of the "Last of the Renshai" series by an author with solid storytelling skills. Reichert's adventure novels are grounded in the real; they lack the "airy-fairy" quality that mars less competent series tales.

Storm Caller, Carol Severence (Del Rey). In this sequel to *Demon Drums*, the Pacific Island setting gives a standard fantasy adventure story the invigorating freshness of a salty island wind.

The Castle of the Silver Wheel, Teresa Edgerton (Ace). The beginning of a new trilogy from a writer whose work is gently magical and romantic. The old tales interspersed with the story are a nice touch.

The Well-Favored Man, Elizabeth Willey (Tor). An entertaining and literate first novel full of dragons, medieval magic, and a baroque plot of family intrigue reminiscent of Roger Zelazny's "Amber" books.

Hart's Hope, Orson Scott Card (Severn House, U.K.). The first hardcover edition of this strange, terrific dark fairy tale by Card, first published in the 1980s.

The Island of the Mighty, Evangeline Walton (Macmillan). A much-needed reprint edition; the conclusion of Walton's gorgeous quartet inspired by the Welsh "Mabinogion." (Though this is the last of the books in sequence, it was actually the first to be published and can be read alone.) This edition includes additional nonfiction by Walton.

Contemporary and Urban Fantasy:

The Thread that Binds the Bones, Nina Kiriki Hoffman (AvoNova). Well-written, enchanting and entertaining, this contemporary fantasy story set in a small Oregon town is as jam-packed with quirky characters as a Dickens novel.

Nevernever, Will Shetterly (Jane Yolen Books/Harcourt Brace). The sequel to last year's wonderful "punk fantasy" novel *Elsewhere*, about a young man who is part wolf in a magical city setting. The novel is part of the ongoing *Borderland* urban fantasy series.

Bedlam Boyz, Ellen Guon (Baen). A light but entertaining addition to the urban fantasy field, a coming-of-age story about a runaway on magical city streets.

Historical Fantasy:

Strange Devices of the Sun and Moon, Lisa Goldstein (Tor). An intriguing novel by an American Book Award winner about the booksellers of Elizabethan England, the English faery court, and a conspiracy involving playwright Christopher Marlowe.

Robin and the King, Parke Godwin (Morrow). The sequel to last year's *Sherwood*, an excellent historical novel with some fantasy elements exploring the Robin Hood legend.

Lord of the Two Lands, Judith Tarr (Tor). A beautifully penned fantasy novel set in Egypt, 336 B.C. by a skillful writer and historian.

The Jaguar Princess, Clare Bell (Tor). A magical fantasy set during the Aztec empire's rule in pre-Columbian Mexico. Notable for its vivid portrayal of a distant time, and for deft handling of power politics and personal trials by a shape-changing novice whose art and private life are pre-empted by the demands of outside forces.

The Rape of Oc, by Michael Baldwin (Houghton Mifflin), blends fantasy and fact into a historical novel about a Joan of Arc-like heroine, set in thirteenth-century France.

The Empress of the Seven Seas, Fiona Cooper (Black Swan, U.K.). Historical fantasy set in seventeenth-century England.

The Hammer and the Cross, Harry Harrison and John Holm (Tor). Historical fantasy set in ninth-century England.

Fantasy from Other Traditions:

Like Water for Chocolate, Laura Esquivel (Doubleday). This beautiful Mexican Magic Realist tale, complete with cooking recipes, was not originally published in 1993 but hit the best-sellers lists in the past year due to the release of the wonderful film version. Highly recommended.

Magic Eyes: Scenes from an Andean Childhood, Wendy Ewald (Bay Press). A magical novel about the real-life Vasquez family in a Colombian village, interspersed with photographs by Ewald who lived for some years in Colombia. Highly recommended. (A 1992 publication not seen until this year.)

The Book of Nights, Sylvie Germain (Godine). Translated from the French, this beautiful novel with Márquezian influences traces the life of the Peniel family from the Franco-Prussian War to World War II.

The Inner Side of the Wind, or The Novel of Hero and Leander, Milorad Pavič (Knopf). A delicious literary fantasy about two lovers from different centuries; it is actually two separate stories, one from each lover's point of view. Translated from the Serbo-Croatian by Christina Pribicevic-Zoric.

Dream Messenger, Masahiko Shimada (Kodansha). A fascinating fantasy novel about a man who can enter other people's dreams, translated from the Japanese by Philip Gabriel.

The Broken Goddess, Hans Bemmann (Roc). A German fantasy novel about a young academic in a fairy tale world, translated by Anthea Bell (published in Germany in 1990).

Walpurgisnacht, Gustav Meyrink (Dedalus). An early twentieth-century literary fantasy novel translated from the German by Mike Mitchell (originally published in Germany in 1917).

Dark Legend, Jamake Highwater (Grove). A peculiar novel inspired by the Germanic "Ring" legends, but set in the tropics of ancient South America.

Humorous Fantasy:
Here Comes the Sun, Tom Holt (Orbit–U.K.). A comic fantasy about the bureaucrats who run the universe.

A Night in the Lonesome October, Roger Zelazny (AvoNova). A humorous Victorian gothic featuring Jack the Ripper, Sherlock Holmes, Frankenstein and more, with illustrations by the wonderful Gahan Wilson.

Fantasy Mysteries:
The Gruband-Stakers House a Haunt, Alisa Craig (Morrow). Another in a delightful series of ghostly mysteries set in a small Canadian town, by Charlotte MacLeod writing under the pen name Alisa Craig.

The Golden, Lucius Shepard (Bantam; also published in a nicely designed limited edition from Ziesing, P.O. Box 76, Shingletown, CA 96088). An intriguing, exotic and erotic entree into the "vampire as detective" genre, by one of the best writers in the speculative fiction field.

Dark Fantasy:
Anno Dracula, Kim Newman (Carroll & Graf). A delightfully odd dark fantasy/vampire/alternate history novel which mixes fictional characters (Dracula, Sherlock Holmes) with historical personages (Queen Victoria, Oscar Wilde, Jack the Ripper) in quite astonishing ways.

The Book of the Mad, Tanith Lee (Overlook). The fourth and final book of Lee's excellent, chilling "Secret Books of Paradys" cycle.

The Werewolves of London by Brian Stableford (Carroll & Graf). First American edition of this terrific dark fantasy set in nineteenth-century London.

Darker Jewels, Chelsea Quinn Yarbro (Tor). Historical vampire novel in Yarbro's well-written Saint-Germaine series, set in the court of Ivan the Terrible.

Fantasy in the Mainstream:
The Moon's Wife, A. A. Attanasio (HarperCollins). The moon comes down from the sky and becomes a man to win the woman he loves. Highly recommended.

The Girl Who Trod on a Loaf, Kathryn Davis (Knopf). Uses the fairy tale of the title as the basis for a story of two women, and the opera, at the beginning of the twentieth century. A lovely little book.

The Glass Mountain, Leonard Wolf (Overlook). This dense fantasy by a literary historian won't be for everyone, but it's a fascinating look at fairy tales in a novel which (like *Damascus Nights* and *Green Grass Running Water*) is told in the form of stories within stories.

Sleeping Beauty, Susanna Moore (Knopf). This skillful mainstream writer mixes Hawaiian legend and myth into a compelling contemporary story. Highly recommended.

The Waking Spell, Carol Dawson (Algonquin Books of Chapel Hill). A beautifully written ghost story using the supernatural to tell a strong feminist tale of a woman's journey as she recreates her life.

Arc d'X, Steve Erickson (Poseidon Press). The first half of the book could be called alternate history fantasy; by the second half it has shifted into science fiction. Whatever category you want to place it in, it's a fascinating, complex work.

Einstein's Dreams, Alan Lightman (Pantheon). An unusual little philosophical novel that explores the nature of time and reality.

The Museum of Happiness by Jesse Lee Kercheval (Faber & Faber). Lyrical Magic Realism set in America and Paris, in the past (the 1920s) and the present.

Dr. Haggard's Disease by Patrick McGrath (Poseidon Press). Gothic literary fantasy, very dark in tone.

Out of Body and Mind, Veronica Jean (Permanent Press). A peculiar black humor New Age satire, the bizarre life story of a woman serving time for the murder of her art teacher.

The Hedge, The Ribbon, Carol Orlock (Broken Moon Press). Winner of the 1993 Western States Award for Fiction, this is a gentle, magical novel about a storyteller, her tales, and the storytelling process.

Don't forget the Young Adult shelves when you're looking for fantasy literature. Fantasy tales are often ageless, and some of the field's best writers have been published in the Young Adult lists (like Robin McKinley, Margaret Mahy, and Susan Cooper). The following are magical novels I would recommend to readers of any age:

The Wizard's Apprentice by S. P. Somtow (Macmillan). An offbeat and charming book that mixes high fantasy and modern shopping mall culture in a delicious way.

Calling on Dragons by Patricia C. Wrede (Jane Yolen Books/Harcourt Brace). Volume III in "The Enchanted Forest Chronicles," a delightful read if you can pry the book out of a ten-year-old's hands (kids adore this series).

The Kingdom of Kevin Malone by Suzy McKee Charnas (Jane Yolen Books/Harcourt Brace). A thoughtful book by an excellent writer mixing the magic of fantastic lands with the hard realities of our own.

A Bone from a Dry Sea by Peter Dickinson (Delacorte). A wonderful tale about modern and ancient Africa from one of the finest writers of our day.

The Books of the Keepers by Ann Downer (Atheneum). A strange and magical Imaginary World fantasy novel full of inventive and surprising characters.

The Promise by Monica Hughes (Simon & Schuster). A lovely story about a young prince who learns the magic of weather.

The Wings of a Falcon by Cynthia Voigt (Scholastic). The third book in a well-written coming-of-age trilogy by this Newbery Award-winning author.

Wren's Quest by Sherwood Smith (Jane Yolen Books/Harcourt Brace). The charming sequel to *Wren to the Rescue*, an entertaining story of two student magicians.

Dragon Sword and Wind Child by Noriko Ogiwara (Farrar, Straus & Giroux). A beautiful Japanese fantasy tale translated by Cathy Hirano (originally published in Japan in 1988).

Himalaya by Nicholas Luard (Century, U.K.). A really wonderful coming-of-age adventure fantasy in the spirit of H. Rider Haggard.

Dakota Dream by James Bennett (Scholastic). Another nice coming-of-age story in which a visionary dream causes a young boy to run away to a Sioux reservation.

The Pirate's Mixed-Up Voyage by Margaret Mahy (Penguin/Dial). A picaresque pirate adventure that reads more like Roald Dahl than Mahy. Highly recommended.

Acquainted with the Night by Hotze Sollace (Houghton Mifflin/Clarion). A terrific gothic ghost story set on an island off the coast of Maine.

Haphazard House by Mary Wesley (Overlook). Quirky British Magic Realism about the family of an unconventional painter.

Others See Us by William Sleator (Dutton). A spooky contemporary fantasy by an original and skillful writer who is one of the best in the children's book field.

There is no lack of good fantasy and Magic Realist short fiction these days. The difficulty lies in finding it all, for it is scattered across numerous mainstream venues and tucked amongst the works of several different genres. Anthologies are still the best place to look, and the place where we find many of the year's best stories. The following anthologies stood out from among the rest and are particularly recommended for lovers of good short fiction:

Xanadu is the first volume of an anthology series by World Fantasy Award-winning editor Jane Yolen (Tor). This excellent collection contains all-original fiction and poetry by the likes of Ursula K. Le Guin, Tanith Lee, Nancy Kress, Gardner Dozois, Steven K. Z. Brust, Pamela Dean and Robert Abel. (We've chosen the Le Guin story for this *Year's Best*—and would have chosen the wonderful Dean piece as well had we room for a story so lengthy.) The anthology is expected to appear more or less annually, and provides a much needed market for good adult fantasy fiction. Let's hope readers of short fiction provide the support to keep this series going.

Touch Wood is another commendable collection of all-original stories. It is Volume II of the "Narrow Houses" anthology series edited by Peter Crowther and published in Britain (Little, Brown & Co., U.K.). While Volume I concentrated on horror fiction, Vol. II delves further into the realm that lies midway between fantasy and horror. Good dark fantasy stories by Adam Corbin Fusco, Garry Kilworth, Neil Gaiman, Charles de Lint and others makes this an anthology series to watch.

Strange Dreams, edited by best-selling fantasy author Stephen R. Donaldson (Bantam), is a terrific reprint anthology that brings together excellent tales by C. J. Cherryh, Greg Bear, Sheri S. Tepper, Harlan Ellison, Rachel Pollack, and many others (along with a lovely story by Patricia A. McKillip that is original to the volume). Donaldson's taste is eclectic and refreshing; he has done a fine job of gathering worthy tales that have not been anthologized a dozen times over. Highly recommended.

The Oxford Book of Modern Fairy Tales, edited by Alison Lurie (Oxford University Press), is also a good reprint collection, in this case gathering works of both the nineteenth and twentieth centuries. All the expected authors are here along with a few unexpected ones. The book begins with an insightful and informative introduction by Lurie.

The Women's Press Book of New Myth and Magic, edited by Helen Windrath (Women's Press, U.K.), looks wonderful and turns out to be a bit disappointing. The best selections in the book are a reprint from Charlotte Watson Sherman's collection *Killing Color* and an original Ellen Kushner story.

Temporary Walls: An Anthology of Moral Fantasy Inspired by John Gardner's On Moral Fiction is edited by Greg Ketter and Robert T. Garcia and published in a slim hardback volume by the 1993 World Fantasy Convention in partnership with Ketter's DreamHaven Books. It's a controversial and thought-provoking premise for an anthology, well-executed with a good introduction by the editors and solid original stories by Patricia A. McKillip, Charles de Lint, John M. Ford, Kristine Kathryn Rusch, Barry N. Malzberg and Kathe Koja. (DreamHaven Books, 1309 4th Street S.E., Minneapolis, MN 55414)

A Wizard's Dozen is a Young Adult collection edited by Michael Stearns (Jane Yolen Books/Harcourt Brace). Featuring entertaining original stories by Patricia C. Wrede, Charles de Lint, Bruce Coville, Tappan King, Will Shetterly, and others, it is recommended to adult readers as well.

Christmas Forever, edited by David G. Hartwell (Tor), is a thoroughly entertaining theme anthology of original holiday stories by fantasy and science fiction writers such as Roger Zelazny, Gene Wolfe, James P. Blaylock, Tim Powers, Joan Aiken, Bruce McAllister, and others.

Chilling Christmas Tales is another holiday theme anthology, this one aimed at younger readers (Scholastic U.K., no editor credited). It's a collection of ten original dark fantasy stories with notable pieces from Joan Aiken and Garry Kilworth.

The Ultimate Witch, edited by Byron Preiss and John Betancourt (Dell Books), is another theme anthology of original stories, the latest volume in a handsomely packaged series from Byron Preiss Visual Publications (*The Ultimate Vampire*, *The Ultimate Werewolf*, etc.). This new volume contains some good dark fantasy, including original stories by Jane Yolen and E. R. Stewart chosen for this *Year's Best*.

The Dedalus Book of 19th Century British Fantasy, edited by Brian Stableford (Dedalus, U.K.), is a thorough reprint anthology including works by Coleridge, Dickens, Keats, Morris, Wilde, Rossetti and others. It's a good reference volume, and the comprehensive introduction by Stableford is excellent. *The Dedalus Book of Dutch Fantasy*, edited and translated by Richard Huijing, is another interesting addition to Dedalus's ongoing classic fantasy reprint series. Dutch fantasy, if this volume is any indication, leans more to surrealism than mythic magic. The story about Bluebeard's daughter was my favorite in the book.

Pleasure in the Word: Erotic Writing by Latin American Women, edited by Margarite Fernandez Olmos and Lizabeth Paravisini-Genert (White Pine Press, 10 Village Square, Fredonia, NY 14063), contains fiction and poems (some of which are fantastic or surrealistic in nature) by María Luisa Bombal, Rosario Ferré, Christina Peri Rossi, Daína Chaviano, Isabel Allende, and others. It's an uneven volume; some of the excerpts are too short, taken out of context, to make for satisfying reading, but the best pieces are luscious.

Mondo Barbie (St. Martin's) is a truly odd anthology edited by Richard Peabody and Lucinda Ebersole of stories and poems inspired by Barbie and Ken dolls (I kid you not). Some fine writers including Marge Piercy, Sandra Cisneros, Alice McDermott, and John Varley contributed work.

Air Fish is a small press anthology of "speculative works" edited by Joy Oestreicher and Richard Singer (Catseye Books, 904 Old Town Court, Cupertino, CA 95014). It's a commendable project in that it provides a publication venue for aspiring writers and noncommercial stories, although the established writers like Bruce Boston provide the strongest pieces in this fat trade-sized paperback.

Full Spectrum 4, edited by Lou Aronica, Amy Stout and Betsy Mitchell, is the latest in the anthology series put together by the former Spectra imprint editors at Bantam Books. These worthwhile volumes, full of good and occasionally great stories, always contain a few strong fantasy pieces mixed in with the science fiction. In number four, the best were by Elizabeth Hand, Danith McPherson, and Martha Soukup.

OMNI Best Science Fiction Three (OMNI Books) edited by Ellen Datlow contains strongly literary science fiction and fantasy stories—some reprinted from the magazine, others original to the collection. Four "short shorts" commissioned by the editor from Joyce Carol Oates, Gahan Wilson, Thomas M. Disch, and John Crowley are particularly recommended.

I'd also like to note *Snow White, Blood Red*, which Ellen Datlow and I edited together (AvoNova). This is an all-original anthology of dark adult fairy tales by Tanith Lee, Elizabeth Lynn, Neil Gaiman, Gahan Wilson, Jane Yolen, Patricia A. McKillip, and others—the first of a series that has grown to three volumes.

As for single-author collections of short fiction, the following is a baker's dozen of the best collections of the past year (in alphabetical order):

A Creepy Company by Joan Aiken (Gollancz). Eleven dark fantasy stories, six of them original, from this master of the genteel ghostly tale. Don't be put off that it's listed as a Young Adult book.

Angels and Insects by A. S. Byatt (Chatto & Windus). Two novellas from a Booker

Prize–winning author. The second tale, "The Conjugal Angel," about the poet Tennyson's sister, is a brilliant fantasy piece.

Dirty Work by Pat Cadigan (Mark V. Ziesing, Box 76, Shingletown, CA 96088). A handsome small press edition that includes fantasy as well as science fiction and horror stories by this prolific and eclectic writer, all highly recommended.

Antiquities by John Crowley (Incunabula, P.O. Box 30146, Seattle, WA 98103). Seven never-before-collected stories by this master of the fantasy form, in an elegant, slim, small press edition. Highly recommended.

Dreams Underfoot by Charles de Lint (Tor). One of the best all-fantasy collections of the year, it gathers together nineteen interconnected urban fantasy stories set in the imaginary city of Newford, including several that were chosen for previous *Year's Best* volumes and nominated for the World Fantasy Award.

Hogfoot Right and Bird-Hands by Garry Kilworth (Edgewood Press, P.O. Box 380264, Cambridge, MA 02238). A terrific small press edition of thirteen fantasy and science fiction stories by this extraordinary storyteller, with an introduction by Robert Holdstock. You might also check out *In the Country of Tattooed Men*, Kilworth's latest British collection (Grafton).

Shoeless Joe Jackson Comes to Iowa by W. P. Kinsella (Southern Methodist University Press). Kinsella is the author whose work was behind the gentle baseball fantasy movie *Field of Dreams*. This collection of stories features a particularly midwestern mixture of the miraculous and the mundane.

Strange Pilgrims, Gabriel García Márquez (Knopf). The title of Márquez's newest collection refers to the strange pilgrimage these stories made into and out of the writer's trash can over a twenty-year period. Rescued and completed and set into print at last, these tales are luminous gems of Magic Realism, set in various locales across South America and Europe, from the master of the form.

Little Kingdoms by Steven Millhauser (Poseidon Press). Macabre and lovely dark fantasy novellas by this literary magician and winner of the World Fantasy Award.

The Elephant Vanishes by Haruki Murakami (Knopf). Seventeen wonderful stories, some of them fantasy, by an author who has twice appeared in *Year's Best* volumes, translated from the Japanese by various translators.

Demons and Shadows: The Ghostly Best of Robert Westall (Farrar, Straus & Giroux). Eleven dark fantasy stories by a master of the form, best known for his award-winning Young Adult novels.

Impossible Things, Connie Willis (Bantam Spectra). An inventive, entertaining collection from this Hugo and Nebula award-winning author.

Here There Be Dragons by Jane Yolen (Harcourt Brace). You'll find this one on the children's book shelves, but Yolen is one of those writers whose enchanting stories, like the old myths and fairy tales, speak to readers of every age.

Other notable collections in 1993:

Siren Songs & Classical Illusions: Fifty Modern Fables by Jascha Kessler (McPherson & Co.). Satirical contemporary stories drawing on mythic roots.

The Man Who Took a Bite Out of His Wife by Bev Jafek (Overlook). Nine surrealistic fantasy and science fiction stories with black humor and some rather violent feminist overtones, from a Pushcart Prize winning author.

Blue Bamboo: Tales of Fantasy and Romance by Osamu Dazai (Kodansha). An English translation by Ralph F. McCarthy of the magical stories by this early 20th century writer sometimes called "Japan's Oscar Wilde."

The Mandarin and Other Stories by Ecade Queiroz (the Dedalus European Classics series). A new translation of a nineteenth century Portuguese writer's satiric fantasy.

Hieroglyphic Tales by Horace Walpole (the Mercury House Neglected Classics series). Walpole's collected gothic and grotesque fairy tales, first published in the eighteenth century. (Other works in this series are by Lewis Carroll, Henry Handel Richardson and I. U. Tarchetti).

Angels and Visitations by Neil Gaiman (DreamHaven Books). A beautifully produced collection of short stories, reviews and essays by a writer best known for his work on the *Sandman* comic book series.

Carnival Aptitude by Greg Boyd (Santa Maria/Asylum Arts, P.O. Box 6203, Santa Maria, CA 93456). Sixty-three surrealistic short-short stories interspersed with Boyd's equally surrealistic photomontages; an interesting, satirical but ultimately bleak view of the world.

Evolution Annie and Other Stories by Rosaleen Love (Women's Press). Idiosyncratic fantasy and science fiction stories.

The Seventh Day and After by Don Webb (Wordcraft, P.O. Box 3235, La Grande, Oregon 97850). Surrealistic stories with illustrations by Roman Scott.

Sexual Chemistry by Brian Stableford (Pocket Books, U.K.). First paperback edition of a truly excellent collection of fantasy and science fiction.

Hostilities: Nine Bizarre Stories by Caroline Macdonald (Scholastic). Dark fantasy tales for Young Adults from an award-winning New Zealand writer.

Please Do Not Touch by Judith Gorog (Scholastic). Dark Y.A. fantasy by one of America's best.

Also of note, on the mainstream shelves:

The Lone Ranger and Tonto Fistfight in Heaven, by Sherman Alexie (Atlantic Monthly Press), is my favorite mainstream collection of the year; this young Native American author occasionally strays into the realms of fantasy, particularly in his exploration of the magic of storytellers ("This is What it Means to Say Phoenix, Arizona") and in the powerful story "Distances," which is included in this *Year's Best*.

Scott Bradfield's *Greetings From Earth* (Picador) is a collection of twenty-one stories by this fine writer, a few of which are fantasy or have fantasy overtones (including stories that were published in *Dream of the Wolf*).

Malingering, by Susan Comp (Faber & Faber), is a dark, trendy "goth-rock" collection that contains some interesting fantasy elements, including a memorable urban angel.

During Mother's Absence, by Michele Roberts (Virago), is another literary collection that strays into areas of dark fantasy.

As for short fiction in the magazines:

At the moment, unlike the horror, mystery, and science fiction fields, there is no professional or semiprofessional magazine specifically for quality fantasy/Magic Realist literature. At the moment there is only one fantasy magazine at all, and that one, *Marion Zimmer Bradley's Fantasy Magazine*, is geared to the specific market of swords-and-sorcery adventure tales. To find fantasy literature on the newsstands, you have to search through a number of different publications: Genre fiction magazines such as *Fantasy & Science Fiction*, *Asimov's Science Fiction*, OMNI, and England's *Interzone* all include good fantasy stories among their other selections. *Weird Tales* includes some fantasy too, although it concentrates more on dark fantasy/horror. Fantasy fiction occasionally pops up in *The New Yorker*, *Esquire*, and *Playboy*; and Magic Realist literature can be found by scouring the literary reviews, particularly *TriQuarterly*, *Grand Street*, *Conjunctions*, and *Glimmer Train*.

The SF and horror fields have spawned a whole underground desktop publishing industry of little magazines; the fantasy field has not. The only consistently readable little 'zine I've yet come across dedicated specifically to fantasy is *Magic Realism*, edited by Julie Thomas and C. Darren Butler (Pyx Press, Box 620, Orem, UT 84059). Thomas and Butler are to be commended for providing a venue for aspiring writers and experimental fiction, although sometimes the art of good storytelling gets a little lost in the surrealist imagery. For a really excellent little magazine of cutting-edge stories, check out the first edition of *Crank!*, edited by Bryan Cholfin. This worhty little magazine contains both SF and fantasy by such talented writers as A. A. Attanasio, Michael Blumlein, Gwyneth Jones, Garry Kilworth and Carter Scholz, and I recommend it highly. (Broken Mirrors Press, P.O. Box 380473, Cambridge, MA 02238.)

The following small magazines also contained interesting fantasy works among their other offerings in 1993: *Aurealis: The Australian Magazine of Fantasy and Science Fiction* (Chimera Publications, P.O. Box 538, Mt. Waverly, Victoria 3149, Australia); *On Spec: The Canadian Magazine of Speculative Writing* (P.O. Box 4727, Edmonton, Alberta, Canada, T6E 5GB); *Pulphouse* (Box 1227, Eugene, OR 97440); *Strange Plasma*, edited by Steve Pasechnick (Edgewood Press, P.O. Box 264, Cambridge, MA 02338); and *The Silver Web* (P.O. Box 38190, Tallahassee, FL 32315).

Various small 'zines contain fantasy-oriented poetry, much of it rather dreadful I'm afraid. *The Magazine of Speculative Poetry*, edited by Roger Dutcher and Mark Rich, is worth taking a look at (P.O. Box 291, Stevens Point, WI 54481), but the best poetry is still to be found in the academic literary journals.

Jane Yolen's anthology *Xanadu* has a high poem-to-story ratio and consistent good quality, as does *Pleasure in the Word*. I consider the standout poetry publication of 1993 to be *The Book of Medicine* by Linda Hogan (Coffee House Press, 27 North Fourth Street, Suite 400, Minneapolis, MN 55401). Hogan's gorgeous poems about our relationship to the earth we walk on are steeped in American mythology and invested with a subtle, cautionary magic. (One of these poems, "The Grandmother Songs," was originally sched-uled to be reprinted in this volume of the *Year's Best*.)

Also of note: Bruce Boston's *Accursed Wives* is a wonderful chapbook of poems about the wives of a shapeshifter, an angel, a brujo, etc., illustrated by Ree Young. Publisher W. Paul Ganley (P.O. Box 149, Buffalo, NY 14226) has produced *Star Songs*, a collection of poems by Nancy Springer, illustrated by Teanna Byerts, which includes some very nice pieces. *Songs of the Maenads* by Jessica Amanda Salmonson is a nicely produced chapbook edition from Salmonson's own Street of Crocodiles Press (Box 20610, Seattle, WA 98102). And I highly recommend the work of Lawrence Schimel's A Midsummer Night's Press (3 Norden Drive, Brookville, NY 11545). Schimel produces beautiful letterpress broadsheets by poets such as Jane Yolen, Nancy Willard, and Marion Zimmer Bradley in signed, one-hundred-copy editions. The poems are excellent; the broadsheets are works of art.

A selection of notable works of nonfiction and folklore published in 1993:

Writers Dreaming: 26 Writers Talk About Their Dreams and the Creative Process, edited by Naomi Epel, contains thoughtprovoking nonfiction by Maya Angelou, Anne Rice, Stephen King, Amy Tan, William Styron, and others discussing their craft and how dream images affect their work (Carol Southern Books/Crown).

Telling Time: Angels, Ancestors and Stories by Nancy Willard. A collection of essays by this exceptional writer (Harcourt Brace).

Michael Moorcock: Death is No Obstacle, by Colin Greenland, is an excellent book-length interview with one of the most fascinating writers working today (plus an introduction by the late Angela Carter). Particularly recommended for aspiring writers (Savoy Books, 279 Deansgate, Manchester M3 4EW U.K.).

Hudson Valley Literary Supplement 1/28/93. Contains an interesting extensive interview with Ian and Betty Ballantine, two editors/publishers who were instrumental in the creation of the modern American fantasy field, among many other things.

Earthsea Revisioned, by Ursula K. Le Guin. A nice little edition that presents the text of her speech at the 1992 Worlds Apart conference on children's literature discussing why she wrote *Tehanu*. This is a fascinating look at the creative process (Children's Literature New England, Norwood Long, 334 Woodland Road, Madison, NJ 07940).

The Rushdie Letters: Freedom to Speak, Freedom to Write, edited by Steve MacDounough, contains twenty-five responses by modern writers to the *fatwa*, plus Rushdie's essay "One Thousand Days in a Balloon" (University of Nebraska Press).

Twentieth Century Fantasists: Essays on Culture, Society and Belief in Twentieth Century Mythopoetic Literature, an informative collection edited by Kath Filmer (St. Martin's).

Off With Their Heads! Fairy Tales and the Culture of Childhood by Maria Tartar, highly recommended. A better study of fairy tales and children than the better-known *The Uses of Enchantment* (Princeton University Press).

The Feminine in Fairy Tales by Marie-Louise von Franz. A republication (revised from the book *Problems of the Feminine in Fairy Tale*) of this excellent Jungian study (Shambala).

The Second Virago Book of Fairy Tales, an excellent collection of unbowdlerized tales edited by Angela Carter, illustrated by Corinna Sargood, highly recommended (Virago, U.K.).

Louisa May Alcott's Fairy Tales and Fantasy Stories, twenty-nine stories with a critical introduction by Daniel Shealy (University of Tennessee Press).

Adventures in Unhistory, Conjectures on the Factual Foundations of Several Ancient Legends by Avram Davidson. An eccentric, unusual collection of fifteen essays which will be of interest to fans of this late author (Owlswick Press, P.O. Box 8243, Philadelphia, PA 19101).

Cinderella retold by C. S. Evans. A reissue of this classic edition with the original Arthur Rackham illustrations (Knopf Everyman Library).

Jewish Mystical Tales retold by Howard Schwartz (Oxford University Press).

Rachel the Clever and Other Jewish Folktales retold by Josepha Sherman (August House).

Jack Always Seeks His Fortune: Appalachian Jack Tales by storyteller Donald Davis (August House).

Shoshone Tales collected by Ann M. Smith (University of Utah Press).

Zulu Fireside Tales by Phyllis Savory (Citadel Press).

American, African and Old European Mythologies and *Asian Mythologies* by Yves Bonnefoy. The final two volumes in a four-volume series (University of Chicago Press).

Persian Myths by Vesta Sarkhosh Curtis (Texas University Press).

Pacific Mythology by Jan Knappert (Aquarian Press).

From Achilles' Heel to Zeus's Shield: A Lively, Informative Guide to More Than 300 Words and Phrases From Mythology by Dale Correy Bibbey (Ballantine).

Children's picture books are an excellent source for magical tales, and for some of the loveliest fantastical artwork created today. I continue to hope that the judges of the World Fantasy Award will keep these books and artists in mind when they choose the Best Fantasy Artist of the year (an award that, contrary to its purpose, seems often to be given for an artist's overall body of work rather than work published in the year of the award).

The most beautiful picture book of 1993 was Nancy Willard's retelling of *The Sorcerer's Apprentice* (Scholastic), with lavish, exuberant paintings by the extraordinary illustration team of Leo and Diane Dillon. I also highly recommend *Mermaid Tales from Around the World*, with stories retold by Mary Pope Osborn and absolutely chock full of beautifully rendered paintings by Troy Howell (Scholastic). My favorite picture book of the year, however, was a more modest one: Janell Cannon's *Stellaluna* (Harcourt Brace), a wonderful and quirky book about a fruit bat raised by birds. I cannot praise this enchanting book too highly; *please* don't miss it, it's an utter delight for adults and children alike—the kind of book you want to buy ten copies of and send to all your friends.

One of the most wickedly peculiar books of the year was William Wegman's latest "Fay's Fairy Tales" edition, *Little Red Riding Hood* (Hyperion). Wegman is a photographer who poses his weimaraner dogs in classic fairy tale scenes, creating macabre, hilarious, and truly one-of-a-kind fairy tale retellings. Another odd one (a 1992 publication not seen till this year) is *The Stinky Cheese Man and Other Fairly Stupid Tales* by Jon Scieszka and Lane Smith (Viking). This Caldecott Honor Book is full of an energetic black humor beloved by kids (and the five-year-old that lurks inside most adults as well). The text is wonderfully stupid, and Lane's illustrations are a treat.

Other picture books of note:

The Princess and the Pea by French artist Dorothee Duntz (North-South) is highly recommended for its skillful Kay Nielsen-like watercolor paintings.

Lauren Mill's *Tatterhood and the Hobgoblins* (Little, Brown) is also recommended; Mill's lovely work is reminiscent of Arthur Rackham and Charles Robinson yet has a distinctive charm all its own. Mill's husband Dennis Nolan also has a couple of beautiful editions out this year: one is a T. H. White volume (mentioned below); the other is a picture book written by Diane Stanley, *The Gentleman and the Kitchen Maid*, an enchanted tale of two Dutch-master portraits who fall in love with each other as they hang in a museum (Dial).

Master bookmaker and illustrator Barry Moser has two handsome children's books out this year: *The Dreamer* (Scholastic), with wonderful text by Cynthia Rylant, and *The Magic Hare* (Morrow), a sweet collection of rabbit tales retold by Lynn Reid Banks.

Chris Van Allsburg's latest is *The Sweetest Fig* (Houghton Mifflin)—beautifully executed as always, but not one of his very best.

The same can be said for Gennady Spirin's version of Jonathan Swift's *Gulliver's Adventures in Lilliput* (Philomel). While not the best of Spirin's work, this Russian artist is so exceptional that even his second best is leagues above most others.

What Rhymes with the Moon (Philomel) is a book of lovely lyrical poems by Jane Yolen with gentle illustrations by Ruth Tietjen Councell.

The Dragons Are Singing Tonight (Greenwillow) contains charmingly silly poems by Jack Prelutsky with even more charming illustrations by Peter Sis. Sis's own book, *A Small Tale from the Far North* (Knopf) is quite wonderful, a surreal adventure tale that I particularly recommend seeking out.

Natalie Babbitt, who is equally talented as a storyteller and as an illustrator, has a touching new book called *Bub: The Very Best Thing* (HarperCollins).

Persephone and the Pomegranate is a magical retelling of the Greek myth with paintings and text by Kris Waldheer, a very talented young illustrator (Dial).

Michael Hague has illustrated the classic *Fairy Tales of Oscar Wilde* in a new edition from Holt, while Gary Kelly has created a sophisticated edition of Washington Irving's *Rip Van Winkle* for Creative Editions. And take a look at *Whales' Song* by Dyan Sheldon (Dial) for the beautiful paintings by Gary Blythe.

Other art publications of note:

The most stunning publication of the year is *The Smithsonian Book of Books*, a thick, comprehensive, gorgeously illustrated volume celebrating books and bookmaking, with text by Michael Olmert (Smithsonian Institute). This sumptuous book is an absolute treasure.

Another strikingly beautiful publication is a new volume dedicated to the works of pre-Raphaelite master *Sir Edward Burne-Jones*, with text by Russell Ash (Abrams). The tall format of the book displays the work to great effect; it is highly recommended.

Ecco Press has published *Dime Store Alchemy: The Art of Joseph Cornell*, an intriguing collection of essays by Charles Simic inspired by Cornell's famous magical boxes.

The Reenchantment of Art, by Suzi Gablik (Thames and Hudson), is a follow-up to her critical work *Has Modernism Failed?*. Gublik's new book is a theoretical discourse about transformative art, myth and renewal.

In 1945, Russian painter Marc Chagall illustrated four magical tales from the Arabian *A Thousand and One Nights* for a sumptuously beautiful edition of only 111 copies. Prestel Verlag of Munich has now published a gorgeous facsimile of the original publication, beautifully produced. Marc Chagall's illustrated Greek romance *Daphnis and Chloe*, first published in Paris in 1961, has also been republished in a stunning facsimile edition by George Braziller of New York. Chilean poet Pablo Neruda's *Twenty Love Poems and a Song of Despair* (translated by W. S. Merwin) has been reissued in a beautiful little edition featuring lovely magical illustrations by Jan Thompson Dicks. (All three titles available through Truepenny Books, 2509 N. Campbell Ave., Tucson, AZ 85719.)

Nick Bantock has published *The Golden Means*, the third (and final? He says so, but who knows . . .) volume of the Griffin and Sabine sequence (Chronicle Books). These extraordinary, beautiful publications document the relationship between a British artist and his possibly mythical South Sea island muse via postcards and letters (the latter actually included in the book in three-dimensional form). The conclusion of the sequence is as mysterious as the beginning. Highly recommended.

I also strongly recommend the new edition of T. H. White's *The Sword in the Stone* (Philomel), chock full of color illustrations by Dennis Nolan, reminiscent of the best of N. C. Wyeth.

The small press Underwood-Miller has published many beautiful editions over the last years. Recent publications include several lavish, beautifully produced art books of interest to fans of fantasy illustration: *The Art of Michael Whelan*; *Dreamquests: The Art of Don Maitz*; *Stephen E. Fabian's Ladies and Legends* and *A Hannes Bok Treasury* (with an introduction by Ray Bradbury). For information on these and other titles write: Underwood-Miller, 708 Westover Drive, Lancaster, PA 17601.

HarperCollins has published *Tolkien's World*, a collection of paintings of Middle Earth by numerous illustrators including Michael Hague, John Howe, and a number of British and European artists whose work will be new to an American audience. The quality of the illustrations is uneven; the volume is likely to be of more interest to fans of Middle Earth than to fans of fine art. The best in the book are by British painter Alan Lee, the master watercolorist who recently illustrated the anniversary edition of *The Lord of the Rings*. Also, look for the new Tolkien Address Book and Tolkien Date Book (published by Grafton, U.K.) with illustrations drawn from the Alan Lee edition; they are beautifully designed, worth seeking out particularly for the exquisite pencil drawings by Lee commissioned expressly for these lovely little volumes.

Despite commercial constraints that severely limit artists working in the area of book jacket design and illustration, there were still some exceptional works that stood out from the rest on the shelves in 1993. To mention just a few of the notable cover treatments in the last year, for which the illustrators and their art directors deserve special commendation: Gervasio Gallardo's Magritte-like surrealism for the anthology *Strange Dreams* (Bantam); Ian Miller's distinctively surreal work (with a touch of Heath Robinson in it) for David R. Bunch's *Bunch!* (Broken Mirrors Press); Thomas Canty's sensual, darkly pre-Raphaelite painting for the anthology *Snow White, Blood Red* (AvoNova); Dawn Wilson's elegant painting (easily mistaken for the work of Robert Gould) on the cover of Robin McKinley's *Deerskin* (Ace); Alan Lee's lovely Celtic watercolor for Evangeline Walton's *The Island of the Mighty* (Macmillan); Jody Lee's gracefully stylized paintings for Mickey Zucher Reichert's *Child of Thunder* (DAW) and for Clare Bell's *The Jaguar Princess* (Tor); Michael Whelan's work in the tradition of Pyle and Wyeth on Tad William's *To Green Angel Tower* (DAW) as well as John Howe's treatment of Roberta Cray's *The Sword and the Lion* (DAW); David Cherry's two very different illustration styles on Judith Tarr's Egyptian *Lord of the*

Two Lands (Tor) and the anthology *Sword and Sorceress* X (DAW); Wayne Barlowe's effective painting and design for Tanith Lee's *The Book of the Mad* (Overlook); Peter Michelena's painterly illustration and design for Kathe Koja's *Skin* (Dell/Abyss); David Chalk's striking, understated treatment of Bradley Denton's *Blackburn* (St. Martin's); and Arnie Fenner's skillful work on the design of the books published by the Mark Ziesing small press.

Traditional folk music is of interest to many fantasy readers because the old ballads, particularly in the Celtic folk tradition, are often based on the same folk and fairy tale roots as fantasy stories. The current generation of worldbeat musicians, like contemporary fantasy writers, are taking ancient, traditional rhythms and themes and adapting them to a modern age.

Listeners new to this kind of music might begin with the new *Narada Celtic Odyssey,* a compilation CD featuring Altan, Capercaille, Scartaglen and other musicians from Ireland, Scotland and America. For those interested in a broader range of traditional music, I recommend the Rhino/Putumayo two-CD set titled *The Best of World Music,* an excellent compilation which includes Johnny Clegg & Saruka, Gregory Issacs, Strunk & Farah, Bela Fleck, Loreena McKennit, The Bhundu Boys, and other musicians from all over the world.

Altan, a Dublin-based sextext who has emerged as one of Ireland's top traditional bands has a beautiful and gutsy new release this year: *Island Angel.* (Altan member Daithi Sproul, a talented singer and guitarist, has also released a solo CD titled *Heart Made of Glass.*) Another top Irish band, Patrick Street, has gone back to their original all-star lineup of musicians (Kevin Burke, Jackie Daly, Arty McGlynn, Andy Irvin) for their latest, *All in Good Time. Barking Mad* and *Shifting Gravel* are two new CDs from Four Men and a Dog, a quirky, cutting edge trad band with the energy of the Pogues. Also from Ireland: Deanta, a new band from County Antrim, debuted with an accomplished release simply titled *Deanta.*

Six superb Irish women musicians (Dolores Keane, Mary Black, Frances Black, Maura O'Connell, Eleanor McEvoy, and Sharon Shannon) teamed up for *A Woman's Heart,* a lovely collection of songs that is highly recommended. Cherish the Ladies, an Irish all-woman band, has a new CD titled *Out and About.* Produced by Johnny Cunningham, it contains gorgeous songs sung by Cathie Ryan backed up with skillful instrumentals. The Heartbeats Rhythm Quartet, an all-woman band from Philadelphia that has been aptly described as "the Bangles meet the Horseflies" has released their eclectic first CD, titled *Spinning World.*

Irish singer/songwriter Robbie O'Connell is backed up by Johnny Cunningham and Seamus Egan on his excellent new release *Never Learned to Dance.* From Green Linnet's Celtic Classics series comes *Will Ye Gang, Love,* featuring many of the best songs of Scottish singer/songwriter Archie Fisher (known to fantasy fans as the writer of the ballad "Witch of Westmorelands," recently turned into an enchanting story by Pamela Dean in *Xanadu*).

Kevin Burke (from the Irish band Patrick Street), Johnny Cunningham (from the Scottish band Silly Wizard), and Christian Lemaitre (from the Breton band Kornog) have released *The Celtic Fiddle Festival,* recorded live on tour. Johnny Cunningham's brother Phil (also a member of Silly Wizard, as well as the composer of the haunting *Last of the Mohicans* soundtrack and a session musician with Bonnie Raitt and Dick Gaughin) released another solo CD in 1993, titled *Rebox.*

Some odder mixes of music to come out recently include Rod Stradling's *Rhythms of the World,* featuring "New Wave Country Dance" music on accordion. The Deighton Family, of South Moluccan/English heritage, mix Celtic, Cajun, bluegrass and rock on their CD, *Rolling Home.* Texas musician Ingrid Karlins mixes Latvian music and American lullabyes with African inspired percussion on her CD, *A Darker Passion*. Ottapasuuna is a band that is part of the New Finnish Folk Music scene, mixing Finnish trad with Celtic, bluegrass and other influences on a broad range of instruments. Their debut release, *Ottapasuuna*, is wild, and highly recommended. Varttina is another interesting New Finnish Folk band: four female vocalists fronting fiddle, guitar, bass, sax and bouzouki. Their CD, *Seleniko*, was number one in the European World Music Charts within days of its release.

Ellipsis Arts has released an unusual boxed set of music rooted in myth and ritual, titled *Voices of Forgotten Worlds: Traditional Music of Indigenous People*. These four CDs contain music from twenty-eight different cultures including Inuit drum songs, Australian Aboriginal didgeridoo, Tibetan chants, and more. Another boxed set called *Global Celebrations* features spiritual and celebratory music from around the world, divided into "Dancing With the Gods," "Earth Spirit," "Passages," and "Gathering." (A portion of all Ellipsis Arts sales goes to the UN Center for Human Rights Fund for Indigenous People.)

I recommend highly Sheila Chandra's *Weaving My Ancestral Voices*—meditative East Indian music mixed with Western music (Irish, Spanish, Persian), all pulled together by Chandra's exquisite voice. Ancient Future, a world music band, has released *Ancient Fusion*, wherein Chinese musician Zhao Hui and Vietnamese musician Bui Huu Nhuit play a truly inspired mix of trad and contemporary, Eastern and Western music.

Geoffrey Oryema sings the achingly haunting folk music of Uganda backed by a blend of African and Western instrumentation on his CD titled *Exile*. Rossy's *One Eye on the Future, One Eye on the Past* features a multi-instrumental trad dance music rooted in the ancient rhythms of Madagascar. *Yekan Imfazwe* from Nati contains traditional music of the Zulu tribe mixed with urban influences (particularly of interest to Johnny Clegg fans). Farafina's *Bolomakote* is a CD of trance-like dance music filled with spirit from Burkina Faso, West Africa. Bajoueou's *Big String Theory* features West African music from guitarists Jalimanda Tounkara and Bouba Sacko as well as the extraordinary vocals of Lafia Diabate.

Inti-Illimani is an ensemble that is part of the "Nuevo Cancion" (New Song) movement in Chile. Their CD, *Andadas*, mixes Andean music with world rhythms and original music played on 16 different instruments, along with wonderful choral harmonies. Conjunto Cespedes is a band that plays the fiery "son" music of Cuba, a type of music so sensual and hot it was once outlawed there; *Una Sola Casa* is their latest release. La Musgana is an unusual band that draws inspiration from the ancient ritualistic music of the Castillian region of Spain and contemporary Carnaval; their release *Lubican* is highly recommended.

On our own native shores, Bill Miller of the Stockbridge-Munsee tribe (a band of Mohicans) has released a really excellent CD titled *The Red Road*, mixing stirring traditional pow-wow music with original songs reminiscent of the work of his friend and occasional songwriting partner Peter Rowan. Rowan has also released an exceptionally beautiful CD this past year titled *Awake Me in the New World*, filled with magical, romantic songs drawing on both North and South American musical roots. Both Miller and Rowan's CDs are highly recommended. Sharon Burch's new *Yazzie Girl* contains original compositions for guitar and voice based on Navajo prayers and chants (including several lovely tracks sung in the Navajo language). Peter Kater and R. Carlos Nakai's soundtrack for the PBS documentary *How the West Was Lost* is absolutely haunting; their music mixes traditional Native American flute with piano, cellos and violin. Nakai also released the beautiful *Native Tapestry*, featuring the music of James DeMars played with the Tos Ensemble on Native American flute, African percussion, and chamber orchestra instruments.

And last but by no means least, two popular writers in the fantasy field, both former members of the band Cats Laughing, have released music CDs this past year—Steven Brust and Emma Bull. Both CDs are musically accomplished and a whole lot of fun. Brust's *A Rose for Iconoclastes* contains bluesy songs by Brust, Adam Stemple (author Jane

Yolen's son), and others. Brust's songwriting style is similar to his fiction style: witty, ironic, thoroughly engaging. "I Was Born About Ten Million Songs Ago," in which the singer demonstrates that he invented rock-and-roll (by Brust and Nate Bucklin), is particularly recommended. Emma Bull (guitarist and vocalist) has teamed up with The Fabulous Lorraine Garland (fiddle player and vocalist) for *The Flash Girls: The Return of Pansy Smith and Violet Jones*, complete with enchanting liner notes by *Sandman* comic book writer Neil Gaiman, and backup instrumentals by three members of the band Boiled in Lead. The original songs, which have a delightfully skewed trad folk edge, are by Bull, Garland, and others; several by Neil Gaiman are particularly intriguing. (Both CDs are available from SteelDragon Press, Box 7253, Minneapolis, MN 55407.)

The World Fantasy Convention, an annual gathering of writers, artists, publishers, and readers, was held in Minneapolis, Minnesota in 1993 (October 28–31). The Guests of Honor were writers Poul Anderson, Roger Zelazny, John Crowley, and Basil Copper, as well as artist Thomas Canty, who was unable to attend. Music was provided by the Flash Girls, Ellen Kushner, and others, with storytelling by Jane Yolen. The World Fantasy Awards ceremony was held at the convention on the 31st. Winners (for work produced in 1992) were as follows: *Last Call* by Tim Powers for Best Novel; "The Ghost Village" by Peter Straub for Best Novella; "Graves" by Joe Haldeman and "This Year's Class Picture" by Dan Simmons for Best Short Story (tie); *The Sons of Noah and Other Stories* by Jack Cady for Best Collection; *Metahorror* edited by Dennis Etchison for Best Anthology; and James Gurney for Best Artist. Special Award/Professional went to Jeanne Cavelos for her work as editor of the Dell/Abyss horror fiction line; Special Award/Nonprofessional went to Doug and Tomi Lewis, publishers of Roadkill Press. The Life Achievement Award was given to Harlan Ellison. The judges for the awards were Roland J. Green, Barbara Hambly, Kathryn Ptacek, Steve Rasnic Tem, and Brian Thomsen. For information on the next World Fantasy Convention, to be held in New Orleans in October 1994, write: Box 91302, New Orleans, LA 70179.

The Fourth Street Fantasy Convention (usually held each June in Minneapolis, Minnesota) was cancelled in 1993 because many of its organizers were busy working on the World Fantasy Convention held in the same city later in the year. For information on future Fourth Street Fantasy Conventions write: David Dyer-Bennett, 4242 Minehaha Avenue S., Minneapolis, MN 55406.

Mythcon was also held in Minneapolis this year, July 30–Aug. 2. Guests of Honor were Jane Yolen, Carol Kendall, and Jack Zipes. For information on the 1994 Mythcon, to be held at American University in Washington, D.C., in August, write: Irv Koch, 5465 N. Morgan St. #106, Alexandria, VA 22312.

The 1993 British Fantasy Awards were presented at the British Fantasy Convention, October 1–3 in Birmingham, U.K. These awards are covered in my co-editor's Summation.

The International Conference on the Fantastic in the Arts was held in Fort Lauderdale, Florida (March 17–21). The Guests of Honor were writers Ursula K. Le Guin and Michael Bishop, scholar Sir Devendra P. Varma, and artist Rodney Marchetti. Susan Palwick, author of *Flying in Place*, was the winner of the Crawford Fantasy Award presented at the conference. Hungarian poet and playwright Casba Laszloffy's dystopian satire *The Heretic, or a Plague of Slugs* had its world premiere performance; and Raymond J. Schneider's chamber theater adaptation of Le Guin's *It Was a Dark and Stormy Night, or Why are We Huddling About the Campfire?* was also performed. For information on next year's conference, write: IAFA, College of the Humanities, 500 N.W. 20th HU-50 B-19, Florida Atlantic University, Boca Raton, FL 33431.

That's a brief summation of the year in fantasy; now on to the stories themselves.

As usual, there are some stories (particularly the lengthy ones) that we do not have room to print even in an anthology as fat as this one. I consider the following tales to be among the year's best along with the stories and poems collected in this volume. I strongly recommend seeking them out if you've not come across them already:

"The Conjugal Angel" by A. S. Byatt from her new book *Angels & Insects*.

"The Night We Buried Road Dog" by Jack Cady from the January issue of *F&SF* magazine.

"Owlswater" by Pamela Dean from Jane Yolen's *Xanadu* anthology #1.

"Mephisto in Onyx" by Harlan Ellison from the October issue of *OMNI* magazine.

"Irene's Song" by Astrid Julian from the March issue of *Interzone* magazine, U.K.

"Xmas Cruise" by Patricia A. McKillip from David Hartwell's holiday anthology *Christmas Forever*. (It's more mainstream than fantasy, but too good to miss regardless.)

"An American Childhood" by Pat Murphy from the April issue of *Asimov's SF* magazine.

"Wall, Stone, Craft," by Walter Jon Williams from the Oct/Nov issue of *F&SF* magazine.

I hope you will enjoy reading the tales gathered in this year's anthology as much as I did. Many thanks to all the gracious authors who allowed us to reprint them here.

—Terri Windling

Comics 1993
by Will Shetterly and Emma Bull
(with help from Laura Poehlman)

Will Shetterly: If you've never been interested in comics but you care about fine writing, there are four names you should know: Alan Moore, Neil Gaiman, Eddie Campbell, and Scott McCloud.

Alan Moore is the author of the best examination yet of the superhero, the *Watchmen* series (still available in a trade paperback from DC Comics). In 1993, Moore was involved in two projects, *1963* (Image Comics), a skewering yet affectionate look at the superhero tradition in the early 1960s, and *From Hell* (Kitchen Sink Press), a series that may prove to be the definitive literary handling of Jack the Ripper.

Neil Gaiman writes *Sandman* (DC Comics), the only comic book to win a World Fantasy Award. DC has been kind enough to issue hardcover and paperback collections as the series progresses. This year saw the release of *A Game of You*, a six-part tale with an introduction by Samuel R. Delany, and *Fables & Reflections*, a collection of short stories, with an introduction by Gene Wolfe. Gaiman also writes *Miracleman* (Eclipse Comics), a deconstructionist superhero series begun by Alan Moore.

Eddie Campbell's work falls into two categories, the overtly fantastical Deadface stories, which tell about Bacchus and other Greek gods who have survived to the present day, and the whimsical adventures of Alec, the author's alter-ego. The earliest Deadface stories have been collected in *Immortality Isn't Forever* from Dark Horse; the earliest Alec stories can be found in *The Complete Alec*. Campbell is also an illustrator; some people find his style sketchy, but I think it delightfully evocative. New Alec and Deadface work continues to be published by Dark Horse.

Scott McCloud created the science-fiction series, *Zot!* (Eclipse Comics), but he's listed here for his nonfiction work. His *Understanding Comics* is a book that uses the comic book form to explain the craft and art of comic book storytelling. Like all good books exploring the creation of a particular thing, it ends up telling the reader something about the nature of creation. Though the section on color is superficial and U.S. comic book lettering conventions are generally accepted without comment, this is a brilliant and insightful work.

For those of you who are reading this because you already like comics or because you think you might like comics, there are a pair of promising newcomers you should seek out. Jeff Smith's *Bone* (Cartoon Books) is fantasy. If Walt Kelly and the Fleisher Studio had collaborated after reading *The Lord of the Rings*, the result might have been much like this. The first six issues of *Bone* have been collected into *The Complete Bone Adventures*.

Terry Moore's *Stranger in Paradise* does not have a supernatural element (not as of the second issue anyway), but if the World Fantasy Award can go to *The Silence of the Lambs*, a fine work of horror that is less fantastic than *Moby Dick* or *Huck Finn*, I'll plug good work, that, like *The Silence of the Lambs*, may not be fantastical but will appeal to most readers of fantasy. This is the story of two young women and their misadventures in love; perhaps Betty and Veronica for Generation X.

Laura Poehlman: Terry LaBan's *Cud* (Fantagraphics) hasn't wrenched my heart like his *Unsupervised Existence* used to, but I laugh so much when I read *Cud* I just don't care.

Lethargic Comics Weakly by Greg Hyland and Steven Remen (Alpha) is deceptively packaged as a spoof of superhero comics. These guys make fun of every part of the comics medium and crack the kind of private jokes that makes the world love "Mystery Science Theatre 3000."

Girlhero, by Megan Kelso (High Drive), is undeniably a Riot Grrl book without any feminist posturing. Obviously, I can't describe this comic. I thought it was *great*. I force people to read it all the time.

Tales of the Beanworld by Larry Marder (Eclipse). I believe *Beanworld* is the best comic book ever done, sometimes. Issue number 20 was one of 'em.

Crap by J. R. Williams (Fantagraphics). I love this guy's cartooning. His stories are improving with every issue, and "Bud Boys" is always a juvenile delight.

Very Vicky, by John E. Mitchell and Jana E. Christy (Meet Danny Ocean), is different, nice to look at, fun to read. No angst, wacky storytelling, kinda doofy, not necessarily funny. Good, good, good.

Emma Bull: What, and I come along at the end with the broom? Humph. Well, I'll happily second all the above recommendations, and add a couple.

Donna Barr's *Stinz* (Mu), the ongoing story of a farming village peopled with Germanic centaurs, remains one of the most imaginative and down-to-earth comics going.

Shade, written by Peter Milligan and drawn by, among others, Chris Bachalo (DC/Vertigo), is always an adventure, full of edgy surrealistic storytelling and starring a character who can do almost anything—and regularly does.

Neil Gaiman and Chris Bachalo's miniseries for DC/Vertigo, *Death: The High Cost of Living*, is an account of the day that Death must spend incarnate among the living every hundred years. It's fast-moving, stylish, and full of delightful surprises, not the least of which is the nature of Death herself.

Phil Foglio's *Xxxenophile* (Palliard Press) is devoted to fantastical and science fictional erotica. It's inventive, amusing, and surprisingly affectionate.

And Allison Bechdel's *Spawn of Dykes to Watch Out For* (Firebrand Books), the latest collection of her "Dykes to Watch Out For" comic strips, may not be overtly fantastical, but it sure is funny, startling, moving, and completely addicting. Her characters are so vivid you'll find yourself gossiping about them.

Summation 1993
Horror

News of the year:

Much of the news continued to be bad for the publishing industry, particularly for those houses considered more "mainstream." There were some major upheavals which have already affected or will before long affect the genre.

Early in 1993, Morgan Entrekin, president and publisher of the recently merged Grove Press/Atlantic Monthly Press laid off the entire Grove editorial staff, with the exception of editor-in-chief Walt Bode. The move fueled speculation that Entrekin planned to cut Grove's frontlist, and to graft its prestigious backlist, which includes the works of Henry Miller, D. H. Lawrence, and Samuel Beckett, among others, onto that of Atlantic Monthly Press; Simon & Schuster announced that Poseidon Press, founded and run by Ann Patty for the last ten years, would be absorbed by Simon & Schuster, losing its independent status, but that Patty's job was "secure." Soon after, Patty departed. S&S president Carolyn Reidy was quoted by *Publishers Weekly* as saying that Patty left by mutual agreement "due to philosophical differences over the Poseidon Press imprint." Patty's attorney said that his client was "abruptly fired and permanently thrown out." Patty is now editing for Crown.

This all came in the wake of accusations leveled against Patty by the V. C. Andrews estate that she accepted money from ghostwriter Andrew Neiderman for services in producing the early, posthumously-published V. C. Andrews novels. Poseidon ceased publishing altogether in spring 1994. In its early days, the press did much to promote horror (albeit not by design) by publishing George R. R. Martin's novel *Armageddon Rag*, *The Books of Blood IV–VI* by Clive Barker (in hardcover, with new titles and surreal Fred Marcellino covers), Mary Gaitskill's collection, *Bad Behavior* and her novel *Two Girls, Fat and Thin*, and all of Patrick McGrath's fiction. Patty also worked with Harry Crews on his most recent novels and *Classic Crews: A Harry Crews Reader* and discovered V. C. Andrews. In its latter days, the house seemed more interested in the "big book" and was publishing less interesting material.

After persistent rumors throughout 1993, Hearst Publishing finally admitted that Avon Books and William Morrow were for sale for the right price. Reportedly, Hearst was approached early in 1993 by at least two companies interested in the book group. Initially, Hearst said that Morrow and Avon were not for sale, but discussions continued, with one offer made and rejected. Sources said the company was asking between $200 and $250 million. In mid-December *The New York Times* announced that MCA, Inc., owned by Matsushita Electric Industrial Company of Japan (and also parent company of Putnam), was close to signing a deal to acquire Avon and Morrow. However, in mid-January 1994, the deal apparently fell through for unknown reasons, leaving employees as perplexed and anxious as ever, despite the urging of the Hearst brass to ignore rumors. Some of their top authors, such as Ken Follett and John Irving, had already left for other publishers.

Random House dropped Joni Evans's two-year-old Turtle Bay Books imprint. Evans declined the offer of another position at Random House; Little, Brown cut thirty-eight jobs, mostly support positions, and closed its children's division New York office. The company is the publisher of John Fowles, author of *The Collector*, *The Magus*, *The French Lieutenant's Woman*, and *A Maggot*.

In contrast there was some good news as Bantam Doubleday Dell announced that it would revive Dial Press under Susan Kamil, formerly of Turtle Bay, who was named editorial director. The imprint will relaunch in 1995, and its mandate is to create "a small, focused list of distinctive fiction and serious nonfiction"; Warner announed the launch of a new imprint named Warner Vision for March 1994 intending to publish one major title per month as a "parallel frontlist imprint." The launch title is P. D. James's genre novel *The Children of Men*; Henry Holt announced it was expanding its adult list by about twenty-five percent in the coming year, so that the total number of books published would be about 175. Holt has published such genre writers as J. G. Ballard, Robert Sheckley, Robert R. McCammon, and Karen Joy Fowler.

January 1994 proved to be particularly bleak as Harcourt Brace announced that it was cutting back on its adult trade program, to concentrate on books that will do well in its Harvest trade paper imprint. About twelve editorial jobs were phased out, including that of Michael Kandel, whose fledgling hardcover line of science fiction was getting positive critical notices for Patricia Anthony's two novels and Jean Mark Gawron's *Dream of Glass*; Houghton Mifflin shut down Ticknor & Fields, a formerly defunct nineteenth century publishing house revived as an imprint of Houghton Mifflin in 1979. The imprint, whose most recent editorial director was John Herman, published about twenty titles a year including books by Robert Stone, Malcolm Bosse, Jimmy Breslin, William Gass, and Roger Kahn; Houghton Mifflin's Joseph Kanon, executive vice-president of trade and reference, then announced the layoff of eleven employees in the trade and reference division. Most of the layoffs are in business, sales and production; Lee Goerner, editor-in-chief at Atheneum, a thirty-five-year-old imprint of Macmillan, was told that the imprint was being discontinued after the spring 1994 list.

Paramount Publishing acquired Macmillan Inc., early in 1994 and officials announced that they would reorganize divisions, reduce the number of imprints and published titles and lay off up to 10 percent of the two companies' combined work force of 10,000. Macmillan had already discontinued the Collier Nucleus SF reprint line edited by James Frenkel. The last title appeared in August. Macmillan was founded in London in 1843 by two Scottish brothers and was bought by British media entrepreneur Robert Maxwell in 1988. After Mr. Maxwell died at sea in 1991, the company declared bankruptcy and was put up for sale.

In other news, Zebra has eliminated the monthly horror title from its Pinnacle imprint as of January 1994. This will reduce its regular horror output to two Zebra titles per month; Pharos Books, publisher of nonfiction books on horror, has been sold to a reference-book publisher; Starmont House, the small press publisher founded by Ted Dikty, ceased publication as of March 1, 1993 and sold selected assets to Robert Reginald's Borgo Press. Upon Dikty's death, his daughter had planned to continue publishing, but a bad automobile accident forced her to terminate the business. Borgo has discontinued the Starmont House name and has merged the company with its own existing series, but will use the imprint "Ted Dikty Books." Items not acquired by Borgo have been declared out-of-print; Spine Tingling Press, publisher of horror audio tapes and of publisher Richard Sutphen's collection, *Sex Punks and Savage Sagas*, is backing away from horror but will continue to publish the New Age and other nonfiction material with which the press started.

Denis Kitchen's Kitchen Sink Press has bought Tundra Publishing. Kitchen Sink publishes a variety of titles including "underground" comics, hardcover trade paperbacks, card sets and other material. Tundra was established in 1990 by Kevin Eastman, co-creator of the Teenage Mutant Ninja Turtles. Horror writer Philip Nutman was editor of Tundra for part of its existence.

John Silbersack, editor-in-chief of the Questar imprint at Warner Books for only about six months, went to HarperCollins as vice-president and editor-in-chief of science fiction and fantasy to launch a program in hardcover, trade and mass market paperbacks. Before joining Warner, Silbersack created the Roc Books program for Penguin in the U.S. and the U.K.; Betsy Mitchell, named editor-in-chief of science fiction at Warner, will be

xl Summation 1993: Horror

relaunching the company's SF/fantasy list in September 1994 with a new name picked by Mitchell—Warner Aspect. The Questar name, started by Brian Thomsen, will be dropped. Mitchell plans to move the line more toward SF than in the past, but there are several horror anthologies in the pipeline, and Warner recently published Dan Simmons's *LoveDeath*, a collection of novellas.

After months of speculation, Lou Aronica finally left his position as deputy publisher at Bantam to become senior vice-president and publisher of the Berkley Publishing Group, where he will be responsible for all creative and marketing activities at Berkley. Aronica founded and ran the Spectra science fiction and fantasy imprint. Bantam announced that Nita Taublib, lately associate publisher of women's fiction, will take Aronica's place as vice-president and deputy publisher. She will work closely with Irwyn Applebaum in directing the editorial department and will oversee the various imprints.

In the U.K., Robinson Publishing has announced the launch of a new mass market horror and fantasy line, to be called Raven Books. The scheduled launch date is May 1994. Editorial director Stephen Jones will head the new imprint, which will initially publish one title per month. The line will be designed to present original novels rather than reprints. Robinson has previously published numerous anthologies in the SF/fantasy/horror field. The first acquisition for the line is Dennis Etchison's *Shadowman*, published in the U.S. by Dell/Abyss; Deborah Beale, publisher of England's Millennium SF imprint at Orion Books, resigned in October. A week later, Charon Wood—her assistant and editor at the line—resigned as well. Caroline Oakley, fiction editor at Headline, moved over near the end of the year to head the Millennium imprint. Beale will retain a part-time role as consultant in copy writing and marketing. Beale and Wood started the line two years ago when they both left Random Century with Anthony Cheetham, who formed the Orion Publishing Group. Working with Cheetham, Beale had previously started and built the very successful Legend imprint there; Headline and Hodder & Stoughton merged to create Hodder Headline. Hodder was a 125-year-old privately owned family publishing house, and is perceived as a publisher of the old school. The house has been suffering financially, and there were many layoffs in 1990 and 1991. Headline, only seven years old in contrast, has been consistently successful over recent years.

Magazine news:
The U.K.'s *Fantasy Tales*, on hiatus since early 1992, will officially cease to exist. The long-lived (sixteen years) small press magazine, co-edited by Stephen Jones and David Sutton, became a paperback anthology after seventeen issues in magazine format. During that period, it won the World Fantasy Award and multiple British Fantasy Awards and was one of the most influential horror magazines in the field. Robinson Publishing began issuing *Fantasy Tales* in 1988 as a paperback original, with four of the seven volumes reprinted in the U.S. by Carroll and Graf. Robinson, under its Magpie imprint, will be bringing out *Fantasy Tales Presents The Giant Book of Fantasy & The Supernatural*, edited by Jones and Sutton, with about forty stories, all bought for *Fantasy Tales*.

Amazing Stories suspended publication with its December 1993 issue. According to editor-in-chief Kim Mohan, "TSR is currently exploring a redesign . . . in terms of format and schedule." Tor Books has contracted for two *Amazing Stories* anthologies, which will be one-third reprint and two-thirds new material edited by Kim Mohan and it has been reported that the magazine is going to publish quarterly digest-sized issues. *Gorezone*, sister publication to *Fangoria*, edited by Anthony Timpone, ceased publication with issue #26 due to lack of sales. Part of the problem was that there was no clearcut difference between the two magazines. Steve Pasechnick's cross-genre magazine, *Strange Plasma*, publishes its last with issue #8. *Aboriginal SF*, published by Charles Ryan, has been granted nonprofit status by the I.R.S., lowering its mailing costs. *Crime Beat*, edited by T.E.D. Klein, folded.

Montilla Publications plans to replace the short-lived but impressive digest-sized nonfiction magazine *Tekeli-li! Journal of Terror*, with *It: The Magazine of Insidious Terror*. The new magazine will reemerge in 8½ × 11 format, and although announced for October 1993, it had still not surfaced by early January 1994. The first issue of *Horror: The News Magazine of the Horror and Dark Fantasy Field* debuted at the World Fantasy Convention in Minneapolis. The monthly is meant to be the equivalent of *Locus* and *Science Fiction Chronicle* in the SF field. It is edited by John and Kim Betancourt and published by The Wildside Press.

Other odds and ends of news:

Warner Books, which was to publish the alleged diary of Jack the Ripper in the fall of 1993 with a first printing of 200,000 copies, decided to cancel the project after the diary's authenticity was challenged by an eleven-page report issued by Kenneth W. Rendell, a British dealer in historical documents. The British publisher Smith Gryphon went ahead with its publication anyway, and Hyperion subsequently published the diary in the U.S.; on April 2, British author/bookseller David Britton was jailed under Britain's Obscene Publication Act in Manchester, England, and ordered to serve a four-month sentence. He has been at odds with Manchester police since the 1989 publication of his novel *Lord Horror* (Savoy). Since the book was ruled obscene, Savoy and Britton have been involved in police raids, court cases, and the threat of destruction of a number of their publications, including a comic based on *Lord Horror*. A 1992 court ruling calling for destruction of the impounded novel was overturned, but the impounded material is still being held by police and the case has yet to come to trial.

Rushdie update: The president of the Norwegian publisher of *The Satanic Verses* was shot in the back outside his home in Oslo in October. This after the 1991 stabbing death of the Japanese translator and an attack on the book's Italian translator the same year. Rushdie continues to make surprise appearances in the U.S., most recently in Boston, Massachusetts, where he appeared after a talk by Susan Sontag.

The British Fantasy Awards were announced. Graham Joyce's novel *Dark Sister* won the August Derleth Award; Nicholas Royle won for his short story "Night Shift Sister" (from *In Dreams*); David Bell and Stuart Hughes won the Best Small Press Award for their magazine *Peeping Tom*; *Darklands 2*, edited by Nicholas Royle, won for Best Collection/ Anthology; Jim Pitts won for Best Artist; Conrad Williams won the Icarus Award for Best Newcomer, and a Special Committee Award was given to Michael Moorcock.

Dan Simmons won the Theodore Sturgeon Memorial Award for best short story for "This Year's Class Picture," from *Still Dead* (Ziesing/Bantam).

Jane Yolen's poem "Will," which was picked up by *The Year's Best Fantasy and Horror: Sixth Annual Collection*, won the Rhysling Award for short poem.

Patricia C. McKissack's *Dark-Thirty: Southern Tales of the Supernatural* (Knopf, 1992) won a 1993 Newbery Honor Medal and the 1993 Coretta Scott King Author Award for young adult literature.

The Horror Writers of America (now The Horror Writers Association) held its annual meeting and Stoker Awards banquet June 18–19, 1993, at the Warwick Hotel in New York City. The keynote speaker was director John Carpenter. The awards were received by Thomas F. Monteleone for his novel *Blood of the Lamb* (Tor); Elizabeth Massie for her first novel *Sineater* (Pan); Stephen Bissette for *Aliens: Tribes* (Dark Horse Comics) tied with Joe R. Lansdale for "The Events Concerning a Nude Fold-Out Found in a Harlequin Romance" (*Dark at Heart*) in the novelette category; Dan Simmons for his short story "This Year's Class Picture" (*Still Dead*); Norman Partridge for his collection *Mr. Fox and Other Feral Tales* (Roadkill Press); Christopher Golden for his nonfiction book *Cut! Writers on Horror Film* (Berkley). The Life Achievement Award was won by Ray Russell. For information on joining this professional organization (there are several different kinds of memberships), write Virginia Aalko, Executive Secretary, Horror Writers Association, 5336 Reef Way, Oxnard, CA 93035.

Following is a biased and eclectic sampling of the novels I read and enjoyed during the year:

The Ice-House, by Minette Walters (St. Martin's Press), is a well written, convoluted mystery. A body is found mutilated in an abandoned icehouse on the property of three women labeled "lesbians and witches" by their neighbors. Ten years past, the master of the manor, from all accounts a despicable man, had disappeared. His wife claimed he simply left when her family's money ran out. Is it his body in the icehouse? Astute portrayals of multi-layered personalities, including detectives and suspects, coupled with revelations of certain old family secrets, make for a dark and enjoyable debut. Highly recommended.

The Sculptress, by Minette Walters (St. Martin's), published later in the year and as good as *The Ice-House*, was honored with the Edgar Award in the Best Novel category. A huge, menacing woman in prison for killing and carving up her mother and sister is known by the other inmates as "Sculptress." A journalist writing a book on the infamous case becomes absorbed, almost obsessed with the case. Did someone else actually commit the murders or is she being manipulated by her subject? What *is* the truth? The twists and turns are completely believable, mostly because of Walters's gift for characterization. A disturbing tale of murder and madness. Highly recommended.

Suckers, by Anne Billson (Atheneum), is an exuberant debut about a not-so-classic romantic triangle in London during the 1980s: Dora, the sardonic heroine, a "creative consultant"; Duncan, a photographer with whom Dora has been infatuated for many years; and Rose Murasaki, who used to be known as Violet, before Duncan and Dora staked her through the heart and chopped her up into several pieces a decade earlier. A dark, gleeful satire about vampires. Highly recommended.

In the Electric Mist with the Confederate Dead, by James Lee Burke (Hyperion), finally gives me the opportunity to praise one of my favorite writers. Burke is best known for his Dave Robicheaux thriller/mysteries, which take place in New Iberia, Louisiana. In each novel the reader learns more about Robicheaux, a cop. The prose is quite fine, the dialogue perfect. Occasionally things bog down while Burke acquaints (or reacquaints) the reader with events from a previous book. *In the Electric Mist . . .* isn't Burke at his best but it's still worth reading. And this particular novel is a ghost story. A movie crew is filming a Civil War epic in New Iberia. The star is a drunk and a psychic (or perhaps hallucinating). In the swamps he finds and shows Robicheaux the skeletal remains of a man wrapped in chains—a murder Robicheaux witnessed over thirty-five years before. In addition, a serial killer is stalking prostitutes. The southern flavor of the fiction and finely wrought characterizations of main and secondary players *make* this series. Some readers feel that Burke's earlier, non-series novels are even better. Read him!

The Golden, by Lucius Shepard (Ziesing/Bantam), is an important addition to vampire literature. With his reputation already established in fantasy and science fiction, Shepard should now garner further acclaim and a whole new audience. *The Golden* is a mature work of significance and beauty. Using the detective story as a base, Shepard explores good and evil as philosophical questions and traces the development of a young vampire (a former Parisian detective in "life"). Bleheim is assigned by the Patriarch to uncover the murderer of the Golden, a specially-bred human meant to enrich the bloodlines of the vampire families both literally and metaphorically. Erotic and visionary, Shepard packs an enormous amount into this short (243 pages), fast-moving novel, substantially adding to vampire arcana. Highly recommended. The Ziesing editions are sold out.

Winter Prey, by John Sandford (G.P. Putnam), is the fifth in the Lucas Davenport series. Sandford's skillful characterizations make for an entertaining page-turner, a must for aficionados of the serial killer/police procedural subgenre of suspense fiction. Davenport, now retired from official police work and living in rural Wisconsin, is drawn from his seclusion by the murder of a family of three. Child porn, the deadly, icy cold of Wisconsin's winter, and a new romantic entanglement for the protagonist are important elements of the plot. Recommended.

Thor, by Wayne Smith (St. Martin's), is a somewhat goofy but engaging werewolf novel. The story is told primarily from the point of view of the family dog, a German shepherd. Something is wrong with one of the family members and only Thor realizes how serious the problem is (although, believably, he doesn't understand what the wrongness means). Smith realistically captures the essence of "dogginess" and the pack mentality of canines, saving the novel from silliness. This is not an anthropomorphic novel wherein the dog behaves in a human manner, such as the much-ballyhooed mystery novel from Turkey, *Felidae* by Akif Pirincci (Villard). While I have mixed feelings about whether *Thor* is entirely successful, I found the story, and Thor himself, quite moving.

In contrast, *Felidae* purports to be from the cat's-eye view yet has this cat quoting philosophy, making erudite comments about classical music, and generally behaving like a snotty human with few if any catlike traits. The only way something like this can work is if it's done as straight satire. *Felidae* can't seem to make up its mind what it is. I read about ninety pages and gave up in irritation.

Close to the Bone by David Wiltse (Putnam, 1992) initially struck me as a typical psycho-terrorist thriller but gradually the protagonist, John Becker, imposed himself on my consciousness. Becker is the F.B.I.'s terrorist stopper extraordinaire, a hunter who can feel what his prey is feeling (sound familiar?). In this prequel to *Prayer for the Dead*, an interesting adult relationship develops between Becker and a novice female agent. Nothing particularly new here but the novel does carry the reader along nicely.

Wiltse's *The Edge of Sleep* (Putnam) is much better. It takes place ten years after *Close to the Bone*. Someone is kidnapping and murdering nine-year-old boys, and Becker, now retired, is back on the job at the behest of his ex-lover and former protégé, Karen Crist. Crist is now second-in-command, and a divorced mother. Working together forces them both to acknowledge the emotional loose ends and lingering charge of their former relationship. And the nature of the case brings up a lot of guilt and fear as Crist realizes just how easy it is to lose control and abuse a child. The portrait of the sociopathic couple responsible for the crimes is a fascinating one. Highly recommended.

Mary, Mary, by Ed McBain (Warner Books), is the newest of the author's Matthew Hope novels, all named after fairy tales. In this one, a reclusive woman with a beautiful but quirky garden is accused of murdering and mutilating three little girls. Several witnesses have seen Mary Barton with each of the girls, and one witness has even seen Mary bury the last girl in her garden. With the overwhelming evidence against her and Mary's odd reluctance to defend herself, her attorney, Matthew Hope, has a tough case on his hands. McBain is never less than readable and this is a good, suspenseful addition to the series.

Drawing Blood, by Poppy Z. Brite (Dell/Abyss), is about the surviving son of a famous underground comic artist of the sixties who murdered his wife and youngest child, then killed himself. Twenty years later, Trevor, the survivor, returns to Missing Mile, the quiet town (from *Lost Souls*) where it all happened to find out why he alone was allowed by his father to live. Trevor draws, too, and fears his own powerful emotions. Meantime, a young hacker on the run from the F.B.I. is moving north from New Orleans and also ends up in Missing Mile. Inevitably, the two, neither of whom has ever loved before, meet and the erotic sparks fly. As in *Lost Souls*, Brite's first novel, the author is dead-on when it comes to teenage and post-teenage angst and her writing is lush and expressive. But the comic art background of Trevor and his father seems wasted and the plot is minimal. Brite occasionally uses "insider" names and details in a forced rather than natural way, distancing the reader rather than drawing her in.

Flight, by Fran Dorf (Dutton), is a fine novel about small-town cruelty, violence, deceit, and redemption. Lana Paluka, a young woman tripping on LSD at Woodstock, is allegedly pushed over a two hundred foot cliff by her boyfriend, but miraculously survives with no physical injury other than broken legs. However, she is catatonic and remains so for twenty years. Now, in the 1990s, she has mysteriously "awakened." Jack Wells, a reporter and former acquaintance of Lana's, unearths inconsistencies while covering this human interest story. Lana's boyfriend, Ethan Skitt, has been in prison most of those twenty years, convicted of her attempted murder and later (during an escape) the murder of one of the witnesses against him. Just as Lana awakes, Ethan has again escaped from prison. What really did happen that day? How did Lana survive the fall? A spellbinding read. Highly recommended.

The Last Magician, by Janette Turner Hospital (Henry Holt), is a fine, darkly mysterious novel about power—sexual, political, and economic—and how that power affects relationships. Lucy, who has given up a life of privilege to become a prostitute, tells the tale of four people whose childhood activities have locked them into an uneasy bondage with one another. The fulcrum is Charlie, a Chinese-Australian photographer/filmmaker who has used his innate alienness to see and interpret the world around him. Charlie is the "last magician," who uses his creative skills as a cudgel to punish one of the four, the one responsible (and unpunished) for a tragedy years earlier. Dark as the "quarry," the warren of caverns and tunnels running beneath Sydney's streets and inhabited by the homeless, this novel is rich, sharp, and magical. My description cannot do it justice. The last twenty pages were so painful I found it difficult to finish the book. Highly recommended.

Exposure, by Kathryn Harrison (Random House), is another dark novel that explores the power of photography. Ann Rogers seems to have it all—she's attractive, smart, loved by her husband, and co-owns a thriving video business in NYC. But as plans for a retrospective of her father's photography come together, Ann's life begins to unravel. After her mother died in childbirth, Ann was raised by her father and his sister. Between the ages of seven and fourteen Ann posed nude for her father (shades of Sally Mann's photographs of her children). Always in fragile health because of diabetes, Ann has become a kleptomaniac and a speed freak. The coming exhibition of her father's disturbing photos (many taken without her knowledge, and not found until after her father's suicide) dredges up forgotten memories of her traumatic childhood. Increasingly self-destructive and out of control, Ann makes a tortuous voyage of self-discovery in this powerful and provocative novel. Highly recommended.

Dr. Haggard's Disease, by Patrick McGrath (Poseidon Press), is a short novel by an expert creator of unreliable narrators. This story is told from the point of view of Dr. Haggard, who fell from grace as a promising young surgeon in a major London teaching hospital to end up as an invalid country doctor just before and during England's entry into World War II. Dr. Haggard's disease is "passion." His short but passionate affair with the wife of one of his superiors has ruined him, physically and emotionally. Throughout more than half of the novel there's no trace of the fantastic or grotesque one associates with McGrath's work. The grotesquerie, or at least strangeness and darkness, begin to permeate the story as it becomes clear that the narrator has become obsessed with the son of the woman he loves, a young man seeking to discover more about this stranger whose presence so obviously intruded into his family. It also becomes clear that Dr. H.'s passion for Fanny Vaughn has never subsided, merely switched gears slightly. I enjoyed the novel but only true fans of McGrath will find it as rewarding as I did. His use of the unreliable narrator is getting stale. It's time for a new voice and new point of view.

Blackburn, by Bradley Denton (St. Martin's), is an exuberant, funny, and original work about a serial killer unlike any other in fact or fiction. Blackburn's murders each comment on the sins and nastiness of Middle America. Only those who deserve it are killed. Wife beaters, dog killers, stealers from the weak—they all get their due. Blackburn is an innocent everyman who wanders America and is probably the most moral person in the book. Highly recommended.

Shella, by Andrew Vachss (Alfred A. Knopf), is an interesting complement to *Blackburn*. I've been a reader of Vachss since his remarkable first novel *Flood*. Unfortunately, I found his subsequent novels increasingly disappointing as his regular cast of characters became more and more saccharine and his agenda more obvious at the expense of fresh storytelling. Each book is about an evil (somehow having to do with child abuse) threatening the "happy family" and that evil's eventual disposal. However, *Shella* is not part of the "Burke" series. The unnamed first person narrator is kind of an idiot savant of murder. Uneducated, but innately bright enough to pick up pointers on any kind of killing, he is in search of his girlfriend Shella, who disappeared while he was in prison. To find her he has to kill various people (none of them very nice—like Blackburn, he seems to pick out those who deserve it) and infiltrate a white supremacist group. It's terse and fast-moving. I never quite believe in this character although he's quite likable.

Skin, by Kathe Koja (Delacorte/Abyss), is one of the best horror novels of the year. There's a lot of mixed opinion about Koja's work—I think she's an ambitious experimenter with language. Her writing demands reader participation: it's dense and jam-packed with images, so you can't just glide along. Each of her novels seems to be reaching toward an idea of what it means to be an artist. *Skin*, her third, is the most direct in asking How far can you go? How far *should* you go? and examines the trendy subject of body modification. Tess Bajac, a metal sculptress, and Bibi Bloss, a dancer and performance artist, together develop Surgeons of the Demolition, a performance art group (modeled on Mark Pauline's Survival Research Laboratory) incorporating Tess's mechanized sculptures with Bibi and her dancers' ritualized bloodletting. The performances increase in intensity, danger, and mayhem until one of the performers accidentally dies. The group fragments. Tess wrestles with her personal and professional relationship with Bibi and her own creative block while Bibi travels with her "acolytes" into her own hellish world of more and more extreme body manipulation. Initially, it bothered me that there was no questioning of Bibi's motivation for her increasingly self-destructive acts in the name of art, but by the end I was convinced that it didn't matter. Koja's prose style perfectly complements the difficult material and I'm amazed at her success at visualizing performance art for the reader. Deeply disturbing and highly recommended.

Created By, by Richard Christian Matheson (Bantam), was accurately described by reviewer Linda Marotta as *"The Player* meets *The Dark Half."* Matheson's reputation as a writer of horrific short-shorts is secure; his novel debut, while perhaps not as dazzling as some of his shorter works, effectively demonstrates his inside knowledge of the entertainment industry. Writer/producer Alan White creates *The Mercenary*, in the words of critic Linda Marotta, "the most violent, exploitative and successful TV program the world has ever seen, and unwittingly unleashes an evil by-product of his id with a life of its own." He then has to choose between fame and fortune from his "child" and killing off the evil twin who is murdering those who cross him. Matheson has Hollywood and Hollywood types down perfectly, but the TV show sounds more intriguing than immoral, so somehow the point gets lost in the shuffle.

Trick of the Eye, by Jane Stanton Hitchcock (Dutton, 1992), is a peculiarly satisfying mystery novel with gothic overtones. Faith Crowell is a specialist in *trompe l'oeil* (the art of using illusion in art) and is commissioned by reclusive grande dame and widow Francis Griffin to recreate, in art, her mysteriously murdered daughter's debutante ball. Faith's hard-earned integrity and independence are threatened by the life of glittery power and privilege shown her by Griffin. Under all the surface elegance and style lies rot and evil. What makes the novel so fresh is that every time I was certain I knew how Faith would behave or react to something, I was surprised by the character's (and so, the author's) ingenuity and commitment to herself. An impressive first novel.

An Incident at Bloodtide, by George C. Chesbro (Mysterious Press), is the new Mongo mystery. Mongo, for those who don't know, is a dwarf who has been a circus performer, but is currently a professor of criminology and a detective. Only a few of the eleven or so mysteries about him have involved the occult, but they're all entertaining. Initially, *An Incident at Bloodtide* seems to contain an occult element when brother Garth's folksinger wife, Mary Tree, is terrorized by a former boyfriend. Sacra Silver claims magical powers and does seem to have a mysterious hold over Mary. But the plot really gets going when an environmental activist dies in the Hudson River near where Garth and Mary live in upstate New York and the two brothers uncover a corporate plot generated by sheer greed.

Loose Among the Lambs, by Jay Brandon (Pocket Books), is an absorbing and highly technical courtroom suspense novel about a San Antonio D.A. up for reelection who gets caught up in the middle of what could be a major political embarrassment. The accused serial child molester is a prominent lawyer with influence throughout the city. The novel is an interesting contrast to Andrew Vachss's Burke novels—both authors deal with the repercussions of various kinds of child abuse. Brandon convincingly shows the immediate psychological effects on an abused child in addition to the long-term effect, as abused becomes abuser in adulthood.

Angel, by Garry Kilworth (Gollancz, U.K.), is the SF and fantasy author's first horror/ suspense novel. It's noteworthy for its fine characterizations of some very troubled individuals as well as for its premise. The year is 1997 and in every large city, all over the world, arson has become the number one crime. San Francisco cop Dave Peters witnesses the unnatural white fire burning up a tenement, and notices a beautiful young man watching the conflagration. It appears that an angel may be the mysterious arsonist/serial killer/mass murderer, and if this is so how does one stop such a creature? Nice horror debut.

Dead Girls, by Richard Calder (HarperCollins, U.K.), is a brilliant but flawed science fiction novel with undertones of horror. The "dead girls" are the aftermath of a plague that struck London—daughters of men who became infected with mutative nanotechnology while enjoying oral sex from Cartier automotons. As they reach puberty, these daughters metamorphize into something both more and less than human. There's intrigue and romance, the whole being imbued with sexual politics unusual in SF or horror. Not for readers exclusively interested in horror but for those with a taste for provocative science fiction.

Brother Termite, by Patricia Anthony (Harcourt, Brace & Co.), is also SF/horror. This one is about the invasion of Earth by a hive mind—to be accurate, sentient giant termites— and the results of the decision made years before to accommodate rather than resist the invaders. Told mostly from the point of view of Brother Reen, chief of staff to the figurehead President of the U.S., it's a political thriller about mind control and interspecies romance. By turns funny, brutal, and depressing, it's also about love, treachery and self sacrifice. A very good read.

Elvissey, by Jack Womack (Tor), is indubitably science fiction yet, like Womack's other novels, it's certainly dark enough and bleak enough for some horror readers. In the grim future, the Western world is ruled by the multinational Dryco Corporation and Elvis Presley is an icon worshipped by an increasingly significant cult. Dryco sends a married couple back to an alternate 1950s America to find and kidnap the *real* Elvis so that he can be installed as a puppet, thereby increasing the corporation's already considerable influence on political affairs. This dark and brilliant novel is part of an ongoing series, but each book reads just dandy on its own. *Elvissey* won the 1993 Philip K. Dick Award.

Smilla's Sense of Snow, by Peter Hoeg (Farrar, Straus & Giroux), is a brilliant novel from Denmark with an unforgettable narrator. Smilla, daughter of an Inuit hunter and a rich Danish scientist, was taken from Greenland to Denmark after her mother's death while hunting. Smilla's bitterness against her father poisons her life; she sees herself as a self-sufficient loner, very much the outsider to both cultures. Only the suspicious death of a young boy she befriended draws her out of her self-imposed loneliness. The language of this multilayered work is rich yet incisive. Perhaps more interesting than the dark suspense aspects (although there actually *is* an horrific/SF element to the mystery) is the protagonist's relationship to snow and ice and her use of mathematics to protect her from feeling. One of the best books of the year, one that deservedly made the N.Y. *Times* bestseller list.

The Food Chain by Geoff Nicholson (Overlook Press) is all about food, glorious food. Rich American wastrel Virgil Marcel, the young owner of L.A.'s trendiest restaurant, is invited to join London's secretive Everlasting Club, where a party has been going nonstop for 350 years. A nasty, funny satire, *The Food Chain* looks at food as "fuel, fad, aphrodisiac, political tool, metaphor, and myth." It's mean-spirited but fun.

Counterparts by Nicholas Royle (Barrington, U.K.) is the first novel by this talented Briton who has been rapidly earning a reputation as a fine short story writer (he had a story in *The Year's Best Fantasy and Horror: Sixth Annual Collection* and is in this year's). A tightrope walker who can't stop mutilating himself and an actor who loses his sense of identity seem to be shifting identities—or are they two aspects of the same personality? The novel is oblique and often opaque, yet there are moments of great clarity and horror. This is a disturbing work that never quite comes into focus.

X, Y, by Michael Blumlein (Dell/Abyss), is the second novel by the author of the acclaimed collection *The Brains of Rats* and the novel *The Movement of Mountains*. Frankie dances topless in New York City while her lout of a boyfriend Terry, a former medical student, works in a bookstore. One night, as a siren blares in the street, something happens as Frankie and a patron of the bar lock eyes and each goes into convulsions, then passes out. The next morning, Frankie wakes to the knowledge that she is a man—despite all physical evidence to the contrary. Terry and Frankie's relationship, not great to begin with, goes downhill from there as Frankie tries desperately to get back to her male body and Terry's initial insensitivity turns into a fullblown mean streak waiting to explode into outright violence. The escalation of the cruelty and savagery that saturates the two characters in this grim story is terrifying, but what is most fascinating is that this is no simple female-seeking-revenge story—it's about a man's realization of the bullshit that women go through, and it's *his* revenge, using the supposed power of the female body, that turns both participants in the relationship into monsters.

Shadow Play, by Frances Fyfield (Pantheon), is an intelligent and surprising crime novel about a strange little man named Mr. Logo. British Crown prosecutor Helen West has failed to convict him on various indecent assault charges for lack of proof that he has actually ever *touched* any of the children. The man has been mad since the mysterious disappearance of his wife and daughter years before. Is he guilty? If so, of what? Meantime, West's long-term relationship with a cop may be falling apart. Fyfield, who also writes under the name Frances Hegerty, is excellent at depicting complex adult relationships. Highly recommended.

Other novels of note: *The Late Man* by James Preston Girard (Atheneum); *Wetwork* by Philip Nutman (Jove); *The Unfinished* by Jay B. Laws (Alyson); *The Stones of Muncaster Cathedral* by Robert Westall (FSG-YA); *The Book of Common Dread* by Brent Monahan (St. Martin's); *7 Steps to Midnight* by Richard Matheson (Tor); *Nightmare, With Angel* by Stephen Gallagher (Ballantine); *The Butcher Boy* by Patrick McCabe (Fromm International); *The Animal Hour* by Andrew Klavan (Pocket); *Shadow Walkers* by Nina Romberg (Pinnacle); *Darkest Day* by Christopher Fowler (Little, Brown, U.K.); *To the White Sea* by James Dickey (Houghton Mifflin); *Wolf Whistle* by Lewis Nordan (Algonquin); *The Unforgiving* by Charlotte Cory (Faber & Faber); *The List of Seven* by Mark Frost (Morrow); *Anno Dracula* by Kim Newman (Carroll & Graf); *A Philosophical Investigation* by Philip Kerr (Farrar, Straus & Giroux); *Due North* by Mitchell Smith (Simon & Schuster); *Black Dogs* by Ian McEwan (Doubleday/Nan A. Talese); *Fan Mail* by Ronald Munson (Dutton); *The Long Lost* by Ramsey Campbell (Headline, U.K.); *Mr. Murder* by Dean R. Koontz

(Putnam); *Savage: From Whitechapel to the Wild West on the Track of Jack the Ripper* by Richard Laymon (Headline, U.K.); *The Last Aerie* by Brian Lumley (Tor); *Making Love* by Melanie Tem and Nancy Holder (Dell/Abyss); *Wild Blood* by Nancy A. Collins (NEL, U.K.); *Facade* by Kristine Kathryn Rusch (Dell/Abyss); *Animals* by John Skipp and Craig Spector (Bantam); *Is Underground* by Joan Aiken (Delacorte); *Complicity* by Iain Banks (Little, Brown, U.K.); *Heart-Beast* by Tanith Lee (Dell/Abyss); *The Darker Saints* by Brian Hodge (Dell/Abyss); *Afterage* by Yvonne Navarro (Bantam); *Half Light* by Frances Hegarty (Pocket); *Among the Dead* by Michael Tolkin (Morrow); *The Book of the Mad* by Tanith Lee (The Overlook Press); *The Vanishing* by Tim Krabbé (Random House); *Montezuma's Man* by Jerome Charyn (Mysterious Press); *Blue Crystal* by Philip Lee Williams (Grove); *The Angel of Pain* by Brian Stableford (Carroll & Graf); *Chimney Rock* by Charlie Smith (Henry Holt); *The Summoning* by Bentley Little (Zebra); *Vanishing Point* by Michaela Roessner (Tor); *The Crocodile Bird* by Ruth Rendell (Crown); *The Horses of the Night* by Michael Cadnum (Carroll & Graf); *Machine* by René Belleto (Grove); *Summer of Fear* by T. Jefferson Parker (St. Martin's); *Cock & Bull* by Will Self (Atlantic Monthly Press); *Juggling the Stars* by Tim Parks (Grove); *Shadow Counter* by Tom Kakonis (Dutton); *The Glass Mountain* by Leonard Wolf (Overlook); *Shadowman* by Dennis Etchison (Abyss); *Kipper's Game* by Barbara Ehrenreich (Farrar, Straus & Giroux); *Until Proven Guilty* by Christine McGuire (Pocket); *Mortal Memory* by Thomas H. Cook (Putnam); *Free* by Todd Komarnicki (Doubleday); *Vindication* by Frances Sherwood (Farrar, Straus & Giroux); *The Angel Carver* by Rosanne Daryl Thomas (Random House); *Agyar* by Steven Brust (Tor); *Irreparable Harm* by Lee Gruenfeld (Warner); *Fishboy: A Ghost's Story* by Mark Richard (Doubleday); *The House of the Toad* by Richard L. Tierney (Fedogan and Bremer); *The Throat* by Peter Straub (Borderland Press, Dutton); *Calling All Monsters* by Chris Westwood (HarperCollins); *The Book of Webster's* by J. N. Williamson (Longmeadow); *In the Garden of Dead Cars* by Sybil Claiborne (Cleis Press); *Beastchild* by Dean R. Koontz (Charnel House); *Twilight* by Peter James (St. Martin's); *The Forbidden Zone* by Whitley Strieber (Dutton); *Angel Kiss* by Kelley Wilde (Dell/Abyss); *The Girl with Kaleidoscope Eyes* by Graham Watkins; and *The Living One* by Lewis Gannett (Random House).

Anthologies:
I'm pleased to note that so far, my fears for the anthology market have been unfounded. Anthologies continue to be published by large and small publishers. 1993 was a bumper year for original anthologies. In no particular order:

Predators, edited by Ed Gorman and Martin H. Greenberg (Roc) opens strongly with a Koontz reprint, and good stories by Joyce Harrington, John Shirley, and Edward Wellen. The Wellen novella is not exactly horror but a mystery solved by an unusual protagonist— a victim of Alzheimer's Disease. The Shirley story makes a perfect fiction companion to last year's nonfiction study on the slasher film, *Men, Women and Chainsaws* by Carol J. Clover. There are also good stories by Richard Laymon, Richard T. Chizmar, Daniel Ransom and Rex Miller, and a wonderfully cynical endgame by John Coyne that is reprinted here. However, in between I found tired ideas and predictable conclusions. Annoyingly, there are no author biographies.

Hottest Blood, edited by Jeff Gelb and Michael Garrett (Pocket) has excellent stories by Nancy Holder, Thomas Tessier, and Bentley Little, some so-so stories, and a few very bad ones. There's one truly disturbing/repellent story by Graham Masterton. In general, there aren't enough stories here from the female character's point of view, and those that are generally treat the woman as victim.

The New Mystery: The International Association of Crime Writers Essential Crime Writing of the Late 20th Century, edited by Jerome Charyn (Dutton). I gather from George C. Chesbro's disappointing metafiction, "Imagine This," that the stories were all meant to be 3,000–5,000 words long. Out of these forty-two stories, sixteen are original and only a handful are first-rate. I suspect it's pretty tough to create a satisfying, multileveled mystery or crime story at that length, so mostly what the reader gets are vignettes. Lawrence Block's piece is the best of the originals. The impressive reprint lineup includes works by Harlan Ellison, Raymond Carver, Angela Carter, Flannery O'Connor, and Joyce Carol Oates. In all, the book is a useful showcase for familiarizing more readers with the writers within.

Journeys to the Twilight Zone, edited by Carol Serling (with Martin H. Greenberg uncredited on cover or title page) (DAW), are all originals except for one reprint by Rod Serling himself. Most of the stories in the anthology lack the kick of the best *TZ* episodes. There are some standouts, by Hugh B. Cave, Jack Dann, Alan Dean Foster, and Karen Haber, but on the whole this anthology just isn't scary.

The Sun Rises Red, edited by Chris Kenworthy (Barrington, U.K., 1992), is a thin but interesting anthology of seven stories that, despite its self-labelling as speculative fiction, contains mostly fantasy and very dark, often horrific stories. The book is plagued by a pretentious introduction proclaiming the contents to herald a new movement in science fiction. Kenworthy further pronounces every story "politically correct," which signals (to me) a passel of boring fiction. Luckily, Kenworthy's creed rarely gets in the way of his editorial judgment, although he *does* include two and a half of his own stories out of a total of seven. There are excellent stories here by Nicholas Royle, Joel Lane, and a collaboration by Mike O'Driscoll and Chris Kenworthy.

Sugar Sleep, edited by Chris Kenworthy (Barrington, U.K.), is another interesting anthology with crossover fiction. All the stories are highly literate, and the roster includes Rick Cadger, D. F. Lewis, Nicholas Royle, Andrew Rollinson, and Joel Lane. Again, though, Kenworthy errs in making grand proclamations in his introduction.

Confederacy of the Dead, edited by Richard Gilliam, Martin H. Greenberg, and Edward E. Kramer (Roc), is an anthology of mostly original Civil War stories. Many of the pieces are from the southern point of view and effectively show the bitterness and misery accompanying the South's defeat. Among the best is a science fiction story by Michael Moorcock (reprinted from *New Worlds* 2), and other excellent originals by Ed Gorman, Nancy A. Collins (reprinted here), Charles L. Grant, Gregory Nicoll, and George Alec Effinger. On the whole, though, there were too many zombies and not enough stories from the Northern point of view, for variety.

Xanadu, edited by Jane Yolen (Tor), has more fantasy than horror but there's a terrific poem by Jane Yolen and wonderful horror stories by Lisa Tuttle and Nancy Kress (the latter reprinted here). Highly recommended for its fantasy and dark fantasy.

After the Darkness, edited by Stanley Wiater (Maclay and Associates), is a non-theme dark crime/thriller/horror anthology. The anthology has a nice range of fiction with especially good stories by Thomas Tessier, Nancy Holder, Gary Raisor, Chet Williamson, Graham Masterton, Ed Gorman, and Joseph A. Citro.

Full Spectrum 4, edited by Lou Aronica, Amy Stout, and Betsy Mitchell (Bantam/Spectra), is a good, solid, mostly science fiction anthology with excellent dark fiction by Martha Soukup and Elizabeth Hand (the latter reprinted here).

Sinistre: An Anthology of Rituals, edited by George Hatch (Noctulpa #7), is a first-rate anthology with varied stories. The bset are by A. R. Morlan, Steve Rasnic Tem, Don D'Ammassa, Stephen M. Rainey, D. R. McBride, Graham Watkins, William Laughlin, James D. Reynolds III, and Connie Hirsch, along with good "psychollages" by t. winterdamon. One of the best anthologies of the year, with two stories chosen for this volume: those by A. R. Morlan and Steve Rasnic Tem. ($8.95 + $1.05 postage from Horror's Head Press, 140 Dickie Avenue, Staten Island, NY 10314.)

Touch Wood: Narrow Houses 2, edited by Peter Crowther (Little, Brown, U.K.), is a bit disappointing compared to *Narrow Houses*, but there are very good stories by Yvonne

Navarro, Steve Lockely, Karl Edward Wagner, Stella Hargreaves, Michael Marshall Smith, and Neil Gaiman.

Dark Voices 5, edited by David Sutton and Stephen Jones (Pan), starts off with a bang, as usual, with some very strong stories, and then it sags in the middle with intermittent energy bolstering the whole package periodically. There are excellent stories here by Dennis Etchison, Roberta Lannes (both reprinted here), as well as by Robert Holdstock, Graham Joyce, Nicholas Royle, Michael Marshall Smith, Kim Newman, and Brian Mooney.

Christmas Forever, edited by David G. Hartwell (Tor), is a mixture of mostly original SF/horror/fantasy Christmas stories. The most disturbing stories are by veteran Gene Wolfe and newcomer Maggie Flinn, and there's an exceptionally moving piece by Charles de Lint. Also, there's good work by Bruce McAllister and Joan Aiken. Overall, it's a charming anthology.

The Ultimate Zombie, edited by Byron Preiss and John Betancourt (Dell trade paperback) is a disappointment, with too much voodoo, not enough variation on the theme but good stories by S. P. Somtow, Lawrence Watt-Evans, and A. R. Morlan.

The Mammoth Book of Zombies, edited by Stephen Jones (Carroll & Graf), by contrast, is an excellent combination of reprints and originals which uses a broad interpretation of "zombie." The selections show intelligence and taste. Terrific originals by Graham Masterton, Nicholas Royle, Michael Marshall Smith, and David Riley are complemented by reprints by Clive Barker, Sheridan Le Fanu, Joe R. Lansdale, Lisa Tuttle, H. P. Lovecraft and others. The Masterton, Royle, and Smith stories are reprinted here.

The Ultimate Witch, edited by Byron Preiss and John Betancourt (Dell trade paperback), is good, with reprints by Ray Bradbury and Dean R. Koontz and notable original stories by Steve Rasnic Tem, Tanith Lee, and Nancy Holder.

Frankenstein: The Monster Wakes, edited by Martin H. Greenberg (DAW), seems to have been put together with no thought to variety or originality. No fewer than three stories take place in the frozen wastes of the north where Mary Shelley's *Frankenstein* ended—with Eskimos or Inuit used as "local color" rather than as three-dimensional characters. Most of the stories focus on the monster itself. Unfortunately, some of the good stories that would stand out otherwise suffer by being in such similar company. The best are by J. N. Williamson, Norman Partridge, William L. DeAndrea, Peter Crowther, Terry Beatty and Wendi Lee, Larry Segriff, and Brian Hodge.

The Weerde Book 2: The Book of the Ancients, devised by Neil Gaiman, Mary Gentle, and Roz Kaveney (Roc, U.K.) is an excellent follow-up to last year's shared world anthology. The best of these stories about mysterious powerful beings living amidst humans are those that stand alone. Most do, including excellent stories by Colin Greenland, Graham Higgins, Liz Holliday, David Langford, Marcus L. Rowland, Michael Ibeji, and Roz Kaveney. Skip the prologue and epilogue because you'll forget the first by the time you get to the end, anyway.

Terror Australis: The Best of Australian Horror, edited by Leigh Blackmore (Coronet, Australia), opens with a useful introduction to horror in general and Australian horror in particular. There are excellent stories in this mostly original anthology. The best originals are those by Terry Dowling (reprinted here), Bill Congreve, Leanne Frahm, Stephen Dedman, and Sharon A. Hansen.

1st Culprit: A Crime Writers' Association Annual, edited by Liza Cody and Michael Z. Lewin (St. Martin's—first pub., U.K. 1992) is a varied anthology of mostly original mystery stories with reprints having appeared only in the U.K. Standouts by James Melville and Susan Moody.

Malice Domestic, presented by Mary Higgins Clark and, as unacknowledged editor, Martin H. Greenberg (Pocket), is another good anthology of mystery stories, some with a dark edginess; the best are by Ed Gorman and Frances Fyfield.

More Whatdunits, edited by Mike Resnick (DAW), is all science fiction, but some of the best stories contain horrific elements. The kicker to this volume is that all the contributors have been involved in editing (a few tenuously) at some time in their careers. Good stories by Barry N. Malzberg and Ginjer Buchanan.

Snow White, Blood Red, edited by Ellen Datlow and Terri Windling (AvoNova), consists of fantasy and dark fantasy stories based on classic fairy tales. The darker stories in the volume include those by Tanith Lee, Esther Friesner, Nancy Kress, Steve Rasnic Tem, Melanie Tem, Wendy Wheeler, Kathe Koja, Lisa Goldstein, Leonard Rysdyk, Neil Gaiman, and a poem by Jane Yolen. The Gaiman and Yolen are reprinted here.

Monsters in Our Midst, edited by Robert Bloch (with Martin H. Greenberg on copyright page), is a follow-up to Bloch's *Psycho-Paths*, has an interesting variety of stories. The best— because most surprising—are those *not* about killers. My favorite stories were authored by John Coyne (reprinted here), Robert E. Vardeman, Ramsey Campbell, Robert Bloch, Chet Williamson, J. N. Williamson, and Steve Rasnic Tem.

In the Fog: The Final Chronicle of Greystone Bay, edited by Charles L. Grant (Tor), closes out the Greystone Bay anthologies in style, with seven consistently literate novellas and novelettes.

Deathport, edited by Ramsey Campbell (Pocket), is the third anthology presented by the Horror Writers of America. I've given my opinion on this series of shared world anthologies in past years and don't want to belabor the point. There are a few very good stories, some good ones, and too many uninteresting ones. I understand that next year's anthology is being edited by Peter Straub with the broad theme of ghost stories. I'm keeping my fingers crossed that the volume will be a far more inventive, original, and worthy showcase for the H.W.A.

Bizarre Sex and Other Crimes of Passion, edited by Stanislaus Tal (Tal Publications), is made up more of vignettes going for the violent surface shock than of real stories that leave disturbing ripples in the reader's consciousness. On the whole, it's disappointing, but with some good stories by Wayne Allen Sallee, Dawn Dunn, and Brad Boucher, and good erotic photo-montages by Róbert Gregory Griffeth. ($8.50 + $1 shipping to *Bizarre Sex and Other Crimes of Passion*, Tal Publications, P.O. Box 1837, Leesburg, VA 22075.)

Dark Seductions, edited by Alice Alfonsi and John Scognamiglio (Zebra), is another entry in the erotic horror sweepstakes and is even less successful. Bad writing, predictable plots, shallow characterizations, and cliché situations mar the stories—as do gender stereotypes. Here and there is a good story—one such by Rick Hautala, and another by J. N. Williamson—but they're few and far between.

Cold Cuts: Tales of Terror, edited by Paul Lewis and Steve Lockley (Alun Boks), is the first Welsh anthology I've seen. The writing quality is high although the stories aren't all that original. A few standouts by Bob Lock, Christopher Evans, Jane Del-Pizzo, Steve Lockley, and Catrin Collier.

A Wizard's Dozen: Stories of the Fantastic, edited by Michael Stearns (Harcourt Brace & Co./Jane Yolen), is an excellent all-original fantasy anthology. Some good, dark stories by Patricia C. Wrede, Charles de Lint, Debra Doyle and James D. MacDonald, and Bruce Coville.

Bizarre Bazaar 93, Volume II, edited by Stanislaus Tal (Tal Publications), is a "magazine anthology" with reprints by Brian Hodge, Joe R. Lansdale, and Stanley Wiater, and good new stories by Julie R. Good, Stephen Mark Rainey, Lucy Taylor, Jack Ketchum, Adam-Troy Castro, and a strong collaboration by Andrew H. Lynch and Wayne Allen Sallee. ($6.95 + $1.55 shipping payable to Tal Publications, *Bizarre Bazaar 93*, address above.)

Crosstown Traffic: Romance, Horror, Fantasy, Sf, Western Invade Crime Fiction, edited by Stuart Coupe, Julie Ogden, and Robert Hood (Five Islands Press Associates, Australia), is an excellent crossover anthology covering all genres. Most of the contributors will be unfamiliar to the American audience except for Robert Hood, Terry Dowling, and Bill Congreve (editor of *Intimate Armageddons*). Worth a look.

The Time Out Book of London Short Stories, edited by Maria Lexton (book editor of *Time Out*) (Penguin, U.K.) has collected a remarkably diverse group of young writers born or living in the U.K. The stories, all originals, are by Clive Barker, Lisa Tuttle, Neil Gaiman, Kim Newman, Anne Billson (*Suckers*), Gordon Burn (*Alma Cogan*), Nicola Barker (*Love Your Enemies*), Lawrence Norfolk (*Lemprière's Dictionary*), Will Self (*Cock and Bull*), and others. Some great crossover material and a few dark stories.

Constable New Crimes 2, edited by Maxim Jakubowski (Constable, U.K.), is a darkly entertaining original anthology with good stories by Kim Newman, Steve Rasnic Tem, and a good collaboration by Sidney G. Williams and Wayne Allen Sallee.

Air Fish: An Anthology of Speculative Works, edited by Joy Oestreicher and Richard Singer (Catseye Books), is a fat, 320-page trade paperback anthology with attractive interior art and a good cover. It features some excellent cross-genre material with a touch of horror; the best darker pieces are by Thomas Metzger, Jeff VanderMeer, Rhonda Eikamp, and Adam-Troy Castro. ($16.95 from Catseye Books, 904 Old Town Court, Cupertino, CA 95014-4024.)

Mondo Barbie, edited by Richard Peabody and Lucinda Ebersole (St. Martin's), contains reprint and original fiction and poetry about this female icon. Among the reprints is John Varley's "The Barbie Murders." There's no real horror (unless you consider Barbie herself a "horror," as some do), but some wonderfully surreal takes on the subject.

Thrillers, edited by Richard Chizmar (CD Press), is the debut volume of a new series in which four writers contribute 20,000 words each of original fiction to one volume. First up are Rex Miller, Nancy A. Collins, Ardath Mayhar, and Chet Williamson. The book is a nice mix of dark suspense, with the two Williamson stories the most successful. Collins does a good job reworking "Freaktent," here called "Freakbabies." Introduction by Joe R. Lansdale and afterwords by each author. The trade edition is $25 + $3 postage; the 500-copy limited is slipcased and signed by all the contributors and artists. The price is $60 + $3 postage, payable to CD Publications, P.O. Box 18433, Baltimore, MD 21237.

OMNI Best Science Fiction Three, edited by Ellen Datlow (OMNI Books) has ten original stories and one reprint from *OMNI*. Several contributions are horrific in nature including a novella by Scott Baker, and stories by Gahan Wilson, Simon Ings, and Ian McDonald (the latter reprinted here).

Danger in DC: Cat Crimes in the Nation's Capital, edited by Martin H. Greenberg and Ed Gorman (Donald I. Fine), has some good stories, all political in some way. Not much horror here, but there's a touch of the dark.

Best of the Midwest's Science Fiction, Fantasy and Horror Volume II, edited by Brian Smart, illustrations coordinated by Katherine Buburuz (ESA Publications), has few horror stories and is not much of a showcase for the writers. It's a sloppy production with too-small margins and an unattractive cover. There's a good horror story by Stephen M. Rainey.

Avant-Pop: Fiction for a Daydream Nation, edited by Larry McCaffery (Black Ice Books/ Fiction Collective Two) has an embarrasing *noir*ish joke introduction by McCaffery. The cover copy is better than the book itself, in which there are only a handful of genuinely interesting and lively originals or reprints by such as Tim Ferret, Kathy Acker, Samuel R. Delany, William T. Vollmann, Mark Leyner, and comic artist John Bergin. But it's a great looking package for $7.

The Dedalus Book of Dutch Fantasy, edited and translated by Richard Huijing (Dedalus), gives readers a rare look at fantasy from another culture, since few of these thirty stories have been translated into English before. The darker stories are the strangest, and I think, the best.

Christmas Ghosts, edited by Mike Resnick and Martin H. Greenberg (DAW), is too gentle to be called a horror anthology, but it has a good story by Terry McGarry and a good collaboration by Kathe Koja and Barry N. Malzberg.

Pulphouse: The Hardback Magazine, the last issue #12, edited by Kristine Kathryn Rusch (Pulphouse), although a couple of years overdue, makes a fitting finale to the series, with an eclectic mixture of fantasy, dark fantasy, and horror. The most powerful horror stories are by David B. Silva, James Dorr, Rory Harper, and Darrell Schweitzer.

Ghosttide, edited by Claudia O'Keefe (Revenant Books), is a new projected anthology series of original horror. Literate and low key, it features good stories by Susan Palwick and David J. Schow. The trade paperback is $12.50 from Revenant Books, P.O. Box 55024, Sherman Oaks, CA 91413.

The Scary Story Reader, collected by Richard and Judy Dockrey Young (August House), is a collection of forty-one urban legends aimed at 10–13 year olds. Entertaining renditions and a good introduction by Jan Harold Brunvand.

The following original anthologies had some horrific fiction: *Writers of the Future IX,* edited by Dave Wolverton—no cover credit (Bridge); *Temporary Walls: An Anthology of Moral Fiction,* edited by Greg Ketter and Robert T. Garcia (World Fantasy Convention/ DreamHaven Books); *New Worlds 3,* edited by David Garnett (Gollancz, U.K.), and *Sword and Sorceress X,* edited by Marion Zimmer Bradley (DAW).

The following original anthologies were not seen by me: *All Hallow's Eve: Tales of Love and the Supernatural,* edited by Mary Elizabeth Allen (Walker), described by *Locus* as sixteen romantic ghost stories, mostly regencies; and *Bruce Coville's Book of Monsters: Tales to Give You the Creeps* (Scholastic), a YA anthology of thirteen stories, eight original.

The following anthologies used mostly reprint material: *Strange Dreams,* edited by Stephen R. Donaldson (Bantam/Spectra), is a gorgeous trade paperback of fantasy stories, reprinting a variety of unfamiliar stories by familiar names in and out of the field: Rudyard Kipling, Orson Scott Card, Lucius Shepard, Jorge Luis Borges, Franz Kafka, Harvey Jacobs, Rachel Pollack, and M. John Harrison, among others. A wonderfully eclectic collection of stories selected by Donaldson out of love for the story—not a bad way to put together an anthology. Highly recommended; *The Oxford Book of Modern Fairy Tales,* edited by Alison Lurie (Oxford University Press), covers stories between 1839 and 1989 and includes reprints by Charles Dickens, Nathaniel Hawthorne, Philip K. Dick, Bernard Malamud, Angela Carter, Tanith Lee, and Jane Yolen. This volume includes "The New Mother," a story by Lucy Lane Clifford which Lurie mentioned in her nonfiction book on fairy tales, *Don't Tell the Children.* A lovely package with the Maxfield Parrish illustration for "The Reluctant Dragon" used as cover art; *Strange Things Sometimes Still Happen: Fairy Tales From Around the World,* edited by Angela Carter with illustrations by Corinna Sargood (Faber & Faber), reprints forty-five feminist fairy tales from twenty-three cultures, from Siberia to Surinam. *Mysterious Cat Stories,* edited by John Richard Stephens and Kim Smith (Carroll & Graf), reprints supernatural cat stories encompassing material from the thirteenth century to the present, with stories by August Derleth, Bram Stoker, Washington Irving, Robert Bloch, H. P. Lovecraft, M. J. Engh, and Nancy Etchemendy's modern classic, "Cat in Glass"; *Shudder Again,* edited by Michele Slung (Roc), reprints erotic horror stories by Thomas Ligotti, Arthur Machen, Harlan Ellison, Robert Aickman, Lisa Tuttle, T. H. White, Arthur Conan Doyle, and includes four originals; *100 Hair-Raising Little Horror Stories,* edited by Al Sarrantonio and Martin H. Greenberg (Barnes & Noble) (not seen); *To Sleep, Perchance to Dream . . . Nightmare: 30 Terrifying Tales,* edited by Stefan R. Dziemianowicz and Martin H. Greenberg (Barnes & Noble Books), is a hefty hardcover with classic stories by Sheridan Le Fanu, Bram Stoker, Ambrose Bierce, C. L. Moore, Richard Matheson, Charles Beaumont, Karl Edward Wagner, Clive Barker, and Bruce McAllister; *Nursery Crimes: 30 Classic Tales of Horror,* edited by Stefan R. Dziemianowicz, Robert Weinberg, and Martin H. Greenberg (Barnes & Noble), reprints stories about children and evil by Theodore Sturgeon, Sarban, Lisa Tuttle, Stephen Gallagher, Margaret St. Clair, and others; *100 Ghastly Little Ghost Stories,* edited by Stefan R. Dziemianowicz, Robert Weinberg, and Martin H. Greenberg (Barnes & Noble), is a great-looking package, with a lovely cover by Jack Eckstein, reprinting stories from 1838 to 1993, and with two original stories by Donald R. Burleson and Stefan Grabinski (the above four anthologies are only available at Barnes & Noble Bookstore chains and are very low-priced); *The Lifted Veil: The Book of Fantastic Literature by Women,* edited and with an introduction by A. Susan Williams (Carroll & Graf), is an important reprint anthology of gothic and horror stories. Considering the self-imposed time limitations of the anthology—it only includes stories originally published between 1806 and W.W. II—the wealth of material is astounding, and clearly demonstrates the relatively unacknowledged influence of female writers during that time on the genre. The book contains stories by Louisa May Alcott, Mary Shelley, Charlotte Brontë, Harriet Beecher Stowe, Edith Wharton, Isak Dinesen, and others less well-known. The only quibble I have is that the editor, in her introduction, seems utterly unaware of horror anthologies outside of Great Britain; *The Mists From Beyond,* edited by Robert Weinberg, Stefan R. Dziemianowicz, and Martin H. Greenberg (Roc), puts together a mix of ghost stories by Charles Dickens, Bram Stoker, Shirley Jackson, John Updike, Davis Grubb, Philip José Farmer, and Peter Straub. Considering the plethora of female writers of short tales, four out of twenty is disappointing in a reprint anthology; *Grifters and Swindlers: Stories from Ellery Queen's Mystery Magazine and Alfred Hitchcock's Mystery Magazine,* edited by Cynthia Manson (Carroll & Graf), with reprints by Donald Westlake, David Morrell, Jim Thompson, and others less well-known; *Hollywood Kills,* edited by the staff of *Mystery Scene* (Carroll & Graf), reprints Fritz Leiber's classic "The Girl With the Hungry Eyes," and stories by Tom Reamy, F. Paul Wilson, Jon L. Breen, Ross MacDonald, and John Jakes, among others; *The Deadliest Games: Tales of Psychological Suspense from EQMM,* edited by Janet Hutchings (Carroll & Graf), has stories by Andrew Vachss, Joyce Carol Oates, Robert Campbell, Bill Pronzini, and Stanley Ellin; *The Gates of Paradise: The Anthology of Erotic Short Fiction,* edited by Alberto Manguel (Clarkson Potter), doesn't have much horror but does include Richard Christian Matheson's (wrongly credited to Matheson, Sr.) chiller "Arousal"; *Four Classic Ghostly Tales,* edited and with an introduction by Anita Miller (Academy Chicago), has four rare novellas by Oliver Onions, Robert Hitchens, Elizabeth Gaskell, and D. K. Broster; *The Year's Best Mystery and Suspense Stories 1993,* edited and with an introduction by Edward D. Hoch (Walker), reprints stories by Ed Gorman, Joyce Carol Oates, Ruth Rendell, Donald Westlake, and inappropriately, one by Hoch himself; *The Year's 25 Finest Crime and Mystery Stories: Second Annual Collection,* edited by the staff of *Mystery Scene* with an introduction by Jon L. Breen (Carroll & Graf), covers 1991 and 1992 with no overlap with the Walker volume. But this one seems to range farther afield, with reprints by Pat Cadigan, Edward Bryant, Lawrence Block, Ed Gorman, Sharyn R. McCrumb, Ruth Rendell, and Norman Partridge from venues as varied as *Pulphouse* and *The Bradbury Chronicles.* Both anthologies list the best novels of the year and list the field's awards; *Best New Horror 4,* edited by Stephen Jones and Ramsey Campbell (Carroll & Graf), only overlaps with Windling and my *Year's Best* with three stories. The book has a generous representation of British writers and classier covers than the first three volumes in the series; *The Year's Best Horror XXI,* edited by Karl Edward Wagner (DAW), is the most eclectic of the three horror *Year's Bests* in its choices, with Wagner choosing more stories from the small press; *The King of the Cats, and Other Feline Fairy Tales,* edited by John Richard Stephens (Faber & Faber), collects variations on "Puss in Boots" by Giovanni Francesco Straparola, Charles Perrault, and Giambattista Basile, variations on "The King of Cats" by William Baldwin and Washington Irving, and other cat fairy tales by Jane G. Austin, Julian Hawthorne (son of Nathaniel), and a host of other writers; *The Best American Short*

Stories 1993, edited by Louise Erdrich (Houghton Mifflin), is notable for its inclusion of stories by Harlan Ellison and Mary Gaitskill; *The Complete Fairy Tales of Charles Perrault*, illustrated by Sally Holmes and newly translated by Neil Philip and Nicoletta Simborowski (Clarion Books), with an introduction and notes on the stories by Neil Philip; *Masterpieces of Terror and the Unknown*, edited by Marvin Kaye (Guild America), is a large collection of rarities and classics, with a few original stories, including a good one by Carole Buggé; *Daughters of Darkness: Lesbian Vampire Stories*, edited by Pam Keesey (Cleis Press), uses reprints (the overused "Carmilla") and excerpts from books by Pat Califia, Jody Scott, Jewelle Gomez, Elaine Bergstrom, and less familiar names in a good-looking trade paper-back package; *Lighthouse Horrors*, edited by Charles G. Waugh (Down East Books), set from the Americas to Great Britain to India (not seen); *Horror by Lamplight* (Chancellor Press, U.K., no editor) forty-two classic horror stories from Sir Walter Scott to Anne Rice (not seen); *Alfred Hitchcock's Tales of the Supernatural and the Fantastic*, edited by Cathleen Jordan (Smithmark), is an instant remainder with thirty-three stories from *Alfred Hitchcock's Mystery Magazine* (not seen); and *The Television Late Night Horror Omnibus*, edited by Peter Haining (Orion, U.K.)—thirty-two stories used as the basis for late night horror shows on TV (not seen).

As in the past, specialty presses published the bulk of the single-author collections during 1993 but the commercial publishers did slightly better than last year. The following collections contain horror or crossover material:

Ace published Joe R. Lansdale's *Bestsellers Guaranteed* with a cute dragon on the cover, undoubtedly surprising buyers unfamiliar with Lansdale's "God of the Razor," "The Fat Man," "My Dead Dog, Bobby," and "Dog, Cat, and Baby," all reprinted in the book. While the stories aren't all-out graphic horror in the best Lansdale tradition they're not for dragon-lovers. This is a reprint of the chapbook originally published by *Pulphouse* as *Stories by Mama Lansdale's Youngest Boy*.

Viking published the late Robert Westall's *The Call and Other Stories*, which appeared in the U.K. in 1989. Despite the copyright notice, I believe this is the collection's first appearance in the U.S. Viking also published Stephen King's 800+ page collection of stories and an essay reprinted from as diverse sources as OMNI, *Cemetery Dance*, *The New Yorker*, various anthologies, and small press chapbooks, titled *Nightmares and Dreamscapes*. Included for the first time in trade edition is the novella "Dolan's Cadillac." King provides brief notes to each story in the back of the book.

Farrar, Straus & Giroux published *Demons and Shadows: The Ghostly Best of Robert Westall*, the first of a projected two volumes. A couple of the eleven stories appeared in *Antique Dust*, an earlier collection. One original story is included.

Tor published four collections in 1993: Ramsey Campbell's *Strange Things and Stranger Places*, which includes the novellas "Needing Ghosts" and "Medusa"; Brian Lumley's *Fruiting Bodies and Other Fungi*, which collects thirteen stories and a novella published between 1962 and 1989, including the British Fantasy Award-winning title story; Terry Bisson's first collection, *Bears Discover Fire*, which reprints most of his short fiction output. While mostly science fiction and fantasy, at least one story, "The Coon Suit," is horror. It appeared in *The Year's Best Fantasy and Horror: Fifth Annual Collection*. Bisson, a novelist who only began selling short stories a few years ago, has a unique voice and swept the science fiction awards with the title story of this collection. It also includes his Nebula award-nominated novelette, "England Underway" (reprinted here); and Charles de Lint's *Dreams Underfoot*, which collects most of his fantasies, both charming and dark, about the imaginary city of Newford, including several reprinted in our *Year's Best Fantasy and Horror* annuals.

Knopf brought out a new collection by Gabriel García Márquez. The twelve stories in

Strange Pilgrims were translated by Edith Grossman and a few (including the darker ones) are original to the collection; also from Knopf, the first collection of eccentric stories by Japanese writer Haruki Murakami, *The Elephant Vanishes.* "TV People" was reprinted in *The Year's Best Fantasy and Horror: Fourth Annual Collection.*

William Morrow and Company published *Some Days You Get the Bear,* a wonderfully varied collection of Lawrence Block's short stories, which originally appeared in venues ranging from *Penthouse* and *Ellery Queen's Mystery Magazine* to the anthologies *Monsters in Our Midst* and *Justice For Hire.*

Dan Simmons's collection of five novellas (two reprints), entitled *LoveDeath* showcases the wide range of Simmons's writing talent. "Entropy's Bed at Midnight" is a mainstream/ horrific masterpiece about memory, loss, and the fear of losing a child (its only previous publication was as an expensive small press item); "Dying in Bangkok," in a different (longer) version than that which appeared in *Playboy* (or herein) is a powerful sexual horror story; "Flashback" is a convincing science fiction/political thriller appearing for the first time; "Sleeping With Teeth Women" puts *Dancing With Wolves* to shame; and "The Great Lover" is a tour de force about death and sensuality on a W.W. I battlefield. Published by Warner Books.

Christopher Fowler's most recent collection, *Sharper Knives,* was published by Warner (U.K.) back in 1992 but I didn't see it until 1993. There's no copyright information distinguishing originals from reprints but some of the stories are familiar to me from other sources. It includes "On Edge," which appeared in last year's *Year's Best.* Nicely illustrated by John Bolton, Graham Humphries, Lee Brimmicombe-Wood, Martin Smith, David Lloyd, and Richard Parker.

Pan's Picador imprint published Scott Bradfield's *Greetings From Earth,* collecting material from his earlier collections and some new stories. Bradfield is respected by the literary as well as the genre scene.

Headline (U.K.) published *Out Are the Lights and Other Tales* by Richard Laymon, a collection of the title novel and five short stories, previously uncollected; *Nightshades,* a new collection by Tanith Lee with the title novella and twelve other stories (including "The Devil's Rose," which appeared in *The Year's Best Fantasy: Second Annual Collection;* and Ramsey Campbell's *Cold Print,* an expanded edition from the one published by Scream/Press in 1985 which contains the entirety of Campbell's first book, *The Inhabitant of the Lake and Less Welcome Tenants.*

Alyson Publications brought out Pat Califia's *Melting Point,* which, like her debut collection *Macho Sluts,* is full of exhilarating and passionate s/m and bondage stories. Two of the stories are science fiction and they all have their dark side.

Northeastern University Press brought out *From Jo March's Attic: Stories of Intrigue and Suspense* by Louisa May Alcott, edited by Madeleine B. Stern with Daniel Shealy, the fifth in a series reprinting the romantic thrillers she wrote anonymously before *Little Women;* the nine tales collected here originally appeared in *Frank Leslie's Lady's Magazine* between 1868 and 1807.

St. Martin's Press brought out *Charles Dickens' Christmas Ghost Stories,* selected and introduced by Peter Haining. The fascinating introduction mentions that Dickens was responsible for perpetrating the tradition of a "white Christmas." And he was the first to link the holiday with the supernatural. The excellent, but uncredited, fine line drawings throughout are those with which the stories were originally published.

Scholastic published three collections aimed at the young adult market. The best is Robert Westall's excellent *In Camera and Other Stories,* which should appeal to all lovers of ghost stories—beautiful, evocative, quirky, and creepy. (The title story is reprinted herewith.) Highly recommended. Also good is Judith Gorog's *Please Do Not Touch,* a collection held together by the conceit of a haunted art gallery. There are some good, scary stories in this one but the collection on the whole is probably a bit tame for the adult market. Jim Murphy's *Night Terrors* is the weakest of the three collections—"horror lite." Mostly trite plots with little suspense and a tendency to talk down to the audience.

Bantam Spectra brought out *Impossible Things*, Connie Willis's second collection of short fiction, which while mostly science fiction, contains a couple of stories with horrific elements, particularly "Jack," about guess who?

Delacorte published *A Fit of Shivers*, Joan Aiken's marvelous new collection for young adults, back in 1992, but I just got hold of it this year. Aiken is one of the few writers (along with Robert Westall and Diana Wynne-Jones) specializing in young adult horror and dark fantasy who doesn't insult the intelligence or taste of that audience and can be enjoyed equally by adults.

And in the U.K., Gollancz published *A Creepy Company*, another collection of Aiken's original ghost/horror stories.

Also from the U.K. comes *Tales My Mother Never Told Me* by Jennie Gray, an original collection of eight supernatural tales published by The Gothic Society, and a facsimile reprint of Ingulphus's *Tedious Brief Tales of Granta and Gramarye*, published by Ghost Story Press.

Grosset and Dunlap published *Ghostly Tales and Eerie Poems of Edgar Allan Poe*, aimed at young adults with full color illustrations by Larry Schwinger.

Faber and Faber—U.S. and U.K.—brought out the refreshing debut collection *Love Your Enemies* by Nicola Barker. Barker writes in a realistic style with occasional flourishes of dark and light fantasy. Highly recommended.

August House brought out two collections: *Queen of the Cold-Blooded Tales*, short ghost stories by professional storyteller Roberta Simpson Brown, and *Rachel the Clever: And Other Jewish Folktales* by Josepha Sherman.

Overlook Press published *The Man Who Took a Bite Out of His Wife*, the first collection by Bev Jafek, a winner of the Pushcart Prize.

The Return of Count Electric and Other Stories, from The Permanent Press, marked the auspicious short fiction debut of the eclectic William Browning Spencer, author of *Maybe I'll Call Anna*. Not much that's horrific here, but worth a look for those interested in crossover material.

Arkham House brought out *Alone with the Horrors: The Great Short Fiction of Ramsey Campbell 1961–1991*, a solid retrospective of a master of the macabre with interiors and cover art by J. K. Potter. Arkham House also published Nancy Kress's collection, *The Aliens of Earth*, which contains an excellent variety of science fiction, fantasy and horror. Interiors by Jane Walker and cover by Ed Paschke. $26.95 payable to Arkham House Publishers, Inc., Sauk City, WI 53583.

Pat Cadigan's third collection, *Dirty Work*, was published by Mark V. Ziesing Books, with a striking cover by Rick Berry and design by Arnie Fenner. Cadigan is one of the best short story writers in any genre and this collection amply demonstrates her versatility. A slipcased signed and numbered edition of 300 copies is available for $65, and a trade edition is available for $29.95. Add $3.00 postage for each, from Mark Ziesing, P.O. Box 76, Shingletown, CA 96088.

Edgewood Press brought out *Hogfoot Right and Bird-Hands*, a trade paperback of Briton Garry Kilworth's short fiction. The gorgeous black & white illustration on the cover is by Ian Miller and the introduction is by Robert Holdstock. Kilworth is one of the most underrated short story writers of his generation. He finally received some deserved attention when his and Holdstock's novella "The Ragthorn" won the World Fantasy Award a couple of years ago. This collects some of Kilworth's work from 1985 to 1992 and includes "Inside the Walled City," "White Noise," and "Island With the Stink of Ghosts." Highly recommended. $9.00 + $1.00 postage to Edgewood Press, P.O. Box 380264, Cambridge, MA 02238.

Silver Salamander Press (published by John Pelan and Michael McLaughlin, the founders of Axolotl Press) is a new imprint specializing in short fiction, novellas, and collections. The first production by the press was Michael Shea's novella, "I, Said the Fly" (see under "Chapbooks"); Silver Salamander also published *Close to the Bone*, Lucy Taylor's second collection. Taylor seems to be making erotic horror her specialty and is a writer to watch and start collecting. Her best stories draw the reader into the lives of her misfits and grotesques. Taylor is good on dialect and the southern gothic sensibility she occasionally shares with Poppy Z. Brite and Elizabeth Massie. Introduction by Edward Bryant. Lovely spot illustrations by Mark Brill and a good cover on the paperback. A 50-copy limited is available in sexy black leather, with red type and the paper cover illustration as a frontispiece ($65), as well as a 300 copy cloth edition ($35); both editions are signed and numbered, while a 500-copy perfectbound trade paperback is $10.

Lost in Booth Nine, by Adam-Troy Castro, also came out in 1993 and is another collection of erotic horror by a talented newcomer. It contains an introduction by Kristine Kathryn Rusch and Dean Wesley Smith. There is a 500-copy trade paperback edition for $10, a 300-copy signed and numbered hardcover for $35, and a 50-copy leatherbound for $65. Silver Salamander Press, 22926 N.E. Old Woodinville-Duval Road, Woodinville, WA 98072.

Dedalus/Hippocrene published Stefan Grabinski's collection *The Dark Domain*. Grabinski's work may be familiar to small press magazine readers as a result of Miroslaw Lipinski's extraordinary effort to bring the work of this author (who died in 1936) to the attention of a wider audience.

Another new publisher, Incunabula, brought out *Antiquities*, collecting seven science fiction, fantasy and ghost stories by John Crowley. The cover and interiors were designed by John D. Berry. The first book Incunabula published was *They Fly at Çiron*, a novel by Samuel R. Delany, with cover and interior design by Olav Martin Kvern. The hardcover editions of 1,000 copies cost $25 and are beautiful objects. A signed and numbered edition of 77 copies of the Crowley is available for $90. The Delany limited is sold out. Incunabula, P.O. Box 30146, Seattle, WA 98103-0146. Add $3 for postage.

Bump in the Night Books published *Voyages into Darkness*, collecting short stories by Stephen Laws and Mark Morris. One Laws is an original. Both are newer horror writers with several novels between them and story publication mostly in the defunct British magazine *Fear*. Signed and limited to 350 copies. At $17.50 it's expensive for such a thin trade paperback (with only five stories). Illustrations by Frank X. Smith. $17.50 to Bump in the Night Books, 133-135 Elfreths Alley, Philadelphia, PA 19106.

Borderlands Press published Poppy Z. Brite's first collection, *Swamp Foetus* with disturbing cover art by Rick Lieder and good interior illustrations by Rodger Gerberding. The material includes everything from *The Horror Show*, where she established her early reputation, up to her most recent short stories and a vignette that appeared in *Gauntlet* in 1993. Good-looking package. The 350-copy signed and numbered limited edition is $50. The trade edition is $20. $3 postage per book. Borderlands Press, Box 3833, Baltimore, MD 21228-0233.

Deadline Press brought out a classy limited edition of Richard Laymon's short stories. Of the twenty stories, about half are original to the collection. The new stories show a greater range in his work. The beautiful jacket, endpapers, and interior illustrations are by Larry Mori. *A Good, Secret Place*, which quickly went out of print, was limited to 574 signed and numbered copies; 26 signed and lettered copies. Deadline Press, 4884 Pepperwood Way, San Jose, CA 95124.

DreamHaven published their second and third books (the first was the poetry collection *Now We Are Sick*), *Temporary Walls*, in honor of the World Fantasy Convention in Minneapolis, and the gorgeous *Angels and Visitations: A Miscellany* by Neil Gaiman. Included are ten stories and several poems, with a striking cover by Dave McKean and interior illustrations by Bill Sienkiewicz, Jill Karla Schwarz, Steve Bissette, Charles Vess, P. Craig Russell, Randy Broecker, and Michael Zulli. The trade edition is $20 + $5 postage. The 400-copy limited will be signed by Gaiman and the artists and numbered. It costs $100 + $5 postage and can be ordered through DreamHaven Books & Comics, 1309 4th St. S.E., Minneapolis, MN 55414.

New Noir by John Shirley was part of the new Black Ice Book series, which also published the *Avant-Pop* anthology. Three stories are reprinted from *Heatseeker*, three are previously uncollected. Good cover and interior illustrations by Ferret. A nice collectible paperback for $7; it can be ordered through Fiction Collective Two, 4950/Publication Unit, Illinois State University, Normal, IL 61761.

Montilla Publications (which also put out the magazine *Tekeli-li!*) published *Driftglider and Other Stories*, written and illustrated by Jeffrey Osier. I've always enjoyed Osier's artistic phantasms and they work well with his stories. In paperback for $9.95 to Montilla Publications, 106 Hanover Avenue, Pawtucket, RI 02861.

Broken Mirrors Press published *Bunch!*, a collection of idiosyncratic crossover fiction. The beautiful black on silver cover is by Ian Miller. Introduction by Barry N. Malzberg. $8.95 payable to Broken Mirrors Press, P.O. Box 380473, Cambridge, MA 02238.

Asylum Arts published *City of Mazes: and Other Tales of Obsession* by Cynthia Hendershot, incredibly hot erotic horror tales with little violence but a lot of sex/mystery/surrealism. Well-written and very enjoyable. $8.95 to Asylum, P.O. Box 6203, Santa Maria, CA 93456.

Macabre, Inc. Press starts off its new series of chapbooks in support of up and coming small press writers with Stephen M. Rainey's *Fugue Devil and Other Weird Horrors*. Illustrated by Augie Weidemann, cover by Philip Reynolds. To be published every nine months in a limited paperback of 1,000 copies at $5.95. For information write to: Macabre, Inc., 454 Munden Avenue, Norfolk, VA 23505.

Earth Prime Productions published *Weird Family Tales*, a collection of five interconnected stories by Ken Wisman, as the first volume of the Solo series. Cover is by Donald W. Schank. $3.75 to *Weird Family Tales*, Earth Prime Productions, P.O. Box 29127, Parma, OH 44129.

Three Stones Press (publisher of the magazine *Heliocentric Net*) led off their Detours line of dark fiction chapbooks with J. N. Williamson's *The Fifth Season*, collecting eight stories, two of which are originals. The introduction is by James Kisner and cover illustration by B. E. Bothell. This numbered and signed paperback is limited to 1,500 copies at $4.95 + $1 shipping to: Three Stones Publications Ltd., P.O. Box 68817, Seattle, WA 98168-0817.

W. Paul Ganley (editor of *Weirdbook*) brought out *Transients and Other Disquieting Stories*, Darrell Schweitzer's first horror collection, with illustrations by Stephen E. Fabian in three editions: Paperback at $8.95; hardcover at $26.50; and deluxe signed at $42.50. W. Paul Ganley: Publisher, P.O. Box 149, Amherst Branch, Buffalo, NY 14226-0149.

Dark Regions Press launched a new chapbook series, intending to publish six a year. The first is *The Odd Lot: The Selected Works of Albert J. Manachino*, illustrated by Larry Dickison and with an introduction by Michael Ambrose. It collects nine stories from various small presses and one original; *Southern Discomfort: The Selected Works of Elizabeth Massie* collects nine stories by the Stoker Award–winning author including "Hooked on Buzzer," the first story to bring Massie attention beyond the small press. Yvonne Navarro introduces the book and H. E. Fassl illustrates it, with his darkly disturbing art; *Needles and Sins: The Selected Works of Michael Arnzen* has an introduction by Karl Edward Wagner, and excellent illustrations by Marge B. Simon. In it are twelve stories by Arnzen, a promising writer from the small horror press who has had stories in Karl Edward Wagner's *Year's Best Horror Stories* series. Single copies $5.95 + (3) .29 stamps or $27.00 a year.

Creation Press in the U.K. brought out *Crawling Chaos: Selected Works 1920–1935* by H. P. Lovecraft, collecting twenty-one Cthulhu Mythos stories. Edited by James Havoc with an introduction by Colin Wilson.

Mystery Scene/Pulphouse published a trade paperback edition of Ed Gorman's *Dark Whispers*, the fifth in a series of single-author collections. The eleven horror and crime stories are mostly from original anthologies published over the last decade. $5.95 from Pulphouse, Box 1227, Eugene, OR 97440.

The Haunted Library (U.K.) published *Supernatural Pursuits*, a collection of three original stories by William I. I. Read, illustrated by Nick Maloret.

Lemon Drops and Other Horrors by Donald R. Burleson has nineteen originals and reprints from a promising writer who has had at least one story in Stephen Jones and Ramsey Campbell's *Best New Horror*. Production is primitive, with a stapled, uneven look but readable type. $6.95 from Hobgoblin Press, Box 806, Bristol, RI 02809.

Bruce Boston had three poetry collections published in 1993. Talisman brought out *Specula: Selected Uncollected Poems: 1968–1993*, a lovely, well-designed item for $6.95, payable to Talisman, Box 321, Beech Grove, IN 46107; and Night Visions brought out the attractive *Accursed Wives*. $3.50 payable to Night Visions, Ree Young, Route 2, Box 357, Troy, NC 27371. Also, from Chris Drumm books, *Night Eyes*, eight stories and poems in a good-looking paperback edition. $4.50 for the trade edition, $8.00 for a signed edition (which comes with a broadside called *The Last Existentialist*) from Chris Drumm Books, P.O. Box 445, Polk City, IA 50226. Boston is an excellent poet of the fantastic.

Bone-Break Psychobilly Stew by Richard L. Levesque was published by Wudge Press. For $3 it has good art by Jeffrey Thomas and blood & guts "poetry." Wudge Press, 2227 Woodglen Drive, Indianapolis, IN 46260.

Jellyfish Mask, written by William Ramseyer and illustrated by Kathryn Otoshi is a lovingly self-published package with SF and surreal vignettes, very fine art and design work, and a terrific full color cover. $12.95 to Buy Yourself Press, P.O. Box 2885, Atascadero, CA 93423-2885.

Wordcraft of Oregon published quirky crossover writer Don Webb's collection of eight stories and a poem, *The Seventh Day and After*, the seventh publication in the publisher's Speculative Writers Series. $7.95 payable to Wordcraft of Oregon, P.O. Box 3235, La Grande, OR 97850.

The Last Rite by Brian Lumley collects six stories spanning 1971–1988, with illustrations by John Borkowski. The reproduction quality of the art isn't great. $8 for the paperback and $35 for the signed and numbered hardcover from Jwindz Publishing, 3812 E. 55th Street, Minneapolis, MN 55417. $1.50 for shipping.

Hate Doom Blood Sex by Wayne Edwards is a selection of poetry. The back and front cover art by Eugene R. Gryniewicz is excellent. $3.00 payable to Merrimack Books, P.O. Box 158, Lynn, IN 47355-0158.

Tal Publications brought out *The Best of D. F. Lewis*, collecting fifteen stories from the ubiquitous British horror writer. Introduction by Ramsey Campbell and very effective cover/interior art by t. winter-damon. $5.95 + $1 shipping payable to Tal Publications, P.O. Box 1837, Leesburg, VA 22075.

Wordcraft of Oregon published Denise Dumars's first collection, *Pangæa*, collecting reprints from various small press publications and originals. The excellent interior art is by Helen Shoenfeld. Published in a 250-copy perfect-bound paperback edition. $7.95 to Wordcraft of Oregon, P.O. Box 3235, La Grande, OR 97850.

I still feel that there are only a few magazines consistently publishing excellent horror and dark fantasy, so the reader will notice that most of my choices for the year's best stories come from anthologies. However, there are exceptions. What follows is a sampling of the professional, semiprofessional, and small press magazines that I feel are publishing the best horror material, whether "horror" magazines or not. The reader should be aware that many small press magazines do not publish on regular schedules, and some go out of business after only a few issues.

Cemetery Dance, edited by Richard Chizmer, is the most consistent and pure *horror* magazine. It keeps a regular schedule, has a readable and attractive design, and the fiction is usually interesting. The fall double issue was chock full of fiction and nonfiction, including a profile of Deadline Press (*The Scream Factory*), an interview with Poppy Z. Brite, and reviews by Douglas E. Winter, Edward Bryant, and Kathryn Ptacek. *Cemetery Dance* published excellent fiction by Nancy Holder, Augustine Bruins Funnell (both included herein), Thomas Tessier, Peter Crowther, Gary A. Braunbeck, Douglas Clegg, and Darrell Schweitzer. The Alan M. Clark covers are exceptionally good, as is the interior art by Allen Koszowski, Keith Minnion, and Alfred Klosterman. Klosterman is the graphics editor. *Cemetery Dance* is getting better and better. Support it. $15 for a one-year subscription (four issues) payable to CD Publications, P.O. Box 18433, Baltimore, MD 21237.

Weird Tales, edited by George Scithers and Darrell Schweitzer is the best dark fantasy-oriented magazine in the field right now. Only two issues came out in 1993, but the editors plan to be back on a quarterly schedule in 1994 (when its title will change to *Worlds of Fantasy and Horror*). There were good stories by newcomer Gordon Jimm, Tanith Lee, R. Chetwynd-Hayes, John Ordover, and Ian Watson. Also, a real sicko clown story by Robert Devereaux and an excellent poem by Bruce Boston (both reprinted here). The Nick Jainschigg cover for spring was effectively weird. $16 for a one year subscription (four issues) payable to Terminus Publishing Co., Inc., P.O. Box 13418, Philadelphia, PA 19101-3418.

Playboy, fiction edited by Alice K. Turner, had a surprising amount of dark fiction during 1993. The only out-and-out horror story was Dan Simmons's novelette "Death in Bangkok," reprinted here as "Dying in Bangkok." But two other excellent dark stories were written by Joe Haldeman and Lawrence Block (the latter story an Edgar nominee).

OMNI, fiction edited by Ellen Datlow, published a lot that could be classified as horror. The dark stories in *OMNI* were by Marc Laidaw, Carol Emshwiller (reprinted here), a collaboration by Barry N. Malzberg and Jack Dann, Harlan Ellison (the latter novella an Edgar and Stoker nominee), and Joyce Carol Oates.

Tomorrow: Speculative Fiction, edited by Algis Budrys, ran some excellent horror stories despite its emphasis on speculative fiction. The magazine has made an impressive start with attractive color covers and good interior illustrations. The only nonfiction so far is a series on how to write by Budrys. Excellent horror stories by Barry Reynolds, Richard Bowes, K. D. Wentworth, Mike Christie, and Annis Shepherd. $18 for a one-year subscription (six issues) payable to The Unifont Company, Inc., Box 6038, Evantson, IL 60204.

Amazing Stories, edited by Kim Mohan, is a glossy with full color. There were some good horror stories by Jack Dann, Carrie Richerson, and David B. Silva.

Pulphouse, edited by Jonathan Bond, had better cover art and better fiction in 1993 than in 1992. The two issues had great covers by Earl W. Morgan and a collaboration by Timothy Caldwell and Rick Lieder, good design and layouts, provocative and entertaining essays by Barry N. Malzberg, and powerful horror fiction by Adam-Troy Castro, Lucy Taylor, Martin Limón, and Kelley Eskridge. One cavil: I do not think *Pulphouse* (or many other magazines) is publishing "dangerous" or "subversive" fiction, as the editor proclaims. A piece of fiction is not dangerous merely because the characters are disgusting and do awful things. I think the horror field needs more discussion on the subject of what *is* dangerous fiction now that so many taboos have been broken. Interestingly, Malzberg brought up the question of taboos in science fiction in an earlier *Pulphouse* column. $39 for thirteen issues. Payable to Pulphouse Publishing, Inc. See address in "Collections." (Only two issues were published in 1993.)

The Magazine of Fantasy & Science Fiction, edited by Kristine Kathryn Rusch, concentrates on those genres mentioned in its title but occasionally publishes horrific stories. In 1993 there was excellent horror by Jack Cady (a novella, nominated for the Nebula), Bridget McKenna (nominated for the Nebula), Mark W. Tiedmann, Marc Laidlaw, Lynn S. Hightower, Elizabeth Hand, Robert Frazier, Ron Savage, and Jane Yolen. $26 for a one-year subscription (eleven issues) payable to Mercury Press, Inc., 143 Cream Hill Road, West Cornwall, CT 06796.

Asimov's Science Fiction, edited by Gardner Dozois, also concentrates more on science fiction and fantasy, with occasional forays into horror. The best horror stories from 1993 were by Rick Wilber, Robert Reed, Gregory Frost, Connie Willis (nominated for the Nebula), Pat Murphy (novella), Patricia Anthony, Sage Walker, Diane Mapes, Tony Daniel, Tanith Lee, Jamil Nasir, Robert Sampson, Steven Utley, Jessica Amanda Salmonson, Nancy Kress (a novella nominated for the Nebula), Neal Barrett, Jr., Kij Johnson, Ian McDowell, Melanie Tem, and David Redd. $39.97 (thirteen issues) for a one-year subscription payable to *Asimov's Science Fiction*, Box 5130, Harlan, IA 51593-5130.

Alfred Hitchcock's Mystery Magazine, edited by Cathleen Jordan occasionally runs horrific material. The best in 1993 was by Charles Ardai, Martin Limón, Esther J. Holt, Stephanie Bendel, Roberta Hall, Dan Crawford, and Don Marshall. $34.97 for a one-year subscription (thirteen issues) payable to *Alfred Hitchcok Mystery Magazine*, PO Box 5124, Harlan, IA 51593-5124.

Ellery Queen's Mystery Magazine, edited by Janet Hutchings usually has quite a bit of dark-edged suspense/horror. The best in 1993 were by Frank McConnell, Clark Howard, Ruth Rendell, R. M. Kinder, Tony Hillerman, Michael Gilbert, Lawrence Treat, Peter Sellers, Kelly Simon, Joyce Harrington, Jackie Walsh, Ruthe Furie, Doug Allyn, Miriam Grace Monfredo (reprinted here), Mauricio-José Schwarz, Barbara Owens, Kate Wilhelm, and Tom Tolnay. $34.97 for a one-year subscription (thirteen issues) payable to *Ellery Queen's Mystery Magazine*, P.O. Box 5127, Harlan, IA 51593-5127.

Interzone, edited by David Pringle, is the United Kingdom's premier science fiction magazine, but on occasion publishes borderline horror material. In 1993 the best dark fiction was by Brian Stableford, Nicola Griffith, Keith Brooke, a collaboration by M. John Harrison and Simon Ings, Peter Crowther, Fergus Bannon, Storm Constantine, Lawrence Dyer, Graham Joyce, and Kim Newman. $52 for a year's subscription (twelve issues) payable to *Interzone*, 217 Preston Drive, Brighton BN1 6FL, U.K.

Science Fiction Age, edited by Scott Edelman, is a good-looking slick magazine of fiction and nonfiction about science fiction. There were some good art portfolios although the color reproduction doesn't quite do justice to the art; a terrific essay by Harlan Ellison on dreams, and an article (surprisingly neutral) on the "fifty most important people in science fiction" by Paul Di Fillippo. Some good horrific fiction by Lois Tilton, Ronald Anthony Cross, and Barry N. Malzberg. $14.95 for a one-year subscription (six issues) payable to *Science Fiction Age*, P.O. Box 749, Herndon, VA 22070-9893.

Tales of the Unanticipated, edited by Eric W. Heideman is an excellent mix of SF, fantasy, dark fantasy, and horror put out at eight-month intervals by the Minnesota Science Fiction Society. Impressive-looking art by Harry O. Morris (cover of #11, although the two-color reproduction isn't great), Erin McKee, Rodger Gerberding, Suzanne Clarke, H. E. Fassl, James Jamison, and incidental art by Peggy Ransom. Good fiction by Kij Johnson, John Harnett, and Christine Beckert. $15 for a four-issue subscription payable to the Minnesota SF Society, *Tales of the Unanticipated*, P.O. Box 8036, Lake Street Station, Minneapolis, MN 55408.

(Un(Real)ity): A Magazine of Fantastic Fiction, edited by David Schindler, has interesting line drawing covers by Karen Kluttz. With its first anniversary issue, the magazine went to an 8 × 10 format and changed its name to *UnReality*. Good fiction by Ken Goldman, Jeffrey Thomas, J. A. Wells, and Robert C. Moore. $11 for a year's subscription (four issues) payable to David Schindler, P.O. Box 1155, Columbia, SC 29202-1155.

Deathrealm, edited by Stephen Mark Rainey, got a new lease on life with Stanislaus Tal taking over as publisher. However, the first new issue (#18) looked confusingly similar to *Bizarre Bazaar*, the sister magazine from Tal Publications, advertised on the back cover. The next two covers, by Harry Fassl and Phillip Reynolds, were less pulpy and more effectively eerie. Clean layouts and attractive design with good interior art by Charles S. Hill. The magazine has a useful "Inside Horror" column, interviews, book reviews, a sometimes rambling column by Karl Edward Wagner, and has published good fiction by Douglas Clegg, Scott Thomas, Sean Doolittle, Mark Rich, D. F. Lewis, Denise Dumars, Don D'Ammassa, and William Bowers. $15.95 for a year's subscription (four issues) payable to Tal Publications. See address under "Anthologies."

The Silver Web: A Magazine of the Surreal, edited by Ann Kennedy is looking better than ever. Two issues were published in 1993. Issue #10 featured artist Jill Bauman's work with a cover and portfolio and interview. There was also good interior art by Cathy Burburz, Rodger Gerberding, t. winter-damon, Michael Shores, H. E. Fassl, and Phil Reynolds. Issue #9 had an overview of the Abyss horror line by Cliff Burns, provoking a couple of the authors whose books were appraised to write in. Good fiction by Juleen Brantingham, Tom Traub, and D. F. Lewis. $10 for a two issue subscription payable to *The Silver Web*, P.O. Box 38190, Tallahassee, FL 32315.

Palace Corbie: the magazine of personal terror, edited by Wayne Edwards, is perfect bound with professional-looking interiors. It has been semi-annual and is going annual with the autumn 1993 issue. The fiction has gotten progressively better with each issue; during 1993 there were good stories by Lenora K. Rogers, Frank Hart, Bentley Little, Sean Doolittle, Lucy Taylor, Wayne Allen Sallee, and a collaboration by Richard L. Levesque and Brad J. Boucher. $7.95 per issue payable to Merrimack Books. See address under "Collections."

Terminal Fright, edited by Ken Abner, a new, all-fiction horror magazine, made its impressive debut with a simple but attractive layout and good stories by Charles M. Saplak and Edward Lodi. $26 for one year's subscription (six issues) payable to *Terminal Fright*, P.O. Box 100, Black River, NY 13612.

Not One of Us, edited by John Benson, only published one issue in 1993, but it had a great cover by Ron Leming and good interior illustrations by Ron Leming and John Borkowski. Powerful stories by Jeffrey Osier, Shelley Moore, Gary A. Braunbeck, and Deidre Cox. $10.50 for a three-issue subscription payable to John Benson, 44 Shady Lane, Storrs, CT 06268.

Grue Magazine, edited by Peggy Nadramia, only put out one issue during 1993, but it had a fine cover by H. E. Fassl and some excellent interiors by Timothy Patrick Butler, Harry O. Morris, and Greg Loudon. A very good issue all around with disturbing fiction by Wayne Allen Sallee, Brett Bogart, and Brian Huff. $13 for a one-year subscription (three issues) payable to Hell's Kitchen Productions, Inc., P.O. Box 370, Times Square Station, New York, NY 10108-0370.

Haunts, edited by Joseph Cherkes is an attractive-looking perfect-bound magazine. Two issues were published in 1993 and they had good stories by Anthony Gael Moral, Harrison Howe, Joseph David Carrabis, and Norman Partridge. $13 for a four-issue subscription payable to Nightshade Publications, P.O. Box 3342, Providence, RI 02906-0742.

The Barrelhouse, edited by Doug Coulson, needs to make the magazine more reader-friendly. The story runover is difficult to find in the back of the book. The best piece of art is a simple yet elegantly stark illustration by Brett Burns. The rest of the art is tough to judge because of poor reproduction quality. However, there is excellent fiction and poetry in this magazine by Ben Pastor, Rhonda Eikamp, and Lisa Lepovesky. $12.50 for a one year subscription (they claim to be a quarterly but I only received a spring 1993 issue and one earlier, on the cusp of 1992/93, so I can't vouch for their timeliness) payable to *The Barrelhouse*, 1600 Oak Creek Drive, Edmond, OK 73034.

Midnight Zoo, edited by Jon L. Herron had better quality fiction in 1993 than in 1992, with good stories by Lillian Csernica, Ken Wisman, Michael Mallory, John Soares, and a poem by Bruce Boston. $40 for a year's subscription (bimonthly) payable to *Midnight Zoo*, 995-H Detroit Avenue, Concord, CA 94518.

Thin Ice, edited by Kathleen Jurgens, has finally, with issue XIV, gotten itself readable typography. Excellent interior illustrations by A. O. Weidemann, and a good cover by H. E. Fassl. The fiction improved overall during 1993 with good stories by Barbara Rosen, Verbena Pastor, and Stephen M. Rainey. $12.50 for a one-year subscription (three issues) payable to Kathleen Jurgens, 379 Lincoln Avenue, Council Bluffs, IA 51503.

Space & Time, edited by Gordon Linzner has been publishing continuously for twenty-seven years but was almost forced to cease publication last year. Luckily, Emerald City Publishing came to the rescue and took over the magazine's sponsorship with its eighty-first issue. The 1993 issues had interesting interior illustrations by Augie Weidemann, Joey Zone, Chet Gottfried, and Mike S. Dunhour and good dark stories by Lillian Csernica and Amy Benesch. $10 for a one-year subscription (two issues) payable to G. Linzner, *Space & Time*, 138 W. 70th St., New York, NY 10023-4432.

Weirdbook and *Weirdbook Encores*, edited by W. Paul Ganley publishes mostly traditional horror. There were good stories by Francis J. Matozzo, Kathleen J. Patterson, and John A. Russell. $25 for a seven-issue subscription (it comes out once or twice a year) payable to W. Paul Ganley, Publisher. See address under "Collections."

On Spec: The Canadian Magazine of Speculative Writing, edited by Catherine Gircyzc, Barry Hammond, Susan MacGregor, Hazel Sangster, Jena Snyder, and Diane L. Walton, is a consistently good digest-sized perfect-bound magazine. The fiction crosses over between SF, fantasy and horror. Most of the covers are excellent, particularly those by Rob Alexander and Kenneth Scott. The spring "over the edge" issue was full of the best fiction I've yet seen in the magazine. Such a theme is always a gamble; in this case it paid off. Three of the best stories were first sales. The best horror stories were by Robert J. Sawyer, Robert Boyczuk, Jason Kapalka, Dirk L. Schaeffer, and J. R. Martel. $18 for a one-year subscription (four issues) payable to *On Spec*, P.O. Box 4727, Edmonton, Alberta, Canada T6E 5G6.

Dementia 13, edited by Pam Creais, is a British magazine that consistently runs literate fiction, interesting art (a good portfolio of "scratchboard" art by Steve Skwarek), and a good variety of nonfiction (e.g., an article about Jorge Luis Borges and a retrospective overview of William Burroughs's fiction). Good stories by John Carter, Julie Akhurst, and Joel Lane. $30 for a one-year subscription (four issues) payable to Pam Creais, *Dementia 13*, 17 Pinewood Avenue, Sidcup, Kent, DA15 8BB, England.

Peeping Tom, edited by Stuart Hughes, just won the British Fantasy Award for Best Small Press Magazine. Despite its cheezy look, *Peeping Tom* is published regularly in the U.K., and consistently runs good horror. The best stories in 1993 were by Joel Lane, Simon Clark, Nicholas Royle, Kevin Mullins, and Ben Leech. $24 for a four-issue subscription payable to Anne Marsden, *Peeping Tom Magazine*, 1052 Calle del Cerro #708, San Clemente, CA 92672-6068.

Aurealis: The Australian Magazine of Fantasy and Science Fiction, edited by Stephen Higgens and Dirk Strasser, is a good-looking digest sized magazine with excellent interior art and articles on SF and fantasy in Australia. There were a couple of strong horror stories by Simon Brown and Bart Meehan. $31 for a four-issue subscription (semiannual) payable to Chimaera Publications, P.O. Box 538, Mt. Waverley, Victoria 3149, Australia.

Eidolon: The Journal of Australian Science Fiction and Fantasy, edited by Jonathan Strahan, Jeremy G. Byrne, and Richard Scriven, is well-designed and highly readable. The snazzy black or white covers make this perfect-bound digest-sized magazine instantly identifiable and the interior artwork is particularly good. Kudos to artists Liesl Yvette,

Shaun Tan, Adam Megow, and James Reston. Good writing and interesting interviews and provocative articles about Australian SF and women in Australian SF. It's literate, with a solid stable of regulars; highly recommended to SF readers and horror readers with broad interests. There were good horror stories by Robert Hood and Sean Williams. $34 for a one-year (four-issue) subscription payable to Richard Scriven, P.O. Box 225, North Perth, West Australia 6006.

Chills, edited by Peter Coleborn and Simon MacCulloch, is published annually by the British Fantasy Society. The 1993 issue was very good with a reprint by Clive Barker and original stories by Nicholas Royle, Tia Travis, and Martin Plumbridge. For information send an s.a.s.e. to the secretary of the British Fantasy Society, Rob Parkinson, 2 Harwood Road, Stockport, SK4 1JJ, U.K.

Dreams & Nightmares, edited by David Kopaska-Merkel, is an excellent source of speculative and dark fantasy poetry. There was a particularly good poem by Corrinne DeWinter. $5 for four issues payable to David Kopaska-Merkel, 1300 Kicker Road, Tuscaloosa, AL 35404.

Skeletal Remains, edited by Richard and Lorrie Levesque, is a new series dedicated to publishing one small press poet's original material per issue. The first three in the series were Jacie Ragan, Wayne Edwards, and Steve Sneyd. $2 payable to Richard or Lorrie Levesque, 2227 Woodglen Drive, Indianapolis, IN 46260.

Other magazines that occasionally published excellent horror during 1993 were *Aboriginal SF, Heliocentric Net, Glimmer Train, The New Yorker, Crossroads, Grotesque, Xenos, Maelstrom, Aberrations, Thunder's Shadows, Doppelganger, Magic Realism, Strange Days, Prisoners of the Night, Dead of Night, Argonaut, Threads, Wicked Mystic, Sunk Island Review, Redcat Magazine, Eldritch Tales, The Tome, Asylum Annual, Black Tears, After Hours, Paper Clips, Eulogy, TriQuarterly, Crank!, New Orleans Stories, Kinesis,* and *Fiction Furnace.*

Single-Author Chapbooks:
"I, Said the Fly," by Michael Shea is a creepy horror novella that originally appeared in a slightly different version several years ago. This first book from the newly-formed Silver Salamander Press has an introduction by Larry Tritten and illustrations by James Burton. Available for $10 in a 500-copy signed edition trade paperback edition, a 300-copy signed and numbered hardcover edition for $35 and a 50-copy signed and numbered leatherbound edition for $65 (see address under "Collections"). Fred Chappell's "The Lodger" (reprinted here) is a strange little tale about possession. The art and cover are by Stephen E. Fabian. $4.50 + .75 postage. And *Two Obscure Tales* by Ramsey Campbell is an odd item. Campbell, in his afterword comments accurately on these two early stories, neither of which is completely successful; he was still finding his voice. Mostly of interest to Campbell collectors. $4.50 + .75 postage. Both from Necornomicon Press, P.O. Box 1304, West Warwick, RI 02893.

"A Flash of White" by Andrew Vachss is an original story, two comic adaptations, one by Rose Bradford and another by David Lloyd, with an introduction by Joe R. Lansdale, and a nonfiction article by Vachss. The cover art is by Mark Masztal. Limited to 300 numbered copies signed by Vachss and Bradford for $12. Available from the same publisher is "Drive-By," an original story by Andrew Vachss, a comic adaptation script by Joe R. Lansdale, comic story with art by Gary Gianni, with an introduction by Neal Barrett, Jr. and cover art by Mark Nelson. Limited to 300 signed and numbered copies at $13. Payable to Thomas Crouss, Crossroads Press, 100 Smyrna Street, West Springfield, MA 01089-1706.

"Wall, Stone, Craft" by Walter Jon Williams is an excellent novella (nominated for the Nebula award), an alternate history story about Mary and Percy Bysshe Shelley, and George

Gordon, Lord Byron, but is not horror. Available in three states, all signed: $10 for a 525-copy limited trade paperback, $35 for a 300-copy limited, numbered hardcover with dustjacket, and $65 for a 75-copy limited, numbered leatherbound edition. Payable to Axolotl Press, Pulphouse Publishing, Box 1227, Eugene, OR 97440.

"La Luz Canyon"/"Going Mobile" are two original stories by Allen H. Royce and Glen E. Cox printed back to back as a paperback double. Illustrations by Melissa Sherman. Signed and limited to 200 copies. $6 + $1 postage payable to Roadkill Press, Little Bookshop of Horrors, 10380 Ralston Rd., Arvada, CO 80004. And from the same publisher, "Aqua Sancta" by Edward Bryant. The publisher calls it "an origami chapbook" or a "signed limited edition greeting card." Whatever, it's an eensy teensy story by Bryant with illustrations by Jennifer Willoughby and lettering and spot illustration by Richard McNeace, designed by Tomi Lewis. Limited to 450 copies. $3 + $1 postage.

"Child of Darkness" and "Bones" by P. C. Hodgell are two attractive paperbacks. "Child of Darkness" is a "lost chapter" that was supposed to appear in the novel *Godstalk*. 111 leatherbound and 333 chapbook copies. All signed and numbered. Both editions are out of print. Hypatia Press, 360 West First, Eugene, OR 97401.

Tal Publications published "Pain Grin" by Wayne Allen Sallee, a powerful memoir by a talented writer, with a self-portrait on the cover and good interior art by H. E. Fassl (signed by writer and artist, $5.95) and *Rex Miller: The Complete Revelations* by t. winter-damon, an everything-you-always-wanted-to-know-about-the-creator-of-Chaingang-Bunkowski kind of rant, for $9.95 each + $1 shipping. For address see "Collections."

"The Turning" by Ron Dee is a 250-copy signed and numbered limited edition vampire story. Good cover collage art by Mark Irwin that would have been better served by not being on red paper. $3 + .75 postage to Simulacran Press-Ozark Triangle Press, Route 1, Box 301, Purdy, MO 65734.

"Going North," a story by Lucy Taylor, was published as a Christmas card chapbook by Rubén Sosa Villegas Publications in a 300-copy numbered and signed limited edition. For information write *Blood Review Journal*, P.O. Box 4394, Denver, CO 80204-9998.

Matthew J. Costello's *Garden*, a sequel to his novel *Wurm* with an introduction by F. Paul Wilson and illustrations by Stephen Honthy was published in three states. A trade paperback, limited to 1,950 copies for $15. A 350-copy signed hardcover for $50 and a 26-copy signed leatherbound edition is $250. $4 shipping for any edition. Order from Twilight Publishing Co., 18 Oaktree Lane, Sparta, NJ 07871.

Other horrific works published by various specialty presses were:

Borderlands Press: A beautiful slipcased 350-copy signed and numbered limited edition of *The Throat* by Peter Straub. The cover is by talented newcomer Ryan Dreimiller. $95 + $3 postage to Borderlands Press. Address under "Collections."

Charnel House: The first hardcover edition of Dean R. Koontz's novel *Beastchild* comes in two editions. A slipcased 750-copy signed and numbered edition with green Japanese fabric and rich-looking green endpapers for $150. And a 26-copy signed and lettered edition bound in lizard in a black traycase for $750. $5 postage per book. Charnel House, P.O. Box 633, Lynbrook, NY 11563.

The Wildside Press: The only hardcover edition and the preferred text of Alan Rodgers's novel, *Night*. A 250-copy trade edition for $35 and a 26-copy lettered hardcover for $75. Add $3 postage. The Wildside Press, 37 Fillmore Street, Newark, NJ 07105. Also, *Swashbuckling Editor Stories*, a trade paperback for $6.99 and a signed hardcover edition $35.

James Cahill Publishing: *Drawing Blood* by Poppy Z. Brite, in a slipcased signed and numbered hardcover edition of 274 copies for $55, and a 26-copy numbered edition for $100. Both editions have french marbled boards (different for each edition). Postage paid. James Cahill Publishing, 9932 Constitution Drive, Huntington Beach, CA 92646.

Fedogan & Bremer published *The House of Toad* by Richard L. Tierney, a poet, writer, editor, and one of the founders of modern Lovecraftian criticism. Jacket and illustration of this hardcover book are by Harry O. Morris. The 100-copy limited signed, numbered, and slipcased edition is $45, and the trade edition is $24. Add $1.50 postage per book. Fedogan & Bremer, 700 Washington Avenue, S.E. Suite 50, Minneapolis, MN 55417.

Mark V. Ziesing Books: Harlan Ellison's novella "Mefisto in Onyx" was published in three states. A 1,000-copy deluxe slipcased edition signed and numbered clothbound for $65 (questionable availability). The black and white and red cover by Frank Miller is unusual and striking. A 40-copy leatherbound signed and lettered edition for $750, encased in a handmade jail cell made of a black brushed aluminum alloy (only 26 for sale). A hardcover trade edition for $16.95 is sold out, but a second edition has been published. The book's design is by Arnie Fenner.

Nonfiction magazines provide news and critical analyses of the field. The best are below. I've included ordering information for those difficult to find on the newsstand.

The Scream Factory, edited by Bob Morrish, Peter Enfantino, and John Scoleri has become *the* important all-around nonfiction magazine of horror. The excellent spring issue (#11) concentrated on "dark suspense" with a thoughtful article by Scott Cupp discussing what is—and isn't—dark suspense; an excellent rundown by Dale Walker of "serial killer" novels up to 1992; Max Allan Collins on Jim Thompson's œuvre; coverage of pre-*Psycho* fiction by Robert Bloch; an article on the early *noir* novels published by Gold Medal Books; and a horror movie column by Gary Braunbeck that made me want to rush out and rent all four movies he writes about—even one I hated first time around. Rounded off by some good fiction and lots of reviews. #12 featured a retrospective of *Whispers*, and an interview with Stuart David Schiff, editor of the now-defunct fiction magazine; an overall look at the Abyss line; Bob Morrish discovers what's up with Jeff Connor and Scream/Press. Another excellent issue. Good art by Alan M. Clark, Greg Weber, Lance Brown, Peter Francis, Harry O. Morris, and Deryck T. Santiago. And for all you zombie cannibal fans, a special issue (sold out) celebrating the twenty-fifth anniversary of *The Night of the Living Dead* containing reviews of zombie films, books and even soundtracks. A four-issue subscription is $21 payable to Deadline Press. See address under "Collections."

Horror: The News Magazine of the Horror and Dark Fantasy Field, edited by John and Kim Betancourt debuted at the 1993 World Fantasy Convention in Minneapolis, although the cover date was January 1994. The magazine will be published monthly, and is modeled upon *Locus* (physically, as well as philosophically), and *SF Chronicle*, which provide extensive coverage of the science fiction and fantasy field. The first 96-page issue had interviews with Peter Straub, Jeanne Cavelos (providentially, both winners of World Fantasy Awards), and Poppy Z. Brite. Fiona Webster writes capsule summaries of mainstream books with horrific elements that were reviewed in *The New York Times* or *The Washington Post*. A promising and much-needed addition to the horror field. A one-year (12-issue) subscription is $36 payable by check to The Wildside Press, 37 Fillmore Street, Newark, NJ 07105.

Necrofile: The Review of Horror Fiction, edited by Stefan Dziemianowicz, S. T. Joshi, and Michael A. Morrison, is the most important regularly published critical journal of the horror field. A 28–32 page quarterly filled with in-depth reviews and capsule reviews, overviews of the field, listings of British and American horror titles, a regular column by Ramsey Campbell, and provocative editorials such as "Has Horror Lost Its Way?" Highly recommended. One-year subscription (four issues), $10 payable to Necronomicon Press. See address under "Single-Author Chapbooks."

Other Dimensions: The Journal of Multimedia Horror #1, edited by Stefan Dziemianow-icz, is a new journal meant to complement *Necrofile*, covering all horror (except for literature) in our culture in a scholarly manner. Michael A. Morrison does a remarkable explication/comparison and analysis of *The Thing*—the original novella, "Who Goes There?" by John W. Campbell, the Howard Hawks film version from the 1950s, and the John Carpenter film version of the early 1980s. Also, Clive Barker writes about his plays, Rob Lathem trashes David J. Skal's book *The Monster Show* (which I loved), and Darrell Schweitzer goes after the various adaptations of Stoker's *Dracula*. Good interior illustrations by Allen Koszowski. $5 + .75 to Necronomicon Press.

Gauntlet: Exploring the Limits of Free Expression #5: Porn in the USA, edited by Barry Hoffman, is always a kick to read even when I don't agree with some of the articles. In this issue there was an interview with sex star Annie Sprinkle and a profile of H. R. Giger plus an original short story by Thomas Tessier and an excerpt from Melanie Tem and Nancy Holder's novel, *Making Love*. Issue #6 focused on black racism. $9.95 payable to *Gauntlet*, Dept. SUB93A, 309 Powell Road, Springfield, PA 19064.

Afraid: The Newsletter for the Horror Professional, edited by Mike Baker. Publishing news, reviews and market reports, and usually at least one provocative column with someone ranting and raving. One-year subscription (twelve issues), $25. Checks payable to *Afraid*, 857 N. Oxford Avenue #4, Los Angeles, CA 90029.

Star*Line: Newsletter of the SF Poetry Assocation, edited by Marge Simon, has invaluable information for the SF/fantasy poet and publishes poetry by its members. $13 for membership (six issues) payable to the Science Fiction Poetry Association, Mike Arnzen, Secretary/Treasurer, P.O. Box 3712, Moscow, ID 83843-1916.

Skinned Alive: The Horror Fiction Fanzine, edited by Rod Williams is an Australian magazine jam-packed with book and magazine reviews with a decidedly splatter bent. Every book is rated on its prose and its splatter quotient. Enjoyable. With the next issue the magazine will be renamed *Sepulchre*. (I'm not sure, but I think you can get it by swapping magazines, I.R.C. coupons, stamps, U.S. cash. It's $2 Australian, whatever that translates into.) Worth a look.

The Gila Queen's Guide to Markets, edited by Kathryn Ptacek, is the most detailed market report around, regularly targeting special markets, and covering trends, writing, and self-promotion, in addition to publishing news. Highly recommended. One-year subscription (twelve issues), $24. Checks payable to Kathryn Ptacek, P.O. Box 97, Newtown, NJ 07860.

Psychotronic Video, a quarterly edited by Michael J. Weldon, is the best magazine for information on low budget, sleazy films. Book, movie, video and record reviews. An interview with Antonio Fargas in #15. Great ads for sleazy movies. Six-issue subscription, $22. Checks payable to *Psychotronic* (Quarterly), 3309 Route 97, Narrowsburg, NY 12764-6126. Highly recommended.

Video Watchdog, edited by Tim and Donna Lucas, is a bimonthly that goes into incredible detail regarding films of the fantastic, including announcing when movies are retitled. It's for devotees to savor, a bit more serious than *Psychotronic Video*. These two are the major magazines on the subject. Generous black and white photos throughout. Issue #29, outlining the seven versions of *Blade Runner*, and written up by Paul Sammon, is particularly good. One-year subscription (six issues), $24. Checks payable to *Video Watchdog*, P.O. Box 5283, Cincinnati, OH 45205-0283. Highly recommended.

Cinefantastique, edited by Frederick S. Clarke, is consistently entertaining and intellectually stimulating. It's the best coverage you can get of major Hollywood movies of the fantastic/horror genre. Some of the mini-coverage is thin, but the cover stories are usually detailed and exhaustive, going at their subjects from every direction. During 1993 it covered Ren & Stimpy, among other subjects. One-year subscription (six issues), $27. Checks payable to *Cinefantastique*, P.O. Box 270, Oak Park, IL 60303.

Fangoria, edited by Anthony Timpone, is the best genre film magazine when it comes to gross-out horror and special effects. The werewolf issue in December was a good one, with an overview of the subgenre, upcoming movies, a retrospective of old ones, an article on *An American Werewolf in London*, and an excellent survey of lyncanthropic literature by Linda Marotta. A good and thorough theme issue. Marotta is one of the best reviewers in the genre and always makes *Fango* worthwhile, as does David J. Schow's regular column.

Filmfax: The Magazine of Unusual Film and Television, edited by Michael Stein and Sharon Lind Williams has lively interviews and profiles of actors and actresses, directors, and producers of past generations' horror films. The black and white photo reproduction is only so-so. Not as quirky as *Video Watchdog* and not as detailed coverage. One year subscription (6 issues) $25. Checks payable to *Filmfax*, 10421/2 Michigan, Evanston, IL 60202.

Scarlet Street: The Magazine of Mystery and Horror, edited by Richard Valley specializes in old mystery films. It feels like some of the interviews are excerpted from books rather than done fresh for the magazine. One year subscription (4 issues) $18. Checks payable to R. H. Enterprises, Inc., 271 Farrant Terrace, Teaneck, NJ 07666.

The New York Review of Science Fiction, edited by David G. Hartwell, Donald G. Keller, Robert K. J. Killheffer, and Gordon Van Gelder only occasionally covers horror but is an important critical monthly. The reviews are eclectic, reflecting the individual tastes of the editors and contributors. One year subscription (12 issues) $30. Checks payable to Dragon Press, P.O. Box 78, Pleasantville, NY 10570.

Science Fiction Eye, edited by Stephen P. Brown also covers horror only intermittently but is an important and entertaining critical magazine. It always has excellent covers and interior art. The most recent issue (summer 1993) has a critical article on Steve Erickson, an interview with Brian Eno, Bruce McAllister on his 1965 stint working at Disneyland, Richard Kadrey on weird music, and myriad reviews of SF, crossover, and some horror fiction. $12.50 for one year (three issues—but they haven't done more than one or two a year for quite some time), payable to *Science Fiction Eye*, P.O. Box 18539, Asheville, NC 28814.

Mystery Scene, edited by Joe Gorman, seems to be getting back on track with #38, and looks much better compared to the year before. Using quality stock for the cover makes a big difference in how a magazine is perceived. It's not heavy on horror coverage, but there's a regular news column by Mike Baker and reviews by Charles de Lint. One-year subscription (six issues), $35. Checks payable to Mystery Enterprises, P.O. Box 669, Cedar Rapids, IA 52406-0669.

Carnage Hall issue 4, edited by David Griffin is irregularly published and isn't afraid to express unpopular opinions. Griffin writes provocative editorials. This issue he attacks Richard Sutphen's advertising campaign for his collection, *Sex Punks and Savage Sagas*. There's a good interview with S. T. Joshi and a raw review that takes on the anthology *The New Gothic*, edited by Patrick McGrath and Bradford Morrow. Fiction by Kim Antieu and excellent interior illustrations. $4.50 payable to David Griffin, *Carnage Hall Magazine*, P.O. Box 7, Esopus, NY 12429.

Graphic Novels:
More prose writers of science fiction and horror are moving into graphic novels. Rachel Pollack, Nancy A. Collins, K. W. Jeter, Karl Edward Wagner, Joe R. Lansdale, Elizabeth Hand and Paul Witcover, are just a few names with whom I'm familiar who have made forays into the medium with varying results. Pollack is writing *Doom Patrol*, Collins has been writing *Swamp Thing* and has created a character for a new series. Jeter wrote *Mr. E*, Wagner wrote *Tell Me Dark*, and Hand and Witcover have created *Anima*.

Vertigo, the ambitious new line from DC aimed at "mature readers," was presented with much fanfare throughout the first half of 1993. Neil Gaiman appeared around the U.S. to publicize Death, his spinoff character from his popular *Sandman* series. According to the editors at Vertigo, the idea behind the imprint is for the writer-driven graphic novels to reach a level of sophistication, with adult content and themes, that most comics don't have. There are elements of horror/dark fantasy and a sophistication in the packaging as well as in the storytelling. Some of the results for the first year:

The Extremist, by Peter Milligan and Ted McKeever, is a darkly erotic thriller in four parts about a young couple who become involved in a secret society of decadence that haunts the underground clubs of San Francisco. The Extremist is the order's "enforcer," dressed in black. But who is the Extremist and who really pulls the strings? Highly recommended.

Skin Graft: The Adventures of a Tattooed Man, by Jerry Prosser and Warren Pleece (covers by Gavin Wilson), is another excellent suspense tale. While in prison, John Oakes allowed Abel Tarrant to tattoo him with arcane symbols and alchemical signs. After his release, Oakes starts up a successful business as a tattoo artist. Then his models start dying horribly. With the Yakuza after him and his tattoos taking on a life of their own, Oakes travels to Kyoto with a beautiful young Japanese woman to meet her grandfather, a master tattooist who he hopes can give him some answers.

Death Gallery is a one-shot with several artists' interpretations of Neil Gaiman's character, Death. Included are some of the best in the field—Dave McKean, Kent Williams, Jill Karla Schwarz, Jon J. Muth, Charles Vess, Gahan Wilson, and Clive Barker. Highly recommended for collectors.

Jonah Hex, by Joe R. Lansdale, Timothy Truman, and Sam Glanzman, is a five-part limited series. Western zombies in a grim, grisly, funny story. Hex, a veteran of the War Between the States, doesn't seek trouble but certainly finds it. Almost everyone he befriends dies. Nasty fun.

Enigma, by Peter Milligan, Duncan Fegredo, and Sherilyn Van Valkenburgh, is an eight-part limited about a failed comic book character who seems to come alive after twenty-five years, causing mayhem in Pacific City. Good characters and good art.

Death: The High Cost of Living by Neil Gaiman and artists Chris Bachalo, Mark Buckingham, and Dave McKean, with an introduction by singer Tori Amos, is a compilation. Death, personified as a perky, attractive young woman dressed in black, is only on earth in corporeal form once per century to feel what it's like to be mortal. She's captivated by life and captivating as a character—as popular, if not more so, than her brother the Sandman.

The Children's Crusade by Neil Gaiman, Chris Bachalo, and Mike Barreiro, is a mystery about forty children gone missing from the peaceful British village of Flaxdown. References to the Pied Piper and the disastrous children's crusade of the middle ages give the first of this two-parter resonance, yet the denouement never fulfills the promise of the first volume.

Fables and Reflections, written by Neil Gaiman and illustrated by various artists, is an entertaining compilation of nine stories.

Apocalypse: The Eyes of Doom, by Juan Gemenez and Roberta Al Prá (Heavy Metal/ Kitchen Sink), is a good-looking, effective adventure yarn with touches of *Scanners.* Vietnam vet, opium smoker, and mystery writer Dan Curry remembers a boy with a strange and dangerous ability from his tour in Vietnam as he watches a TV report about grotesque mystery deaths in Los Angeles's Chinatown. Are they related?

The Upturned Stone by Scott Hampton (Heavy Metal/Kitchen Sink) is a perfect Halloween tale about four boys who decide to avenge a murder ten years past. The boys have been haunted by nightmares since digging up a huge pumpkin near a young boy's grave and these nightmares lead them to the murderer. The illustrations are in a beautiful, dreamy style.

Blood Club by Charles Burns (Kitchen Sink) came out in 1993 although it has a '92 copyright. Another story appropriate to Halloween, this one stars Big Baby, takes place at summer camp, and has the distinctive Burns art.

From Hell, volumes two and three, by Alan Moore and Eddie Campbell (Mad Love/ Tundra), continue the brilliant, diligently researched story of Jack the Ripper. In volume three, the plot thickens when the four prostitutes who eventually are murdered try to blackmail Prince Albert regarding his illegitimate daughter. Polly Nichols is stalked and murdered in volume three. As interesting as the graphic novel itself, the wealth of material and speculation by Moore in each volume's appendix is an extra delight.

Signal to Noise, by Neil Gaiman and Dave McKean (Victor Gollancz, Dark Horse, 1992) with an introduction by Jonathan Carroll. A film director at the pinnacle of his career is diagnosed with cancer but refuses treatment. He is determined to create his masterpiece before he dies. In this dark meditation on death and art, the art and text complement each other beautifully.

Hardboiled, by Frank Miller and Geoff Darrow (Dark Horse, Dell), is about a mild-mannered insurance agent, seemingly happily married with two kids. The victim of persistent nightmares, the man doesn't know that he's actually a machine, and an assassin. Funny, violent, with a cyberpunk feel to it.

Dark Horse has started a bi-monthly anthology series called *Underground*, created by Andrew Vachss, which has both graphic novels and stories. The first is excellent, with a Harry O. Morris cover. The stories are written by Vachss and Steve Rasnic Tem, and illustrated by John Bergin, Jeff Dickinson and others.

Hard Looks #6 and #7, by Andrew Vachss (Dark Horse), are comic adaptations of Vachss's short fiction. His stories, always more vignettes than fully realized stories, lend themselves well to this format. Artists such as Harry O. Morris and John Bergin illustrate, Neal Barrett, Jr. did some of the adaptations.

The Best of Dark Horse Presents 3 is a compilation of twenty stories, some of which stand alone. An eclectic mixture worth a look.

True Crime—Eclipse Noir 1 is the first in a new series of graphic novel adaptations from Eclipse of "real cases of actual crimes." The first comic has "The Made Man" about John Gotti's first hit and "The Aileen Wuornos Story." Included is a "spotlight on forensics" section which features an article on genetic fingerprinting.

System Shock: Graphic Tales of Horror (Tuscany Press) debuts with stories by Dan Simmons, John Skipp, and Richard Laymon. Labeled "for mature readers," this series seems to be going for the guts with little subtlety or grace. Blood and guts and death all over. Planned as a ten-issue horror anthology series coming out three times a year.

Other graphic novels of note: *The Thing and Climate of Fear* by Chuck Pfaffer, John Higgins, John Arcudi, Jim Somerville, Robert Jones, and Brian Garvey (Dark Horse); *The Last One* by J. M. Matteis and Dan Sweetman (Vertigo), a six-part limited with lovely art by Dan Sweetman; *Aliens: Hive, The Collected Edition* (Dark Horse) by Jerry Prosser and Kelley Jones; *Batman: Legends of the Dark Night, Halloween Special,* by Jeph Loeb and Tim Sale (DC), has a pallid villain in the Scarecrow; *Trapped,* by Dean R. Koontz, adapted by Ed Gorman and illustrated by Anthony Belau (Eclipse), is notable for being the first graphic novel adaptation of Koontz's work; *Sebastian O,* by Grant Morrison and Steve Yeowell (Vertigo), a three-part series, seems to take place in Victorian England, except for those computers. . . . and has some very unpleasant characters; *Revelations* and *Babel's Children* by Clive Barker (Eclipse)—*Revelations* is adapted by Steve Niles and illustrated by Lionel Talaro, while *Babel's Children* is adapted by Steve Niles and illustrated by Hector Gomez; *Like a Velvet Glove Cast in Iron*, by Daniel Clowes (Fantagraphics Books), is a surreal story about pornography with no sex, but instead rife with mutilation and monsters; and *Lève ta jambe mon Poisson est Mort!* by Julie Doucet (Drawn & Quarterly)—translated literally as *Lift Your Leg My Fish is Dead!*—is a compilation of this popular Canadian graphic novelist's work. Fresh, raw, dirty, funny—very female.

Nonfiction:
The Day of the Dead and Other Mortal Reflections, by F. Gonzalez-Crussi (Harcourt, Brace) is a lively book of short essays by a professor of pathology. The B.B.C. asked to

make a documentary based on Gonzalez-Crussi's writings and in doing so followed him around on a whirlwind tour to Chicago to visit an embalmer and film an autopsy, to cemeteries and pathology labs, and to Crussi's native Mexico for the annual Day of the Dead celebration. This book, delving into history, literature, film, and his own memories, is Dr. Gonzalez-Crussi's attempt "to cast into literary form the varied reflections or meditations sparked along the way and the experiences incurred . . . in the course of the production." The author is a marvelous storyteller and a meticulous observer. A section was published in *The New Yorker*.

Murder in the 1940s, from Colin Wilson's True Crime Files (Carroll & Graf), is an entertaining book of case studies (by Wilson and others) of the more sordid murders of the era, including London's "Blackout Ripper," the case of "The Black Dahlia," and the "Acid Bath Murderer."

Murder Guide to London, by Martin Fido (Academy Chicago), is a great walking-tour guide to murders in London, organized by area. Wonderfully detailed, with maps, illustrations, bibliography, and index to victims, murderers, and locations, this is a handy little book for the tourist with more macabre tastes. Highly recommended.

The Chronicle of Crime: The Infamous Felons of Modern History and Their Hideous Crimes, by Martin Fido (Little, Brown–U.K., Carroll & Graf), is an oversized hardcover illustrated with over 450 photographs, collected and presented in a year-by-year newspaper format from the beginning of the nineteenth century to 1993.

The Illustrated Vampire Movie Guide, by Stephen Jones (Titan, U.K.), is an oversized trade paperback filmography liberally laced with photographs from many vampire films, obscure and famous, from the silents to the nineties. Jones includes *any* movie with a vampire in it, whether the movie is about vampires or not, and gives ratings for all films. It's a good book to dip into, with excellent design and photo reproduction; its companion volume, *The Illustrated Dinosaur Movie Guide* has an introduction by Ray Harryhausen and profiles him, Willis O'Brien (the head technician in charge of creating King Kong), and others involved in building the great ape. Same format, just as entertaining.

The Transylvanian Library: A Consumer's Guide to Vampire Fiction by Greg Cox (Borgo) is a bibliography and reader's guide to vampire fiction, novels, and short stories. It covers the material in chronological order, putting the literature in a historical context. However, this format makes it difficult to look up specific writers or their work without checking the index. Entertaining and useful, with bats as a rating guide.

Androids, Humanoids, and Other Science Fiction Monsters: Science and Soul in Science Fiction Films by Per Schelde (N.Y.U. Press). The author treats most of the movies herein as "monster movies" rather than using any kind of SF criteria. His thesis—that SF film represents a kind of modern folklore—forces all science fiction movies into the same boot, whether it fits or not, making for a very peculiar book. I get the feeling he hasn't actually seen some of the movies he analyzes, but rather, has read about them. He confuses the two female characters/actresses in *Brainstorm*; his analysis of *Alien* being about monstrous vs. natural motherhood neglects the popular interpretation of what those penile appendages did to a couple of the unfortunate crew of the *Nostromo*; and in his bibliography he describes *A Clockwork Orange* as "an upbeat, happy movie."

Looking at Death, by Barbara P. Norfleet (David R. Godine), is a collection of 107 photographs of death between 1850 and the present culled from the archives of Harvard University and Radcliffe College. The material ranges from grisly post-mortem photographs of Mussolini, mummies, murder victims, and dead soldiers to the quite peaceful-looking infants posed in death for their memorial photographs. In the past, photography was a way to help people come to terms with the devastation of losing a young loved one. Norfleet's essay puts the photographs in a context, but the photos themselves are the stars of the show. Highly recommended for those with a taste for the macabre.

Encyclopedia of Death: Myth, History, Philosophy, Science—The Many Aspects of Death and Dying, by Robert Kastenbaum and Beatrice Kastenbaum (Avon), is a very peculiar book in that it seems almost random in its entries. While each alphabetized subject seems meticulously researched and some of the entries are fascinating—such as Black Death, The Dance of Death (Danse Macabre) and great deathbed scenes—others are way too long, too dry, or given no context or explanation as to why they are included. Why Jim Jones and no other mass murderers? Why cover suicide but not murder?

The Vampire Encyclopedia, by Matthew Bunson (Crown), is a useful guide to the undead, with more than 2,000 entries covering in detail methods of finding, identifying, and destroying vampires; the origin and meaning of the accepted ways of resisting vampires; the importance of blood in vampiric lore; and the psychological-medical view on vampirism. It makes interesting reading. The appendix of novels and anthologies is a hit-and-miss affair, though; some of the misses being Barbara Hambly's classic novel *Those Who Hunt the Night*, my second vampirism anthology *A Whisper of Blood*, and a mistaken attribution of the editing of the anthology *The Ultimate Dracula* to Leonard Wolf.

The Encyclopedia of Ghosts and Spirits, by Rosemary Ellen Guiley (Facts on File), is an oversized 350+ page paperback. Thorough, entertaining, and seemingly exhaustive, its entries include ghosts and spirits from all cultures, hauntings, and descriptions of various types of psychic phenomena. Fascinating little tidbits for those interested—Mark Twain purportedly witnessed an "arrival case," in which he saw a person hours before the person actually appeared at an event. Great for browsing.

News from the Fringe: True Stories of Weird People and Weirder Times, by John J. Kohut and Roland Sweet with illustrations by Drew Friedman (Plume), is a compendium of strange but (supposedly) true craziness. The fourth volume in the series, this one notes sightings of Jesus and Mary, a Thai gang of transvestite robbers who forced victims to suck their drugged nipples in order to tranquilize them, and a man who blew himself up in Corsica while fishing with explosives. Fun for the whole family.

Bloody Business: An Anecdotal History of Scotland Yard, by H. Paul Jeffers (Pharos Books), is an informative and entertaining history of Scotland Yard and police detection in Great Britain. In addition to actual murder cases, the book includes fascinating material—such as the fact that Henry Fielding, initially a playwright, gave up that profession because of censorship pressure and instead became a lawyer and magistrate of London (during which period he wrote *Tom Jones*). Highly recommended.

Without Conscience: The Disturbing World of the Psychopaths Among Us, by Dr. Robert D. Hare (Pocket), is a chilling book for the layman about psychopathology and how to identify it. A professor of psychology in Canada, Hare defines the term and discusses the characteristics of psychopaths. They can be of any age (think of *The Bad Seed*, or some of the crimes committed by children today). An important tip-off is an inability to feel emotions. These people simulate what they think they are supposed to feel. The really bad news is that there is no answer at this time to what causes the syndrome or how to cure those who suffer from it (and inflict themselves on other people).

Bones: A Forensic Detective's Casebook, by Dr. Douglas Ubelaker and Henry Scammell (HarperCollins), is for those interested in forensics and the identification of skulls and skeletons (similar to *Witnesses From the Grave* by Joyce and Stover, covered a couple of years ago). Ubelaker is curator of anthropology at the Smithsonian. He and Scammell give a basic history of forensic anthropology and relate various case histories. Annoyingly, they never tell the outcome—who was murdered and how.

Rack, Rope and Red Hot Pincers: A History of Torture and its Instruments by Geoffrey Abbott (Headline, U.K.) is a disturbing compendium of various tortures through the ages (although Abbott avoids more contemporary ones). Repellent and very difficult to read in one sitting.

The Video Watchdog Book, by Tim Lucas with foreword by Joe Dante (Video Watchdog), is a collection of columns written by Lucas between 1985 and 1992. The column began in response to his viewing a video of *Hercules* and discerning differences between it and the version he had previously taped from a telecast; Lucas then realized aficionados would want to know if they were seeing cut or uncut movies. The columns reprinted in the book originally appeared in *Video Times* or *Gorezone*. In the book, Lucas gives updates on each column when appropriate. Now, of course, he publishes the magazine *Video Watchdog*. A must for genre video connoisseurs.

Lon Chaney: The Man Behind the Thousand Faces, by Michael F. Blake (Vestal Press), is a biography of the actor whose remarkable ability to change his appearance radically from film to film enabled him to create an enormous gallery of colorful and grotesque characters. Chaney played a legless gangster, the Hunchback of Notre Dame, the Phantom of the Opera, and Dr. Jekyll and Mr. Hyde. (He played dual roles in many movies.) Even more interesting than the actual biography are the articles in the afterword about makeup problems, and prison reform. Loads of photos of the actor in and out of makeup; he was a fascinating man. In place of hard data are numerous review notices and interview material from such magazines as *Photoplay*. One wonders about the accuracy of a life story drawn from these sources.

The Monster Show, by David J. Skal (Norton), is an engrossing cultural history of horror in which Skal's love and respect for the genre shines through. The book opens with an imaginary scene involving photographer Diane Arbus's epiphany at discovering Tod Browning's movie *Freaks*. Skal goes on to discuss the early horror movies and their censorship problems at home and abroad, Lon Chaney and his many roles (interestingly, Skal and Blake—Chaney's biography—disagree on how the star "created" the nose for Erik, the Phantom of the Opera). Skal's analysis of the post-W.W. II popularity among young horror fans of the gruesome *Tales From the Crypt* and other EC comics is brief yet fascinating. He feels the comic books were greatly influenced by war casualties more hideous in their physical destructiveness than in any earlier war. Personal revenge was an important theme and, according to Skal, ". . . morality was a state of grace attainable only by the living dead and the murderously insane." Another great quote of Skal's, about the horror-show hostess: "Vampira was a souped-up hearse . . . with headlights." Entertaining, compulsively readable, and highly recommended.

Pictures at an Execution: An Inquiry into the Subject of Murder, by Wendy Lesser (Harvard), is a fascinating book about murder in life and art. According to Lesser, "We are all interested in murderers these days. They are our truth and our fiction; they are our truth *as* fiction, and vice versa." The book centers on a groundbreaking legal case in California, in which a federal court judge was asked to decide whether a gas chamber execution would be broadcast on public television. The decision at that time was negative. Lesser uses literature, film, and theater to paint an intricate portrait of contemporary society and its views on death, murder, and justice.

The Fine Art of Murder: The Mystery Reader's Indispensible Companion, edited by Ed Gorman, Martin H. Greenberg, and Larry Segriff with Jon L. Breen (Carroll & Graf), is a must for every mystery and dark suspense reader. It's an oversized paperback that looks from several different directions at mystery fiction of all kinds—from the cozy to the police procedural to the serial killer novel, from regional views to gay detectives to comic book detectives. The volume is full of overviews, interesting articles, and lists for each kind of mystery. There should be an equivalent for horror fiction. Nominated for the Edgar Award. Highly recommended.

A Prescription For Murder: The Victorian Serial Killings of Dr. Thomas Neill Cream, by Angus McLaren (University of Chicago), is a detailed account of a series of murders by strychnine poisoning. In addition to providing an account of the murders by Dr. Cream,

McLaren does a good job putting the crimes in a social context. The victims were all prostitutes or women seeking abortions at a time (the mid-1860s) when abortions were becoming more difficult to get. Also, the marriage laws and women's status in general was changing. The victims were considered guilty because they were bad (although I can't see much difference today), and the police didn't go out of their way to look into "suspicious" deaths of prostitutes. Highly readable. Recommended.

The History of Hell, by Alice K. Turner (Harcourt, Brace), is an attractive, informative, and entertaining 4000-year survey of how religious leaders, poets, painters, and ordinary people have visualized Hell—its location, architecture, furnishings, purpose, and inhabitants. Our ideas of Hell have changed over history but one thing seems sure—most of us find it a lot more interesting than Heaven. From the painterly images of Hieronymus Bosch, Gustav Doré, William Blake, and Auguste Rodin to, in the Age of Freud, the more literary images of Hell by such writers as Joseph Conrad, Joseph Heller, Günther Grass, and Jerzy Kozinski.

Other notable nonfiction titles: *The Diary of Jack the Ripper: the Discovery, the Investigation, the Debate* (Hyperion) one of the big brouhahas of 1993. Is it authentic? People I trust think not; *Horror and the Holy: Wisdom-Teachings of the Monster Tale* by Kirk J. Schneider (Open Court); *Once Around the Bloch: An Unauthorized Autobiography of Robert Bloch* (Tor); *A Critical Edition of the War of the Worlds: H. G. Wells's Scientific Romance*, introduction and notes by David Y. Hughes and Harry M. Geduld (Indiana University Press); *The Invisible Man: The Life and Liberties of H. G. Wells* by Michael Coren (Bloomsbury/Atheneum); *Brave New World: History, Science, and Dystopia* by Robert S. Baker (Macmillan/Twayne); *Lord Dunsany: A Bibliography* by S. T. Joshi and Darrell Schweitzer (Scarecrow Press); *Stephen King: Man and Artist* by Carroll F. Terrell (Northern Lights); *(Vampires) An Uneasy Essay on the Undead in Film* by Jalal Toufic (Station Hill); *Classic Horror Writers*, edited by Harold Bloom (Chelsea House); *On Poe: The Best from American Literature*, edited by Louis J. Budd and Edwin H. Cady (Duke University Press); *The Essential Frankenstein: The Definitive Annotated Edition of Mary Shelley's Classic Novel*, edited by Leonard Wolf (Plume) the original 1818 text; *H. P. Lovecraft Letters to Robert Bloch*, edited by David E. Schultz and S. T. Joshi (Necronomicon Press); *Irony and Horror: The Art of M. R. James* by Samuel D. Russell (The Ghost Story Society, U.K.); *Salem Is My Dwelling Place: A Life of Nathaniel Hawthorne* by Edwin Haviland Miller (University of Iowa Press); *Off With Their Heads: Fairy Tales and the Culture of Childhood* by Maria Tatar (Princeton University Press); *Hot Schlock Horror!* by John Wooley (Dreamtrip), wherein each of forty-three drive-in movies gets an illustrated chapter, ranging from *Anatomy of a Psycho* to *The Wizard of Gore* (P.O. Box 580932, Tulsa, OK 74158); *Poverty Row Horrors!: Monogram, PRC and Republic Horror Films of the Forties* by Tom Weaver (McFarland); *Vampires and Violets: Lesbians in Film* by Andrea Weiss (Penguin); *Horror Film Directors, 1931–1990* by Dennis Fischer (McFarland); *Fantastic Cinema Subject Guide* by Bryan Senn and John Johnson (McFarland); *Obsession: The Films of Jess Franco* by Lucas Balbo, Peter Blumenstock, and Christian Kessler (Videodram, Germany); *Creepers: British Horror and Fantasy in the Twentieth Century* by Clive Bloom (Pluto Press); *The Vampire Companion: The Official Guide to Anne Rice's The Vampire Chronicles* by Katherine Ramsland (Ballantine); *Movie Psychos and Madmen: Film Psychopaths From Jekyll and Hyde to Hannibal Lecter*, by John McCarty (Citadel); *Songs of Love and Death: The Classic American Horror Film of the 1930s* by Michael Sevastakis (Greenwood Press); *Fear to the World: Eleven Voices in a Chorus of Horror* by Kevin E. Proux (Starmont House)—previously unpublished interviews with Clive Barker, Ramsey Campbell, Chelsea Quinn Yarbro, F. Paul Wilson, and others; *Mary Shelley's Early Novels: "This Child of Imagination and Misery"* by Jane Blumberg

(University of Iowa Press); *James Branch Cabell and Richmond-in-Virginia* by Edgar Mac-Donald (University Press of Mississippi); *The Laserdisc Film Guide* by Jeff Rovin (St. Martin's); *Death: The Trip of a Lifetime* by Greg Palmer (Harper San Francisco); *Sade: A Biography of Maurice Lever* (Farrar, Straus & Giroux); *William Burroughs* by Barry Miles (Hyperion); *Among the Thugs* by Bill Buford (Vintage); *Broadsides From the Other Orders: A Book of Bugs* by Sue Hubbell (Random House); *On Poe: The Best From* American Literature, edited by Louis J. Budd and Edwin H. Cady (Duke University Press); *The Essential Dracula: The Definitive Annotated Edition of Bram Stoker's Classic Novel*, edited by Leonard Wolf (Plume); *The Birth of Modernism: Ezra Pound, T. S. Eliot, W. B. Yeats and the Occult* by Leon Surette (McGill-Queen's University Press); *Dracula: The Ultimate, Illustrated Edition of the World-Famous Vampire Play*, edited and annotated by David J. Skal (St. Martin's); *The Count of Thirty: A Tribute to Ramsey Campbell*, edited by S. T. Joshi (Necronomicon Press); and *The Invention of Pornography: Obscenity and Origins of Modernity, 1500-1800*, edited by Lynn Hunt (Zone Books).

Art Books:

Ranch, by Michael Light (Twin Palms Publishers) with an afterword by Rebecca Solnit, is a simple and stark evocation in black-and-white photographs of contemporary American life on a western ranch—the tools, the cattle, and the eventual completion of the process, the dead cow. A look at a vanishing lifestyle.

Diane Keaton's *Mr. Salesman*, also published by Twin Palms, views a lifestyle alien to anyone under forty. Keaton has collected training filmstrips of salesmen being taught to hook suckers on the American Dream. The eerie black and white photographs create the impression of a zombified citizenry. Terrifying.

Faces, by Nancy Burson (Twin Palms), is different from the book of the same title published in 1992 by the Contemporary Arts Museum in Houston. I hesitate to cover this book under the rubric of a "horror" anthology but I think it's important that Burson's extraordinary photography receive as much exposure as possible. An outgrowth of her evolving interest in the "face," the book consists of uncaptioned photographs of families afflicted with craniofacial conditions, as well as people who have been burned, and children with progeria (the rare and mysterious disease that accelerates aging and death). The afterword is by Jeanne McDermott, a woman who is the mother of Nathaniel, a child with Apert's syndrome, who was one of the first children to be photographed by Burson. McDermott justifies other people's staring "as the time required by the brain to make sense of the unexpected. . . . Watching others react to Nathaniel was like having a telescope aimed into the deep space of the human heart." A powerful study in humanity.

Aperture Fall 1993—On Location is about the working processes of seven well-established photographers including Joel-Peter Witkin's, whose photograph, *John Herring: Person With Aids, Posed as Flora with Lover and Mother, New Mexico 1992*, is on the cover. Witkins explains his working methods; how he put together the elements that make up a particular photograph just finished—*Raping Europa*. A new Witkin book, postponed from 1993, should be out from Twin Palms around now. Other photographers in the Aperture issue are Cindy Sherman, Annie Leibovitz, Lorna Simpson, Susan Meiselas, Adam Fuss, and Jon Goodman.

Heavy Light: The Art of De Es (Morpheus International) is a visual survey of the development of the Austrian artist's work between 1963 and 1989. His earlier work, strongly influenced by the Viennese School of Fantastic Realism which produced Ernst Fuchs and Rudolf Hausner, is imaginative and varied. His middle period, featuring boulder-like humanoids, was often used in *OMNI* magazine during the early '80s. Over the years, De Es Schwertberger's work has concentrated more on texture and less on actual content or context.

Horripilations: The Art of J. K. Potter (Paper Tiger, U.K.), with introduction by Stephen King, is a beautiful visual retrospective of Potter's career with commentary by Potter. Potter's text illuminates; in contrast, some of the text by Nigel Suckling is stilted and irrelevant (e.g., he rambles on about "cyberpunk" for several pages). The book showcases Potter's commissioned and personal art from 1985 on. His private work is obviously closer to his heart and as such is more interesting. The reproduction quality is generally excellent, with the exception of two pieces upon which King comments in the introduction—the reproductions are too dark to discern what King is referring to in them.

Baudelaire's Voyages: The Poet and His Painters, by Jeffrey Coven with an essay by Dore Ashton (Little, Brown/Bullfinch), is a smallish coffee table book about how the darker art of Bruegel, Delacroix, Goya, James Ensor, among others, influenced Baudelaire's poetry, which in turn influenced Munch and Redon. The book, with 65 color and 49 black and white illustrations was published in conjunction with an exhibition organized by the Heckscher Museum in Huntington, New York.

Monsters and Aliens From George Lucas, by Bob Carrau, foreword by George Lucas (Abrams), is an amusing art book of beings created and drawn by the artists at Lucasfilm. Some of the creatures have made it onto film, others not. Drawings, photographs, sketches along with witticisms, poems, recipes, diaries, etc. No individual credit is given to any of the artists.

The Disney Villain by Ollie Johnston and Frank Thomas (Hyperion), with a hologram of the evil queen from *Snow White* on the cover, is a retrospective of the villains created for the studio as well as a beautiful coffee table book. The authors were formerly two of the head animators at the Walt Disney Studio for more than forty years. Villains are often more colorful than heroes and the Disney villains are no exception. The wicked queen from *Snow White*, the stepmother in *Cinderella*, Captain Hook, Cruella De Vil, and all the animal villains (often cats) are here in all their glory. For all the bad press Walt Disney and his cartoon versions of classic fairy tales have gotten in the last decade, he was still a master animator and a visionary, and the Disney versions brightened a lot of kids' lives.

Grotesque: Natural Historical & Formaldehyde Photography (Fragment) is for those who can't wait for the next Joel-Peter Witkin or Rosamund Purcell. This handsome pocket-sized trade paperback includes excellent reproductions of photographs by several artists working with dead animal parts and people. In addition to the better known work of Witkin and Purcell are pig snouts by Akin & Ludwig (whose work appears in the Mütter Calendar), a storage room filled with stuffed, dead birds looking alive and peaceful by Roger Wagner, some overly arty color compositions by Paul den Hollander, and a confusion of feathers titled "Rhode Island Red Hits the Sack" by Olivia Parker. $12.95 + $2.50 postage. Can be ordered through the American distributor, Distributed Art Publishers, 636 Broadway, New York, NY 10012. DAP also has a toll-free number: 1-800-338-BOOK.

Odds and Ends:

The Three Little Wolves and The Big Bad Pig, by Eugene Trivizas and Helen Oxenburg (McElderberry Books), is a charming turnaround wherein the pig—a pretty nasty-looking character—victimizes three innocent wolves who first build a house of brick, then of concrete, then of plate armor.

The Sweetest Fig, by Chris Van Allsburg (Houghton Mifflin), is another beauty by World Fantasy Award-winner and creator of *The Mysteries of Harris Burdick*, *The Polar Express*, *The Wretched Stone*, etc. A mean-spirited dentist is given two magic figs for services rendered. The dentist, Monsieur Bibot, and his long-suffering dog Marcel act out a morality play of poetic justice in the author/artist's memorable color style.

The Sorcerer's Apprentice by Nancy Willard and illustrated by Leo and Diane Dillon (Blue Sky/Scholastic). The art is delightful and the poetry graceful. A new version of the classic made famous by Disney. By the creators of last year's *Pish, Posh, Said Hieronymous Bosch*.

Halloween, written and with photographs selected by Katherine Leiner (Atheneum), is by turns charming and sinister. Some of the contemporary photographers represented are William Wegman, Mary Ellen Mark, Matt Mahurin, Arthur Tress, and Sally Mann. A few photographs are original to the book. A nice Halloween gift for children, with all the profits and royalties going to the Pediatric AIDS Foundation.

The Nightmare Before Christmas, by Tim Burton (Hyperion), makes a better book than movie, particularly if you hated, as I did, the light operatic ditties throughout the film. Horror readers will find the book a gas (as will subversive children), as Santa Claus is kidnapped so that the denizens of Halloweenland can contribute their services to Christmas Town. The story seems truncated, but the illustrations by Burton are terrific.

The Mushroom Man, by Ethel Pochocki and Barry Moser (Green Tiger), is a charming children's book about an unattractive, solitary little man who makes an unexpected friend. His job, harvesting mushrooms, seems to fit him well—he looks like a mushroom. Illustrated by one of the finest contemporary illustrators—Moser has illustrated more than one hundred books for adults and children, his wonderful wood-engravings gracing *Moby-Dick*, *Alice's Adventures in Wonderland*, *The Wonderful Wizard of Oz*, and last year's *Beauty and the Beast*.

Cinderella, by William Wegman (Hyperion), starts off a series of "Fay's Fairy Tales." Fay is Fay Wray, Wegman's star Weimaraner who has posed for her master in costume and out. Here, she plays the evil stepmother to her daughter Battina's Cinderella. The second in the series is *Little Red Riding Hood*. Battina plays the title character. In these doggy tales, everyone lives happily ever after, even the wolf and the evil stepsisters. If you like dogs dressed in wigs and costumes (I know *I* do), these books are for you.

Mexico: The Day of the Dead is a little box put out by Shambhala/Redstone Editions, which consists of an anthology on the subject compiled and edited by Chloe Sayer and designed by Julian Rothenstein. The small hardcover contains essays, poems, illustrations, memorial photographs of the dead, *calaveras* (witty fake epitaphs), a piece on Sergei Eisenstein's ambitious but unfinished Mexican film project, and extracts by Malcolm Lowry and Octavio Paz. With the book comes a color print of a detail from a mural by Diego Rivera, a tin skeleton, and a postcard-sized print of a skeletal couple. A great gift.

From the same publisher comes *The Paradox Box*, with foreword by Jonathan Miller, a charming and fun assemblage of optical illusions and puzzling pictures—twenty-three full-color cards and five black-and-white cards, three "hold-to-the-light" images, four with folds or moving parts, and two little books, one a reproduction of *Spectropia*, a color booklet of "after-image" pictures, and the second an anthology of verbal paradoxes and words at play, compiled by artist Patrick Hughes. This too, would make a great gift. Both are highly recommended.

Barron Storey: The Marat/Sade Journals (Tundra) is a beautifully designed hardcover with four-color illustrations and black-and-white pencil sketches. As an art book, it's terrific. I've read de Sade, Beckett, Hesse (all of whom Storey quotes liberally), and seen *Marat/Sade* the play and movie, and I still have no idea what Storey's trying to accomplish. Ignore the postmodern gibberish of the text and buy it as an art collectible.

Bad Girls Do It!: An Encyclopedia of Female Murderers, by Michael Newton (Loompanics Unlimited), uses the same format as *Hunting Humans*. Case histories of 182 women who have committed multiple murders. Women still have a long way to go to catch up with men in the murder racket, but we're getting there, and many seem to have the same motives as men.

Bob Flanagan: Supermasochist, People Series: Volume One (Re/Search), is the first book in a series that will be focusing on unusual people. It is a fascinating profile/autobiography of a man who has suffered from cystic fibrosis since birth, and at forty-one has lived far longer than anyone else with the disease. According to editors Andrea Juno and V. Vale, "The physical pain of his childhood suffering was principally alleviated by masturbation and sexual experimentation, wherein pain and pleasure became inextricably linked, resulting in his lifelong practice of extreme masochism." This is a series of interviews with Flanagan about his obsession, and his relationship with Sheree Rose, his long-time partner and mistress. There is a wonderful rant about "Why?" and it really *does* give the outsider a hint at the answers. The numerous photographs taken by Rose show Flanagan in all his glory— pierced, tattooed, whipped, and branded, during his shows, in the hospital, during his childhood. A life story of pain and dealing with that pain. Flanagan has a great sense of humor and irony, and seems like a really sweet and interesting guy. Highly recommended.

Incredibly Strange Music, Volume I, was also published by Re/Search in 1993. It's a comprehensive guide to little-known yet amazing vinyl recordings, and features the following kinds of music: outer space, belly-dancing and lurid stripping, Moog, whistling, harmonica, exotica, celebrity (and *sub*-celebrity).

Encyclopedia of Unusual Sex Practices, by Brenda Love (Barricade Books), is an entertaining foray into the world of weird and not-so-weird sex. One of the weirdest is the guy who has "a doll fetish who shaved the hair from Barbie doll heads and then swallowed the heads to produce sexual arousal. X-rays showed six doll heads in his intestines. Once these passed through the digestive tract he would boil them and repeat the process." Aside from the book's entertainment value, it's a useful fount of knowledge about sexual terminology, a how-to, and has helpful illustrations. Highly recommended.

MicroAliens: Dazzling Journeys with an Electron Microscope, by Howard Tomb and Dennis Kunkel (Farrar, Straus & Giroux), is aimed at young adults and shows ordinary objects photographed in black and white through an electron microscope. You've got bees, ladybugs, fleas, dust mites, etc., looking like monsters from outer space; even hair cut with scissors looks mutilated as it is "squashed" rather than "sliced."

Higham's House of Horrors is a mail order business specializing in the gruesome, the morbid, the icky, or—as George Higham calls it—Macabrebilia. Featured in his most recent catalog is the dead fetus line: "Bizarre and controversial! Gothic and truly macabre, these lifesize hydro-stone sculptures are both practical and ornamental." A "sleeping dead fetus candy dish/incense holder" is $60; "decayed fetal corpse in bondage" bookends are $100 for the pair. The b&w catalog doesn't do justice to the sculptures. I've seen color photographs. $1 to Higham's House of Horrors, PO Box 180-204, Brooklyn, NY 11218. For all you out there with a taste for the grotesque.

Jerk, by Nayland Blake and Dennis Cooper (Artspace), is a beautifully produced and quite disturbing product made to look like a children's book with a "this book belongs to" section on the inside cover. The subject is Dean Corll's serial killings of young boys, done in the form of a puppet show. The story is told from the point of view of David Brooks, one of Corll's two young accomplices. The two boys brought back other boys to the Corll house where they tortured, raped, and murdered them. Blake created "marionettes and puppets to examine ritual, addiction, cultural iconography, and fetishism." A powerful piece of work that will offend many. Cooper is the author of the dark and violent books *Closer* and *Frisk*.

The Deluxe Transitive Vampire: The Ultimate Handbook of Grammar for the Innocent, the Eager, and the Doomed, by Karen Elizabeth Gordon (Pantheon), is a beautiful new edition of the book (along with the *Well-Tempered Sentence*) that made thousands of readers look at grammar in a new way—as fun. Gordon uses pop culture for her colorful images, particularly the horrific and the fantastic. As she says in her introduction, she "is smuggling the injunctions of grammar into your cognizance through a ménage of revolting lunatics kidnapped into this book." Vampires, lamias, trolls, and gargoyles, bound through these pages, in the text, and in the imaginative collage art by Marc Yankus. Gordon's use of language makes one sit up and take note: e.g., "the subject . . . is what the sentence's other words are gossiping about" and "the verb is the heartthrob of a sentence."

Broadsides From the Other Orders: A Book of Bugs, by Sue Hubbell (Random House), is an absorbing mixture of facts and reflections by a bug lover. There are two kinds of people: those who are terrified and/or hate bugs, and those like Hubbell, who are fascinated by them. Throughout her life she has been intrigued by all kinds of bugs and has visited different entomologists, questioning them and sometimes working with them. Each chapter, about a different kind of bug, is informative and entertaining. Even bugs no one has a good word for, like the black fly, which plagues northern states and Canada during the late spring and early summer, have to be studied in case their eradication damages the health of the trout that feed off their larvae. And according to the experts, the African "killer bees" inching up the United States are more victims of a political propaganda campaign than an actual threat. Indeed, these sturdy honey bees may be the best thing ever to happen to American beekeeping, because of their resistance to disease.

A lovely little tidbit: Vladimir Nabokov "studied the mountain blues so thoroughly that he patterned his descriptions of Lolita after one of them: certain phrases—such as 'fine downy limbs'—come from technical descriptions of this butterfly." Highly recommended.

Katan Doll Retrospective by Katan Amano photographed by Ryoichi Yoshida plus: *Katan Doll, Katan Doll: Fantasm,* and *Anatomic Doll* by Ryoichi Yoshida (all the above from Treville). The retrospective was first brought to my attention by K. W. Jeter in San Francisco last year, and I knew I had to procure a copy for myself. The text is in Japanese, so I suppose there can be some misinterpretation here, but still . . . what you've got are lush color photographs of beautiful, tortured-looking dolls (presumably made by Katan Amano) with glass eyes that make them look real; battered, melancholic, sexy children, some dressed in Victorian velvets, some half-naked, others Brian Froud-like—elfin. This is doll-porn, somewhat reminiscent of Hans Bellmar but much more sexual and evil-looking. There are also some evil-looking cats, grotesque sculptures of strange creatures, and a Bosch reproduction in sculpture form. But it's those eerie dolls. . . . The three books are small and overlap somewhat with the Retrospective. Highly recommended.

Classic Crews: A Harry Crews Reader (Poseidon) collects his novels *Car* and *The Gypsy's Curse,* his memoir, *A Childhood: The Biography of a Place,* and three essays. A must for those readers interested in the southern gothic tradition of Flannery O'Connor and Carson McCullers.

The Trials and Tribulations of Little Red Riding Hood, edited by Jack Zipes (Routledge, second ed.), traces the story's evolution from its first tellings as a folktale, to its written renderings by authors such as the Brothers Grimm, Walter De La Mare, James Thurber, Anne Sexton, and Angela Carter. Zipes uses thirty-five of the best versions to explore questions of Western culture, sexism, and politics. A new preface, epilogue and expanded bibliography are included.

Freaks: Myths and Images of the Secret Self, by Leslie Fiedler (Anchor), is a reissue of the classic study of the nature of man's fascination with freaks from classical times to the present. Highly recommended.

Trading cards:

Windows on the Unspeakable, by Robert Williams (Kitchen Sink), are 36 "adults only" cards, colorful, beautifully rendered dream and nightmare images in a kind of psychedelic style; *Dinosaur Nation: Seventy Years of Saurian Cinema* (Kitchen Sink) are 36 color movie posters compiled and annotated by Michael Barson from 1919 up to the late sixties; *Chicago Mob Wars,* by Max Allan Collins and George Hagenauer (Kitchen Sink) are 36 sepia-toned cards about the conflict between Eliot Ness and Al Capone; *Human Freaks and Oddities*

IV, texts written by Zack Umagat and Roger Worsham (Mother Productions), looks better than the Freakards, from a different company a few years ago. The photographs are clearer, and bordered in a deep pink that brings out the images better. Some cards I was unfamiliar with include the "headless girl illusion" and "the largest mouth."

Cold Blooded Killers: A Collection of Madmen (Mother Productions) has a variety of art by Samatha Harrison, Dan Sauerwold, and Roger L. Worsham ranging from psychedelia to cartoons. The box cover art is by Paul Leblanc. The forty full color cards cover less familiar slayers as well as the expected ones, and are labeled "For mature audiences." *Nazi Cards* (Mother Productions), with box cover art by Roger L. Worsham contains forty cards of Nazi propaganda poster art, mini-bios with photographs of Hitler, samples of propaganda booklet covers, postcards, portraits of Hitler, and German war posters (not specifically Nazi). Interesting perspective not usually seen in the U.S.

The Hollywood Dead (Mother Productions) set of trading cards comes in a little cardboard coffin. Each card has a photo of a star's tombstone. Photographs by Roger L. Worsham, Artie Freedman, and Zack Umagat. *Bloody Visions: Mass Murderers and Serial Killers II,* by Michael H. Price and Todd Camp (Shel-Tone), 36 cards in full color, a follow-up to last year's *Bloody Visions.*

Clive Barker Trading Cards, art by Clive Barker, written by Michael Brown and designed by Jim Whiting (Fantaco) are 50 striking black and white and gold cards of characters and scenes from Barker's movies, novels, stories, and plays; each card is a gorgeous miniature piece of art. *True Crime Series Four: Serial Killers and Mass Murderers* (Eclipse), text by Valerie Jones and Peggy Collier, art by Paul Lee. Beautifully rendered, as are the earlier cards in the series. Now you can get the first two volumes in the series as little paperback booklets for $4.95 each. Just as attractive as the trading cards.

Some interesting calendars:

The Mütter Museum Calendar once again "presents the work of a distinguished group of photographers who have turned their attention to the unexpected art inherent in the study of medical science." The photographers are Rosamund Purcell, Scott Lindgren, Gwen Akin and Allan Ludwig, Max Aguilera-Hellweg, Shelby Lee Adams, and Arne Svenson. The Mütter Museum of the College of Physicians of Philadelphia has, from all accounts, a remarkable collection of wax models of diseased limbs and faces, preserved human skulls, fetuses, skeletons, and other oddities of interest to medicine. Some bookstores carry the calendar or write to 19 South 22nd Street, Philadelphia, PA 19103, for ordering information.

The Autonomedia Calendar of Jubilee Saints: Radical Heros for the Millenium is a 15-month wall calendar with 500 images and thousands of dates of events in world history. The credo is "everyday a high holiday," so celebrate with this goofy and colorful (not to mention useful) calendar. And you can nominate your own saints for the next year's calendar. $6 to Autonomedia, P.O. Box 568, Williamsburgh Station, Brooklyn, NY 11211.

Charles Burns Calendar has a full-color cover and twelve black-and-white pieces of classic Burns art including the cover of *Hard Boiled Defectives,* a portrait of William S. Burroughs, and a Jim Jones caricature. The events noted on this calendar are more of the "hipper" ones, including the day the patent for the toothpick was awarded. (Last Gasp of San Francisco, 2180 Bryant Street, San Francisco, CA 94111). *The Psychotronic Movie Calendar* by Michael Weldon has black & white movie posters of trash movies and all kinds of events relating to films (St. Martin's Press); *H. R. Giger Calendar of the Fantastique* is beautiful with an eerie red-orange set of lips on the front and a multitude of dead babies on the back. The dates are done in pale blue, salmon, and lilac on a black background (not a calendar to write on). Literary and artistic events noted (Morpheus International).

—Ellen Datlow

Horror and Fantasy in the Media: 1993
by Edward Bryant

There was good news and there was bad news. I could quote from that famous first line from Charles Dickens and *The Tale of Two Cities*, but I don't feel like being so terribly formal this year. Let's just say that 1993 was a wonderful year for Hollywood, a terrific year for a few films of the fantastic, but certainly no bed of hot gross receipts for most of them. To put it succinctly, all the really big bucks clotted around one summer blockbuster and one holdover from 1992. The holdover was Disney's *Aladdin*, which grossed nearly $118 million in 1993 alone. That was enough to set it in sixth place overall for the year's top ten, and in second place in the genre film category. Oh yeah, and the video release did indeed bowdlerize the music under the opening credits to make the lyrics less objectionable to Arab audiences.

The big kahuna for the year, though, was Steven Spielberg's *Jurassic Park*, adapted from the Michael Crichton best-seller. This T. Rex of popcorn features raked in close to $340 million in North America. Count the rest of the global markets, all the merchandising deals, the eventual video release, and you'll have the kind of staggering numbers with which you could launch a whole new Air Force bomber program. Never mind the odder spinoffs . . . did you know the movie has triggered a run on mineral dealers and the world supply of amber?

I hate to be a grinch, but I sometimes wonder, in the deep, dark shadows of my own psychic Jurassic thicket, if perhaps the movie's success wasn't so much due to its being a consummate masterpiece of cinema as it was to that oddly sapient fascination with dinosaurs. Regardless, zillions of people, young and old, went out to see *Jurassic Park*. And so what did they see? Well, they saw something of a reworking of Crichton's film, *Westworld*. Amusement park critters turn on the humans in each case.

The knockout part comes with the special effects. Seeing Yul Brynner play a robot was one thing; viewing a quantum leap forward in dinosaur puppetry and computer animation is yet another. Though not always consistently convincing, the dinosaur effects, a seamless blend of physical gimmickry and digital simulations, were generally astonishing. Along with various big lizards in supporting roles, the Tyrannosaurus Rex was awesome, particularly in his pursuit of the good guys in their Land Rover, and the smaller, faster, velociraptors were properly terrifying when put through their paces. They tended to upstage Sam Neill and Laura Dern as the paleo folk, and even Jeff Goldblum as something like the Bob Bakker of chaos math.

Jurassic Park was a lot of fun. Is it one of the greatest pictures of all time? Only financially. But it will go down in the film histories as one of the major signposts toward the future of cinematic technology. Along with TV's *Babylon 5* this year, *Jurassic Park* suggests just how convincingly filmmakers can now begin to fabricate and manipulate outright visual lies through the magic of computer simulation. Jurassic beasts today; recreating Bogie and Marilyn and James Dean tomorrow. Oh yeah, and tapes for blackmailing political candidates. . . .

Okay, so what about the rest of the film field that only made sixty or seventy million or less? In most cases, *much* less? Here are some feature films I thought pulled their own weight and more. These are not *all* the pictures of virtue; in fact, some aren't that virtuous at all. But they are the ones in our field I thought added something important to my viewing year:

1. Demolition Man
2. Tim Burton's Nightmare Before Christmas
3. Addams Family Values
4. The Dark Half
5. Batman: Mask of the Phantasm
6. Dead Alive
7. Alferd Packer: The Musical

Actually this list is pretty arbitrary. I'll mention some pictures later on that could just as appropriately hang out with the pack above. And maybe I have some second thoughts—secretly, of course—about the list, but this book's deadline is hard upon me and I've gotta say *something*.

Demolition Man's something of a guilty pleasure. I think of it somewhat as Sylvester Stallone's good picture of 1993. The bad one is, of course, *Cliffhanger*. It's not that *Demolition Man* is really top of the line science fiction. It's more that the movie's genuinely amusing, and deliberately so. The plot's not exactly fresh. An unjustly imprisoned cop (Stallone) is pulled out of cryogenic storage to do battle with a demented killer (Wesley Snipes) who, like Stallone, has been in the deep freeze since the late twentieth century. The future is a fairly humanist (read "wimpo") extrapolation of California New Age tendencies. A real old-fashioned macho dude is needed to kick some psycho butt. Snipes, by the way, does a great crazed job with his hair bleached blond. The action is furiously fast-paced. The product placement is superb (we have seen the future and the food is fast and Taco Bell). But what the film mainly has going for it is the humor. The satiric tongue's planted firmly in cheek throughout, sometimes broadly, sometimes with a nastily pointed wit. Hey, there's even a revolution of the poor and bored being led by people like Denis Leary. It works.

Tim Burton gave us *Nightmare Before Christmas* as a holiday present. This animated feature showed what would happen if all the bizarre denizens of Halloween decided to muscle in on the Christmas holiday action. Burton's design and realization of his vision is absolutely breathtaking. The story didn't come across as enthralling as one would have hoped, though the evolving love relationship between Jack Skellington (the voice of Chris Sarandon), the pumpkin prince, and Sally (the voice of Catherine O'Hara), the patchwork girl, was romantically macabre. Sally's performance was disjointed—but only literally. Directed by Henry Selick, scripted by Caroline Thompson, scored by Danny Elfman, this is a gorgeous dark fantasy.

Barry Sonnenfeld's *Addams Family Values* also looked great. I think this live-action sequel was a bit funnier than *The Addams Family*. In this one, Morticia and Gomez have their third child, Pubert. But their search for a nanny who'll stay longer than one night brings them a Black Widow killer (Joan Cusack) who's set her sights on poor Uncle Fester. Anjelica Huston, Raul Julia, Christopher Lloyd, and the rest do a splendid job realizing Charles Addams's creations. But the real high point of this picture is Christina Ricci's Wednesday. She flatly steals the picture. Or maybe it's just that she has all the best lines, not to mention the very best deadpan (and I use the word deliberately) delivery.

The pictures caught in Orion's bankruptcy are slowly creeping toward release. One of those painful survivors happens to be the best Stephen King adaptation of the year. That's George A. Romero's version of *The Dark Half*. Starring Timothy Hutton and Michael Rooker, the story treats a novelist whose dark alter ego comes literally to life. Murder and menace result. Part suspense shocker, part commentary on creativity and writing, *The Dark Half* is effective, but is not one of King's most polished achievements. But the film still is one of the most faithful and accomplished of his adaptations for the screen.

Along with the above-noted *Nightmare Before Christmas*, the other most interesting animated feature of the year was *Batman: Mask of the Phantasm*. A creation of the same creative team who do the syndicated TV series, the feature is certainly one of the hardest-edged G-rated movies in my experience. The look—very deco—is fabulous. Unlike most Saturday morning animation, people in this movie die, and then stay dead. Another fascinating element is the sight of animated adults actually performing a love scene. Whooee! The plot has Batman dealing with his old love, Andrea Beaumont, as well as dealing with a new anonymous killer in Gotham City who's doing in top-level gangsters. The phraseology of the title never actually appears in the script. Kevin Conroy provides the voice of the Batman, Dana Delany does the honors for Andrea, and Mark Hamill is wonderful as the Joker. This is first-rate work, and beats anything you could have seen in *Tom and Jerry: The Movie* or *We're Back! A Dinosaur's Story*.

For a horror movie both utterly uncompromising and totally berserk, you had to see Peter Jackson's *Dead Alive*. Take all your favorite zombie gross-out epics, crank 'em up to hyperdrive, then set the result in 1950s New Zealand as the deadly Sumatran rat-monkey (the result of mutant rats interbreeding with local simians) sets loose a grisly transformative plague. The ooze and guck budget on this one was considerable. It's all sublimely manic in a way that Sam Raimi and many others would do well to study carefully. This is a picture that ferociously gnaws your funnybone.

Another seriously comedic achievement that hit the festival circuit in 1993, and may yet find its way to general distribution, is *Alferd Packer: The Musical*. Based (loosely) on the actual historical event of guide Alferd Packer's becoming America's only convicted cannibal in the 1870s (terrible things happened to the five gold-hungry dudes he was hired to escort through Colorado's mountain winter), this unlikely musical was filmed by four University of Colorado film school graduates. One of those cool ideas, it escalated to full featuredom. And it works. The conceit is that the feature has been reassembled today after being produced back in 1954, then dropping out of sight after being overshadowed in the public eye by such films as *Paint Your Wagon*. The spark of this all is Trey Parker, a young man who wrote, directed, scored and stars in this singing, dancing, murdering extravaganza. Produced on a shoestring, it has a lavish look bred of its location filming in the Rockies. Though the production numbers are polished, it's the goofy details that help it work. A Mountain Ute encampment is populated by Indians played by Japanese. And Japanese is what they speak. Sometimes a minuscule budget, high production values, genuine talent, and inspired madness all happily come together. *Alferd Packer: The Musical* is one of those times. Whether at your local art theater, an unusual mallplex, or your favorite video store, check it out.

Okay, so those are some of the more interesting features. So what else was playing? Well, on the fantasy side of the ledger, you could see Bill Murray and Andie MacDowell in *Groundhog Day*, a comedy directed by Harold Ramis from a script by Danny Rubin and Ramis. Murray plays a churlish Pittsburgh weatherman who goes to Punxsatawney to cover the annual groundhog ceremony. Because of some unknown metaphysical mechanism, he finds himself living Groundhog Day day over and over. Apparently endlessly. Adaptable, at first he exploits the repetitive situation for ignoble aims (like learning to psych out a resistant woman he wants to bed). Later he cottons to the moral lesson the situation suggests. Alas, the whole proceedings are not exactly sprightly. Much in keeping with the metaphor of the whole shebang, *Groundhog Day* is very similar to *12:01 A.M.*, an Oscar-winning short feature based on a 1973 Richard A. Lupoff short story. With the title truncated to *12:01*, the Lupoff story was turned into a cable feature film last year.

Fantasy, but of a wildly different sort, is a touchstone for Guy Maddin's third feature, *Careful*. You may recall Maddin's bizarre *Tales from the Gimli Hospital* a couple of years back. This time the Canadian writer/director recreates a German expressionist look with cardboard sets and an eerily colorized version of black-and-white sequences. All is set in a little Alpine village where the avalanche danger is so acute, all inhabitants must remain very, very quiet. Kids are gagged until they're old enough to remain hushed on their own. Even the local dogs have to be debarked. Convoluted love and family relationships, visiting ghosts—all contribute to the outrageously funny surrealism. Très cool.

Now for some of the cheaper, but more conventional films. *Leprechaun* has its moments, though not many. Mark Jones wrote and directed this slight, but adequately gory, melodrama of an authentic Irish leprechaun come to America in search of a bag of stolen gold coins. Warwick Davis gets to eat a fair amount of scenery—as well as much fake flesh—as the magically vicious little feller with an attitude and a shoe fetish. Newcomer Jennifer Aniston has a good turn as a southern California princess unhappily marooned for a summer in North Dakota.

Sam Raimi's *Army of Darkness (Evil Dead III)* was a disappointment. This time with Bruce Campbell marooned in the Olden Times, the whacked-out humor of the first two *Evil Dead* films seemed to be spread mighty thin. The manic pace was still there, but somehow the energy seemed to have leached out. The humor was thin as well in *Coneheads*, though in a somewhat different sense. Dan Aykroyd and Jane Curtin's lovable extraterrestrial family worked fine as a series of skits on *Saturday Night Live*. But when expanded into a full feature-length treatment for Steve Barron's film, well, let's just say that animator Phil Tippett's Garthok monster was pretty terrific.

RoboCop 3, helmed by Fred Dekker, was another long-suffering survivor from Orion's shelf. Robert Burke takes over the cyborg role here from Peter Weller, cop sidekick Nancy Allen gets blasted, and Atlanta stands in for future Detroit. The appealing mix of humor and action is still present, though not nearly so over-the-top as in Paul Verhoeven's original feature. There's a real feeling of restraint, as though this version of Robo's man/machine identity crisis is aimed more at a younger, family audience.

New Line's *Man's Best Friend*, directed by John Lafia, attempts to set up a nice family horror movie about an experimentally altered mastiff designed to be the ultimate security device. Unfortunately, even though the dog is quite capable of (and does) kill and bury the mailman and chase a cat up a tree and swallow it whole, it still isn't nearly as frightening as a huge white shark that can't even make it up onto the beach. Ally Sheedy does her best to play a concerned mom; the always interesting Lance Henriksen phones in his role as the nasty scientist attempting to create superdogs.

It must be no fun for Stephen King to see a decent story strung up like a piñata, then subjected to a series of lame talents taking wild swings with a stick. 1993 saw *Children of the Corn II: The Final Sacrifice*. This was basically a rehash of the first version, right down to the bad script and the bad acting. Terrence Knox doesn't do too badly as a bimbo tabloid reporter—at least he looks the part. And there are a few nice touches such as a disenchanted small-town native capping a 15-year decision to leave by jacking up her big old frame farmhouse so she can take it with her. This almost leads to a witty nod to *The Wizard of Oz*, but then drops the ball when it drops the house. Then there's one cool scene when a bunch of murderous kids return their all-day suckers to the condescending local sawbones who gave them all lollipops earlier in the movie. David Price directs. North Carolina stands in for Nebraska. The production's silly, sexist, ageist, anti-environment, and, worst of all, anticlimactic when the One Who Walks Behind the Rows never troubles Himself to appear on camera. This is one that could give F.F.A. and 4-H a bad name.

Rather better, though not quite an Oscar competitor either, is *Needful Things*, adapted from Stephen King's thick novel about the final days of Castle Rock, Maine. As in the book, the devil comes to town, opens a store of heart's desire, and gives the locals an object lesson about the soul-searing dangers of getting what they wish for. Ed Harris has a good turn as the local sheriff. The pivotal character is, of course, Satan, but alas, the distinguished Max von Sydow can't seem to bring him to life. And the apocalyptic climax never seems quite apocalyptic enough. Or perhaps one should be a more devout Christian than is your Faithful Critic to enjoy this morality play properly.

Something rather more prepossessing is *Meteor Man*, a science fiction feature directed, written, and acted by Robert Townsend. He plays a mild-mannered school teacher who develops super-hero powers after getting clobbered with a meteor. A little reminiscent of Joe Morton's role in John Sayles' *Brother From Another Planet*, Townsend's portrayal represents both a solid black perspective and a funny, affecting, humanist view of neighborhood problems in the '90s.

Let's not forget Arnold and *Last Action Hero*. Though treated as a major disaster by Hollywood, it wasn't *that* bad. In this self-mocking treatment of the dynamic tension between theatrical action and real-life violence, Schwarzenegger probably went just a little too far into self-parody for his fans' taste. But when the movie worked, it was genuinely amusing. Probably those moments, as when Arnie does Hamlet, didn't happen often enough. But not to worry, those of you who were warned off by savage reviews—go ahead and rent the tape. This is no *Ishtar*.

Hmm. *Super Mario Brothers*? It had marginally more plot than the video game. That's no recommendation. It also had Bob Hoskins in the cast. That *is* a recommendation—up to a point. *Fire In The Sky*? Really only for latter-day Whitley Strieber fans. *Look Who's Talking Now*? No comment. *Jason Goes to Hell*? I'd sort of hoped this would be the crossover between Jason and Freddy Krueger. I was wrong. Not the worst of the *Friday the 13th* movies. But not the best either. And I guess the crossover feature's still on the way.

Then there was the special edition of *The Abyss*, James Cameron's 1989 epic of undersea first-contact. Twenty-something minutes of material cut from the initial theatrical release have been restored, ranging from some welcome character-fleshing-out stuff, to special effects sequences in which the marine aliens use super-science to menace human coastal cities in the interests of peace. The fascination of the film is still the character interrelationships and the spectacular underwater melodrama. The more obviously SF stuff still doesn't quite integrate or convince, but it was wonderful to see the more complete movie on a huge screen and with good sound.

There were two Hollywood remakes of European films that probably should never have been attempted. George Sluizer, the original director, remade *The Vanishing* with Jeff Bridges and Kiefer Sutherland, Americanizing the obsessive, claustrophobic original. They didn't do badly. The only viewers, I suspect, who felt deep outrage at seeing the movie ripped off and heavily diluted in effect were the folks who'd seen the 1988 version. Little do the '93 viewers know what they missed. John Badham remade Luc Besson's 1990 *La Femme Nikita* as *Point of No Return*. This grim *1984/Clockwork Orange*-ish tale of the brainwashing of a young female assassin succeeds as well as it does mostly because of Bridget Fonda's presence. But she's still not quite as magnetic a character as Anne Parrilaud was in the original. A solid reason to see the picture, though, is Harvey Keitel's depiction of Victor the Cleaner, the agent whose job it is to fix up the messes other agents carelessly generate. Bleakly funny stuff.

An interesting small horror film making the festival rounds is George Hickenlooper's *Grey Knight* (also known as *The Killing Box*). Set in Tennessee in 1863 at the height of the Civil War, it follows a Union mission to find out what weird force is killing soldiers from both North and South in terrifying ways. Adrian Pasdar, Corbin Bernsen, and Cynda Williams star. The film has a real multiple-personality problem since the script and plot can never quite reconcile whether the real supernatural force is vampirism or the more intriguing possibility of African mojo, but it's still fascinating for its setting and atmosphere.

Some odd stuff: *The Sandlot* is a sports movie for all of us who usually don't like sports movies. It's a boyhood baseball fantasy about the nature of friendship and growing up, and coping with the monster dog (literally) that lives next door in the junkman's (James Earl Jones) yard. If Bill Murray is something of a waste in *Groundhog Day*, he gets a much more challenging role in *Mad Dog and Glory*, John McNaughton's more-or-less main-stream follow-up to *Henry, Portrait of a Serial Killer*. Murray gets to play a darkly comic gangster to Robert De Niro's doofus cop. And for sheer fun, I hope you caught Robert Rodriguez's *El Mariachi*. Originally planned as a super-low budget feature for Spanish-language cable (it cost a few pennies over $7,000), Warner Bros. picked it up after a rave critical reception and put it into general release. It's funny, sharp, and conducted with witty conviction. You might think of it as something of a Sergio Leone movie for the nineties.

Over on the turf staked out by more realistic horror, *Kalifornia* raised some neck-hairs. *The X Files's* David Duchovny and Michelle Forbes play somewhat twittish yuppies who, to save a few bucks on gas, share a cross-country ride with a stone killer (Brad Pitt) and his sophistication-challenged girlfriend (Juliette Lewis). Naturally Duchovny and Forbes discover this to be a rather bad idea. At the same time, the unfolding revelations do help Duchovny, since his big idea for the trip route is to investigate sites of notorious mass murders for a book he's writing. His wife is photographing this Ed Geinoid odyssey. The best research is, indeed, experience. Pitt and Lewis do a particularly wonderful job por-traying white trash at its most crafty and slackjawed. The movie has a lot to say about the impulse toward violence and generally does so successfully. It is only—literally—in the final shot of the final scene that the director and writer drop the ball. A potentially chilling afterimage is reduced to the merely conventional.

I trust you all caught Jennifer Lynch's *Boxing Helena*. The media certainly gave you every opportunity to be alerted to the debut directorial effort by the second generation of Lynches to make strange movies. Probably the biggest related story was Kim Basinger's allegedly backing out of a verbal deal to star, and eventually getting socked in court for millions. The story itself was about an obsessed surgeon (Julian Sands) capitalizing on a traffic accident to keep the ever more immobilized (two limbs at a time) bitch-goddess Helena (Sherilyn Fenn) as a very private acquisition for his home. This supremely grotesque idea unfortunately became all effect, triggering little visceral response. One can only speculate how things might have turned out with the previously announced cast of Basinger and Ed Harris.

Then there's the matter of real-life horror ultimately presented as uplifting and even inspirational. I speak of Frank Marshall's film version of Piers Paul Read's account of the Uruguayan soccer team disaster, *Alive*. These were the young people who, along with their coaches and some of their families, found themselves trapped for seventy-two days in the Andes after a plane crash. A large part of their survival was ultimately due to their acceptance of the need to cannibalize the bodies of their dead fellows. Marshall and screen-writer John Patrick Shanley tread very carefully, almost reverently. This is a movie about faith and endurance as well as cannibalism. It also starts with one of the most harrowing depictions of a plane crash ever on film. The only real problem is that the cast is thoroughly North American: Ethan Hawke, Vincent Spano, etc. I guess the implicit thought was that our domestic audience wouldn't warm to identifiably Latino actors. Now *that's* horrifying.

Speaking of horrifying, here are a couple of remarkable features that are not, strictly speaking, horror movies. The thing is, though, if they walk like a duck, and talk like a duck, and scare the bejeezus out of you like a duck . . . well, maybe I ought to mention them.

Abel Ferrara's *Bad Lieutenant* is an intense little rough gem of a movie that will cause the Manhattan Tourist Authority to throw up its collective hands in utter dismay and severe disapproval. Harvey Keitel executes a supremely over-the-top role as a corrupt New York detective whose immersion in the case of a particularly nasty rape of a nun leads him to re-examine his own lapsed Catholicism and plumb the depths of twisted forgiveness. This is an ugly, ugly picture—and also a genuinely affecting one. But certainly not for every taste.

Then there's Tony Scott's *True Romance*. With a script by Quentin Tarantino, the writer/director of *Reservoir Dogs*, this is one manic inferno of a '90s *noir* crime movie. The cast is amazing: Christian Slater and Patricia Arquette as a young white-trash couple who meet over a Sonny Chiba triple-bill; Gary Oldman as a wanna-be-black pimp; Val Kilmer, Brad Pitt, Chris Penn, Dennis Hopper, Christopher Walken, and on and on. Slater and Arquette light out from Detroit to L.A. in a purple Caddy convertible with a suitcase full of unasked-for cocaine. A lot of people eventually want them—in custody for some, dead for the rest. It's all funny, sentimental, and brutally, casually violent. Call it a highly uneasy entertainment. And yes, there is indeed a fantasy element. Or perhaps realistic, depending on your particular brand of pop culture metaphysics. Slater's character keeps getting spirit messages from, well, the King of Kings. Yes, Elvis himself. *True Romance* isn't for kids; but it certainly is a treat for the weird kid in all grownups.

And now for something completely different. Sort of. I've been grousing, now and then, about the deplorable state of affairs as regards treatment of the fantastic on television. TV does make such an easy target. And I've been a bit disappointed in the proliferation of cable services and the looming specter of the info-pike not having really materialized much significant creative work in terms of high-quality, creatively written, low-budget video production. Well, things *are* creeping along, it seems. Or maybe I'm just starting to look in the right corners. Actually quite a lot is happening.

ABC aired something remarkable, exciting, and genuinely significant, even if most of us seemed still to be ultimately disappointed. I'm speaking of the Oliver Stone-backed miniseries, *Wild Palms*. Here were six hours of near-future SF written by Hollywood maverick Bruce Wagner. Check out his novel *Force Majeure* for a suitably nasty *Player*-like depiction of the film industry. The series aired in four episodes directed by a variety of talents including Peter Hewitt, Kathryn Bigelow, and Keith Gordon. James Belushi plays a poor dweeb who finds himself soon sucked into a maelstrom of surreal sociopolitical intrigue shortly after the cusp of the coming century. There's sex, violence, virtual reality, hardball politics as a valiant resistance group attempts to thwart an authoritarian power-grab, a thinly veiled—and none too flattering—view of L. Ron Hubbard and Scientology, lots of cyberpunk touches, a cameo by William Gibson, secret tunnels linking most of the important back yards of Beverly Hills, and a dream rhino at the deep end of Jim Belushi's empty swimming pool. Robert Loggia and Angie Dickinson seem to have an enormous amount of fun being absolutely vicious villains. So does it all work? Fascinated, I watched hour by hour and kept a mental log. The first four hours set up a completely intriguing world. In the fifth hour, things start to come undone. In the sixth and final hour, all comes disappointingly to naught. Part of the problem may be that James Belushi makes a convincing "before" portrait of a revolutionary. But when he becomes radicalized, it's a little hard to take his character seriously. The winning of the revolution is just a touch hard to swallow. Perfunctory is what it is. Too bad. But even as a partial success, *Wild Palms* was brave and exciting. It's the kind of financial and artistic risk the broadcast networks will have to take increasingly if they ever hope to compete with the indies and syndicated stations, and all the cable services.

Owned by the USA Network, the Sci-Fi Channel chugged along. Their ether was crowded with endless reruns of fairly undistinguished SF moldy-oldies. The "Sci-Fi Buzz" news show is briskly entertaining, thinly informative, and has renewed Harlan Ellison's deliciously provocative commentary feature. Unfortunately, the Sci-Fi Channel's market penetration is still a peculiar checkerboard that's leaving a variety of markets across the United States out in the cold. Mine, for example. Denver's just out of luck. I have to go to L.A. to watch the channel and to catch Harlan's no-holds-barred stand-up routines.

There's quite a bit one can watch in terms of dramatic series. Paramount continues to build its *Star Trek* projects, in part in preparation for the launch of its own network. Warner's doing the same thing with its projected Prime Time Entertainment Network, a staple of which will be J. Michael Straczynski's long-awaited *Babylon 5*. *Star Trek: The Next Generation* will, I believe, be extended another half-season, be followed by a feature film starring the TV cast, and then will ascend to franchise Valhalla. *Deep Space Nine* continues to slouch along. Every once in a while, I could swear I saw Hawk striving and sweating to break through Avery Brooks's incredibly humane exterior. The original *Star Trek* episodes continue to air just about everywhere in the known universe. And apparently a fourth *ST* series is in prep. Will it never end? Neither in my time nor in yours, matey.

There are other, less grandiose, series to be seen. Lifetime Cable still gives us *The Hidden Room*, a weekly half-hour anthology series of suspense-sometimes-with-fantastic-overtones. I had the pleasure of seeing one of my own stories dramatized in the summer with Stephanie Zimbalist starring. Other continuing series include the time-travelling bounty hunter action melodrama, *Time Trax*, and the low-brain-challenged but often diverting *Highlander*. And there was occasional amusement value in ABC's *Lois and Clark*, the latest seriocomic interpretation of the *Superman* legend. Over on NBC, Roy Scheider and the merry crew of *SeaQuest DSV* continue to limp along in the ratings. But Steven Spielberg wanted a family adventure show, and that's what he's got.

Cable also gave us a variety of in-house feature films. HBO's *Attack of the 50 Ft. Woman* gave us Daryl Hannah in a remake of the '50s, well, *classic* is probably too high-falutin' a word. Daniel Baldwin played Hannah's two-timing husband. Director Christopher Guest achieved some wonderfully lit scenes that looked as if they really *were* out of a '50s cheapie. It was a painless entertainment with an interesting, but not wholly convincing, '90s coda.

An HBO original production I had considerable hopes for was the cop-werewolf thriller, *Full Eclipse*. The script was by Michael Reeves and Richard Christian Matheson. Mario Van Peebles plays a cop who discovers there's a clandestine unit of lycanthropic officers existing secretly within the department. Before you can say "Patsy Kensit," his fellow cop and developing love interest (lupine to the core, she enjoys sex doggie style) shanghais Van Peebles into werewolfery. The pack leader and villain is Bruce Payne, the wonderful villain of *Passenger 57*. He gets the best line in the script, leering maniacally at Van Peebles as Payne withdraws a huge syringe needle from his head and goes through a "This is my brain, this is you on my brain, any questions?" routine. The effects and abundant violence never quite distract the viewer sufficiently from the nagging feeling that the plot and characters fall short of making as much sense as they could. And yes, I know this is a B movie; but that doesn't preclude ambition and intelligence. This was a film I really wanted to work.

Cinemax gave us Mark Hamill doing a number as Earth's last hope in *Time Runner*, coming back through a wormhole to alter things in the present so as to save future humankind from alien invasion. Don't tell me if you've encountered that plot before. The effects aren't bad, the script's a little unfocused, but the high point is seeing Brion James cast as the President of the World. About time, I'd say.

Cable also gave us some psycho horror movies too. A good example was *Slaughter of the Innocents*, in which FBI agent Scott Glenn and his incredibly precocious hacker kid (Jesse Cameron-Glickenhaus, apparently the son of the writer and director, James Glickenhaus) track down a religious zealot and serial killer in deepest, darkest Utah. The scene where we discover that the murderous nut has built a *Texas Chainsaw Massacre*–style full-size Ark in a cave high in the Utah mountains is definitely amusing. But poor Darlanne Pfluegle has a thankless role as wife and mother to the cop and kid. This ends up pretty much being a boys' movie.

I must admit, though, that my personal favorite among all the offerings on the small screen has not been *Picket Fences*, *The Simpsons* or the animated *Batman*, not even *Northern Exposure* or *Beavis and Butt-Head*. No, what I tune into religiously every week, or at least set the VCR timer for, is the Fox double feature of *The Adventures of Brisco*

County, Jr. and *The X Files*. What a blast. If you haven't seen it, *Brisco County* is something of a mutant hybrid between *The Wild, Wild West* and *Doc Savage*, set in 1898 in the far west. It stars Bruce Campbell and shows there is indeed life after *Evil Dead* movies. Creators Jeffrey Boam and Carlton Cuse have done a fine job setting up some genuine entertainment. And if the humor's generally as broad as the Mississippi, it's still good-humored in the extreme, and possesses a warmth not found in many series these days.

The X Files is a nifty series that can be credited to executive producer Chris Carter. There's a real *Night Stalker* sensibility about this one. David Duchovny and Gillian Anderson play an FBI team assigned to evaluate and investigate cases the Bureau doesn't want to get mired in—things like genetic monsters, UFO abductions, paranormal phenomena and the like. Duchovny's Fox Mulder is generally the believer, sometimes too much so. Anderson's Dana Scully is the skeptic. The show has allowed the mutual tension between Scully and Mulder to evolve throughout the season. One particularly adroit episode starred Brad Dourif doing a bizarre Mr. Rogers-ish interpretation of a death-row psychic trying to bargain with the government for his life. Jerry Hardin plays a mysterious Deep Throat bureaucrat who helps our protagonists from time to time. This being the nineties and life being complex, they usually need that help. The show manages to balance freestanding episodes with an allover story arc in a pleasing manner. Along with the characterizations, suspense and unexpected twists raise this show above the average. I can honestly say I hope this one makes it at least another season.

As ever, my coverage of the fantastic in music is haphazard. Remember, I do take suggestions for checking out performers and albums. Feel free to write me in care of this book. At any rate, the last year saw the usual proliferated number of metal albums replete with all sorts of darkly suggestive titles and dark fantasy package art. At the suggestion of Siobhan Keleher, a staffer at the Tattered Cover Bookstore, I'll pass on to you a citation for Ministry's *Psalm 69* (Sire/Warner Bros.). Better than the usual run of music designed to enrage parents. Consider this one a good compilation of tongue-in-cheek Satanic mass tracks.

Writer Norman Partridge turned me on to *Buck Naked and the Bare Bottom Boys* (Heyday Records), the self-titled memorial album for old Buck himself. Buck's tragic story is the stuff of which rock 'n' roll legends are made. On November 21, 1992, Buck, the front man for the Bay Area bar band that bears his moniker, was walking his dog in Golden Gate Park very early in the morning. It would seem that he was accused by a homeless man of molesting some pigeons. The homeless man held quite proprietary feelings about those birds. Also he was packing heat. He shot Buck dead (although the *San Francisco Chronicle* coverage of the trial couldn't seem to fix on whether Buck died by gunshot or stabbing). Early this year, the accused killer was brought to trial and convicted on a count of manslaughter. Now is that bizarre end comparable to Bobby Fuller's demise, or what? At any rate, *Buck Naked and the Bare Bottom Boys* boasts a full-color photo cover of the band with Buck using a plumber's friend as a codpiece, along with a dozen or so high-energy tracks good for manic listening, cranked-up dancing, or just for jump-starting a party. "Horny Pig" and "Enema Party" are two distinctive tracks. The SF part comes in with "Teenage Pussy From Outer Space." Sample: "They got no bodies and they got no face/They're teenage pussy from outer space." Hey, you were expecting Dylan? Anyhow, this is a fine goodtime album, albeit with a sad undertone.

Norm also recommended *The Forbidden Dimension* by Calgary's Sin Gallery (Cargo Records). This demented group boasts names such as Jackson Phibes, Lars Bonfire, and Larry Van Halen, and is clearly influenced by a vastly misspent childhood. "Carnival of Souls" and "Atomic Cannibal" are two of the cuts. "Martian Death Saucer" is another. Sold up-tempo stuff oozing with '50s SF/horror pop culture. Sin Gallery's version of "In the Pines" is not to be believed—or missed.

Musician and writer Trey Barker suggested a truly varied selection of *Nite Flights* by David Bowie; "I Do Miracles," "Morphine Tango I," and "Where You Are" from the Broadway soundtrack of *Kiss of the Spider Woman*; *Postman* by Living Colour; "Snowbound," "Trans-Island Skyway," and "Tea-House and the Tracks" from *Kamakiriad* by Donald Fagan; and *Renaissance Man* by Midnight Oil. That gets a prize for eclecticism.

And let us not forget Billy Idol's *Cyberpunk* album. It's not Warren Zevon and *Transverse City*, but what the heck.

Last year I reported on that peculiarly literary supergroup, the Rock Bottom Remainders, and their spectacular performance at the American Booksellers Association annual trade show. Well, they returned for a follow-up appearance at the 1993 A.B.A. in Miami Beach, once again having a great time (and treating the audience to a similarly great time) and demonstrating why most writers really shouldn't give up their day jobs.

Actually the concert wasn't just that—it was the capstone of a mini-tour. This supergroup composed primarily of literature's superstars was climaxing a two-week, eight-city, East Coast "3 Chords & an Attitude" tour on behalf of a variety of worthy literacy and free-speech causes. Still under the musical direction of classic blues-rocker Al Kooper, the Remainders performed two sets at the Club Paragon (where the unisex restrooms featured vending machines for condom earrings and condom lollipops). Most of the music was rock standard covers, occasionally doctored with varietal lyrics. The primary group consists of guitarists Dave Barry (lead), Stephen King (rhythm), Ridley Pearson (bass), along with Robert Fulghum on mando cello and Barbara Kingsolver playing keyboards, and non-writer ringers Josh Kelly on drums and Jerry Peterson wailing on sax. Backup singers Amy Tan, Tad Bartimus, and Kathi Kamen Goldmark (San Francisco literary escort and Remainders founder) distinguished themselves. The Critics Chorus, Dave Marsh, Greil Marcus, Matt Groening, and others, were distinguished for their off-key rowdiness. *Backlash's* Susan Faludi unfortunately had to cancel out as a go-go girl. This year's most pleasant surprise was Barbara Kingsolver's greater opportunity to display her musical ability and stage poise. Novelist Amy Tan's high point came in a very funny cover of "These Boots Are Made for Walking" when some of the crowd seemed a bit taken aback as the platinum-wigged Tan energetically tackled a whip-and-discipline rendition of Nancy Sinatra's hit.

The show was introduced by Larry King, ably demonstrating a real ability as a stand-up comic. The entertainment between sets was a British invasion group, the Hard Covers, consisting of Douglas Adams on guitar, Ken Follett on bass, and bookseller Dick Jude on percussion. Thriller writer Follett demonstrated that he was maybe the only male writer/musician on stage who occasionally lived in his body. In other words, he had a sense of rhythm. The musical accomplishment was not exactly Grammy quality, but the crowd didn't care. The idea for the evening was to have fun and support good works. And the whole night *was* a great deal of fun.

The Remainders will return yet again for this year's A.B.A. in Los Angeles. They'll play the Hollywood Palladium. It won't be Altamont, but that's probably just as well.

And finally . . . A book, a live performance, and a last picture show. The book is *Lon Chaney: the Man Behind the Thousand Faces* by Michael F. Blake. This is a beautifully produced hardback from a smaller publisher called Vestal Press. It costs a sawbuck and a half or so, but it's worth it. This is the definitive biography of Lon Chaney, Sr. Blake, a professional makeup artist himself, knows whereof he writes. The book is exhaustively researched, finely detailed, fun to read, and includes copious photographs, some of which are unobtainable elsewhere. It's a perfect reference text for one of the fantastic cinema's greatest talents.

The live performance is Jim Rose and the Jim Rose Circus Sideshow. Not for the squeamish, Rose and his show got a big boost from touring with Lollapalooza '92. Now he and his colleagues are on their own. This is a circus freak show for our time. No physical deformities here, though. Rose's performers look pretty much like me and thee. They just *do* weird things. Matt "the Tube" Crowley rams several feet of clear tubing down his throat into his stomach and demonstrates force-feeding and the reversal of that process, using beer and other ingredients. The Enigma is tattoed in a jigsaw puzzle pattern from head to foot and eats some disgusting things. The Torture King licks the flame of a blowtorch and sticks meat skewers through his cheeks. Everyone's favorite, though, is Mr. Lifto, a gentleman who suspends—and swings—heavy weights from piercings in various parts of his body. Those parts include both nipples and his penis. Most of us guys in the crowd did wince. All of this and more is emceed by Jim Rose in an accomplished carnival barker patter. Part visceral sensation (ohmigod, he's not gonna do that, not *really*), part old-fashioned circus hokum, these performances are unlike anything else currently on the road. And if Jim Rose isn't coming to your town soon, there's a 35-minute video of performance highlights available.

The last picture show I'm going to mention this year is Joe Dante's *Matinee*. This is not, strictly speaking, a science fiction, fantasy, or horror film. But it is *about* all those things. Set in Key West during the Cuban missile crisis, it's sweet and nostalgic, and about the crossing of a Rubicon of innocence, both for a group of young people and our society. This one's PG. It's about a high school student (Simon Fenton) whose Navy dad is suddenly and worrisomely gone during the U.S. faceoff with Castro and the Soviet Union. Our hero is also an incredible movie buff—films have evidently filled in his life and given him a fantasy buffer as the real world starts to close in. At the same time that American forces are standing on alert, a William Castle-like movie producer/promoter (John Goodman) comes to Key West with his blonde girlfriend (Cathy Moriarty). Goodman's Lawrence Woolsey is opening his new SF thriller *MANT*, a big-screen adventure about a half-man, half-insect creature presented in Atomo Vision and Rumble-Rama. The film-within-the-film sequences are completely terrific. Maybe HBO will commission the complete 90 minutes of *MANT*. Probably not.

At any rate, *Matinee* recaptures a time and place now gone, and documents both the disabling terror of the Cold War and the disconcerting signs of what was then to come. This is not a leave-'em-gasping-in-the-aisles movie; it is a very warm picture that will trigger considerable smiles. For today's young audience, it's just as dated as *Johnny Tremaine* or *The Red Badge of Courage*. But for those of us staring all too close into the rheumy eyes of our declining years, this is an important past now recaptured. Isn't that one of the things art does?

See you next year.

Obituaries

As cataclysmic a year as 1993 was in terms of natural disasters, death seemed to take it all in stride, calling no more or fewer people from the scene of their creative endeavors than in other years. Nonetheless, it seems that this year witnessed the passing of an inordinate number of fine, important writers, as well as talented, creative people from all other branches of the arts. Their works, their creative acts, remain with us to remind us of what we've lost and to inspire us with their gifts of words and images.

Sir William Golding, 81, was the Nobel Prize-winning author of highly crafted novels, including the famous *Lord of the Flies*. His work was imbued with an almost frenzied intensity, and frequently was possessed of a fevered, obsessive quality which marked it as his alone. He was in love with the sea, which was the setting of much of his work, including the remarkable tour de force, *Pincher Martin*.

Vincent Price, 82, was perhaps the best known actor in horror films in the 1950s and 1960s. His career began with him playing handsome southern gentlemen, but his portrayal of the bitter, brilliant, but mad sculptor in *House of Wax* began a career in horror movies that made him famous through a succession of often low-budget but entertaining films, including a number of adaptations of the works of Edgar Allan Poe, among many others. He was extremely articulate and cultured, known as a capable critic of fine art, and as a gourmet cook.

Lester del Rey, 77, was at one time or another a writer, editor, book reviewer, and critic of science fiction and fantasy. He was known first for a number of fine short stories, including such SF classics as "Helen O'Loy," "For I Am a Jealous People," and others. His best known novel is *Nerves*, a nuclear-accident thriller based on the short story of the same name. He edited various magazines in the '40s and '50s, and reached his peak as an editor when he worked with his fourth and last wife, Judy-Lynn (Benjamin) del Rey. Together, they took over Ballantine's SF and fantasy line and revolutionized the publication and marketing of SF and fantasy books. Lester discovered and developed such bestselling authors as Terry Brooks, Stephen R. Donaldson, David Eddings, and Barbara Hambly, among others. He felt his roots were in pulp fiction, and to the end considered editors to be the final arbiters of an author's work. Some authors bridled at this attitude and avoided him; others flourished under his stern tutelage. There's never been one like him, and likely will never be another.

Avram Davidson, 70, was an extraordinarily literate and eclectic writer whose fantasy and science fiction defied categorization. Author of more than 300 stories and a number of novels, he won the Hugo Award for his story, "Or All the Seas with Oysters." He was editor of *The Magazine of Fantasy & Science Fiction* from 1962 to 1964, and won the Hugo Award as Best Editor during that period. Much of his work was influenced by his interest in Jewish scholarship; he served in the Israeli Army during the Arab-Israeli war of 1948–49. His fantasy was sometimes densely allegorical, and always fascinating. One suspects that his true genius has yet to be fully recognized by the literary world at large.

Anthony Burgess, 74, was the British author of more than fifty novels, including *A Clockwork Orange* (1962), which was hugely popular, partly due to the film of the novel made by Stanley Kubrick in 1971, which became a symbol of the growing alienation and violence in society. Burgess was a lover of language, and his novels reflected that love. He translated as well as wrote, and also composed music, but his fame will always rest on his novels, which remain intelligent, passionately intense, and committed to a humanistic political agenda. His novel *The Wanting Seed*, also 1962, was an early speculative novel about overpopulation; since then his novels ranged to different locales, including Malaya, where he taught when he was a young man. His fantasies include *Tremor of Intent* (1966), *Any Old Iron* (1989), and *The Eve of Saint Venus* (1964).

Kobo Abé, 68, was a noted novelist, playwright and poet whose works frequently inhabited the realm of the surreal. His novel *The Woman in the Dunes* (1962), was made into a prize-winning Japanese film in 1964. His work has been described variously as Kafka-esque and grotesque. He counted Lewis Carroll and Edgar Allan Poe as among his greatest influences.

Robert Westall, 63, was a writer whose work ranged across many fields and was beloved to readers young and old alike. Perhaps best known for his young adult fiction, his writings, supernatural and otherwise, were subtle and psychologically complex in nature, as in his 1989 collection *Antique Dust*.

Fred Gwynne, 66, was best known as the actor who portrayed Herman Munster on the popular 1960s television series, *The Munsters*. He played many other roles in a film and television career that spanned four decades. He had another career, as a writer and illustrator of children's books, the style of which tended toward a gentle, warm comedy.

Thomas Dean Clareson, 68, was an academic who had a lifelong passion for science fiction and fantasy. He was the prime mover behind the creation of the Science Fiction Research Association, an academic group dedicated to scholarship about the field. For twenty years he was editor of *Extrapolation*, the journal of that organization. The S.F.R.A. grew out of sessions he and others organized under the aegis of the Modern Language Association from 1956 through the 1960s. In 1977 he was honored by the S.F.R.A. with the Pilgrim Award for lifetime contribution to and achievement in scholarship. He wrote and edited critical material about SF and fantasy, and also wrote fiction himself, scripting a number of issues of the comic *Sheena, Queen of the Jungle* in the years after World War II. He taught from the mid-sixties until his retirement in 1993 at the College of Wooster (Ohio). More than any other single person, he was responsible for bringing science fiction and fantasy into the world of academia, despite the howls of many who thought it shouldn't be there.

Harvey Kurtzman, 68, cartoonist for William Gaines's EC Comics, including *Mad*, which then became *Mad Magazine*. Some credited him with inventing the character who became the symbol of *Mad*, Alfred E. Neuman. He founded several magazines after leaving *Mad*, including *Trump*, *Humbug*, and *Help!* Later he drew the "Little Annie Fanny" comic strip that ran in *Playboy*. He also wrote a history of the comics, entitled *From Aargh! to Zap: Harvey Kurtzman's History of the Comics*.

Gustav Hasford, 45, was the author of several novels, including *The Short-Timers*, which was filmed as *Full Metal Jacket*, and the sequel, *The Phantom Blooper*, which had fantasy elements. He also wrote works in other veins, including *A Gypsy Good Time*, a hardboiled mystery. **Cyril Cusack**, 82, was best known for his marvelously droll performance in the stage and television productions of *Peter Pan*. He acted in many other stage, film, and television productions. **William Pené du Bois**, 76, was the Newbery Award-winning author of many elegantly whimsical children's books, including the award-winning *The Twenty-One Balloons*.

River Phoenix, 23, was a highly regarded, gifted and popular young actor. He made a big impression in every film in which he acted, from early work in *Stand by Me*, the adaptation of the Stephen King short story, "The Body," to *My Own Private Idaho*, an idiosyncratic comedy in which he starred with Keanu Reeves, and other films. Phoenix was from a counter-culture family (all his siblings had similarly unusual names; e.g., Summer, Leaf) and seemed to have everything going for him. He was someone whom the camera loved, and had been successful in all his roles, including his most popular, as the young Indiana Jones in *Indiana Jones and the Last Crusade*. Unfortunately, he succumbed to the pressures of fame, and died very publicly from complications due to illicit drug use. His death at such a tender age was particularly sad, and spurred comparisons between him and another film icon who died too young, James Dean.

Chad Oliver, 65, was known primarily as a science fiction writer who drew upon his knowledge of anthropology to infuse his writing with a certain degree of background texture missing in much of his contemporaries' work. All of his work was possessed of an emotional warmth that made it more memorable than that of other writers with otherwise comparable imagination and narrative skills. This quality endears him still to readers, despite the relative scarcity of his fiction over the past twenty years. His final novel, *The Cannibal Owl*, had elements of dark fantasy. He was a professor of anthropology for many years, and lived much of his life in the southwest, which was the setting for much of his work, including two western novels. He was the winner of the Western Writers of America's Golden Spur Award. **Fletcher Knebel**, 81, was co-author with Charles W. Bailey III of *Seven Days in May*. Knebel was a journalist and columnist based in Washington, which provided the background for the bestseller that later became a highly-charged film starring Burt Lancaster and Kirk Douglas. The story involved a plot by high-ranking military officials to overthrow the United States government and seize control. **Keith Laumer**, 67, was a prolific author known most for his science fiction, which ranged from humorous adventure to more serious suspense. His best known books were *The Great Time Machine Hoax, The House in November, The Persistence of Memory*, and his Retief series. Some of his work was within the realm of fantasy; certainly his view of man's exalted place among sentient beings could be considered fantasy. He was a rugged individualist, a tough-minded writer who fought through a stroke to continue his career for another twenty years. **Leslie Charteris**, 85, was the creator and author of "The Saint" mysteries featuring Simon Templar, and other works, some of which contained fantasy elements.

Baird Searles, 59, was a critic and bookseller who worked within the field for more than twenty years, encouraging new talent and spreading the word about fantasy and science fiction in all his activities. He ran, with Martin Last, New York's first SF/fantasy specialty bookstore, The Science Fiction Shop, for many years, and reviewed books for *Isaac Asimov's Science Fiction Magazine* for over ten years. Above all else, Searles loved books, and loved to share his joy in books with others. He had no pretension in this regard, freely admitting that a certain book might have a flaw or two, or three, but nonetheless was enjoyable for the right reader. There should be more like him. **Claire Parman Brown**, 28, was a young writer who had just sold her first fantasy story to Jane Yolen's *Xanadu* series before she was killed in a car crash in Nepal. Among those within the professional community who knew her, she was considered to be a fine and very promising writer; sadly, she never lived to see her work in print. **Chris Steinbrunner**, 59, was a film historian, author, and fan in the New York area. In the days before VCRs, his position as film director at WOR-TV enabled him to provide many films to science fiction conventions. He was co-editor, with Otto Penzler, of *The Encyclopedia of Mystery and Detection* (1976), which won the Mystery Writers of America's Edgar Award. Among other books, he wrote *Cinema of the Fantastic* (1972). **Ron Nance**, 42(?), was a fantasy short story writer and poet who had stories published in a number of different anthologies, many of them published by small press publishers. **Walter Breen**, 63, was a longtime fan, and the husband of Marion Zimmer Bradley. An avid and somewhat famous coin collector, he was at times involved in controversy within the realm of SF convention fandom.

Gordon W. Fawcett, 81, was one of four brothers who founded Fawcett Publications, which started with the mildly notorious magazine *Captain Billy's Whiz-Bang* and grew to be a vast publishing company that included a number of magazines and Fawcett Books, and ultimately was sold to CBS in 1977, and subsequently acquired by Random House. **Scott Meredith**, 69, was a major literary agent representing fantasy and science fiction writers. His agency, begun in 1946, grew into one of the largest literary agencies in the world, representing dozens of writers in all fields, with a special strength in science fiction and fantasy authors born of Meredith's origins in the field. Many current agents got their start at the Meredith agency, and a number of authors worked for him to supplement their income while gaining experience.

In addition to those mentioned above, a number of creative and productive people involved in theater arts and film died in 1993. Those whose careers touched on fantasy or horror included the following: Japanese film director **Inishiro Honda**, 81, directed the 1954 film *Gojira*, which was released in the U.S. as *Godzilla, King of the Monsters*. Based on Japanese folkloric legend, the Godzilla films, of which he directed a number, were extremely popular both in Japan and here. He also directed a number of other popular films, including *Rodan* and other science fiction and fantasy films. **Sam Rolfe**, 69, was the creator and producer of the extremely popular tongue-in-cheek *Man from U.N.C.L.E.* television series about a pair of super-spies, played by Robert Vaughn as "Napoleon Solo" and David McCallum as "Ilya Kiryakin." Rolfe worked on a number of other shows on television as well. **Ken Englund**, 79, was a screenwriter whose credits included the 1947 Danny Kaye classic, *The Secret Life of Walter Mitty*, based on the famous James Thurber story, and *The Unseen*, 1945, among others. British actor **James Donald**, 76, starred in the 1967 film *Five Million Years to Earth*, the third *Quatermass* film. He was best known for his role as the doctor in *The Bridge Over the River Kwai*. **Bernard Bresslaw**, 59, was a British actor whose many credits included *Blood of the Vampire*, *Jabberwocky*, and many other film and TV roles. **Christian Nyby**, 80, was a cinematographer and director whose work included directing the original 1951 classic *The Thing*. He also worked in television, including the original *Twilight Zone* series. It's not exactly fantasy or horror, but **Charles Fraser-Smith**, 88, was the man upon whom Ian Fleming based the character "Q" in the James Bond novels. He was responsible for designing disguisable miniature tools used by escaping allied POWs. **John Beck**, 83, was the producer of the film fantasy *Harvey*, as well as *One Touch of Venus* and many other films. **Nan Grey**, 75, was an actress in many films, including *Dracula's Daughter*, *The Tower of London*, *The Invisible Man Returns*, and *The House of Seven Gables*, among many in a long career dating from the 1930s. **Zita Johann**, 89, was a film actress who played, among her many credits, the role of Helen Grosvenor opposite Boris Karloff in *The Mummy*.

Others who died last year in the fields of fantasy and horror included people of varied accomplishments. **T(erry) L(ee) Parkinson**, 43, was the author of the novel *The Man Upstairs* (1991) and a number of dark fantasy stories. **Chandler Brossard**, 71, edited, with Vincent Price, *Eighteen Best Stories of Edgar Allan Poe*. He was also an author in his own right. **Herbert R. Reaver, Jr.**, 57, was an Edgar Award-winning novelist and fantasy writer. His novel *Mote* won the Edgar. **Kiyoshi Hayakawa**, 80, was the founder and publisher of Hayakawa Shobo, the largest publisher in Japan and a major publisher of fantasy and science fiction in that country. **Lenore Marie Nier**, 48, was a poet and writer who had several fantasy poems published before her death. She was married to fantasy author F. Gwynplaine MacIntyre. **Ralph P. Wattley**, 67, was an art director who worked at Ballantine Books in the 1950s, for Ian and Betty Ballantine, on many SF and fantasy covers. He subsequently worked at other houses, including Signet. **Maurice Dolbier**, 81, was a children's book author, actor, and former book editor for the New York *Herald-Tribune*. His books included *The Magic Shop*, *The Half-Pint Jinnie and Other Stories*, and others. **Drew Whyte**, 53(?) was a bibliographer active in the fantasy and science fiction fields from the 1960s until he married and left the U.S. to live with his wife in Brazil in the early 1980s. He wrote a column for *Galileo* magazine, and before that was quite active in the organization of early Boston-based science fiction conventions. Known for his careful scholarship and gentle demeanor, Whyte was also a contributor to early indexes compiled by the New England Science Fiction Assocation.

—James Frenkel

THE POACHER
Ursula K. Le Guin

Ursula K. Le Guin is widely considered to be one of the world's finest writers of fantasy and science fiction. Her books include *The Dispossessed, The Left Hand of Darkness, Always Coming Home,* and the four *Earthsea* volumes. (The latter are particularly recommended for fantasy readers.) Her stories have been collected in *The Wind's Twelve Quarters* and *The Compass Rose*; her illuminating essays and speeches have been collected in *The Language of the Night* and *Dancing at the Edge of the World*. Le Guin has won the National Book Award as well as the Hugo and Nebula Awards. She lives in Oregon.

"The Poacher" (from Jane Yolen's new anthology series, *Xanadu*), is a fairy tale penned with a poet's touch. The prose is gorgeous, the story enchanting. Once again, Ursula K. Le Guin shows us that her sterling reputation is well deserved.

—T.W.

> . . . *And must one kiss*
> *Revoke the silent house, the birdsong wilderness?*
> SYLVIA TOWNSEND WARNER

I was a child when I came to the great hedge for the first time. I was hunting mushrooms, not for sport, as I have read ladies and gentlemen do, but in earnest. To hunt without need is the privilege, they say, of noblemen. I should say that it is one of the acts that make a man a nobleman, that constitute privilege itself. To hunt because one is hungry is the lot of the commoner. All it generally makes of him is a poacher. I was poaching mushrooms, then, in the King's Forest.

My father had sent me out that morning with a basket and the command, "Don't come sneaking back here till it's full!" I knew he would beat me if I didn't come back with the basket full of something to eat—mushrooms at best, at this time of year, or the fiddleheads of ferns that were just beginning to poke through the cold ground in a few places. He would hit me across the shoulders with the hoe handle or a switch, and send me to bed supperless, because he was hungry and disappointed. He could feel that he was at least better off than somebody if he made me hungrier than himself, and sore and ashamed as well. After a while my stepmother would pass silently by my corner of the hut and leave on my pallet

or in my hand some scrap she had contrived or saved from her own scant supper—
half a crust, a lump of pease pudding. Her eyes told me eloquently, Don't say
anything! I said nothing. I never thanked her. I ate the food in darkness.

Often my father would beat her. It was my fate, fortunate or misfortunate, not
to feel better off than her when I saw her beaten. Instead I felt more ashamed
than ever, worse off even than the weeping, wretched woman. She could do
nothing, and I could do nothing for her. Once I tried to sweep out the hut when
she was working in our field, so that things would be in order when she came
back, but my sweeping only stirred the dirt around. When she came in from
hoeing, filthy and weary, she noticed nothing, but set straight to building up the
fire, fetching water, and so on, while my father, as filthy and weary as she, sat
down in the one chair we had with a great sigh. And I was angry because I had,
after all, done nothing at all.

I remembered that when my father first married her, when I was quite small,
she had played with me like another child. She knew knife-toss games, and taught
me them. She taught me the ABC from a book she had. The nuns had brought
her up, and she knew her letters, poor thing. My father had a notion that I might
be let into the friary if I learned to read, and make the family rich. That came
to nothing, of course. She was little and weak and not the help to him at work
my mother had been, and things did not prosper for us. My lessons in reading
ended soon.

It was she who found I was a clever hunter and taught me what to look for—
the golden and brown mushrooms, woodmasters and morels and other fungi, the
wild shoots, roots, berries, and hips in their seasons, the cresses in the streams;
she taught me to make fish traps; my father showed me how to set snares for
rabbits. They soon came to count on me for a good portion of our food, for
everything we grew on our field went to the Baron who owned it, and we were
allowed to cultivate only a mere patch of kitchen garden, lest our labors there
detract from our work for the Baron. I took pride in my foraging, and went
willingly into the forest, and fearlessly. Did we not live on the very edge of the
forest, almost in it? Did I not know every path and glade and grove within a mile
of our hut? I thought of it as my own domain. But my father still ordered me to
go, every morning, as if I needed his command, and he laced it with distrust—
"Don't come sneaking back until the basket's full!"

That was no easy matter sometimes—in early spring, when nothing was up
yet—like the day I first saw the great hedge. Old snow still lay greyish in the
shadows of the oaks. I went on, finding not a mushroom nor a fiddlehead.
Mummied berries hung on the brambles, tasting of decay. There had been no
fish in the trap, no rabbit in the snares, and the crayfish were still hiding in the
mud. I went on farther than I had yet gone, hoping to discover a new fernbrake,
or trace a squirrel's nut hoard by her tracks on the glazed and porous snow. I was
trudging along easily enough, having found a path almost as good as a road, like
the avenue that led to the Baron's hall. Cold sunlight lay between the tall beech
trees that stood along it. At the end of it was something like a hedgerow, but
high, so high I had taken it at first for clouds. Was it the end of the forest? the
end of the world?

I stared as I walked, but never stopped walking. The nearer I came the more amazing it was—a hedge taller than the ancient beeches, and stretching as far as I could see to left and right. Like any hedgerow, it was made of shrubs and trees that laced and wove themselves together as they grew, but they were immensely tall, and thick, and thorny. At this time of the year the branches were black and bare, but nowhere could I find the least gap or hole to let me peer through to the other side. From the huge roots up, the thorns were impenetrably tangled. I pressed my face up close, and got well scratched for my pains, but saw nothing but an endless dark tangle of gnarled stems and fierce branches.

Well, I thought, if they're brambles, at least I've found a lot of berries, come summer!—for I didn't think about much but food when I was a child. It was my whole business and chief interest.

All the same, a child's mind will wander. Sometimes when I'd had enough to eat for supper, I'd lie watching our tiny hearth fire dying down, and wonder what was on the other side of the great hedge of thorns.

The hedge was indeed a treasury of berries and haws, so that I was often there all summer and autumn. It took me half the morning to get there, but when the great hedge was bearing, I could fill my basket and sack with berries or haws in no time at all, and then I had all the middle of the day to spend as I pleased, alone. Oftenest what pleased me was to wander along beside the hedge, eating a particularly fine blackberry here and there, dreaming formless dreams. I knew no tales then, except the terribly simple one of my father, my stepmother, and myself, and so my daydreams had no shape or story to them. But all the time I walked, I had half an eye for any kind of gap or opening that might be a way through the hedge. If I had a story to tell myself, that was it: There is a way through the great hedge, and I discover it.

Climbing it was out of the question. It was the tallest thing I had ever seen, and all up that great height the thorns of the branches were as long as my fingers and sharp as sewing needles. If I was careless picking berries from it, my clothes got caught and ripped, and my arms were a net of red and black scratches every summer.

Yet I liked to go there, and to walk beside it. One day of early summer, some years after I first found the hedge, I went there. It was too soon for berries, but when the thorns blossomed, the flowered sprays rose up and up one above the other like clouds into the sky, and I liked to see that, and to smell their scent, as heavy as the smell of meat or bread, but sweet. I set off to the right. The walking was easy, all along the hedge, as if there might have been a road there once. The sun-dappling arms of the old beeches of the forest did not quite reach to the thorny wall that bore its highest sprays of blossom high above their crowns. It was shady under the wall, smelling heavily of blackberry flowers, and windlessly hot. It was always very silent there, a silence that came through the hedge.

I had noticed long ago that I never heard a bird sing on the other side, though their spring songs might be ringing down every aisle of the forest. Sometimes I saw birds fly over the hedge, but I never was sure I saw the same one fly back.

So I wandered on in the silence, on the springy grass, keeping an eye out for the little russet-brown mushrooms that were my favorites, when I began to feel something queer about the grass and the woods and the flowering hedge. I thought I had never walked this far before, and yet it all looked as if I had seen it many times. Surely I knew that clump of young birches, one bent down by last winter's long snow? Then I saw, not far from the birches, under a currant bush beside the grassy way, a basket and a knotted sack. Someone else was here, where I had never met another soul. Someone was poaching in my domain.

People in the village feared the forest. Because our hut was almost under the trees of the forest, people feared us. I never understood what they were afraid of. They talked about wolves. I had seen a wolf's track once, and sometimes heard the lonely voices, winter nights, but no wolf came near the houses or fields. People talked about bears. Nobody in our village had ever seen a bear or a bear's track. People talked about dangers in the forest, perils and enchantments, and rolled their eyes and whispered, and I thought them all great fools. I knew nothing of enchantments. I went to and fro in the forest and up and down in it as if it were my kitchen garden, and never yet had I found anything to fear.

So, whenever I had to go the half mile from our hut and enter the village, people looked askance at me, and called me the wild boy. And I took pride in being called wild. I might have been happier if they had smiled at me and called me by my name, but as it was, I had my pride, my domain, my wilderness, where no one but I dared go.

So it was with fear and pain that I gazed at the signs of an intruder, an interloper, a rival—until I recognised the bag and basket as my own. I had walked right round the great hedge. It was a circle. My forest was all outside it. The other side of it was—whatever it was—inside.

From that afternoon, my lazy curiosity about the great hedge grew to a desire and resolve to penetrate it and see for myself that hidden place within, that secret. Lying watching the dying embers at night, I thought now about the tools I would need to cut through the hedge, and how I could get such tools. The poor little hoes and mattocks we worked our field with would scarcely scratch those great stems and branches. I needed a real blade, and a good stone to whet it on.

So began my career as a thief.

An old woodcutter down in the village died; I heard of his death at market that day. I knew he had lived alone, and was called a miser. He might have what I needed. That night when my father and stepmother slept, I crept out of the hut and went back by moonlight to the village. The door of the cottage was open. A fire smouldered in the hearth under the smoke hole. In the sleeping end of the house, to the left of the fire, a couple of women had laid out the corpse. They were sitting up by it, chatting, now and then putting up a howl or two of keening when they thought about it. I went softly in to the stall end of the cottage; the fire was between us, and they did not see or hear me. The cow chewed her cud, the cat watched me, the women across the fire mumbled and laughed, and the old man lay stark on his pallet in his winding-sheet. I looked through his tools, quietly, but without hurrying. He had a fine hatchet, a crude saw, and a mounted, circular grindstone—a treasure to me. I could not take the mounting, but stuck the handle in my shirt, took the tools under my arm and the stone in both hands, and walked out again. "Who's there?" said one of the women, without interest, and sent up a perfunctory wail.

The stone all but pulled my arms out before I got it up the road to our hut, where I hid it and the tools and the handle a little way inside the forest under a bit of brushwood. I crept back into the windowless blackness of the hut and felt my way over to my pallet, for the fire was dead. I lay a long time, my heart beating hard, telling my story: I had stolen my weapons, now I would lay my siege on the great thorn hedge. But I did not use those words. I knew nothing of sieges, wars, victories, all such matters of great history. I knew no story but my own.

It would be a very dull one to read in a book. I cannot tell much of it. All that summer and autumn, winter and spring, and the next summer, and the next autumn, and the next winter, I fought my war, I laid my siege: I chopped and hewed and hacked at the thicket of bramble and thorn. I cut through a thick, tough trunk, but could not pull it free till I had cut through fifty branches tangled in its branches. When it was free I dragged it out and then I began to cut at the next thick trunk. My hatchet grew dull a thousand times. I had made a mount for the grindstone, and on it I sharpened the hatchet a thousand times, till the blade was worn down into the thickness of the metal and would not hold an edge. In the first winter, the saw shivered against a rootstock hard as flint. In the second summer, I stole an ax and a handsaw from a party of travelling woodcutters camped a little way inside the forest near the road to the Baron's hall. They were poaching wood from my domain, the forest. In return, I poached tools from them. I felt it was a fair trade.

My father grumbled at my long absences, but I kept up my foraging, and had so many snares out that we had rabbit as often as we wanted it. In any case, he no longer dared strike me. I was sixteen or seventeen years old, I suppose, and though I was by no means well grown, or tall, or very strong, I was stronger than he, a worn-out old man, forty years old or more. He struck my stepmother as often as he liked. She was a little, toothless, red-eyed old woman now. She spoke very seldom. When she spoke, my father would cuff her, railing at women's chatter, women's nagging. "Will you never be quiet?" he would shout, and she would shrink away, drawing her head down in her hunched shoulders like a turtle. And yet sometimes when she washed herself at night with a rag and a basin of water warmed in the ashes, her blanket would slip down, and I saw her body was fine-skinned, with soft breasts and rounded hips shadowy in the firelight. I would turn away, for she was frightened and ashamed when she saw me looking at her. She called me "son," though I was not her son. Long ago she had called me by my name.

Once I saw her watching me as I ate. It had been a good harvest, that first autumn, and we had turnips right through the winter. She watched me with a look on her face, and I knew she wanted to ask me then, while my father was out of the house, what it was I did all day in the forest, why my shirt and vest and trousers were forever ripped and shredded, why my hands were callused on the palms and crosshatched with a thousand scratches on the backs. If she had asked I would have told her. But she did not ask. She turned her face down into the shadows, silent.

Shadows and silence filled the passage I had hacked into the great hedge. The thorn trees stood so tall and thickly branched above it that no light at all made its way down through them.

As the first year came round, I had hacked and sawn and chopped a passage of about my height and twice my length into the hedge. It was as impenetrable as ever before me, not allowing a glimpse of what might be on the other side nor a hint that the tangle of branches might be any thinner. Many a time at night I lay hearing my father snore and said to myself that when I was an old man like him, I would cut through the last branch and come out into the forest—having spent my life tunnelling through nothing but a great, round bramble patch, with nothing inside it but itself. I told that end to my story, but did not believe it. I tried to tell other ends. I said, I will find a green lawn inside the hedge . . . A village . . . A friary . . . A hall . . . A stony field. . . . I knew nothing else that one might find. But these endings did not hold my mind for long; soon I was thinking again of how I should cut the next thick trunk that stood in my way. My story was the story of cutting a way through an endless thicket of thorny branches, and nothing more. And to tell it would take as long as it took to do it.

On a day near the end of winter, such a day as makes it seem there will never be an end to winter, a chill, damp, dark, dreary, hungry day, I was sawing away with the woodcutter's saw at a gnarled, knotted whitethorn as thick as my thigh and hard as iron. I crouched in the small space I had and sawed away with nothing in my mind but sawing.

The hedge grew unnaturally fast, in season and out; even in midwinter thick, pale shoots would grow across my passageway, and in summer I had to spend some time every day clearing out new growth, thorny green sprays full of stinging sap. My passage or tunnel was now more than five yards long, but only a foot and a half high except at the very end; I had learned to wriggle in, and keep the passage man-high only at the end, where I must have room enough to get a purchase on my ax or saw. I crouched at my work, glad to give up the comfort of standing for a gain in going forward.

The whitethorn trunk split suddenly, in the contrary, evil way the trees of that thicket had. It sent the saw blade almost across my thigh, and as the tree fell against others interlaced with it, a long branch whipped across my face. Thorns raked my eyelids and forehead. Blinded with blood, I thought it had struck my eyes. I knelt, wiping away the blood with hands that trembled from strain and the suddenness of the accident. I got one eye clear at last, and then the other, and blinking and peering, saw light before me.

The whitethorn in falling had left a gap, and in the maze and crisscross of dark branches beyond it was a small clear space, through which one could see, as through a chink in a wall: and in that small bright space I saw the castle.

I know now what to call it. What I saw then I had no name for. I saw sunlight on a yellow stone wall. Looking closer, I saw a door in the wall. Beside the door stood figures, men perhaps, in shadow, unmoving; after a time I thought they were figures carved in stone, such as I had seen at the doors of the friary church. I could see nothing else: sunlight, bright stone, the door, the shadowy figures. Everywhere else the branches and trunks and dead leaves of the hedge massed before me as they had for two years, impenetrably dark.

I thought, if I was a snake I could crawl through that hole! But being no snake, I set to work to enlarge it. My hands still shook, but I took the ax and struck and struck at the massed and crossing branches. Now I knew which branch to cut, which stem to chop: whichever lay between my eyes and that golden wall, that door. I cared nothing for the height or width of my passage, so long as I could force and tear my way forward, indifferent to the laceration of my arms and face and clothing. I swung my dull ax with such violence that the branches flew before me; and as I pushed forward, the branches and stems of the hedge grew thinner, weaker. Light shone through them. From winter-black and hard they became green and soft, as I hacked and forced on forward, until I could put them aside with my hand. I parted the last screen and crawled on hands and knees out onto a lawn of bright grass.

Overhead the sky was the soft blue of early summer. Before me, a little downhill from the hedge, stood the house of yellow stone, the castle, in its moat. Flags hung motionless from its pointed towers. The air was still and warm. Nothing moved.

I crouched there, as motionless as everything else, except for my breath, which came loud and hard for a long time. Beside my sweaty, blood-streaked hand a little bee sat on a clover blossom, not stirring, honey-drunk.

I raised myself to my knees and looked all round me, cautious. I knew that this must be a hall, like the Baron's hall above the village, and therefore dangerous to anyone who did not live there or have work there. It was much larger and finer than the Baron's hall, and infinitely fairer; larger and fairer even than the friary church. With its yellow walls and red roofs it looked, I thought, like a flower. I had not seen much else I could compare it to. The Baron's hall was a squat keep with a scumble of huts and barns about it; the church was grey and grim, the carved figures by its door faceless with age. This house, whatever it was, was delicate and fine and fresh. The sunlight on it made me think of the firelight on my stepmother's breasts.

Halfway down the wide, grassy slope to the moat, a few cows lay in midday torpor, heads up, eyes closed; they were not even chewing the cud. On the farther slope, a flock of sheep lay scattered out, and an apple orchard was just losing its last blossoms.

The air was very warm. In my torn, ragged shirt and coat, I would have been shivering as the sweat cooled on me, on the other side of the hedge, where winter was. Here I shrugged off the coat. The blood from all my scratches, drying, made my skin draw and itch, so that I began to look with longing at the water in the moat. Blue and glassy it lay, very tempting. I was thirsty, too. My water bottle lay back in the passage, nearly empty. I thought of it, but never turned my head to look back.

No one had moved, on the lawns or in the gardens around the house or on the bridge across the moat, all the time I had been kneeling here in the shadow of the great hedge, gazing my fill. The cows lay like stones, though now and again I saw a brown flank shudder off a fly, or the very tip of a tail twitch lazily. When I looked down I saw the little bee still on the clover blossom. I touched its wing curiously, wondering if it was dead. Its feelers shivered a little, but it did not stir. I looked back at the house, at the windows, and at the door—a side door—which I had first seen through the branches. I saw, without for some while knowing that I saw, that the two carved figures by the door were living men. They stood one on each side of the door as if in readiness for someone entering from the garden or the stables; one held a staff, the other a pike; and they were both leaning right back against the wall, sound asleep.

It did not surprise me. They're asleep, I thought. It seemed natural enough, here. I think I knew even then where I had come.

I do not mean that I knew the story, as you may know it. I did not know why they were asleep, how it had come about that they were asleep. I did not know the beginning of their story, nor the end. I did not know who was in the castle. But I knew already that they were all asleep. It was very strange, and I thought I should be afraid; but I could not feel any fear.

So even then, as I stood up, and went slowly down the sunny sward to the willows by the moat, I walked, not as if I were in a dream, but as if I were a dream. I didn't know who was dreaming me, if not myself, but it didn't matter. I knelt in the shade of the willows and put my sore hands down into the cool water of the moat. Just beyond my reach a golden-speckled carp floated, sleeping. A waterskater poised motionless on four tiny dimples in the skin of the water. Under the bridge, a swallow and her nestlings slept in their mud nest. A window was open, up in the castle wall; I saw a silky dark head pillowed on a pudgy arm on the window ledge.

I stripped, slow and quiet in my dream-movements, and slid into the water. Though I could not swim, I had often bathed in shallow streams in the forest. The moat was deep, but I clung to the stone coping; presently I found a willow root that reached out from the stones, where I could sit with only my head out, and watch the golden-speckled carp hang in the clear, shadowed water.

I climbed out at last, refreshed and clean. I rinsed out my sweaty, winter-foul shirt and trousers, scrubbing them with stones, and spread them to dry in the hot sun on the grass above the willows. I had left my coat and my thick, strawstuffed clogs up under the hedge. When my shirt and trousers were half dry, I put them on—deliciously cool and wet-smelling—and combed my hair with my fingers. Then I stood up and walked to the end of the drawbridge.

I crossed it, always going slowly and quietly, without fear or hurry.

The old porter sat by the great door of the castle, his chin right down on his chest. He snored long, soft snores.

I pushed at the tall, iron-studded, oaken door. It opened with a little groan. Two boarhounds sprawled on the flagstone floor just inside, huge dogs, sound asleep. One of them "hunted" in his sleep, scrabbling his big legs, and then lay still again. The air inside the castle was still and shadowy, as the air outside was still and bright. There was no sound, inside or out. No bird sang, or woman; no voice spoke, or foot stirred, or bell struck the hour. The cooks slept over their cauldrons in the kitchen, the maids slept at their dusting and their mending, the king and his grooms slept by the sleeping horses in the stableyard, and the queen at her embroidery frame slept among her women. The cat slept by the mousehole, and the mice between the walls. The moth slept on the woollens, and the music slept in the strings of the minstrel's harp. There were no hours. The sun slept in the blue sky, and the shadows of the willows on the water never moved.

I know, I know it was not my enchantment. I had broken, hacked, chopped, forced my way into it. I know I am a poacher. I never learned how to be anything else. Even my forest, my domain as I had thought it, was never mine. It was the King's Forest, and the king slept here in his castle in the heart of his forest. But it had been a long time since anyone talked of the king. Petty barons held sway all round the forest; woodcutters stole wood from it, peasant boys snared rabbits in it; stray princes rode through it now and then, perhaps, hunting the red deer, not even knowing they were trespassing.

I knew I trespassed, but I could not see the harm. I did, of course, eat their food. The venison pastry that the chief cook had just taken out of the oven smelled so delicious that hungry flesh could not endure it. I arranged the chief cook in a more comfortable position on the slate floor of the kitchen, with his hat crumpled up for a pillow; and then I attacked the great pie, breaking off a corner with my hands and cramming it in my mouth. It was still warm, savoury, succulent. I ate my fill. Next time I came through the kitchen, the pastry was whole, unbroken. The enchantment held. Was it that as a dream, I could change nothing of this deep reality of sleep? I ate as I pleased, and always the cauldron of soup was full again and the loaves waited in the pantry, their brown crusts unbroken. The red wine brimmed the crystal goblet by the seneschal's hand, however many times I raised it, saluted him in thanks, and drank.

As I explored the castle and its grounds and outbuildings—always unhurriedly, wandering from room to room, pausing often, often lingering over some painted scene or fantastic tapestry or piece of fine workmanship in tool or fitting or furniture, often settling down on a soft, curtained bed or a sunny, grassy garden nook to sleep (for there was no night here, and I slept when I was tired and woke when I was refreshed)—as I wandered through all the rooms and offices and cellars and halls and barns and servants' quarters, I came to know, almost as if they were furniture too, the people who slept here and there, leaning or sitting or lying down, however they had chanced to be when the enchantment stole upon them and their eyes grew heavy, their breathing quiet, their limbs lax and still. A shepherd up on the hill had been pissing into a gopher's hole; he had settled down in a heap and slept contentedly, as no doubt the gopher was doing down in the dirt. The chief cook, as I have said, lay as if struck down unwilling in the heat of his art, and though I tried many times to pillow his head and arrange his limbs more comfortably, he always frowned, as if to say, "Don't bother me now, I'm busy!" Up at the top of the old apple orchard lay a couple of lovers, peasants like me. He, his rough trousers pulled down, lay as he had slid off her, face buried in the blossom-littered grass, drowned in sleep and satisfaction. She, a short, buxom young woman with apple-red cheeks and nipples, lay sprawled right out, skirts hiked to her waist, legs parted and arms wide, smiling in her sleep. It was again more than hungry flesh could endure. I laid myself down softly on her, kissing those red nipples, and came into her honey sweetness. She smiled in her sleep again, whenever I did so, and sometimes made a little groaning grunt of pleasure. Afterwards I would lie beside her, a partner to her friend on the other side, and drowse, and wake to see the unfalling late blossoms on the apple boughs. When I slept, there inside the great hedge, I never dreamed.

What had I to dream of? Surely I had all I could desire. Still, while the time passed that did not pass, used as I was to solitude, I grew lonely; the company of the sleepers grew wearisome to me. Mild and harmless as they were, and dear as many of them became to me as I lived among them, they were no better companions to me than a child's wooden toys, to which he must lend his own voice and soul. I sought work, not only to repay them for their food and beds but because I was, after all, used to working. I polished the silver, I swept and reswept the floors where the dust lay so still, I groomed all the sleeping horses, I arranged the books on the shelves. And that led me to open a book, in mere idleness, and puzzle at the words in it.

I had not had a book in my hands since that primer of my stepmother's, nor seen any other but the priest's book in the church when we went to Mass at Yuletime. At first I looked only at the pictures, which were marvelous, and entertained me much. But I began to want to know what the words said about the pictures. When I came to study the shapes of the letters, they began to come back to me: *a* like a cat sitting, and the fat-bellied *b* and *d*, and *t* the carpenter's square, and so on. And *a-t* was *at*, and *c-a-t* was *cat*, and so on. And time enough to learn to read, time enough and more than enough, slow as I might be. So I came to read, first the romances and histories in the queen's rooms, where I first had begun to read, and then the king's library of books about wars and kingdoms and travels and famous men, and finally the princess's books of fairy tales. So it is that I know now what a castle is, and a king, and a seneschal, and a story, and so can write my own.

But I was never happy going into the tower room, where the fairy tales were. I went there the first time; after the first time, I went there only for the books in the shelf beside the door. I would take a book, looking only at the shelf, and go away again at once, down the winding stair. I never looked at her but once, the first time, the one time.

She was alone in her room. She sat near the window, in a little straight chair. The thread she had been spinning lay across her lap and trailed to the floor. The thread was white; her dress was white and green. The spindle lay in her open hand. It had pricked her thumb, and the point of it still stuck just above the little thumb joint. Her hands were small and delicate. She was younger even than I when I came there, hardly more than a child, and had never done any hard work at all. You could see that. She slept more sweetly than any of them, even the maid with the pudgy arm and the silky hair, even the rosy baby in the cradle in the gatekeeper's house, even the grandmother in the little south room, whom I loved best of all. I used to talk to the grandmother when I was lonely. She sat so quietly as if looking out the window, and it was easy to believe that she was listening to me and only thinking before she answered.

But the princess's sleep was sweeter even than that. It was like a butterfly's sleep.

I knew, I knew as soon as I entered her room, that first time, that one time, as soon as I saw her I knew that she, she alone in all the castle, might wake at any moment. I knew that she, alone of all of them, all of us, was dreaming. I knew that if I spoke in that tower room she would hear me: maybe not waken, but hear me in her sleep, and her dreams would change. I knew that if I touched her or even came close to her I would trouble her dreams. If I so much as touched that spindle, moved it so that it did not pierce her thumb—and I longed to do that, for it was painful to see—but if I did that, if I moved the spindle, a drop of red blood would well up slowly on the delicate little cushion of flesh above the joint. And her eyes would open. Her eyes would open slowly; she would look at me. And the enchantment would be broken, the dream at an end.

I have lived here within the great hedge till I am older than my father ever was. I am as old as the grandmother in the south room, grey-haired. I have not climbed the winding stair for many years. I do not read the books of fairy tales any longer, nor visit the sweet orchard. I sit in the garden in the sunshine. When the prince comes riding, and strikes his way clear through the hedge of thorns— my two years' toil—with one blow of his privileged, bright sword, when he strides up the winding stair to the tower room, when he stoops to kiss her, and the spindle falls from her hand, and the drop of blood wells like a tiny ruby on the white skin, when she opens her eyes slowly and yawns, she will look up at him. As the castle begins to stir, the petals to fall, the little bee to move and buzz on the clover blossom, she will look up at him through the mists and tag ends of dream, a hundred years of dreams; and I wonder if, for a moment, she will think, "Is that the face I dreamed of seeing?" But by then I will be out by the midden heap, sleeping sounder than they ever did.

ENGLAND UNDERWAY

Terry Bisson

Terry Bisson is the talented and idiosyncratic author of four delightful novels that defy genre categorization: *Wyrldmaker, Talking Man, Fire on the Mountain,* and *Voyage to the Red Planet*. The title story in his short fiction collection, *Bears Discover Fire and Other Stories,* won the Nebula, Hugo, and Theodore Sturgeon Awards.

Bisson is a native of Kentucky who now lives with his wife and six children in New York City, where he has worked as an editor and copywriter in the publishing industry. Though Bisson's stories are often imbued with the folksy lyricism of his rural Kentucky background, the following tale ventures farther afield, depicting the British nation as it sets out to sea with quintessential British aplomb. It comes from the July issue of *OMNI* magazine.

—T.W.

Mr. Fox was, he realized afterward, with a shudder of sudden recognition like that of the man who gives a cup of water to a stranger and finds out hours, or even years later, that it was Napoleon, perhaps the first to notice. Perhaps. At least no one else in Brighton seemed to be looking at the sea that day. He was taking his constitutional on the Boardwalk, thinking of Lizzie Eustace and her diamonds, the people in novels becoming increasingly more real to him as the people in the everyday (or "real") world grew more remote, when he noticed that the waves seemed funny.

"Look," he said to Anthony, who accompanied him everywhere, which was not far, his customary world being circumscribed by the Boardwalk to the south, Mrs. Oldenshield's to the east, the cricket grounds to the north, and the Pig & Thistle, where he kept a room—or more precisely, a room kept him, and had since 1956—to the west.

"Woof?" said Anthony, in what might have been a quizzical tone.

"The waves," said Mr. Fox. "They seem—well, odd, don't they? Closer together?"

"Woof."

"Well, perhaps not. Could be just my imagination."

Fact is, waves had always looked odd to Mr. Fox. Odd and tiresome and sinister. He enjoyed the Boardwalk but he never walked on the beach proper, not only because he disliked the shifty quality of the sand but because of the waves with their ceaseless back and forth. He didn't understand why the sea had to toss about so. Rivers didn't make all that fuss, and they were actually going somewhere. The movement of the waves seemed to suggest that something was stirring things up, just beyond the horizon. Which was what Mr. Fox had always suspected in his heart, which was why he had never visited his sister in America.

"Perhaps the waves have always looked funny and I have just never noticed," said Mr. Fox. If indeed *funny* was the word for something so odd.

At any rate, it was almost half past four. Mr. Fox went to Mrs. Oldenshield's, and with a pot of tea and a plate of shortbread biscuits placed in front of him, read his daily Trollope—he had long ago decided to read all forty-seven novels in exactly the order, and at about the rate, in which they had been written— then fell asleep for twenty minutes. When he awoke (and no one but he knew he was sleeping) and closed the book, Mrs. Oldenshield put it away for him, on the high shelf where the complete set, bound in Morocco, resided in state. Then Mr. Fox walked to the cricket ground, so that Anthony might run with the boys and their kites until dinner was served at the Pig & Thistle. A whisky at nine with Harrison ended what seemed at the time to be an ordinary day.

The next day it all began in earnest.

Mr. Fox awoke to a hubbub of traffic, footsteps, and unintelligible shouts. There was, as usual, no one but himself and Anthony (and of course, the Finn, who cooked) at breakfast; but outside, he found the streets remarkably lively for the time of year. He saw more and more people as he headed downtown, until he was immersed in a virtual sea of humanity. People of all sorts, even Pakistanis and foreigners, not ordinarily much in evidence in Brighton off season.

"What in the world can it be?" Mr. Fox wondered aloud. "I simply can't imagine."

"Woof," said Anthony, who couldn't imagine either, but who was never called upon to do so.

With Anthony in his arms. Mr. Fox picked his way through the crowd along the Kings Esplanade until he came to the entrance to the Boardwalk. He mounted the twelve steps briskly. It was irritating to have one's customary way blocked by strangers. The Boardwalk was half-filled with strollers who, instead of strolling, were holding onto the rail and looking out to sea. It was mysterious; but then the habits of everyday people had always been mysterious to Mr. Fox; they were much less likely to stay in character than the people in novels.

The waves were even closer together than they had been the day before; they were piling up as if pulled toward the shore by a magnet. The surf where it broke had the odd appearance of a single continuous wave about one and a half feet high. Though it no longer seemed to be rising, the water had risen during the night: It covered half the beach, coming almost up to the sea wall just below the Boardwalk.

The wind was quite stout for the season. Off to the left (the east) a dark line was seen on the horizon. It might have been clouds but it looked more solid, like land. Mr. Fox could not remember ever having seen it before, even though he had walked here daily for the past forty-two years.

"Dog?"

Mr. Fox looked to his left. Standing beside him at the rail of the Boardwalk was a large, one might even say portly, African man with an alarming hairdo. He was wearing a tweed coat. An English girl clinging to his arm had asked the question. She was pale with dark, stringy hair, and she wore an oilskin cape that looked wet even though it wasn't raining.

"Beg your pardon?" said Mr. Fox.

"That's a dog?" The girl was pointing toward Anthony.

"Woof."

"Well, of course it's a dog."

"Can't he walk?"

"Of course he can walk. He just doesn't always choose to."

"You bloody wish," said the girl, snorting unattractively and looking away. She wasn't exactly a girl. She could have been twenty.

"Don't mind her," said the African. "Look at that chop, would you."

"Indeed," Mr. Fox said. He didn't know what to make of the girl but he was grateful to the African for starting a conversation. It was often difficult these days; it had become increasingly difficult over the years. "A storm off shore, perhaps?" he ventured.

"A storm?" the African said. "I guess you haven't heard. It was on the telly hours ago. We're making close to two knots now, south and east. Heading around Ireland and out to sea."

"Out to sea?" Mr. Fox looked over his shoulder at the King's Esplanade and the buildings beyond, which seemed as stationary as ever. "Brighton is heading out to sea?"

"You bloody wish," the girl said.

"Not just Brighton, man," the African said. For the first time, Mr. Fox could hear a faint Caribbean lilt in his voice. "England herself is underway."

England underway? How extraordinary. Mr. Fox could see what he supposed was excitement in the faces of the other strollers on the Boardwalk all that day. The wind smelled somehow saltier as he went to take his tea. He almost told Mrs. Oldenshield the news when she brought him his pot and platter; but the affairs of the day, which had never intruded far into her tea room, receded entirely when he took down his book and began to read. This was (as it turned out) the very day that Lizzie finally read the letter from Mr. Camperdown, the Eustace family lawyer, which she had carried unopened for three days. As Mr. Fox had expected, it demanded that the diamonds be returned to her late husband's family. In response, Lizzie bought a strongbox. That evening, England's peregrinations were all the news on BBC. The kingdom was heading south into the Atlantic at 1.8 knots, according to the newsmen on the telly over the bar at the Pig & Thistle, where Mr. Fox was accustomed to taking a glass of whisky with Harrison the barkeep, before retiring. In the sixteen hours since the phenomenon had first been detected, England had gone some thirty-five miles, beginning a long turn around Ireland which would carry it into the open sea.

"Ireland is not going?" asked Mr Fox.

"Ireland has been independent since 19 and 21," said Harrison, who often hinted darkly at having relatives with the IRA. "Ireland is hardly about to be chasing England around the seven seas."

"Well, what about, you know . . . ?"

"The Six Counties? The Six Counties have always been a part of Ireland and always will be," said Harrison. Mr. Fox nodded politely and finished his whisky. It was not his custom to argue politics, particularly not with barkeeps, and certainly not with the Irish.

"So I suppose you'll be going home?"

"And lose me job?"

For the next several days, the wave got no higher but it seemed steadier. It was not a chop but a continual smooth wake, streaming across the shore to the east as England began its turn to the west. The cricket ground grew deserted as the boys laid aside their kites and joined the rest of the town at the shore watching the waves. There was such a crowd on the Boardwalk that several of the shops, which had closed for the season, reopened. Mrs. Oldenshield's was no busier than usual, however, and Mr. Fox was able to forge ahead as steadily in his reading as Mr. Trollope had in his writing. It was not long before Lord Fawn, with something almost of dignity in his gesture and demeanour, declared himself to the young widow Eustace and asked for her hand. Mr. Fox knew Lizzie's diamonds would be trouble, though. He knew something of heirlooms himself. His tiny attic room in the Pig & Thistle had been left to him in perpetuity by the innkeeper, whose life had been saved by Mr. Fox's father during an air raid. A life saved (said the innkeeper, an East Indian, but a Christian, not a Hindu) was a debt never fully paid. Mr. Fox had often wondered where he would have lived if he'd been forced to go out and find a place, like so many in novels did. Indeed, in real life as well. That evening on the telly there was panic in Belfast as the headlands of Scotland slid by, south. Were the Loyalists to be left behind? Everyone was waiting to hear from the King, who was closeted with his advisors.

The next morning, there was a letter on the little table in the downstairs hallway at the Pig & Thistle. Mr. Fox knew as soon as he saw the letter that it was the fifth of the month. His niece, Emily, always mailed her letters from America on the first, and they always arrived on the morning of the fifth.

Mr. Fox opened it, as always, just after tea at Mrs. Oldenshield's. He read the ending first, as always, to make sure there were no surprises. "Wish you could see your great-niece before she's grown," Emily wrote; she wrote the same thing every month. When her mother, Mr. Fox's sister, Clare, had visited after moving to America, it had been his niece she had wanted him to meet. Emily had taken up the same refrain since her mother's death. "Your great-niece will be a young lady soon," she wrote, as if this were somehow Mr. Fox's doing. His only regret was that Emily, in asking him to come to America when her mother died, had asked him to do the one thing he couldn't even contemplate; and so he had been unable to grant her even the courtesy of a refusal. He read all the way back to the opening ("Dear Uncle Anthony") then folded the letter very small, and put it into the box with the others when he got back to his room that evening.

The bar seemed crowded when he came downstairs at nine. The King, in a brown suit with a green and gold tie, was on the telly, sitting in front of a clock in a BBC studio. Even Harrison, never one for royalty, set aside the glasses he was polishing and listened while Charles confirmed that England was, indeed, underway. His words made it official, and there was a polite "hip, hip, hooray" from the three men (two of them strangers) at the end of the bar. The King and his advisors weren't exactly sure when England would arrive, nor, for that matter, where it was going. Scotland and Wales were, of course, coming right along. Parliament would announce time-zone adjustments as necessary. While His Majesty was aware that there was cause for *concern* about Northern Ireland and the Isle of Man, there was as yet no cause for *alarm*.

His Majesty, King Charles, spoke for almost half an hour, but Mr. Fox missed much of what he said. His eye had been caught by the date under the clock on the wall behind the King's head. It was the fourth of the month, not the fifth; his niece's letter had arrived a day early! This, even more than the funny waves or the King's speech, seemed to announce that the world was changing. Mr. Fox had a sudden, but not unpleasant, feeling almost of dizziness. After it had passed, and the bar had cleared out, he suggested to Harrison, as he always did at closing time: "Perhaps you'll join me in a whisky"; and as always, Harrison replied, "Don't mind if I do."

He poured two Bells'. Mr. Fox had noticed that when other patrons "bought" Harrison a drink, and the barkeep passed his hand across the bottle and pocketed the tab, the whisky was Bushmills. It was only with Mr. Fox at closing, that he actually took a drink, and then it was always scotch.

"To your King," said Harrison. "And to plate tectonics."

"Beg your pardon?"

"Plate tectonics, Fox. Weren't you listening when your precious Charles explained why all this was happening? All having to do with movement of the Earth's crust, and such."

"To plate tectonics," said Mr. Fox. He raised his glass to hide his embarrassment. He had in fact heard the words, but had assumed they had to do with plans to protect the household treasures at Buckingham Palace.

Mr. Fox never bought the papers, but the next morning he slowed down to read the headlines as he passed the news stalls. King Charles's picture was on all the front pages, looking confidently into the future.

> ENGLAND UNDERWAY AT 2.9 KNOTS;
> SCOTLAND, WALES
> COMING ALONG PEACEFULLY.
> CHARLES FIRM AT 'HELM'
> OF UNITED KINGDOM

read the *Daily Alarm*. The *Economist* took a less sanguine view:

> CHUNNEL COMPLETION DELAYED
> EEC CALLS EMERGENCY MEETING

Although Northern Ireland was legally and without question part of the United Kingdom, the BBC explained that night, it was for some inexplicable reason apparently remaining with Ireland. The King urged his subjects in Belfast and Londonderry not to panic; arrangements were being made for the evacuation of all who wished it.

The King's address seemed to have a calming effect over the next few days.

The streets of Brighton grew quiet once again. The Esplanade and the Boardwalk still saw a few video crews which kept the fish-and-chips stalls busy; but they bought no souvenirs, and the gift shops all closed again one by one.

"Woof," said Anthony, delighted to find the boys back on the cricket ground with their kites. "Things are getting back to normal," said Mr. Fox. But were they really? The smudge on the eastern horizon was Brittany, according to the newsmen on the telly; next would be the open sea. One shuddered to think of it. Fortunately, there was familiarity and warmth at Mrs. Oldenshield's, where Lizzie was avoiding the Eustace family lawyer, Mr. Camperdown, by retreating to her castle in Ayr. Lord Fawn (urged on by his family) was insisting he couldn't marry her unless she gave up the diamonds. Lizzie's answer was to carry the diamonds with her to Scotland in a strongbox. Later that week, Mr. Fox saw the African again. There was a crowd on the old West Pier, and even though it was beginning to rain, Mr. Fox walked out to the end, where a boat was unloading. It was a sleek hydrofoil, with the Royal Family's crest upon its bow. Two video crews were filming, as sailors in slickers passed an old lady in a wheelchair from the boat to the pier. She was handed an umbrella and a tiny white dog. The handsome young captain of the hydrofoil waved his braided hat as he gunned the motors and pulled away from the pier; the crowd cried "hurrah" as the boat rose on its spidery legs and blasted off into the rain.

"Woof," said Anthony. No one else paid any attention to the old lady, sitting in the wheelchair with a wet, shivering dog on her lap. She had fallen asleep (or perhaps even died!) and dropped her umbrella. Fortunately it wasn't raining. "That would be the young Prince of Wales," said a familiar voice to Mr. Fox's left. It was the African. According to him (and he seemed to know such things) the Channel Islands, and most of the islanders, had been left behind. The hydrofoil had been sent to Guernsey at the Royal Family's private expense to rescue the old lady, who'd had a last-minute change of heart; perhaps she'd wanted to die in England. "He'll be in Portsmouth by five," said the African, pointing to an already far-off plume of spray.

"Is it past four already?" Mr. Fox asked. He realized he had lost track of the time.

"Don't have a watch?" asked the girl, sticking her head around the African's bulk.

Mr. Fox hadn't seen her lurking there. "Haven't really needed one," he said.

"You bloody wish," she said.

"Twenty past, precisely," said the African. "Don't mind her, mate." Mr. Fox had never been called "mate" before. He was pleased that even with all the excitement, he hadn't missed his tea. He hurried to Mrs. Oldenshield's, where he found a fox hunt just getting underway at Portray, Lizzie's castle in Scotland. He settled down eagerly to read about it. A fox hunt! Mr. Fox was a believer in the power of names.

The weather began to change, to get, at the same time, warmer and rougher. In the satellite pictures on the telly over the bar at the Pig & Thistle, England was a cloud-dimmed outline that could just as easily have been a drawing as a photo. After squeezing between Ireland and Brittany, like a restless child slipping from the arms of its ancient Celtic parents, it was headed south and west, into the open Atlantic.

The waves came no longer at a slant but straight in at the sea wall. Somewhat to his surprise, Mr. Fox enjoyed his constitutional more than ever, knowing that he was looking at a different stretch of sea every day, even though it always looked the same. The wind was strong and steady in his face, and the Boardwalk was empty. Even the newsmen were gone—to Scotland, where it had only just been noticed that the Hebrides were being left behind with the Orkneys and the Shetlands. "Arctic islands with their own traditions, languages, and monuments, all mysteriously made of stone," explained the reporter, live from Uig, by remote. The video showed a postman shouting incomprehensibly into the wind and rain.

"What's he saying?" Mr Fox asked. "Would that be Gaelic?"

"How would I be expected to know?" said Harrison.

A few evenings later, a BBC crew in the Highlands provided the last view of the continent: the receding headlands of Brittany seen from the 3,504-foot summit of Ben Hope, on a bright, clear day. "It's a good thing," Mr. Fox joked to Anthony the next day, "that Mrs. Oldenshield has laid in plenty of Hyson." This was the green tea Mr. Fox preferred. She had laid in dog biscuits for Anthony as well. Lizzie herself was leaving Scotland, following the last of her guests back to London, when her hotel room was robbed and her strongbox was stolen, just as Mr. Fox had always feared it would be. For a week it rained. Great swells pounded at the sea wall. Brighton was almost deserted. The faint-hearted had left for Portsmouth, where they were protected by the Isle of Wight from the winds and waves that struck what might now be properly called the *bow* of Britain.

On the Boardwalk, Mr. Fox strolled as deliberate and proud as a captain on his bridge. The wind was almost a gale, but a steady gale, and he soon grew used to it; it simply meant walking and standing at a tilt. The rail seemed to thrum with energy under his hand. Even though he knew that they were hundreds of miles at sea, Mr. Fox felt secure with all of England at his back. He began to almost enjoy the fulminations of the water as it threw itself against the Brighton sea wall. Which plowed on west, into the Atlantic.

With the south coast from Penzance to Dover in the lead (or perhaps it should be said, at the bow) and the Highlands of Scotland at the stern, the United Kingdom was making almost four knots, 3.8 to be precise.

"A modest and appropriate speed," the King told his subjects, speaking from his chambers in Buckingham Palace, which had been decked out with nautical maps and charts, a lighted globe, and a silver sextant. "Approximately equal to that of the great ships-of-the-line of Nelson's day."

In actual fact, the BBC commentator corrected (for they will correct even a king), 3.8 knots was considerably slower than an 18th century warship. But it was good that this was so, Britain being, at best, blunt; indeed, it was estimated that with even a half-knot more speed, the seas piling up the Plymouth and Exeter channels would have devastated the docks. Oddly enough, it was London, far from the headwinds and bow wave, that was hardest hit. The wake past Margate, along what used to be the English Channel, had sucked the Thames down almost two feet, leaving broad mud flats along the Victoria Embankment and under the Waterloo Bridge. The news showed treasure seekers with gum boots tracking mud all over the city, "a mud as foul-smelling as the ancient crimes they unearth daily," said BBC. Not a very patriotic report, thought Mr. Fox, who turned from the telly to Harrison to remark, "I believe you have family there."

"In London? Not hardly," said Harrison. "They've all gone to America."

By the time the Scottish mountain tops should have been enduring (or perhaps "enjoying" is the word, being mountains, and Scottish at that) the first snow flurries of the winter, they were enjoying (or perhaps "enduring") subtropical rains as the United Kingdom passed just to the north of the Azores. The weather in the south (now west) of England was springlike and fine. The boys at the cricket ground, who had usually put away their kites by this time of year, were out every day, affording endless delight to Anthony, who accepted with the simple, unquestioning joy of a dog, the fact of a world well supplied with running boys. *Our Day's Log*, the popular new BBC evening show, which began and ended with shots of the bow wave breaking on the rocks of Cornwall, showed hobbyists with telescopes and camcorders on the cliffs at Dover, cheering "Land Ho!" on sighting the distant peaks of the Azores. Things were getting back to normal. The public (according to the news) was finding that even the mid-Atlantic held no terrors. The wave of urban seasickness that had been predicted never materialized. At a steady 3.8 knots, Great Britain was unaffected by the motion of the waves, even during the fiercest storms: It was almost as if she had been designed for travel, and built for comfort, not for speed. A few of the smaller Scottish islands had been stripped away and had, alarmingly, sunk; but the only real damage was on the east (now south) coast, where the slipstream was washing away house-sized chunks of the soft Norfolk banks. The King was seen on the news, in muddy hip boots, helping to dike the fens against the wake. Taking a break from digging, he reassured his subjects that the United Kingdom, wherever it might be headed, would remain sovereign. When a reporter, with shocking impertinence, asked if that meant that His Majesty *didn't know* where his Kingdom was headed, King Charles answered coolly that he hoped his subjects were satisfied with his performance in a role that was, after all, designed to content them with *what was*, rather than to shape or even predict *what might be*. Then, without excusing himself, he picked up his silver shovel with the Royal Crest, and began to dig again.

Meanwhile, at Mrs. Oldenshield's, all of London was abuzz with Lizzie's loss. Or supposed loss. Only Lizzie (and Messrs. Fox and Trollope) knew that the diamonds had been not in her strongbox but under her pillow. Mr. Fox's letter from his niece arrived a day earlier still, on the third of the month, underscoring in its own quiet manner that England was indeed underway. The letter, which Mr. Fox read in reverse, as usual, ended alarmingly with the words "looking forward to seeing you." Forward? He read on backward and found "underway toward America." America? It had never occurred to Mr. Fox. He looked at the return address on the envelope. It was from a town called, rather ominously, Babylon.

Lizzie was one for holding on. Even though the police (and half of London society) suspected that she had engineered the theft of the diamonds in order to avoid returning them to the Eustace family, she wasn't about to admit that they had never been stolen at all. Indeed, why should she? As the book was placed back up on the shelf day after day, Mr. Fox marveled at the strength of character of one so able to convince herself that what was in her interest, was in the right. The next morning there was a small crowd on the West Pier, waving Union Jacks and pointing toward a smudge on the horizon. Mr. Fox was not surprised to see a familiar face (and hairdo) among them.

"Bermuda," said the African. Mr. Fox only nodded, not wanting to provoke the girl, whom he suspected was waiting on the other side of the African, waiting to strike. Was it only his imagination, that the smudge on the horizon was pink? That night and the two nights following, he watched the highlights of the Bermuda Passage on the telly over the bar. The island, which had barely been visible from Brighton, passed within a mile of Dover, and thousands turned out to see the colonial policemen in their red coats lined up atop the coral cliffs, saluting the Mother Country as she passed. Even where no crowds turned out, the low broads of Norfolk, the shaley cliffs of Yorkshire, the rocky headlands of Scotland's (former) North Sea coast, all received the same salute. The passage took nearly a week, and Mr. Fox thought it was quite a tribute to the Bermudans' stamina, as well as their patriotism.

Over the next few days, the wind shifted and began to drop. Anthony was pleased, noticing only that the boys had to run harder to lift their kites, and seemed to need a dog yipping along beside them more than ever. But Mr. Fox knew that if the wind dropped much further, they would lose interest altogether. The Bermudans were satisfied with their glimpse of the Mother Country, according to BBC; but the rest of the Commonwealth members were outraged as the United Kingdom turned sharply north after the Bermuda Passage, and headed north on a course that appeared to be carrying it toward the USA. Mr. Fox, meanwhile, was embroiled in a hardly unexpected but no less devastating crisis of a more domestic nature: For Lizzie had had her diamonds stolen—for real this time! She had been keeping them in a locked drawer in her room at the loathsome Mrs. Carbuncle's. If she reported the theft, she would be admitting that they hadn't been in the strongbox stolen in Scotland. Her only hope was that they, and the thieves, were never found.

COMMONWEALTH IN UPROAR
CARIBBEAN MEMBERS REGISTER
SHARP PROTEST
BRITS TO BASH BIG APPLE?

The British and American papers were held up side by side on BBC. Navigation experts were produced, with pointers and maps, who estimated that on its current course, the south (now north) of England would nose into the crook of New York harbor, where Long, Island meets New Jersey, so that Dover would be in sight of the New York City skyline. Plymouth was expected to end up off Montauk, and Brighton somewhere in the middle, where there were no place names on the satellite pictures. Harrison kept a map under the bar for settling bets, and when he pulled it out after *Our Daily Log*, Mr. Fox was alarmed (but not surprised) to see that the area where Brighton was headed was dominated by a city whose name evoked images too lurid to visualize:

Babylon.

On the day that Lizzie got her first visit from Scotland Yard, Mr. Fox saw a charter fishing boat holding steady on the shore, making about three knots. It was the *Judy J* out of Islip, and the rails were packed with people waving. Mr. Fox waved back, and waved Anthony's paw for him. An airplane flew low over the beach towing a sign. On the telly that night, Mr. Fox could see on the satellite picture that Brighton was already in the lee of Long Island; that was why the wind was dropping. The BBC showed clips from *King Kong*. "New York City is preparing to evacuate," said the announcer, "fearing that the shock of collision with ancient England will cause the fabled skyscrapers of Manhattan to tumble." He seemed pleased by the prospect, as did the Canadian earthquake expert he interviewed, as, indeed, did Harrison. New York City officials were gloomier; they feared the panic more than the actual collision. The next morning there were two boats off the shore, and in the afternoon, five. The waves, coming in at an angle, looked tentative after the bold swells of the mid-Atlantic. At tea, Lizzie was visited for the second time by Scotland Yard. Something seemed to have gone out of her, some of her fight, her spunk. Something in the air outside the tea room was different too, but it wasn't until he and Anthony approached the cricket ground that Mr. Fox realized what it was. It was the wind. It was gone altogether. The boys were struggling to raise the same kites that had flown so eagerly only a few days before. As soon as they stopped running the kites came down. Anthony ran and barked wildly, as if calling on Heaven for assistance, but the boys went home before dark, disgusted.

That night, Mr. Fox stepped outside the Pig & Thistle for a moment after supper. The street was as still as he had always imagined a graveyard might be. Had everyone left Brighton, or were they just staying indoors? According to *Our Daily Log*, the feared panic in New York City had failed to materialize. Video clips showed horrendous traffic jams, but they were apparently normal. The King was . . . but just as the BBC was about to cut to Buckingham Palace, the picture began to flicker and an American game show came on. "Who were the Beatles," said a young woman standing in a sort of bright pulpit. It was a statement and not a question.

"The telly has arrived before us," said Harrison, turning off the sound but leaving the picture. "Shall we celebrate with a whisky? My treat tonight."

Mr. Fox's room, left to him by Mr. Singh, the original owner of the Pig & Thistle, was on the top floor under a gable. It was small; he and Anthony shared a bed. That night they were awakened by a mysterious, musical scraping sound. "Woof," said Anthony, in his sleep. Mr. Fox listened with trepidation; he thought at first that someone, a thief certainly, was moving the piano out of the public room downstairs. Then he remembered that the piano had been sold twenty years before. There came a deeper rumble from far away—and then silence. A bell rang across town. A horn honked; a door slammed. Mr. Fox looked at the time on the branch bank across the street (he had positioned his bed to save the cost of a clock): It was 4:36 a.m., Eastern Standard Time. There were no more unusual sounds, and the bell stopped ringing. Anthony had already drifted back to sleep, but Mr. Fox lay awake, with his eyes open. The anxiety he had felt for the past several days (indeed, years) was mysteriously gone, and he was enjoying a pleasant feeling of anticipation that was entirely new to him.

"Hold still," Mr. Fox told Anthony as he brushed him and snapped on his little tweed suit. The weather was getting colder. Was it his imagination, or was the light through the window over the breakfast table different as the Finn served him his boiled egg and toast and marmalade and tea with milk? There was a fog, the first in weeks. The street outside the inn was deserted, and as he crossed the King's Esplanade and climbed the twelve steps, Mr. Fox saw that the Boardwalk was almost empty, too. There were only two or three small groups, standing at the railing, staring at the fog as if at a blank screen.

There were no waves, no wake; the water lapped at the sand with nervous, pointless motions like an old lady's fingers on a shawl. Mr. Fox took a place at the rail. Soon the fog began to lift; and emerging in the near distance, across a gray expanse of water, like the image on the telly when it has first been turned on, Mr. Fox saw a wide flat beach. Near the center was a cement bathhouse. Knots of people stood on the sand, some of them by parked cars. One of them shot a gun into the air; another waved a striped flag. Mr. Fox waved Anthony's paw for him.

America (and this could only be America) didn't seem very developed. Mr. Fox had expected, if not skyscrapers, at least more buildings. A white lorry pulled up beside the bathhouse. A man in uniform got out, lit a cigarette, looked through binoculars. The lorry said GOYA on the side.

"Welcome to Long Island," said a familiar voice. It was the African. Mr. Fox nodded but didn't say anything. He could see the girl on the African's other side, looking through binoculars. He wondered if she and the GOYA man were watching each other. "If you expected skyscrapers, they're fifty miles west of here, in Dover," said the African.

"West?"

"Dover's west now, since England's upside down. That's why the sun rises over Upper Beeding."

Mr. Fox nodded. Of course. He had never seen the sun rising, though he felt no need to say so.

"Everyone's gone to Dover. You can see Manhattan, the Statue of Liberty, the Empire State Building, all from Dover."

Mr. Fox nodded. Reassured by the girl's silence so far, he asked in a whisper, "So what place is this; where are we now?"

"Jones Beach."

"Not Babylon?"

"You bloody wish," said the girl.

Mr. Fox was exhausted. Lizzie was being harried like the fox she herself had hunted with such bloodthirsty glee in Scotland. As Major Mackintosh closed in, she seemed to take a perverse pleasure in the hopelessness of her situation, as if it bestowed on her a vulnerability she had never before possessed, a treasure more precious to her than the Eustace family diamonds. "Mr. Fox?" asked Mrs. Oldenshield.

"Mr. Fox?" She was shaking his shoulder. "Oh, I'm quite all right," he said. The book had fallen off his lap and she had caught him sleeping. Mrs. Oldenshield had a letter for him. (A letter for him!) It was from his niece, even though it was only the tenth of the month. There was nothing to do but open it. Mr. Fox began, as usual, at the ending, to make sure there were no surprises, but this time there were. "Until then," he read. As he scanned back through, he saw mention of "two ferries a day," and he couldn't read on. How had she gotten Mrs. Oldenshield's address? Did she expect him to come to America? He folded the letter and put it into his pocket. He couldn't read on.

That evening BBC was back on the air. The lights of Manhattan could be seen on live video from atop the cliffs of Dover, shimmering in the distance through the rain (for England had brought rain). One-day passes were being issued by both governments, and queues were already six blocks long. The East (now West) Kent Ferry from Folkestone to Coney Island was booked solid for the next three weeks. There was talk of service to Eastbourne and Brighton as well. The next morning after breakfast, Mr. Fox lingered over his tea, examining a photograph of his niece which he had discovered in his letter box while putting her most recent (and most alarming) letter away. She was a serious-looking nine-year-old with a yellow ribbon in her light brown hair. Her mother, Mr. Fox's sister, Clare, held an open raincoat around them both. All this was thirty years ago but already her hair was streaked with grey. The Finn cleared the plates, which was the signal for Mr. Fox and Anthony to leave. There was quite a crowd on the Boardwalk, near the West Pier, watching the first ferry from America steaming across the narrow sound. Or was "steaming" the word? It was probably powered by some new type of engine. Immigration officers stood idly by, with their clipboards closed against the remnants of the fog (for England had brought fog). Mr. Fox was surprised to see Harrison at the end of the pier, wearing a windbreaker and carrying a paper bag that was greasy, as if it contained food. Mr Fox had never seen Harrison in the day, nor outside, before; in fact, he had never seen his legs. Harrison was wearing striped pants, and before Mr. Fox could speak to him, he sidled away like a crab into the crowd. There was a jolt as the ferry struck the pier. Mr. Fox stepped back just as Americans started up the ramp like an invading army. In the front were teenagers, talking among themselves as if no one else could hear; older people, almost as loud, followed behind them. They seemed no worse than the Americans who came to Brighton every summer, only not as well dressed.

"Woof, woof!"

Anthony was yipping over his shoulder, and Mr. Fox turned and saw a little girl with light brown hair and a familiar yellow ribbon. "Emily?" he said, recognizing his niece from the picture. Or so he thought. "Uncle Anthony?" The voice came from behind him again. He turned and saw a lady in a faded Burberry. The fog was blowing away and behind her he could see, for the first time that day, the drab American shore.

"You haven't changed a bit," the woman said. At first Mr. Fox thought she was his sister, Clare, just as she had been thirty years before, when she had brought her daughter to Brighton to meet him. But of course Clare had been dead for twenty years; and the woman was Emily, who had then been almost ten, and was now almost forty; and the girl was her own child (the great-niece who had been growing up inexorably) who was almost ten. Children, it seemed, were almost always almost something.

"Uncle Anthony?" The child was holding out her arms. Mr. Fox was startled, thinking she was about to hug him; then he saw what she wanted and handed her the dog. "You can pet him," he said. "His name is Anthony, too."

"Really?"

"Since no one ever calls us both at the same time, it creates no confusion," said Mr. Fox.

"Can he walk?"

"Certainly he can walk. He just doesn't often choose to."

A whistle blew and the ferry left with its load of Britons for America. Mr. Fox saw Harrison at the bow, holding his greasy bag with one hand and the rail with the other, looking a little sick, or perhaps apprehensive. Then he took his niece and great-niece for a stroll along the Boardwalk. The girl, Clare—she was named after her grandmother—walked ahead with Anthony, while Mr. Fox and his niece, Emily, followed behind. The other Americans had all drifted into the city looking for restaurants, except for the male teenagers, who were crowding into the amusement parlors along the Esplanade, which had opened for the day.

"If the mountain won't come to Mahomet, and so forth," said Emily, mysteriously, when Mr. Fox asked if she'd had a nice crossing. Her brown hair was streaked with grey. He recognized the coat now; it had been her mother's, his sister's, Clare's. He was trying to think of where to take them for lunch. The Finn at the Pig & Thistle served a pretty fair shepherd's pie, but he didn't want them to see where he lived. They were content, however, with fish and chips on the Boardwalk; certainly Anthony seemed pleased to have chips fed to him, one by one, by the little girl named for the sister Mr. Fox had met only twice: once when she had been a student at Cambridge (or was it Oxford? he got them confused) about to marry an American; and once when she had returned with her daughter for a visit.

"Her father, your grandfather, was an Air Raid Warden," Mr. Fox told Emily. "He was killed in action, as it were, when a house collapsed during a rescue; and when his wife (well, she wasn't exactly his wife) died giving birth to twins a week later, they were each taken in by one of those whose life he had saved. It was a boarding house, all single people, so there was no way to keep the two together, you see—the children, I mean. Oh dear, I'm afraid I'm talking all in a heap."

"That's okay," said Emily.

"At any rate, when Mr. Singh died and his Inn was sold, my room was reserved for me, in accordance with his will, *in perpetuity*, which means as long as I remain in it. But if I were to move, you see, I would lose my patrimony entire."

"I see," said Emily. "And where is this place you go for tea?"

And so they spent the afternoon, and a rainy and an English afternoon it was, in the cozy tea room with the faded purple drapes at the west (formerly east) end of Moncton Street where Mrs. Oldenshield kept Mr. Fox's complete set of Trollope on a high shelf, so he wouldn't have to carry them back and forth in all kinds of weather. While Clare shared her cake with Anthony, and then let him doze on her lap, Mr. Fox took down the handsome leather-bound volumes, one by one, and showed them to his niece and great-niece. "They are, I believe, the first complete edition," he said. "Chapman and Hall."

"And were they your father's?" asked Emily "My grandfather's?"

"Oh no!" said Mr. Fox. "They belonged to Mr. Singh. His grandmother was English and her own great-uncle had been, I believe, in the postal service in Ireland with the author, for whom I was, if I am not mistaken, named." He showed Emily the place in *The Eustace Diamonds* where he would have been reading that very afternoon, "were it not," he said, "for this rather surprisingly delightful family occasion."

"Mother, is he blushing," said Clare. It was a statement and not a question.

It was almost six when Emily looked at her watch—a man's watch, Mr. Fox noted—and said, "We had better get back to the pier, or we'll miss the ferry." The rain had diminished to a misty drizzle as they hurried along the Boardwalk.

"I must apologize for our English weather," said Mr. Fox, but his niece stopped him with a hand on his sleeve. "Don't brag," she said, smiling. She saw Mr. Fox looking at her big steel watch and explained that it had been found among her mother's things; she had always assumed it had been her grandfather's. Indeed, it had several dials, and across the face it said: "Civil Defense, Brighton." Across the bay, through the drizzle as through a lace curtain, they could see the sun shining on the sand and parked cars.

"Do you still live in, you know . . ." Mr. Fox hardly knew how to say the name of the place without sounding vulgar, but his niece came to his rescue. "Babylon? Only for another month. We're moving to Deer Park as soon as my divorce is final."

"I'm so glad," said Mr. Fox. "Deer Park sounds much nicer for the child."

"Can I buy Anthony a goodbye present?" Clare asked. Mr. Fox gave her some English money (even though the shops were all taking American) and she bought a paper of chips and fed them to the dog one by one. Mr. Fox knew Anthony would be flatulent for days, but it seemed hardly the sort of thing one mentioned. The ferry had pulled in and the tourists who had visited America for the day were streaming off, loaded with cheap gifts. Mr. Fox looked for Harrison, but if he was among them, he missed him. The whistle blew two warning toots. "It was kind of you to come," he said.

Emily smiled. "No big deal," she said. "It was mostly your doing anyway. I could never have made it all the way to England if England hadn't come here first. I don't fly."

"Nor do I." Mr Fox held out his hand but Emily gave him a hug and then a kiss and insisted that Clare give him both as well. When that was over, she pulled off the watch (it was fitted with an expandable band) and slipped it over his thin, stick-like wrist. "It has a compass built in," she said. "I'm sure it was your father's. And Mother always . . ."

The final boarding whistle swallowed her last words. "You can be certain I'll take good care of it," Mr. Fox called out. He couldn't think of anything else to say. "Mother, is he crying," said Clare. It was a statement and not a question. "Let's you and me watch our steps," said Emily.

"Woof," said Anthony, and mother and daughter ran down (for the pier was high, and the boat was low) the gangplank. Mr. Fox waved until the ferry had backed out and turned, and everyone on board had gone inside, out of the rain, for it had started to rain in earnest. That night after dinner he was disappointed to find the bar unattended. "Anyone seen Harrison?" he asked. He had been looking forward to showing him the watch.

"I can get you a drink as well as him," said the Finn. She carried her broom with her and leaned it against the bar. She poured a whisky and said, "Just indicate if you need another." She thought indicate meant ask. The King was on the telly, getting into a long car with the President. Armed men stood all around them. Mr. Fox went to bed.

The next morning, Mr. Fox got up before Anthony. The family visit had been pleasant—indeed, wonderful—but he felt a need to get back to normal. While taking his constitutional, he watched the first ferry come in, hoping (somewhat to his surprise) that he might see Harrison in it; but no such luck. There were no English, and few Americans. The fog rolled in and out, like the same page on a book being turned over and over. At tea, Mr. Fox found Lizzie confessing (just as he had known she someday must) that the jewels had been in her possession all along. Now that they were truly gone, everyone seemed relieved, even the Eustace family lawyer. It seemed a better world without the diamonds.

"Did you hear that?"

"Beg your pardon?" Mr. Fox looked up from his book. Mrs. Oldenshield pointed at his teacup, which was rattling in its saucer. Outside, in the distance, a bell was ringing. Mr. Fox wiped off the book himself and put it on the high shelf, then pulled on his coat, picked up his dog, and ducked through the low door into the street. Somewhere across town, a horn was honking. "Woof," said Anthony. There was a breeze for the first time in days. Knowing, or at least suspecting what he would find, Mr. Fox hurried to the Boardwalk. The waves on the beach were flattened, as if the water were being sucked away from the shore. The ferry was just pulling out with the last of the Americans who had come to spend the day. They looked irritated. On the way back to the Pig & Thistle Mr. Fox stopped by the cricket ground, but the boys were nowhere to be seen, the breeze being still too light for kiting, he supposed. "Perhaps tomorrow," he said to Anthony. The dog was silent, lacking the capacity for looking ahead.

That evening, Mr. Fox had his whisky alone again. He had hoped that Harrison might have shown up, but there was no one behind the bar but the Finn and her broom. King Charles came on the telly, breathless, having just landed in a helicopter direct from the Autumn White House. He promised to send for anyone who had been left behind, then commanded (or rather, urged) his subjects to secure the kingdom for the Atlantic. England was underway again. The next morning the breeze was brisk. When Mr. Fox and Anthony arrived at the Board-walk, he checked the compass on his watch and saw that England had turned during the night, and Brighton had assumed its proper position, at the bow. A stout headwind was blowing and the sea wall was washed by a steady two-foot curl. Long Island was a low, dark blur to the north, far off the port (or left).

"Nice chop."

"Beg pardon?" Mr. Fox turned and was glad to see a big man in a tweed coat, standing at the rail. He realized he had feared the African might have jumped ship like Harrison.

"Looks like we're making our four knots and more, this time."

Mr. Fox nodded. He didn't want to seem rude, but he knew if he said anything the girl would chime in. It was a dilemma.

"Trade winds," said the African. His collar was turned up, and his dreadlocks spilled over and around it like vines. "We'll make better time going back. If indeed we're going back. I say, is that a new watch?"

"Civil Defense chronometer," Mr. Fox said. "Has a compass built in. My father left it to me when he died."

"You bloody wish," said the girl.

"Should prove useful," said the African.

"I should think so," said Mr. Fox, smiling into the fresh salt wind; then, saluting the African (and the girl), he tucked Anthony under his arm and left the Boardwalk in their command. England was steady, heading south by south east, and it was twenty past four, almost time for tea.

THE WOMAN IN THE PAINTING

Lisa Goldstein

Lisa Goldstein is one of the very best of the current generation of fantasists. This Bay Area writer won the American Book Award with her first novel, *The Red Magician*, and went on to follow up that early promise with *The Dream Years*, *A Mask for the General*, *Tourists*, and other fascinating stories that imbue the real world with surrealism and magic. Her most recent novels are *Strange Devices of the Sun and Moon*, about Christopher Marlowe, and *Summer King, Winter Fool*.

The following epistolary tale concerns a wholly imaginary group of artists, yet it evokes the romantic images of nineteenth-century London's pre-Raphaelite painters, as well as distinctively Victorian ideas about the nature of women. It comes from the July issue of *F & SF* magazine.

—T.W.

25 June, 1858
My Dear Henry—

You will not believe what a treasure I found yesterday. As you know, I had been trying to finish the painting I began last January, but it grows no closer to completion, and indeed I sometimes feel that it will never be done, that I will still be attempting it when I have grown too old and feeble to hold a brush. And yesterday I had an additional problem: the light was poor, a sooty, sunless London day. As the painting proved impossible I resolved instead to take a walk to clear my brain, and I headed toward the shops in Leicester Square.

And that is where I saw her, in a milliner's shop. At first, as I gazed at her through the dusty window, I thought her quite plain, with pallid brown hair and a thin ungenerous mouth. To be honest I don't know why I stared for so long except that she posed a minor sort of mystery: she was not a shop-girl, and in some indefinable way I knew that she was not one of the ladies patronizing the store.

Then she turned and saw me. Do you know how some women seem to change their appearance in an instant? I cursed myself for thinking her plain. Her hair was not brown but long and thick and black; her mouth was red, her skin so white it seemed luminous.

I have thought about our first meeting several times since then, but I cannot explain the first glimpse I had of her. Perhaps when she turned to me my soul understood her as she truly is; perhaps (more likely, I admit) I had first seen her through a distortion in the glass.

I must have stared for several seconds, longer, I fear, than propriety allows. But when I came to my senses I saw that she was not offended. There was a dreamy expression on her face, a vague sort of confusion; everything in the store seemed equally a mystery to her, the hats, the shop-girls, the other ladies present. I yearned to paint her.

I went into the store, lifted my hat to her, and asked if I could be of assistance. She looked vastly startled, as if she had worked out that the store was inhabited only by women; my presence there threatened to pose a further mystery. Then her lips moved a little—I cannot describe so slight a motion as a smile—and she said, "You are very kind, sir."

When she first spoke to me she had a faint accent, a way of pronouncing her words as if she were more used to singing than speaking. Now, a day later, the accent is quite gone. I cannot account for this. Everything about her is a mystery.

She would have said more, I believe, but at that moment she collapsed into a dead faint.

Bustle, commotion, ladies stepping back in horror, shop-girls hurrying to offer her smelling salts. At length her eyes fluttered open—they were a deep blue—and she moaned a little. The confusion had returned to her eyes.

The shop-girls were concerned, of course, but when she managed to stand, aided by two or three of them, they could not think what to do with her. One suggested that she rest in a chair provided for the patrons of the store, but the others quickly demurred—the owner of the shop would return soon, and the owner, it seemed, was a terrible dragon.

And there matters would have stayed, had I not lifted my hat a second time and offered to find the woman's family. The girls turned to me gratefully, and in a short time I was leading this extraordinary woman through the streets of London.

Not knowing what else to do, I took her to a good restaurant and watched, amazed, as she ate a meal large enough for several stevedores. Her problem, then, had been simple hunger, as I had hoped; I had feared consumption, or worse.

And there my tale ends. She dropped off to sleep on my couch as soon as I brought her back to the studio, woke briefly this morning for another of her gargantuan meals, and is at present sleeping again. I have been able to find out next to nothing about her; she does not seem to know who her family is, or where she came from, or what she did before her collapse. I recited several names to her—Mary, Elizabeth, Jenny—and she responded strongest to Jenny, so that is what I call her.

She seems a gift from the gods. I wanted nothing more than to paint her, and here she is, delivered to my studio as if by heavenly messenger. I have abandoned the painting I had struggled with for so long and have started several preliminary sketches, hoping to use her as a model when she grows strong enough.

I trust that you and Kate are well. I know you both will understand if I ask you not to visit my studio for a few weeks—I am anxious to begin the new painting, and I work best with no distractions. I will write you as often as I can; our mail system, the best in the world, will see to it that I keep in touch with you.

Your loving friend,
John

26 June, 1858

Dear John—

I must admit that your letter disturbed me very much. For one thing, I would like the opportunity to examine this woman. I speak not only as a doctor but as one who has seen the ravages of consumption at close hand—or surely you remember when Kate's poor sister Anna died of the disease. From what you tell me it seems quite possible that this unfortunate woman, this Jenny, is also a victim of consumption. Like many laymen you seem to think that you have enough medical knowledge to make a diagnosis, and such belief is dangerous, both to you and to her.

But you put yourself in moral danger as well. Surely you must see that it is quite impossible for her to live with you. If she is an honest woman who was lost her memory you compromise her to the extent that she may no longer be able to make her way in society. Even if you act the perfect gentleman with her your situation is one that is bound to cause talk. And no doubt she has friends and family who are frantic with worry about her—think of them, and of what the loss of their loved one must mean to them.

And if she is not a lady—well, then, in that case I fear you compromise yourself. In either circumstance you must stop your painting and make every effort to find this woman's family. Failing that, you must put her in a hospital. In any case, I would like to see her and make a diagnosis.

> Your most sincere friend,
> Henry

26 June, 1858

Dearest John,

I would like to add my voice to that of my husband, to ask you to allow us to come call on you at the studio. Henry and I have never forgotten your kindnesses to us during the dreadful year when my sister was ill, and we would consider it an honor to be allowed to repay you.

> Your loving friend,
> Kate

27 June, 1858

Henry—

It is not surprising that you abandoned painting when we were together at university. The surprise is that you became a doctor instead of a prating literal-minded clerk; you have the very soul of a clerk. Why must you constantly prostrate yourself before the god Propriety? There is nothing unseemly about my sharing the studio with this creature: she is ill, and cannot be moved for days, perhaps weeks.

You are my doctor, true, but you are not my conscience. Really, Henry, the accusations you make! I must confess myself surprised you did not go on to call me a white slaver. Please believe me when I say that she is as safe here as she would be in any house in England. And I am doing everything in my power to find her family.

And tell me, O keeper of my conscience, what would you have done with her?

Where would you have taken her? She has still not remembered her family, or her occupation if she had one. I am afraid she is a prostitute, one of the many women who have come to London and have been unable to find work in more honest trades. And if that is the case then it is an act of mercy for me to use her as my model. Though society frowns on women who model for artists we both know that this is honorable work, and far more worthy of her than her former profession.

You will be happy to hear that I have started a new painting, one inspired by her beauty. She has lost the confused expression she had when I found her; she now seems regal, unmoved, as remote as an allegorical figure or an ancient queen. Of course I must paint her as Guinevere, waiting for Lancelot. I believe strongly that it will be the best thing that I have ever done.

Please do not come visit, as I cannot afford the time to receive you. I must take advantage of every minute of the day until the light fails. And even then, with the help of dozens of lamps, I am able to work, to paint in the background while She sleeps.

—John

28 June, 1858
My Dear John—

I am sorry if my letter offended you—you must know that I was only trying to offer my help. If you will not let me see this woman I hope you will tell me more about her. What are her symptoms? Does she grow stronger or weaker? Does she speak of her family at all? What was she wearing when you met her?

I hope that you are well.

Your sincere friend,
Henry

29 June, 1858
My Dear Henry—

I am happy to see that you have climbed down from your high horse, that you are able to discuss the matter of Jenny calmly. And you must know I never truly opposed you, my dear friend; of course she must be found lodgings as soon as possible. But, as I said before, she is far too ill to be moved now.

You ask about her clothes. They are of surprisingly good quality. I know next to nothing about women's clothing but even I can see that hers are made of good fabric, with fine lace at the throat and wrists. Upon reading this you will, I know, return immediately to your earlier suspicions and tell me that she is a great lady, but I am now entirely convinced, for reasons I will tell you later, that this is not the case. It is far more likely, I think, that she had the patronage of some wealthy lord, and lost it again.

Besides, it no longer matters to me who she is. She is Guinevere.

She is also, unfortunately, quite mad, and this is why I do not believe she is a lady; no family of high birth would let their daughter wander the streets in her condition. She wakes several times a night and goes to the windows; once there she looks out at the stars for minutes, sometimes hours. If she were not so clearly a human woman I would think her an angel, longing for heaven. And she asks questions about the most ordinary things—What is a pen? What is a butter knife? She seems a blank slate, a canvas on which I may paint anything.

Yours,
John

30 June, 1858
My Dear Henry—

I write you in a state of high excitement. Before I can continue, though, I must ask you not to repeat, under any circumstances, what I am about to tell you.

I would also ask you not to judge me. I know you are worried about the possibility that I might corrupt this woman, but I must assure you that she was as eager for what happened as I.

She is, as I mentioned before, ignorant about things of the world; there is no guilt for her in matters of the flesh. Unlike most women she showed no coy hesitation as she removed her dress; rather, she seemed curious as to what might come next.

I write you not to boast about my conquest but to ask your professional advice as a doctor. For I have to tell you that when she removed her undergarments it seemed for a moment that her parts were not formed as are those of other women. For the space of an instant I saw nothing but a smooth expanse of skin between her legs. And then this skin seemed to unfold as I watched, petaling like a flower, or opening like an eye . . .

So quickly did this happen that once or twice since I wondered if I imagined it. But I know beyond a doubt that it did take place.

My question to you, of course, is—Is such a thing possible? Have you ever come across such a thing in your practice?

Yours sincerely,
John

2 July, 1858
John—

No doubt you believe I should apologize for my sudden visit to your studio. I will not apologize, however. I believe I was right to call on you when I did, that your extraordinary letter absolved me of all blame. It is impossible for a friend of long standing to stand by while another follows a course harmful to himself and to others.

And now that I have seen the woman you call Jenny I know that I have a reason for my concern. You called her remote, disinterested, but having heard her story I could not see her as anything but a woman in the greatest distress. Several times, while you were not watching, I was certain that she looked at me with the most pitiable expression, as if she asked me to rescue her from the impossible situation which entangled her. She looked, in fact, a little like my wife Kate, though younger.

What have you done to her, to this innocent, unfortunate woman? I must confess that I cannot forget the contents of your last letter to me, and that I shudder whenever I remember how you used her. You must stop. You must remember that she is not in her right mind.

I even thought of severing all ties with you, of refusing to speak to you until the woman is returned to the bosom of her family. I feel, however, that her interests would be best served if I continued to press you to give her up. Kate and I would be happy to have her in our house until her family is found.

My father is ill; I am leaving for the country tomorrow to tend to him. Kate will remain in London. I urge you to write to her, to tell her how you are getting on with your search. It is unfortunate that women of good breeding cannot visit artists' studios alone, or I would have her call on you.

> Yours most sincerely,
> Henry

3 July, 1858

Dearest Kate–

You must not believe a word your husband says about me. I am, in fact, healthier than I have been in years. I feel renewed, almost reborn. I am working harder than I have ever done in my life.

I have finished the painting of Guinevere, but I grew dissatisfied with it the moment it was done. How could I have thought her remote, unattainable? She is a woman like any other. I am painting her meeting with Lancelot—she will be the very personification of Carnality. It is my best painting so far.

I hope you are well, and that Henry will return soon.

> Your sincere friend,
> John

4 July, 1858

Dearest Kate–

Did I call her Guinevere? She is Morgan le Fay, the temptress, the sorceress, the lamia. She has ensorcelled me; I cannot rid my thoughts of her.

I have started another painting. I am determined to capture her, to fix her forever on canvas *as she truly is*. I am devouring her. No—she is devouring me. But if I can capture one iota of her beauty my paintings will be the talk of London.

> —John

5 July, 1858

My Dearest Husband–

I must confess that I have visited John in his studio today. Please do not be angry—I am sending you his latest letter to me, and I am certain that when you read it you will understand my concern.

You told me that when you called on him he did not want to let you inside. I am afraid that he is now so obsessed with this woman that he is indifferent to visitors—he opened the door without asking for my name, murmured a few words and nodded absently, and then motioned me in. Once I was inside the studio, however, he seemed to forget my presence entirely, and paid no more attention to me than he did to his furniture—less, in fact, since he painted his furniture.

His studio was lit by dozens of lamps and candles, all of them artfully arranged to show his Jenny in the best light. Do you remember that horrible gargoyle candelabrum, the one he displayed proudly at a dinner party until we all begged him to hide it away? That was there, resting on the floor, the wax dripping slowly into its open mouth.

Against the wall I saw a half-finished painting of Eve offering the apple to Adam, and another of a sorceress luring a figure, possibly Merlin, into a cave. The canvas on his easel held the barest outline of a tall dark-haired woman. The colors were astonishing, vibrant and strong. He said in the letter I enclose that his paintings will be the talk of London, and I do believe that if he shows them they will not be soon forgotten.

I must tell you I was very alarmed by his appearance. His face was pale, his eyes sunken; his clothes, which were stained with paint, were as rumpled as if he had worn them for a week or more.

If I was worried by him, however, I became even more concerned about the woman Jenny. You said that she seemed pitiable, uncertain. At first I did not find her so at all; she looked hard, all glittering surface, a little cruel. But after a while—No, I will tell you the story in the order in which it occurred.

She lay against his divan, dressed in white and green. Golden jewelry glinted against her neck and at her fingers. As he worked the sun came out, shining so brightly through his windows that I had to squint to see against it, but he did not pause to douse the lamps. I remember what you told me, that he is in great want because he has not sold (or indeed completed) a painting in quite some time, and I was alarmed at his profligacy.

He stopped for a moment and looked around him. He swore horribly—I will not repeat what he said. Then he looked at Jenny and said, "Where is my other paintbrush?"

She said nothing. I truly believe she did not know. He paced up and down the room, agitated. "Answer me!" he said. "What do you have to say for yourself? Nothing—I assumed so. You were nothing before I found you. Where did you put my paintbrush?"

I had to speak in her defense. "She doesn't know," I said, timidly enough. "Can't you see that?"

"Hold your tongue!" he said to me. "Don't defend her to me. You don't know what she is."

I could not think what to say to this. Before I could answer, however, he left the room, still cursing, to look for his paintbrush.

I took advantage of his absence to study the woman Jenny. And at that moment the most extraordinary thing happened. She seemed to—to change her shape. She was no longer the woman of his paintings, aloof, cold, cruel, but fragile, thin and pale. She looked like nothing so much as my sister Anna before she died.

I asked her her name and the name of her family. She seemed not to regard me at first, but gradually I thought she warmed to me; she even tilted her head to the side as Anna used to do when she wanted to concentrate on something.

I think it is true that she is quite mad. She told me that she had come from the heavens, that when night fell she could point out the very star that is her home. I asked her if she thought she was an angel.

"An angel!" John said, coming back into the room. I turned to him, startled by his sudden entrance. He laughed. "Where are the other angels, then, all the heavenly host?"

She shook her head. "Lost," she said. "All lost, and I have forgotten much—"

"An angel," John said, laughing again. "You do not know her, or you would not say such a thing. She is a very devil, a devil from Hell."

"She is nothing of the sort," I said. "She is a poor harmless woman, a lost soul. She deserved better than to be found by you."

"Nonsense," he said. "I rescued her. If I had not taken her to my studio she would have—well, you know what happens to women of her sort. She is lucky to be here."

He wiped his face, which was wet with perspiration. We were all terribly hot— the heat blazed from the windows, and the candles and lamps, as I said, still burned around the room. I forced myself to become calm.

"John, my good friend," I said, trying to speak in soothing tones. "How can you say she is evil? You know nothing about her, nothing at all, not even her station in life."

"She is a temptress," he said. "She will be the death of me yet."

"Come—look at her, see her how she really is. Don't you think she resembles my sister Anna?"

He turned to her—we both turned to her. And there, on his divan, was the image of my poor dead sister. How could I have thought her cold, cruel?

His face changed in an instant. "Dear God," he said. He wiped his face again on his sleeve. Then he hurried to one of the pieces of paper scattered around the room and began to sketch.

I looked over his shoulder and saw a drawing of Anna, her large eyes, the pale skin with the two red spots of consumption on her cheeks. As I watched he drew several bold lines, and then several more—wings. He had made Anna an angel.

I remembered that he had regarded my sister as a saint, especially in the last terrible days of her illness. "I see," he said, talking as if to himself. "I see it all now. I will capture her yet—she will not escape me."

Once again I did not know what to say. I was certain that he was mad, as mad as she—a *folie à deux*. I turned and left quickly.

I agree with you that the woman should be placed in a better situation as soon as possible. Your suggestion that she live with us until her family is found seems to me a good one, and good-hearted as well—you are, as always, a charitable man.

I hope that you are well, and that your father is improving. I would like to have you home again, so that we may do something about this dreadful situation.

Your loving wife,
Kate

7 July, 1858

Kate–

I cannot thank you enough for your insight into Jenny's character. There is a brilliance about her that is hers alone; when I fixed a strand of pearls at her neck they kindled into light, as if they caught fire from her. She is an angel—that explains the innocence I saw in her when I first rescued her. I need her, need that innocence, to start afresh, to be reborn. She makes me see everything in a new light.

—J.

20 July, 1858
Dearest Henry–

These past two weeks I have felt the most terrible apprehension for John. I waited anxiously each day for the morning and afternoon post, but nothing arrived from him. My worry grew to such a pitch that I felt I must visit him again, despite your prohibition.

Accordingly I called on him at his studio today. (You must forgive my shaking handwriting—I am still terribly alarmed by what I saw there.) My dear Henry, I am sorry to tell you that the situation is worse than ever. He is emaciated, his face sunken, his eyes huge. Flies buzz around the remains of his meals, rotting meat and vegetables, and the room has a terrible smell. I do not think he has eaten in several days. And she—she is thinner and paler than ever. My heart goes out to her, poor creature.

The room was dim, shadowy—all of the lamps were out, and the candles were nearly extinguished, leaving pale clots of wax on the floor. The sun, which had burned so brightly the last time I visited, had gone behind a cloud, and a thin rain fell. Dusty fans and feathers and tin crowns lay scattered about the floor.

And yet there was a strange light in the room. I hope you will not think me as mad as he is if I tell you that the light seemed to come from her, from her lambent face and skin. She was still pale, still thin, her eyes huge—she seemed to be consuming herself, spending her life, as Anna did. I cannot tell you how horrible it was to see this woman suffering so—it was as if I were condemned to watch Anna die twice.

When I looked away from her I could see small lights gleam in the shadowy corners. Some of the light came from the facets of the paste gems with which he had draped her, but others—oh, how I longed to leave, to simply turn and run out the door!—I fear some of the other light came from the glint of rats' eyes in the darkness. They came out to eat the food, and neither John nor Jenny had the strength to chase them away.

Despite the odd light he continued to paint, pausing only once to coil a chain of gold around her arm. "She is ill," I said. "She must be seen by a doctor."

At first he did not hear me. He moved away from her, overturning the gargoyle candelabrum at his foot, and studied his model. Then he said, "She is not ill, though she may seem that way to you."

"How can you say that? She—"

"She is changing, becoming something new. Haven't you noticed?—she appears in a new light from day to day." He lit a match and the light flared up briefly in the darkness. The smell of sulfur lingered for a moment in the room. He bent and lifted a candle, lit it.

"What do you mean?"

"She was remote, a queen of antiquity," he said. He began to pace. The candle lit his face from beneath, made his eyes into hollows, his eyebrows into spread wings. "Then she became carnal, a fleshy woman. And an evil sorceress, and an angel . . . I don't know how she does it, but she—she responds to me somehow. And to you as well—to everyone. You changed her into Anna, didn't you? Your husband thought she resembled you."

"What do you mean?" I asked again, backing away. Nothing I had seen in this room had prepared me for this lunacy.

"But what is she?" he asked. His pacing grew agitated. "She is mystery, an unknowable mystery. You feel it too, you must. She blazes like a fire, but what will happen if she begins to fade, to gutter out like a candle? I must discover the answer before she dies, before we both die. And I will discover it—I will burn her down to her core."

"You're mad," I said, and turned and fled.

My dearest Henry, I have thought of nothing but that poor woman since I left John's studio. I pray that your father regains his health soon, and that you return to me, and that together we may take Jenny from him and place her in our care.

Sometimes—sometimes I wake in the night, and see the stars from our bedroom window, and I wonder if John could be right. What if we each see in this woman what we want to see? It's true that she appeared to me as my sister, and you as me, and to John, it seems, as every woman he has ever desired.

What if she did come from the sky, as she told me? What better way to ensure her safety among us than to appear as the thing we most love? But then who is she, what is her true appearance ? What will happen if John does as he threatens and burns her down to her core?

> Your loving wife,
> Kate

27 July, 1858
Dearest Henry–

I am sending you the last letter I received from John. I became alarmed even before I read it, and if you but glance at it you will see why. The handwriting is chaotic, unruly—as he says he wrote the last part completely in the dark.

After I read the letter I hurried to his studio. I found him motionless and dazed, but—God be thanked!—still alive. All his candles had gone out, and only a fitful light came in through the window. Heaps of things lay scattered across the room— in the dim light they were no more than shadows. There was no sign of Jenny.

I brought him home with me, not caring what the neighbors might think, and I fed him. After a little while he responded to my ministrations. He refuses to speak of Jenny—all I know comes from the letter I enclose.

> Your loving wife,
> Kate

K.–

I have no more food. I have no more candles. For our old friendship's sake I beg you to come to my studio and give me what you can.

And yet I am not in the dark, for the light that comes from her is strong enough to guide me, grows stronger as I watch. I do not know what she is. I know she is changing one last time, and that I am changing as well. Perhaps this last change is death.

Look!—She is—she is shedding everything, all the costumes and jewelry I gave her, all her disguises. She is shedding her skin as well, she is emerging—

And I see—I see Her. She flares, she shines! I know—I understand—But she is gone.

How can I tell you what I saw? I understand now that she was not unknown, but unknowable. She never changed at all, in all the time I knew her—it was I who changed in my efforts to understand her. She was everything, illumination. And my mind could not grasp what she was, and so I put a familiar face on it, called her Jenny, as you called her Anna.

Her light has gone out, extinguished like a candle. But it is enough for me to have understood her for a single second, for her to have illuminated the entire world for me. It is enough to know that for a moment I partook of mystery. Because I am truly in the dark now, with only my pictures and my memories.

—J.

THE DAEMON STREET GHOST-TRAP

Terry Dowling

Terry Dowling is a lecturer in English at a large Sydney business college and is one of the most respected writers of speculative fiction in Australia. His short fiction has appeared in Australian magazines such as *Aphelion, Eidolon,* and *Australian Short Stories,* in U. S. magazines *Strange Plasma* and *The Magazine of Fantasy & Science Fiction,* and in the anthologies *Urban Fantasies, Matilda at the Speed of Light,* and *Intimate Armageddons.* His novels include *Rynosseros* and *Blue Tyson,* and his collection *Wormwood* won the Readercon Small Press Award for Best Collection of 1991. A collection of his horror stories is in preparation.

All the stories by Dowling I'd previously read have been science fiction, so I was unprepared for "The Daemon Street Ghost-Trap," an elegant and quietly chilling ghost story in the tradition of horror's earlier days. The story first appeared in the anthology *Terror Australis.*

—E.D.

I first heard of the Daemon Street ghost-trap from Jarvis Henry on the day after he lost his aide of six years to an interstate posting.

I was doing my Honors year, and the retired academic had been giving some honorary lectures and a completely optional series of seminars on perceptual anomalies. I enjoyed the classes, participated readily in the discussions, and received an invitation to stay back after the three o'clock meeting on that momentous Friday. Jarvis Henry's words were gently spoken, but they exploded in my mind.

"Jack, I wonder if you would like to accompany me this evening to see a Renfeld ghost-trap in Daemon Street?"

We'd all heard the news of his assistant's departure, so I spent the next hour daring to hope I was being considered as a replacement for the job—the Sorcerer's Apprentice.

All through the class, I watched Jarvis (as he preferred to be known), his bushy eyebrows flicking about on that pink, scrubbed-looking teddy-bear face, studying the small blue eyes for some sign. But no. He seemed jovial, excited, and determined to leave me in suspense.

While he listened patiently to a question from Megan Hatford, I reviewed all I knew about the Sorcerer (our name for him), trying to distinguish fact from rumor.

This small neatly-scrubbed-looking man in a worn tan suit, for all his qualifications, had made a name for himself searching out ghost-traps and spirit-foils across the world. He'd already examined forty-seven, but as I was later to discover, the one in Daemon Street had always been the one he most wanted to see.

When the class finally ended I approached him.

"I'd love to . . . Jarvis," I said, as though the previous hour hadn't existed, only his invitation.

"Good man," he replied, then spent ten minutes with me talking about the visit.

All through the next lecture I thought about what Jarvis Henry had said relating to Daemon Street. I looked out of the window at the fading autumn light, hoping my friends wouldn't mind me cancelling our plans for this evening. As I tried to take notes, Jarvis's words kept coming back to me.

Daemon Street. What a name. What a rare joke.

For a start, he suspected it was a real ghost-trap, not just a foil for keeping ghosts away like the Baxter's staircase-to-nowhere, or the Talbot's Blank Door, the false Red Room at Cromer, the Rot Bottle or the Blackfriar's Eat-Yourself Spiral Maze. According to Jarvis's most reliable source, the Crane residence in Daemon Street probably had token versions of those too, but it was the doorless room in the center of the ground floor that had Jarvis so excited. It was not a modification, Jarvis had said, not some afterthought added later, but part of the house's original design. Someone had set out to catch and hold something.

I marvelled at it too. It wasn't just that someone had had the determination and commitment to give over a dining-room-sized space to catching a family ghost. There was also the healthy respect that kept the succeeding generations from breaking the thing open and putting it to more immediate use. As Jarvis said, it took a strong haunting tradition, recurring manifestations, to do that.

These people believed.

I arrived at Jarvis's office in the Whiting Building at six. It was a brightly lit room, with the same twinkling, neatly scrubbed quality that Jarvis had. Amid the drab functional greys of filing cabinets and bookshelves, there was a collection of small curios and talismans.

I took the sound equipment and cameras Jarvis handed me and we went down to his car in the staff carpark.

"I wish I had time to show you more of the Private Listings, Jack; the Bellerton and Dutton breakdown released last year, the Getier monograph. You only got to browse them in class and you would be interested. Oh, I am so excited!"

There was no need for the street directory. Jarvis had plotted the route in advance, had no doubt driven down Daemon Street many times just to look at the house. He put some of the heavier things on the back seat, gave me the Pentax to hold, and started the engine.

"It's a real one, Jack. I am convinced!" he said as we reversed out of the carpark.

"Are there many fakes, Jarvis?"

"Oh yes, Jack. It's like mazes and topiaries. You make their existence public and everyone wants to see them. They become tourist attractions, even status symbols. The fakes soon appear. It's understandable with the television shows and magazines paying so well for coverage."

While Jarvis discussed the next week's parking arrangements with a university security guard I had time to savor what was happening, to glance at the traffic moving under a chill blue evening sky, and know that this was a special time.

I was the Sorcerer's Apprentice. For tonight at least, I was it.

To my knowledge Jarvis had seen two fakes: the Garden Trap at Higgs, and the Wentletrap-in-a-Well at Barstow. Campus talk had it that he had exposed many others, always in the same urbane, thoroughly civilized way, always avoiding legal action with his celebrated and quite damning line: "There is nothing for me here."

"How did you persuade Mr. Crane?" I asked, wondering why he had never been able to visit the Daemon Street site before now.

"Ah, Jack," Jarvis said, turning left and heading towards the city. "Ever since I heard about Tesserley Crane seventeen years ago I've been trying to get in to see it. Phone calls and letters every other month for a while. Polite refusals every time. He's a widower, but one of his sons Bradlan or young Roderick, or Tesserley himself, would point out that publicity wasn't wanted. I promised discretion but they refused. Every other month became every other year. Now this phone call. The old man claims he has trapped a ghost—a Renfeld Four—and apparently he's going to breach the room. He invited me to be there."

"A Four?" I said, deciding to show my ignorance up front.

"Yes, Jack. You've heard me mention Eugene Renfeld's *Ghostings: A Taxonomy* in class. Remind me to show you the extracts I have, if you like apprenticing for me."

And he winked. I definitely saw him wink.

"It's a limited edition, published in 1934. Very much a vanity press thing; none of the respectable publishers would touch it. The mutual friend who first told me about Crane's room also mentioned that Crane has a copy and from what he says, probably believes in Renfeld's four types. This is a marvellous opportunity if this is the case."

I went to comment but Jarvis spoke first.

"Forgive me, Jack, if I leave it to Crane to tell you what the four kinds of ghosts are. I'm hoping to hear how the old man handles it, and your detachment may be useful. I'm even thinking he may have been a student of Renfeld at some time. But you may remember the concept of the Red Room. I mentioned it at our first class when I showed my slides of Cromer."

"Yes, I do," I said, trying to remember what I had heard in class, and what Jarvis had told me that afternoon.

"Well, Renfeld fixed on that as the best way to hold the ghost. I'm thinking that the room in Daemon Street is a Renfeld trap."

"A Red Room?"

"Yes."

We turned into Parkhill, then did a sharp left into Makinson.

"What's the reasoning there, Jarvis?"

"It's straightforward, Jack. Blood memory, I should think, though I prefer to leave that sort of theorizing to people like Renfeld. Honorary lectureships are worth a degree of circumspection. Off the record though" (and again there was a wink) "the ghost essence once occupied a living body. Whatever life is—or was—is drawn to that color. Red and darkness. Renfeld gives ten cases in my extracts from *Ghostings* where Red Rooms attracted and neutralized Fours."

The car's headlights fell on a metal sign fixed to the brick wall of a corner terrace house: Daemon Street. I was startled by the archaic spelling

The Crane house was halfway down the street. A large three-storeyed dwelling, it was set back behind some pin oaks, appearing smaller than it was because of even larger houses closely adjoining it on either side.

The evening had turned cold. The pin oaks shook in the sudden chill wind, and the warm light spilling out of the stained-glass fantail above the front door was a welcome sight. Through the ragged, autumn-stripped trees we could see more light falling from the long shades of the first-storey windows.

A butler answered the door, a dour sallow-skinned elderly man in formal black, who admitted us to a lit hallway. At the end of the hall, a stairway went up into darkness. The rest of the ground floor was in gloom.

"Mr. Crane is upstairs, gentlemen, if you would be so kind. First door on the left. He is expecting you, of course. Dinner will be in twenty minutes."

Both Jarvis and I had been studying the panelled wall to the right of the staircase.

"That's it," the butler said, and moved off towards the kitchen at the back of the house.

We left our gear on a hall table and found Crane waiting for us at the door of an upstairs drawing room.

He was a tall, gaunt, bespectacled man in a mulberry-colored lounge jacket and dark trousers, who was so pale and ancient that he made Jarvis seem robust and youthful by comparison.

Crane was in his early eighties, but even allowing for the rough usage of years his haggard appearance had to be the result of some affliction, though Jarvis clearly had no knowledge of it. He gave me a look of puzzled surprise as we were ushered into the large room which combined the functions of a study, library and dining room.

It was a splendid room, obviously loved and much lived in, occupying most of the first floor. Deep, comfortable armchairs were set before a crackling fire; high bookcases reached to the ceiling, holding thousands of volumes; a chandelier and fine crystal bent the firelight into sudden brilliant flecks and glimmers. To one side, a mahogany dining table was laid for three.

"This is very good of you, Mr. Crane," Jarvis said when the introductions were completed.

"It's a pleasure, Dr. Henry. Andrew and I keep to this part of the house while the boys are away."

He asked me to pour sherry while he and Jarvis discussed the house, which the Crane family had lived in for generations. I joined them by the fireside, waiting for Jarvis to steer the conversation on to the subject of the room.

It didn't happen, not then. Andrew called us to the table and served soup and croutons followed by a casserole. Crane ate sparingly, then settled back with his eyes closed as if he had fallen asleep. There was no sound other than the crackle of the fire and the tick-tick of our eating utensils.

Just when I felt that Jarvis would suggest we return another time, the old man's head came up and his eyes flashed with new life.

"I am doing the right thing!" he said. "The story bears telling and I've procrastinated long enough."

He spoke in a vigorous, forthright voice, as if the conversation had been proceeding all along.

"I chose you, Dr. Henry, because you make no coin out of this. Like me, you are the genuine article, and you remind me a little of Eugene Renfeld as he's been described to me. Set your recorder going, Mr. Obern."

Our things had been brought upstairs, so I placed the machine on the table and switched it on. Crane nodded with approval.

"I have trapped something, a ghost, a horrifying and utterly cruel Four, the very worst of them. Downstairs is a closed room. You passed it when you came in. Tonight, with your help, we shall breach the room. Then you will rewrite the books, Dr. Henry, should you have the courage. Or you will, Mr. Obern, because it's a sensational new viewpoint But, like poor Renfeld, and like my forebears, you will have the story and the truth, and that seems the very least I owe myself and my family and my faithful Andrew here."

Andrew created a silence by serving sherry, then went back to reading a book by the fire.

"Why are you doing it, Mr. Crane?" Jarvis asked when the silence became unbearable. "Why you?"

The old man sipped his sherry, then cleared his throat.

"Do you know of the Alderson house at Port Savine? Of Janie Alderson, the woman who for years added to her house, room by room, believing that so long as she kept adding new rooms, new corridors, that a ghost would not kill her? It's somewhat like that here. We have auspicious relatives all over the world, Dr. Henry. In law, in politics, in commerce, and the arts. We're well represented, quite wealthy, and long-lived.

"It fell to the Daemon Street Cranes to safeguard the rest, you see. Some forebear rightly divined that our family was especially prone to the destructive force of ghostings; so he established this house. At first, the occupancy was rotated among less accomplished, less promising cousins, for a handsome stipend and the privilege of living here rent-free. They had nothing whatever to do for it, they could just live their lives peaceably, so long as the room remained intact. It was a powerful family superstition. These are more enlightened times, but I suppose I'm still the poorer line of the family." He laughed.

"But it's coming to an end?" Jarvis said.

"Oh yes. It's time. The Cranes can fend for themselves."

"Your sons don't wish to keep up the tradition?" I said.

"Partly correct, Mr. Obern. I live alone but for Andrew here." Crane gave an unreadable frown, one that might have hinted at recalcitrance and obduracy in Bradlan and his younger brother, Roderick, but which might have meant other things too.

"But it's more to do with something I have discovered, some research I've carried out on the Daemon Street Cranes."

"May we ask what that is?" Jarvis said.

"I wish to tell you. My father discovered that a great percentage of the Cranes who resided here in Daemon Street—men, women, young and old—all died of what is commonly diagnosed these days as carcinogens. Living here, they fell prey to cancer in all its hideous forms."

I could see why Bradlan and Roderick Crane had left. The rumor alone would be enough to set me packing.

"I had difficulty verifying much of this, of course. Cancer is very much a modern discovery by that name. But the coincidence was striking, especially in view of the Crane longevity elsewhere. Naturally my father suspected the ghost-trap downstairs, some deleterious by-product of its working through the years."

I glanced at Andrew sitting with his book by the fire, looked again at the ruined man at the head of the table but could not bring myself to ask Crane if he were suffering from cancer.

Jarvis spoke carefully. "You suggest that such disease is ghost-related?"

"It's more than that." Crane poured us both more sherry and stood up, indicating with a gesture that we should join him at the fire.

Jarvis and I sat down in two of the deep armchairs, but Crane remained standing.

"It occurred to me shortly after my father's death that ghosts had to be homotropic in every sense. They only have half-life energy to draw on, sometimes very weak and fleeting, sometimes remarkably powerful and enduring. But it seemed natural then that the ghost would be directed to that end—which may account for conditions like possession and schizophrenia. Or, failing that, they would seek the strongest material things we ever own, houses, rooms, objects, as fixing points. But people first. They would try to get back to people first; relatives, friends, the impressionable young, unsuspecting tenants, doctors at the bedsides of dying patients."

"Hence your closed room," I said, welcoming the fire of the wine, relying on the act of drinking it to keep me from being too impatient.

Jarvis, however, seemed the very soul of patience, relaxing back in his chair, as if prepared to let Crane talk all evening.

I hadn't learned the Sorcerer's ways yet. I was impatient to see the room, to break it open and look upon what Jarvis had probably seen many times.

Crane began to move slowly to and fro in front of the tall bookcases. He laid a finger on the spine of a red-bound volume.

"This is Renfeld. He classifies the ghost as four types—according to power vectors and how they manifest the tropism. Do you know Renfeld, Dr. Henry? Mr. Obern?"

"Of him," Jarvis said "Yes. I don't have my own copy, and I have never read it. Only extracts."

"This will be yours soon," Crane said. "I'll see to it. No! Here! Take it now." And he passed it over.

Jarvis accepted it, his mouth open in amazement at the unexpected generosity. Crane gave him no time to express his thanks.

"The Ones, Renfeld suggests, and I believe him, are the barest echoes, all non-specific residues. Premonitions and *frissons*. The conviction of something under the bed. The *déjà-vus* and *cauchemars*."

"*Cauchemars?*" I said, and instantly recalled the French word and regretted the interruption.

"The nightmare, Mr. Obern. The ghost as nightmare. Intruding into our consciousness when the mind is at rest and vulnerable. Most specters are Ones. Quite weak, ineffectual, diluted, just as many personalities are average, un-dynamic. Very tenuous life-echoes.

"The Twos are more powerful versions of these, still subjective experiences, private, solitary things, phenomenological rather than phenomenal, but more defined. With characteristics and features, identities, behavior. You would agree, Dr. Henry? Most ghostings, over ninety-five percent, are Ones and Twos. There is never anything to find; it all happens within the perceiver. Objectively, they do not harm us overly much."

Jarvis nodded, encouraging Crane with attentive silence.

"Exasperating for you two," Crane said, and smiled weakly. "The only haunted house is the self."

"The Bogeyman," I said, giving in to the flush of the sherry, needing to speak.

"The very worst of the Bogeymen, Jack," Jarvis said, and I appreciated his use of my name. "The ones children take with them when families move house."

"Absolutely," Crane said. "Renfeld's Threes, on the other hand, mark the cross-over. The subjective experience becomes the phenomenal one, measurable at last. External manifestations. Recordable bumpings and groanings. Visible signs and stigmata. Traceable energy surges. With enough power for the ghosting to sustain itself out-of-body, haunting a space, a locality, a house, a closet . . ."

"A sealed room?"

"No, Mr. Obern. My sealed room is not where a ghost would ever *want* to be. It's where it is forced to be. By techniques which are not completely understood but which were discovered by chance and refined by repeated effective use. Cargo cult empiricism. A cause and effect."

"Mr. Crane's point, Jack," Jarvis said, "is that with a Three, the ghost haunts the artifact rather than a person's unconscious, and different individuals will experience the ghost both subjectively *and* objectively, and with the same characteristics."

I didn't say anything. The wine was making me eager and I was coming over as foolish. Thankfully, Jarvis didn't seem to mind.

Crane continued. "The Four is the really dangerous one. It has enough power to haunt a house for many, many years, a whole town or neighborhood, a lake, a beach, but it aims that power at a living person, directs all of its force to returning to an in-life state."

Jarvis leaned forward in his chair.

"What are you telling us, Mr. Crane?"

Crane stopped pacing. "Just this, Doctor. The ghost-trap in this house has been catching ghosts since my great-grandfather's time."

And killing you with cancer, I thought. Jarvis too was busy trying to fathom what Crane had told us. The room downstairs was full of Fours?

"You are opening it tonight, Mr. Crane," Jarvis said. "Tell us again why that is."

"I am dying, Doctor, as you have guessed. I am riddled with cancers, and I know I have less than the few months the doctors have allowed. It will be sooner, I know. Much sooner.

"The Fours are not common, but statistically many exist. The Fours in our ghost-trap here at Daemon Street have all been focused there and neutralized long ago, consumed in the panelled darkness of the Red Room. I love Renfeld's writing, don't you? Except for one that arrived three nights ago and prompted my call to you, and the one I believe will appear tonight when the room is breached.

"I want to share my family's legacy now. People resist the idea of ghosts because they sense the harm; they seem to know intuitively that the ghostings accrue about the preoccupied and the sensitive among us. They come so quickly to any receptive person, bringing physical harm not just psychological. It takes courage to think of the discontinued identities trying to get back in, trying to be bodies again, trying to be people, trying to be what they cannot be. But they cannot stop.

"Tomorrow Andrew will deliver all my papers to your office at the university, Dr. Henry. My other legacy to you; the legacy of the Daemon Street Cranes. We've done our share of ghost-hunting. Let the others try."

"Your sons will sell the house then?" Jarvis asked.

"My sons are abroad, Doctor. They want no part of this. And why should they? Why should anyone bring ghosts together, work at such a task, bear such a burden and die for it? It's better that we disregard these displaced forces, let them remain free radicals sullying our more susceptible moments. Acknowledging them focuses their energy, directs it. It is folly."

"Is your ghost-trap a Red Room, Mr. Crane?"

The ruined old man smiled and moved away from the bookcases. "Why don't I show you? Come, gentlemen. And Mr. Obern, if you and Andrew would be so good as to bring those heavy crowbars by the hearth; we will need them. This is a momentous occasion."

We left the cosy room and went downstairs to the blind wall at the end of the entrance hall. Crane switched on the lights as we went, far more lights than were needed. The lower floor was ablaze with warm yellow light when we reached it.

Then he began feeling the panelled walls, striking panels to find joists and sections.

"Some sealed rooms have spy-holes which, of course, render them useless," Crane told us. "Modern ones are totally sealed but have light-fittings and video cameras inside so the interior can be lit and observed. None of that foolishness here. This room has not seen light for one hundred and sixteen years. It is the no-place."

"Is it furnished?" Jarvis said.

"Oh yes. In a sense," Crane answered. "With enough people-things to draw the Threes and Fours."

The last words prompted a thought, one that suddenly grew to worry me in this overlit corridor.

"You said a Four arrived three nights ago, Mr. Crane. Is it in there now then?"

Crane looked at us again in a wholly unreadable way, giving a strange lop-sided smile, his long hands planted on the panels like two parchment spiders. He reminded me of a creature about to spring, or of a thief listening for the fall of tumblers in a hidden wall safe.

"The Four is in the trap, Mr. Obern. But it will not harm you. It is otherwise engaged. Its days, too, are numbered. But another will come when the walls are broken. If this troubles either of you, please . . ."

"No, Mr. Crane," Jarvis said. "Jack and I wouldn't miss this."

"Good. I doubt the exercise would be advisable for me. Or for Andrew. Mr. Obern, if you would strike here, here and here,"—he indicated the spots with his white spider hands—"we can begin to make the breach."

I struck where he said, struck again and again until the panelling split and could be wrenched back, exposing some joists which formed a door that had never been finished as one. Jarvis took some photographs.

"In the middle of the room, Dr. Henry, there is a table. On it is a large porcelain bowl."

"A water-trap!" Jarvis cried. "Your ancestor used a water-trap?"

"Initially," the old man said. "It's basic and it works. Please, when the wall is sundered, shine that hand-light on the bowl immediately. Mr. Obern can then bring those other lights in from the hall. The room must be lit."

Jarvis began taking photographs again while I pounded at the wood, shattering more of the panelling, ruining beautiful old timber that would have cost a fortune now. I had cleared the false door from this side. Only the inner panelling remained. I found I was trembling with anticipation and fear looking at it, aware only of the broken wood and the steady flash of Jarvis's Pentax.

Obviously the whole south wall had been fitted as a pre-fabricated section, with the outer panels added once the frame was bolted in place. It must have cost a great sum; the finishing was flawless, a true fourth wall, not just a partition.

"This is your moment, gentlemen," Mr. Crane said. "Andrew, goodnight to you. It's time you were out of this. I am in good hands."

Jarvis and I were surprised to see the men embrace, to see the tears of a painful and final farewell on their faces.

"Bless you, Mr. Crane," the butler said. He made no further fuss, just nodded a goodnight to us, took up a small suitcase, and went out of the front door.

It had a sense of unreality about it, how suddenly it happened. It seemed comical in its intensity and abruptness: the embrace, the door opening, the windy street beyond, the click of the lock.

Jarvis went to speak but did not.

"Let us continue," Crane said. "And thank you for forbearing with your questions. We can proceed."

I struck the inner panels a resounding blow, turning my anxiety into hard action. I struck and struck until the timber burst, and stale chill air engulfed me. I swooned a little at it, trying not to breathe, and kept up the blows, while Crane stood to my left and Jarvis took his pictures.

"Stop!" Crane hissed, and suddenly there was a parchment claw closing on my shoulder. I froze, stopped mid-strike, and lowered the crowbar.

"What is it, Mr. Crane?" Jarvis said.

The hand relaxed its terrible grip.

"Not yet!" the old man said. "Proceed! Proceed!"

Again I put my fear into the blows. Like someone whistling past the graveyard or shouting at the devil, I made my big brash noises to hide the deathly silence, to distract me from the dread I felt growing within.

Splinters flew, whole sections of shattered oak fell inwards. I hit and pounded and poleaxed any part that resisted, until only the joists stood and the sealed room was no longer any part of that.

"Bring the lights!" Crane said. "Light everywhere!"

In my haste, I dropped the crowbar so it clanged against the wooden floor. Jarvis helped me set up the portable floodlights. We aimed them into the room and switched them on.

We saw striped wallpaper, polished wainscoting and panels, a featureless plastered ceiling. There was a wooden chair by one wall, with a book resting on the chair. On the mantelpiece of the blind fireplace directly opposite there was a clock with no hands. In the middle of the room was a narrow wooden table and on it a large white bowl.

"It's not a Red Room!" Jarvis said, but the words were lost as Crane gasped, gave a soft cry of agony, and staggered against the wall. His face was a white mask, as if all the skin had yellowed cords underneath suddenly drawn tight. His hand was on his chest.

"Mr. Crane!" Jarvis cried.

In a moment we had him, holding him steady between us, trying to ease him away from the trap to a chaise longue we saw near the front door.

"I can take it," he muttered, breathing deeply. "I can do it." Then: "It's all right now. Dr. Henry, examine the room."

Jarvis did so, while I brought in yet another light. Crane sat in the hall while we moved about the panelled space.

"It's not a Red Room," Jarvis said to me. He moved to the bowl, empty of water for the best part of a century. "This is not painted red either."

Behind us, Crane had recovered and was climbing gingerly between the joists of the door frame, throwing long distorted shadows about the room as he came to us, crossing a floor unused before our intrusion.

"No, it isn't," he said, looking as if he would collapse at any moment. Jarvis steadied him.

"You said there was a Four here."

"There is. Now there is. And other ghostings. They know what I am doing. And they are vicious and blindly angry things. Powerful, vicious and quite desperate. They want to live again so much. A tropism . . ." The old man paused, grimaced.

We held him again. Jarvis got the room's wooden chair and we sat him in it. He nodded his thanks, then looked up.

"You know the story of Dorian Grey?" he said, panting, obviously in great pain. "The painting ages while the man . . ."

Jarvis nodded. "Of course."

"Yes," I said, seeking the connection.

Jarvis leaned in close. "Are you saying, Tesserley . . . ?"

"Not Tesserley," Crane gasped. "Not Tesserley. I am Roderick, the youngest. I am thirty-two."

We stared at eighty-two, ninety, and more; at wasted diseased parchment. At the mouth working to speak. At a dying man.

"Tesserley, Bradlan . . . died full of ghosts. Both filled up . . . choked with them. We are the ghost-traps! We never knew. The room only focuses them; they leak out into us. The Fours become living tissue. That is what cancer is, what ghosts become. So many of us . . . so full of ghosts. It happens more quickly once you know. You cannot stop thinking of it, drawing them to you . . ."

Jarvis stood wide-eyed beside me, saying nothing, but understanding as I was just beginning to.

"The room was never it at all," I said, marvelling and horrified at the same instant.

Roderick Crane seemed not to hear.

"You only have to know, to think of them, to focus them somewhere." His voice was very soft, filled with his agony. "Then you cannot stop them." He gave a ratcheting, bleating laugh. "But the irony! We destroy them only by dying. And now I have Tesserley and Bradlan both. Now I have them."

"Here?" I cried, needing to be sure.

"Oh yes, I have them now," Crane said, at the edge of death, and jerked a thumb up to his chest.

"In the Red Room!"

MEMO FOR FREUD

Daína Chaviano

Daína Chaviano, born in Cuba in 1957, is part of a younger generation of Cuban writers challenging the secondary literary roles assigned to women in that country. Among her published works, which include science fiction, are *Historias de hadas para adultos* and *Fabulas de una abuela extraterrestre.*

The following dark erotic fantasia (translated from the Spanish by Heather Rosario-Sievert) comes from the Latin American anthology *Pleasure in the Word.* It was translated into English for Chaviano's unpublished poetry manuscript titled *Confesiones eroticas y otros hechizos,* which received Honorable Mention in Mexico's Concurso Plural.

—E.D. and T.W.

> *In the center of the lake was an island*
> *full of castles inhabited by ants.*
> *Each rainy night*
> *came the warriors to spawn*
> *their spears of light*
> *that I frightened away by the cries of a vampire.*
> *Slowly I stretched out on the grass*
> *and you rolled over me.*
> *Over and again you plunged a smooth stake*
>   *into my vulva*
> *Like a silver nail*
>
>   *and you smiled,*
>
> *I don't know why*
> *when I fall in love I have nightmares.*

THE SUNDAY-GO-TO-MEETING JAW

Nancy A. Collins

Nancy A. Collins is a native of Arkansas who now lives in New York. Her vampire novel *Sunglasses After Dark*, won the 1989 Bram Stoker Award for first novel. Her three subsequent novels are *Tempter,* and a follow-up to *Sunglasses, In the Blood,* and a "grunge" werewolf novel entitled *Wild Blood*. She has been writing *Swamp Thing* for DC Comics for the past two years and has recently created a new graphic novel series for DC, to be called *Wick.*

"The Sunday-Go-To-Meeting Jaw," from *Confederacy of the Dead,* reflects her southern upbringing, as do several of her other stories (including "Freaktent," which was reprinted in *The Year's Best Fantasy and Horror: Fourth Annual Collection*). Its portrait of a family in the aftermath of the War Between the States is powerful and poignant.

—E.D.

The hungry man squatted in the shadows of the tree-line marking the boundary of the Killigrew land, never once taking his eyes off the back of the house. His hot, bloodshot eyes followed the handful of chickens scratching haphazardly in the dirt. Although he had not eaten in three days, the chickens had nothing to fear from him. His hunger could no longer be appeased in such a simple fashion.

He hugged his bony knees with broomstick arms and studied the faded lace curtains that hung in the long, narrow windows of the two-story clapboard house. He stiffened as he caught a glimpse of a woman dressed in black. He began to sweat and shiver at the same time. Had the fever come back? Or was it something else this time?

The back door slammed open and an elderly Negro woman, her head wrapped in a worn kerchief, stepped out on the porch, drying her wrinkled hands on a voluminous apron that hung all the way down to her ankles. After studying the coming twilight, the old Negress descended the stairs and hobbled toward a small, neatly kept two-room cabin near the house.

From the looks of the rest of the half-dozen slave quarters, the old mammy was the only remaining servant on the place.

It was getting dark. The family inside the house was no doubt gathered around the dinner table. If he was going to do what he planned, he'd have to move from his hiding place soon. The starving man's stomach tightened even further.

Hester Killigrew pushed the food on her plate with her fork. Collard greens, roast sweet potatoes, and corn pone. Again. White trash food. Nigger food. Least that's what Fanny Walchanski said.

Fanny's father, Mr. Walchanski, owned the dry goods store in Seven Devils. He was one of a handful of merchants who had benefited from the arrival of the railroad in Seven Devils last year. Mr. Walchanski was very well-to-do, Fanny was fond of pointing out to anyone within earshot. Hester could just imagine what Fanny would have to say if she discovered the Killigrews took their meals in the kitchen instead of the dining room.

Hester looked at her mother, seated at the head of the table, then at her little brother. Francis was busy shoveling food into his rosebud mouth. Francis was only two and a half and couldn't remember how it'd been before the war. Back when there'd been more than just Mammy Joella to see to them. Back when they ate in the dining room every day on proper china.

Hester knew better than to complain about their situation. It was sure to make her mother scold her or, worse, break into tears. Hester realized they weren't as bad off as other folks in Choctaw County. They still had a roof over their heads and ate on a regular basis. There wasn't as much red meat as before, and they had a goat for milk instead of a cow, but there were plenty of chickens and eggs.

She remembered how Old Man Stackpole sat in his big old empty mansion until he went crazy and set it on fire before shooting himself in the head. Maybe he got sick of eating greens and corn pone all the time, too.

There was a knock on the back door. Since Mammy Joella had gone back to her cabin for the night, Mama answered it herself.

Hester craned her neck to see around her mother's skirts. A tall, thin raggedy man stood on the stoop, his hair long and grimy. He looked—and smelled—like he hadn't washed in weeks. For some reason Hester was reminded of the nutcracker soldier she'd seen in the window of Walchanski's Dry Goods.

"If you want work, I don't have any to give you—and no money to pay you with, if I did," Penelope Killigrew said tersely. In the year since the war ended, ragged hungry strangers looking for food or temporary work were common. Most were trying to make their way back home the best they could. Others, however, were trouble looking for a place to happen.

The stranger spoke in a slobbering voice that reminded Hester of the washerwoman down the road's idiot son.

"Nell—don't you know me?"

Penelope Killigrew started to cry and shake her head "no." Francis, who'd been happily crumbling corn pone with his pudgy little hands, looked up at the sound of his mother's sobs.

Hester thought the funny-looking stranger had done something. She jumped from her chair and hurried to the door.

"What did you do to my mama?!" she demanded.

Penelope Killigrew turned and grabbed her daughter's shoulders. She was smiling and crying at the same time, like the time she wouldn't put Francis down. Hester started to get scared.

"It's alright, honey! Everything's going to be alright! Daddy's come home!"

Confused, Hester stared at the half-starved stranger dressed in the tatters of a Confederate uniform. He stared back, his rheumy eyes blinking constantly. Now that she had a good look at him, she realized why he'd reminded her of the nutcracker soldier.

He had a wooden jaw.

Hester slammed the door to her room as hard as she could. She didn't care if it shook the whole house. She didn't care if it knocked the house to the ground, for that matter! Mama made her go to her room. Well, that's just fine! She could be just as mad as Mama!

Mama lost her temper because she refused to kiss him. Hester didn't care if she got switched for it later. She wasn't going to kiss him! She didn't care what Mama or anyone else might say!

That man wasn't her daddy!

Everyone kept insisting that Hester was too young to remember things from before the war. That was stupid. If she could remember their ole dog, Cooter, why not Daddy? She certainly could remember the war—leastways the occasions it wandered into their lives. Hester didn't know why Mama kept telling the Nutcracker she didn't know better. Maybe it made her feel better about having a stranger in the house. But why did Mama have to pretend he was Daddy?

Daddy was the handsomest man in Arkansaw. At least Choctaw County, anyway. He was big and strong, with shoulders like a bull. He had dark hair with deep blue eyes. He laughed a lot and had a charming smile. Even other men said so.

Hester remembered how she used to sit on the floor in the parlor, playing with her rag doll, listening for the sound of his boots in the hall. Then he'd sweep her up in his arms, swinging her high in the air. Sometimes the top of her head brushed the chandelier and made the crystal drops shake and dance. It sounded just like angels singing.

She'd squeal and giggle and Daddy would laugh, too—the sound booming out of his chest like thunder. Mama didn't approve of such tomfoolery, though. Hester supposed she was afraid they'd break the chandelier.

Hester was six when Daddy went off to fight for President Davis. Mama cried a lot, but Daddy said it was something he had to do. Hester didn't really understand what was going on at the time, but she thought Daddy looked handsome in his gray uniform.

They all went down to Mr. Potter's daguerreotype palace down near the train depot and Daddy had his picture taken. Mama kept it in the family Bible, pressed between the pages like a dried flower.

Daddy left in 1861 to go help General Lyon fight General McCulloch at Oak Hills, near Missouri. He wrote letters every day, and Mama would read them aloud in the parlor before going to bed. Most of the time he wrote about how much he missed them and how bad the army food was.

In 1862, Daddy's unit joined with General Van Dorn's to keep the Yankees from pushing the Confederacy out of Missouri. That was Pea Ridge. The Confederates lost and the Yankees ended up marching all the way to Helena. Daddy came home for a visit after that. He was skinny and had a beard, but as far as Hester could tell, he was still Daddy. He hugged her so hard Hester thought her ribs would bust. He smelled bad, but she pretended not to notice so he wouldn't get hurt feelings. When Mama saw him, she started to cry, but Daddy shook his head at her.

"Hush, Nell. Not in front of the child."

He left two days later.

Just before Christmas of that year, Daddy fought with General Hindman at Prairie Grove. When they had to retreat to Fort Smith, Daddy was one of the men who didn't desert. He kept writing home, but sometimes they didn't get the letters until a long time after he mailed them. Hester knew sometimes he never got the letters Mama sent him, like the one telling him about Francis being born that winter.

The last letter Daddy wrote said he was going with General Holmes to kick the Yankees out of Helena. That was 1863.

They didn't get news of what happened at Helena until a month or two later. Mama found out first. It was a massacre. That's how Mama said it. A regular massacre. Hester didn't know what that meant at the time, but judging from how everyone was carrying on, she figured it had to be real bad. Mama cried a lot and carried Francis around and wouldn't put him down or let Mammy Joella take him.

Mammy Joella got upset and begged Mama to eat something. If not for herself, then for "the chirren's sake." All that did was make Mama cry even more.

Things changed after that. Mama took to wearing black and made Hester wear it too, even though it was way too hot for that time of year. Mama cut her hair real short and was sad most of the time. Although they never got an official notice from the army, she was convinced Daddy was dead. Or as good as.

Things at home got hard. Most of the niggers ran off when they heard about the proclamation Mr. Lincoln made freeing the slaves. Not that Hester's family had a lot of slaves to begin with, unlike Old Man Stackpole's plantation up the road. The only nigger that stayed behind was Mammy Joella, who claimed she was too old to start someplace new.

Mama sold off several parcels of Killigrew land to keep from being thrown out on the road. After General Lee surrendered, she sold almost all of her fancy dresses, saying she'd never have anything worth celebrating ever again. She also sold off the dining room set and the good china and silverware.

At first Hester thought Mama was joking about the dirty, foul-smelling man being Daddy. Then Mammy Joella came out of her cabin to see what all the fuss was about. She took one look at the Nutcracker and gave a little scream like she'd just seen a ghost.

"It's Mr. Ferris! Mr. Ferris!"

Mammy Joella helped Grandma Killigrew deliver Daddy, long time ago. She'd known Ferris Killigrew longer than anyone outside his own family. But she was old and didn't see or think as well as she used to. Everyone knew that.

Penelope Killigrew sat on a chair in the kitchen, a clean towel folded in her lap, and silently watched Mammy Joella scrub what was left of her husband. She stared at her long-lost husband's back. His vertebrae looked like the beads on a necklace.

The numbness was beginning to fade, like it had years ago, when she'd thought Ferris was dead. Part of her felt guilty for having surrendered hope and resigned herself to widow's weeds so prematurely.

Ferris Killigrew, her husband of fifteen years and father of her two children, was, like Lazarus before him, back from the land of the dead he'd been so hurriedly consigned to.

Wasn't he?

Steam rose from the dented metal tub, wrapping the gaunt figure in a damp haze. Penelope blinked the tears from her eyes and looked away.

Mammy Joella moved purposefully about her former master, scrubbing his grayish skin, occasionally pouring warm water over his tangled hair with a ladle, clucking under her tongue.

Killigrew realized he should have undone the leather straps that held his jaw in place before bathing, but he was not ready to subject Nell to that yet. She'd had a bad enough shock as it was, what with him showing up unannounced on the back stoop.

The smell of Mammy Joella's skin and the touch of her calloused hands on his naked flesh reminded Killigrew of how she used to bathe him as a child. The memory was so sharp, so unexpected, he began to cry.

He was both surprised and disgusted by the hot tears rolling down his cheeks and how his sides shook and shuddered from the force of his sobs. He'd never cried in front of Nell before, not even when his mother died. He squeezed his eyes shut, too ashamed to look at his wife.

Mammy Joella's voice whispered in his ear. "Go 'head an' cry, Mister Ferris. You have yourself a good cry. If anyone deserves one, it's you."

Hester woke up when her mother screamed.

Although it was dark, the moon outside her window cast a cold, dim light into the room. Hester lay on her bed and held her breath. What was happening? Was the house on fire? Had something happened to Francis?

Then she remembered the Nutcracker, and she leapt from her bed and hurried across the narrow hall to her mother's room. She grabbed the doorknob, but it refused to turn in her hand.

Hester pounded her fists against the door, shrieking at the top of her lungs. "What are you doing to my mother!?! Leave her alone! Get out of our house! Get out! Go away! Leave us alone!"

The door jerked open so quickly Hester nearly fell headfirst into her mother's room. Mrs. Killigrew stood in the doorway, her face white and tense—whether from anger or shock Hester could not tell.

"Hester, what are you doing up at this hour? Return to your room, immediately!"

Hester could make out the rail-thin form of the Nutcracker seated on the edge of her parents' bed, his face hidden by shadows. "I heard you yell, Mama . . ."

"Nonsense, child! You must have been having a bad dream."

"It *wasn't* a dream! I *heard* you." She scowled and pointed at the Nutcracker. "What's *he* doing here, Mama?"

Mrs. Killigrew frowned and glanced over her shoulder. Her grip tightened on the doorknob. "Come along, honey. Be quiet, or you'll wake up Francis! I'll tuck you back in bed," she whispered, pulling the door shut behind her.

"But Mama, you *did* scream! I *heard* you!" Hester protested as her mother herded her back into her room.

"I told you to hush once already, child!" Mrs. Killigrew hissed. "You'll have the whole house up if you're not careful!"

Hester crawled into bed and looked into her mother's face. "Is that man *really* Daddy?"

"Yes, honey. It's really him." Mrs. Killigrew drew a quilt over her daughter and smoothed it with trembling hands.

"But why does he look so—funny?"

Mrs. Killigrew took a deep breath, like a woman preparing to jump into a cold stream. "When your father went with General Holmes to try and chase the Yankees out of Helena, he ended up getting himself captured. They sent him to a camp somewhere up North, where they kept Confederate soldiers. He was in that place over a year.

"A couple of weeks before . . . before General Lee surrendered, your daddy led a protest for more food and decent clothing for the prisoners. He got smashed in the face with a Yankee rifle butt for his trouble. The Yankee doctors ended up cutting off his lower jaw to keep the gangrene from spreading. So they gave him a wooden one to replace it and let him go. He's been working his way back home ever since."

"Is he going to stay here with us?"

"Yes, darling. Forever and ever."

"Do people have to see him?"

The slap came so suddenly Hester was too stunned to react. Mrs. Killigrew spun on her heel without another word and slammed the door behind her, leaving her daughter alone in the dark.

Hester lay in her bed, refusing to cry. She pressed her red, stinging cheek against Grandma Killigrew's patchwork quilt and wondered what was wrong with grownups.

She felt like she was trapped inside a bad dream and that she was the only one who knew she was asleep. It was like everyone was crazy but her. But maybe that was what being an adult was all about: believing things you know aren't so.

Like the Nutcracker being Daddy.

Hester had seen the lie in her mother's eyes when she'd assured her that the Nutcracker was her father. She knew in her heart, just as Hester did, that whoever this gaunt scarecrow might be, he *wasn't* Ferris Killigrew. So why did Mama keep pretending?

Penelope Killigrew stood shivering in the hallway.

She realized she shouldn't have screamed like that, but she just couldn't help herself. When he'd exposed his wounds to her she'd been so overwhelmed. . . . Her relief at discovering Ferris still alive had prevented her from recognizing just how severe her husband's wounds really were. But now there was no turning away from it.

The half-starved creature that had found its way back home was not the man she'd loved before the war. The Ferris Killigrew that had returned was a mangled, incomplete copy of the husband that had marched off to war four years ago. But she owed it to the memory of the man she'd adored to see to it that what was left be looked after and treated well. It was the least she could do.

Hester was walking home from school when she caught sight of the wagon in her family's front yard. As she drew closer, Hester recognized it as belonging to the man in town who bought used furniture; the one who'd bought their old dining room set the year before.

"Mama! Mama!"

Hester hurried through the front door, nearly knocking down her mother. Mrs. Killigrew stood in the narrow foyer, Francis resting on one hip.

"Land's sakes, child! What is it *now*?" she sighed.

"What are these men doing here?" Hester demanded, pointing at the two men in the parlor. One of the men was laying thin blankets on the floor, while the second prepared a heavy wooden crate filled with excelsior.

"They've come to haul off some furnishings I've sold to Mr. Mercer, that's all."

"What are they taking *this* time?"

"Don't use that tone of voice with me, Hester Annabelle Killigrew!"

Just then there was the sound of a hundred angels laughing, and Hester spun around in time to see one of the packing men lower the crystal chandelier, winding the old-fashioned pulley Grandpa Killigrew had had installed decades ago.

"No! No! I won't let you sell it!" shrieked Hester, throwing her books to the floor.

"Hester! Hester, what's gotten into you?!?"

Hester propelled herself at the workman lowering the chandelier, hammering her doubled fists against his ribs. "I won't let you take it! I won't! I *won't*!"

"*Hester!*"

The second workman grabbed the girl and pulled her away from his companion. He cast an anxious look over his shoulder at the child's mother. "Mebbe we oughta come round later, Miz Killigrew, after she's calmed down some. . . ."

Penelope Killigrew's face was livid. "You'll do no such thing! You'll take the chandelier with you, just as I promised Mr. Mercer! Now if you'll kindly unhand my daughter . . ."

The workman let go and Mrs. Killigrew snatched her daughter's left ear, twisting it viciously.

"*Mama!* Owww! You're *hurting* me!"

"And you're *embarrassing* me, young lady!" Mrs. Killigrew dragged her daughter down the hall, away from Mr. Mercer's hired men. "How *dare* you act such a way in front of strangers!" she hissed. "People will think you were raised in a *barn*! I sold that chandelier to Mr. Mercer to help pay for your father's needs! We have another mouth to feed, and it will be some time before your father is well enough to contribute to the family's welfare! Now, would you care to explain yourself, young lady, as to what brought on that outburst?"

Hester shook her head, her tears finally catching up with her hurt. Francis, distressed by his older sister's sobs, began to whimper.

"Oh, don't you start in as well!" groaned Mrs. Killigrew. "Hester, go to your room! I don't want to see your face until supper time! Is that clear?"

Hester stormed up the stairs, clamping her hands over her ears to keep from hearing the chandelier's angel-song as it was packed away. She paused and gave her parents' bedroom a venomous look. Before she realized what she was doing, she'd kicked open the door and was shrieking at the Nutcracker.

"It's all *your* fault! She sold it because of *you*! I hate you! Why don't you go back where you came from and leave us *alone*?!?"

Mammy Joella sprang from the corner of the bed, moving faster than Hester had ever seen her move before. "Chile, get outta this room for I bust yore haid!" She flapped her apron at the girl as if she was an errant chicken, a wooden spoon clutched in one arthritic hand. Hester stumbled backward into the hall, but not before she caught a glimpse of the Nutcracker.

He was sitting up in bed, surrounded by pillows, one of Francis's old diapers knotted around his neck. A bowl of yellow grits and a pitcher of goat's milk rested on the dresser next to the bed. A length of rubber tubing hung from the middle of his face, a small metal funnel fixed to its end. A mixture of grits and milk dribbled from what passed for the Nutcracker's mouth.

The tube dangling from the Nutcracker's face reminded Hester of something she'd seen at the traveling circus in Arkansaw City before the war.

"He looks like an elephant!" she giggled.

Mammy Joella smacked her with the spoon, leaving a smear of porridge on Hester's forehead. "Don't you be callin' yore pappy names!"

Hester was taken aback by this new affront. As far back as she could remember, Mammy Joella had been a pleasant, if slightly decrepit, servant: loving, forgiving, and slow to anger. "You can't hit me! You're just a nigger!"

"I'm a nigger, awright; but I'm the only nigger y'all got!" Mammy Joella hissed back. With that, she returned her attention to the Nutcracker, closing the door in Hester's face.

The next day, Mrs. Killigrew loaded her husband into the buckboard and went in to town to see Doc Turner. Doc Turner measured Ferris Killigrew's head with a pair of calipers and studied the extent of his patient's wounds before showing them a catalog from a company up north.

"There's nothing they can't make nowadays," he explained cheerily. "Wooden legs, hook arms, glass eyes, tin noses. . . . Course it helps there's such a large demand! Now, what can I do you for, Ferris?"

The Sunday-go-to-meeting jaw came in the mail a month later. The Killigrew children watched as their mother unwrapped the parcel in the kitchen. While Francis was more interested in playing with the cast-off stamps and string, Hester's attention was riveted on the package's contents.

The Nutcracker's new jaw had its own special case that reminded Hester of the box Mama used to keep her emerald necklace and pearl brooch in, back when she used to have jewelry. The jaw rested on a maroon velvet lining, a network of straps and buckles that resembled a dog's muzzle folded underneath it.

Mrs. Killigrew had sent the artificial limb company one of the few photographs she had of Mr. Killigrew from before the war. The custom-fitting cost more, but Doc Turner had assured them it was worth it. Seeing the replica jaw displayed like a watch in a jeweler's window flustered Mrs. Killigrew somewhat. Outside of noticing it had been painted to mimic European skin tones and was of a distinctly masculine cast, it was difficult to judge how closely the people at the artificial limb company had hewed to the photograph.

"Ferris, look! It's here!"

Ferris Killigrew stared at the gleaming piece of hard wood on its velvet cushion but did not move to touch it.

"Let's try it on," Mrs. Killigrew urged.

Killigrew grunted and slowly unfastened the straps that held his army-issue wooden jaw in place. Mrs. Killigrew did not allow her smile to slip as she averted her eyes.

When he'd finished adjusting the new straps, he shuffled over to the cheval glass his wife keep in the corner of the room and studied his new jaw.

He had to admit that it didn't look nearly as fake as the old one. It fit a damn sight better than his old one, too. However, its unnaturally rosy pigmentation made it look like he'd never washed his face above the jawline.

"Oh, Ferris! It's better than I thought it would be!" Mrs. Killigrew smiled. "It makes you look—like you!" She slid her arms around her husband's waist, pressing her head against his shoulder, like she did in their courting days. "Now you can go to church this Sunday!"

Killigrew clumsily returned her hug, trying hard not to cry again.

"I love you, Ferris," she whispered.

He wanted to tell her that he loved her, too; that it had been that love that kept him alive in the prisoner of war camp all those horrible months; that his love for her had drawn him back across four states, despite harsh weather, harsher treatment, and the threat of death by starvation or disease.

He wanted to tell her all these things, but that was impossible now.

As Doc Turner had warned them, weeks ago, the model Mrs. Killigrew had chosen for her husband, while expensive, was purely ornamental. All it was good for was looking natural.

"But Mama! Everyone will be *looking* at us!"

"So let them look, then," sighed Mrs. Killigrew, who was busy taking in a pair of her husband's old pants. She frowned at her handiwork. Even after all she'd done, Ferris would still need to wear suspenders *and* a belt.

"Mama! You don't understand!" The very idea of walking into the First Methodist Church of Seven Devils, Arkansaw, with the Nutcracker made Hester's stomach knot up.

"You're right I don't understand!" Mrs. Killigrew barked. "I don't understand why you're acting like such an ungrateful little monster! Here the Good Lord brings your daddy back from the war—"

"He's not Daddy! He's *not!*"

"See here, young lady! You're not so grown up I can't take you over my knee! If I hear another outburst like that, I'll cut myself a switch and lash you bloody! You're going to church with us tomorrow even if I have to drag you behind the buckboard like a heifer bound for market!"

"You don't care! You don't care about me at all!" Hester bellowed, knocking her mother's sewing basket off the kitchen table with one sweep of her hand. "All you're interested in is that, that *Nutcracker!* You think you can turn him into Daddy and make everything like it used to be! But you can't! Daddy's dead!"

"*Hester!*" Mrs. Killigrew grabbed her daughter with her left hand, twisting Hester's right arm behind her back. "That's it, young lady! That's all I'm going to take out of you!" she spat, raising her right hand.

"Go ahead! Hit me! Slap me!" Hester taunted through her tears. "Beat on me all you like! It's still the truth!"

Mrs. Killigrew hesitated for a moment then lowered her hand, pulling her daughter to her bosom. Hester struggled for a moment, but her mother's grip was firm. After a few seconds, she began to cry—great, wracking sobs—while Mrs. Killigrew held her daughter tight, rocking her like she used to do, not so many years ago.

The Killigrew family always sat in the third pew on the left-hand side of the aisle. It was a tradition that dated back before Hester's birth. For as long as she could remember, her family always sat there during Sunday services.

As they walked down the aisle, everybody turned and *looked.* Hester's cheeks glowed like hot coals. She could feel Fanny Walchanski's greedy eyes on them, devouring every detail for later recitation. The thought of what she would have to face at school the next day made Hester tighten her grip on Francis' hand. Her little brother began to whine, but she quickly hushed him.

She could hear the members of the congregation mumbling amongst themselves; the ladies agitating the still air with their fans as they craned their necks for a better look.

Reverend Cakebread watched from behind the pulpit as the Killigrews approached the front of the church. He was a round, pink-faced man with heavy eyebrows the size and shape of caterpillars. Right then, the caterpillars looked like they were trying to crawl into his hair.

Aside from being keenly aware that everybody was watching them, the service went as usual; Francis curling up on the bench for a nap next to his sister halfway into Reverend Cakebread's sermon.

Bored by the minister's nasal drone, Hester found herself looking at the Nutcracker and was startled to glimpse the faint outline of her father's profile. Without realizing what she was doing, she brushed her fingers against his sleeve.

The Nutcracker turned his head and looked at her, breaking the illusion. The sadness in his eyes reminded Hester of the time she found a rabbit in the snare.

And then Reverend Cakebread was saying, ". . . and if there are any announcements any of you in the congregation would care to make right now?"

Mrs. Killigrew stood up, nervously straightening the shawl around her shoulders. "I would like to make an announcement, if I could, Reverend."

The minister nodded his agreement, and Mrs. Killigrew turned to face the congregation.

"As you no doubt already heard, my husband—Captain Ferris Killigrew, who I had thought lost to this world—has been returned to his rightful home, thanks to Our Lord. He is now once more fit to reclaim his place in society. I would like to extend an open invitation to all of you here today to stop by our place after church and help my family celebrate God's mercy. There will be food and drink for everyone."

After Mrs. Killigrew sat down, Mr. Eichorn stood up and announced that there would be a Ku Klux meeting that night at the ruins of Old Man Stackpole's plantation house, then they sang the benediction and church was over.

There was a fly walking on the potato salad; Mrs. Killigrew waved a hand at the intruder, only to have it land on one of the deviled eggs.

"Mama, can't we eat yet?"

"You know better than to ask me that, Hester! You know we've got company coming!" She gave her son's hand a quick slap, forcing him to let go of an oatmeal cookie. "Francis! No!"

Francis plopped down on the floor and began to cry, sucking on his chastised fingers.

Ferris Killigrew sat on the parlor love seat, looking like a well-dressed scarecrow, his hands folded in his lap. He could not bring himself to meet his wife's eyes.

Mrs. Killigrew massaged her forehead, trying to stall the sick headache she knew was coming. *All the money I spent on food. Killing one of my best chickens. And no one has the decency to show up. Not one.* She retreated into the kitchen, where Mammy Joella was grinding Ferris' evening allotment of grits and black-strap molasses into a fine mush.

"An' one show up yet?"

"Not yet. No, I take that back. Reverend Cakebread came by just after church."

"Tha's a preacher-man's job; payin' visits on folks no one else wants t' mess wif."

"That's not true! Ferris was born and raised in Seven Devils! He has plenty of friends! You now that!"

The old woman sighed wearily but did not halt grinding the grits into babyfood. "Tha's 'fore the war. Things different now. Folks herebouts usta thinkin' Mr. Ferris daid. They mo' comfortable wif him that way, I reckon."

"What are you babbling about?" hissed Mrs. Killigrew.

"If'n he'd come back whole stead'a crippled-up, things might be different. Mebbe. But he ain't. He reminds folks things ain't ne'er gonna be th' same. Like us black folks. He's embarassin'. He reminds folks of what they done lost."

Mrs. Killigrew stared, dumbstruck, at the gnarled negress. In the fifteen years since she'd become a member of the Killigrew home, this was the only time Mammy Joella had spoken to her about something besides housework and childcare.

The moment his mother left the room, Francis Killigrew walked across the floor and helped himself to the oatmeal cookies. After satisfying his hunger, he waddled over to his father and offered him a cookie.

Killigrew accepted the offering, nodding his thanks and trying his best to smile around the jaw. It wasn't easy. He ruffled his son's curls and allowed his hand to linger, caressing the boy's cheeks and smooth brow with his trembling fingers.

When he looked up, he saw Hester standing in the parlor door, watching him the way you'd look at a bug.

He was found the next morning, hanging from the chandelier hook in the parlor, still dressed in his nightshirt. His face was darkened with congested blood while his lower jaw seemed to glow with rosy health. Although the Sunday-go-to-meeting jaw wasn't any good for eating or talking, it had proved adequate for suicide.

Mrs. Killigrew found him. She stared at her husband's body for a long moment, then went upstairs and woke Hester. She told her daughter to take the mule and ride into town and fetch Mr. Mouzon, Seven Devil's undertaker.

After she made sure Hester had left by the back door, Mrs. Killigrew went to her room and dressed. When she returned to the parlor to await the undertaker's arrival, she discovered Mammy Joella standing in the doorway, staring up at her former master.

"Mammy Joella?"

The old woman grunted to herself and turned, brushing past her employer without looking at her.

"Joella!"

Her only answer was the slamming of the back door.

Hester sat on the love seat and watched the wax trickle down the sides of the thick white candles burning at either end of the Nutcracker's coffin. She was dressed in her best black dress, her hair fixed with a black velvet ribbon. She swung her feet back and forth, watching the tips of her shoes disappear then reappear from under the hem of her skirt.

She could hear her mother talking in hushed tones with Reverend Cakebread and Mr. Mouzon in the kitchen.

Francis was crawling on his hands and knees on the worn Persian carpet, pushing his little wooden train round and round in circles. Hester knew she should tell him to stop grubbing around on the floor in his good suit, but she also knew that would only make him cry, and she really didn't want to deal with that right now.

Hester wished Mamy Joella was still around so she wouldn't be expected to keep an eye on her little brother all the time. But Mammy Joella had disappeared the same day the Nutcracker hanged himself, walking away from her cabin with nothing but the clothes on her back, a gunnysack full of bread and goat's cheese, and a fruit jar full of sassafras tea.

Mama had complained to Sheriff Cooper about it, but he hadn't been of much help.

"What do you expect me to do about it, Nell? Set th' hounds on her? Niggers can leave whene'er they see fit, now."

Still, Hester thought her mother was holding up well, under the circumstances. In many ways, she seemed more tired than grief-stricken. To Hester's knowledge, her mother had yet to shed a tear. Whenever she responded to the condolences offered her, there was a hollowness in her voice. Hester knew that, secretly, her mother was relieved that it was all over; that she no longer had to pretend that the Nutcracker was her husband. Better to bury him and get on with the business of living. She wondered what new schoolyard taunt Fanny Walchanski would dream up to commemorate the event and was surprised to discover she no longer really cared what Fanny Walchanski thought or did.

Hester stared at the Nutcracker, stretched out in his narrow pine box, a lily clamped to his motionless chest. Mr. Mouzon had done a good job, for once. The Nutcracker's face was now the same color as his jaw, giving his appearance a continuity it had lacked in life.

As she stared at the Nutcracker's profile, a weird feeling crept over her, like the one in church two days earlier. For a moment she found herself looking at the face of her father, Ferris Killigrew. Then the vision wavered and was gone. In its place was the dead Nutcracker; only now the rabbit was free of the snare.

Hester felt something on her face and touched her cheek. She stared at the tears for a long time before she realized she was crying.

BREATH

Adam Corbin Fusco

Adam Corbin Fusco works in the film and television industry in Maryland, and has published short fiction in *Cemetery Dance, Young Blood,* and *Expanse.* "Breath" is an unusual and memorable short story that comes from *Touch Wood: Volume Two of Narrow Houses* (the excellent British anthology series edited by Peter Crowther). Like many of its companion stories in *Touch Wood,* Fusco's story does not fall easily into either camp of horror or fantasy but fuses the language of both into a tale that is chilling, yet ultimately redemptive.

—T.W.

Dale Cunningham woke to find the cat standing on his chest, sucking the breath right out of him.

He jerked; he shoved; he flung the cat off him and wiped his mouth to rid himself of the stink of fish and the feel of that furry muzzle.

My God, it's happening again.

Golden flecks blinked at him, then disappeared. Dale sat up, breathing hard. Blue light from the street lamps glowed in the louvered blinds. Daney remained asleep, thank goodness. A fall of frizzled hair hid her face. He saw by the clock that it was five fifteen. He wouldn't be getting any more sleep tonight.

It had happened before, yes. A number of times. He remembered his sister Jessica sitting at the green-lacquered kitchen table when he was seven as she snapped peanut shells and, after scolding him for chewing with his mouth open, told him that when he was a baby they had found Mr. Smits, their silver tabby, in the crib with him, sucking on his mouth. "That's not true," he had said. "Mmm-hmmm. It is," said Jessica. "I saw it. I saw it three times. But it was okay. We swatted him away just in time." She teased him with it whenever she wanted to be mean. He knew she had made it up—until he was eight.

Just in time for what?

Dale peeled the sheet away from his body. His legs were sweaty with shock. He looked toward the doorway to see if the cat had returned. The cat was black with white paws; maybe he'd be able to see the paws as they approached.

He had been living with Daney for half a year, and this was the second time the cat had jumped on him. He never told her about the first time. She'd scold him for being crazy; she'd accuse him of hating the cat. She knew he hated cats. He wouldn't tell her, no, but tonight was one of the worst. Every time it had happened it was the edge of a nightmare that lingered into waking—lingered because the cat was still there. He wanted to wake Daney and tell her; maybe they could make love.

He floundered in the bed, lying on one side to gaze at Daney's sweet form and then on the other to watch the floor and wait for the cat to return. Was it the second time or the third? In six months? Numbers, numbers, too many numbers. The cat must have left the room by now. What the hell time was it anyway? Seven thirty. He got up to shower and shave.

After he had dressed in his uniform he went into the kitchen. Daney was already awake. Though definitely not a morning person she was an early riser. She sat at the kitchen table in the pair of his flannel pajamas she had heisted early in their relationship. In the mornings, with eyes puffy and dry lips slack, he found her irresistible. She poured milk over a bowl of Peanut Butter Captain Crunch. The cat sat in his seat eating peanut butter nuggets Daney had laid out for it.

"Morning," he said.

"Howdy."

He slid the pan on to the stove. He broke a couple of eggs into a bowl, whisked them with a fork. He didn't want to look at the cat; its nonchalant attitude made him shiver. Maybe it didn't remember, but he did. And this habit of having the cat sit at breakfast infuriated him. But no, the morning was the last place to confront Daney about something.

He threw pepper and cheddar cheese into the bowl. "That sugar stuff is bad for it."

"Oh?" Holding the spoon with her fist, she shoveled a heap of Crunch into her mouth. "He likes it. It's his favorite." She fished a piece from her bowl, held it aloft. "Here, Snowshoes. Munchies." The cat snatched it.

She must have seen the look on his face because her eyebrows meshed as if to say, "What the hell's the matter with you?"

The eggs sizzled in the pan. "It's not good for you either."

"Well, thank you for your diagnosis, Dr. Cunningham, Mr. Clogged-Artery of the Week."

"I'm just looking out for you."

"I can look out for myself." Not mean, just a statement of fact.

Dale approached the table with his cooked eggs. Daney scooped the cat into her lap so he could sit.

"He says it's bad for you, but it isn't, is it, precious?" she cooed at the cat, scratching its ears. "You like the milk, that's all." She let the cat dip its muzzle into the bowl. Dale cringed. "I want to paint the apartment, 'kay?" she said brightly.

"Paint the apartment?"

"Yeah. I think we should. How about Robin's Egg Blue?"

"Robin's Egg?"

"Blue. You know what blue is."

"You want to paint the apartment? What's wrong with what we have?"

"What's *wrong*? Don't you see how dingy it is? Oh, c'mon. I feel like it. You *like* blue."

"I like blue."

"Great. I can get the paint for free." She tickled the cat under its chin. "Oh, don't be sour, Dale. You'll like it. It'll be fun."

"Yeah, I know, but—"

"*Gawd*, you're so sour in the morning."

The eggs turned to silvery mush in his mouth. "No, I'm not. Yes, it'll be fun. I'm just tired right now."

"Will you help me paint? Snowshoes will help too."

Dale didn't want to finish his eggs. He wasn't good with decisions in the morning, like this painting thing, and his brain was still addled by the encounter with the cat. She had sprung it on him so suddenly. He didn't notice things like blank walls. Theirs were laundry white; maybe they did need some color. He felt bad for being such a bump on a log. Now he had got Daney mad at him, and if he had wanted to say that he liked blue but not "Robin's Egg" blue, he had missed his chance.

To put a smile on things, he said, "All right, I'll paint. But you have to wear your tool belt."

"I always wear my tool belt."

"Nah. I mean, *only* your tool belt."

She rested her chin in her hand and winked. "Well, we'll just have to see about that."

All done. Fixed. No more argument. Relieved, he rinsed off his plate in the sink and deposited it in the dishwasher. "Time to hit the coal mines."

"Dig me a diamond."

He turned and she was there behind him, holding one of the cat's white paws and waving with it. "Have a nice day," she said with irony; she had always hated that phrase.

He wanted to kiss her goodbye but that meant getting near the cat. Instead, he brushed her hair off her forehead. "I'll have a day at least," he said.

She smiled sweetly. "See ya."

Rain speckled the windshield as he pulled out of the parking lot. He would call it love, if pressed. He had met her on his lunch hour outside the post office where he worked. She was pacing frantically in front of the mailboxes. She had just popped in a scathing letter to a former boyfriend and now that it was irretrievable she wanted to retrieve it. He said that it wouldn't be right to meddle with the mail that way. She pouted. He was lost. He got the keys and nabbed the letter. His invitation for a cup of coffee was met with an askance look and a why-not nod. The coffee warmed a place in him that needed warming; they were living together four weeks later.

He had to flick the wipers on by the time he turned on to Frederick Road. Daney was a painter. Not the artist type but the industrial type. She did houses, both outside and inside, and a school once in a while. She worked at ABC Painting and hoped one day to add her name to continue the alphabet. Her real hope was to be an artist type but she despised the tiny brushes; Daney liked big strokes.

What he couldn't figure was why she was attracted to him. He was sure attracted to her. He had always liked "dangerous" women. Daney was dangerous; she had an edge: fickle, indeterminate, ambiguous. She was fiery and fiercely attractive, especially when swaying that tool belt and peeking through a bundle of straw hair under a painter's cap. Maybe it was the opposites thing: he had an affection for stasis, which marooned him in a postal clerk job, and she didn't.

When he learned that she owned a cat it didn't bother him. He had to weigh the advantages and disadvantages anyway, and Daney was a big advantage. Besides, Snowshoes wasn't one of *those* cats, wasn't one of his family cats. He figured it would be different. He should have known better. But it had been months since Snowshoes had leapt on him. Maybe it wasn't the same thing; maybe it was a mistake.

Rain spat at him as he crossed the parking lot. Big Ed opened the door into the sorting room.

"Bingo!"

R & B burbled from the radio on top of the bins. Dale ease on to a stool and shuffled his feet in the dust coating the checkerboard floor. Big Ed always made the back room a bastion of rhythm and laughter, but that didn't take away the government green walls or the dingy yellow lights.

Big Ed balanced a stack of mail on his pot belly, launch pad into the bins. "You okay, Dale-man? Somethin' got you down?"

"Nah," Dale said. "Just one of those days."

"Bingo!"

Dale sorted mail. Maybe Ed was somebody he could confide in, tell about the cats. Maybe he would have some advice, or know just how to solve it, have a cousin with the same problem. Or maybe he would listen, sucking on his beard, and call out "Bingo!"—the solution to everything. Dale had never told anyone.

When he was eight and they had moved to the Baltimore backwater, Mr. Smits was thirteen years old and mangy. It couldn't keep its fur ruffled; it was, instead, matted and damp. It prowled the rowhouse with wide chocolate eyes as if the new territory were a personal indignity visited upon it. Jessica had graduated from pigtails to ponytails which she fastened from a drawerful of dayglo barrettes that she accused her little brother of stealing to make catapults every time one was missing. It was a cottony August night when Dale opened the window and lay atop his sheets—the air conditioning never seemed to pump into his room—and fell into a fitful sleep only to realize the cat was on top of him. Snuzzling. Sucking. He pushed it to the floor, catching his breath. The cat stared at him a moment, accusing Dale of being mean. Dale shuddered. What his sister told him about what happened in his crib was true. A tendril of nightmare gloomed the walls. The sensation of cat paws on his chest, the wet muzzle, the sucking sound were familiar, like a dream you know you've had before while dreaming it, then upon waking aren't quite sure. When Mr. Smits was pounded by a Good Humor truck in late autumn Dale celebrated.

"Gotta take a leak," said Big Ed. "Hold down the fort, McHenry."

"Okay."

When he was thirteen his sister was well into teasing other boys in other ways. They had a new cat, a red Persian longhair, that Jessica had cajoled their parents into purchasing. She named it "Mr. Bits" but occasionally called it "Mr. Shits" in deference to the dead one. It was a summer marked by the giant rock piles at Patapsco State Park. A guy could make the best forts there. He and his friends would gather discarded wood and metal slats and make a fort, one on each pile, and have mud fights As the leaves turned they would find the detritus left by the nighttime visits of the older kids: cigarette butts, smashed cans of Bud, paper bags with gobs of glue, all charred by some bonfire. And bits of dirty magazines. They came in pockets of five or ten pages, torn, moist from the earth, burned on their edges, and a few would have some amber-colored nudey lady torn just below her stomach, the mystery beneath forever hidden by a line of black ash. Dale would feel his face flush when he found one of those pictures. His loins would tingle with the thrill of unearthing a secret, knowing that he wanted something but not knowing what. He hid the pictures in the rocks. He wouldn't take them to his room for fear of them being discovered by his parents, or worse, by his sister; but he would think about them at night, and on a few of those nights he would be caught in a fever of sweat half-asleep, dreaming of red soft flesh, and reaching up would encounter the brittle fur of Mr. Bits as it stood on his chest. Disgusted, he would shove the animal away. It was a maelstrom of feelings that summer, of tantalizing ladies hiding their most tantalizing parts, and that blasted cat secretly flicking its tongue between his lips.

Dale shuddered. The mail piled into the bins, was carted away, piled some more. Big Ed twisted the dial to classical in the downslope of the day. Four o'clock. Dale headed home.

When he opened the door he saw a pyramid of paint cans atop a splattered canvas. The sides of the cans were streaked with blue. Leftovers.

Jeez, she really means it.

He thought of the work involved in painting the apartment and groaned. Why did she always have to have these little projects, and why did they always have to involve him? The cans squatted in front of him like a dare, expecting him to pop their tops and dip in a brush and start that disruptive chore that people try to make fun but always turns into aggravation. Moving furniture, covering things up, getting paint in your hair, cleaning the brushes, the smell—he didn't want those things to be happening now; he just didn't want his spare time eaten up.

The cat was nowhere to be found, thankfully. Fuming with frustration, exhausted from the boredom of work, he turned toward the bedroom. The door opened and Daney stepped out.

"Howdy," she said, smiling. She was wearing the tool belt. Nothing else. He smiled back.

The frustration and exhaustion drained from his spine. They had a marvelous time.

The paint cans lay dormant for two days. On the third day one wall had been turned into a canvas. A huge face in Robin's Egg Blue had been painted there, a woman's face with Picasso nose, with doves and porpoises dancing around her.

A painter's cap slouched on Daney's head. She stood with hip cocked and paint roller dripping. "Do you like it?"

She was being her artist self, and now expected him to accept a painting of hers to cover one of their walls. "Well, how long do you want to have it up there?"

"Oh, forever." She mashed the roller into the paint can, then looked at him. "I'm just *kidding*. Gawd. I just wanted to see what I could do. It's not permanent." She proceeded to cover her painting with the roller.

Irritable, Dale noticed that his stereo was only half covered by a tarp. He bent to see if any paint had splattered on it. "Daney, my stereo—"

"I'm not painting over there yet."

"But you still have to protect it from—"

"Jezuz, Dale, I'm not gonna wreck it. All you can think about is yourself."

Selfish? Him? With the place all disoriented, covered in plastic and canvas, the furniture piled in the middle of the room, just so she can entertain herself with painting? He *hated* that damned color.

She puffed a lank of hair from her forehead. A patch of Robin's Egg had smudged her nose. "I thought you were gonna help me," she said softly. "You tired from work and all?" As if she didn't expect him to be.

He was being selfish. He wanted her to be an artist, to let herself go free. Was he holding her back? If he were a drag on her she'd just leave and fly away, wouldn't she. He wished he could give her the self-esteem to get some canvas and do *real* paintings. Maybe this was the first step for her, doing the apartment walls. Guilt fluttered his stomach.

"I'm sorry," he said. "Just tired. Got another cap somewheres?"

She whipped one out from her back pocket and tossed it. "Betcha I do."

Snowshoes ignored the proceedings. The cat pranced daintily over the canvas, careful not to step in any wet spots, sidling up to Daney's legs to rub them. Dale eyed the creature with contempt, hoping it would think the pan of paint was filled with water and drink its filthy muzzle full of poison.

Teeny darts pricking his nipple. *Suck, suck, slurp.* Silent elfin weight on his chest. Wet nose on his tongue, dipping . . .

He shot upright. The cat rolled on to the floor. It swished its tail, gleamed golden eyes into his, waiting.

Dale stretched his lungs with air. His head felt stuffed with cotton. His temples throbbed.

Goddamned cat.

Paint fumes stuck needles up his nose. He couldn't get comfortable, lay on his side instead. His legs were wet with sweat, quivering. He must still be half asleep to feel so muzzy. He was glad Daney was still asleep; he didn't want her to think he was freaking out.

He leaned his head over the side of the bed to feel the cooler air. The blue pearl-light from the window cast no illumination on the objects of the room, simply made their indistinct outlines throb. A balled outline near the door moved. Or had he imagined it? He could work up quite an imagination, he knew. If he concentrated hard enough he could imagine that ball pacing back and forth. Phosphenes in his eyes made it dance with amber pinpoints.

He mustn't play this kind of game with himself. He'd scare himself to death. The cat had left, certainly. Imagining things moving in the room wasn't like counting sheep; if he kept trying to see something moving he'd never get to sleep.

The outline's white paw took a step nearer.

My God, the thing's stalking me.

He eased back into the pillows and held himself still. Soft *plomp* as a weight landed on the bed. The bedspread crimped along his calves, his thigh. It was getting nearer.

Dale sat up and the form disappeared. Was he never to get to sleep? Was it not going to let him lie down? The thing was relentless tonight.

Anger and fear roiled in his belly. What did it want? Where was it now? He searched the shadows but saw nothing. As an experiment he lay flat on his back. *I'm not going to move,* he thought. *Let's wait and see.*

He didn't know how many minutes it took. Did it see that his eyes were open? What was it *doing*? If he had to stay up all night—

Sleet, sleet, slip, the brush of claws on the bedspread. The fabric indented between him and Daney. He held his arms at his sides. He didn't move. It paused at his hand. There was a shift in weight. *It must have one paw raised,* he thought. *It's deciding. I don't dare close my eyes. I don't dare.*

Light white footfall, closer. Dale flung the bedspread and heard a plop as the cat landed on the floor. *Goddamn.* This was downright frustrating. It was going to keep coming after him.

Raging, he flopped back on to the bed. *I'm going to go to sleep, goddammit,* he thought. *To hell with that cat.* He scrunched over on his side and closed his eyes.

Paw pads making tracks along his legs.

Dale arched his back, kicked, flung his arm through the air. It connected with something soft. The cat screeched and plummeted to the floor.

"Wha?" Daney raised her head from the pillow.

"Oh, jeez, go back to sleep." Dale shivered.

"What happened? Was that Snowy?"

Irritable, Dale said, "That cat keeps jumping on me."

"Jumping on you."

"It jumped on me while I was asleep." He couldn't tell her all of it.

"So?"

"Daney, it won't get off the bed."

She hunched herself on to an elbow and switched on the light. "He likes you." Snowshoes stood by the doorway, back ruffled.

"What did you do to him?" asked Daney.

"What did I—?"

"Oh, come here, precious." Daney scrabbled her finger on the covers. Snowshoes leapt to gnaw playfully at it. Dale gulped back a shudder.

"It's what it did to me."

"Oh, come on." Daney gathered the cat in her arms rocked it. "Poor baby," she said to it. "What did the mean man do to you?" She rubbed her cheek against the cat's head. "Did he hurt my precious boy?" She smiled at Dale. "He just wants to snuggle. You're a big Daddy Cat to him."

"I'm not his Daddy Cat."

"Oooh, yes you are." Daney lifted the cat's paws and walked them towards Dale. "Aren't you a Daddy Cat?" she said in a little girl voice. She stroked the cat affectionately.

Dale lay down. Daney turned out the light and turned her back to him, curling up with the cat. He looked at the clock. Five thirty. Might as well stay up all night.

The next evening they finished the walls of the living room and started the trim. Dale wore the painter's hat like a dunce cap. Snowshoes padded over the room and Dale did his best to avoid it, and did his best to hide his fear of the cat from Daney.

Drained from too little sleep and the toil of meticulous painting, he prepared for bed gratefully. As he was slipping under the sheets Daney entered the bedroom dragging behind her the paisley pillow that was Snowshoes' bedding.

"What's that?"

"What do you think? I can't have Snowy sleeping in the fumes. He'll sleep with us tonight. Cozy, huh?"

"Cozy."

Snowshoes stretched, pounced on the pillow. Daney closed the door. He couldn't believe it. He was hoping to close the door against the fumes *and* the cat tonight, something he'd missed the night before, but now he was trapped. His eyes were wide open. Daney looked at him for an extra second. He wasn't going to say a word, not against the cat. He had been getting on her nerves for days and if he started complaining about something as simple as letting the cat sleep in the bedroom she would rail at him for sure. Then she might leave him. She would just pack up and leave and then where would he be? That would be the worst. He wouldn't be able to stand the loss. *It's only for one night,* he told himself. *Do it for her. Just don't fall asleep.*

He smiled and nodded. He watched as she slunk into her pajamas. She winked at him, scrunched under the covers, planted a goodnight kiss on his cheek, then buried her face in the pillow after turning out the light.

He lay still. And waited. Maybe it wasn't going to do it tonight. Maybe it was all random, just a fluke. He settled his shoulders into the mattress, tried to relax. The paint fumes made his breath catch in his lungs; he could only manage shallow breaths. He fidgeted, fixated by the light vibrating in the blinds.

Soft pad near his feet. *Jesus, here it comes.*

He waited. He felt something press his thigh. A whiteness pressed his stomach.

He pushed the cat off the bed, exasperated. He wasn't going to sleep tonight. He wasn't going to sleep *ever.*

So let it come, he thought. *Come on, you. I'm going to give you what you want. If I just lie still and close my eyes it will come to me, and if I let it get to my mouth and let it do* whatever the hell it wants, *if I wait long enough I'll find out what it's about after all these years.*

Buoyed by the strength of desperation he lay down and closed his eyes. *It'll come if I lie still. It'll come if I close my eyes.* He wished he could look at the clock; its numbers would be a beacon of sanity as he waited. But he kept his eyes closed.

Footfall. Paw pad. Near his shin. *Come on and get me.* At his knee, a hesitation. *It's looking me over, looking into my eyes with those slits, those unblinking wide slits, to see if my eyes are closed, to see if I might be asleep. It comes when I'm asleep.*

Sleety-slit, slip, along his thigh. Pause. Pounce to his chest. A paw flexed on his sternum, gaining purchase.

Dale's feet sweated. An awful tingling began in his loins. The horrid anticipation. If the tingling didn't stop he was going to shudder uncontrollably.

A susurrant slip of paws echoed along his ribs and jangled nerve endings at the base of his stomach. *Hurry up. Just get it over with. My heart's pounding; I can hear it in my ears. It's going to know. It's going to know I'm awake 'cause it can feel my heartbeat through its claws.*

He wanted to look. He wanted to open his eyes. Where was it? His breath came in and out. With a sixth sense he could feel the cat's face angling toward his own. His shoulders wanted to tense. His legs wanted to kick. His back wanted to arch and fling the thing off his chest.

Snuffling. The cat muzzled into his mouth. He could hear its rapid breathing. The cold, wet nose touched his teeth. Whiskers burred his lips. The tongue—

Oh God, no, stop it. Just stop it!

It sucked on him. A fishy bite to the air mingled with acrid fumes of paint. The cat nuzzled into his mouth, its movements quickening, becoming desperate. It wanted to get deeper. It drew in its breath to take the breath out of him. The claws tensed.

I can't stand it, what the hell do you want—

He could feel the heat of its fur. The snout snuzzled deeper. The cat clung to him like a child, cloying, needful.

In quick breaths it sucked. And its breaths became fuller. The fuller they became the less air he had to breathe. He was suffocating. The cat drew the air out of his lungs until they throbbed.

He lay paralyzed. Such a sense of loss. He was empty. His lungs were flat. The breath of life had left him, stolen. The ache that began in his lungs leapt to his heart.

Don't take it away. Don't take it away from me.

His spine arched. Dizzy, he spun back to the other times he had been assaulted in this way, back to his sister telling him about the cat in his crib. *We swatted him away just in time.*

Just in time?

It came back to him then: *We swatted him away just in time, before you started to cry.*

His stomach muscles bunched. His back whipcracked him upright. The cat fell away. And drawing a deep breath he felt such an aching loneliness that a sob escaped his lips, then choking. Tears formed in his eyes. His lungs hurt. They hurt bad. He cried from the hurt. He couldn't remember crying before.

Great choking sobs struck his chest. Loss. And anger.

Daney stirred awake. "What is it?"

Dale drove his fist into his thigh. "I don't like that goddamned color."

"What the—"

"I hate it. Can't you see? Haven't you noticed?"

"Noticed?"

"I don't *want* to paint the apartment. It's a *stupid* color. It's *ugly*. Why don't you *know* that?"

"Know what?"

"I *hate* it. And all of your *teasing*. You're so condescending to me."

Her voice whispered. "No, I'm not."

"To *me* you are. God*damn*."

"Dale, Dale, what's the matter?"

"If you don't like me what the hell are you doing here?"

"Why would—but I do—"

He held his knees to his chest, rocking. "And why, why do you love that goddamned *fucking* cat more than me?"

She was fully awake now, brushing her hair out of her eyes. "I don't love the fucking cat more than you." She put her hand on his back, rubbed it gently. "What brought all this on? You *idiot*, I love you."

His gasps eased. He looked her in the eye. Oh, irresistible, as always.

"Why didn't you tell me you didn't like the color?" she said. "Or painting?"

"It isn't just that."

"Obviously not."

"I'm just really upset."

"I can see that. You have to tell me these things."

"I know."

"Why didn't you?"

His breathing slowed. His nose was running. "I was afraid you'd—you'd get mad. Leave me. I don't know. Find some guy painter who did like it."

"I don't want some guy painter. Jesus, Dale, I *like* you, okay? I'm stuck on you. Get it?"

"I get it." He was shocked at all that had poured out of him. His eyes hurt from the pressure that was behind them. He wiped the tears from his face and took a deep breath, filling his lungs. He put his arms around her, kissed her.

The cat swished its tail and curled into its bed. It seemed content to leave him alone.

KNIVES

Jane Yolen

This poem, from the anthology *Snow White, Blood Red*, is a dark, adult interpretation of the fairy tale, "Cinderella."

—E.D.

Love can be as sharp
as the point of a knife,
as piercing as a sliver of glass.
My sisters did not know this.
They thought love was an old slipper:
pull it on and it fits.
They did not know this secret of the world:
the wrong word can kill.
It cost them their lives.

Princes understand the world,
they know the nuance of the tongue,
they are bred up in it.
A shoe is not a shoe:
it implies miles, it suggests length,
it measures and makes solid.
It wears and is worn.
Where there is one shoe, there must be a match.
Otherwise the kingdom limps along.

Glass is not glass
in the language of love:
it implies sight, it suggests depth,
it mirrors and makes real,
it is sought and is seen.
What is made of glass reflects the gazer.
A queen must be made of glass.

I spoke to the prince in that secret tongue,
the diplomacy of courting,

he using shoes, I using glass,
and all my sisters saw was a slipper,
too long at the heel,
too short at the toe.
What else could they use but a knife?
What else could he see but the declaration of war?

Princes understand the world,
they know the nuance of the tongue,
they are bred up in it.
In war as in life they take no prisoners
And they always marry the other shoe.

MRS. JONES

Carol Emshwiller

Carol Emshwiller's stories have been published in literary, feminist, and science fiction magazines. Her stories are collected in *Joy in Our Cause*, *Verging on the Pertinent*, and *The Start of the End of It All*. Her first novel, *Carmen Dog*, was published in 1990. She is finishing her second novel.

"Mrs. Jones" can be considered a domestic drama, a tale of two sisters, and a monster story. It was originally published in *OMNI* Magazine.

—E.D.

Cora is a morning person. Her sister, Janice, hardly feels conscious till late afternoon. Janice nibbles fruit and berries and complains of her stomach. Cora eats potatoes with butter and sour cream. She likes being fat. It makes her feel powerful and hides her wrinkles. Janice thinks being thin and willowy makes her look young, though she would admit that—and even though Cora spends more time outside doing the yard and farm work—Cora's skin does look smoother. Janice has a slight stutter. Normally she speaks rapidly and in a kind of shorthand so as not to take up anyone's precious time, but with her stutter, she can hold people's attention for a moment longer than she would otherwise dare. Cora, on the other hand, speaks slowly and if she had ever stuttered would have seen to it that she learned not to.

Cora bought a genuine kilim rug to offset, she said, the bad taste of the flowery chintz covers Janice got for the couch and chairs. The rug and chairs look terrible in the same room, but Cora insists that her rug be there. Janice retaliated by pawning Mother's silver candelabras. Cora had never liked them, but she made a fuss anyway, and she left Janice's favorite silver spoon in the mayonnaise jar until, polish as she would, Janice could never get rid of the blackish look. Janice punched a hole in each of Father's rubber boots. Cora wears them anyway. She hasn't said a single word about it, but she hangs her wet socks up conspicuously in the kitchen.

They wish they'd gotten married and moved away from their parent's old farm house. They wish . . . desperately that they'd had children, though they know nothing of children—or husbands for that matter. As girls they worked hard at domestic things: canning, baking bread and pies, sewing . . . waiting to be good wives to almost anybody, but nobody came to claim them.

Janice is the one who worries. She's worried right now because she saw a light out in the far corner of the orchard—a tiny, flickering light. She can just barely make it out through the misty rain. Cora says, "Nonsense." (She's angry because it's just the sort of thing Janice would notice first.) Cora laughs as Janice goes around checking and rechecking all the windows and doors to see that they're securely locked. When Janice has finished, and stands staring out at the rain, she has a change of heart. "Whoever's out there must be cold and wet. Maybe hungry."

"Nonsense," Cora says again. "Besides, whoever's out there probably deserves it."

Later, as Cora watches the light from her bedroom window, she thinks whoever it is who's camping out down there is probably eating her apples and making a mess. Cora likes to sleep with the windows open a crack even in weather like this, and she prides herself on her courage, but, quietly, so that Janice, in the next room, won't hear, she eases her windows shut and locks them.

In the morning the rain has stopped though it's foggy. Cora goes out (with Father's walking stick, and wearing Father's boots and battered canvas hat) to the far end of the orchard. Something has certainly been there. It had pulled down perfectly good, live, apple branches to make the nests. Cora doesn't like the way it ate apples, either, one or two bites out of lots of them, and then it looks as if it had made itself sick and threw up not far from the fire. Cora cleans everything so it looks like no one has been there. She doesn't want Janice to have the satisfaction of knowing anything about it.

That afternoon, when Cora has gone off to have their pickup truck greased, Janice goes out to take a look. She, also, takes Father's walking stick, but she wears Mother's floppy, pink hat. She can see where the fire's been by the black smudge, and she can tell somebody's been up in the tree. She notices things Cora hadn't: little claw marks on a branch, a couple of apples that had been bitten into still hanging on the tree near the nesting place. There's a tiny piece of leathery stuff stuck to one sharp twig. It's incredibly soft and downy and has a wet-dog smell. Janice takes it, thinking it might be an important clue. Also she wants to have something to show that she's been down there and seen more than Cora has.

Cora comes back while Janice is upstairs taking her nap. She sits down in the front room and reads an article in the *Reader's Digest* about how to help your husband communicate. When she hears Janice come down the stairs, Cora goes up for her nap. While Cora naps, Janice sets out grapes and a tangerine, and scrambles one egg. As she eats her early supper, she reads the same article Cora has just read. She feels sorry for Cora who seems to have nothing more exciting than this sort of thing to read (along with her one hundred great books) whereas Janice has been reading: *How Famous Couples Get the Most Out of Their Sex Lives*, just one of many such books that she keeps locked in her bedside cabinet. When she finishes eating, she cleans up the kitchen so it looks as if she hadn't been there.

Cora comes down when Janice is in the front parlor (sliding doors shut) listening to music. She has it turned so low Cora can hardly make it out. Might be Vivaldi. It's as if Janice doesn't want Cora to hear it in case she might enjoy it. At least that's how Cora takes it. Cora opens a can of spaghetti. For desert she takes a couple of apples from the "special" tree. She eats on the closed-in porch, watching the clouds. It looks as if it'll rain again tonight.

About eight-thirty they each look out their different windows and see that the flickering light is there again. Cora says, "Damn it to hell," so loud that Janice hears from two rooms away. At that moment Janice begins to like the little light. Thinks it looks inviting. Homey. She forgets that she found that funny piece of leather and those claw marks. Thinks most likely there's a young couple in love out there. Their parents disapprove and they have no place else to go but her orchard. Or perhaps it's a young person. Teenager, maybe, cold and wet. She has a hard time sleeping, worrying and wondering about whoever it is, though she's still glad she locked the house up tight.

The next day begins almost exactly like the one before, with Cora going out to the orchard first and cleaning up—or trying to—all the signs of anything having been there, and with Janice coming out later to pick up the clues that are left. Janice finds that the same branch is scratched up even more than it was before, and this time Cora had left the vomit (full of bits of apple peel) behind the tree. Perhaps she hadn't noticed it. Apples—or at least so many apples aren't agreeing with the lovers. (In spite of the clues, Janice prefers to think that it's lovers.) She feels sorry about the all-night rain. There's no sign that they had a tent or shelter of any kind, poor things.

By the third night, though, the weather finally clears. Stars are out and a tiny moon. Cora and Janice stand in the front room, each at a different window looking out towards where the light had been. An old seventy-eight record is on, Fritz Kreisler playing a Bach Chaconne. Janice says, "You'd think, especially since it's not raining. . . ."

Cora says, "Good riddance," though she, too, feels a sense of regret. At least something unusual had been happening. "Don't forget," Cora says, "the state prison's only ninety miles away."

Little light or no little light, they both check the windows and doors and then recheck the ones the other had already checked, or at least Cora rechecks all the ones Janice had seen to. Janice sees her do it and Cora sees her noticing, so Cora says, "With what they're doing in genetic engineering, it could be anything at all out there. They make mistakes and peculiar things escape. You don't hear about it because it's classified. People disapprove so they don't let the news get out." Ever since she was six years old, Cora has been trying to scare her younger sister, though, as usual, she ends up scaring herself.

But then, just as they are about to give up and go off to bed, there's the light again. "Ah." Janice breathes out as though she had been holding her breath. "There it is, finally."

"You've got a lot to learn," Cora says. She'd heard the relief in Janice's big sigh. "Anyway, I'm off to bed, and you'd better come soon, too, if you know what's good for you."

"I know what's good for me," Janice says. She would have stayed up too late just for spite, but now she has another, secret reason for doing it. She sits reading an article in Cosmopolitan about how to be more sexually attractive to your husband. Around midnight, even downstairs, she can hear Cora snoring. Janice goes out to the kitchen. Moves around it like a little mouse. She's good at that. Gets out Mother's teakwood tray, takes big slices of rye bread form Cora's stash, takes a can of Cora's tunafish. (Janice knows she'll notice. Cora has them all counted up.) Takes butter and mayonnaise from Cora's side of the refrigerator. Makes three tunafish sandwiches. Places them on three of Mother's gold-rimmed plates along with some of her own celery, radishes and grapes Then she sits down and eats one plateful herself. She hasn't let herself have a tunafish sandwich, especially not one with mayonnaise and butter and rye bread, in quite some time.

It's only when Janice is halfway out in the orchard that she remembers what Cora said about the prison and thinks maybe there's some sort of escaped criminal out there—a rapist or a murderer, and here she is, wearing only her bathrobe and nightgown, in her slippers, and without even Father's walking stick. (Though the walking stick would probably just have been a handy thing for the criminal to attack *her* with.) She stops, puts the tray down, then moves forward. She's had a lot of practice creeping—creeping up on Cora ever since they were little. Used to yell, "Boo," but now shouts out anything to make her jump. Or not even shouting. Creeping up and standing very close and suddenly whispering right by her ear can make Cora jump as much as a loud noise. Janice sneaks along slowly. Has to step over where whoever it is has already thrown up. Something is huddling in front of the fire wrapped in what at first seems to be an army blanket. Why it *is* a child. Poor thing. She'd known it all the time. But then the creature moves, stretches, makes a squeaky sound, and she sees it's either the largest bat, or the smallest little old man she's ever seen. She's wondering if this is what Cora meant by genetic engineering.

Then the creature stands up and Janice is shocked. He has such a large penis that Janice thinks back to the horses and bulls they used to have. It's a Pan-type penis, more or less permanently erect and hooked up tight against his stomach, though Janice doesn't know this about a Pan's penis, and, anyway, this is definitely not some sort of Pan.

The article in *Cosmopolitan* comes instantly to her mind, plus the other, sexier books that she has locked in her bedside cabinet. Isn't there, in all this, some way to permanently outdo Cora? Whether she ever finds out about it or not? Slowly Janice backs up, turns, goes right past her tray (the gleam of silverware helps her know where it is), goes to the house and down into the basement.

They'd always had dogs. Big ones. For safety. But Mr. Jones (called Jonesy) had only died a few months ago and Cora is still grieving, or so she keeps saying. Since the dog had become blind, diabetic, and incontinent in his last years, Janice is relieved that he's gone. Besides, she has her heart set on something small and more tractable, some sort of terrier, but now she's glad Jonesy was large and difficult to manage. His metal choke collar and chain leash are still in the cellar. She wraps them in a cloth bag to keep them from making any clanking noises and heads back out, picking up the tray of food on the way.

As she comes close to the fire, she begins to hum. This time she wants him to know she's coming. The creature sits in the tree now and watches her with red glinting eyes. She puts the tray down and begins to talk softly as though she were trying to calm old Jonesy. She even calls the thing Mr. Jones. At first by mistake and then on purpose. He watches. Moves nothing but his eyes and big ears. His wings, folded up along his arms and dangling, are army-olive drab like that piece she found, but his body is a little lighter. She can tell that even in this moonlight.

Now that she's closer and less startled than before, she can see that there's something terribly wrong. One leathery wing is torn and twisted. He's helpless. Or almost. Probably in pain. Janice feels a rush of joy.

She breaks off a bit of tunafish sandwich and slowly, talking softly all the time, she holds it towards his little, clawed hand. Equally slowly, he reaches out to take it. She keeps this up until almost all of one plateful is eaten. But suddenly the creature jumps out of the tree, turns around and throws up.

Janice knows a vulnerable moment when she sees one. As he leans back on his heels between spasms, she fastens the choke collar around his neck, and twists the other end of the chain leash around her wrist.

He only makes two attempts to escape: tries to flap himself into the air, but it's obviously painful for him; then he tries to run. His legs are bowed, his gait rocking and clumsy. After these two attempts at getting away, he seems to realize it's hopeless. Janice can see in his eyes that he's given up—too sick and tired to care. Probably happy to be captured and looked after at last.

She leads him back to the house and down into the basement. Her own quiet creeping makes him quiet, too. He seems to sense that he's to be a secret and that perhaps his life depends on it. It was hard for him to walk all the way across the orchard. He doesn't seem to be built for anything but flying.

There is an old coal room, not used since they got oil heat. Janice makes a nest for him there, first chaining him to one of the pipes. She gets him blankets, water, an empty pail with lid. She makes him put on a pair of her underpants. She has to use a cord around his waist to make them stay up. She wonders what she should leave him to eat that would stay down? Then brings him chamomile tea, dry toast, one very small potato. That's all. She doesn't want to be cleaning up a lot of vomit.

He's so tractable through all this that she loses all fear of him. Pats his head as if he were old Jonesy. Strokes the wonderful softness of his wings. Thinks: If those were cut off, he'd look like a small old man with long, hard fingernails. Misshapen, but not much more so than other people. And clothes can hide things. Without the dark wings, he'd look lighter. His body is that color that's always described as café au lait. She would have preferred it if he'd been clearly a white person, but, who knows, maybe a little while in the cellar will make him paler.

After a last rubbing of his head behind his too-large ears, Janice padlocks the coal room and goes up to her bedroom, but she's too excited to sleep. She reads a chapter in *Are You Happy with Your Sex Life?*, the one on "How to Turn Your Man into a Lusting Animal." ("The feet of both sexes are exquisitely sensitive," and, "Let your eyes speak, but first make sure he's looking at you." "Surrender. When he thinks he's leading, your man feels strong in *every* way.") Janice thinks she will have to be the one to take the initiative, though she'll try to make him feel that he's the boss—even though he'll be wearing the choke collar.

For a change, Janice wakes up just as early as Cora does. Earlier, in fact, and she lies in bed making plans until it is late enough to get up. She gets a lot of good ideas. She comes downstairs whistling Vivaldi—off key, as usual, but she's not doing it to make Cora angry this time. She really can't whistle on key. Cora knows that Janice knows Cora hates the way she whistles. Cora thinks that if Janice really tried, she could be just as in tune as Cora always is. Cora thinks Janice got up early just so she could spoil Cora's breakfast by sitting across from her and looking just like Mother used to look when she disapproved of Father's table manners. And Cora notices, even before she makes her omelet, that one can of tunafish is missing, and that her loaf of rye bread has gone down by several slices. She takes a quart of strawberries from Janice's side of the refrigerator and eats them all, not even bothering to wash them.

Janice doesn't say a word, or even do anything. She doesn't care, except that Jonesy might have wanted some. Janice is feeling magnanimous and powerful. She feels so good she even offers Cora some of her herb tea. Cora takes the offer as ironic, especially since she knows that Janice knows she never drinks herb tea. She retaliates by saying that, since they're both up so early, they should take advantage of it and go out to the beach to get more lakeweed for the garden.

Janice knows that Cora decided this just to make her pay for the tunafish and mayonnaise and such, but she still feels magnanimous—kindly to the whole world. She doesn't even say that they'd already done that twice in the spring, and that what they needed now were hay bales to put around the foundations of the house for the winter. All she says is, "No."

It's never been their way to shirk their duties no matter how angry they might be with each other. When it comes to work, they've always made a good team. But now Janice is adamant. She says she has something important to do. She's not ever said this before nor has she ever had something important to do. Cora has always been the one who did important things. This time Cora can't persuade Janice to change her mind, nor can she persuade her that there's nothing important to be done—or nothing more important than lakeweed.

Finally Cora gives up and goes off alone. She hadn't meant to go. She's never gone off to get lakeweed by herself, but she goes anyway, hoping to make Janice feel guilty. Except Cora knows something is going on. She's not sure what, but she's going to be on her guard.

As soon as Janice hears the old pick-up crunch away on the gravel drive, she goes down in the basement, bringing along Father's old straight razor (freshly sharpened), rubbing alcohol and bandages. Also, to make it easier on him, a bottle of sherry.

Cora comes back, tired and sandy, around six-thirty. Her face is red and she has big, dried, sweat marks on her blue farmer's shirt, across the back and under the arms. She smells fishy. She's so tired she staggers as she climbs the porch steps. Even before she gets inside, she knows odd things are still going on. There's the smells . . . of beef stew or some such, onions, maybe mince pie, and there, on the hall table, a glass of sherry is set out for her. Or seems to be for her. Or looks like sherry. Though the day was hot, these fall evenings are cool, and Janice has laid a fire in the fireplace, and not badly done. Cora always knew Janice could do it properly if she really tried. Cora takes the sherry and sits on the footstool of Father's big chair. It's one of the ones Janice had covered in a flowery pattern— looks like pinkish-blue hydrangea. Cora turns away from it and looks at the fire. Thinks: All this has got to be because of something else. Or maybe it's going to be a practical joke. If she lets down her guard she'll be in for big trouble. But even if it's a joke, might as well take advantage of it for as long as she can. The sherry relaxes her. She'll go up and shower—if, that is, Janice has left her any hot water.

For several days, Mr. Jones is in pain. Janice is glad of it. She knows how a wild thing—or even a not so wild thing—appreciates being nursed back to health. She hopes Mr. Jones was too drunk to remember about the . . . removal . . . amputation . . . whatever you'd call it. (Funny, he only has four fingers on each hand. She'd not noticed that at first.)

As soon as he's better, she hopes to bond him to her in a different way.

Cora is still suspicious, but doesn't know what to be suspicious about. The good food is going on and on. After supper Janice cleans up and doesn't ask Cora for help even though Janice has done all the cooking. And Janice disappears for hours at a time. Goes up to take her nap—or so she says, but Cora knows for a fact that she's not in her bedroom. After the dishes are cleaned up in the evenings, Janice sews or knits. It's not hard to see that she's knitting a child-sized sweater, sewing a child-sized pair of trousers. At the same time, she's working on a white dress, lacy and low necked. Cora thinks much too low necked for someone Janice's age. But perhaps it's not for Janice. Maybe Janice has some news she's keeping from Cora. That would be just like her. Someone is getting married or coming for a visit. Or maybe both: someone getting married and a child is coming to visit.

Mr. Jones is getting better, eating soup, nuts and seeds and keeping everything down, finally. Janice is happy to see that his skin has faded some. He might pass for a gnarled, little Mexican, or maybe a fairly light India Indian. And he's beginning to understand some words. She's been talking to him a lot, more or less as she used to talk to old Jonesy. He knows: good boy and bad boy, and sit, lie down, be quiet. . . . She thinks he even has the concept of, "I love you." She'd never said that to any other creature ever before, not even to the pony they'd had when they were little. She's been doing a lot of patting, back rubbing, scratching under the chin and behind the ears. Though he's always wearing a pair of her underpants tied up around his waist, every now and then she notices his penis swelling up even larger than it already is, though she hasn't even tried the stroking of the exquisitely sensitive feet yet.

One night, after reading over again the chapter, "How to Turn Your Man into a Lusting Animal," she puts on her flowery summer nightgown (even though the nights are colder than ever and they haven't started up the furnace yet). She puts on lipstick, eyeshadow, perfume, combs her hair out and lets it hang over her shoulders. . . . (She's only graying a little bit at the temples. Thank God not like Cora; she's almost completely gray.) She goes down into the cellar with a glass of sherry for each of them. Not too much, though. She's read about alcohol and sex. She tells him she loves him several times, kisses him on the cheeks and then on the neck, just below the choke collar. Finally she kisses his lips. They are thin and closed tight. She can feel the teeth behind them. Then she rolls her nightgown up to her chin. She hopes he likes what he sees even though she's not young anymore. (If anything, he looks surprised.) But no sooner has she lain herself down beside him, than it's over. She's even wondering, Did it really happen? Except, yes, there's blood and it did hurt. But this isn't at all like the books said it would be or should be. She's read about premature ejaculation. This must be it. Maybe later, when he knows more words, they can go for sex therapy. But— oops—there he goes again, and just as fast as before. After that he falls asleep. She not only didn't get any real foreplay, but no afterplay either. She's wondering: Where's the romance in all this?

Well, at least she's a real woman now. She hasn't missed all of life. She may have missed a lot, but no one can say she missed all, which is more than Cora

can say about herself. Janice thinks she is, and probably permanently—at least
she hopes so—one up on Cora. She has joined the human race in a way Cora
probably never will, poor thing. Janice will be kind.

Janice hardly ever drives. She has always left that to Cora. She knows how, but
she's out of practice. Now she has several errands to do. She wants a nice pin-
striped suit, though she wonders if they come in boys' sizes—a suit like her father
never would have worn. She wants a good suitcase. Not one from the five and
ten. Shiny shoes big enough for rough claws, though she's cut those claws as
short as she could, using old Jonesy's nail clippers. Since Mr. Jones looks sort of
Mexican, she'll get him a south-of-the-border, Panama-type hat and dark glasses.

It only takes a couple of days for Janice to get her errands done and then a couple
more to get the guest room ready: aired out, curtains washed, bed made. (Good
it's a double bed.) She whistles all the time and doesn't even remember that it
always bothers Cora.

Cora watches the preparation of the guest room, but refuses to give Janice the
satisfaction of asking her any questions. It's easy to see that Janice wonders why
Cora isn't asking. Once Janice started to tell her something, but then turned red
to her collar bone and shut up fast.

Janice has continued making good suppers of Cora's favorite foods. Cora is still
waiting for the practical joke to come to its finale, but even—or especially if it
doesn't end, she knows something's up. She hasn't let down her guard and she's
snooped around—even in the basement, but not in the coal room. She didn't
notice the padlock on the door. But in the attic she did find a large—*very* large
piece of stiff leather, dried blood along its edges. So brittle she couldn't unfold it
to see what it was. It gave her the shivers. Pained her to see it, though she couldn't
say why. Perhaps it was the two toenails or claws that were attached to each corner.
She'd thought of throwing the dead-looking thing out in the garbage, but after she
saw those claws that were part of it, she couldn't bring herself to touch it again.

Everything is ready, but Janice knows Jonesy needs a little more experience and
training. She wants to pretend to go down and pick him up at the airport in
Detroit. Cora, if she hears about it, will never let Janice go there by herself. But
Cora mustn't be there. For lots of reasons, not the least of which that Janice wants
the trip to be like a honeymoon. They could sneak out in the middle of the night
and they could take two or three or even more days getting down there, and two
or three or more days coming back. Maybe a couple of days enjoying Detroit.
Jonesy could learn a lot.

Janice has never dared to even think of going on a trip like this before, but
with Jones she wouldn't be alone. She sees herself, dressed in her best, sitting
across from him (he'll be wearing his pin-striped suit) in restaurants, going to
motels—movies, even. . . . She'd *look* right doing these things. Like all the other
couples. They'd hold hands in the movies. They'd stroll in the evenings after
their long drive. Can he stroll? She'll get him a walking stick in Detroit. Better
than Father's. Silver handled. He may be a cripple, but he'll look like a gentleman.
And the better he looks the more jealous Cora will be.

* * *

And it started out to be a wonderful honeymoon. Janice kept the choke collar on under Jones's necktie and shirt, running the chain down inside his left sleeve so that when she held his hand she could also hold the chain just to make sure. She also found a way to hold the back of his shirt so she could give a little pull on it, but she seldom had to use any of these techniques. And how could he try to escape, hobbling as he does? Unless he learns to drive the pickup? But Janice wouldn't be a bit surprised if he could learn to drive it. Even before they get to Detroit, Jonesy is dressing himself, uses the right fork in fancy restaurants, can eat a lobster just as neatly as anyone can.

Janice keeps a running conversation going, just as if they were communicating. She keeps saying, "Don't you think so, dear?" hoping nobody will notice that he doesn't nod. Except she's sure that lots of husbands are like that. Even Father often didn't answer Mother, lost in his own thoughts all the time. But Mr. Jones doesn't look lost in his thoughts. And he doesn't look as if he feels hopeless anymore. He looks out at everything with such intelligence that Janice is considering calling him *Doctor* Jones.

In Detroit (they are staying at the Renaissance Center) Janice gets the good idea that they should get married right there at City Hall. Before she even tries to do it, she calls up Cora. "I got married," she says, even though it hasn't happened yet, but, anyway, whether it does or not, Cora will never know the difference. "And isn't it funny, I'm Mrs. Jones, and I call him Jones, just like Old Jonesy."

Cora can't answer. She just sputters. She's been lonelier without Janice there than she ever thought she would be. She had even wished the little light was still flickering in the orchard. She'd gone out there, hoping to find another nest. Partly she'd been just looking for company. She'd even left the doors unlocked, her window open. But then she'd put two and two together. She's had all these days to wonder and worry and wait, and she's been down in the basement where the coal-room door had been carelessly left open. She's seen the pallet on the floor, the bowl of dusty water, the remains of a last meal (Mother's china, wine glasses), three pairs of Janice's underpants, badly soiled. And she remembered that piece of folded leather with the dried blood all over it that she'd found in the attic and she'd gotten the shivers all over again. Cora knows she's been out-maneuvered by Janice, which she never thought could ever come about, but she suddenly realizes that she doesn't care about that anymore.

She sputters into the phone and then, for the first time—at least that Janice ever knew about—Cora bursts into tears. Janice can tell even though Cora is trying to hide it. All of a sudden Janice wants to say something that will make Cora happy, but she doesn't know what. "You'll like him," she says. "I know you will. You'll *love* him, and he'll love you, too. I know him well enough to know he will. He *will*."

Cora keeps on trying to hide that she's crying, but she doesn't hang up. She's glad, at last, to be connected to Janice however tenuously.

"I'll bring you something nice from Detroit," Janice says.

Cora still doesn't say anything, though Janice can hear her ragged breathing.

"I'll be back real soon." Janice, also, doesn't want to break the connection, but she can't think of anything else to say. "I'll see you in two days."

*   *   *

It takes four. Janice comes home alone by taxi, after a series of buses. (The pick-up is going to be found two weeks later up in Canada, north of Thunder Bay. Men's clothes will be found in it, including Panama hat, dark glasses, and silver-handled cane. The radio will have been stolen. There will be maps, and a big dictionary that had never belonged either to Cora or Janice.)

As Janice staggers up the porch steps, Cora rushes down, her arms held out, but Janice flinches away. Janice is wearing a wedding ring and a large, phony diamond engagement ring. She has on a new dress. Even though it's wrinkled and is stained with sweat across the back, Cora can see it was expensive. Janice's hair is coming loose from its psyche knot and now she's the one who's crying and trying to pretend she's not.

Cora tries to help Janice up the steps. Even though Janice stumbles, she won't let her, but she does let Cora push her on into the living room. Janice collapses onto the couch, tells Cora, "Don't hover." Hovering is something Cora never did before. It's more like something Janice would do.

Even after Cora brings Janice a strong cup of coffee, Janice won't say a single word about anything. Cora says she'll feel better if she talks about it, but she won't. She looks tired and sullen. "You'd like to know everything, wouldn't you just," she says. (What other way to stay one up than not to tell? . . . than to have secrets?)

Cora almost says, "Not really," but she doesn't want to be, anymore, what she used to be. Janice hasn't had the experience of being in the house all alone for several days. There's a different secret now that Janice doesn't know about yet. Maybe never will unless Cora goes off someplace. But why would she go anyplace? And where? Besides, being one up or being even doesn't matter to Cora anymore. She doesn't care if Janice understands or not. She just wants to take care of her and have her stay. Maybe, after a while, Janice will come to see that things have changed.

Cora goes to the kitchen to make a salad that she thinks Janice will like. She sets the dining room table the way she thinks Janice would approve of with Mother's best dishes, and with the knives and forks in all the right places and both water glasses and wine glasses, but Janice says she'll eat later in the kitchen and alone and on paper plates. Meanwhile she'll take a bath.

After Cora eats and is cleaning up the last of her dishes, Janice comes in, wearing her nightgown and Mother's bathrobe. As she leans to get a pan from a lower shelf, the bathrobe falls away. When she straightens up again, she sees Cora staring at her. "What are you ogling!" she says, holding the frying pan like a weapon.

"Nothing," Cora says, knowing better than to make a comment. She's seen more than she wants to see. There are big red choke collar marks all around Janice's neck.

But something *must* be done or said. Cora wonders what Father would have done? She usually knows exactly what he'd do and does it without even thinking about it. Now she can't imagine Father ever having to deal with something like this. She can't say anything. She can't move, finally she thinks: No secrets. She says, "Sister." And then . . . but it's too hard. (Father never would have said it.) She starts. She almost says it. "Sister, I love. . . ."

At first it looks as if Janice *will* hit her with the frying pan, but then she drops it and just stares.

SNOW MAN
John Coyne

John Coyne has written twenty-three books, including *The Piercing, Hobgoblins*, and *Child of Shadows*. His most recent book, *Going Up Country*, is a collection of travel essays by former Peace Corps volunteers, edited by Coyne.

Coyne, himself a former member of the Peace Corps, uses his experience as a volunteer in Africa to good effect. In this subtle story about a teacher and his students, it only becomes apparent late in the tale why it is appropriate that "Snow Man" was published in the anthology *Monsters in Our Midst*.

—E.D.

When Marc entered the classroom, "Peace Corps Go Home" had already been written on the blackboard. It was neatly done, and that eliminated all but two of the Ethiopian students.

They were watching him, but he only laughed. Stepping up to the board, he erased the words, deliberately sending a spray of dust into the room. The girls near the windows waved their arms to keep the dust away, and Kelemwork stood and opened one of the windows.

Nothing was said.

Marc arranged his books on the teacher's desk, making sure he looked busy and important before them. The second bell rang and he looked up at the class. A few faces turned away. They were unsure of what he'd do and that made him feel better. Still, he had to take a couple of deep breaths to put a stopper on a wave of his own fear.

"You're unhappy about the quiz," he began, speaking slowly. Even though they were in the third year of secondary school, they still had a hard time understanding English. He spoke slowly, too, because it helped to calm his nerves. "All right! I'm unhappy, too! A teacher must set standards. You understand, don't you?"

He wondered how much they did understand. He crossed the front of the room, pacing slowly. No one was watching him.

"What do you want from me?" he shouted. "All hundreds? What good will that do you? Huh? How far will you get? Into fourth year? So what!" He kept shouting. He couldn't stop himself. His thin voice bounced off the concrete walls.

Still they sat unmoved. A few glanced in his direction, their brown eyes sweeping past his eyes. In the rear of the classroom Tekele raised his hand and stood.

"We want you to be fair, Mr. Marc."

"Am I not fair?"

Tekele hesitated.

"Go ahead, Tekele, speak up." Marc lowered his voice.

"You are difficult."

"Oh, I'm difficult. First I am unfair, now I am difficult."

Tekele did not respond. He looked out the window, and then sat down.

They kept silent. Marc stared at each one, letting the silence intensify. He could feel it swell up and fill his eardrums.

"All right," he told them. "We will have another test."

They stirred immediately, whispering fiercely in Amharic. Marc opened the folder on his desk and taking the mimeographed sheets began to pass them out, setting each one face-down on a desk, telling them not to start until they were told. When he came back to the front of the room he announced, "You have thirty minutes. Begin."

No one moved.

He walked slowly among the rows, down one, then the next, and when he reached the far left rear corner of the room, he said, "If you do not begin, I will fail everyone. You will all get zeros."

They did not move.

He went again to the front of the room, letting them have plenty of time.

"All right!" he said again, pausing. If just one of them would weaken, look at the quiz, he would have them. "That's all!" he announced. "You all get zeros. No credit for the quiz and I am counting it as an official test." He gathered his books into his arms and left the classroom.

As the door closed, the room ignited. Desks slammed. Students shouted. He turned from the noise and went along the second floor corridor and into the faculty room. Helen was there grading papers. She glanced at her watch when Marc entered and smiled, asking, "Did you let your class go?"

He shook his head.

"What, then?" She watched as he went to the counter and made himself a cup of tea.

"They won't take my quiz."

She waited for his explanation.

"I left them in the room."

"Marc!"

"They wrote 'Peace Corps Go Home' on the blackboard."

"My, they're out to get you." She smiled, sipping her tea and watching him over the rim of the cup. She had a small round face, much like a smile button, and short blond hair.

Marc wanted to slap her.

He heard footsteps on the stairs, voices talking in Amharic, and then silence as the class walked by the open door of the faculty room. The students were headed for the basketball court.

"What are you going to do?" Helen asked. She was trying to be nice.

"Nothing."

"Aren't you going to talk to Ato Asfaw?"

"Why should I? He said discipline was our problem." Helen put down her cup. "Marc, you're making a mistake."

"You're the one who thinks it's so goddamn funny."

"Okay! I'm sorry I made light of your tragedy." She began again to correct her students' papers.

Marc sat with her, waiting for something to happen. The faculty room was hot. The dry, hot early morning of an African winter. Through the open windows, Marc could feel the hot winds off the Ogaden Desert. He was from Michigan and that morning he had heard on the shortwave radio that the American Midwest was having a blizzard. He tried to remember snow. Tried to remember the wet feel of it under his mittens when he was only ten and walking home from where the school bus left him on the highway.

He was still sitting staring out at the desert when the school guard came and said in Amharic that the Headmaster wanted to see him. Walking to the office, Marc glanced again at the arid lowlands and thought of snow blowing against his face. It made him feel immensely better.

"Mr. Marc," Ato Asfaw asked, "why are 3B on the playground?" The small, slight headmaster was standing behind his desk.

"I left them in class. They refused to take my test." Marc sat down and made himself comfortable. He knew his casualness upset the Headmaster; it was an affront to the Ethiopian culture. In the two years that he had been in Ethiopia, he had learned what offended Ethiopians and he enjoyed annoying them.

"But you gave them a quiz last week." The Headmaster sat down behind his enormous desk, nearly disappearing from sight. With his high, pronounced forehead and the finely sculptured face of an Amharia, he looked like the emperor Haile Selassie.

"Yes, I gave them a quiz. They did poorly, so I decided to give them another one."

Asfaw nodded, hesitated a moment, then said, "3B has other complaints. They say you are not fair. They say you call them monkeys, tell them they are stupid."

"They're lying."

"They say you left the classroom, is this true?"

"They refused to take my quiz."

"Perhaps you may give them another chance."

"Why?"

"Because they are children, Mr. Marc. And you are their teacher." He spoke quickly, showing his impatience.

His desk was covered with papers typed in Amharic script. Stacks of thin sheets fastened together with small straight pins. How could he help a country that couldn't even afford paperclips, Marc wondered.

"I don't see them as children," he told the Headmaster. "Some of those 'boys' are older than I am. They know what they're doing. They wrote 'Peace Corps Go Home' on the blackboard." Marc stopped talking. He knew it sounded like a stupid complaint. Helen was right, yet he wouldn't back down in front of the Ethiopian. Americans never back down, he reminded himself.

"You have been difficult with them," the Headmaster went on, still speaking softly, as if discussing Marc's sins. "They are not American students; you are being unjust, treating them as such." He stood again, as if to gain more authority by standing.

"I am not treating them as American students or any other kind of student, except Ethiopians," Marc answered back. He crossed his legs, knowing it was another sign of disrespect.

"Mr. Marc, your classes in Peace Corps training taught you Ethiopian customs. Am I correct?"

Marc nodded, watching Ato Asfaw, waiting for the catch.

"You learned that we have our own ways. Your teaching methods are, what do you call it, 'culture shock'?" He smiled.

Marc shrugged. They had all been told about culture shock, how everything in the new country would disorient them. But he had weathered "culture shock" of his own, he reminded himself, and said to the Headmaster, "This country has a history of school strikes, am I right?"

"Not a history, no. There have been some strikes. But over nothing as trivial as this! This quiz!" His voice rose as he finished the sentence.

"Well, what are you going to do?" Marc asked. He hooked his arm over the back of the chair.

Asfaw picked up a sheet of paper off his desk.

From where he sat, Marc saw the paper was full of handwritten Amharic notes.

"There are many complaints on this paper," the Headmaster said again. "The students are sending a copy to the Ministry of Education in Addis Ababa. Did I mention that?" He looked over at Marc, enjoying the moment. He had the brown saucer eyes of all Ethiopians. In the women, Marc found the eyes made them timid-looking and lovely. The same eyes made the men look weak.

"These complaints are lies. You know that!" Marc stood. "I want an apology before consenting to teach that class again." He turned and walked out of the Headmaster's office without being dismissed. It made him feel great, like the protagonist of his own life story.

The students in 3B were still on strike at the end of the week. Marc kept out of sight. He stayed in the faculty room when not teaching his other classes, spending his time reading old copies of *Time* magazine. None of the teachers, including the other Peace Corps Volunteers, ever mentioned the strike. The Volunteers stationed at the school were the Olivers, a married couple from Florida, who lived out near the school, and Helen Valentino, who had an apartment next to his place.

The town was called Diredawa and it was built at the edge of the Ogaden. There was an old section which was all Ethiopian, mostly Somalis and Afars, and the newer quarter where the French had lived when they built the railway from Djibouti across the desert and up the escarpment to Addis Ababa in the Ethiopian highlands.

Marc never saw his students in town. He had no idea where they lived. Unlike the other Volunteers, he had never been asked to any of their homes for Injera and Wat. He thought about that when he was killing time in the faculty lounge waiting out his striking class period.

He did see the students from his class, saw them as they passed along the open hallways, going and coming from one another class. They watched him with their brown eyes and said nothing, did not even take a sudden breath, as was the Ethiopian custom when making a silent note of recognition.

He thought of them as brown rabbits. Like the brown rabbits he hunted every fall back home on the farm. He liked to get close to the small animals, to see quivering brown bodies burrowing into the snow, and then he'd cock his .22 and fire quickly, catching the fleeing whitetail in mid-hop, splattering blood on the fresh whiteness.

Marc raised his hand and aimed his forefinger at his students lounging in the shade of trees beyond the makeshift basketball courts. He silently popped each one of them off with his make-believe pistol.

"Singh has had classes with 3B for the last week," Helen told him. "I just found out."

It was the second week of the strike when she came over to his apartment with the news. He was dressed in an Arab skirt and sitting on his bed chewing the Ethiopian drug chat. The chat gave him a low-grade high and a slight headache, but it was the only drug he could get at the edge of the desert.

"That bastard," Marc said.

"Singh is telling the students that they can't trust the Peace Corps Volunteers. He's telling them we're not real teachers."

"That bastard," Marc said again.

"What are you going to do about it?" she demanded.

Marc shrugged. The chat had made him sleepy.

"We're all in trouble because of you," Helen told him. She was pacing the bedroom, moving in and out of the sunlight filtering through the metal shutters. The only way to keep the apartment cool was to lower the shutters during the long hot days.

"It's my class," he told her, grinning.

They had been lovers in training at UCLA, and during the first few months in Diredawa.

"Yes, but we're all Peace Corps!"

"Screw the Peace Corps."

"Marc, be serious!" She was in tears, and she was holding herself, trying to keep from crying.

"I am serious. I don't give a damn."

"I'm calling Morgan in Addis. I'm getting him down here," she shouted back.

He wanted to pull away the mosquito netting and ask her climb into bed with him, but he didn't have the nerve.

"I don't want him here. I'll handle this," he told Helen.

"You just said you're not going to do anything. Look at you sitting here all day chewing chat!" She waved dismissively.

"Want some?" he asked, grinning through the thick netting.

Helen left him in his apartment. The chat had made him too listless to keep arguing, to go running after her, to pull her back to his bed and make love to her. Besides, he knew she would call Morgan. She was always trying to run his life.

Marc went to the airport to meet the Peace Corps Director. It might have been more dramatic to let Brent Morgan find him, to track him down in one of the bars, to come in perspiring from the heat with his suit crumpled, his tie loosened. But then Helen would have had first chance at him, and Marc didn't want that.

The new airport terminal was under construction and there was nowhere to wait for the planes, so Marc parked the Peace Corps jeep in the shade of palm trees and watched the western horizon for the first glimpse of the afternoon flight from Addis.

He himself had first arrived in Diredawa on the day train. It was their second week in Ethiopia and all the Volunteers were leaving Addis Ababa for their assignments. They were the only ones traveling by train.

The long rains were over and they could see the clouds rolling away from the city, leaving a very pure blue on the horizon. It was still chilly, but not the piercing cold they had felt when they first arrived in country. No one had told them Ethiopia, or Africa, could be so cold. But they were going now, everyone said, to a beautiful climate, to warm country, to what Africa was really like.

It had been their first trip out of the city. They did not know anyone, and everything was new and strange. They sat together on metal benches and watched the plains stretch away towards the mountains as they dropped rapidly into the Great Rift Valley.

The land, after the long rains, was green and bright with yellow meskal flowers. On the hillsides were mushroom-shaped tukul huts, thick brown spots on the green hillside, in among the yellow flowers. There were few trees and they were tall, straight eucalyptus which grew in tight bunches near the tukul compounds.

In the cold of early morning, Ethiopians were going off to church. They moved in single file across the low hills towards the Coptic church set in a distant grove of eucalyptus. A few Ethiopians rode small, short-legged horses and mules, all brightly harnessed, and everyone on the soft hills wore the same white shammas dress and white jodhpurs.

Marc had never been so happy in his life.

Now, sitting in the shade, he saw the Ethiopian Airlines plane come into sight; and, spotting it, he realized his eyes were blurry and that he was crying.

Marc wondered why he was crying, but also he knew that lately he was always finding tears on his face and having no idea why he was crying.

The Peace Corps Director was the first off the plane. His coat and tie were already off and his collar was open. From the hatch of the small craft, he waved, then bounded down the ramp, swinging his thick brown briefcase from one hand to the other. He came over to where Marc sat in the front seat of the open jeep.

Marc reached forward and turned over the engine.

"Tenastelign," Brent said, jumping into the front seat.

"Iski. Indemin aderu," Marc answered in Amharic and spun the vehicle out of the dirt lot.

Brent grabbed the overhead frame as the small jeep swayed.

"Where do you want to go?" Marc shouted, glancing at the Peace Corps Director.

"School . . . ?"

Marc nodded, and spun the jeep abruptly toward the secondary school.

Brent kept trying to make conversation, shouting to Marc over the roar of the engine, asking about the others, telling Marc news from Addis. Marc kept quiet.

He was being an asshole, he knew, but he couldn't help himself. He wanted Brent to have a hard time. It was crazy, but he couldn't stop.

When they reached the school, a few students were standing in the shade of the building, leaning up against the whitewashed wall and holding hands, as Ethiopian men did. Brent straightened his tie and put on his coat as they went to the Headmaster's office.

Asfaw stood when they entered the office, and he came around his desk to shake hands with them both, gesturing for them to sit. Brent began to talk at once in his quick, nervous way, telling the school director why he had come to Diredawa, explaining that the Ministry of Education, as well as the Peace Corps, was concerned about the situation with Marc's class.

Asfaw listened hard, frowned, nodded, agreeing with everything, as Marc had known he would. He nodded to Brent's vague generalizations about the Headmaster supporting the faculty, and the Ministry supporting both.

Marc wondered if Brent really believed all this bullshit.

"Of course, Mr. Marc has been very strict with his pupils," Asfaw finally said, not following up on what Brent had said.

"Well, perhaps," Brent answered, gesturing with both hands, as if he were trying to fashion some meaning of the situation from the hot desert breeze. "But that really isn't the question. I mean, in the larger sense." He pulled himself forward on the chair, straining to make himself clear. Then he stopped, saw Asfaw was not comprehending, saw a film of confusion cross the Headmaster's brown eyes, and asked, as if in defeat, "What do you think is the solution?"

"Mr. Marc is not very patient with our people. They are not used to his ways."

"There are certain universal ways of good behavior," Marc interrupted, raising his voice. "They deliberately did not take my test. That's an insult! And you! They know you're too afraid to do anything."

"All right! All right!" Brent spoke quickly, halting Marc.

Asfaw nodded, then began. "If you do not mind, Mr. Brent Morgan, I would like to say something." He looked for agreement and Brent nodded, gesturing with both hands.

"We have a strike in our school. Now this is something not unknown in our country. We have had many strikes. I have been in strikes when I was a student. I say this because I do not want Mr. Marc to feel he is being subjected to prejudice by his students. So, we must not say why do the students strike, but how can we bring them back to school."

"For Mr. Brent, you have said education is the most important for Ethiopia. We must not be so hidden by these petty problems, and look instead towards the larger issues. Do you not agree? Is this not what you have said?" He glanced at both of them, his face as alert as a startled rabbit's.

"Why, yes," Brent answered hesitantly. "We can certainly agree, but let's not dismiss some basic educational principles."

"And what is this?"

"That a teacher commands a position of authority within the community, that the students respect this authority," the Peace Corps Director answered quickly.

"A teacher, I was told when I studied at Ohio University, achieved respect by proving to his students that he deserved it."

"Yes, this is very true, but it is difficult to achieve when the students know the teacher is alone in his authority," Morgan answered.

"Or when they would rather have a passing grade than an education," Marc butted in.

Asfaw smiled at Marc and said softly, like a caring parent, "To be truly honest, Mr. Marc, you, too, were probably concerned mostly with point averages, I believe the term is, when you were in school."

"Let us try," Brent began slowly, "to look at this issue again." He maintained a smile, adding, "We have been missing the main point. The strike must cease. The students must return to school. Now what avenues are open to us?"

"But I have made my decision!" Asfaw seemed surprised. He looked from face to face, his brown eyes widening.

"Certainly, but do you really think Marc should return to class without an apology from the students?"

"Oh, an apology is such a deceiving thing. Yes, perhaps in America, it is important, but you must remember this is Ethiopia. We have our own ways, don't we, Mr. Marc?" The Headmaster smiled, and then shrugged, as if it were all beyond his power.

"And in Ethiopia the mark of a clever man is his ability to outwit another person," Brent answered. "You must realize if Marc returns to his classroom without an apology, or some form of disciplinary action taken, he will be ineffective as a teacher."

The small man leaned forward, putting his elbows on the desk. "I will first lecture the class. I will tell them such demonstrations will not be tolerated. And Mr. Marc, if he wishes, can have them write an essay, which I will also see is done."

"And what happens the next time I give a test?"

"I should think, Mr. Marc, as a clever person, you will review your teaching methods. I think you are aware none of the other teachers, including the Peace Corps, are having difficulty with their classes."

"I have to remain in authority in my class."

"I think Marc is correct. We must be united on this point. Take a firmer position," Brent added, making a fist with one hand.

"How might you handle it?" Asfaw asked Marc.

"Give them some manual work."

"They cannot do coolie work! They are students!"

"That's the point! They don't deserve to be students. A little taste of hard labor will prove my point. They won't mouth off again."

"It could be symbolic, I should think," Brent suggested. "You could arrange a clean-up of the compound, perhaps. It would be very instructive, actually."

"Nothing less than three days. The first day it will be all a joke, but the next two they'll work up a little sweat!" Marc smiled in anticipation.

"You are asking very much." Asfaw shook his head. "It is against their culture to work with their hands."

"I'm asking only enough to let me return to that classroom with the respect given a teacher."

Brent kept glancing at Marc, who in turn, kept avoiding Morgan's eyes. He liked pushing the Headmaster up against the wall.

"If you have them do at least three days of work around the school," Marc finally said, surrendering to the pressure of the moment, "I'll forget about the apology and go back to teaching."

Brent glanced quickly at Asfaw.

The Headmaster hesitated.

He was thinking of what all that meant, Marc knew. He wasn't going to be outwitted by this ferenji.

"It is not completely satisfactory," the Headmaster responded slowly, "but the students are not learning. I must put away my personal feelings for the betterment of education in Ethiopia. I will call the boys together and explain the require-ments." He smiled.

Brent slapped the knees of his lightweight suit and stood. He was beaming with relief even before he reached across the Headmaster's desk and shook the small man's hand.

Marc drove back into town after he dropped Brent at the airport. He drove past the Ras Hotel where they went to swim, and where they ate lunch and dinner on Sundays, the cook's day off. He turned at the next block and went by the open-air theater, then slowly drove along the street which led to their apartments and the piazza.

The street was heavily shaded from trees and the houses with big compounds, built up to the sidewalks. It was one of the few towns in Ethiopia which resembled a city, with geometric streets, sidewalks, traffic signs. But the bush was present. Somalis walked their camels along the side streets, herded small flocks of sheep and goats between the cars and up to the hills. Behind the taming influences of the foreign houses was Africa. Marc felt as if it were beating against his temples.

The apartment the Peace Corps had rented was not what Marc had imagined he'd be living in. He had visions of mud huts, of seamy little villages along the Nile. But not Diredawa. It was a small town with pavement, sidewalks, warm evenings filled with the smell of bougainvillea bushes, and bars with outside tables. It was a little French town in the African desert.

He parked the jeep in front of the apartment building, then walked over to Helen's apartment and, going onto the porch, knocked on the door. When she didn't answer, he walked in and went into her bedroom, whispering her name. When she still didn't answer, he walked in and sat on the edge of her bed and watched her sleep. She had taken a nap, as always, after her last afternoon classes.

She continued to sleep, breathing smoothly, her arms stretched out at her sides. He could see she was naked under a white cotton sheet, and he watched her in silence for awhile before leaning forward and kissing her softly on the cheek. She stirred and blinked her eyes.

"What time is it?" she asked, waking and pulling the sheet closer.

"After three. Morgan's gone. I took him to the afternoon plane."

"Why didn't you wake me?" She turned on her side.

"I didn't know you wanted to see him."

She shook her head, pressing her lips together.

"You want to have dinner?" he asked, not responding to her anger.

"I can't. I'm going out."

Marc watched her for a moment, and then said, "Do you want me to ask with whom?"

"I have a date with Tedesse. We're going to the movies."

"When did this start?" He kept his eyes on her.

"Nothing has started." She shifted again on the bed sensing her own nakedness under the sheet.

"What about us?" he asked weakly, wanting her to feel his pain.

"Marc, I have no idea what our relationship is, not from one moment to the next." She was staring at him. "Sometimes, you're great. You can't do enough for me. The next day, you know, you barely say hello. What do you expect?" Her eyes glistened.

"The school's bugging me, that's all. You know that. Can't you understand, for chrissake!"

"There's nothing wrong with the school," she answered. "You've created half the problems yourself." She had pulled herself up and was wide awake.

"And you top it off by dating some Ethiopian!"

"Marc, quit all this self-pity. It's very unattractive."

"I wanted to go to the movies."

"Then go!"

"Sure, and have you there with Tedesse?"

"Do what you want." She turned her face toward the whitewashed bedroom wall. "Now please leave. I want to get some sleep."

"Are you in love with him?"

"I don't want to talk about it."

"I need to know."

"Marc, don't badger me."

He slammed the apartment door, leaving, and a Somali knife on the living room wall fell down with a crash.

The students began to move rock on Monday. Marc walked out to the field behind the school and watched them work. It was malicious of him, he knew, but he enjoyed it.

He stood on a mound overlooking the work area and did not speak, but he knew they were aware of him. He saw them glancing at him, whispering to themselves.

They continued to work and after a few minutes he turned and started back toward the school. It was almost two o'clock, time for his afternoon classes.

The first stone flew over his head. Marc didn't react to it. He wasn't even sure where it came from. The second one clipped his shoulder, and the next hit him squarely in the back. He wheeled about, ducked one aimed at his head, and started back at the students.

There were no obvious attackers. He saw no upraised arms. They were working as docilely as before. He stopped and cursed them, but no one looked his way, no satisfying smirks flashed on any of their brown faces.

He stayed away from the work site for the next two days, but watched them from the second floor corridor making sure they saw him, standing there, grinning while they sweated under the hot sun.

On the Thursday morning the class was to return, he decided to begin teaching immediately, not to dawdle on their punishment, or the rock tossing. He planned to teach just as Mr. Singh, the Indian, did, with no class discussion, nothing but note taking. He would fill the blackboard and let them copy down the facts. No more following the question where it led. No more trying to make his classroom exciting and interesting. He didn't care if they learned anything more than what they could memorize.

He rode his bike out to school early, getting there before the students or teachers, and went upstairs to the faculty room to wait for the first bell.

A few of the teachers said hello as they arrived, but when Helen arrived on her bike shortly after seven, she asked what was wrong with their students.

Marc didn't know what she was talking about. Helen went to the front windows and watched the compound.

The students were too quiet, she told him. Something was wrong.

Marc stepped onto the breezeway and looked up at the three stories of class-rooms. The railings were crowded. The students stood quietly, waiting and watch-ing. A few, mostly girls from the lower grades, were playing on the basketball court. The others in the compound were in small groups of three and four. There was a little talking, but only in whispers. Gradually they turned and noticed Marc, and watched him without expression, their soft brown eyes telling him nothing.

He stepped back into the faculty room.

The Sports Master, an Ethiopian, had just come in. He scanned the teachers until he spotted Marc and came directly to him.

He had once played football for the country's national team and had a small, well-built body. Around his neck a whistle dangled from a cord. The man was sweating.

"We're having a strike," he told Marc. "Asfaw has sent for the army."

As he spoke, two Land Rovers swung into the compound and a half-dozen soldiers tumbled out. The students' reaction was immediate. The passive, quiet assembly rose up clamoring. Those students on the three tiers of the breezeway began to beat the iron railing. Girls began the strange high shrills they usually saved for funerals. And then rocks began to fly.

The windows of the Land Rovers were broken first. The officer was caught halfway between the school and the Rovers; he hesitated, not sure whether to keep going or rejoin his men.

And then the barrage escalated. From all sides, from everywhere, came the stones and rocks. One soldier was hit hard, faltered, and grabbed his buddy. From the second floor faculty room, Marc could see the blood on the man's face. And then from everywhere in the school compound came the stones and rocks.

The officer ran back to the Land Rover and grabbed his Uzi. Spinning around, he opened fired on the students, spraying them with a quick burst of bullets. The small bodies of boys and girls bounced backwards, smashed up against the whitewashed walls of the school.

Time magazine was sold at a barber shop near the apartment. The barber saved Marc a copy when it came in on the Friday plane and he picked it up on Saturday, the day after the shooting at school, to read in the Ras Makonnen Bar. There were soldiers in the piazza, loitering in the big square facing the bar.

Occasionally a jeep would careen through the open square, its tires squealing. There were no students in the piazza, but periodically Marc heard gunfire coming from across the gully. He wondered if it had to do with the students. Were they catching more of them, chasing them down in the dark alley of the Moslem section? He smiled, thinking that might be happening while he had a peaceful breakfast.

He ordered orange juice, pastry, and opened *Time*, flipping rapidly through the pages for articles about the Midwest.

There had been another ice storm in Chicago, he read, that had closed down O'Hare Airport, caused a forty-five-car pile up on I-94. Marc read the article twice, lingering over familiar names and the details of the storm.

He kept smiling, thinking of home, wishing he were there for the storm. He imagined what his Michigan town might looked like, buried deep in ice and snow. He could feel the sharp pain of the wind on his cheeks, feel the biting cold. He looked up, stared through the thick, bright, lush bougainvillea bushes.

There were tears in his eyes. Cold tears on his face. He didn't know that he was crying.

He wiped his face with the small, waxy paper napkin, and looked out at the bright square and the loitering soldiers, who had found shade at the base of several false banana trees. They had abandoned their rifles, left them propped against a tree. He wondered why the soldiers weren't cold.

He thought again of the killings at the school, how the officer with the Uzi had killed eight in the first burst of gunfire.

Helen has begun to scream. She was holding her ears, trying not to hear the students' cries, but still she couldn't look away from the slaughter.

He couldn't either. Several of his students, long, lanky kids, jumped and jerked when they were hit. The bullets tossed them around, made them hop and dance, before they were slammed back against the whitewashed walls of the school where they splattered like eggs, breaking bright red yolks.

Helen wouldn't stop screaming, even after silence fell in the school yard, after the lieutenant stopped firing, after the students scattered, those who were still alive.

She was standing at the windows, screaming. Marc couldn't go to her; he couldn't figure out how to walk. Mr. Singh finally seized her, pulled her away from the window as the Headmaster began screaming in Amharic at the soldiers.

Marc walked out the door then and down the stairs. He walked straight by the soldiers as if what had happened meant nothing to him. He walked away from the school, went across the open brush land to the dry gully river, which he knew he could follow into town. From the river bed, he heard the sounds of an ambulance coming out from the French hospital.

He walked to his apartment and locked himself inside, then crawled into bed and slept through the heat of the day. Helen came to get him after dark. She had told him martial law had been proclaimed and that she and the Olivers were leaving, going up to Addis Ababa on the night train. It was no longer safe in town, she told him. But he wouldn't leave, he told her. He wouldn't let the students drive him out of Diredawa.

Marc stood and walked out of the cafe bar and into the piazza. It was empty except for the soldiers. He wondered where everyone had gone, why no one was on the streets. He was lonely, knowing that he was the only Peace Corps Volunteer in Diredawa. He thought that perhaps he was the only white man left in town.

But it wasn't true. There were French doctors at the hospital, missionaries from the Sudan Interior Mission, French workers with the railway. Tourists. Yes, the desert town was full of white people.

Still he hurried, cut across the open square, going home, back to his apartment where behind locked doors he'd be safe until the Peace Corps staff came to get him. They wouldn't leave him alone, he knew. This was a mistake, he thought at the same moment, crossing the empty street. He shouldn't have left his apartment and taken a chance on the streets. There might be students around.

He broke into a run.

A rock hit him on the side of the head and bounced off like a misplayed golf shot. He stumbled forward, but knew he was okay. It had only been a rock. They couldn't kill him with rocks. He was too tough. Too much of an American. These were just people in some godawful backward Third World country, half starving to death every few years.

He pulled his hand away from the side of his face and his fingers looked bright with blood.

"Shit!" he said, thinking of the mess to his clothes. And he hated the smell of blood. He stumbled forward, finding his feet, knowing he had to keep running. They couldn't catch him in the middle of the street.

A half-dozen soldiers were still loitering by the entrance of the movie theater, less than a dozen yards from him. He waved to get their attention and shouted out in Amharic. Another rock hit him in the mouth.

He tumbled over on his back and rolled in the dirt, coughing up pieces of his teeth and globs of blood and spit. Marc raised his hand and tried to shout at the soldiers. Why weren't they helping him?

He crawled forward, still going toward the apartment, thinking only that if he could get to the gate and behind the iron fence, he would be safe.

He coughed up more blood and in his tears and pain knew he had to run, that they might swarm out of the trees, or wherever they were hiding deep in the palm-lined street, and seize him, take him back into the Old City, where it was another tribal law that would deal with him. An eye for an eye.

He got to his feet and ran.

There were more rocks, coming from the right and left, showering him, bashing his head, knocking him over once more. He fell forward, into the gutter and smashed his head against the concrete.

If he stopped he was dead. His only hope was to reach the iron gates. Gebra, his zebagna, would keep out the crowd of students.

Why weren't the soldiers helping him? They hadn't hesitated to shoot when they were pelted, why couldn't they protect him?

He burst through the metal compound gate, startling Gebra. Marc shouted at him to bolt the compound door. It was the guard's job to protect him now.

He ran up the stairs to the second floor apartment and slammed the back door, locking it behind him. Running from room to room, he pulled the side cords that dropped the heavy old metal shutters, shutting out the sunlight and sealing the apartment in the shadowy dark.

He fell in a corner, sweating from fear and exhaustion. Then he reached up and touched his forehead, felt for the rock bruise. When he took away his hand, he couldn't see his bloody fingers in the darkened room.

His hands were shaking. And he was freezing. He crept across the floor, going toward the bed, keeping himself below the windows, afraid the students might figure out which ones were his. The shutters were metal, but he couldn't be too careful, he told himself.

His whole body was trembling. It was funny, he thought. How could he be so cold in the middle of Africa? At the edge of the desert?

He thought of when he was in school, waiting on the road for the school bus and standing in the freezing cold. He shivered, and crawled under the mosquito netting, covering himself with the sheets. He would be okay soon, once he was warm. Why didn't he have a blanket, he wondered.

He watched the slanting sunlight filter through the metal window shades. The sunlight stirred the dust off the desert. It lit the room with shafts that looked like prison bars. He felt his face and wondered why there was no blood. He waited for the rocks to begin again. He thought about waking in the warmth and comfort of his farmhouse in Michigan, where he knew everyone and everything, where he was safe, and no one was different. He shivered, freezing from the cold. He opened his eyes again and saw that it had begun to snow in Africa. The flakes falling through the sunlight filtered into the room.

He would be all right, he knew. He understood cold weather and deep snow. Ethiopians knew nothing of snow. He smiled, thinking: let them try to shovel snow! They'd need him. He knew about snow. It was part of his heritage. He would teach the students how to make a snow man, he thought, grinning, and realized that everything was going to be okay. He was in the Peace Corps, and he had a job to do.

ONE NIGHT, OR SCHEHERAZADE'S BARE MINIMUM

Thomas M. Disch

Thomas M. Disch is one of the most acclaimed writers working in the field of speculative fiction today. His work includes the science fiction novels *Camp Concentration*, *334*, and *On Wings of Song*; the delightful children's fantasies *The Brave Little Toaster* and *The Brave Little Toaster Goes to Mars*; and *Neighboring Lives* (highly recommended), an historical novel about Victorian London written in collaboration with Charles Naylor. Disch's award wining short fiction has appeared in numerous magazines and collections. He has also edited influential anthologies and has been the theater critic for *The Nation*. Disch lives in New York City. His most recent novel is *The M.D.*, and his next novel, *The Priest*, is coming soon.

The following "short short" story is a sharp modern take on the old Arabian saga of the Thousand and One Nights. It comes from the anthology OMNI *Science Fiction Three*, edited by Ellen Datlow.

—T.W.

"And this," Sara's abductor explained, throwing open the French doors of a room filled with potted plants and hanging ferns, "is the oda."

"An 'oda,' like in crossword puzzles?" Sara marveled.

"I wouldn't know about that." He sounded miffed.

Sara shuffled over to the barred window. With each step the delicate golden chain hobbling her ankles clinked on the marble parquet. In the distance, silhouetted against the lavender twilight, was the dome of the Taj Mahal.

"So this is Agra! That's another word that's always cropping up in crossword puzzles."

"And *this*, my little gazelle"—-He unsheathed the long curved sword that dangled from the sash about his waist. "—is a scimitar. The number of wives and concubines who have been beheaded by this blade is many as the stars in the firmament."

"I'll remember that in case you ever propose."

"The Emir of Bassorah does not solicit the favor of his beloved. The arrows of his desire fly directly to their target. The moment I saw you pass through customs at the Rome airport, I said to my vizier: That one! I must possess her for my pleasure tonight. Hijack the plane, abduct her, dress her in costly raiments and bring her to my divan. I spoke, and he obeyed."

"Okay, but before you possess me or have me beheaded, aren't I entitled to tell a story? I've never been a hostage before, and I don't know a lot about Middle Eastern culture, but that's the basic tradition here, right?"

When the Emir of Bassorah heard his abductee speak in this impudent manner he smote hand upon hand and cried, "There is no Majesty and there is no Might save in Allah the Glorious, the Great." And he sat down on the biggest pillow on the oda's floor and folded his legs into a half-lotus position, which was quite an accomplishment for someone of his girth, but people in traditional societies where there is nothing to sit on (not even in the bathroom!) have to learn to be flexible. And he said to Sara, grudgingly: "All right, those are the rules. Tell me a story, like unto the tale of the loves of Al-Hayfa and Yusuf, and if it amuses I may let you live one night longer. Mind you, I'm not promising anything. I'm merciful, but I'm also capricious."

"Well," said Sara, trying to get comfortable on another pillow without ripping the delicate gauze of her harem pants, "I don't know the story you mention, but in the creative writing course I took at NYU our instructor told us that basically there are only a few stories that anyone can tell. It's all a matter of ascending action and descending action, and how they relate to the objectives of the protagonist. He drew some diagrams that made each archetype clear: if I had my notebook here—"

"Listen, my little American pomegranate, I want a story, not a lecture. A tale full of marvels and wonders and sex and violence."

"Okay, okay, I'll tell you a story about . . . um . . . Ed Walker and Sally Morton. Ed was a marketing executive for a major manufacturer of . . . um . . . " Sara cast about for inspiration. "Ceramic tiles! And Sally was a young woman he'd met at a party in . . . Babylon (the Babylon on Long Island, not your Babylon in the Middle East)."

"And she was very beautiful?" the Emir inquired.

"Stunning. On the street people often confused her with Vanna White."

"And her breasts?"

"Her breast were watermelons."

The Emir licked his thick lips. "Ah, very good! Continue."

Sara continued her tale, which was freely adapted from a story she'd written for her creative writing class at NYU. It had a minimal plot, but her instructor had praised it for the way it revealed the hollowness at the center of Ed's and Sally's lives and for its moments of low-key humor and its accurate observation of everyday life in a business-oriented environment.

As Sara's story unfolded with all deliberate speed, the pointy toes of her listener's golden shoes began to beat time to a faster tempo. At last he broke out: "By the beard of the Prophet, enough of this doleful twaddle! This is not fiction, this is accountancy!"

Sara glared at the Emir and, in a tone of ill-concealed resentment, said: "Sire?"

"I want romance! Mystery! Adventure!"

"Your word is my command," said Sara, and she bethought herself. The Emir of Bassorah was, as might be expected of someone in his position, a male chauvinist pig. The story she had been telling, though it had got her an A in the creative writing course and received some highly complimentary rejection slips from major quarterlies, was probably not suited to the emotional needs of a man of his temperament and social position.

So, instead of telling her own story, Sara began to retell, as well as she could remember it, "The Ballad of Jim Beam," a story by Barry McGough that had appeared in a Pushcart Press annual. It was about a famous short story writer in Oregon who had writer's block and whose marriage was on the rocks because of his alcoholism. On the surface of the story nothing appears to happen—-the man and his wife go fishing for bass, without success, drink a bottle of bourbon, and argue about their autistic child—-but underneath the surface McGough was opening a whole supermarket of cans of worms.

As an indictment of American culture in the '80s, "The Ballad of Jim Beam" was scathing, but the Emir of Bassorah, unlike so many of his Middle Eastern compatriots, seemed indifferent to the framing of such an indictment, for he yawned a mighty yawn, and scratched his crotch, and began to reach for his scimitar, which he'd placed on another pillow beside the one on which he was sitting, for it's hard enough for a fat man to assume the half-lotus position in an unencumbered state, but to do so with a scimitar lodged in his cummerbund is virtually impossible. Just try it some time.

"Wait!" Sara said, sensing the Emir's displeasure, "I've just thought of another story you might like better. About a magician."

"And is he afflicted with arthritis?" the Emir demanded. "And does he cringe like a beaten dog before his wife's rebukes?"

"No, a real magician, who is extremely rich and has strange powers, called Shahbankhan the Munificent. He can shrink down as small as a pea and swell up to the size of a . . . I don't know, something enormous. And he can fly anywhere in the world on the back of hummingbird."

"How could he do that?" The Emir's hand drew back from the jeweled pommel of the scimitar.

"The hummingbird had a teeny-tiny saddle."

"Yes. Go on."

Sara continued her tale, throwing in some new wonder or marvel whenever the Emir showed signs of restlessness or inattention. When his eyes drifted to the window's view of the Taj Mahal, she introduced a veiled maiden who ministered with great skill to the pleasures of Shahbankhan and then mysteriously disappeared. When he began to scrape at the dirt under his fingernails with a golden nail-clipper, she had Shahbankhan fall into a pit of vipers.

All the while the klepsydra, or waterclock, on the wall was dribbling away the minutes of the night. One o'clock found Shahbankhan contending against an army of invisible skeletons. At one-fifteen he was in Samarkand in pursuit of the legendary Blue Scarab of Omnipotence. At one-thirty in Zagzig being plied with a love elixir by an Egyptian enchantress. The Emir listened to it all like a drowsy but querulous child, and the night dripped on endlessly.

It was only a few minutes before dawn, but Sara was at her wit's end. Had it been like this for the original Scheherazade? If so, it was small wonder that so many other wives and concubines had chosen the scimitar to such tiresome and demeaning service. Sara would have much preferred just to give the old fart a blowjob and be done with it. But when she hinted at this possibility, in a narrative aside, the Emir's hand edged toward his damned scimitar. He had a rapist's mentality, unable to conceive of sex as other than a metaphor for murder.

A thousand and one nights of Barry McGough would be bad enough, but a thousand and one nights of rehashing superhero cartoons was an intolerable prospect. Enough! Sara thought, for she was a woman of resourcefulness and courage though not really a great storyteller, notwithstanding her A in creative writing. That had been a tribute more to her looks than any gift for narrative.

She knelt down beside the Emir. Her crimson lips brushed the immense pearl popping from the flesh of his earlobe like a nacreous wart. "And then," she whispered, "the fair enchantress removed the veil from her swanlike neck and, ever so gently, covered the eyes of the guileless magician, so that he was blindfolded now by silk as well as by love." Deftly, Sara demonstrated how this was done with the veil that swathed her own swanlike neck. Then, quick as a mongoose, her hand grasped the pommel of the Emir's scimitar. She lifted it from the pillow on which it rested and raised it high above her head—not an easy thing to do, for scimitars weigh more than you might think, but Sara worked out regularly at Jack La Lanne's and was surprisingly strong. And then, with a sense that she was revenging the grievances of every hack writer who'd ever lived, she beheaded the Emir of Bassorah.

After she'd cleaned up the mess and hidden the Emir's body under a pile of pillows in the oda's farthest corner and found a vase big enough to accommodate his severed head, she tested the various keys on his keyring in the locks of the various locked doors of the harem until she found what she was sure must be there, the "Bluebeard" room in which he had stored the personal possessions of his earlier victims. Sara's own clothes were uppermost in the heap. It was a great relief to change from the constricting and *scratchy* harem clothes into something sensible.

Then she looked through the numerous purses arranged on a malachite display case and took those credit cards that hadn't yet expired.

And then, feeling just like a princess in a fairy tale (but also a bit like the nameless wife in Barry McGough's novella "Born to Shop") she took a taxi to Agra's main bazaar and had the spree of her life.

DEAD MAN'S SHOES
Charles de Lint

Canadian author Charles de Lint is both prolific and versatile. His long list of publications includes works of adult fantasy fiction, children's fiction, horror, poetry, and critical nonfiction; he is also a Celtic musician with the band Jump at the Sun. He is best known, however, as a pioneer of contemporary Urban Fantasy, bringing myth and folklore motifs into a modern-day urban context. *Memory and Dream* and *The Wild Wood* (in collaboration with British painter Brian Froud) are his most recent works in this vein. Other recommended works include *Spirit Walk, The Little Country,* and his collection of Newford stories *Dreams Underfoot.* A second Newford collection is forthcoming.

The Newford stories are de Lint's best work to date: interconnected Magic Realist tales set in an imaginary North American city. The following piece is a poignant tale about the Grasso Street Angel and a murdered man's ghost. It comes from *Touch Wood,* volume two of the British anthology series *Narrow Houses,* edited by Peter Crowther.

—T.W.

> There are people who take the heart out of you,
> and there are people who put it back.
> —Elizabeth David

In her office, her head rests upon her arms, her arms upon the desk. She is alone. The only sound is that of the clock on the wall monotonously repeating its two-syllable vocabulary and the faint noise of the street coming in through her closed windows. Her next appointment isn't until nine P.M.

She meant merely to rest her eyes for a few moments; instead, she has fallen asleep.

In her dream, the rain falls in a mist. It crouches thicker at knee-level, twining across the street. The dead man approaches her through the rain with a pantherish grace he never displayed when alive. He is nothing like Hollywood's shambling portrayals of animated corpses; confronted by the dead man, she is the one whose movements are stuttered and slow.

Because she is trapped in flesh, she thinks.

Because in this dreamscape, he is pure spirit, unfettered by gravity or body

weight, while she still carries the burden of life. The world beyond this night's
dreams retains a firm grip, shackling her own spirit's grace with the knowledge of
its existence and her place in it.

Not so the dead man.

The rain has pressed the unruly thicket of his hair flat against his scalp. His
features are expressionless, except for the need in his eyes. He carries a somewhat
bulky object in his arms, bundled up in wet newspapers. She can't quite identify
what it is. She knows what he carries is roundish, about the size of a soccer ball,
but that is all. All other details have been swallowed in the play of shadow that
the rain has drawn from the neon signs overhead and the streetlight on the corner.

She is not afraid of the dead man, only puzzled. Because she knows him in
life. Because she has seen him glowering from the mouths of alleyways, sleeping
in doorways. He has never been truly dangerous, despite his appearance to the
contrary.

What are you doing here? she wants to ask him. What do you want from me?
But her voice betrays her as much as her body and what issues forth are only
sounds, unrecognizable as words.

She wakes just as he begins to hand her what he is carrying.

The dream was very much upon Angel's mind as she looked down at the pathetic
bundle of rag-covered bones Everett Hoyle's corpse made at the back of the alley.
But since she had always believed that the supernatural belonged only to the
realm of fiction and film and the tabloids, she refused to allow it to take root.

Jilly would call what she had experienced prescience; she thought of it only as
an unhappy coincidence and let it go no further. Instead she focused her attention
on the latest addition to the city's murder victim statistics.

No one was going to miss Everett, she thought, least of all her. Still, she
couldn't help but feel sorry for him. It was an alien reaction insofar as Everett
was concerned.

The streets were filled with angry individuals, but the reasons behind their
anger usually made sense: lost homes, lost jobs, lost families. Drink, or drugs.
Institutions turning out their chronic psychiatric patients because the government
couldn't afford their care. Victims of neglect or abuse who discovered too late
that escaping to a life on the street wasn't the answer.

But Everett was simply mean-spirited.

He had a face that would make children cry. He wasn't deformed, he simply
wore a perpetual look of rage that had frozen his features into a roadmap of constant
fury. He stood a cadaverous six-four that was more than merely intimidating to
those from whom he was trying to cadge spare change; it could be downright
frightening. With that manner, with his matted shock of dirty grey hair and
tattered clothing, he didn't seem so much a man down on his luck as some
fearsome scarecrow that had ripped itself free from its support pole and gone out
to make the world around him as unpleasant as he felt himself. Which put him
about one step up from those men who had to kill their families before they put
the gun in their own mouth and pulled the trigger.

No, Angel corrected herself. Think in the past tense now because Everett had
terrorized his last passer-by.

Surprisingly, death had brought a certain calm to his features, smoothing away the worst of the anger that normally masked them. This must be what he looked like when he was sleeping, Angel thought. Except he wasn't asleep. The blood pooled around his body bore stark testimony to that. She'd already checked for a pulse and found none. Having called the police before she left the office, now it was simply a matter of waiting for them to arrive.

The scene laid out before her held an anomaly that wouldn't stop nagging her. She took a step closer and studied the body. It was like a puzzle with one piece missing and it took her a few minutes before she could finally pinpoint what was bothering her. She turned to the young white boy who'd come to her office twenty minutes ago and brought her back to where he'd found the body.

"What happened to his boots, Robbie?" she asked.

Everett's footwear had been distinctive: threadbare Oxfords transformed into boots by stitching the upper half of a pair of Wellingtons on to the leather of each of the shoes. Olive green with yellow trim on the left; black with red trim on the right. The Oxfords were so old and worn that they were devoid of any recognizable colour themselves.

"I guess Macaulay took 'em," the boy replied.

"You never said Macaulay was here with you."

Robbie shrugged.

She waited for him to elaborate, but Robbie simply stood beside her, face washed pale by the streetlight coming in from the mouth of the alley, thin shoulders stooped, one Doc Marten kicking at the trash underfoot. His dirty blond hair was so short it was no more than stubble. He wouldn't meet her gaze.

Angel sighed. "All right," she said. "I'll bite. Why did Macaulay take the boots?"

"Well, you know what the homes are saying, Miz Angel. Man gets nined, you got to take away his shoes or he's gonna go walkin' after he's dead. He'll be lookin' for who took him down, usually, but Everett now—he's so mean I suppose anybody'd do."

With all her years of working with street people, dealing with the myriad superstitions that ran rampant through the tenements and squats, Angel thought she'd heard it all. But this was a new one, even on her.

"You don't believe that, do you?" she asked.

"No, ma'am. But I'd say Macaulay surely do."

Robbie spoke casually enough, but Angel could tell there was more to what had happened here tonight than he was letting on. He was upset—a natural enough reaction, considering the circumstances. Keeping Everett's corpse company until the police arrived had upset her as well. But the tension underlying Robbie's seeming composure spoke of more.

Before she could find just the right way to persuade him to open up to her, one of the sirens that could be heard at all hours of the day or night in this part of the city disengaged itself from the general hubbub of night sounds and became more distinct. Moments later, a cruiser pulled up, blocking the mouth of the alley. The cherry red lights of its beacons strobed inside the alley, turning the scene into a macabre funhouse. Backlit, the two officers who stepped out of the cruiser took on menacing shapes: shadows, devoid of features.

At Angel's side, Robbie began to tremble and she knew she wouldn't get anything from him now. Hands kept carefully in view, she went to meet the approaching officers.

Angelina Marceau ran a youth distress centre on Grasso Street, from which she got her nickname, the Grasso Street Angel. She looked like an angel as well: heart-shaped face surrounded by a cascade of dark curly hair, deep warm eyes, next to no make-up because she didn't need it with her clear complexion. Her trim figure didn't sport wings and she leaned more towards baggy pants, T-shirts and high tops than she did harps and white gowns, but that didn't matter to those living on the streets of Newford. So far as they were concerned, all she lacked was a visible halo.

Angel wasn't feeling particularly angelic by the time three A.M. rolled around that night. She sat wearily in her Grasso Street office, gratefully nursing a mug of coffee liberally spiked with a shot of whiskey that Jilly had handed to her when she walked in the door.

"I appreciate your looking after the place while I was at the precinct," she said.

"It wasn't a problem," Jilly told her. "No one showed up."

Angel nodded. Word on the street moved fast. If the Grasso Street Angel was at the precinct, *no one* was going to keep their appointment and take the chance of running into one of the precinct bulls. The only one of her missed appointments that worried her was Patch. She'd spent weeks trying to convince him to at least look into the sponsorship program she administrated, only to have this happen when she'd finally gotten him to agree. Patch was so frail now that she didn't think the boy would survive another beating at the hands of his pimp.

"So how'd it go?" Jilly asked.

It took Angel a moment to focus on what she'd been asked. She took a sip of her coffee, relaxing as the warmth from the whiskey reached her stomach.

"We were lucky," she said. "It was Lou's shift. He made sure they went easy on Robbie when they took our statements. They've got an APB out on Macaulay."

"Robbie. He's the skinny little peacenik that looks like a skinhead?"

Angel smiled. "That's one way of putting it. There's no way he could have killed Everett."

"How *did* Everett die?"

"He was stabbed to death—a half-dozen times at least."

Jilly shivered. "They didn't find the knife?"

"They didn't find the weapon and—I find this really odd—they didn't find Everett's boots either. Robbie says Macaulay took them so that Everett's ghost wouldn't be able to come after anyone." She shook her head. "I guess they just make them up when they haven't got anything better to do."

"Actually, it's a fairly old belief," Jilly said.

Angel took another sip of her whiskey-laced coffee to fortify herself against what was to come. For all her fine traits, and her unquestionable gift as an artist, Jilly had a head filled with what could only charitably be called whimsy. Probably it was *because* she was an artist and had such a fertile imagination, Angel had eventually decided. Still, whatever the source, Jilly was ready to espouse the oddest theories at the drop of a hat, everything from Victorian-styled fairies living in refuse dumps to Bigfoot wandering through the Tombs.

Angel had learned long ago that arguing against them was a fruitless endeavor, but sometimes she couldn't help herself.

"Old," she said, "and true as well, I suppose."

"It's possible," Jilly said, plainly oblivious to Angel's lack of belief. "I mean, there's a whole literature of superstition surrounding footwear. The one you're talking about dates back hundreds of years and is based on the idea that shoes were thought to be connected with the life-essence, the soul, of the person to whom they belonged. The shoes of murdered people were often buried separately to prevent hauntings. And sorcerers were known to try to persuade women to give them their left shoes. If the woman did, the sorcerer would have power over her."

"Sorcerers?" Angel repeated with a cocked eyebrow.

"Think what you want," Jilly told her, "but it's been documented in old witch trials."

"Really?"

"Well, it's been documented that they were accused of it," Jilly admitted.

Which wasn't quite the same thing as being true, Angel thought, but she kept the comment to herself.

Jilly put her feet up on a corner of Angel's desk and started to pick at the paint that freckled her fingernails. There were always smudges of paint on her clothes, or in her tangled hair. Jilly looked up to find Angel watching her work at the paint and shrugged unselfconsciously, a smile waking sparks of humor in her pale blue eyes that made them seem as electric as sapphires.

"So what're you going to do?" Jilly asked.

"Do? I'm not going to do anything. I'm a counselor, not a cop."

"But you could find Macaulay way quicker than the police could."

Angel nodded in agreement. "But what I do is based on trust—you know that. If I found Macaulay and turned him over to the police, even though it's just for questioning, who's going to trust me?"

"I guess."

"What I am going to do is have another talk with Robbie," Angel said. "He's taken all of this very badly."

"He actually liked Everett?"

Angel shook her head. "I don't think anyone liked Everett. I think it's got to do with finding the body. He's probably never seen a dead man before. I have, and I'm still feeling a little queasy."

She didn't mention that Robbie had seemed to be hiding something. That was Robbie's business and even if he did share it with her, it would still be up to him who could know about it and who could not. She just prayed that he hadn't been any more involved in Everett's death than having stumbled upon the body.

"Actually," she said after a moment's hesitation, "there was another weird thing that happened tonight."

Although she knew she'd regret it, because it was putting a foot into the strange world Jilly inhabited where fact mixed equally with fantasy, she told Jilly about her dream. As Angel had expected, Jilly accepted what she was told as though it were an everyday occurrence.

"Has this ever happened to you before?" she asked.

Angel shook her head. "And I hope it never happens again. It's a really creepy feeling."

Jilly seemed to be only half listening to her. Her eyes had narrowed thoughtfully. Chewing at her lower lip, her head was cocked and she studied the ceiling. Angel didn't know what Jilly saw up there, but she doubted it was the cracked plaster that anybody else would see.

"I wonder what he wanted from you," Jilly finally said. Her gaze dropped and focused on Angel's. "There has to be a reason he sent his spirit to you."

Angel shook her head. "Haven't you ever dreamed that someone you know died?"

"Well, sure. But what's that—"

"And did they turn out to be dead when you woke?"

"No, but—"

"Coincidence," Angel said. "That's all it was. Plain and simple coincidence."

Jilly looked as though she was ready to argue the point, but then she simply shrugged.

"Okay," she said, swinging her feet down from the desk. "But don't say you weren't warned when Everett's spirit comes back to haunt you again. He wants something from you and the thing with ghosts is they can be patient forever. He'll keep coming back until you figure out what he wants you to do for him and you do it."

"Of course. Why didn't I think of that?"

"I'm serious, Angel."

Angel smiled. "I'll remember."

"I just bet you will," Jilly said, returning her smile. She stood up. "Well, I've got to run. I was in the middle of a new canvas when you called."

Angel rose to her feet as well. "Thanks for filling in."

"Like I said, it was no problem. The place was dead." Jilly grimaced as the word came out of her mouth. "Sorry about that. But at least a building doesn't have shoes to lose, right?"

After Jilly left, Angel returned to her desk with another spiked coffee. She stared out the window at Grasso Street where the first touch of dawn was turning the shadows to grey, unable to get Everett's stockinged feet out of her mind. Superimposed over it was an image of Everett in the rain, holding out a shadowed bundle towards her.

One real, one from a dream. Neither made sense, but at least the dream wasn't supposed to. When it came to Everett's boots, though . . .

She disliked the idea of someone believing superstitions almost as much as she did the superstitions themselves. Taking a dead man's shoes so he wouldn't come back seeking revenge. It was so patently ludicrous.

But Macaulay had believed enough to take them.

Angel considered Jim Macaulay. At nineteen, he was positively ancient compared to the street kids such as Robbie whose company he kept, though he certainly didn't look it. His cherubic features made him seem much younger. He'd been in and out of foster homes and juvie hall since he was seven, but the experiences had done little to curb his minor criminal ways, or his good humor. Macaulay always had a smile, even when he was being arrested.

Was he good for Everett's murder? Nothing in Macaulay's record pointed to it. His crimes were always non-violent: B&Es, minor drug dealing, trafficking in stolen goods. Nothing to indicate that he'd suddenly upscaled to murder. And where was the motive? Everett had carried nothing of value on his person—

probably never had—and everyone knew it. And while it was true he'd been a royal pain in the ass, the street people just ignored him when he got on a rant.

But then why take the boots?

If Macaulay believed the superstition, why would he be afraid of Everett coming after him unless he *had* killed him?

Too tired to go home, Angel put her head down on the desk and stared out the window. She dozed off, still worrying over the problem.

Nothing has changed in her dream.

The rain continues to mist. Everett approaches her again, no less graceful, while she remains trapped in the weight of her flesh. The need is still there in Everett's eyes, the mysterious bundle still cradled against his chest as he comes up to her. But this time she finds enough of her voice to question him.

Why is he here in her dream?

"For the children," he says.

It seems such an odd thing for him to say: Everett who's never had a kind word for anyone, so far as Angel knows.

"What do you mean?" she asks him.

But then he tries to hand the bundle to her and she wakes up again.

Angel sat up with a start. She was disoriented for a long moment—as much by her surroundings as from the dream—before she recognized the familiar confines of her office and remembered falling asleep at her desk.

She shook her head and rubbed at her tired eyes. Twice in the same night. She had to do something about these hours, but knew she never would.

The repetition of the dream was harder to set aside. She could almost hear Jilly's voice, I-told-you-so plain in its tone.

Don't say you weren't warned when Everett's spirit comes back to haunt you again.

But it had just been a dream.

He wants something from you and the thing with ghosts is they can be patient forever.

A disturbing dream. That shadowed bundle Everett kept trying to hand to her and his enigmatic reply, "For the children."

He'll keep coming back until you figure out what it is he wants you to do for him and you do it.

She didn't need this, Angel thought. She didn't want to become part of Jilly's world where the rules of logic were thrown out the door and nothing made sense anymore. But this dream . . . and Macaulay taking those damn boots . . .

She remembered Jilly asking her what she was going to do and what her own reply had been. She still didn't want to get involved. Her job was helping the kids, not playing cop. But the image of the dream Everett flashed in her mind, the need in his eyes and what he'd said when she'd asked him why he was there in her dream.

For the children.

Whether she wanted it or not, she realized that she was involved now. Not in any way that made sense, but indiscriminately, by pure blind chance, which seemed even less fair. It certainly wasn't because she and Everett had been friends. For God's sake, she'd never even *liked* Everett.

For the children.

Angel sighed. She picked up her mug and looked down at the cold mixture of whiskey and coffee. She started to call Jilly, but hung up before she'd finished dialing the number. She knew what Jilly would say.

Grimacing, she drank what was left in her mug, then left her office in search of an answer.

Macaulay had a squat in the same abandoned tenement where Robbie lived, just a few blocks north of Angel's office on the edge of the Tombs. Angel squinted at the building, then made her way across the rubble-strewn lot that sided the empty tenement. The front door was boarded shut, so she went around the side and climbed in through a window the way the building's inhabitants did. Taking a moment to let her eyes adjust to the dimmer light inside, she listened to the silence that surrounded her. Whoever was here today was obviously asleep.

She knew Macaulay's squat was on the top floor, so she found the stairwell by the boarded-up entrance and climbed the two flights to the third floor. She looked in through the doorways as she passed by the rooms, heart aching with what she saw. Squatters, mostly kids, were curled up in sleeping bags, under blankets or in nests of newspaper. What were they going to do when winter came and the coolness of late summer nights dropped below the freezing mark?

Macaulay's room was at the end of the hall, but he wasn't in. His squat had a door, unlike most of the other rooms, but it stood ajar. Inside it was tidier than Angel had expected. Clean, too. There was a mattress in one corner with a neatly folded sleeping bag and pillow on top. Beside it was an oil lamp, sitting on the wooden floor, and a tidy pile of spare clothes. Two crates by the door held a number of water-swelled paperbacks with their covers removed. On another crate stood a Coleman stove, a frying pan and some utensils. Inside the crate was a row of canned goods while a cardboard box beside it served to hold garbage.

And then there were the shoes.

Although Angel didn't know Macaulay's shoe size, she doubted that any of them would fit him. She counted fifteen pairs, in all shapes and sizes, from a toddler's tiny sneakers to a woman's spike-heeled pumps. They were lined up against the wall in a neat row, a miniature mountain range, rising and falling in height, with Everett's bizarre boots standing like paired peaks at the end closer to the door.

It was a perfectly innocent sight, but Angel felt sick to her stomach as she stood there looking at them. They were all the shoes of children and women—except for Everett's. Had Macaulay killed all of their—

"Angel."

She turned to find him standing in the doorway. With the sun coming through the window, making his blond hair look like a halo, he might have been describing himself as much as calling her name. Her gaze shifted to the line of shoes along the wall, then back to his face. His blue eyes were guileless.

Angel forwent the amenities

"These . . . these shoes . . . ?" she began.

"Shoes carry the imprint of our souls upon their own," he replied. He paused, then added, "Get it?"

All she was getting was a severe case of the creeps. What had she been thinking to come here on her own? She hadn't told anyone where she was going. Her own hightops could be joining that line of shoes, set in place beside Everett's.

Get out while you can, she told herself, but all she could do was ask, "Did you kill him?"

"Who? Everett?"

Angel nodded.

"Do I look like a killer to you?"

No, he looked as though he was on his way to mass—not to confess, but to sing in the choir. But the shoes, something about the way the shoes stood in their tidy, innocuous line, said different.

"Why did you take them?"

"You're thinking they're souvenirs?"

"I . . . I don't know what to think."

"So don't," he said with a shrug, then disconcertingly changed the subject. "Well, it's a good thing you're here. I was just going out to look for you."

"Why?"

"Something terrible's happened to Robbie."

The flatness of his voice was completely at odds with his choir boy appearance. Angel's gaze dropped to his hands, but they were empty. She'd been expecting to see him holding Robbie's shoes.

"What . . . ?"

"You'd better come see."

He led the way down to the second floor, on the other side of the building, then stood aside at the open door to Robbie's room. It was as cluttered as Macaulay's was tidy, but Angel didn't notice that as she stepped inside. Her gaze was drawn and riveted to the small body hanging by a rope from the overhead light fixture. It turned slowly, as though Robbie's death throes were just moments past. On the floor under him, a chair lay on its side.

Angel turned to confront Macaulay, but he was gone. She stepped out into the hallway to find it empty. Part of her wanted to run him down, to shake the angelic smugness from his features, but she made herself go back into Robbie's room. She righted the chair and stood on it. Taking her penknife from the back pocket of her jeans, she held Robbie against her as she sawed away at the rope. When the rope finally gave, Robbie's dead weight proved to be too much for her and he slipped from her arms, landing with a thud on the floor.

She jumped down and straightened his limbs. Forcing a finger between the rope and his neck, she slowly managed to loosen the pressure and remove the rope. Then, though she knew it was too late, though his skin was already cooling, body temperature dropping, she attempted CPR. While silently counting between breaths, she called for help, but no one stirred in the building around her. Either they were sleeping too soundly, or they just didn't want to get involved. Or maybe, a macabre part of her mind suggested, Macaulay's already killed them all. Maybe she hadn't walked by sleeping runaways and street kids on her way to Macaulay's room, but by their corpses . . .

~~She forced the thought out of her mind, refusing to let it take hold.~~

She worked until she had no more strength left. Slumping against a nearby wall, she stared at the body, but couldn't see it for the tears in her eyes.

It was a long time before she could get to her feet. When she left Robbie's room, she didn't go downstairs and leave the building to call the police. She went upstairs, to Macaulay's room. Every room she passed was empty, the sleeping figures all woken and fled. Macaulay's room was empty as well. It looked the same as it had earlier, with one difference. The sleeping bag and the clothes were gone. The line of shoes remained.

Angel stared at them for a long time before she picked up Everett's boots. She carried them with her when she left the building and stopped at the nearest payphone to call the police.

There was no note and the coroner ruled it a suicide. But there was still an APB out on Macaulay and no longer only in connection with Everett's death. Two of the pairs of shoes found in his squat were identified as belonging to recent murder victims; they could only assume that the rest did as well. The police had never connected the various killings, Lou told Angel later, because the investigations were handled by so many different precincts and, other than the missing footwear, the M.O. in each case was completely different.

Behind his cherubic features, Macaulay proved to have been a monster.

What Angel didn't understand was Robbie's suicide. She wouldn't let it go and finally, after a week of tracking down and talking to various street kids, she began to put together another picture of Macaulay. He wasn't just a killer; he'd also made a habit of molesting the street kids with whom he kept company. Their sex made no difference—just the younger the better. Coming from his background, Macaulay was a classic case of "today's victim becoming tomorrow's predator"— a theorem put forth by Andrew Vachss, a New York lawyer specializing in juvenile justice and child abuse with whom Angel had been in correspondence.

Even more startling was the realization that Macaulay probably hadn't killed Everett for whatever his usual reasons were, but because Everett had tried to help Robbie stand up to Macaulay. In a number of recent conversations Angel had with runaways she discovered that Everett had often given them money he'd panhandled, or shown them safe places to flop for a night.

Why Everett had needed to hide this philanthropic side of himself, no one was ever going to find out, but Angel thought she now knew why Robbie had killed himself: it wasn't just the shame of being abused—a shame that kept too many victims silent—but because Everett had died trying to protect him. For the sweet soul that Robbie had been, Angel could see how he would be unable to live with himself after what had happened that night.

But the worst was that Macaulay was still free. Two weeks after Everett's death he still hadn't been apprehended. Lou didn't hold out much hope of finding him.

"A kid like that," he told Angel over lunch the following Saturday, "he can just disappear into the underbelly of any big city. Unless he gets picked up someplace and they run his sheet, we might never hear from him again."

Angel couldn't face the idea of Macaulay in some other city, killing, sexually abusing the runaways on its streets, protected by his cherubic features, his easy smile, his guileless eyes.

"All we can hope," Lou added, "is that he picks himself the wrong victim next time—someone meaner than he is, someone quicker with a knife—so that when we do hear about him again, he'll be a number on an ID tag in some morgue."

"But this business of his taking his victims' shoes," Angel said.

"We've put it on the wire. By this time, every cop in the country has had their duty sergeant read it to them at roll call."

And that was it. People were dead. Kids already feeling hopeless carried new scars. She had a dead man visiting her in her dreams, demanding she do she didn't know what. And Macaulay went free.

Angel couldn't let it go at that, but there didn't seem to be anything more that she could do.

All week long, as soon as she goes to sleep, Everett haunts her dreams.

"I know what you were really like," she tells him. "I know you were trying to help the kids in your own way."

For the children.

"And I know why Macaulay killed you."

He stands in the misting rain, the need still plain in his eyes, the curious bundle held against his chest. He doesn't try to approach her anymore. He just stands there, half swallowed in mist and shadow, watching her.

"What I don't know is what you want from me."

The rain runs down his cheeks like tears.

"For God's sake, *talk* to me."

But all he says is, "Do it for the children. Not for me. For the children."

"Do *what?*"

But then she wakes up.

Angel dropped by Jilly's studio on the Sunday night. Telling Jilly she just wanted some company, for a long time she simply sat on the Murphy bed and watched Jilly paint.

"It's driving me insane," she finally said. "And the worst thing is, I don't even believe in this crap."

Jilly looked up from her work and pushed her hair back from her eyes, leaving a streak of Prussian blue on the errant locks.

"Even when you dream about him every night?" she asked

Angel sighed. "Who knows what I'm dreaming, or why."

"Everett does," Jilly said.

"Everett's dead."

"True."

"And he's not telling."

Jilly laid down her brush and came over to the bed. Sitting down beside Angel, she put an arm around Angel's shoulders and gave her a comforting hug.

"This doesn't have to be scary," she said.

"Easy for you to say. This is all old hat for you. You like the fact that it's real."

"But—"

Angel turned to her. "I don't want to be part of this other world. I don't *want* to be standing at the check-out counter and have seriously to consider which of the headlines are real and which aren't. I can't deal with that. I can barely deal with this . . . this haunting."

"You don't have to deal with anything except for Everett," Jilly told her. "Most people have a very effective defensive system against paranormal experiences. Their minds just automatically find some rational explanation for the unexplainable that allows them to put it aside and carry on with their lives. You'll be able to do the same thing. Trust me on this."

"But then I'll be just denying something that's real."

Jilly shrugged. "So?"

"I don't get it. You've been trying to convince me for years that stuff like this is real and now you say just forget it?"

"Not everybody's equipped to deal with it," Jilly said. "I just always thought you would be. But I was wrong to keep pushing at you about it."

"That makes me feel inadequate."

Jilly shook her head. "Just normal."

"There's something to be said for normal," Angel said.

"It's comforting," Jilly agreed. "But you do have to deal with Everett, because it doesn't look like he's going to leave you alone until you do."

Angel nodded slowly. "But do what? He won't tell me what he wants."

"It happens like that," Jilly said. "Most times spirits can't communicate in a straightforward manner, so they have to talk in riddles, or mime, or whatever. I think that's where all the obliqueness in fairy tales comes from: they're memories of dealing with real paranormal encounters."

"That doesn't help."

"I know it doesn't," Jilly said. She smiled. "Sometimes I think I just talk to hear my own voice." She looked across her studio to where finished paintings lay stacked against the wall beside her easel, then added thoughtfully, "I think I've got an idea."

Angel gave her a hopeful look.

"When's the funeral?" Jilly asked.

"Tomorrow. I took up a collection and raised enough so that Everett won't have to be buried in a pauper's grave."

"Well, just make sure Everett's buried with his boots on," Jilly told her.

"That's *it*?"

Jilly shrugged. "It scared Macaulay enough to take them, didn't it?"

"I suppose. . . ."

For all she's learned about his hidden philanthropic nature, she still feels no warmth towards the dead man. Sympathy, yes. Even pity. But no warmth.

The need in his eyes merely replaces the anger they wore in life; it does nothing to negate it.

"You were buried today," she says. "With your boots on."

The slow smile on the dead man's face doesn't fit well. It seems more a borrowed expression than one his features ever knew. For the first time in over a week, he approaches her again.

"A gift," he says, offering up the newspaper-wrapped bundle. "For the children."

For the children.

He's turned into a broken record, she thinks, stuck on one phrase.

She watches him as he moves into the light. He peels away the soggy newspaper, then holds up Macaulay's severed head. He grips it by the haloing blond hair, a monstrous, bloody artifact that he thrusts into her face.

Angel woke screaming. She sat bolt upright, clutching the covers to her chest. She had no idea where she was. Nothing looked right. Furniture loomed up in unfamiliar shapes, the play of shadows was all wrong. When a hand touched her shoulder, she flinched and screamed again, but it was only Jilly.

She remembered then, sleeping over, going to bed, late, late on that Sunday night, each of them taking a side of the Murphy bed.

"It's okay," Jilly was telling her. "Everything's okay."

Slowly, Angel felt the tension ease, the fear subside. She turned to Jilly and then had to smile. Jilly had been a street kid once—she was one of Angel's success stories. Now it seemed it was payback time, their roles reversed.

"What happened?" Jilly asked.

Angel trembled, remembering the awful image that had sent her screaming from her dream. Jilly couldn't suppress her own shivers as Angel told her about her dream.

"But at least it's over," Jilly said.

"What do you mean?"

"Everett's paid Macaulay back."

Angel sighed. "How can you *know* that?"

"I don't know it for sure. It just feels right."

"I wish everything was that simple," Angel said.

The phone rang in Angel's office at mid-morning. It was Lou on the other end of the line.

"Got some good news for you," he said.

Angel's pulse went into double-time.

"It's Macaulay," she said. "He's been found, hasn't he? He's dead."

There was a long pause before Lou asked, "Now how the hell did you know that?"

"I didn't," Angel replied. "I just hoped that was why you were calling me."

It didn't really make anything better. It didn't bring Robbie back, or take away the pain that Macaulay had inflicted on God knew how many kids. But it helped.

Sometimes her dreams still take her to that street where the neon signs and streetlights turn a misting rain into a carnival of light and shadow.

But the dead man has never returned.

THE LODGER
Fred Chappell

Fred Chappell is one of the most talented writers working today, blithely ignoring boundaries drawn between mainstream and genre fiction in his six novels, two collections of stories, and twelve volumes of poetry. He has received the Award in Literature from the National Institute of Arts and Letters, the Best Foreign Novel prize from the French Academy, and the Bollingen Prize in Poetry. His short fiction has been cited in *Best American Short Stories* and has won the World Fantasy Award. Chappell, a native of North Carolina, currently teaches at the University of North Carolina. His most recent book is a collection of essays on poetry, *Plowing Naked.*

"The Lodger" is a wonderfully wry novella about the unusual relationship between a young librarian (living) and a decadent poet (deceased). It comes from a small press chapbook, published as part of the short fiction series from Necronomicon Press (Warwick, Rhode Island), edited by Stefan Dziemianowicz.

—T.W.

1.

We better understand Robert Ackley's character and temperament when we recall that he referred to the presence that had recently usurped so large a part of his mind as The Lodger. He was a great admirer of Alfred Hitchcock's movies, and his assiduity in pursuing his interests had led him to read the novel from which the film was adapted, though with a dash of disappointment. He found the book clumsily cobbled together.

His judgement was generally trustworthy because he read a great deal. Poe's familiar phrase describes the tenor of his booklist—"many a quaint and curious volume of forgotten lore"—and he had lifelong opportunity to pursue arcane interests because he was a librarian at Bryan University in Plattsborough, North Carolina. His ongoing daily task in these years was to transfer titles from the card catalogue into the computer; the twentieth century had waited until its last decade to overtake Bryan University.

And to overtake Robert Ackley also. He was not altogether willing to be a modern person, even though he was still in his early thirties, sound of body and mind (until these latter nine months, at least), wholesome in his appetites, wryly humorous in disposition. He was a slight man with dark hair cut straight across his forehead, a gauzy swatch of moustache, and bright inquisitive eyes as black as licorice. Not exactly prepossessing, we might say, but those lively eyes often attracted the notice of females in whom Robert took a pleasant casual interest.

Bryan University was not one of the largest, and its library, the David Shelton Greene Library, included only some two million volumes. In these days that number may fairly be described as a modest one, yet five zeroes with an integer comprise an obese magnitude when it comes to counting books. It is hard to be convinced that human beings have ever known or needed to know two million different ideas. There were surely enough *curious* volumes among the ones he recatalogued to keep Ackley's lazy connoisseurship fastidious. He decided early on that he would have to forego reading such promised delights as a three-volume history of Burmese marriage customs, a *soi disant* "Tantric" interpretation of the *Kaballah*, a duodecimo treatise on the engineering feats of the Mongols, and even the newly discovered translation of the *Satyricon* by Sir Richard Burton.

Even so, the shelves and tables and chairs and floors of his snug three-room apartment on Granby Street were stacked, strewn, and scattered with all sorts of titles that Ackley had turned up in the catalogue, books that had aroused no interest other than his own in years, pages that had not felt the pressure of human gaze since their first publication. There must have been a good one hundred fifty of these, and if we are constrained to choose one title to serve as an index to Ackley's taste and to represent the multitude of these volumes we might single out Annie Francé's *Die Tragödie des Paracelsus*, published by Seifert in 1924 at Stuttgart.

He was a dillettante—as we see. For the Francé opus is reckoned by those who are renowned in judging such things as of little value as science, history, drama, or poetry. Even for Ackley its main attraction was that it was obscure; for though he did profess an interest in alchemy and some other occult sciences, he had only opened the play in the middle, jogged along for a few pages with one finger in his German dictionary, and then laid it aside, perhaps to look into it more closely later on, perhaps to return it to the library with the regretful conviction that life is devastatingly *brevis* and a mastery of German excruciatingly *longa*.

The book that afflicted him, the book that brought on the advent of The Lodger, was not a striking volume in the least. It was poetry and as slender as those volumes usually are. Its salient features, according to Ackley's judgement, were that it was published privately in Asheville, North Carolina, in 1934, and that it had been written by Lyman Scoresby. It was entitled *Chants of a Wander-Star*.

In light of later developments, we might make a lame joke by saying that Lyman Scoresby was hardly a name to conjure with. It is true that his name is but barely known to scholars of American literature and nowhere appears in the anthologies or histories and that he never even supplied subject matter for journal articles. A lonesome footnote in one book review or another mentions him, usually in parentheses, and to trace his name in literary history is rather like trying to outline the flight of a firefly on the far side of a lake. There are occasional gleams at random points but little hint of coherent pattern.

He attracted Robert Ackley's notice because he had once been associated with that strange group of artists and writers who had gathered in Cleveland in the 1920s: Samuel Loveman the poet and William Sommers the painter, the artist and architect William Lescaze, Hart Crane and his philosopher friend Sterling Croydon, the stage designer Richard Rychtarik and his wife Charlotte, the accomplished pianist. There were others too. H. P. Lovecraft, though not a resident of Cleveland, was once a visitor among them, as was the blind mathematical theorist who called himself "Dormouse," and the taciturn, ever patient observer of the group, the book designer E. Warburton, to whose later casual memoir, "Songsters in a Flock," we owe our knowledge of his friends.

They were never formally organized—being too anarchical for that—and so they never gave their group a name. And after the baffling disappearance of Sterling Croydon in 1923, these artists and thinkers scattered themselves across America, keeping so far apart from one another that it seemed their conscious plan to do so. But intermittently for the three years earlier they had met and rejoiced in each other's company.

E. Warburton implies in his account that it was the poet Lyman Scoresby who acquainted this homegrown Cleveland avant garde with the use of drugs. Scoresby was a mysterious figure even to them, a vagabond who claimed to have extensive knowledge of such things as European movements in painting, of the group of decadent poets currently raising bourgeois eyebrows in San Francisco, of the sexual practices of Lafcadio Hearn, of the most abstruse oriental philosophies. He had written, and published at his own expense, a sonnet sequence, *Spindrift Twilights*, which Hart Crane had praised as being "pretty unusual, after all—at least not the usual wagonload of horseshit."

But even for the redoubtable Crane Scoresby's personal habits were too bizarre to permit a close friendship to develop. Scoresby as a general practice engorged a number of obscure and poisonous-smelling drugs at once, draped himself in a diaphanous silk robe shoulder to toe, and sat for hours on a scrap of Ispahan carpet in his apartment bedroom, chanting incomprehensible phrases, incantations in no known language. Crane enjoyed Scoresby's drugs, the cocaine and the various cannabis derivatives, but could not put up with the man himself, considering him a poseur. "As phony as a glass eye on a bulldog," he said.

In artistic terms, at least, the description seemed accurate. There was nothing original about such poems as "Meditation of the Lycanthrope," "Etude in Puce and Nacre," and "Secret Glances." The sonnet beginning "Though vile thy kisses, drawn am I to thee" was easy material for one of Hart Crane's obscene parodies, one that he improvised at a party while being so hilariously inebriated he did not notice Scoresby's presence in the room. Scoresby's reaction to the incident is not recorded, but it is likely that he simply shrugged it off.

As far as Robert Ackley could discern—at a distance of some sixty years—that weary sardonic careless shrug had characterized Scoresby's attitude toward life. Though he had died (according to fairly reliable rumor) in Buenos Aires in 1945, he wrote to the end the kind of verse which was already fading from fashion when the century began. Lines rubbly with semiprecious stones—agates, onyxes, beryls, and the like; quatrains fetid with headaching perfumes and incenses; sonnets that mentioned, but did not describe, "unspeakable desires," "sable impurities," "unnameable caresses," and so forth. All this was Scoresby's stock in trade, the images he lived for, the phrases he died among.

What gave Scoresby the confidence to shrug life off like a lightly dozing sleeper brushing away a fly was his steady conviction that he was immortal. So reports Warburton in his "Songsters" account. The names of Guillaume Apollinaire, T. S. Eliot, Arthur Symons, J.J. Fleury, and the others would blaze in the firmament like ruptured stars but then—like those same stars—would fade and disperse to filmy rags. The name of Lyman Scoresby, the name that soulless injustice had treated as a mere tattered ghost during his earthly years, would come to life again and burn with a strong steady light.

But it took a long time for Robert Ackley to understand that the life Scoresby was trying to assume was Ackley's own. The struggle began when he woke one morning with a strong craving for nicotine. He had once been a smoker for a short time, but that had been seven years ago, and when he decided to give up the habit he was able to do so without fuss or fret. But now that he felt such desire for a cigarette to accompany his customary single cup of Maxwell House he tried to think why. There had been a dream, one of those vivid morning dreams that occur when the mind is on the edge of waking. There had been tobacco smoke in it and . . . water. There had been water in it. When he pondered the fact of the water, a word came to his mouth and he said it aloud: "Hookah." Then he smiled and nodded; he remembered reading Lyman Scoresby's poem just before he dropped asleep last night. "The Hookah" was the opening poem in *Chants of a Wander-Star*.

He fetched the volume from his bedside table to his breakfast bar, perched on a stool with his coffee, and read through the poem with desultory curiosity. In the cool morning light it seemed even less notable than before.

> *Strange visions in the smoke are gliding*
> *Like dusky isles in eastern seas*
> *Where foreign constellations sliding*
> *Suggest most ancient memories!*

The latter seven stanzas of the poem bore out the lack of promise displayed in the first. Ackley found it a vapid production entirely.

But his severe judgement did not quell his desire for tobacco and all day long he found that he had to keep pushing this desire to the back of his mind. The end result was a deafening headache and so he stopped by Keeler's Drug Store on his way home after work and picked up a package of Old Golds. He was startled by the expense; when last he smoked, cigarettes had cost fifty cents a package.

In his apartment he did not light up immediately but began to rummage through the clothes in his closet for a piece of apparel he could not at first put a name to. Vexed at a palpable absence, vexed with himself, he dropped into his one armchair, smoked the cigarette he didn't like, and tried to understand what was wrong.

In the first place, what had he been seeking in his closet?

He smoked down to the filter before it came to him that he had been trying to find his smoking jacket. He gasped at this revelation, then giggled. He had never owned a smoking jacket, had never felt the least impulse to buy one. At work he wore jacket and tie and blue jeans and his only concern about fashion otherwise was to make sure he didn't wear a T-shirt with an offensive slogan. To Robert Ackley a smoking jacket was as alien a concept as fuzzy pink bedroom slippers— and most particularly the sort of jacket of which he had formed an image: a burgundy velvet creation with scarlet silk lapels and wide cuffs and a gold cord sash.

Good Lord, he thought. What in the world has got into me?

He determined to puzzle it out. He went into the kitchen, took a Budweiser from the refrigerator, popped it and came back into the living room. Abruptly he rose again from the armchair and after a moment's search returned with a glass. That was odd enough, for he was used to sipping from the can, but then he poured it up, a scrap of poetry flashing into his head: *liqueur jaune qui fait suer.* Where had he ever heard that? And how had he memorized it? His French was not even as good as his pitiable German.

The one clue he had to the distress of this day was Lyman Scoresby. He had thumbed about in *Chants of a Wander-Star* last night in bed and wondered about the career of that marginal versifier—born out of his proper time and now remembered by Ackley in an era even less proper. He got the book from where it sat by his cold coffee cup on the breakfast bar and riffled through it. There must have been a particular poem here that had brought about his restless sleep, his restless day.

But all of Scoresby's strophes were so vague and pastel that they misted into one another. Ackley could not remember whether he had drowsed off over "Assignation at Midnight" or "Vampire Kisses" or "The Wine of the Unforgotten" or "Violet Eyes." Still he persisted. He did not want to take up smoking again and he was determined to suppress savagely any budding passion for velvet smoking jackets.

The centerpiece of *Chants* was a longish effort entitled "The Incantation." It was divided into four parts, of which the first was comprehensible enough and conventional enough too, a poet's ordinary boast that his work shall outlast marble and bronze. The remaining sections surpassed Scoresby's usual vagueness. Part II began with these lines:

> *Sylphs of elements aethereal,*
> *In all contiguous shades and properties,*
> *Numinous and nominal, employ*
> *To every corner of the universe*
>
> *Might and power and ebon puissance*
> *In service to thy servant proud and humble,*
> *His willing spirit joining to your strength*
> *Infernal, and his soul to subterranean*
>
> *Dis indentured and the compact signed*
> *Eternally in blood, eternally,*
> *Indissolubly bound, admixtured, mingled. . . .*

Mere blather, mere daft natter.

But then Ackley thought he noticed something and took a closer look. Sure enough: his half forgotten knowledge of Latin had picked out an acrostic. The initial letters of the lines spelled it out: *Sint mihi dei Acherontii propitii! Ignei, aerii, aquatici, spiritus salvete! Orientis Princeps Beelzebub,* etc.

Etc.

Etc.: It was a classic invocation for the appearance of Beelzebub, or Mephistophilis, or Satan . . . What's in a name? Scoresby had designed his poem to call up the Prince of Darkness by whatever cognomen he might care to be hailed.

Supposing that notion to be true, for what purpose had he done so?

Why, for the same reason that any weakminded ne'er-do-well poetaster would sign to such a stupid ruinous association—to insure the longevity of his work.

But in Scoresby's case the terms of the contract must have been a little different; he must have secured an agreement for the reanimation of his spirit in the mind and body of another person, someone who would be living after he died, someone sympathetic to his poetic ambitions and exotic philosophies. He would enter this victim—whom he had to count upon as being more or less willing—and begin a campaign to rescue his stanzas from oblivion. Only a poet or an utter idiot would be willing to strike such a bargain, giving up as hostage his immortal soul.

And yet Scoresby might have had reason to consider himself lucky. We know poets as a puling, equivocal, and feeble race of beings, do we not? Over the centuries some hundreds or even thousands of them must have called upon the Tyrant of Shadows to pocket their souls and preserve their phrases and Satan had rejected them. Perhaps the Evil One felt momentary pity for a mankind long overburdened with verses, or perhaps he knew that these spirits were already forfeit to him on other grounds. Or maybe he considered these particular souls too dingy and cheapjack to be worth the collecting.

But for whatever reason he must have appeared to Scoresby and taken an interest in his proposal.

Robert Ackley regarded this train of thought rather as if he were reading a detective story and trying to discover the author's solution. Or like someone trying to diagnose and repair an ailing kitchen appliance. For though he probably did not truly believe in Satan, his powers and dominion, he did not entirely disbelieve, either. In this matter, as in so many others, he was strongly neutral.

So the situation presented itself to him in pragmatic terms: the spirit of the dead poet Lyman Scoresby had been summoned by Ackley's reading of "The Incantation" to take over the young librarian in order to work his posthumous stratagem. It was as if he were a bright new duplex apartment infested by a ghost. The task at hand was simply to get rid of this unwelcome lodger, to drive him away.

Then occurred the incident that removed the problem from the provenance of the suppositional. A voice spoke in Ackley's mind, cool and unmistakable. Its timbre was almost precisely that of Vincent Price in one of his sinister roles—unctuousness soaked in sarcasm. And the voice said:

Drive me out! What makes you think you can do that, you pustulant inconsequential little turd?

2.

With these words began the struggle of Robert Ackley for his life. It was not epic in proportion, nor cosmic in its philosophic terms, but for the young man it was in deadly earnest. His mettle and his cunning were tested thoroughly. And so was his temper. The moment he heard those first two sentences in his mind, he no longer thought of Lyman Scoresby as The Lodger but as The Squatter, and he determined to evict the dead poet, even if it meant standing against Satan and all his legions.

Scoresby broke into these valiant resolvings. "As for Satan," he said, "that notion is all putrid claptrap. The simple anagram is present merely as a red herring to draw attention away from the truly effective mechanism of the poem. There are other, more complex, anagrams in the lines that spell out in letter symbols Sterling Croydon's mathematical formulae for the manipulation of temporal-spatial emplacement. It is science, not hoodoo."

"That is valuable information to have," Ackley said.

"Not for you," replied Scoresby. "I have observed your mind at extremely close range for three days now and a more muddled swamp of puerility and incoherence would be impossible to discover. There is no way you could comprehend the information. You possess no strength of character, no sense of purpose, no true love of learning, no aptitude for luxury, no capacity for logic, no taste in literature."

"No taste in literature? You say that to a man who is engrossed in your *Chants of a Wander-Star?*"

Ackley's attempt at sarcasm made no impression upon Scoresby. "I would almost prefer to be devoured by hogs than read by Robert Ackley. I watched your perusal of 'Evanescent Crepuscule.' You caught not the least glimmer of even one of its beauties. There is a delicate nimbus of nuance about every line of that sonnet, yet you worked through it like a groom mucking out a stable. You have no ear for assonance, no eye for filigree. A poet must clout you with a brickbat to catch your attention."

"Well then, if I'm such unpromising material, why don't you go take over someone else's mind?"

A dark bitterness suffused Scoresby's reply. "Since my death you are the first to look into my poems. The only one! Can you comprehend that? I was Hart Crane's unacknowledged mentor, his greatest influence. I talked with Emile Verhaeren in a cafe in Bruges one rainy September afternoon, learning the secret of his music. My long correspondence with George Sterling is lost now, but it changed the whole complexion of his work. It was from me that J.J. Fleury purloined that famous line: *'Bateau des rêves, blessé par la lune!'* Yet fifty years have passed since anyone even so much as opened *Chants of a Wander-Star,* and here I am, called by my 'Incantation' from that zone of silent oblivion, to greet my savior—a tin-eared slovenly tasteless little nincompoop in tennis shoes!"

Ackley was so addled by the acridity of this outburst that he could only ask, "What's wrong with tennis shoes?"

"They're called Nikés, for God's sake! Can even that hamhanded irony be lost upon you?"

"No," Ackley said defensively. Then: "Yes." Then: "I don't know."

Scoresby continued in a tone resonant with suppressed malevolence. "But I do not despair. The situation seems impossible. It is not that I must make a silk purse from a sow's ear; it is more like having to fashion a Venus de Milo from a lump of wet cow dung. But I believe that I can persevere and triumph."

"You'll have to do it without my help," Ackley said. "And so far you haven't given me cause to be happy with our relationship."

"Oh, but I shall," Scoresby said. "I have many gifts to confer. I am privy to confidences you cannot yet imagine. I know things about life and love and literature that talented poets would kill to learn. The greatest part of my knowledge lies far beyond the tiny purview of your acquaintance."

"Maybe you know a lot of stuff I don't care to know."

"Once you glimpse the vistas I can provide, once you taste the hidden knowledge I have acquired, you will find my outlook irresistible."

This prediction turned out to be lacking in accuracy. Ackley discovered that his attraction to literary obscurities was never so strong as he had imagined. Scoresby related encounters with poets and writers from nations that had long disappeared from the maps, but Ackley could not respond with enthusiasm. He had heard of hardly any of these scribblers; sometimes he had not even heard of the cities they inhabited. Now and then some famous spot would be mentioned, the Cafe Deux Magots or the Catalán or the Cafe Royal or The Fabulous Pickwick—but the writers with whom Scoresby had conversed, argued, and brought to heel in these legendary rooms were unknown to Ackley.

"It is no use trying to educate you," Scoresby said, his tone pale with disappointment. "The completely ignorant are ineducable. Knowledge has to find some little niche to serve as toehold. But you—you are a blank page."

"I am a more widely read fellow than almost anyone else you could have latched onto," Ackley said.

"So you say. And yet you know nothing of Montalini's ballet, *Schisma*, or the cycle of Onotrio's poems that suggested it."

"No."

"You never heard of Henri Dollé's scandalous novel, *Les Liaisons Scabreuses.*"

"No."

"You never even heard of that legendary literary review from the Four Oaks group in Texas, *Hashish Cayuse.*"

"Never."

"I have returned too soon," Scoresby said. "I have arrived in a new Dark Age when literature and art and music are unknown. I suppose the best minds of your generation are preoccupied with television wrestling shows and the Roller Derby."

"Well—not the *very* best."

"I despair of ever intriguing your intellectual curiosity or your aesthetic sensibility. You have neither." The tone of his words sharpened then and Ackley heard a hint of threat. "But there are other means to my ends."

"What are you referring to?"

"You'll understand. Soon."

But Ackley did not at first understand; he only began to experience jittery days and excited sleep. His mind was distracted and his body incapable of repose. When he sat he twiddled his fingers and when he stood he twisted in his shoes. His condition was just the same as it had been during the day he had been plagued by a craving for cigarettes. He knew that he wanted something, that Scoresby had worked upon his sleeping mind to produce this powerful desire in him, but he could not say what it was that he desired.

He knew that when he was asleep he was almost defenseless, that the vengeful poet could exacerbate his nerves dreadfully. Yet clear understanding did away with the artificial desire as easily as light devours shadow. As soon as Ackley comprehended that Scoresby had planted in his psyche an artificial need for tobacco, he threw away those cigarettes and had not craved them since.

Of course, as soon as Ackley figured out the process, Scoresby, inhabiting his mind, also knew. Therefore, Scoresby was producing in him a strong craving for something or other but would not say what, because when Ackley knew the object of his enforced desire he would be able to disregard that desire.

So he only grew more anxious and more wildly nervous. Scoresby operated in his mind at night and was silent when he was awake. When his colleagues at the library remarked upon the state of his nerves, Ackley replied that he was trying to give up coffee. He had decided long ago that he could speak frankly to no one about the truth of his situation. They would neither believe nor understand.

So he tried to figure out what Scoresby was causing him to desire by analyzing the sensations he felt. It was something liquid, probably a liquor of some sort, and he detected in his mouth the faint anticipatory taste of licorice and in his soft palate the strong odor of gymnasium floors.

This latter olfactory clue was tantalizing and when he tried to put it together with what he knew of Scoresby's life and personality he at first drew a blank. Only the chance occurrence of Pablo Picasso's name in a newspaper article reminded him: *The Absinthe Drinkers*. Scoresby was trying to work up in his host a thirst for absinthe.

Ackley sat in his armchair and laughed aloud and when he did so the voice which had not spoken in actual words for two days returned. Scoresby's tone was sour and disappointed. "I do not find this situation amusing."

"Oh, come on," Ackley said. "Absinthe. You've got to be kidding. In the first place, it's been illegal for decades. And in the *real* first place, this is America. We don't drink absinthe here. I know you know better than that. What the hell are you trying to do?"

"I'm only trying to make myself comfortable. I find that I am forced to inhabit, as it were, a shabby suite of rooms in a particularly seedy hotel. I am only trying to furnish the locus with a few civilized amenities."

"Well, you can stop trying to get me hooked on all the vices you used to enjoy. I've got enough of my own, thank you."

"Your boasting is pointless," Scoresby replied. "You worry about having three beers instead of two in the evening. You fear you'll become overweight. You fret endlessly about something called cholesterol and what it will do to your arteries. Can you possibly conceive how humiliating it is for me to be trapped in the psyche of a man who worries about the inner walls of his arteries? Do you realize what disgusting subliminal images are thrown at me when you think about eating a hamburger sandwich?"

"I hadn't thought," Ackley said. "I hadn't known you could see my subconscious thoughts so clearly." He fell silent under the force of a presentiment. "Oh my God. That means you can see into my sexual fantasies too."

"Let us please not go into this subject. The whole matter is stomach-wrenching."

"Well, you're a dirty old man by vocation. I'll bet you're enough of a voyeur to get turned on."

"*Turned on*. The mechanical nature of your metaphor gives you away completely. Do you realize that you're about to fall in love with a female gym teacher? That your most daring fantasy only involves this woman and a trampoline. Bounce bounce bounce—like a windup toy. Have you happened to notice that this gym-creature has freckles?"

"I think they're cute," Ackley said.

"Cute? Cute! This conversation is utterly nauseating. I really cannot put up with it. A female gym teacher . . . Oh, this is hell, nor are we out of it."

"Well," said Ackley, "I'm sorry my sex life isn't sordid enough for you."

"It isn't even sex, not in the true sense—and I'm not convinced it's a life, either."

"I'm sure you have better ideas."

"I believe so," the poet said, and then there began to take shape in Ackley's mind a face and afterward a figure. Cold blue eyes, and a complexion fair and unblemished, a careless lock of ash-blond hair falling over a low forehead, and a full and petulant mouth that hinted cruelty. This face looked over a naked white shoulder, and then the figure turned slowly, presenting itself full length.

"Not my type, I'm afraid," Ackley said. "An Etonian, I presume?"

"He is The Love that Dare Not Speak Its Name," Scoresby said. "You would know him at first as a mere wanton, but once you became intimate you would find unexpected shadows in his character, surprising profundities."

"No I wouldn't."

"You would be taught," Scoresby promised. "You need to realize that each of the appetites can be developed into a wild access of poetic inspiration, of dark correspondences and revelatory hours of ecstasy."

"I've got no interest in playing with boys whether they speak their names or not." Ackley's voice was firm. "I'm not interested in burning incense or smoking hashish or buying a lot of haberdashery in mauve and puce. You've got the wrong guy, that's all. I'm never going to change."

"You spend half your life in sleep," Scoresby said. "That's when I work my will. We have a long way to go together, you and I."

3.

Next afternoon Ackley began his counteroffensive. In the supermarket he bought a case of beer, economy-size packages of potato chips, Fritos, and fried pork rinds. For reading matter he picked up a *TV Guide* and a tabloid newspaper that informed him in its lead story that Elvis Presley was one of Siamese twins separated at birth and taught to sing by angels sent to warn him against drug abuse.

He had planned a full evening for himself and his Squatter. He ate most of the junk food, got squidgy on twelve cans of Budweiser, and sat through a loud television session in which a hairy wrestler in silver lamé trunks and cape promised dire revenge upon his personal nemesis, a surly fellow who was billed as The Eviscerator but found the pronunciation of his sobriquet a tricky proposition.

There Ackley sat in his armchair, munching, guzzling, and stunned, while his brain cells committed suicide. After an hour he switched to a political talk show; its format seemed identical to the wrestling show, shrieking blusterers trading insults. He then watched four sitcoms in a row, foreseeing the punchlines and mouthing them along with the actors. Finally he turned to the C-Span channel and watched the public workings of the government; this spectacle seemed to combine all the qualities of the programming he had watched earlier: hysteria, predictability, illogic, swagger, decibel worship, and hollow threats. Two hours he spent with the Senate before he went to bed convinced that he must have struck his Squatter a telling blow, perhaps a fatal one.

He had certainly dealt sorely with himself. He woke with a dull red headache, grainy eyes, a tongue as shaggy as an angora cat, and a painful bladder. He tended his urgencies as best he could and hoped that this coming day would not be molested by those unsettling nonspecific yearnings with which Scoresby had been attacking him. Maybe he had crippled the poet's powers.

"What a dolt you are," the voice said. "Do you think I could find mere simpleminded vulgarity threatening? Don't you understand that poets develop early in their lives armor to protect themselves from the babble of mass idiocy? You'll have to try harder than that, little fellow. If you can. For I believe that such a regimen as you propose will be harder on you than on me."

Ackley, heavyheaded and with trembling hands, could only agree with his adversary. It was a trial to get his coffee made this morning, and after he had poured a cup and added his skim milk he could not bear to taste it. He left it standing on the breakfast bar and went off to work bloated and crapulous.

His condition was such that he could not even attempt to formulate a new plan of attack and he was resigned to the idea that Scoresby would punish his sleep again tonight, worming some silly craving deeper into his psyche, undermining his strength even more.

He knew that he had to hit the poet swiftly and forcibly, but his tenderest spot, his overawing vanity, seemed impossible to reach. It was only too bad that *Spindrift Twilights* and *Chants of a Wander-Star* had been so thoroughly ignored by critics. If they had not been, Ackley could read Scoresby's unfavorable notices again and again until the plummy scribbler shriveled to a prune.

His aesthetic sensibilities also seemed immune. The temperament that could withstand an evening of World Championship Wrestling and *The National Enquirer* could take any brutal punishment . . . But perhaps that choice of poisons had been mistaken; perhaps it was not popular vulgarity that would debilitate Scoresby but an entirely different aesthetic philosophy.

At work he raided the library shelves and brought home a box full of poetry books of widely varying sorts. He took them out of the box immediately after clearing away his frugal supper and stacked them by his faithful armchair—which he had begun to think of as his "command post." Here he laid out poets beatnik, bleatnik, and fruitnik; propaganda poets of every persuasion, Marxist, feminist, environmentalist, animal rightist, animal leftist, fetishist, capitalist, elitist, anti-elitist, pacifist, militarist, pessimist, and even optimist; poets heterosexual, homosexual, bisexual, pansexual, neuter, and undecided; poets advocating revolution in Haiti, the U.S.S.R., Chile, Bosnia, France, Canada, the Solomon Islands, Nebraska, and Antarctica; poets for and against, beneath and above, behind and beyond; cowboy poets and poets playing Indian; regional poets and universal poets; poets pragmatic or mystic or merely helpless; love poets and hate poets and

indifferent poets; poets who wrote in nonstop blocks of print and others who
brought out books filled with blank pages.

Ackley served himself soda water on the rocks and gritted his teeth and began.
The first book he picked up was called *Bustin' on the Brazos* and the poem he
turned to was "Old Red."

> *Well, they said Old Red was a helluva horse,*
> *But me and the boys didn't feel no remorse*
> *And my nerve didn't flag*
> *When I roped that nag*
> *And swore I'd ride her to hell or worse!*

This poet was named Willie "Tex" Brannigan and he was powerful partial to
exclamation points.

After twenty pages or so Ackley began to feel saddle sore, so he switched to a
chapbook of wild typography called *Werewolf Amoco Gas Station Sutra* by someone who signed himself "Loper." This poet had raised the art of poetry to pure
interjection; his lines were made up of transliterated animal cries: "Wooaugh!
Rrrrr! Wuhwuhwoo! Ahaagh" and so on. Now and then he would return to the
minor theme announced in his title and throw in a phrase like "Next gas 100
mi." and "unleaded" and "high test." Loper's lines were hard to concentrate on,
Ackley found, and when he tried to read them aloud he couldn't stop giggling.

Next up was Gerald Greyforth and his *Autobiography Regarded as a Species of
Refracted Flourish*. Reading the poem called "Weeds" (in which weeds were not
mentioned), Ackley could not decide whether Greyforth had visited the Alps or
not. Those mountains were often named but never described, yet it seemed at
least possible that some sort of sexual act had taken place among three people on
skis. But it was not clear in the least how Titian, Thelonius Monk, and the
elephant were involved. Ackley became impatient and flipped over to a poem
called "Lenox Avenue: 2:43 P.M., 1948 or '72."

> *I said did you see Lady Day was she really*
> *and Frank said Pardon me in that way he used to*
> *and nobody knew they would die then*
> *because after all he was Frank and she was*
> *Lady Day and how it all happened was beyond*
> *the taxis and the glare and Lenox even out to*
> *124th Street.*

Greyforth seemed to have trouble in concentrating on his subject matter, and his
way of muttering lines on the page made Ackley feel nervous and ashamed, as if
he were overhearing some poor deranged homeless person in the street and had
no way to give aid.

He found no relief in the next effort either, a book-length poem called *Squall*.
It was about "angel-headed hipsters" and incestuous impulses and unfortunate
gustatory experiences. Ackley turned from scanning the middle of the poem back
to the opening lines, then snapped the book shut. If this poet really had seen the

best minds of his generation, it was obvious that none of them had spoken to him.

And so on through the night till two A.M. Robert Ackley ran the gauntlet of contemporary poetry, feeling more and more dislocated with every page he turned.

When he rose on the morrow he still felt dislocated; he was lightheaded and forgetful and divined that some part of his morning was missing, even though he had kept to his usual routine. Then he realized that the presence of Lyman Scoresby was in some measure diminished in him. He could feel that the poet was still there—it was a sensation like standing in front of an open refrigerator—but he knew that he must be on the right track. Scoresby had suffered a hit, a palpable hit. Ackley wished that he knew which of the books had wreaked the most damage so that he could seek out that poet's *Collected Works* and deliver his Squatter a destroying barrage.

But such a tactic might not work. It was possible that Scoresby might develop an immunity to the ravages of contemporary poetry. Ackley had known two persons in his lifetime who claimed not only to read the stuff frequently but even to enjoy it. Now that he had given over a long evening to this experience, he did not know whether to admire his friends' fortitude or to doubt their veracity. Still, he would take no chances; he would move on to the next stage of his plan, escalating the ferocity of his attack.

It was the weekend, two days of promised October sunshine that Ackley would ordinarily have spent cycling or playing softball or fishing at Platt Lake. But he had his task before him and he felt, carrying another boxful of books home from the library on this lovely Friday evening, that he had acquired the ammunition necessary to make this onslaught upon Scoresby the final one.

He took pains to set a nourishing table: a small steak, baked potato, green salad, and a thawed slab of apple pie. He ate at his kitchen table, lonesome and somber, sipping iced tea and trying to clear his mind. When he felt sufficiently prepared, he marched to his command post, kicked his way through the books of poetry, cleared a space for the book-box, and set it down beside him. He leaned back in the armchair, closed his eyes and breathed deeply. He paused for a long dramatic moment, summoning his powers. Then he plunged his hand into the box and took out the first volume he touched.

It was Rhoda Taylor-Smythe-Bernstein's *Shakespeare and Other Crimes Against Women,* and it lived up to the promise of its title. This scholar had more grudges against the male animal than she had names for. Ackley learned to his surprise that the high regard Elizabethan male poets avowed for their sovereign was a plot to put womankind on a pedestal, thus making the gender more vulnerable to attack. He was astonished to find that the practice of using boys in female roles was a conspiracy designed to keep women away from the stage and therefore less important in the later history of English literature. But this eager savant did not stint in giving praise to Francis Bacon, after first advancing the thesis that the prim philosopher was a transvestite lesbian.

Ackley's consciousness had been raised by these pages to such a towering height that he experienced a brief attack of vertigo. So he put aside Taylor-Smythe-Bernstein's latter chronicle of the acts of the martyrs and took up an English translation of Guillaume Aride's famous *Of Syntactology.* Plunging into it at reckless speed, he soon mired and turned back to the title page to assure himself that he was indeed reading English and not some *bêche-de-mer* that combined English, French, and all the classical languages. "The *poikonos*," he read, "represents neither place nor time, person nor thing, vegetable nor mineral; neither a speech-particle nor a non-particle of incipient *discours*; neither consummation nor indifference; neither the primary state nor any state dependent upon sense-aporia *hors de soi en soi* in either of its possible tendencies toward *l'exergué* or *le propre*."

This was the real stuff—the kind of writing Ackley had heard about but had never looked into. He didn't understand it, of course, but then he hadn't expected to. He had counted upon its notorious silliness, its self-important pomposity, its disdain for human intelligence, and above all its barbarous macaronic cacophony of sound to drive the ghost of Scoresby out of both minds—his mind and the dead poet's own. He had counted most of all upon the versifier's hatred of bad French.

Ackley acquitted himself against Aride with real honor. When his attention slid around the text like a live escargot avoiding a diner's fork he would begin reading aloud. When he came to paragraphs impossible to pronounce he would place his fingertip upon each word as he went along and murmur the syllables slowly. Sometimes he found himself reduced to spelling the individual words letter by letter. He was valiant, he was determined, and he was confident of victory.

No fewer than 120 pages *Of Syntactology* were gone through in this way and Ackley felt that he had earned some refreshment. He visited the washroom and the kitchen, replenishing his iced tea, then rested himself and took out of the box his blind choice, Natterjee-Renaud's *Despotic Signifiers and the Babylonian Antireactionary Episteme*. He began the first paragraph with a soldierly feeling of duty but finished its perusal in white-faced alarm:

> Aride's post-signifying regime of subjectification struggles with an after-image of the regime of significance in the figure of some (absent) guarantor and guarantee of stable meaning, its only resource and solace being the delusion of individual subjectivity. Desire is either blocked, as by the meaninglessness of existence in the Sartrean "Absurd," bouncing off the blank wall onto the desolate subject; or surrendered, as in the Lacanian metonymy of desire for the lost object, falling into the black hole of tragic subjectivity.

Robert Ackley snapped the book shut. There was a film of sweat on his forehead and he stared in sheer terror into the space before him. Surely he must be mistaken in his impression. He opened the book again, turned over fifty pages, and once more began to read: "Lacan would say we are subjectified in language as a signifying system from which the signified has dropped out as the unapproachable Real, or we are subjectified in the Symbolic Order in which we are irremediably divided and condemned by desire to slip along the two poles of language (metaphor-condensation and metonymy-displacement) in the chain of signification."

This time he closed the book gently. Tiredly he leaned back into his armchair, rested his head on the cushion, and closed his eyes. It was no mistake. *He actually comprehended the sentence he had just read.* He wasn't able to paraphrase it; perhaps, like the sounds of static heard during a radio transmission, it was unparaphrasable. Yet it made sense to him; it spoke to him with an authority that had no use for logic, no need for communication in the normal sense of the word. There was an overmastering attitude attached to these words. In some implicit but undeniable fashion, and despite its froufrou of qualification and professorial persnickitiness, this sentence snapped an arm's-length salute, clicked its heels smartly, and barked *Heil!*

Slowly now and tentatively, Ackley began to search his mind for the presence of Scoresby. But he was only making sure of his conclusion, for he felt he already knew the truth. The poet had been driven off never to return. Ackley was free at last.

While he felt relief at this knowledge—it was rather like paying the last installment of a twenty-year house mortgage—he also felt let down, a bit disappointed. He had been so divided by Scoresby's presence and then later so intent on driving him away that he had not noticed how much the struggle had taken out of him. He was exhausted and felt darkly displaced. He knew he was a very different person from what he had been before.

He returned to the bathroom and rinsed his face with cold water and looked at himself in the mirror. He saw that he *had* changed and as he observed his features and attempted to study out the changes that had taken place, a sentence popped whole and unbidden in his mind as clearly as if it had spoken in his ear: "This signifying object (the face) is characterized by mere *relative* deterritorialization, for though its physicality is posited as a typological genome, its *difference* can be endlessly reproduced by other mirrors, as in any capitalist mass-production signification-web."

There are worse horrors than being haunted by ghosts. Scoresby had posed a threat to the integrity and sanity of his unwilling host. Yet it was Ackley's own defense that did him in.

Almost all of us have succeeded in exorcising the poet from ourselves, and we are forever afterward different persons than we imagined we could be. But the doom that came in later years to Robert Ackley was so terrible that Nature drew a merciful veil over his mind, causing him to imagine that he enjoyed his new situation and that he served some useful purpose in the scheme of things. He observed the fact but could not comprehend its truth: he had become the leading literary critic of the post-postmodernist generation. His first volume, *The Spirit Killeth: The Lost Signifier in the "Forgotten Poems" of Lyman Scoresby,* is reckoned a classic of its kind.

THE ERL-KING
Elizabeth Hand

Elizabeth Hand is the gifted author of the novels *Winterlong*, *Æstival Tide*, and *Icarus Descending*, as well as numerous works of short fiction. Her most recent novels are *Waking the Moon* and *Black Light*, the latter a dark fantasy about Andy Warhol's Factory. Hand, who hails from New York, studied acting and anthropology and worked for a number of years at the National Air and Space Museum, Smithsonian Institute in Washington, D.C. She now lives on the Maine coast with novelist Richard Grant and their children.

"The Erl-King" draws inspiration from the folk legend of the same name about a fey, seductive creature who imprisons women's souls. Hand has deftly turned the story into a dark modern fairy tale which is one of the very best novellas of the year. It is reprinted from the anthology *Full Spectrum 4*.

—T.W.

The kinkajou had been missing for two days now. Haley feared it was dead, killed by one of the neighborhood dogs or by a fox or wildcat in the woods. Linette was certain it was alive; she even knew where it was.

"Kingdom Come," she announced, pointing a long lazy hand in the direction of the neighboring estate. She dropped her hand and sipped at a mug of tepid tea, twisting so she wouldn't spill it as she rocked back and forth. It was Linette's turn to lie in the hammock. She did so with feckless grace, legs tangled in her long peasant skin, dark hair spilled across the faded canvas. She had more practice at it than Haley, this being Linette's house and Linette's overgrown yard bordering the woods of spindly young pines and birches that separated them from Kingdom Come. Haley frowned, leaned against the oak tree, and pushed her friend desultorily with one foot.

"Then why doesn't your mother call them or something?" Haley loved the kinkajou and justifiably feared the worst. With her friend exotic pets came and went, just as did odd visitors to the tumbledown cottage where Linette lived with her mother, Aurora. Most of the animals were presents from Linette's father, an elderly Broadway producer whose successes paid for the rented cottage and Linette's occasional artistic endeavors (flute lessons, sitar lessons, an incomplete course in airbrushing) as well as the bottles of Tanqueray that lined Aurora's bedroom. And, of course, the animals. An iguana whose skin peeled like mildewed wallpaper, finally lost (and never found) in the drafty dark basement where the girls held annual Hallowe'en seances. An intimidatingly large Moluccan cockatoo that escaped into the trees, terrorizing Kingdom Come's previous owner and his garden-party guests by shrieking at them in Gaelic from the wisteria. Finches and fire weavers small enough to hold in your fist. A quartet of tiny goats, Haley's favorites until the kinkajou.

The cockatoo started to smell worse and worse, until one day it flopped to the bottom of its wrought-iron cage and died. The finches escaped when Linette left the door to their bamboo cage open. The goats ran off into the woods surrounding Lake Muscanth. They were rumored to be living there still. But this summer Haley had come over every day to make certain the kinkajou had enough to eat, that Linette's cats weren't terrorizing it; that Aurora didn't try to feed it crème de menthe as she had the capuchin monkey that had fleetingly resided in her room.

"I don't know," Linette said. She shut her eyes, balancing her mug on her stomach. A drop of tea spilled onto her cotton blouse, another faint petal among faded ink stains and the ghostly impression of eyes left by an abortive attempt at batik. "I think Mom knows the guy who lives there now, she doesn't like him or something. I'll ask my father next time."

Haley prodded the hammock with the toe of her sneaker. "It's almost my turn. Then we should go over there. It'll die if it gets cold at night."

Linette smiled without opening her eyes. "Nah. It's still summer," she said, and yawned.

Haley frowned. She moved her back up and down against the bole of the oak tree, scratching where a scab had formed after their outing to Mandrake Island to look for the goats. It was early August, nearing the end of their last summer before starting high school, the time Aurora had named "the summer before the dark."

"My poor little girls," Aurora had mourned a few months earlier. It had been only June then, the days still cool enough that the City's wealthy fled each weekend to Kamensic Village to hide among the woods and wetlands in their Victorian follies. Aurora was perched with Haley and Linette on an ivied slope above the road, watching the southbound Sunday exodus of limousines and Porsches and Mercedes. "Soon you'll be gone."

"Jeez, Mom," laughed Linette. A plume of ivy tethered her long hair back from her face. Aurora reached to tug it with one unsteady hand. The other clasped a plastic cup full of gin. "No one's going anywhere, I'm going to Fox Lane,"— that was the public high school—"you heard what Dad said. Right, Haley?"

Haley had nodded and stroked the kinkajou sleeping in her lap. It never did anything but sleep, or open its golden eyes to half-wakefulness oh so briefly before finding another lap or cushion to curl into. It reminded her of Linette in that, her friend's heavy lazy eyes always ready to shut, her legs quick to curl around pillows or hammock cushions or Haley's own battle-scarred knees. "Right," said Haley, and she had cupped her palm around the soft warm globe of the kinkajou's head.

Now the hammock creaked noisily as Linette turned onto her stomach, dropping her mug into the long grass. Haley started, looked down to see her hands hollowed as though holding something. If the kinkajou died she'd never speak to Linette again. Her heart beat faster at the thought.

"I think we should go over. If you think it's there. And—" Haley grabbed the ropes restraining the hammock, yanked them back and forth so that Linette shrieked, her hair caught between hempen braids—"it's—*my*—turn—*now*."

They snuck out that night. The sky had turned pale green, the same shade as the crystal globe wherein three ivory-bellied frogs floated, atop a crippled table. To keep the table from falling Haley had propped a broom handle beneath it for a fourth leg—although she hated the frogs, bloated things with prescient yellow eyes. Some nights when she slept over they broke her sleep with their song, high-pitched trilling that disturbed neither Linette snoring in the other bed nor Aurora drinking broodingly in her tiny shed-roofed wing of the cottage. It was uncanny, almost frightening sometimes, how nothing ever disturbed them: not dying pets nor utilities cut off for lack of payment nor unexpected visits from Aurora's small circle of friends, People from the Factory Days she called them. Rejuvenated junkies or pop stars with new careers, or wasted beauties like Aurora Dawn herself. All of them seemingly forever banned from the real world, the adult world Haley's parents and family inhabited, magically free as Linette herself was to sample odd-tasting liqueurs and curious religious notions and lost arts in their dank corners of the City or the shelter of some wealthier friend's up-county retreat. Sleepy-eyed from dope or taut from amphetamines, they lay around the cottage with Haley and Linette, offering sips of their drinks, advice about popular musicians and contraceptives. Their hair was streaked with gray now, or dyed garish mauve or blue or green. They wore high leather boots and clothes inlaid with feathers or mirrors, and had names that sounded like the names of expensive perfumes: Liatris, Coppelia, Electric Velvet. Sometimes Haley felt that she had wandered into a fairy tale, or a movie. *Beauty and the Beast* perhaps, or *The Dark Crystal*. Of course it would be one of Linette's favorites; Linette had more imagination and sensitivity than Haley. The kind of movie Haley would choose to wander into would have fast cars and gunshots in the distance, not aging refugees from another decade passed out next to the fireplace.

She thought of that now, passing the globe of frogs. They went from the eerie interior dusk of the cottage into the strangely aqueous air outside. Despite the warmth of the late summer evening Haley shivered as she gazed back at the cottage. The tiny bungalow might have stood there unchanged for five hundred years, for a thousand. No warm yellow light spilled from the windows as it did at her own house. There was no smell of dinner cooking, no television chattering. Aurora seldom cooked, Linette never. There was no TV. Only the frogs hovering in their silver world, and the faintest cusp of a new moon like a leaf cast upon the surface of the sky.

The main house of the neighboring estate stood upon a broad slope of lawn overlooking the woods. Massive oaks and sycamores studded the grounds, and formal gardens that had been more carefully tended by the mansion's previous owner, a New York fashion designer recently dead. At the foot of the long drive a post bore the placard on which was writ in spidery silver letters KINGDOM COME.

In an upstairs room Lie Vagal perched upon a windowsill. He stared out at the same young moon that watched Haley and Linette as they made their way through the woods. Had Lie known where to look he might have seen them as well; but he was watching the kinkajou sleeping in his lap.

It had appeared at breakfast two days earlier. Lie sat with his grandmother on

the south terrace, eating Froot Loops and reading the morning mail, *The Wall
Street Journal* and a quarterly royalty statement from BMI. His grandmother
stared balefully into a bowl of bran flakes, as though discerning there unpleasant
intimations of the future.

"Did you take your medicine, Gram?" asked Lie. A leaf fell from an overhanging
branch into his coffee cup. He fished it out before Gram could see it as another
dire portent.

"Did you take yours, Elijah?" snapped Gram. She finished the bran flakes and
reached for her own coffee, black and laced with chicory. She was eighty-four
years old and had outlived all of her other relatives and many of Lie's friends. "I
know you didn't yesterday."

Lie shrugged. Another leaf dropped to the table, followed by a hail of bark and
twigs. He peered up into the greenery, then pointed.

"Look," he said. "A squirrel or cat or something."

His grandmother squinted, shaking her head peevishly. "I can't see a thing."

The shaking branches parted to show something brown attached to a slender
limb. Honey-colored, too big for a squirrel, it clung to a branch that dipped lower
and lower, spattering them with more debris. Lie moved his coffee cup and had
started to his feet when it fell, landing on top of the latest issue of *New Musical
Express*.

For a moment he thought the fall had killed it. It just lay there, legs and long
tail curled as though it had been a doodlebug playing dead. Then slowly it opened
its eyes, regarded him with a muzzy golden gaze, and yawned, unfurling a tongue
so brightly pink it might have been lipsticked. Lie laughed.

"It fell asleep in the tree! It's a—a what-you-call-it, a sloth."

His grandmother shook her head, pushing her glasses onto her nose. "That's
not a sloth. They have grass growing on them."

Lie stretched a finger and tentatively stroked its tail. The animal ignored him,
closing its eyes once more and folding its paws upon its glossy breast. Around its
neck someone had placed a collar, the sort of leather-and-rhinestone ornament
old ladies deployed on poodles. Gingerly Lie turned it, until he found a small
heart-shaped tab of metal.

KINKAJOU
My name is Valentine
764–0007

"Huh," he said. "I'll be damned. I bet it belongs to those girls next door."
Gram sniffed and collected the plates. Next to Lie's coffee mug, the compart-
mented container holding a week's worth of his medication was still full.

The animal did nothing but sleep and eat. Lie called a pet store in the City
and learned that kinkajous ate insects and honey and bananas. He fed it Froot
Loops, yogurt and granola, a moth he caught one evening in the bedroom.
Tonight it slept once more, and he stroked it, murmuring to himself. He still
hadn't called the number on the collar.

From here he could just make out the cottage, a white blur through dark leaves
and tangled brush. It was his cottage, really; a long time ago the estate gardener

had lived there. The fashion designer had been friends with the present tenant in the City long ago. For the last fourteen years the place had been leased to Aurora Dawn. When he'd learned that, Lie Vagal had given a short laugh, one that the realtor had mistaken for displeasure.

"We could evict her," she'd said anxiously. "Really, she's no trouble, just the town drunk, but once you'd taken possession—"

"I wouldn't *dream* of it." Lie laughed again, shaking his head but not explaining. "Imagine, having Aurora Dawn for a neighbor again. . . ."

His accountant had suggested selling the cottage, it would be worth a small fortune now, or else turning it into a studio or guest house. But Lie knew that the truth was, his accountant didn't want Lie to start hanging around with Aurora again. Trouble; all the survivors from those days were trouble.

That might have been why Lie didn't call the number on the collar. He hadn't seen Aurora in fifteen years, although he had often glimpsed the girls playing in the woods. More than once he'd started to go meet them, introduce himself, bring them back to the house. He was lonely here. The visitors who still showed up at Aurora's door at four A.M. used to bang around Lie's place in the City. But that was long ago, before what Lie thought of as The Crash and what *Rolling Stone* had termed "the long tragic slide into madness of the one-time *force majeur* of underground rock and roll." And his agent and his lawyer wouldn't think much of him luring children to his woodland lair.

He sighed. Sensing some shift in the summer air, his melancholy perhaps, the sleeping kinkajou sighed as well, and trembled where it lay curled between his thighs. Lie lifted his head to gaze out the open window.

Outside the night lay still and deep over woods and lawns and the little dreaming cottage. A Maxfield Parrish scene, stars spangled across an ultramarine sky, twinkling bit of moon, there at the edge of the grass a trio of cottontails feeding peacefully amidst the dandelions. He had first been drawn to the place because it looked like this, like one of the paintings he collected. "Kiddie stuff," his agent sniffed; "fairy tale porn." Parrish and Rackham and Nielsen and Clarke. Tenniel prints of Alice's trial. The DuFevre painting of the Erl-King that had been the cover of Lie Vagal's second, phenomenally successful album. For the first two weeks after moving he had done nothing but pace the labyrinthine hallways, planning where they all would hang, this picture by this window, that one near another. All day, all night he paced; and always alone.

Because he was afraid his agent or Gram or one of the doctors would find out the truth about Kingdom Come, the reason he had really bought the place. He had noticed it the first time the realtor had shown the house. She'd commented on the number of windows there were—

"South-facing, too, the place is a hundred years old but it really functions as passive solar with all these windows. That flagstone floor in the green room acts as a heat sink—"

She nattered on, but Lie said nothing. He couldn't believe that she didn't notice. No one did, not Gram or his agent or the small legion of people brought in from Stamford who cleaned the place before he moved in.

It was the windows, of course. They always came to the windows first.

The first time he'd seen them had been in Marrakech, nearly sixteen years ago.

A window shaped like a downturned heart, looking out onto a sky so blue it
seemed to drip; and outside, framed within the window's heavy white curves, Lie
saw the crouching figure of a young man, bent over some object that caught the
sun and flared so that he'd had to look away. When he'd turned back the young
man was staring up in amazement as reddish smoke like dust roiled from the
shining object. As Lie watched the smoke began to take the shape of an immense
man. At that point the joint he held burned Lie's fingers and he shouted, as much
from panic as pain. When he looked out again the figures were gone.

Since then he'd seen them many times. Different figures, but always familiar,
always fleeting, and brightly colored as the tiny people inside a marzipan egg.
Sinbad and the Roc; the little mermaid and her sisters; a brave little figure carrying
a belt engraved with the words SEVEN AT A BLOW. The steadfast tin soldier and a
Christmas tree soon gone to cinders; dogs with eyes as big as teacups, as big as
soup plates, as big as millstones. On tour in Paris, London, Munich, L.A., they
were always there, as likely (or unlikely) to appear in a hotel room overlooking a
dingy alley as within the crystal mullions of some heiress's bedroom. He had
never questioned their presence, not after that first shout of surprise. They were
the people, *his* people; the only ones he could trust in what was fast becoming a
harsh and bewildering world.

It was just a few weeks after the first vision in Marrakech that he went to that
fateful party; and a few months after that came the staggering success of *The Erl-
King*. And then The Crash, and all the rest of it. He had a confused memory of
those years. Even now, when he recalled that time it was as a movie with too
much crosscutting and no dialogue. An endless series of women (and men) rolling
from his bed; dark glimpses of himself in the studio cutting *Baba Yaga* and *The
Singing Bone*; a few overlit sequences with surging crowds screaming soundlessly
beneath a narrow stage. During those years his visions of the people changed. At
first his psychiatrist was very interested in hearing about them. And so for a few
months that was all he'd talk about, until he could see her growing impatient.
That was the last time he brought them up to anyone.

But he wished he'd been able to talk to someone about them; about how
different they were since The Crash. In the beginning he'd always noticed only
how beautiful they were, how like his memories of all those stories from his
childhood. The little mermaid gazing adoringly up at her prince; the two children
in the cottage made of gingerbread and gumdrops; the girl in her glass coffin
awakened by a kiss. It was only after The Crash that he remembered the *other*
parts of the tales, the parts that in childhood had made it impossible for him to
sleep some nights and which now, perversely, returned to haunt his dreams. The
witch shrieking inside the stove as she was burned to death. The wicked queen
forced to dance in the red-hot iron shoes until she died. The little mermaid's
prince turning from her to marry another, and the mermaid changed to sea foam
as punishment for his indifference.

But since he'd been at Kingdom Come these unnerving glimpses of the people
had diminished. They were still there, but all was as it had been at the very first,
the myriad lovely creatures flitting through the garden like moths at twilight. He
thought that maybe it was going off his medication that did it; and so the full
prescription bottles were hoarded in a box in his room, hidden from Gram's eyes.

That was how he made sure the people remained at Kingdom Come. Just like in Marrakech: they were in the windows. Each one opened onto a different spectral scene, visual echoes of the fantastic paintings that graced the walls. The bathroom overlooked a twilit ballroom; the kitchen a black dwarf's cave. The dining room's high casements opened onto the Glass Hill. From a tiny window in the third-floor linen closet he could see a juniper tree, and once a flute of pale bone sent its eerie song pulsing through the library.

"You hear that, Gram?" he had gasped. But of course she heard nothing; she was practically deaf.

Lately it seemed that they came more easily, more often. He would feel an itching at the corner of his eyes, Tinkerbell's pixie dust, the Sandman's seed. Then he would turn, and the placid expanse of new-mown lawn would suddenly bc transformed into gnarled spooky trees beneath a grinning moon, rabbits holding hands, the grass frosted with dew that held the impressions of many dancing feet. He knew there were others he didn't see, wolves and witches and bones that danced. And the most terrible one of all—the Erl-King, the one he'd met at the party; the one who somehow had set all this in motion and then disappeared. It was Lie's worst fear that someday he would come back.

Now suddenly the view in front of him changed. Lie started forward. The kinkajou slid from his lap like a bolt of silk to lie at his feet, still drowsing. From the trees waltzed a girl, pale in the misty light. She wore a skirt that fetched just above her bare feet, a white blouse that set off a tangle of long dark hair. Stepping onto the lawn she paused, turned back and called into the woods. He could hear her voice but not her words. A child's voice, although the skirt billowed about long legs and he could see where her breasts swelled within the white blouse.

Ah, he thought, and tried to name her. Jorinda, Gretel, Ashputtel?

But then someone else crashed through the brake of saplings. Another girl, taller and wearing jeans and a halter top, swatting at her bare arms. He could hear what *she* was saying; she was swearing loudly while the first girl tried to hush her. He laughed, nudged the kinkajou on the floor. When it didn't respond he bent to pick it up and went downstairs.

"I don't think anyone's home," Haley said. She stood a few feet from the haven of the birch grove, feeling very conspicuous surrounded by all this open lawn. She killed another mosquito and scratched her arm. "Maybe we should just call, or ask your mother. If she knows this guy."

"She doesn't like him," Linette replied dreamily. A faint mist rose in little eddies about them. She lifted her skirts and did a pirouette, her bare feet leaving darker impressions on the gray lawn. "And it would be even cooler if no one was there, we could go in and find Valentine and look around. Like a haunted house."

"Like breaking and entering," Haley said darkly, but she followed her friend tiptoeing up the slope. The dewy grass was cool, the air warm and smelling of something sweet, oranges or maybe some kind of incense wafting down from the immense stone house.

They walked up the lawn, Linette leading the way. Dew soaked the hem of her skirt and the cuffs of Haley's jeans. At the top of the slope stood the great main house, a mock-Tudor fantasy of stone and stucco and oak beams. Waves of ivy and cream-colored roses spilled from the upper eaves; toppling ramparts of hollyhocks grew against the lower story. From here Haley could see only a single light downstairs, a dim green glow from behind curtains of ivy. Upstairs, diamond-paned windows had been pushed open, forcing the vegetation to give way and hang in limp streamers, some of them almost to the ground. The scent of turned earth mingled with that of smoke and oranges.

"Should we go to the front door?" Haley asked. Seeing the back of the house close up like this unnerved her, the smell of things decaying and the darkened mansion's *dishabille*. Like seeing her grandmother once without her false teeth: she wanted to turn away and give the house a chance to pull itself together.

Linette stopped to scratch her foot. "Nah. It'll be easier to just walk in if we go this way. If nobody's home." She straightened and peered back in the direction they'd come. Haley turned with her. The breeze felt good in her face. She could smell the distant dampness of Lake Muscanth, hear the croak of frogs and the rustling of leaves where deer stepped to water's edge to drink. When the girls turned back to the big house each took a step forward. Then they gasped, Linette pawing at the air for Haley's hand.

"Someone's there!"

Haley nodded. She squeezed Linette's fingers and then drew forward.

They had only looked away for an instant. But it had been long enough for lights to go on inside and out, so that now the girls blinked in the glare of spotlights. Someone had thrown open a set of French doors opening onto a sort of patio decorated with tubs of geraniums and very old wicker porch furniture, the wicker sprung in threatening and dangerous patterns. Against the brilliance the hollyhocks loomed black and crimson. A trailing length of white curtain blew from the French doors onto the patio. Haley giggled nervously, and heard Linette breathing hard behind her.

Someone stepped outside, a small figure not much taller than Haley. He held something in his arms, and cocked his head in a way that was, if not exactly welcoming, at least neutral enough to indicate that they should come closer.

Haley swallowed and looked away. She wondered if it would be too stupid just to run back to the cottage. But behind her Linette had frozen. On her face was the same look she had when caught passing notes in class, a look that meant it would be up to Haley, as usual, to get them out of this.

"Hum," Haley said, clearing her throat. The man didn't move. She shrugged, trying to think of something to say.

"Come on up," a voice rang out; a rather high voice with the twangy undercurrent of a Texas accent. It was such a cheerful voice, as though they were expected guests, that for a moment she didn't associate it with the stranger on the patio. "It's okay, you're looking for your pet, right?"

Behind her Linette gasped again, in relief. Then Haley was left behind as her friend raced up the hill, holding up her skirts and glancing back, laughing.

"Come on! He's got Valentine—"

Haley followed her, walking deliberately slowly. Of a sudden she felt odd. The too-bright lights on a patio smelling of earth and mandarin oranges; the white curtain blowing in and out; the welcoming stranger holding Valentine. It all made her dizzy, fairly breathless with anticipation; but frightened, too. For a long moment she stood there, trying to catch her breath. Then she hurried after her friend.

When she got to the top Linette was holding the kinkajou, crooning over it the way Haley usually did. Linette herself hadn't given it this much attention since its arrival last spring. Haley stopped, panting, next to a wicker chair, and bent to scratch her ankle. When she looked up again the stranger was staring at her.

"Hello," he said. Haley smiled shyly and shrugged, then glanced at Linette.

"Hey! You got him back! I told you he was here—"

Linette smiled, settled onto a wicker loveseat with Valentine curled among the folds of her skirt. "Thanks," she said softly, glancing up at the man. "He found him two days ago, he said. This is Haley—"

The man said hello again, still smiling. He was short, and wore a black T-shirt and loose white trousers, like hospital pants only cut from some fancy cloth. He had long black hair, thinning back from his forehead but still thick enough to pull into a ponytail. He reminded her of someone; she couldn't think who. His hands were crossed on his chest and he nodded at Haley, as though he knew what she was thinking.

"You're sisters," he said; then when Linette giggled shook his head, laughing. "No, of course, that's dumb: you're just friends, right? Best friends, I see you all the time together."

Haley couldn't think of anything to say, so she stepped closer to Linette and stroked the kinkajou's head. She wondered what happened now: if they stayed here on the porch with the stranger, or took Valentine and went home, or—

But what happened next was that a very old lady appeared in the French doors that led inside. She moved quickly, as though if she slowed down even for an instant she would be overtaken by one of the things that overtake old people, arthritis maybe, or sleep; and she swatted impatiently at the white curtains blowing in and out.

"Elijah," she said accusingly. She wore a green polyester blouse and pants patterned with enormous orange poppies, and fashionable eyeglasses with very large green frames. Her white hair was carefully styled. As she stood in the doorway her gaze flicked from Linette and the kinkajou to the stranger, then back to Linette. And Haley saw something cross the old woman's face as she looked at her friend, and then at the man again: an expression of pure alarm, terror almost. Then the woman turned and looked at Haley for the first time. She shook her head earnestly and continued to stare at Haley with very bright eyes, as though they knew each other from somewhere, or as though she had quickly sized up the situation and decided Haley was the only other person here with any common sense, which seemed precisely the kind of thing this old lady might think. "I'm Elijah's grandmother," she said at last, and very quickly crossed the patio to stand beside the stranger.

"Hi," said Linette, looking up from beneath waves of dark hair. The man smiled, glancing at the old lady. His hand moved very slightly toward Linette's head, as though he might stroke her hair. Haley desperately wanted to scratch her ankle again, but was suddenly embarrassed lest anyone see her. The old lady continued to stare at her, and Haley finally coughed.

"I'm Haley," she said, then added, "Linette's friend." As though the lady knew who Linette was.

But maybe she did, because she nodded very slightly, glancing again at Linette and then at the man she had said was her grandson. "Well," she said. Her voice was strong and a little shrill, and she too had a Texas accent. "Come on in, girls. *Elijah.* I put some water on for tea."

Now this is too weird, thought Haley. The old lady strode back across the patio and held aside the white curtains, waiting for them to follow her indoors. Linette stood, cradling the kinkajou and murmuring to it. She caught Haley's eye and smiled triumphantly. Then she followed the old lady, her skirt rustling about her legs. That left Haley and the man still standing by the wicker furniture.

"Come on in, Haley," he said to her softly. He extended one hand toward the door, a very long slender hand for such a short man. Around his wrist he wore a number of thin silver- and gold-colored bracelets. There came again that overpowering scent of oranges and fresh earth, and something else too, a smoky musk like incense. Haley blinked and steadied herself by touching the edge of one wicker chair. "It's okay, Haley—"

Is it? she wondered. She looked behind her, down the hill to where the cottage lay sleeping. If she yelled would Aurora hear her? Would anyone? Because she was certain now that something was happening, maybe had already happened and it was just taking a while (as usual) to catch up with Haley. From the woods edging Lake Muscanth came the yapping of the fox again, and the wind brought her the smell of water. For a moment she shut her eyes and pretended she was there, safe with the frogs and foxes.

But even with her eyes closed she could feel the man staring at her with that intent dark gaze. It occurred to Haley then that the only reason he wanted her to come was that he was afraid Linette would go if Haley left. A wave of desolation swept over her, to think she was unwanted, that even here and now it was as it always was: Linette chosen first for teams, for dances, for secrets, and Haley waiting, waiting.

"Haley."

The man touched her hand, a gesture so tentative that for a moment she wasn't even sure it was him: it might have been the breeze, or a leaf falling against her wrist. She looked up and his eyes were pleading, but also apologetic; as though he really believed it wouldn't be the same without her. And she knew that expression—now who stared at her just like that, who was it he looked like?

It was only after she had followed him across the patio, stooping to brush the grass from her bare feet as she stepped over the threshold into Kingdom Come, that she realized he reminded her of Linette.

The tea was Earl Grey, the same kind they drank in Linette's kitchen. But this kitchen was huge: the whole cottage could practically have fit inside it. For all that it was a reassuring place, with all the normal kitchen things where they should be—microwave, refrigerator, ticking cat clock with its tail slicing back and forth, back and forth.

"Cream and sugar?"

The old lady's hands shook as she put the little bowl on the table. Behind her Lie Vagal grinned, opened a cabinet and took out a golden jar.

"I bet she likes *honey*," he pronounced, setting the jar in front of Linette.

She giggled delightedly. "How did you know?"

"Yeah, how did you know?" echoed Haley, frowning a little. In Linette's lap the kinkajou uncurled and yawned, and Linette dropped a spoonful of honey into its mouth. The old lady watched tight-lipped. Behind her glasses her eyes sought Haley's, but the girl looked away, shy and uneasy.

"Just a feeling I had, just a lucky guess," Lie Vagal sang. He took a steaming mug from the table, ignored his grandmother when she pointed meaningfully at the pill bottle beside it. "Now, would you girls like to tour the rest of the house?"

It was an amazing place. There were chairs of brass and ebony, chairs of antlers, chairs of neon tubes. Incense burners shaped like snakes and elephants sent up wisps of sweet smoke. From the living room wall gaped demonic masks, and a hideous stick figure that looked like something that Haley, shuddering, recalled from *Uncle Wiggly*. There was a glass ball that sent out runners of light when you touched it, and a jukebox that played a song about the Sandman.

And everywhere were the paintings. Not exactly what you would expect to find in a place like this: paintings that illustrated fairy tales. Puss in Boots and the Three Billy Goats Gruff. Aladdin and the Monkey King and the Moon saying goodnight. Famous paintings, some of them—Haley recognized scenes from books she'd loved as a child, and framed animation cells from *Pinocchio* and *Snow White* and *Cinderella*.

These were parceled out among the other wonders. A man-high tank seething with piranhas. A room filled with nothing but old record albums, thousands of them. A wall of gold and platinum records and framed clippings from *Rolling Stone* and *NME* and *New York Rocker*. And in the library a series of Andy Warhol silk-screens of a young man with very long hair, alternately colored green and blue, dated 1972.

Linette was entranced by the fairy-tale paintings. She walked right past the Warhol prints to peruse a watercolor of a tiny child and a sparrow, and dreamily traced the edge of its frame. Lie Vagal stared after her, curling a lock of his hair around one finger. Haley lingered in front of the Warhol prints and chewed her thumb thoughtfully.

After a long moment she turned to him and said, "I know who you are. You're, like, this old rock star. Lie Vagal. You had some album that my babysitter liked when I was little."

He smiled and turned from watching Linette. "Yeah, that's me."

Haley rubbed her lower lip, staring at the Warhol prints. "You must've been really famous, to get him to do those paintings. What was that album called? The Mountain King?"

"*The Erl-King*." He stepped to an ornate ormulu desk adrift with papers. He shuffled through them, finally withdrew a glossy pamphlet. "Let's see—"

He turned back to Haley and handed it to her. A CD catalog, opened to a page headed ROCK AND ROLL ARCHIVES and filled with reproductions of album cover art. He pointed to one, reduced like the others to the size of a postage stamp. The illustration was of a midnight landscape speared by lightning. In the foreground loomed a hooded figure, in the background tiny specks that might have been other figures or trees or merely errors in the printing process. *The Erl-King*, read the legend that ran beneath the picture.

"Huh," said Haley. She glanced up to call Linette, but her friend had wandered into the adjoining room. She could glimpse her standing at the shadowed foot of a set of stairs winding up to the next story. "Awesome," Haley murmured, turning toward Lie Vagal. When he said nothing she awkwardly dropped the catalog onto a chair.

"Let's go upstairs," he said, already heading after Linette. Haley shrugged and followed him, glancing back once at the faces staring from the library wall.

Up here it was more like someone had just moved in. Their footsteps sounded louder, and the air smelled of fresh paint. There were boxes and bags piled against the walls. Amplifiers and speakers and other sound equipment loomed from corners, trailing cables and coils of wire. Only the paintings had been attended to, neatly hung in the corridors and beside windows. Haley thought it was weird, the way they were beside all the windows: not where you usually hung pictures. There were mirrors like that too, beside or between windows, so that sometimes the darkness threw back the night, sometimes her own pale and surprised face.

They found Linette at the end of the long hallway. There was a door there, closed, an ornate antique door that had obviously come from somewhere else. It was of dark wood, carved with hundreds of tiny figures, animals and people and trees, and inlaid with tiny mirrors and bits of glass. Linette stood staring at it, her back to them. From her tangled hair peeked the kinkajou, blinking sleepily as Haley came up behind her.

"Hey," she began. Beside her Lie Vagal smiled and rubbed his forehead.

Without turning Linette asked, "Where does it go?"

"My bedroom," said Lie as he slipped between them. "Would you like to come in?"

No, thought Haley.

"Sure," said Linette. Lie Vagal nodded and opened the door. They followed him inside, blinking as they strove to see in the dimness.

"This is my inner sanctum." He stood there grinning, his long hair falling into his face. "You're the only people who've ever been in it, really, except for me. My grandmother won't come inside."

At first she thought the room was merely dark, and waited for him to switch a light on. But after a moment Haley realized there *were* lights on. And she understood why the grandmother didn't like it. The entire room was painted black, a glossy black like marble. It wasn't a very big room, surely not the one originally intended to be the master bedroom. There were no windows. An oriental carpet covered the floor with purple and blue and scarlet blooms. Against one wall a narrow bed was pushed—such a small bed, a child's bed almost—and on the floor stood something like a tall brass lamp, with snaky tubes running from it.

"Wow," breathed Linette. "A hookah."

"A what?" demanded Haley; but no one paid any attention. Linette walked around, examining the hookah, the paintings on the walls, a bookshelf filled with volumes in old leather bindings. In a corner Lie Vagal rustled with something. After a moment the ceiling became spangled with lights, tiny white Christmas-tree lights strung from corner to corner like stars.

"There!" he said proudly. "Isn't that nice?"

Linette looked up and laughed, then returned to poring over a very old book with a red cover. Haley sidled up beside her. She had to squint to see what Linette was looking at—a garishly tinted illustration in faded red and blue and yellow.

The colors oozed from between the lines, and there was a crushed silverfish at the bottom of the page. The picture showed a little boy screaming while a long-legged man armed with a pair of enormous scissors snipped off his thumbs.

"Yuck!" Haley stared open-mouthed, then abruptly walked away. She drew up in front of a carved wooden statue of a troll, child-sized. Its wooden eyes were painted white, with neither pupil nor iris. "Man, this is kind of a creepy bedroom."

From across the room Lie Vagal regarded her, amused. "That's what Gram says." He pointed at the volume in Linette's hands. "I collect old children's books. That's *Struwwelpeter*. German. It means Slovenly Peter."

Linette turned the page. "I love all these pictures and stuff. But isn't it kind of dark in here?" She closed the book and wandered to the far end of the room where Haley stared at a large painting. "I mean, there's no windows or anything."

He shrugged. "I don't know. Maybe. I like it like this."

Linette crossed the room to stand beside Haley in front of the painting. It was a huge canvas, very old, in an elaborate gilt frame. Thousands of fine cracks ran through it. Haley was amazed it hadn't fallen to pieces years ago. A lamp on top of the frame illuminated it, a little too well for Haley's taste. It took her a moment to realize that she had seen it before.

"That's the cover of your album—"

He had come up behind them and stood there, reaching to chuck the kinkajou under the chin. "That's right," he said softly. "The Erl-King."

It scared her. The hooded figure in the foreground hunched towards a tiny form in the distance, its outstretched arms ending in hands like claws. There was a smear of white to indicate its face, and two dark smudges for eyes, as though someone had gouged the paint with his thumbs. In the background the smaller figure seemed to be fleeing on horseback. A bolt of lightning shot the whole scene with splinters of blue light, so that she could just barely make out that the rider held a smaller figure in his lap. Black clouds scudded across the sky, and on the horizon reared a great house with windows glowing yellow and red. Somehow Haley knew the rider would not reach the house in time.

Linette grimaced. On her shoulder the kinkajou had fallen asleep again. She untangled its paws from her hair and asked, "The Erl-King? What's that?"

Lie Vagal took a step closer her.

> "—'Oh father! My father! And dost thou not see?
> The Erl-King and his daughter are waiting for me?'
> —'Now shame thee, my dearest! Tis fear makes thee blind
> Thou seest the dark willows which wave in the wind.' "

He stopped. Linette shivered, glanced aside at Haley. "Wow. That's creepy—you really like all this creepy stuff. . . ."

Haley swallowed and tried to look unimpressed. "That was a song?"

He shook his head. "It's a poem, actually. I just ripped off the words, that's all." He hummed softly. Haley vaguely recognized the tune and guessed it must be from his album.

" 'Oh father, my father,' " he sang, and reached to take Linette's hand. She joined him shyly, and the kinkajou drooped from her shoulder across her back.

"Lie!"

The voice made the girls jump. Linette clutched at Lie. The kinkajou squealed unhappily.

"Gram." Lie's voice sounded somewhere between reproach and disappointment as he turned to face her. She stood in the doorway, weaving a little and with one hand on the doorframe to steady herself.

"It's late. I think those girls should go home now."

Linette giggled, embarrassed, and said, "Oh, we don't have—"

"Yeah, I guess so," Haley broke in, and sidled toward the door. Lie Vagal stared after her, then turned to Linette.

"Why don't you come back tomorrow, if you want to see more of the house? Then it won't get too late." He winked at Haley. "And Gram is here, so your parents shouldn't have to worry."

Haley reddened. "They don't care," she lied. "It's just, it's kind of late and all."

"Right, that's right," said the old lady. She waited for them all to pass out of the room, Lie pausing to unplug the Christmas-tree lights, and then followed them downstairs.

On the outside patio the girls halted, unsure how to say goodbye.

"Thank you," Haley said at last. She looked at the old lady. "For the tea."

"Yeah, thanks," echoed Linette. She looked over at Lie Vagal standing in the doorway. The backlight made of him a black shadow, the edges of his hair touched with gold. He nodded to her, said nothing. But as they made their way back down the moonlit hill his voice called after them with soft urgency.

"Come back," he said.

It was two more days before Haley returned to Linette's. After dinner she rode her bike up the long rutted dirt drive, dodging cabbage butterflies and locusts and looking sideways at Kingdom Come perched upon its emerald hill. Even before she reached the cottage she knew Linette wasn't there.

"Haley. Come on in."

Aurora stood in the doorway, her cigarette leaving a long blue arabesque in the still air as she beckoned Haley. The girl leaned her bike against the broken stalks of sunflowers and delphiniums pushing against the house and followed Aurora.

Inside was cool and dark, the flagstones' chill biting through the soles of Haley's sneakers. She wondered how Aurora could stand to walk barefoot, but she did: her feet small and dirty, toenails buffed bright pink. She wore a short black cotton tunic that hitched up around her narrow hips. Some days it doubled as nightgown and daywear; Haley guessed this was one of those days.

"Tea?"

Haley nodded, perching on an old ladderback chair in the kitchen and pretending interest in an ancient issue of *Dairy Goat* magazine. Aurora walked a little unsteadily from counter to sink to stove, finally handing Haley her cup and then sinking into an overstuffed armchair near the window. From Aurora's mug the smell of juniper cut through the bergamot-scented kitchen. She sipped her gin and regarded Haley with slitted eyes.

"So. You met Lie Vagal."

Haley shrugged and stared out the window. "He had Valentine," she said at last.

"He still does—the damn thing ran back over yesterday. Linette went after it last night and didn't come back."

Haley felt a stab of betrayal. She hid her face behind her steaming mug. "Oh," was all she said.

"You'll have to go get her, Haley. She won't come back for me, so it's up to you." Aurora tried to make her voice light, but Haley recognized the strained desperate note in it. She looked at Aurora and frowned.

You're her mother, you bring her back, she thought, but said, "She'll be back. I'll go over there."

Aurora shook her head. She still wore her hair past her shoulders and straight as a needle; no longer blonde, it fell in streaked gray and black lines across her face. "She won't," she said, and took a long sip at her mug. "He's got her now and he won't want to give her back." Her voice trembled and tears blurred the kohl around her eyelids.

Haley bit her lip. She was used to this. Sometimes when Aurora was drunk, she and Linette carried her to bed, covering her with the worn flannel comforter and making sure her cigarettes and matches were out of sight. Linette acted embarrassed, but Haley didn't mind, just as she didn't mind doing the dishes sometimes or making grilled cheese sandwiches or French toast for them all, or riding her bike down to Schelling's Market to get more ice when they ran out. She reached across to the counter and dipped another golden thread of honey into her tea.

"Haley. I want to show you something."

The girl waited as Aurora weaved down the narrow passage into her bedroom. She could hear drawers being thrown open and shut, and finally the heavy thud of the trunk by the bed being opened. In a few minutes Aurora returned, carrying an oversized book.

"Did I ever show you this?"

She padded into the umber darkness of the living room, with its frayed kilims and cracked sitar like some huge shattered gourd leaning against the stuccoed wall. Haley followed, settling beside her. By the door the frogs hung with splayed feet in their sullen globe, their pale bellies turned to amber by the setting sun. On the floor in front of Haley glowed a rhomboid of yellow light. Aurora set the book within that space and turned to Haley. "Have I shown you this?" she asked again, a little anxiously.

"No," Haley lied. She had in fact seen the scrapbook about a dozen times over the years—the pink plastic cover with its peeling Day-Glo flowers hiding newspaper clippings and magazine pages soft as fur beneath her fingers as Aurora pushed it towards her.

"He's in there," Aurora said thickly. Haley glanced up and saw that the woman's eyes were bright red behind their smeared rings of kohl. Tangled in her thin fine hair were hoop earrings that reached nearly to her shoulder, and on one side of her neck, where a love bite might be, a tattoo no bigger than a thumbprint showed an Egyptian Eye of Horus. "Lie Vagal—him and all the rest of them—"

Aurora started flipping through the stiff plastic pages, too fast for Haley to catch more than a glimpse of the photos and articles spilling out. Once she paused, fumbling in the pocket of her tunic until she found her cigarettes.

YOUTHQUAKER! the caption read. Beside it was a black-and-white picture of a girl with long white-blonde hair and enormous, heavily kohled eyes. She was standing with her back arched, wearing a sort of bikini made of playing cards. MODEL AURORA DAWN, BRIGHTEST NEW LIGHT IN POP ARTIST'S SUPERSTAR HEAVEN.

"Wow," Haley breathed. She never got tired of the scrapbooks: it was like watching a silent movie, with Aurora's husky voice intoning the perils that befell the feckless heroine.

"That's not it," Aurora said, almost to herself, and began skipping pages again. More photos of herself, and then others—men with hair long and lush as Aurora's; heavy women smoking cigars; twin girls no older than Haley and Linette, leaning on a naked man's back while another man in a doctor's white coat jabbed them with an absurdly long hypodermic needle. Aurora at an art gallery. Aurora on the cover of *Interview* magazine. Aurora and a radiant woman with shuttered eyes and long, long fishnet-clad legs—the woman was really a man, a transvestite Aurora said; but there was no way you could tell by looking at him. As she flashed through the pictures Aurora began to name them, bursts of cigarette smoke hovering above the pages.

"Fairy Pagan. She's dead.

"Joey Face. He's dead.

"Marletta. She's dead.

"Precious Bane. She's dead.

"The Wanton Hussy. She's dead."

And so on, for pages and pages, dozens of fading images, boys in leather and ostrich plumes, girls in miniskirts prancing across the backs of stuffed elephants at F.A.O. Schwartz or screaming deliriously as fountains of champagne spewed from tables in the back rooms of bars.

"Miss Clancy deWolff. She's dead.

"Dianthus Queen. She's dead.

"Markey French. He's dead."

Until finally the clippings grew smaller and narrower, the pictures smudged and hard to make out beneath curls of disintegrating newsprint—banks of flowers, mostly, and stiff faces with eyes closed beneath poised coffin lids, and one photo Haley wished she'd never seen (but yet again she didn't close her eyes in time) of a woman jackknifed across the top of a convertible in front of the Chelsea Hotel, her head thrown back so that you could see where it had been sheared from her neck neatly as with a razor blade.

"Dead. Dead. Dead," Aurora sang, her finger stabbing at them until flecks of paper flew up into the smoke like ashes; and then suddenly the book ended and Aurora closed it with a soft heavy sound.

"They're all dead," she said thickly; just in case Haley hadn't gotten the point.

The girl leaned back, coughing into the sleeve of her T-shirt. "What happened?" she asked, her voice hoarse. She knew the answers, of course: drugs, mostly, or suicide. One had been recent enough that she could recall reading about it in the *Daily News*.

"What *happened?*" Aurora's eyes glittered. Her hands rested on the scrapbook as on a Ouija board, fingers writhing as though tracing someone's name. "They sold their souls. Every one of them. And they're all dead now. Edie, Candy, Nico, Jackie, Andrea, even Andy. Every single one. They thought it was a joke, but look at it—"

A tiny cloud of dust as she pounded the scrapbook. Haley stared at it and then at Aurora. She wondered unhappily if Linette would be back soon; wondered, somewhat shamefully because for the first time, exactly what had happened last night at Kingdom Come.

"Do you see what I mean, Haley? Do you understand now?" Aurora brushed the girl's face with her finger. Her touch was ice cold and stank of nicotine.

Haley swallowed. "N-no," she said, trying not to flinch. "I mean, I thought they all, like, OD'd or something."

Aurora nodded excitedly. "They did! *Of course* they did—but that was after-ward—that was how they *paid*—"

Paid. Selling souls. Aurora and her weird friends talked like that sometimes. Haley bit her lip and tried to look thoughtful. "So they, like, sold their souls to the devil?"

"Of course!" Aurora croaked triumphantly. "How else would they have ever got where they did? Superstars! Rich and famous! And for what reason? None of them had any talent—*none* of them—but they ended up on TV, and in V*ogue*, and in the movies—how else could they have done it?"

She leaned forward until Haley could smell her sickly berry-scented lipstick mingled with the gin. "They all thought they were getting such a great deal, but look how it ended—famous for fifteen minutes, then *pfffttttt!*"

"Wow," Haley said again. She had no idea, really, what Aurora was talking about. Some of these people she'd heard of, in magazines or from Aurora and her friends, but mostly their names were meaningless. A bunch of nobodies that nobody but Aurora had ever even cared about.

She glanced down at the scrapbook and felt a small sharp chill beneath her breast. Quickly she glanced up again at Aurora: her ruined face, her eyes; that tattoo like a faded brand upon her neck. A sudden insight made her go *hmm* beneath her breath—

Because maybe that was the point; maybe Aurora wasn't so crazy, and these people really *had* been famous once. But now for some strange reason no one remembered any of them at all; and now they were all dead. Maybe they really were all under some sort of curse. When she looked up Aurora nodded, slowly, as though she could read her thoughts.

"It was at a party. At the Factory," she began in her scorched voice. "We were celebrating the opening of *Scag*—that was the first movie to get real national distribution, it won the Silver Palm at Cannes that year. It was a fabulous party, I remember there was this huge Lalique bowl filled with cocaine and in the bathroom Doctor Bob was giving everyone a pop—

"About three A.M. most of the press hounds had left, and a lot of the neophytes were just too wasted and had passed out or gone on to Max's. But Candy was still there, and Liatris, and Jackie and Lie Vagal—all the core people—and I was sitting by the door, I really was in better shape than most of them, or I thought I was, but then I looked up and there is this *guy* there I've never seen before. And, like, people wandered in and out of there all the time, that was no big deal, but I was sitting right by the door with Jackie, I mean it was sort of a joke, we'd been asking to see people's invitations, turning away the offal, but I swear I never saw this guy come in. Later Jackie said *she'd* seen him come in through the fire escape; but I think she was lying. Anyway, it was weird.

"And so I must have nodded out for a while, because all of a sudden I jerk up and look around and here's this guy with everyone huddled around him, bending over and laughing like he's telling fortunes or something. He kind of looked like that, too, like a gypsy—not that everyone didn't look like that in those days, but with him it wasn't so much like an act. I mean, he had this long curly black hair and these gold earrings, and high suede boots and velvet pants, all black and red and purple, but with him it was like maybe he had *always* dressed like that. He was handsome, but in a creepy sort of way. His eyes were set very close together and his eyebrows grew together over his nose—that's the mark of a warlock, eyebrows like that—and he had this very neat British accent. They always went crazy over anyone with a British accent.

"So obviously I had been missing something, passed out by the door, and so I got up and staggered over to see what was going on. At first I thought he was collecting autographs. He had this very nice leather-bound book, like an autograph book, and everyone was writing in it. And I thought, God, how tacky. But then it struck me as being weird, because a lot of those people—not Candy, she'd sign *anything*—but a lot of the others, they wouldn't be caught dead doing anything so bourgeois as signing autographs. But here just about everybody was passing this pen around—a nice gold Cross pen, I remember that—even Andy, and I thought, Well this I got to see.

"So I edged my way in, and that's when I saw they *were* signing their names. But it wasn't an autograph book at all. It wasn't like anything I'd ever seen before. There was something printed on every page, in this fabulous gold and green lettering, but very official-looking, like when you see an old-fashioned decree of some sort. And they were all signing their names on every page. Just like in a cartoon, you know, 'Sign here!' And, I mean, everyone had done it—Lie Vagal had just finished and when the man saw me coming over he held the book up and flipped through it real fast, so I could see their signatures. . . ."

Haley leaned forward on her knees, heedless now of the smoke and Aurora's huge eyes staring fixedly at the empty air.

"What was it?" the girl breathed. "Was it—?"

"It was *their souls*." Aurora hissed the last word, stubbing out her cigarette in her empty mug. "Most of them, anyway—because, *get it*, who would ever want *their* souls? It was a standard contract—souls, sanity, first-born children. They all thought it was a joke—but look what happened." She pointed at the scrapbook as though the irrefutable proof lay there.

Haley swallowed. "Did you—did *you* sign?"

Aurora shook her head and laughed bitterly. "Are you crazy? Would I be here now if I had? No, I didn't, and a few others didn't—Viva, Liatris and Coppelia, David Watts. We're about all that's left, now—except for one or two who haven't paid up. . . ."

And she turned and gazed out the window, to where the overgrown apple trees leaned heavily and spilled their burden of green fruit onto the stone wall that separated them from Kingdom Come.

"Lie Vagal," Haley said at last. Her voice sounded hoarse as Aurora's own. "So he signed it, too."

Aurora said nothing, only sat there staring, her yellow hands clutching the thin fabric of her tunic. Haley was about to repeat herself, when the woman began to hum, softly and out of key. Haley had heard that song before—just days ago, where was it? and then the words spilled out in Aurora's throaty contralto:

> "—'Why trembles my darling? Why shrinks she with fear?'
> —'Oh father! My father! The Erl-King is near!
> 'The Erl-King, with his crown and his hands long and white!'
> —'Thine eyes are deceived by the vapors of night.' "

"That song!" exclaimed Haley. "He was singing it—"

Aurora nodded without looking at her. "*The Erl-King*," she said. "He recorded it just a few months later. . . ."

Her gaze dropped abruptly to the book at her knees. She ran her fingers along its edge, then as though with long practice opened it to a page towards the back. "There he is," she murmured, and traced the outlines of a black-and-white photo, neatly pressed beneath its sheath of yellowing plastic.

It was Lie Vagal. His hair was longer, and black as a cat's. He wore high leather boots, and the picture had been posed in a way to make him look taller than he really was. But what made Haley feel sick and frightened was that he was wearing makeup—his face powdered dead white, his eyes livid behind pools of mascara and kohl, his mouth a scarlet blossom. And it wasn't that it made him look like a woman (though it did).

It was that he looked exactly like Linette.

Shaking her head, she turned towards Aurora, talking so fast her teeth chattered. "You—does she—does he—does he know?"

Aurora stared down at the photograph and shook her head. "I don't think so. No one does. I mean, people might have suspected, I'm sure they talked, but—it was so long ago, they all forgot. Except for *him*, of course—"

In the air between them loomed suddenly the image of the man in black and red and purple, heavy gold rings winking from his ears. Haley's head pounded and she felt as though the floor reeled beneath her. In the hazy air the shining figure bowed its head, light gleaming from the unbroken ebony line that ran above its eyes. She seemed to hear a voice hissing to her, and feel cold sharp nails pressing tiny half-moons into the flesh of her arm. But before she could cry out the image was gone. There was only the still dank room, and Aurora saying,

". . . for a long time thought he would die, for sure—all those drugs—and then of course he went crazy; but then I realized he wouldn't have made that kind of deal. Lie was sharp, you see; he *did* have some talent, he didn't need this sort of—of *thing* to make him happen. And Lie sure wasn't a fool. Even if he thought it was a joke, he was terrified of dying, terrified of losing his mind—he'd already had that incident in Marrakech—and so that left the other option; and since he never knew, I never told him; well it must have seemed a safe deal to make. . . ."

A deal. Haley's stomach tumbled as Aurora's words came back to her—*A standard contract—souls, sanity, first-born children.* "But how—" she stammered.

"It's time." Aurora's hollow voice echoed through the chilly room. "It's time, is all. Whatever it was that Lie wanted, he got; and now it's time to pay up."

Suddenly she stood, her foot knocking the photo album so that it skidded across the flagstones, and tottered back into the kitchen. Haley could hear the clatter of glassware as she poured herself more gin. Silently the girl crept across the floor and stared for another moment at the photo of Lie Vagal. Then she went outside.

She thought of riding her bike to Kingdom Come, but absurd fears—she had visions of bony hands snaking out of the earth and snatching the wheels as she passed—made her walk instead. She clambered over the stone wall, grimacing at the smell of rotting apples. The unnatural chill of Linette's house had made her forget the relentless late-August heat and breathless air out here, no cooler for all that the sun had set and left a sky colored like the inside of a mussel shell. From the distant lake came the desultory thump of bullfrogs. When she jumped from the wall to the ground a windfall popped beneath her foot, spattering her with vinegary muck. Haley swore to herself and hurried up the hill.

Beneath the ultramarine sky the trees stood absolutely still, each moored to its small circle of shadow. Walking between them made Haley's eyes hurt, going from that eerie dusk to sudden darkness and then back into the twilight. She felt sick, from the heat and from what she had heard. It was crazy, of course, Aurora was always crazy; but Linette *hadn't* come back, and it had been such a creepy place, all those pictures, and the old lady, and Lie Vagal himself skittering through the halls and laughing. . . .

Haley took a deep breath, balled up her T-shirt to wipe the sweat from between her breasts. It was crazy, that's all; but still she'd find Linette and bring her home.

On one side of the narrow bed Linette lay fast asleep, snoring quietly, her hair spun across her cheeks in a shadowy lace. She still wore the pale blue peasant's dress she'd had on the night before, its hem now spattered with candle wax and wine. Lie leaned over her until he could smell it, the faint unwashed musk of sweat and cotton and some cheap drugstore perfume, and over all of it the scent of marijuana. The sticky end of a joint was on the edge of the bedside table, beside an empty bottle of wine. Lie grinned, remembering the girl's awkwardness in smoking the joint. She'd had little enough trouble managing the wine. Aurora's daughter, no doubt about that.

They'd spent most of the day in bed, stoned and asleep; most of the last evening as well, though there were patches of time he couldn't recall. He remembered his grandmother's fury when midnight rolled around and she'd come into the bedroom to discover the girl still with him, and all around them smoke and empty bottles. There'd been some kind of argument then with Gram, Linette shrinking into a corner with her kinkajou; and after that more of their laughing and creeping down hallways. Lie showed her all his paintings. He tried to show her the people, but for some reason they weren't there, not even the three bears drowsing in the little eyebrow window in the attic half-bath. Finally, long after midnight, they'd fallen asleep, Lie's fingers tangled in Linette's long hair, chaste as kittens. His medication had long since leached away most sexual desire. Even before The Crash, he'd always been uncomfortable with the young girls who waited backstage for him after a show, or somehow found their way into the recording studio. That was why Gram's accusations had infuriated him—

"She's a friend, she's just a *friend*—can't I have any friends at all? Can't I?" he'd raged, but of course Gram hadn't understood, she never had. Afterwards had come that long silent night, with the lovely flushed girl asleep in his arms, and outside the hot hollow wind beating at the walls.

Now the girl beside him stirred. Gently Lie ran a finger along her cheekbone and smiled as she frowned in her sleep. She had her mother's huge eyes, her mother's fine bones and milky skin, but none of that hardness he associated with Aurora Dawn. It was so strange, to think that a few days ago he had never met this child; might never have raised the courage to meet her, and now he didn't want to let her go home. Probably it was just his loneliness; that and her beauty, her resemblance to all those shining creatures who had peopled his dreams and visions for so long. He leaned down until his lips grazed hers, then slipped from the bed.

He crossed the room slowly, reluctant to let himself come fully awake. But in the doorway he started.

"Shit!"

Across the walls and ceiling of the hall huge shadows flapped and dove. A buzzing filled the air, the sound of tiny feet pounding against the floor. Something grazed his cheek and he cried out, slapping his face and drawing his hand away sticky and damp. When he gazed at his palm he saw a smear of yellow and the powdery shards of winge.

The hall was full of insects. June bugs and katydids, beetles and lacewings and a Prometheus moth as big as his two hands, all of them flying crazily around the lights blooming on the ceiling and along the walls. Someone had opened all the windows; he had never bothered to put the screens in. He swatted furiously at the air, wiped his hand against the wall and frowned, trying to remember if he'd opened them; then thought of Gram. The heat bothered her more than it did him—odd, considering her seventy-odd years in Port Arthur—but she'd refused his offers to have air conditioning installed. He walked down the corridor, batting at clouds of tiny white moths like flies. He wondered idly where Gram had been all day. It was strange that she wouldn't have looked in on him; but then he couldn't remember much of their argument. Maybe she'd been so mad she took to her own room out of spite. It wouldn't be the first time.

He paused in front of a Kay Nielsen etching from *Snow White*. Inside its simple white frame the picture showed the wicked queen, her face a crimson O as she staggered across a ballroom floor, her feet encased in red-hot iron slippers. He averted his eyes and stared out the window. The sun had set in a wash of green and deep blue; in the east the sky glowed pale gold where the moon was rising. It was ungodly hot, so hot that on the lawn the crickets and katydids cried out only every minute or so, as though in pain. Sighing, he raised his arms, pulling his long hair back from his bare shoulders so that the breath of breeze from the window might cool his neck.

It was too hot to do anything; too hot even to lie in bed, unless sleep had claimed you. For the first time he wished the estate had a pool; then remembered the Jacuzzi. He'd never used it, but there was a skylight in there where he'd once glimpsed a horse like a meteor skimming across the midnight sky. They could take a cool bath, fill the tub with ice cubes. Maybe Gram could be prevailed upon to make some lemonade, or he thought there was still a bottle of champagne in the fridge, a housewarming gift from the realtor. Grinning, he turned and paced back down the hall, lacewings forming an iridescent halo about his head. He didn't turn to see the small figure framed within one of the windows, a fair-haired girl in jeans and T-shirt scuffing determinedly up the hill towards his home; nor did he notice the shadow that darkened another casement, as though someone had hung a heavy curtain there to blot out the sight of the moon.

Outside the evening had deepened. The first stars appeared, not shining so much as glowing through the hazy air, tiny buds of silver showing between the unmoving branches above Haley's head. Where the trees ended Haley hesitated, her hand upon the smooth trunk of a young birch. She felt suddenly and strangely reluctant to go further. Before her, atop its sweep of deep green, Kingdom Come glittered like some spectral toy: spotlights streaming onto the patio, orange and yellow and white gleaming from the window casements, spangled nets of silver and gold spilling from some of the upstairs windows, where presumably Lie Vagal had strung more of his Christmas lights. On the patio the French doors had been flung open. The white curtains hung like loose rope to the ground. In spite of her fears Haley's neck prickled at the sight: it needed only people there moving in the golden light, people and music. . . .

As though in answer to her thought a sudden shriek echoed down the hill, so loud and sudden in the twilight that she started and turned to bolt. But almost immediately the shriek grew softer, resolved itself into music—someone had turned on a stereo too loudly and then adjusted the volume. Haley slapped the birch tree, embarrassed at her reaction, and started across the lawn.

As she walked slowly up the hill she recognized the music. Of course, that song again, the one Aurora had been singing a little earlier. She couldn't make out any words, only the wail of synthesizers and a man's voice, surprisingly deep. Beneath her feet the lawn felt brittle, the grass breaking at her steps and releasing an acrid dusty smell. For some reason it felt cooler here away from the trees. Her T-shirt hung heavy and damp against her skin, her jeans chafed against her bare ankles. Once she stopped and looked back, to see if she could make out Linette's cottage behind its scrim of greenery; but it was gone. There were only the trees, still and ominous beneath a sky blurred with stars.

She turned and went on up the hill. She was close enough now that she could smell that odd odor that pervaded Kingdom Come, oranges and freshly turned earth. The music pealed clear and sweet, an insidious melody that ran counterpoint to the singer's ominous phrasing. She *could* hear the words now, although the singer's voice had dropped to a childish whisper—

> "—'Oh Father! My father! And dost thou not hear
> 'What words the Erl-King whispers low in mine ear?'
> —'Now hush thee, my darling, thy terrors appease.
> 'Thou hearest the branches where murmurs the breeze.' "

A few yards in front of her the patio began. She was hurrying across this last stretch of lawn when something made her stop. She waited, trying to figure out if she'd heard some warning sound—a cry from Linette, Aurora shrieking for more ice. Then very slowly she raised her head and gazed up at the house.

There was someone there. In one of the upstairs windows, gazing down upon the lawn and watching her. He was absolutely unmoving, like a cardboard dummy propped against the sill. It looked like he had been watching her forever. With a dull sense of dread she wondered why she hadn't noticed him before. It wasn't Lie Vagal, she knew that; nor could it have been Linette or Gram. So tall it seemed that he must stoop to gaze out at her, his face enormous, perhaps twice the size of a normal man's and a deathly yellow color. Two huge pale eyes stared fixedly at her. His mouth was slightly ajar. That face hung as though in a fog of black, and drawn up against his breast were his hands, knotted together like an old man's—huge hands like a clutch of parsnips, waxy and swollen. Even from here she could see the soft glint of the spangled lights upon his fingernails, and the triangular point of his tongue like an adder's head darting between his lips.

For an instant she fell into a crouch, thinking to flee to the cottage. But the thought of turning her back upon that figure was too much for her. Instead Haley began to run towards the patio. Once she glanced up: and yes, it was still there, it had not moved, its eyes had not wavered from watching her; only it seemed its mouth might have opened a little more, as though it was panting.

Gasping, she nearly fell onto the flagstone patio. On the glass tables the remains of this morning's breakfast sat in congealed pools on bright blue plates. A skein of insects rose and trailed her as she ran through the doors.

"*Linette!*"

She clapped her hand to her mouth. Of course it would have seen where she entered; but this place was enormous, surely she could find Linette and they could run, or hide—

But the room was so full of the echo of that insistent music that no one could have heard her call out. She waited for several heartbeats, then went on.

She passed all the rooms they had toured just days before. In the corridors the incense burners were dead and cold. The piranhas roiled frantically in their tank, and the neon sculptures hissed like something burning. In one room hung dozens of framed covers of *Interview* magazine, empty-eyed faces staring down at her. It seemed now that she recognized them, could almost have named them if Aurora had been there to prompt her—

Fairy Pagan, Dianthus Queen, Markey French . . .

As her feet whispered across the heavy carpet she could hear them breathing behind her, *dead, dead, dead.*

She ended up in the kitchen. On the wall the cat-clock ticked loudly. There was a smell of scorched coffee. Without thinking she crossed the room and switched off the automatic coffee maker, its glass carafe burned black and empty. A loaf of bread lay open on a counter, and a half-empty bottle of wine. Haley swallowed: her mouth tasted foul. She grabbed the wine bottle and gulped a mouthful, warm and sour; then coughing, found the way upstairs.

Lie pranced back to the bedroom, singing to himself. He felt giddy, the way he did sometimes after a long while without his medication. By the door he turned and flicked at several buttons on the stereo, grimacing when the music howled and quickly turning the levels down. No way she could have slept through *that.*

He pulled his hair back and did a few little dance steps, the rush of pure feeling coming over him like speed.

> " *'If you will, oh my darling, then with me go away,*
> *My daughter shall tend you so fair and so gay . . .'* "

He twirled so that the cuffs of his loose trousers ballooned about his ankles. "Come, darling, rise and shine, time for little kinkajous to have their milk and honey—" he sang. And stopped.

The bed was empty. On the side table a cigarette—she had taken to cadging cigarettes from him—burned in a little brass tray, a scant half-inch of ash at its head.

"Linette?"

He whirled and went to the door, looked up and down the hall. He would have seen her if she'd gone out, but where could she have gone? Quickly he paced to the bathroom, pushing the door open as he called her name. She would have had to pass him to get there; but the room was empty.

"Linette!"

He hurried back to the room, this time flinging the door wide as he entered. Nothing. The room was too small to hide anyone. There wasn't even a closet. He walked inside, kicking at empty cigarette packs and clothes, one of Linette's sandals, a dangling silver earring. "Linette! Come on, let's go downstairs—"

At the far wall he stopped, staring at the huge canvas that hung there. From the speakers behind him the music swelled, his own voice echoing his shouts.

> " *'My father! My father! Oh hold me now fast!*
> *He pulls me, he hurts, and will have me at last—'* "

Lie's hands began to shake. He swayed a little to one side, swiping at the air as though something had brushed his cheek.

The Erl-King was gone. The painting still hung in its accustomed place in its heavy gilt frame. But instead of the menacing figure in the foreground and the tiny fleeing horse behind it, there was nothing. The yellow lights within the darkly silhouetted house had been extinguished. And where the hooded figure had reared with its extended claws, the canvas was blackened and charred. A hawkmoth was trapped there, its furled antennae broken, its wings shivered to fragments of mica and dust.

"*Linette.*"

From the hallway came a dull crash, as though something had fallen down the stairs. He fled the room while the fairy music ground on behind him.

In the hall he stopped, panting. The insects moved slowly through the air, brushing against his face with their cool wings. He could still hear the music, although now it seemed another voice had joined his own, chanting words he couldn't understand. As he listened he realized this voice did not come from the speakers behind him but from somewhere else—from down the corridor, where he could now see a dark shape moving within one of the windows overlooking the lawn.

"Linette," he whispered.

He began to walk, heedless of the tiny things that writhed beneath his bare feet. For some reason he still couldn't make out the figure waiting at the end of the hallway: the closer he came to it the more insubstantial it seemed, the more difficult it was to see through the cloud of winged creatures that surrounded his face. Then his foot brushed against something heavy and soft. Dazed, he shook his head and glanced down. After a moment he stooped to see what lay there.

It was the kinkajou. Curled to form a perfect circle, its paws drawn protectively about its elfin face. When he stroked it he could feel the tightness beneath the soft fur, the small legs and long tail already stiff.

"Linette," he said again; but this time the name was cut off as Lie staggered to his feet. The kinkajou slid with a gentle thump to the floor.

At the end of the hallway he could see it, quite clearly now, its huge head weaving back and forth as it chanted a wordless monotone. Behind it a slender figure crouched in a pool of pale blue cloth and moaned softly.

"Leave her," Lie choked; but he knew it couldn't hear him. He started to turn, to run the other way back to his bedroom. He tripped once and with a cry kicked aside the kinkajou. Behind him the low moaning had stopped, although he could still hear that glottal voice humming to itself. He stumbled on for another few feet; and then he made the mistake of looking back.

The curved staircase was darker than Haley remembered. Halfway up she nearly fell when she stepped on a glass. It shattered beneath her foot; she felt a soft prick where a shard cut her ankle. Kicking it aside, she went more carefully, holding her breath as she tried to hear anything above that music. Surely the grandmother at least would be about? She paused where the staircase turned, reaching to wipe the blood from her ankle, then with one hand on the paneled wall crept up the next few steps.

That was where she found Gram. At the curve in the stairwell light spilled from the top of the hallway. Something was sprawled across the steps, a filigree of white etched across her face. Beneath Haley's foot something cracked. When she put her hand down she felt the rounded corner of a pair of eyeglasses, the jagged spar where she had broken them.

"Gram," the girl whispered.

She had never seen anyone dead before. One arm flung up and backwards, as though it had stuck to the wall as she fell; her dress raked above her knees so that Haley could see where the blood had pooled onto the next riser, like a shadowy footstep. Her eyes were closed but her mouth was half-open, so that the girl could see how her false teeth had come loose and hung above her lower lip. In the breathless air of the passageway she had a heavy sickly odor, like dead carnations. Haley gagged and leaned back against the wall, closing her eyes and moaning softly.

But she couldn't stay like that. And she couldn't leave, not with Linette up there somewhere; even if that horrible figure was waiting for her. It was crazy: through her mind raced all the movies she had ever seen that were just like this, some idiot kid going up a dark stairway or into the basement where the killer waited, and the audience shrieking *No!*; but still she couldn't go back.

The hardest part was stepping over the corpse, trying not to actually *touch* it. She had to stretch across three steps, and then she almost fell but scrabbled frantically at the wall until she caught her balance. After that she ran the rest of the way until she reached the top.

Before her stretched the hallway. It seemed to be lit by some kind of moving light, like a strobe or mirror ball; but then she realized that was because of all the moths bashing against the myriad lamps strung across the ceiling. She took a step, her heart thudding so hard she thought she might faint. There was the doorway to Lie Vagal's bedroom; there all the open windows, and beside them the paintings.

She walked on tiptoe, her sneakers melting into the thick carpeting. At the open doorway she stopped, her breath catching in her throat. But when she looked inside there was no one there. A cigarette burned in an ashtray next to the bed. By the door Lie Vagal's stereo blinked with tiny red and green lights. The music went on, a ringing music like a calliope or glass harp. She continued down the hall.

She passed the first window, then a painting; then another window and another painting. She didn't know what made her stop to look at this one; but when she did her hands grew icy despite the cloying heat.

The picture was empty. A little brass plate at the bottom of the frame read *The Snow Queen*; but the soft wash of watercolors showed only pale blue ice, a sickle moon like a tear on the heavy paper. Stumbling, she turned to look at the frame behind her. *La Belle et La Bête*, it read: an old photograph, a film still, but where two figures had stood beneath an ornate candelabra there was only a whitish blur, as though the negative had been damaged.

She went to the next picture, and the next. They were all the same. Each landscape was empty, as though waiting for the artist to carefully place the principals between glass mountain and glass coffin, silver slippers and seven-league boots. From one to the other Haley paced, never stopping except to pause momentarily before those skeletal frames.

And now she saw that she was coming to the end of the corridor. There on the right was the window where she had seen that ghastly figure; and there beneath it, crouched on the floor like some immense animal or fallen beam, was a hulking shadow. Its head and shoulders were bent as though it fed upon something. She could hear it, a sound like a kitten lapping, so loud that it drowned out even the muted wail of Lie Vagal's music.

She stopped, one hand touching the windowsill beside her. A few yards ahead of her the creature grunted and hissed; and now she could see that there was something pinned beneath it. At first she thought it was the kinkajou. She was stepping backwards, starting to turn to run, when very slowly the great creature lifted its head to gaze at her.

It was the same tallowy face she had glimpsed in the window. Its mouth was open so that she could see its teeth, pointed and dulled like a dog's, and the damp smear across its chin. It seemed to have no eyes, only huge ruined holes where they once had been; and above them stretched an unbroken ridge of black where its eyebrows grew straight and thick as quills. As she stared it moved its hands, huge clumsy hands like a clutch of rotting fruit. Beneath it she could glimpse a white face, and dark hair like a scarf fluttering above where her throat had been torn out.

"*Linette!*"

Haley heard her own voice screaming. Even much later after the ambulances came she could still hear her friend's name; and another sound that drowned out the sirens: a man singing, wailing almost, crying for his daughter.

Haley started school several weeks late. Her parents decided not to send her to Fox Lane after all, but to a parochial school in Goldens Bridge. She didn't know anyone there and at first didn't care to, but her status as a sort-of celebrity was hard to shake. Her parents had refused to allow Haley to appear on television, but Aurora Dawn had shown up nightly for a good three weeks, pathetically eager to talk about her daughter's murder and Lie Vagal's apparent suicide. She mentioned Haley's name every time.

The nuns and lay people who taught at the high school were gentle and understanding. Counselors had coached the other students in how to behave with someone who had undergone a trauma like that, seeing her best friend murdered and horribly mutilated by the man who turned out to be her father. There was the usual talk about satanic influences in rock music, and Lie Vagal's posthumous career actually was quite promising. Haley herself gradually grew to like her new place in the adolescent scheme of things, half-martyr and half-witch. She even tried out for the school play, and got a small part in it; but that wasn't until spring.

With apologies to Johann Wolfgang von Goethe

THE CHRYSANTHEMUM SPIRIT

Osamu Dazai

Osamu Dazai is something of a cult figure in Japan, known as much for his brief and flamboyant life as for his witty, stylistic modern fairy tales that have been compared to Hans Andersen's and Oscar Wilde's. Longer, semiautobiographical works, such as *The Setting Sun* and *No Longer Human*, assured Dazai's reputation as a major twentieth-century Japanese writer, but it was in his tales of fantasy and romance that the writer shone with warmth, wit and inventiveness. Born in 1909, Dazai died in a double suicide shortly before his thirty-ninth birthday in 1948.

"The Chrysanthemum Spirit" comes from *Blue Bamboo*, an English translation of Dazai's fantasy tales published in 1993. Translator Ralph F. McCarthy, an American writer living in Tokyo, has also published *Self Portraits*, another collection of stories by Dazai, as well as 69 by Ryu Murakami.

—T.W.

Once upon a time, in Mukôjima in Edo, there lived a man with the rather silly name of Mayama Sainosuke. Sainosuke was very poor, and was still a bachelor at the age of thirty-two. Chrysanthemums were the great love of his life. If told of an excellent strain of chrysanthemum seedlings being grown in some corner of the land, he would go to the most absurd lengths to search them out and purchase a few for his own garden. It's said that he'd undertake such a mission though it meant a journey of more than two thousand miles, which ought to give you some idea of just how far gone he was.

One year in early autumn Sainosuke received word of an extraordinary variety of mums in the town of Numazu in Izu, and no sooner had he heard the news than he changed into his traveling clothes and set out with a strange gleam in his eye. He crossed the mountains of Hakone, swept into Numazu, and tramped through the streets until he located the object of his desire and acquired a couple of truly splendid seedlings. After carefully wrapping these treasures in oilpaper he smiled smugly to himself and set out for home.

As he was crossing back over the mountains of Hakone, with the city of Odawara just coming into view below, he became aware of the clip-clop of a horse's hooves on the road behind him. Euphoric over the purchase of his precious mums,

Sainosuke thought nothing of this at first, but when the animal continued to follow him at the same distance, neither drawing nearer nor falling behind, clopping along at the same leisurely rhythm for five, eight, ten miles, it began to strike him as somewhat odd, and finally he turned to look back. Not more than twenty paces behind him was a youth with strikingly lovely features, mounted upon an emaciated old horse. The boy flashed a smile when their eyes met, and Sainosuke, not wanting to appear impolite, returned the smile and stopped to wait for him. The youth rode up, dismounted, and said: "Lovely day, isn't it?"

"It is a lovely day," Sainosuke agreed.

And with that they continued walking along side by side, the youth leading the horse by the reins. Looking his companion over, Sainosuke could see that, though clearly not of samurai stock, the lad possessed a certain elegance of bearing; he was neatly dressed and had an easy, confident way about him.

"Headed for Edo?" the youth asked in a disarmingly familiar manner, and Sainosuke responded in kind.

"Yep. Going back home."

"Oh, you live there, then. And where have you been to?"

Small talk between travelers is always the same. In the course of exchanging the usual information, Sainosuke divulged the purpose of his trip to Numazu, and at the mention of chrysanthemums the young man's eyes lit up.

"You don't say! It's always a pleasure to meet someone who loves mums. I know a thing or two about them myself, you see. I must say, though, that it's not so much the quality of the seedlings as how you care for them." He was beginning to describe his own method of cultivation when Sainosuke interrupted him excitedly.

"Well, I can't agree with you there." Chrysanthemum fanatic that he was, no topic of conversation could have stimulated him more. "If you ask me, it's absolutely vital to have the best seedlings. Let me give you an example," he said and proceeded to launch into quite a lecture, drawing upon the extensive knowledge he'd acquired over the years. The youth didn't contest Sainosuke's opinions in so many words, but his occasional muttered interjections of *Oh?* and *H'mm* and so forth made it clear that he was in less than full agreement and somehow seemed to hint at an uncommon depth of experience, the upshot of which was that the more zealously Sainosuke prattled on, the less confident he felt of himself, and finally, in a voice that was nearly a sob, he said: "Enough! I won't say another word. Theory will get us nowhere. The only way to convince you I'm right would be to show you the mums in my garden."

"Well, I suppose that's true," the boy said, nodding rather indifferently. Sainosuke, for his part, had worked himself into quite a state. He was so anxious to show this young man his chrysanthemums and make him gasp in awe that he was literally trembling.

"All right, then," he said, throwing all sense of discretion to the winds, "what do you say to this: Come with me straight to my house in Edo and see my mums for yourself. One quick look, that's all I ask."

The youth laughed and said: "Unfortunately I'm in no position to oblige you there. As soon as we reach Edo I've got to start looking for work."

"Don't be ridiculous." Sainosuke was not about to take no for an answer now.

"You can look for a job after you've come to my house and rested up. You've simply got to see my chrysanthemums."

"I'm afraid you're putting me on the spot here," said the youth, no longer smiling. He walked along for some time with his head bowed in thought, then finally looked up and said in a rather doleful tone of voice: "Allow me to explain. My name's Tômoto Saburô. My elder sister and I have been living alone in Numazu ever since our parents died some years ago, but a while back my sister took a sudden disliking to the place and began to insist we move to Edo. Finally we disposed of our belongings and, well, here we are, on our way to the city. It's not as if we have any prospects waiting for us in Edo, however, and I don't mind telling you that this is far from being a carefree, lighthearted journey for me. It's certainly no time to be engaging in some silly argument about chrysanthemums. I shouldn't have opened my mouth at all, and wouldn't have, except that I'm rather partial to mums myself. If you don't mind, I'd rather just drop the subject. Please forget I ever brought it up. We've got to be moving along anyway. Perhaps we'll meet again under more favorable circumstances."

The youth nodded goodbye and was about to climb back on the horse when Sainosuke clutched tightly at his sleeve.

"Wait a minute. If that's how it is, then all the more reason for you to come to my house. What are you so worried about? I'm a poor man myself, but not so destitute that I can't put you up for a while. Just leave everything to me. You say you're with your sister? Where is she?"

Glancing around, Sainosuke noticed for the first time a girl in red traveling attire peeking over at him from the other side of the horse. He blushed when their eyes met.

In the end, unable to rebuff his ardent appeal, the two young people agreed to be Sainosuke's guests at his humble home in Mukôjima. When they arrived and saw that the cottage Sainosuke lived in was even more dilapidated than his professions of poverty had led them to imagine, they looked at each other and sighed. Sainosuke, however, merely ushered them straight to his garden, not even pausing first to change his clothes. After delivering a long, boastful spiel about his prized mums, he showed the pair to a little shed in the rear and explained that this was where they were to stay. Cramped as the shed was, they could see that it was at least preferable to Sainosuke's ramshackle cottage, which was so filthy and filled with trash that one hesitated even to step inside.

"Well, Sis, this is a fine state of affairs," the younger Tômoto whispered as he undid his traveling gear inside the shed. "Guests of a madman."

"He is a bit strange," the sister replied with a smile. "But he seems harmless enough. I'm sure we'll be comfortable here. And the garden is certainly spacious. You must plant some nice chrysanthemums for him, to show our appreciation."

"What? Don't tell me you want to stay here for any length of time?"

"Why not? I like it here," she said, her cheeks flushing slightly. The sister was about twenty, with a lovely, slender figure and skin as smooth and white as the purest wax.

By the following morning, Sainosuke and Saburô were already having the first of many arguments. The lean old horse, which the youth and his sister had taken turns riding all the way from Numazu, had disappeared. They'd left it tethered to a stake in the garden the night before, but when Sainosuke went out to check on his mums first thing in the morning it had vanished, having first left a path of destruction through his chrysanthemum patch. Sainosuke took one look at the trampled, gnawed, and uprooted plants and flew into a rage. He pounded on the door of the shed.

Saburô opened it at once and said: "What is it? Something wrong?"

"See for yourself. That bandy-legged horse of yours has gone and destroyed my garden. It's enough to make me want to lie down and die!"

"You're right," said the youth calmly. "And the horse?"

"Who cares? He's run off, I guess."

"But that's terrible."

"What are you talking about? A rickety old nag like that!"

"I beg your pardon. That happens to be an extremely clever horse. We must go and find him immediately. The devil take your silly chrysanthemums."

"What! What did you say?" Sainosuke shouted, his face turning ghostly pale. "Are you belittling my mums?"

Just then Saburô's sister stepped out of the shed with a demure smile on her face.

"Saburô," she said, "apologize to the gentleman. That skinny horse of ours is no great loss. I let it go myself. The thing to do now is to fix up the chrysanthemum patch. It's a perfect chance to express our gratitude for all the kindness we've been shown."

"Oh, so that's it," Saburô groaned. "You planned this, didn't you?"

Saburô heaved a deep sigh but grudgingly began to tend to the damaged plants. Watching him, Sainosuke couldn't help but marvel at how even those mums that were nearly dead from having been trampled or nibbled on sprang back to life as the youth replanted them. The roots soaked up moisture from the soil in great draughts, the stems swelled, the buds grew plump and heavy, and the wilted leaves stretched out firm and erect, pulsating with vitality. Sainosuke wasn't about to let on how astonished he was, however; as a man who'd spent his life growing mums, he had his pride to maintain.

"Well, do what you can here," he said as coolly as possible, then strode into his cottage to climb in bed and bury himself beneath the quilt. Soon he was back on his feet, however, peeping out at the garden through a crack in the shutters. Sure enough, all the plants Saburô tended to were springing miraculously to life.

That night Saburô came smiling to the cottage and said: "Sorry about this morning. But, listen, my sister and I were talking things over, and, well, if you'll pardon my saying so, you don't seem to be leading a very comfortable life. We were thinking that if you'd lend me half your garden, I could grow you some really first-rate mums, and then you could take them down to the market in Asakusa or somewhere and sell them. I'd be happy to do it."

Sainosuke, whose self-esteem as a grower of chrysanthemums had been severely shaken that morning, was not in the best of moods. Seeing this as a chance to even the score, he twisted his lips in a contemptuous sneer.

"Out of the question," he said. "Of all the vulgar ideas! And here I thought you were a man of taste and breeding. I'm shocked. To even think of selling one's beloved flowers simply to put food on the table! It's too outrageous for words. Why, it's a violation of the very spirit of chrysanthemums! To turn a nobleminded pastime into a scheme to make money is, why it's, it's obscene, that's what it is. I'll have nothing to do with it."

Sainosuke spewed out this rebuke in the gruff and guttural tones of a samurai issuing a challenge, and Saburô, understandably enough, took offense. His reply was rather heated.

"Using one's god-given talent to put food on the table hardly qualifies as greed, and to sneer at me and accuse me of being vulgar for wishing to do so is appallingly wrongheaded. It's arrogant and childish—the attitude of a spoiled little brat. A man shouldn't be overly covetous of riches, true, but to take undue pride in one's poverty is every bit as base and mean."

"When have I ever boasted of my poverty? Look, my ancestors left me with a small inheritance, and it's all I've ever needed. I want for nothing. And I'll thank you not to meddle in my affairs."

Once again their exchange had blossomed into a full-blown row.

"You're being awfully narrowminded, you know."

"Fine. Call me narrowminded. Call me a spoiled brat. Call me anything you like. I simply prefer to carry on as I always have, sharing the joys and sorrows of life with my mums."

"All right, all right," said Saburô, nodding and smiling ruefully. "You win. But listen: There's a small plot of bare ground behind the shed. Would you consider lending that to us for the time being?"

"You must realize by now that I'm not a man who's attached to worldly possessions. I don't imagine you'll find such a tiny plot sufficient to your needs. Half of my garden remains unplanted: take all of that if you like. Do with it as you see fit. Allow me to make one thing clear, however: I will not associate with anyone who would grow mums with the intention of offering them for sale. From this day on, I want you to consider me a complete stranger."

Saburô gaped at him incredulously for a moment, then shook his head in exasperation.

"So be it," he said. "I won't refuse such a generous offer. In fact, if I might further impose upon your generosity, I noticed that you've discarded a number of old chrysanthemum seedlings behind the shed . . ."

"You needn't bother me with requests for every little trifle. Take them."

And thus they parted, on the worst of terms. The next day Sainosuke divided his garden in two and erected a tall fence along the border, obstructing the view from either side. Relations between the two households were severed.

As autumn advanced, all of Sainosuke's chrysanthemums burst into beautiful bloom. Satisfying as this was, he couldn't help wondering how his neighbors' flowers had fared, and finally one day his curiosity got the best of him and he decided to peek over the fence. What he saw left him agog. The other half of the garden was ablaze from end to end with the largest and most spectacular blooms Sainosuke had ever seen. And that wasn't the only surprise. The shed had been rebuilt and was now a charming and cozy little cottage. This was hardly a sight to soothe Sainosuke's soul. His own chrysanthemums were clearly no match for Saburô's. What's more, the upstart had built himself an elegant little home. No doubt he'd made a small fortune selling his mums. It was an outrage! Determined to teach the youth a lesson, he scrambled over the fence, his heart wracked with an insufferable mixture of righteous indignation and sheer envy. Close up, Saburô's mums were even more impressive. The flowers were blooming for all they were worth; each individual petal was extraordinarily long and thick and throbbing with vital force. Adding insult to injury was the fact that, as Sainosuke soon realized, the plants were none other than the worthless seedlings he'd discarded behind the shed. He let out a gurgle of despair, and just as he did so a voice called to him from behind.

"Welcome! We've been waiting for you to drop by."

Flustered, Sainosuke spun around to see Saburô standing there grinning at him.

"You've won!" he nearly shouted in frustration. "I know when I'm beaten, and I'm man enough to admit it, too. Listen, I'm . . . I'm here to ask you to take me on as your apprentice. Everything that's passed between us . . ." He paused to unload a great sigh of relief. "It's all just water under the bridge. We'll let bygones be bygones. However, I . . ."

"Wait. Please don't say what I think you're going to say. I'm not a man of your moral fiber. As you've probably guessed, I've been selling off the chrysanthemums little by little. Please don't look down on us for that. My sister, for one, is always fretting about what you'll think. But we're only doing what we need to do to survive. Unlike yourself, we have no inheritance to fall back on—it's either sell the mums or die of starvation. Please be so indulgent as to overlook that, and let us be friends again."

The sincerity of Saburô's plea and the sad droop of his head melted Sainosuke's heart.

"Don't be silly," he said meekly and bowed. "I'm not worthy of your apology. I feel no enmity toward either of you. Besides, I'm the one who's asking you be my teacher. If anyone should apologize, it's me."

And so they were reconciled, at least for the time being. Sainosuke dismantled the fence in the garden, and the members of the two households resumed relations, although, to be sure, dissension continued to arise between them now and then.

"You seem to have some secret to raising these mums."

"Nothing of the sort. I've already taught you everything I know. The rest is in the fingertips, but that's where it gets a bit mysterious. I simply seem to have a certain touch, and since it's something I'm not really conscious of, I can't very well teach it to you in words. It's a genius of sorts, I suppose."

"Oh, I get it. So you're a genius and I'm a nincompoop, right? Not much hope of teaching anything to a nincompoop, right?"

"You needn't put it like that. Let's just say that my life depends on getting the best blooms I can. If they don't sell, I don't eat. Perhaps that's why the flowers get so big—because I'm driven by necessity. People like yourself, on the other hand, who grow mums as a hobby, are motivated more by simple curiosity, or the desire to satisfy their pride."

"Oh, I see. You're telling me I should sell my mums, too, is that it? Do you really think I'd stoop so low? How dare you say such a thing!"

"That's not what I'm saying at all. Why must you be this way?"

The relationship, in short, lacked a certain harmony.

As time went by, the Tômotos' fortune only increased. When the new year came along they hired a team of carpenters and, without so much as consulting Sainosuke, began construction of a sizable mansion that extended from the rear of the garden to within an inch or so of his cottage. Sainosuke had just begun to consider severing relations again when, one day, Saburô came calling with a pensive and serious expression on his face.

"Please accept my sister as your bride," he said somberly.

Sainosuke blushed. From the first time he'd laid eyes on the sister he'd been unable to dispel that image of tenderness and purity from his mind. But, true to form, his manly pride forced him to launch into a queer sort of argument.

"I can't afford a betrothal gift, and I'm not qualified to take a bride like that anyway. You're rich people now, you know." Far from expressing his true feelings, he'd resorted to sheer sarcasm.

"Not at all. Everything we have is yours. That was how my sister intended it to be from the beginning. And there's no need to worry about a betrothal gift. All you have to do is move in with us, just as you are. My sister is in love with you."

Sainosuke shook his head, trying his best to feign composure. "Not interested. I have my own house. You won't catch me marrying into money. Not that I have anything against your sister, mind you," he said and laughed what he hoped was a hearty, manly laugh. "But to marry for money is the greatest shame a man can bring upon himself. I refuse. Go back and tell your sister that. And tell her that if she doesn't mind living in honest poverty, she can come move in with me."

Thus they parted once again on less than amicable terms. That night, however, a delicate white butterfly came fluttering into Sainosuke's room on a gentle breeze.

"I don't mind living in honest poverty," the sister said with a giggle. Her name was Kié.

For a while the two of them passed their days and nights within the confines of Sainosuke's ramshackle cottage, but eventually Kié opened a hole in the rear wall and another in the adjoining wall of the Tômoto mansion, allowing her to go freely from one to the other. And, to Sainosuke's great dismay, she also began to bring along whatever furnishings or utensils she needed.

"This won't do. That hibachi, that vase . . . all these things are from your house. Don't you realize how it sullies a man's honor to use his wife's possessions? I want you to stop carting this junk over here."

Kié would only smile when he scolded her like this and continue to bring the things she needed. Sainosuke, who fancied himself a man of incorruptible integrity, finally resorted to purchasing a large ledger in which he wrote: "This is to acknowledge receipt of the following items, to be temporarily retained by the undersigned." He started trying to list every article Kié had brought from the mansion, but found to his chagrin that there was now nothing in the cottage that didn't fit that description. Realizing that he might fill any number of ledgers without completing the task, he gave up all hope. He continued to resent what was happening, however, and one night he turned to Kié and said: "Thanks to you I've ended up being a kept man. To acquire wealth through marriage is the greatest disgrace a man can suffer. For thirty years I've lived in noble, honest poverty, and now it's all been for nothing, thanks to you and that brother of yours."

The bitterness in his voice stung Kié's heart, and she looked at him sadly and said: "It's all my fault, I suppose. It's just that I wanted to do everything I could to find some way to repay you for your kindness. I'm afraid I didn't realize how deeply committed you were to that honest poverty of yours. Let's do this: We'll sell all my things, and the new house as well. Then you can take the money and use it any way you like."

"Don't be stupid. You think a man like myself would accept your filthy money?"

"Well, then, what *is* to be done?" Kié pleaded with a sob in her voice. "Saburô, too, feels a great debt of gratitude to you. That's why he works so hard to get money by growing the mums and delivering them all over town. What are we to do? We just don't see eye to eye on this at all, do we?"

"There's only one thing we can do: separate." Sainosuke's own highminded pronouncements had backed him into a corner, and now he found himself having to utter these painful words, which were nowhere in his heart. "Let the pure live in purity and the corrupt in corruption. There's no other way. I'm not qualified to order anyone else about; I'll leave this place to you, build a little hut in the corner of the garden, and pass my days enjoying the solitary pleasures of honest poverty."

It was all quite ridiculous, but once a man has spoken there's no turning back. First thing the following morning Sainosuke slapped together a little lean-to in the corner of the garden. He moved into this tiny space that night and sat there on his knees, shivering from the cold. After he'd spent a mere two nights enjoying his honest poverty, however, the freezing weather began to take its toll, and on the third night he stole back to his cottage and tapped lightly on the rain shutter. The shutter opened a crack and Kié's fair, smiling face appeared.

"So much for moral fiber," she said with a giggle.

Sainosuke was deeply ashamed. From that night on, not a single obstinate demand was ever again to escape his lips.

By the time the cherry trees along the Sumida River began to bloom, construction of the Tômoto mansion was complete. It was now connected to the cottage in such a way that there was no distinction between the two. Sainosuke, however, uttered not a word of complaint. He left the household affairs entirely up to Kié and Saburô, and spent his days playing Chinese chess with friends from the neighborhood.

One day the three members of the household set out for the Sumida to view the cherry blossoms. They settled down with their lunch at a suitable spot on the riverbank, and Sainosuke lost no time in breaking out the saké he'd brought and urging Saburô to join him. Kié shot a forbidding glance at her brother, but he calmly accepted a cup.

"Sis," he said, "it's all right if I drink a little saké today. We've saved up enough now so that you and Sainosuke can take it easy for the rest of your lives, even if I'm not around. I'm tired of growing chrysanthemums."

And with this mysterious declaration he began guzzling saké at an alarming rate. He was soon thoroughly drunk, and finally he lay down and stretched out on the grass. And then, right before their eyes, Saburô's body melted away and disappeared in a puff of smoke, leaving nothing behind but his kimono and sandals. Flabbergasted, Sainosuke snatched up the kimono only to find, growing out of the earth where it had lain, a fresh, bright green chrysanthemum seedling. Now, for the first time, he realized that Saburô and Kié were not human beings. But Sainosuke, who by this time had come to truly appreciate the young pair's wisdom and affection, felt not in the least horrified at the realization but only grew to love Kié, his poor chrysanthemum fairy, all the more deeply.

When autmn came, Saburô's seedling, which Sainosuke had replanted in his garden, produced a single blossom. The flower was faintly rouge, like a drinker's blush, and gave off a light scent of saké. As for Kié, tradition tells us there was "no change forever." In other words, she lived as a human being to the end of her days.

ANGEL
Mary Ellis

Mary Ellis, who has lived in Wisconsin for most of her life, has had short fiction published in various magazines and reviews. A strong sense of place infuses the following story, lending it a special quality that is rare in any fiction.

"Angel" is a beautifully written fantasy story about the nature of love, and its tenacity. It comes from the Winter 1993 issue of *Glimmer Train* magazine.

—T.W.

Of course we have had our differences which at times turned into bitter arguments; then I would bite my lip so as to not cry out. That is natural, human: love is a series of scars. "No heart is as whole as a broken heart," said the celebrated Rabbi Nahman of Bratzlav.
—Elie Wiesel, *The Fifth Son*

angel (ānj'əl) n. 2. A guardian spirit or guiding influence
5. *Military*. Enemy aircraft
—*American Heritage Dictionary*

Ernie Morriseau knew the exact moment that Jimmy Lucas had died.

It was late January in 1969. The sunset had been an unusually spectacular orange-red, like the sunsets of late summer, and was streaked with clouds shaped like scattered fleece. He had been shoveling manure for about an hour behind the barn, adding to the pile already banked up against the outside wall, when he stopped to have a smoke and ponder the sunset. Northern Wisconsin had been experiencing a freak midwinter thaw and the temperatures during the day had reached the low forties for the past week. But now dusk was rapidly taking over and the temperature was dropping. Ernie put out his cigarette and hurried to get the job done because in another half hour he wouldn't be able to see or feel his hands on the shovel. As he worked, he could hear the family dog inspecting and exploring through the thick wet snow around the barn.

Ernie was straining to lift an enormous shovelful when he heard the dog stop prowling and give a quick snort. Thinking the dog had just found an unlucky mouse under the snow, Ernie tossed the manure onto the pile and was about to shovel up some more when he realized that the dog had stopped moving completely. He straightened up and was trying to locate the dog when he heard him instead. A long, high howl broke the farmyard quiet. Ernie shivered and involuntarily dropped the shovel. Then the dog streaked right past him, jumping over the shovel and running about three hundred yards into the snowcrusted field behind the barn. Ernie turned in the direction the dog had taken, wondering what had spooked him, when he saw that the large black animal had stopped again and stood rigidly still with his head and nose held high. He looked beyond the dog and that was when he saw Jimmy Lucas.

At first, Ernie thought that Jimmy had been discharged early from the army and was finally home from fighting in Vietnam. But he was wearing his combat helmet and fatigues, and carrying a rifle. Ernie stepped forward, sinking into the snow, and raised his arm.

"Jimmy!" he yelled and waved his hand.

Jimmy Lucas didn't answer and instead reached up and took off his helmet, dropping it into the snow. The helmet rolled as though it had hit hard ground instead of snow and Ernie noticed that Jimmy was standing on top of the snow instead of sinking into it as Ernie and the dog had. Suddenly Ernie knew it was and wasn't Jimmy Lucas, and why he was standing in the Morriseaus' eighty-acre field behind the barn. Ernie sank to his knees.

"Oh no, Jimmy," he whispered. "No, no Jimmy."

As Ernie watched, Jimmy dropped his rifle, too, and slowly turned around. The dog snorted again but did not move. Then Jimmy walked away from them and continued walking until he reached the big swamp that bordered the Morriseau and Lucas farms. The very moment that Jimmy disappeared into the swamp, the dog howled again and took off running, floundering through the snow until he, too, reached the swamp.

An hour went by before Ernie was able to rise to his feet. He threw the shovel into the toolshed and reluctantly approached the house. Methodically and silently he ate dinner before trudging up the stairs to bed. Thinking it was exhaustion, his wife only asked where the dog was, and didn't question her husband's decision to go to sleep early.

Two days later the official news came. James Lucas had been killed in action in an unspecified location near the DMZ.

It's July. The dog lies on the porch, catching the hot July wind in his mouth, tasting it between his pink tongue and the roof of his mouth before panting it out again. I watch him determine in a second what the messages are in the wind— who's coming, who's been where, who's alive, who's dead—and then he sends his own message when he lets the wind go, to whatever animal will savor and understand it as he does. Angel's done this a million times. He's an old dog. So I imagine he has much to say.

I'm washing the supper dishes, listening to some old records, watching the dog, and ignoring the heat. The records are stacked like a vinyl layer cake, losing a layer every time a record falls and is played on the stereo. Right now, Roy Orbison is singing one of my favorite songs. "Blue Angel."

"Hey!" I yell, rapping the kitchen window with a soapy knuckle. "He's singing your song."

Angel briefly looks up at me, and then, swatting a horsefly away from his mangled ear with his front paw, resumes his panting. I stare at the dog, stretched out on the porch floor. And I remember the day we found him twelve years ago.

We were driving home from a Friday night fish fry when I thought I saw something moving in the shadows beside the road. Ernie slowed the truck down. I motioned for him to stop and rolled down my window.

Something big and dark was trying to drag itself back into the ditch, away from the headlights. At first I thought it was a bear cub and looked up at the trees along the road for the sow. Ernie opened his door and stepped out. Then he stood there, leaning against the open door and taking long drags on his cigarette. I waited. My husband continued to just stare at the ditch. Finally, I leaned over in the seat.

"Are you meditating or what? You want me to check it out?" I whispered.

Ernie dropped his cigarette and smashed it with the heel of his boot.

"Wait a minute," he said. "I think it's a dog."

He slowly walked around the front of the truck and to the edge of the ditch. I poked my head out of the window just in time to hear a low growl. My scalp tingled.

"Be careful! He might have rabies," I whispered again, and grabbed the flashlight out of the glove compartment. I got out of the truck and shined the light down into the ditch.

Ernie was right. There, in the watery mud of spring, was a dog, his breath whistling through his blood-caked nose. He was about six months old but was already a big animal. The light caught the glistening blood running down the side of his head and he weakly pulled himself around so that he faced us. He was as black as a night without stars. Blue-black. One eye shined white and luminous in the light but the other was swollen shut and covered with clotting blood. Ernie stepped forward for a better look. The dog barked and tried to lunge forward.

"Christ!" Ernie said, stepping back. "It looks like he's been shot in the head and shot in his left hip . . . and I think he caught some buckshot in his chest. Whoever it was couldn't shoot straight. That's why he's still alive . . . and in one piece. Goodlookin' dog though, huh Rose? Think he's part Lab?"

The dog looked away from Ernie and focused on me with his one good eye before I could answer. I stared at that dog. He stared at me. His eye burned a path through all the hidden memories in my head. Standing on that dusky gravel road, I felt the sudden chill of knowing what the reality of his wounds meant. The same meaning that accompanies a calf born too deformed to live, or a piglet whose back has been broken by the carelessness of its mother's bulky roll in the pen. It is not a mean decision but one that comes with the harshness of rural life and expensive veterinarian bills. Ernie had anticipated what was coming and had already retrieved the shotgun from the back of the truck. I ignored the gun and squatted, resting on the balls of my feet.

"You're right. Looks like almost all Lab. Poor fella," I crooned.

He stopped growling and whimpered. Then Ernie cautiously moved toward him again. His good eye left me and zeroed in on Ernie. He growled, this time baring his teeth. That's how I knew it was a man that shot him and threw him into that ditch. His head must have been searing with pain, like someone stuck a knife into it, but he could still tell a woman from a man.

I loved him in that instant.

"Nope," I said. "Not this time. I can fix him up."

"Oh Lord, Rose," Ernie said. "It's pretty bad. He's never gonna be the same. He's gotta be in a helluva lot of pain, too."

I started to get up and prepare myself for a good fight with Ernie. But as I stood up, a sudden warm infused me from my belly up to my chest that felt almost blessed. I am not a religious person but I can't think of any other way to describe it. It was like that circular feeling I had when I anticipated being a mother and remembered what it was like to be mothered; that feeling of having been chosen without having to ask. And this dog chose me.

"Well?" my husband asked, turning to face me. Then the name just popped into my head.

"Angel," I said. "We're going to take him home and call him Angel."

"Angel?" Ernie said, giving me a funny look. "He looks more like a Bruno to me."

"Angel," I repeated.

Ernie shrugged and walked to the bed of the truck for some twine. Angel's good ear stood up like a small wing. I kept talking to him until he slumped back into the mud. He gazed into the flashlight beam and became mesmerized enough by both the pain and the light so that Ernie could grab his muzzle, tying the twine around it so he wouldn't bite us. Then we took him home.

I don't know how he lived. Whoever tried to blow his brains out missed the best part, the telling part. Angel has fits every now and then, chasing his tail around and around, and sometimes he gallops in his sleep, his legs scissoring through the air and going nowhere. His head appears a little lopsided when you look at him straight on, and the shredded remains of his one ear wave in the breeze. They are soft though, when you touch them, like strips of black chamois cloth. He let me touch him from the very beginning. But it took Angel a long time to trust Ernie. I've always been secretly proud that Angel took to me right off. I'm good with animals and children, but Ernie's better.

Angel's memory is whole and enduring. I don't think any of the buckshot got into that part of his brain even though I can feel with my fingertips the round bumps of lead coming to the surface when I rub his head. When he loves, he loves completely, recognizing someone he trusts even after years of not seeing them. He lopes down the driveway in an easy way, his big tongue hanging out. This is the way he greets women and children. Yet his hatred is just as complete, just as absolute. He hates men, all men, except for Ernie and our neighbor Bill Lucas and his brother Jimmy; even though Bill's a grown man now and not the little boy who spent so much time visiting us; even though Jimmy's been dead for twelve years, bombed into a hillside in Vietnam.

Angel's my dog. He sits in the cab of the truck with his big muzzle poking out of the window, tasting the wind as we fly down the road.

*   *   *

I'm almost done with the dishes. It's seven o'clock, it's hotter than hell, and I've got the blues really bad. I look out of the window in the hope that I'll think of something else besides crying when a flash of color catches my eye from the Lucas field. Then I see Bill Lucas, tall and hunched, walking along the edge of the field that borders the big swamp and our field. Angel sees him too and scrambles to his feet. His good ear rises like a flag, but he doesn't bark.

"There goes your friend," I say softly, but of course the dog can't hear me through the window.

Bill stops then. Just stops and stands there and faces the big swamp. Angel continues to silently watch him. He lifts his nose. I turn my head for just a minute and that's when Angel barks, once. I look back just in time to see Bill get swallowed into the thick cover of those swamp cedars. This is the fifth time this summer I've seen him disappear like that into the swamp. I stand up on my toes to catch a glimpse of him but he's gone and the only thing I see now is my husband by the toolshed, watching Bill just like me, just like the dog.

Once last summer I saw Bill up close at the Standard station where he works, and was shocked by the oily stubble and savage look of his face. His eyes are no longer the soft gray color they were when he was a kid. They are a rock gray now, and like a split rock they are small but with jagged edges.

We wait and watch, but nothing. Ernie's shoulders sag when he realizes that Bill will not reappear and he trudges off toward the barn, sixty years of exhaustion in every step.

We will not talk about this. My husband does not know that I know he watches the Lucas place, looking for signs of life—a vigorous wave of a hand or the yellow halo of the yard light when night falls. The little boy who used to visit our farm, eat dinner with us, and play with the dog has grown into a remote and painfully shy young man. We see him rarely and almost always at a distance. And the oddest thing is that his name is never spoken between us . . . as though he were dead instead of his brother Jimmy. Which is nonsense because we do *see him*, working, walking, or driving, even if it isn't often. It hurts Ernie that Bill does not come to our place anymore or accept visits easily from us. But Ernie doesn't talk about that either. He deals with his pain like most men, treating it as though it doesn't exist, and therefore, cannot be talked about.

I, on the other hand, have never been known to stay quiet. When I'm in pain I cry a blue streak, and when I'm angry I yell like hell. And when something is bothering me, I talk. A lot.

But I don't have another person to talk to easily outside of Ernie, who's been punishing me with silence for the past two weeks, and who has even struggled to keep his feet from touching mine while we sleep. I don't even know what I'm being punished for, that's how nonexistent our conversations have been. I've given up trying, fearful that I might use the most intimate details that people who have lived together for a long time can carry like swords. But I still need to talk to somebody. Most of our neighbors are a good two, three miles away and busy farmers like us. So I talk to the dog whose eyes have taken on a kind of old-man wisdom to match his graying muzzle.

Some days it's hilarious. Angel patiently trails behind me as I do the housework, ducking behind a chair when I vacuum, sitting by the bathroom door as I scrub the toilet and floor, or lying on the porch while I peel vegetables or count eggs, all the while listening to the constant run of my mouth.

It is only at night when I let Angel out of the house that he leaves me for a few hours, running out the door and into the nearest patch of woods with the determination of a reconnaissance pilot, his black coat giving him a natural camouflage at night. In the past I had only an inkling of what he did on these forays; what any male dog would do, and him especially, pent up all day in the house with me. But lately I've suspected that Angel's nightly journeys are not meaningless wanderings or chance matings, and if he could talk he would tell me things that my husband never does. It frightens me. Other women who are isolated and lonely drink or pick fights with their silent husbands, or take up with other men, or maybe just suffer silently. I talk to the dog. And watch a little boy who was never mine and who has long since grown up and abandoned me.

Then this morning at breakfast my husband, who has borne like a Buddhist monk the hardships of being a WW II veteran, a farmer, and a mixed-blood man in northern Wisconsin, did talk to me, only to hurt me. He put down his coffee cup and said, "I just can't do it anymore, Rose. I used to be able to lift a bale of hay in each hand, and now I can barely lift one with two hands. I can't sleep worth a shit, and things that used to mean so much to me don't anymore. I just don't give a damn."

What could I say? For other people the meaning of life does not rest on being able to lift a bale of hay. But we're farmers. Everything rests on that bale of hay. Actually, it was the look on his face, not what Ernie said, that did me in this morning. The message was loudly broadcast with those dark brown, bloodshot, and tired eyes. That bale of hay should have been passed onto younger hands. We are Rosemary and Ernest Morriseau—good farmers, but farmers *without children*.

I sat as though slapped speechless. My lips moved but no sound came out. Ernie stood up as though he didn't notice, maybe he didn't care, and walked out the kitchen door.

I give a damn, is what I couldn't spit out. *I tried*. And it got worse as the day went on. I could barely keep my head up, could barely talk for fear of tears.

Now the dishes are done and the dog is scratching at the door to be let in. I open the door and Angel strolls through the doorway, his nails tapping like drumsticks on the linoleum. Then he sits and looks up at me, my only friend.

Suddenly I can't look at the dog and I can't breathe. I stumble out of the kitchen and into the living room, but Angel trails me. When I reach for, and slump into, the old brown recliner by the window, I am temporarily relieved of the burden of Ernie's words, of Ernie's silence. I cry, hiccuping and sputtering like a three-year-old. I cry for hours until it gets dark, until my eyes become puffy and my head aches. Angel rubs his scarred head against my knee for a while before settling down next to the chair. I'm grateful for even that amount of touch.

I love this dog and this dog loves me. But when did my husband and I stop doing the dance of love? What have I done, what crime have I committed that warrants being ignored? That justifies not being touched? And when will I stop being punished, however slightly, for the children I could not give birth to?

*   *   *

I met Ernie at a Legion party in Milwaukee. I was an army nurse who had just finished my tour of duty in the Philippines, and Ernie was a shrapnel-filled soldier. I was sipping my favorite drink of depression, a gin and tonic, and spiraling downward when I smelled cedar. I turned around to stare into a pair of the most velvety brown eyes I'd ever seen. He had a chest like a gladiator and hair the color of my most recent dreams. Black. But his voice was warm and soft.

"War's over. Wanna dance?" he asked, and smiled that enormous slow smile that made me put down my drink, suddenly crazed to wrap my arms around that huge, cedar-smelling chest and hold on for as long as I could.

We both held on like two long-lost buddies from childhood. He was from northern Wisconsin like me. We got married and left Milwaukee to take on his family farm in Olina. Then I tried having babies.

The doctor said my uterus was damaged but he couldn't figure out how. I told him that I'd been sick, on and off, in the Philippines with what was thought to be some kind of intestinal flu.

"Well," he commented nonchalantly, "maybe that did it," and motioned for me to get dressed. Then he said to quit trying. But I tried.

Just when I would start to think that this one was going to hold, and get ready to shop for baby clothes, I'd feel that damn ache in my lower back. Then the contractions would come on fast, and before I could get to the hospital twenty miles away, my lovely baby would slip and fall out, looking like clotted peony petals shaken from the stem into a pool of blood.

I remember the last baby. I was in the bathroom, feeling that downward pull and squeezing my thighs together to hold it in.

"Don't leave me. Don't leave me," I kept saying. Chanting it, Ernie said, long after the baby was gone and he'd taken me to the hospital. Ernie had been kind enough after the first three miscarriages. But as they continued, he made love to me as though he were pouring precious seed onto waterless ground.

Then Ernie and I got two sons by default, at least for a short time, and my husband and the ghosts of our own children were temporarily appeased. First Jimmy and then Bill began to visit us, driven out of their house by their father's rageful drinking and their mother's mental descent into another world. I didn't give a damn about Jon Lucas, but Claire was like too many women I'd seen and grown up with. Women with brains three times the size and depth of their fathers' and husbands', but trapped and nowhere to go with that kind of intelligence but sideways or down. I tried for a long time to get close to Claire, but she avoided me as though I were painful to her. I used to watch her walk in one continuous circle around the edge of their back forty acres while Jimmy was in the army and Billy was at school, her hands talking to the air, and her face slanted toward the sky.

"She's losing it," I said to Ernie once when we watched her discreetly from behind our barn.

"You don't know that for sure," my husband said, surprising me. "Maybe she really is talking to someone."

"Do you see anybody else out there?" I asked sarcastically.

"I'm just sayin' there's alotta things we don't know about," Ernie answered and shrugged.

"Especially in that family," I cracked, and even Ernie had to nod.

But I felt lousy saying it and shut up after that, not wanting to tempt the spirits. *There but for the grace of God*, I thought, *go I.* I rationalized it away, thinking that Claire probably needed a break from the kids, and opened up our house and my arms to Jimmy and Bill, letting the love pour. But that was not enough. Jimmy became a teenager so hell-bent on escaping his old man that enlisting in the army looked like a sure chance in a million-dollar lottery in comparison to his life in Olina. Then Jimmy lost the lottery. In her grief, Claire Lucas woke up and realized that she had another son, keeping little Bill close to home after that. And Ernie and I lost both of them. I don't know who I cried more for, Ernie and I, or Jimmy and Bill.

Then when Bill was sixteen, his father died of a heart attack. I could not find any warmth in that kid's hand when I shook it after the funeral mass. It was as though he didn't know or remember me. But the look on his face was one that couldn't be mistaken. While Claire appeared bewildered and exhausted, her son was obviously relieved instead of sad.

"You'd be relieved too! He won't have that stinkin' mean drunk for a father anymore," Ernie commented bitterly on the drive home.

When Bill turned eighteen, he inherited the farm and Claire gratefully moved to a small house across from the church in Olina, becoming a receptionist for the Forest Service. She seems much better now but she still won't accept my friendship.

I'm almost ready to drift off to sleep when I hear the steps creak. Angel wakes up and cocks his head toward the staircase. I wait and watch. My husband's shuffling body fills the doorway. He is wearing what he always wears to bed, a pair of blue pajama bottoms and nothing else. It's too dark for me to see his face, but I know something is wrong by the way his big shoulders are slumped forward.

"You know," he begins quietly, "my grandma Morriseau told me before I was shipped out to the Pacific that I would know if anyone close to me had died. Here at home or over there. I told her I didn't wanna know. She said, want to or not, I would just know, especially if I kept my mind open to it. I thought it was just old Indian superstition. Nothin' ever happened during my service that made me think about what she said. Except my buddy, Frank. His old French-Canadian, Catholic mother told him almost the same thing. We laughed about it."

I'm either so tired or it's really been a strange day. This morning he tells me he doesn't care anymore, and now it's almost midnight and he's telling me about his reservation grandmother who's been dead for almost thirty years.

"But," he says, his voice dropping an octave, "I had a bad feeling when Jimmy left for basic training."

I am instantly wide awake.

"Jimmy?" I ask. "What about Jimmy?"

Ernie went on as though he didn't hear what I said.

"I didn't pay any attention to it," he says. "I figured I felt that way because of the kind of war it was. But when I saw him, I knew I had done a bad thing. I could've invited him over to dinner with Billy that night, remember? Before he shipped out the next day? But I didn't 'cause of what he did to that turtle with that stupid-ass Schwartz kid he used to hang out with. I could've went after him, talked to him about what he was getting himself into. I could've talked him out of it. I came so close," he says and then repeats, "so close."

"Ernie," I say. "Don't you remember? We didn't know that Jimmy had even enlisted until that night Billy came over for dinner. Remember when Jon came over to pick up Billy, he told us. Remember you were so mad because Jon was *proud* of it, and you said he was just getting rid of his son before the kid took him down. Don't you remember?"

"I *saw* Jimmy," he says, his voice dropping to a whisper, "two days before we heard about him. Remember, it was so warm that winter? I was shoveling manure. Well . . . that's when I saw him. Angel," he gestures toward the dog, "saw him first and howled like crazy. Jimmy was standing in the back field. But he didn't say a word, not a word. He just took off his helmet and dropped his gun. Then," Ernie swallows, "he turned around and walked into the swamp. That's when I knew . . . that Jimmy had died."

My husband, by nature, does not exaggerate. Still, I find his words hard to believe until I remember that Ernie didn't cry like I did when we heard the news. At the time, I thought it was because he had accepted it as a consequence of war. He'd fought. He knew the chances. Now it all makes sense. For the past twelve years, he has been trudging through his daily life, not silenced by hard solitary work, but by grief.

"I wanted to tell you," he says, suddenly shaking so much that the air seems to crack around him. "Then this morning when I saw the look on your face . . . so lonely, *so lonely*, it hit me what a goddamn bastard I've been. I'm sorry, Rose. I'm so sorry."

Then Ernie covers his face with his hands, and hunching over, lets out a long, deep sob that echoes through the room. My heart hits the wall of my chest.

I don't remember the last time Ernie cried. It must have been years ago. I've cried plenty and I've heard lots of other women cry, too. But women cry, even in their worst pain, with hope and relief. They cry like wolves and coyotes do, howling to talk to their mates as well as to the rest of the pack. But there is something about the way men cry that sounds so hopeless, so anguished, as though the very act of crying is killing them.

I could feel the tears start up fresh in my eyes.

"C'mere," I say, and open my arms to stop the waters.

My husband stumbles toward me. The recliner moans under our weight as Ernie sinks into my arms. Angel bolts up and trots over by the TV. He hunkers down in front of it, alert but oddly calm. He lifts his nose to sniff the air, then opens his mouth to taste it. Our big black dog, satisfied with what his nose and tongue read, lowers his lopsided head to rest in a pool of moonlight on the floor. I wrap my arms tighter around Ernie, touching with my fingertips the scars and pointed shrapnel still under his skin. He nuzzles his face deep into the crook of my neck to hide it while he cries.

I wish there were some way I could tell Jimmy that Ernie cries for him. I wonder if Jon Lucas ever grieved so for what was his flesh-and-blood son. We thought not at the time. He'd brag in town about Jimmy being a war hero and tell stories as though he'd actually been there with Jimmy, fighting in the jungle. Ernie and the other veterans in town never talked like that. They'd done it. They knew war wasn't a movie. It was hell personified, and for them to talk about it was to give it new life, to raise the dead. And I covered up so many shattered bodies in the hospital in the Philippines that I had dreams. Terrible dreams that lasted for twenty years. I dreamt that my limbs were being torn off or that I was being shot into the air by the force of an exploding bomb, or that I was being held at gunpoint, unable to speak Japanese, and finally, being bayoneted through the chest. My worst dream, though, was of a large white sheet descending on me from above, and I was still alive and fighting to keep that endless white cotton from smothering me. Jon Lucas just couldn't know. Whatever it was that made him drink, it wasn't the crap of war.

The dog exhales a deep lungful of air, but his eyes stay open, luminescent in the white light. I stare at him until I realize that I have forgotten to let him out for his nightly wandering. Then it dawns on me that he has not made the slightest familiar sign of wanting to go outside.

My head suddenly clears from years of shameful and cloudy debris, and my skin prickles.

Oh yes, I want to say out loud. *Yes, yes, yes.*

Grandma Morriseau was right about such things.

Up until now, I would've traded Angel to have had at least one child come out of my rickety womb. I was at one of the lowest points in my life when we found Angel lying in that ditch. I believed, since the first time I saw him all shot up, and spared him an early death, that I had saved him. That all my stored-up and unused maternal love and care could at least save him, a mere dog. I was *determined* to save him. But all the tears in the world can't hide the truth.

If anyone was saved, it was me.

When I have given and given and danced with love until I am exhausted, when my husband remained as silent, and some days, as bitter and brittle, as a winter's day, this dog has given to me. When I have felt fragile and vulnerable; when I have wondered if Ernie would still fight for me and over me, over an aging, fifty-seven-year-old farm wife instead of the once svelte and long-legged beauty that I was, it is Angel who sits beside me in the cab of the truck while I sell eggs to homes on some of the worst back roads in this county. It is Angel who guards the farm and me from aggressive salesmen, from all the possible evil that people are capable of bestowing out of the blue. It is Angel who has kept me from talking to the air like Claire Lucas, and whose very presence has kept at a distance the haunting ghosts of my never-born children. It is Angel who circles the perimeter of the farm at night, black and mysterious, who tastes the wind and listens for sounds that we cannot hear. And it was Angel who saw Jimmy Lucas first, and who I suspect, because I will never really know, is able to talk to Bill Lucas because Ernie and I cannot. It is this big, black, scarred-up dog lying in front of us that has carried for years a spirit that is not his own.

My husband has stopped crying but makes no move to uncoil himself from my arms. Someday I will tell Ernie what I know, that it was a good thing, not a bad thing, that he saw Jimmy. That Jimmy chose him. That we cannot save anyone. That we choose to be saved ourselves.

Love, I will tell my silent husband, is never wasted.

And I will tell him, looking at Angel now sleeping by the TV, that we have never been alone.

THE TAKING OF MR. BILL

Graham Masterton

Graham Masterton is the author of more than twenty novels of horror and suspense, including *Walkers*, *Death Trance*, *Prey*, and *The Manitou*, which was adapted for film. His most recent novel is *Burial*, a sequel to *The Manitou*. He is the editor of the anthology series *Scare Care* as well.

"The Taking of Mr. Bill" uses two characters from Peter Pan in an extraordinary way that could never have been envisioned by their creator. This chiller was originally published in *The Mammoth Book of Zombies*.

—E.D.

It was only a few minutes past four in the afternoon, but the day suddenly grew dark, thunderously dark, and freezing-cold rain began to lash down. For a few minutes, the pathways of Kensington Gardens were criss-crossed with bobbing umbrellas and au-pairs running helter-skelter with baby-buggies and screaming children.

Then, the gardens were abruptly deserted, left to the rain and the Canada geese and the gusts of wind that ruffled back the leaves. Marjorie found herself alone, hurriedly pushing William in his small navy-blue Mothercare pram. She was wearing only her red tweed jacket and her long black pleated skirt, and she was already soaked. The afternoon had been brilliantly sunny when she left the house, with a sky as blue as dinner-plates. She hadn't brought an umbrella. She hadn't even brought a plastic rain-hat.

She hadn't expected to stay with her Uncle Michael until so late, but Uncle Michael was so old now that he could barely keep himself clean. She had made him tea and tidied his bed, and done some hoovering while William lay kicking and gurgling on the sofa, and Uncle Michael watched him, rheumy-eyed, his hands resting on his lap like crumpled yellow tissue-paper, his mind fading and brightening, fading and brightening, in the same way that the afternoon sunlight faded and brightened.

She had kissed Uncle Michael before she left, and he had clasped her hand between both of his. "Take good care of that boy, won't you?" he had whispered. "You never know who's watching. You never know who might want him."

"Oh, Uncle, you know that I never let him out of my sight. Besides, if anybody wants him, they're welcome to him. Perhaps I'll get some sleep at night."

"Don't say that, Marjorie. Never say that. Think of all the mothers who have said that, only as a joke, and then have wished that they had cut out their tongues."

"Uncle . . . don't be so morbid. I'll give you a ring when I get home, just to make sure you're all right. But I must go. I'm cooking chicken chasseur tonight."

Uncle Michael had nodded. "Chicken chasseur . . . ," he had said, vaguely. Then, "Don't forget the pan."

"Of course not, Uncle. I'm not going to burn it. Now, make sure you put the chain on the door."

Now she was walking past the Round Pond. She slowed down, wheeling the pram through the muddy grass. She was so wet that it scarcely made any difference. She thought of the old Chinese saying, "Why walk fast in the rain? It's raining just as hard up ahead."

Before the arrival of the Canada geese, the Round Pond had been neat and tidy and peaceful, with fluttering ducks and children sailing little yachts. Now, it was fouled and murky, and peculiarly threatening, like anything precious that has been taken away from you and vandalized by strangers. Marjorie's Peugeot had been stolen last spring, and crashed, and urinated in, and she had never been able to think of driving it again, or even another car like it.

She emerged from the trees and a sudden explosion of cold rain caught her on the side of the cheek. William was awake, and waving his arms, but she knew that he would be hungry by now, and that she would have to feed him as soon as she got home.

She took a short cut, walking diagonally through another stand of trees. She could hear the muffled roar of London's traffic on both sides of the garden, and the rumbling, scratching noise of an airliner passing overhead, but the gardens themselves remained oddly empty, and silent, as if a spell had been cast over them. Underneath the trees, the light was the colour of moss-weathered slate.

She leaned forward over the pram handle and cooed, "Soon be home, Mr. Bill! Soon be home!"

But when she looked up she saw a man standing silhouetted beside the oak tree just in front of her, not more than thirty feet away. A thin, tall man wearing a black cap, and a black coat with the collar turned up. His eyes were shaded, but she could see that his face was deathly white. And he was obviously waiting for her.

She hesitated, stopped, and looked around. Her heart began to thump furiously. There was nobody else in sight, nobody to whom she could shout for help. The rain rattled on the trees above her head, and William let out one fitful yelp. She swallowed, and found herself swallowing a thick mixture of fruit-cake and bile. She simply didn't know what to do.

She thought: there's no use running. I'll just have to walk past him. I'll just have to show him that I'm not afraid. After all, I'm pushing a pram. I've got a baby. Surely he won't be so cruel that he'll—

You never know who's watching. You never know who might want him.

Sick with fear, she continued to walk forward. The man remained where he was, not moving, not speaking. She would have to pass within two feet of him, but so far he had shown no sign that he had noticed her, although he must have done; and no sign at all that he wanted her to stop.

She walked closer and closer, stiff-legged and mewling softly to herself in terror. She passed him by, so close that she could see the glittering raindrops on his coat, so close that she could *smell* him, strong tobacco and some dry, unfamiliar smell, like hay.

She thought: thank God. He's let me pass.

But then his right arm whipped out and snatched her elbow, twisted her around, and flung her with such force against the trunk of the oak that she heard her shoulder-blade crack and one of her shoes flew off.

She screamed, and screamed again. But he slapped her face with the back of his hand, and then slapped her again.

"What do you want?" she shrieked. "What do you want?"

He seized the lapels of her jacket and dragged her upright against the harsh-ribbed bark of the tree. His eyes were so deep-set that all she could see was their glitter. His lips were blue-grey, and they were stretched back across his teeth in a terrifying parody of a grin.

"What do you want?" she begged him. Her shoulder felt as if it were on fire, and her left knee was throbbing. "I have to look after my baby. Please don't hurt me. I have to look after my baby."

She felt her skirt being torn away from her thighs. Oh God, she thought, not that. Please not that. She started to collapse out of fear and out of terrible resignation, but the man dragged her upright again, and knocked her head so hard against the tree that she almost blacked out.

She didn't remember very much after that. She felt her underwear wrenched off. She felt him forcing his way into her. It was dry and agonizing and he felt so *cold*. Even when he had pushed his way deep inside her, he still felt cold. She felt the rain on her face. She heard his breathing, a steady, harsh *hah! hah! hah!* Then she heard him swear, an extraordinary curse like no curse that she had ever heard before.

She was just about to say "My baby," when he hit her again. She was found twenty minutes later standing at a bus-stop in the Bayswater Road, by an American couple who wanted to know where to find Trader Vic's.

The pram was found where she had been forced to leave it, and it was empty.

John said, "We should go away for a while."

Marjorie was sitting in the window-seat, nursing a cup of lemon tea. She was staring across the Bayswater Road as she always stared, day and night. She had cut her hair into a severe bob, and her face was as pale as wax. She wore black, as she always wore black.

The clock on the mantelpiece chimed three. John said, "Nesta will keep in touch—you know, if there's any development."

Marjorie turned and smiled at him weakly. The dullness of her eyes still shocked him, even now. "Development?" she said, gently mocking his euphemism. It was six weeks since William had disappeared. Whoever had taken him had either killed him or intended to keep him forever.

John shrugged. He was a thick-set, pleasant-looking, but unassertive man. He had never thought that he would marry; but when he had met Marjorie at his younger brother's twenty-first, he had been captivated at once by her mixture of shyness and wilfulness, and her eccentric imagination. She had said things to him that no girl had ever said to him before—opened his eyes to the simple magic of everyday life.

But now that Marjorie had closed in on herself, and communicated nothing but grief, he found that he was increasingly handicapped; as if the gifts of light and colour and perception were being taken away from him. A spring day was incomprehensible unless he had Marjorie beside him, to tell him why it was all so inspiring.

She was like a woman who was dying; and he was like a man who was gradually going blind.

The phone rang in the library. Marjorie turned back to the window. Through the pale afternoon fog the buses and the taxis poured ceaselessly to and fro. But beyond the railings, in Kensington Gardens, the trees were motionless and dark, and they held a secret for which Marjorie would have given anything. Her sight, her soul, her very life.

Somewhere in Kensington Gardens, William was still alive. She was convinced of it, in the way that only a mother could be convinced. She spent hours straining her ears, trying to hear him crying over the bellowing of the traffic. She felt like standing in the middle of Bayswater Road and holding up her hands and screaming "Stop! Stop, for just one minute! Please, stop! I think I can hear my baby crying!"

John came back from the library, digging his fingers into his thick chestnut hair. "That was Chief Inspector Crosland. They've had the forensic report on the weapon that was used to cut your clothes. Some kind of gardening-implement, apparently—a pair of clippers or a pruning-hook. They're going to start asking questions at nurseries and garden centres. You never know."

He paused, and then he said, "There's something else. They had a DNA report."

Marjorie gave a quiet, cold shudder. She didn't want to start thinking about the rape. Not yet, anyway. She could deal with that later, when William was found.

When William was found, she could go away on holiday and try to recuperate. When William was found, her heart could start beating again. She longed so much to hold him in her arms that she felt she was becoming completely demented. Just to feel his tiny fingers closing around hers.

John cleared his throat. "Crosland said that there was something pretty strange about the DNA report. That's why it's taken them so long."

Marjorie didn't answer. She thought she had seen a movement in the gardens. She thought she had seen something small and white in the long grass underneath the trees, and a small arm waving. But—as she drew the net curtain back further—the small, white object trotted out from beneath the trees and it was a Sealyham, and the small waving arm was its tail.

"According to the DNA report, the man wasn't actually alive."

Marjorie slowly turned around. "What?" she said. "What do you mean, he wasn't actually alive?"

John looked embarrassed. "I don't know. It doesn't seem to make any sense, does it? But that's what Crosland said. In fact, what he actually said was, the man was dead."

"*Dead*? How could he have been dead?"

"Well, there was obviously some kind of aberration in the test results. I mean, the man couldn't have been *really* dead. Not clinically. It was just that—"

"Dead," Marjorie repeated, in a whisper, as if everything had suddenly become clear. "The man was *dead*."

John was awakened by the telephone at five to six that Friday morning. He could hear the rain sprinkling against the bedroom window, and the grinding bellow of a garbage truck in the mews at the back of the house.

"It's Chief Inspector Crosland, sir. I'm afraid I have some rather bad news. We've found William in the Fountains."

John swallowed. "I see," he said. Irrationally, he wanted to ask if William were still alive, but of course he couldn't have been, and in any case he found that he simply couldn't speak.

"I'm sending two officers over," said the chief inspector. "One of them's a woman. If you could be ready in—say—five or ten minutes?"

John quietly cradled the phone. He sat up in bed for a while, hugging his knees, his eyes brimming. Then he swallowed, and smeared his tears with his hands, and gently shook Marjorie awake.

She opened her eyes and stared up at him as if she had just arrived from another country. "What is it?" she asked, throatily.

He tried to speak, but he couldn't.

"It's William, isn't it?" she said. "They've found William."

They stood huddled together under John's umbrella, next to the grey, rain-circled fountains. An ambulance was parked close by, its rear doors open, its blue light flashing. Chief Inspector Crosland came across—a solid, beef-complexioned man with a dripping mustache. He raised his hat, and said, "We're all very sorry about this. We always hold out hope, you know, even when it's pretty obvious that it's hopeless."

"Where was he found?" asked John.

"Caught in the sluice that leads to the Long Water. There were a lot of leaves down there, too, so he was difficult to see. One of the maintenance men found him when he was clearing the grating."

"Can I see him?" asked Marjorie.

John looked at the chief inspector with an unspoken question: how badly is he decomposed? But the chief inspector nodded, and took hold of Marjorie's elbow, and said, "Come with me."

Marjorie followed him obediently. She felt so small and cold. He guided her to the back of the ambulance, and helped her to climb inside. There, wrapped in a bright red blanket, was her baby, her baby William, his eyes closed, his hair stuck in a curl to his forehead. He was white as marble, white as a statue.

"May I kiss him?" she asked. Chief Inspector Crosland nodded.

She kissed her baby and his kiss was soft and utterly chilled.

Outside the ambulance, John said, "I would have thought—well, how long has he been down there?"

"No more than a day, sir, in my opinion. He was still wearing the same Babygro that he was wearing when he was taken, but he was clean and he looked reasonably well nourished. There were no signs of abuse or injury."

John looked away. "I can't understand it," he said.

The chief inspector laid a hand on his shoulder. "If it's any comfort to you, sir, neither can I."

All the next day, through showers and sunshine, Marjorie walked alone around Kensington Gardens. She walked down Lancaster Walk, and then Budge's Walk, and stood by the Round Pond. Then she walked back beside the Long Water, to the statue of Peter Pan.

It had started drizzling again, and rainwater dripped from the end of Peter's pipes, and trickled down his cheeks like tears.

The boy who never grew up, she thought. Just like William.

She was about to turn away when the tiniest fragment of memory scintillated in her mind. What was it that Uncle Michael had said, as she left his flat on the day that William had been taken?

She had said, "I'm cooking chicken chasseur tonight."

And *he* had said, "Chicken chasseur . . ." and then paused for a very long time, and added, "Don't forget the pan."

She had assumed then that he meant saucepan. But why would he have said "don't forget the pan?" After all, he hadn't been talking about cooking before. He had been warning her that somebody in Kensington Gardens might be watching her. He had been warning her that somebody in Kensington Gardens might want to take William.

Don't forget the Pan.

He was sitting on the sofa, bundled up in maroon woollen blankets, when she let herself in. The flat smelled of gas and stale milk. A thin sunlight the colour of cold tea was straining through the net curtains; and it made his face look more sallow and withered than ever.

"I was wondering when you'd come," he said, in a whisper.

"You expected me?"

He gave her a sloping smile. "You're a mother. Mothers understand everything."

She sat on the chair close beside him. "That day when William was taken . . . you said 'don't forget the Pan.' Did you mean what I think you meant?"

He took hold of her hand and held it in a gesture of infinite sympathy and infinite pain. "The Pan is every mother's nightmare. Always has been, always will be."

"Are you trying to tell me that it's not a story?"

"Oh . . . the way that Sir James Barrie told it—all fairies and pirates and Indians—*that* was a story. But it was founded on fact."

"How do you know that?" asked Marjorie. "I've never heard anyone mention that before."

Uncle Michael turned his withered neck toward the window. "I know it because it happened to my brother and my sister and it nearly happened to me. My mother met Sir James at a dinner in Belgravia, about a year afterwards, and tried to explain what had happened. This was in 1901 or 1902, thereabouts. She thought that he might write an article about it, to warn other parents, and that because of his authority, people might listen to him, and believe him. But the old fool was such a sentimentalist, such a fantasist . . . he didn't believe her, either, and he turned my mother's agony into a children's play.

"Of course, it was such a successful children's play that nobody ever took my mother's warnings seriously, ever again. She died in Earlswood Mental Hospital in Surrey in 1914. The death certificate said 'dementia,' whatever that means."

"Tell me what happened," said Marjorie. "Uncle Michael, I've just lost my baby . . . you have to tell me what happened."

Uncle Michael gave her a bony shrug. "It's difficult to separate fact from fiction. But in the late 1880s, there was a rash of kidnappings in Kensington Gardens . . . all boy babies, some of them taken from prams, some of them snatched directly from their nannies' arms. All of the babies were later found dead . . . most in Kensington Gardens, some in Hyde Park and Paddington . . . but none of them very far away. Sometimes the nannies were assaulted, too, and three of them were raped.

"In 1892, a man was eventually caught in the act of trying to steal a baby. He was identified by several nannies as the man who had raped them and abducted their charges. He was tried at the Old Bailey on three specimen charges of murder, and sentenced to death on June 13, 1893. He was hanged on the last day of October.

"He was apparently a Polish merchant seaman, who had jumped ship at London Docks after a trip to the Caribbean. His shipmates had known him only as Piotr. He had been cheerful and happy, as far as they knew—at least until they docked at Port-au-Prince, in Haiti. Piotr had spent three nights away from the ship, and after his return, the first mate remarked on his 'moody and unpleasant mien.' He flew into frequent rages, so they weren't at all surprised when he left the ship at London and never came back.

"The ship's doctor thought that Piotr might have contracted malaria, because his face was ashy white, and his eyes looked bloodshot. He shivered, too, and started to mutter to himself."

"But if he was hanged—" put in Marjorie.

"Oh, he was hanged, all right," said Michael. "Hanged by the neck until he was dead, and buried in the precincts of Wormwood Scrubs prison. But only a year later, more boy-babies began to disappear from Kensington Gardens, and more nannies were assaulted, and each of them bore the same kind of scratches and cuts that Piotr had inflicted on his victims.

"He used to tear their dresses, you see, with a baling-hook."

"A baling-hook?" said Marjorie, faintly.

Uncle Michael held up his hand, with one finger curled. "Where do you think that Sir James got the notion for Captain Hook?"

"But I was scratched like that, too."

"Yes," nodded Uncle Michael. "And that's what I've been trying to tell you. The man who attacked you—the man who took William—it was Piotr."

"What? That was over a hundred years ago! How could it have been?"

"In the same way that Piotr tried to snatch me, too, in 1901, when I was still in my pram. My nannie tried to fight him off, but he hooked her throat and severed her jugular vein. My brother and my sister tried to fight him off, too, but he dragged them both away with him. They were only little, they didn't stand a chance. A few weeks later, a swimmer found their bodies in the Serpentine."

Uncle Michael pressed his hand against his mouth, and was silent for almost a whole minute. "My mother was almost mad with grief. But somehow, she *knew* who had killed her children. She spent every afternoon in Kensington Gardens, following almost every man she saw. And—at last—she came across him. He was standing amongst the trees, watching two nannies sitting on a bench. She approached him, and she challenged him. She told him to his face that she knew who he was; and that she knew he had murdered her children.

"Do you know what he said? I shall never forget my mother telling me this, and it still sends shivers down my spine. He said, 'I never had a mother, I never had a father. I was never allowed to be a boy. But the old woman on Haiti said that I could stay young forever and ever, so long as I always sent back to her the souls of young children, flying on the wind. So that is what I did. I kissed them, and sucked out their souls, and sent them flying back to Haiti on the wind.'

"But do you know what he said to my mother? He said 'Your children's souls may have flown to a distant island, but they can still live, if you wish them to. You can go to their graves, and you can call them, and they'll come to you. It only takes a mother's word.'

"My mother said, 'Who are you? *What* are you?' And he said 'Pan,' which is nothing more nor less than Polish for 'Man.' That's why my mother called him 'Piotr Pan.' And that's where Sir James Barrie got the name from.

"And here, of course, is the terrible irony—Captain Hook and Peter Pan weren't enemies at all, not in real life. They were one and the same person."

Marjorie stared at her Uncle Michael in horror. "What did my great-auntie do? She didn't *call* your brother and sister, did she?"

Uncle Michael shook his head. "She insisted that their graves should be covered in heavy slabs of granite. Then—as you know—she did whatever she could to warn other mothers of the danger of Piotr Pan."

"So she really believed that she could call her children back to life?"

"I think so. But—as she always said to me—what can life amount to, without a soul?"

Marjorie sat with her Uncle Michael until it grew dark, and his head dropped to one side, and he began to snore.

She stood in the chapel of rest, her face bleached white by the single ray of sunlight that fell from the clerestory window. Her dress was black, her hat was black. She held a black handbag in front of her.

William's white coffin was open, and William himself lay on a white silk pillow, his eyes closed, his tiny eyelashes curled over his deathly-white cheek, his lips slightly parted, as if he were still breathing.

On either side of the coffin, candles burned; and there were two tall vases of white gladioli. Apart from the murmuring of traffic, and the occasional rumbling of a Central Line tube train deep beneath the building's foundations, the chapel was silent.

Marjorie could feel her heart beating, steady and slow.

My baby, she thought. My poor sweet baby.

She stepped closer to the coffin. Hesitantly, she reached out and brushed his fine baby curls. So soft, it crucified her to touch it.

"William," she breathed.

He remained cold and still. Not moving, not breathing.

"William," she repeated. "William, my darling, come back to me. Come back to me, Mr. Bill."

Still he didn't stir. Still he didn't breathe.

She waited a moment longer. She was almost ashamed of herself for having believed Uncle Michael's stories. Piotr Pan indeed! The old man was senile.

Softly, she tiptoed to the door. She took one last look at William, and then she closed the door behind her.

She had barely let go of the handle, however, when the silence was broken by the most terrible high-pitched scream she had ever heard in her life.

In Kensington Gardens, beneath the trees, a thin dark man raised his head and listened, and listened, as if he could hear a child crying in the wind. He listened, and he smiled, although he never took his eyes away from the young woman who was walking towards him, pushing a baby-buggy.

He thought, *God bless mothers everywhere.*

THE SAINT
Gabriel García Márquez

Gabriel García Márquez was born in Aracataca, Colombia, and studied at the University of Bogotá before working as a newspaper foreign correspondent in Rome, Paris, Barcelona, Caracas, and New York. He currently lives in Mexico City.

García Márquez is widely regarded as the premier writer of Latin American magical realist fiction, and was awarded the Nobel Prize for Literature in 1982. His splendid novels, published internationally, include *One Hundred Years of Solitude*, *Love in the Time of Cholera*, *The Autumn of the Patriarch*, and *The General in his Labyrinth*. He is also the author of numerous collections of short fiction, including *Leaf Storm and Other Stories* and *No One Writes to the Colonel*.

"The Saint" was published in his brilliant 1993 collection *Strange Pilgrims* (as well as in the *Paris Review*), translated from the Spanish by Edith Grossman. Set among the boarders in a Rome *pensione*, the author spins a typical Márquezian tale in which the fabulous and the miraculous are simply part of fabric of everyday life.

—T.W.

I saw Margarito Duarte after twenty-two years on one of the narrow secret streets in Trastevere, and at first I had trouble recognizing him, because he spoke halting Spanish and had the appearance of an old Roman. His hair was white and thin, and there was nothing left of the Andean intellectual's solemn manner and funereal clothes with which he had first come to Rome, but in the course of our conversation I began, little by little, to recover him from the treachery of his years and see him again as he had been: secretive, unpredictable, and as tenacious as a stonecutter. Before the second cup of coffee in one of our bars from the old days, I dared to ask the question that was gnawing inside me.

"What happened with the Saint?"

"The Saint is there," he answered. "Waiting."

Only the tenor Rafael Ribero Silva and I could understand the enormous human weight of his reply. We knew his drama so well that for years I thought Margarito Duarte was the character in search of an author that we novelists wait for all our lives, and if I never allowed him to find me it was because the end of his story seemed unimaginable.

He had come to Rome during that radiant spring when Pius XII suffered from an attack of hiccups that neither the good nor the evil arts of physicians and wizards could cure. It was his first time away from Tolima, his village high in the Colombian Andes—a fact that was obvious even in the way he slept. He presented himself one morning at our consulate carrying the polished pine box the shape and size of a cello case, and he explained the surprising reason for his trip to the consul, who then telephoned his countryman, the tenor Rafael Riberto Silva, asking that he find him a room at the *pensione* where we both lived. That is how I met him.

Margarito Duarte had not gone beyond primary school, but his vocation for letters had permitted him a broader education through the impassioned reading of everything in print he could lay his hands on. At the age of eighteen, when he was village clerk, he married a beautiful girl who died not long afterward when she gave birth to their first child, a daughter. Even more beautiful than her mother, she died of an essential fever at the age of seven. But the real story of Margarito Duarte began six months before his arrival in Rome, when the construction of a dam required that the cemetery in his village be moved. Margarito, like all the other residents of the region, disinterred the bones of his dead to carry them to the new cemetery. His wife was dust. But in the grave next to hers, the girl was still intact after eleven years. In fact, when they pried the lid off the coffin, they could smell the scent of the fresh-cut roses with which she has been buried. Most astonishing of all, however, was that her body had no weight.

Hundreds of curiosity-seekers, attracted by the resounding news of the miracle, poured into the village. There was no doubt about it: The incorruptibility of the body was an unequivocal sign of sainthood, and even the bishop of the diocese agreed that such a prodigy should be submitted to the judgment of the Vatican. And therefore they took up a public collection so that Margarito Duarte could travel to Rome to do battle for the cause that no longer was his alone or limited to the narrow confines of his village, but had become a national issue.

As he told us his story in the *pensione* in the quiet Parioli district, Margarito Duarte removed the padlock and raised the lid of the beautiful trunk. That was how the tenor Ribero Silva and I participated in the miracle. She did not resemble the kind of withered mummy seen in so many museums of the world, but a little girl dressed as a bride who was still sleeping after a long stay underground. Her skin was smooth and warm, and her open eyes were clear and created the unbearable impression that they were looking at us from death. The satin and artificial orange blossoms of her crown had not withstood the rigors of time as well as her skin, but the roses that had been placed in her hands were still alive. And it was in fact true that the weight of the pine case did not change when we removed the body.

Margarito Duarte began his negotiations the day following his arrival, at first with diplomatic assistance that was more compassionate than efficient, and then with every strategy he could think of to circumvent the countless barriers set up by the Vatican. He was always very reserved about the measures he was taking, but we knew they were numerous and to no avail. He communicated with all the religious congregations and humanitarian foundations he could find, and they listened to him with attention but no surprise and promised immediate steps that were never taken. The truth is that it was not the most propitious time. Everything having to do with the Holy See had been postponed until the Pope overcame the attack of hiccuping that proved resistant not only to the most refined techniques of academic medicine, but to every kind of magic remedy sent to him from all over the world.

At last, in the month of July, Pius XII recovered and left for his summer vacation in Castel Gandolfo. Margarito took the Saint to the first weekly audience, hoping he could show her to the Pope, who appeared in the inner courtyard on a balcony so low that Margarito could see his burnished fingernails and smell his lavender scent. He did not circulate among the tourists who came from every nation to see him, as Margarito had anticipated, but repeated the same statement in six languages and concluded with a general blessing.

After so many delays, Margarito decided to take matters into his own hands, and he delivered a letter almost sixty pages long to the Secretariat of State but received no reply. He had foreseen this, for the functionary who accepted his handwritten letter with all due formality did not deign to give more than an official glance at the dead girl, and the clerks passing by looked at her with no interest at all. One of them told him that in the previous year they had received more than eight hundred letters requesting sainthood for intact corpses in various places around the globe. At last Margarito requested that the weightlessness of the body be verified. The functionary verified it but refused to admit it.

"It must be a case of collective suggestion," he said.

In his few free hours, and on the dry Sundays of summer, Margarito remained in his room, devouring any book that seemed relevant to his cause. At the end of each month, on his own initiative, he wrote a detailed calculation of his expenses in a composition book, using the exquisite calligraphy of a senior clerk to provide the contributors from his village with strict and up-to-date accounts. Before the year was out he knew the labyrinths of Rome as if he had been born there, spoke a fluent Italian as laconic as his Andean Spanish, and knew as much as anyone about the process of canonization. But much more time passed before he changed his funereal dress, the vest and magistrate's hat which in the Rome of that time were typical of certain secret societies with unconfessable aims. He went out very early with the case that held the Saint, and sometimes he returned late at night, exhausted and sad but always with a spark of light that filled him with new courage for the next day.

"Saints live in their own time," he would say.

It was my first visit to Rome, where I was studying at the Experimental Film Center, and I lived his calvary with unforgettable intensity. Our *pensione* was in reality a modern apartment a few steps from the Villa Borghese. The owner occupied two rooms and rented the other four to foreign students. We called her Bella Maria, and in the ripeness of her autumn she was good-looking and temperamental and always faithful to the sacred rule that each man is absolute king of his own room. The one who really bore the burden of daily life was her older sister, Aunt Antonietta, an angel without wings who worked for her hour after hour during the day, moving through the apartment with her pail and brush, polishing the marble floor beyond the realm of the possible. It was she who taught us to eat the little songbirds that her husband, Bartolino, caught—a bad habit left over from the war—and who, in the end, took Margarito to live in her house when he could no longer afford Bella Maria's prices.

Nothing was less suited to Margarito's nature than that house without law. Each hour had some surprise in store for us, even the dawn, when we were awakened by the fearsome roar of the lion in the Villa Borghese zoo. The tenor Ribero Silva had earned this privilege: The Romans did not resent his early morning practice sessions. He would get up at six, take his medicinal bath of icy water, arrange his Mephistophelean beard and eyebrows, and only when he was ready, and wearing his tartan bathrobe, Chinese silk scarf, and personal cologne, give himself over, body and soul, to his vocal exercises. He would throw open the window in his room, even when the wintry stars were still in the sky, and warm up with progressive phrasings of great love arias until he was singing at full voice. The daily expectation was that when he sang his *do* at top volume, the Villa Borghese lion would answer him with an earth-shaking roar.

"You are the reincarnation of Saint Mark, *figlio mio*," Aunt Antonietta would exclaim in true amazement. "Only he could talk to lions."

One morning it was not the lion who replied. The tenor began the love duet from *Otello*—"*Già nella notte densa s'estingue ogni clamor*"—and from the bottom of the courtyard we heard the answer, in a beautiful soprano voice. The tenor continued, and the two voices sang the complete selection to the delight of all the neighbors, who opened the windows to sanctify their houses with the torrent of that irresistible love. The tenor almost fainted when he learned that his invisible Desdemona was no less a personage than the great Maria Caniglia.

I have the impression that this episode gave Margarito Duarte a valid reason for joining in the life of the house. From that time on he sat with the rest of us at the common table and not, as he had done at first, in the kitchen, where Aunt Antonietta indulged him almost every day with her masterly songbird stew. When the meal was over, Bella Maria would read the daily papers aloud to teach us Italian phonetics, and comment on the news with an arbitrariness and wit that brought joy to our lives. One day, with regard to the Saint, she told us that in the city of Palermo there was an enormous museum that held the incorruptible corpses of men, women, and children, and even several bishops, who had all been disinterred from the same Capuchin cemetery. The news so disturbed Margarito that he did not have a moment's peace until we went to Palermo. But a passing glance at the oppressive galleries of inglorious mummies was all he needed to make a consolatory judgment.

"These are not the same," he said. "You can tell right away they're dead."

After lunch Rome would succumb to its August stupor. The afternoon sun remained immobile in the middle of the sky, and in the two-o'clock silence one heard nothing but water, which is the natural voice of Rome. But at about seven the windows were thrown open to summon the cool air that began to circulate, and a jubilant crowd took to the streets with no other purpose than to live, in the midst of backfiring motorcycles, the shouts of melon vendors, and love songs among the flowers on the terraces.

The tenor and I did not take a siesta. We would ride on his Vespa, he driving and I sitting behind, and bring ices and chocolates to the little summer whores who fluttered under the centuries-old laurels in the Villa Borghese and watched for sleepless tourists in the bright sun. They were beautiful, poor, and affectionate, like most Italian women in those days, and they dressed in blue organdy, pink poplin, green linen, and protected themselves from the sun with parasols damaged by storms of bullets during the recent war. It was a human pleasure to be with them, because they ignored the rules of their trade and allowed themselves the luxury of losing a good client in order to have coffee and conversation with us in the bar on the corner, or take carriage rides around the paths in the park, or fill us with pity for the deposed monarchs and their tragic mistresses who rode horseback at dusk along the *galoppatoio*. More than once we served as their interpreters with some foreigner gone astray.

They were not the reason we took Margarito Duarte to the Villa Borghese: We wanted him to see the lion. He lived uncaged on a small desert island in the middle of a deep moat, and as soon as he caught sight of us on the far shore he began to roar with an agitation that astonished his keeper. The visitors to the park gathered around in surprise. The tenor tried to identify himself with his full-voiced morning *do*, but the lion paid him no attention. He seemed to roar at all of us without distinction, yet the keeper knew right away that he roared only for Margarito. It was true: Wherever he moved the lion moved, and as soon as he was out of sight the lion stopped roaring. The keeper, who held a doctorate in classical literature from the University of Siena, thought that Margarito had been with other lions that day and was carrying their scent. Aside from that reasoning, which was invalid, he could think of no other explanation.

"In any event," he said, "they are roars of compassion, not battle."

And yet what most affected the tenor Ribero Silva was not that supernatural episode, but Margarito's confusion when they stopped to talk with the girls in the park. He remarked on it at the table, and we all agreed—some in order to make mischief and others because they were sympathetic—that it would be a good idea to help Margarito resolve his loneliness. Moved by our tender hearts, Bella Maria pressed her hands, covered by rings with imitation stones, against her bosom worthy of a doting biblical matriarch.

"I would do it for charity's sake," she said, "except that I never could abide men who wear vests."

That was how the tenor rode his Vespa to the Villa Borghese at two in the afternoon and returned with the little butterfly he thought best able to give Margarito Duarte an hour of good company. He had her undress in his bedroom, bathed her with scented soap, dried her, perfumed her with his personal cologne, and dusted her entire body with his camphorated aftershave talc. And then he paid her for the time they had already spent, plus another hour, and told her step by step what she had to do.

The naked beauty tiptoed through the shadowy house, like a siesta dream, gave two gentle little taps at the rear bedroom door, and Margarito Duarte appeared, barefoot and shirtless.

"*Buona sera, giovanotto*," she said, with the voice and manners of a schoolgirl. "*Mi manda il tenore.*"

Margarito absorbed the shock with great dignity. He opened the door wide to let her in, and she lay down on the bed while he rushed to put on his shirt and shoes to receive her with all due respect. Then he sat beside her on a chair and began the conversation. The bewildered girl told him to hurry because they only had an hour. He did not seem to understand.

The girl said later that in any event she would have spent all the time he wanted and not charged him a cent, because there could not be a better behaved man anywhere in the world. Not knowing what to do in the meantime, she glanced around the room and saw the wooden case near the fireplace. She asked if it was a saxophone. Margarito did not answer, but opened the blind to let in a little light, carried the case to the bed, and raised the lid. The girl tried to say something, but her jaw was hanging open. Or as she told us later: "*Mi si gelò il culo*." She fled in utter terror, but lost her way in the hall and ran into Aunt Antonietta, who was going to my room to replace a light bulb. They were both so frightened that the girl did not dare leave the tenor's room until very late that night.

Aunt Antonietta never learned what happened. She came into my room in such fear that she could not turn the bulb in the lamp because her hands were shaking. I asked her what was wrong. "There are ghosts in this house," she said. "And now in broad daylight." She told me with great conviction that during the war a German officer had cut the throat of his mistress in the room occupied by the tenor. As Aunt Antonietta went about her work, she often saw the ghost of the beautiful victim making her way along the corridors.

"I've just seen her walking naked down the hall," she said. "She was identical."

The city resumed its autumn routine. The flowering terraces of summer closed down with the first winds, and the tenor and I returned to our old haunts in Trastevere, where we ate supper with the vocal students of Count Carlo Calcagni, and with some of my classmates from the film school, among whom the most faithful was Lakis, an intelligent, amiable Greek whose soporific discourses on social injustice were his only fault. It was our good fortune that the tenors and sopranos almost always drowned him out with operatic selections that they sang at full volume, but which did not bother anyone, even after midnight. On the contrary, some late-night passersby would join in the chorus, and neighbors opened their windows to applaud.

One night, while we were singing, Margarito tiptoed in so as not to interrupt us. He was carrying the pine case that he had not had time to leave at the *pensione* after showing the Saint to the parish priest at San Giovanni in Laterano, whose influence with the Holy Congregation of the Rite was common knowledge. From the corner of my eye I caught a glimpse of him putting it under the isolated table where he sat until we finished singing. As always, just after midnight, when the trattoria began to empty, we would push several tables together and sit in one group—those who sang, those of us who talked about movies, and all our friends. And among them Margarito Duarte, who was already known there as the silent, melancholy Colombian whose life was a mystery. Lakis was intrigued and asked him if he played the cello. I was caught off guard by what seemed to me an indiscretion too difficult to handle. The tenor was just as uncomfortable and could not save the situation. Margarito was the only one who responded to the question with absolute naturalness.

"It's not a cello," he said. "It's the Saint."

He placed the case on the table, opened the padlock, and raised the lid. A gust of stupefaction shook the restaurant. The other customers, the waiters, even the people in the kitchen with their bloodstained aprons, gathered in astonishment to see the miracle. Some crossed themselves. One of the cooks, overcome by a feverish trembling, fell to her knees with clasped hands and prayed in silence.

And yet when the initial commotion was over, we became involved in a shouting argument about the lack of saintliness in our day. Lakis, of course, was the most radical. The only clear idea at the end of it was that he wanted to make a critical movie about the Saint.

"I'm sure," he said, "that old Cesare would never let this subject get away."

He was referring to Cesare Zavattini, who taught us plot development and screenwriting. He was one of the great figures in the history of film, and the only one who maintained a personal relationship with us outside class. He tried to teach us not only the craft but a different way of looking at life. He was a machine for inventing plots. They poured out of him, almost against his will, and with such speed that he always needed someone to help catch them in mid-flight as he thought them up aloud. His enthusiasm would flag only when he had completed them. "Too bad they have to be filmed," he would say. For he thought that on the screen they would lose much of their original magic. He kept his ideas on cards arranged by subject and pinned to the walls, and he had so many they filled an entire room in his house.

The following Saturday we took Margarito Duarte to see him. Zavattini was so greedy for life that we found him at the door of his house on the Via Di Sant'-Angela Merici, burning with interest in the idea we had described to him on the telephone. He did not even greet us with his customary amiability, but led Margarito to a table he had prepared, and opened the case himself. Then something happened that we never could have imagined. Instead of going wild, as we expected, he suffered a kind of mental paralysis.

"*Ammazza!*" he whispered in fear.

He looked at the Saint in silence for two or three minutes, closed the case himself, and without saying a word led Margarito to the door as if he were a child taking his first steps. He said good-bye with a few pats on his shoulder. "Thank you, my son, thank you very much," he said. "And may God be with you in your struggle." When he closed the door he turned toward us and gave his verdict.

"It's no good for the movies," he said. "Nobody would believe it."

That surprising lesson rode with us on the streetcar we took home. If he said it, it had to be true: The story was no good. Yet Bella Maria met us at the *pensione* with the urgent message that Zavattini was expecting us that same night, but without Margarito.

We found the maestro in one of his stellar moments. Lakis had brought along two or three classmates, but he did not even seem to see them when he opened the door.

"I have it," he shouted. "The picture will be a sensation if Margarito performs a miracle and resurrects the girl."

"In the picture or in life?" I asked.

He suppressed his annoyance. "Don't be stupid," he said. But then we saw in his eyes the flash of an irresistible idea. "What if he could resurrect her in real life?" he mused, and added in all seriousness:

"He ought to try."

It was no more than a passing temptation, and then he took up the thread again. He began to pace every room, like a happy lunatic, waving his hands and reciting the film in great shouts. We listened to him, dazzled, and it seemed we could see the images, like flocks of phosphorescent birds that he set loose for their mad flight through the house.

"One night," he said, "after something like twenty popes who refused to receive him have died, Margarito grown old and tired goes into his house, opens the case, caresses the face of the little dead girl, and says with all the tenderness in the world: 'For love of your father, my child, arise and walk.'"

He looked at all of us and finished with a triumphant gesture:

"And she does!"

He was waiting for something from us. But we were so befuddled we could not think of a thing to say. Except Lakis the Greek, who raised his hand, as if he were in shock, to ask permission to speak.

"My problem is that I don't believe it," he said, and to our surprise he was speaking to Zavattini: "Excuse me, Maestro, but I don't believe it."

Then it was Zavattini's turn to be astonished.

"And why not?"

"How do I know?" said Lakis in anguish. "But it's impossible."

"*Ammazza!*" the maestro thundered in a voice that must have been heard throughout the entire neighborhood. "That's what I can't stand about Stalinists: They don't believe in reality."

For the next fifteen years, as he himself told me, Margarito carried the Saint to Castel Gandolfo in the event an opportunity arose for displaying her. At an audience for some two hundred pilgrims from Latin America, he managed to tell his story, amid shoves and pokes, to the benevolent John XXIII. But he could not show him the girl because, as a precaution against assassination attempts, he had been obliged to leave her at the entrance along with the knapsacks of the other pilgrims. The Pope listened with as much attention as he could in the crowd, and gave him an encouraging pat on the cheek.

"*Bravo, figlio mio,*" he said. "God will reward your perseverance."

But it was during the fleeting reign of the smiling Albino Luciani that Margarito really felt on the verge of fulfilling his dream. One of the Pope's relatives, impressed by Margarito's story, promised to intervene. No one paid him much attention. But two days later, as they were having lunch at the *pensione,* someone telephoned with a simple, rapid message for Margarito: He should not leave Rome, because sometime before Thursday he would be summoned to the Vatican for a private audience.

No one ever found out whether it was a joke. Margarito did not think so and stayed on the alert. He did not leave the house. If he had to go to the bathroom he announced: "I'm going to the bathroom." Bella Maria, still witty in the dawn of her old age, laughed her free woman's laugh.

"We know, Margarito," she shouted, "just in case the Pope calls."

Early one morning the following week Margarito almost collapsed when he saw the headline in the newspaper slipped under the door: *Morto il Papa.* For a moment he was sustained by the illusion that it was an old paper delivered by mistake, since it was not easy to believe that a pope would die every month. But it was true: The smiling Albino Luciani, elected thirty-three days earlier, had died in his sleep.

I returned to Rome twenty-two years after I first met Margarito Duarte, and perhaps I would not have thought about him at all if we had not run into each other by accident. I was too depressed by the ruinous weather to think about anybody. An imbecilic drizzle like warm soup never stopped falling, the diamond light of another time had turned muddy, and the places that had once been mine and sustained my memories were strange to me now. The building where the *pensione* was located had not changed, but nobody knew anything about Bella Maria. No one answered at the six different telephone numbers that the tenor Ribero Silva had sent me over the years. At lunch with new movie people, I evoked the memory of my teacher, and a sudden silence fluttered over the table for a moment until someone dared to say:

"Zavattini? Mai sentito."

That was true: No one had heard of him. The trees in the Villa Borghese were disheveled in the rain, the *galoppatoio* of the sorrowful princesses had been devoured by weeds without flowers, and the beautiful girls of long ago had been replaced by athletic androgynes cross-dressed in flashy clothes. Among all the extinct fauna, the only survivor was the old lion, who suffered from mange and a head cold on his island surrounded by dried waters. No one sang or died of love in the plastic trattorias on the Piazza di Spagna. For the Rome of our memory was by now another ancient Rome within the ancient Rome of the Caesars. Then a voice that might have come from the beyond stopped me cold on a narrow street in Trastevere:

"Hello, Poet."

It was he, old and tired. Four popes had died, eternal Rome was showing the first signs of decrepitude, and still he waited. "I've waited so long it can't be much longer now," he told me as he said good-bye after almost four hours of nostalgia. "It may be a matter of months." He shuffled down the middle of the street, wearing the combat boots and faded cap of an old Roman, ignoring the puddles of rain where the light was beginning to decay. Then I had no doubt, if I ever had any at all, that the Saint was Margarito. Without realizing it, by means of his daughter's incorruptible body and while he was still alive, he had spent twenty-two years fighting for the legitimate cause of his own canonization.

August 1981

COTTAGE

Bruce McAllister

Bruce McAllister is a professor of English at the University of Redlands in California. He is the author of numerous stories and of two novels, *Humanity Prime* and the acclaimed Vietnam fantasy *Dream Baby*.

"Cottage" is a mysterious, disturbing, yet beautiful tale examining a myth that will be very familiar to most readers. It comes from the magical holiday collection *Christmas Forever*, edited by David G. Hartwell.

—T.W.

She was standing near the small window in their study. She was looking out at their white picket fence—which was as pretty as a picture, and which could have easily been a soft painting tacked to the other side—when it began. It began with the tiniest of reindeer, antlers like twigs, hooves the blur of a bee's wings, though they didn't have wings. As it began, it seemed to her that the air of the study, an air so pleasantly heavy with aromas of his perfect pipe tobaccos and the leather of his big chair, actually picked up speed. If not the air of the study, then perhaps the air right outside the closed window. *Somewhere* the air was picking up speed as if someone somewhere were running. She could feel her legs beginning to move, though it wasn't *her* legs.

The tiny wingless deer with its pin-size bells on a thread-thick harness flew over the picket fence—a dark spot no one else would have noticed had they not already understood it—up over the rose bushes that were pruned so perfectly, and, zigzagging, began to follow the flagstones up to the cottage.

It rose like a small black hole in the universe to the edge of the roof, disappearing from her sight, dropping back down before her vision again, banking to the right, approaching the small window and hovering on motionless hooves. She could see it clearly now and she moved in closer to the glass. The antlers with their perfect velvet did a little dance for her, buffeting the glass two or three times before veering away to the branches of the big elm. She pressed her nose against the pane and followed it as long as she could. When it was gone, she relaxed. Maybe it wouldn't happen again. Maybe she wouldn't have to try to talk to him again about it.

She looked straight ahead at nothing, but could still feel her legs trying to move.

Something . . . somewhere . . . was happening.

Beyond the pickets something broke in and she squinted to see it. It was the little cloud, so familiar as she watched it sway to the left, sway to the right, puffing itself up larger, rising at last over the fence like a brown fog, then flowing through the rose bushes, dappling with tiny shadows—like the dark little memories that obediently kept to their corners in the past—the green of the leaves and the royal-red of the petals she and her husband felt such affection for. The cloud came closer, clearing in her eyes to become once again a swarm of little horned heads and hooves like those of the first deer, the one that had been marking out a path, though there was nothing special about *its* nose. The special one was somewhere else, and even thinking about him made her uneasy . . .

The cloud followed the path. It followed it *exactly*. She smiled and sighed. It felt so right, despite the whisper of fear that came with it. The storm came on and only now were her old eyes hurting, working to see the individual heads and twigs and tiny bells she would never be able to hear through the glass.

Every little deer was a part of the cloud that swept toward her, spinning in a funnel up to the edge of the roof, dipping back down again, turning to the right like something molten—white-hot silver or icicles melting in the sun—and arriving at her window at last.

When it touched the glass and every velvety pair of twigs buffeted it at once, the entire cottage shook. It rocked from wall to wall, the windowpane cracked, and she stepped back, waiting for the shards to fall in, to shatter on their burgundy carpet, to cut her toes, her face.

It didn't happen. The windowpane remained cracked, but held, like ice on a pond where children skated on brand-new skates on a cold winter's morning.

"I had a dream last night," she announced without turning to him. She would try again, though he still wouldn't hear.

"What was it about, dear?" He had moved up behind her and placed his arms, which were quite manly, around her waist, which was still youthfully trim. He had lost so much weight since the last of the Little People—who without their work, without the purpose they had been called into being for, had fallen ill so quickly, becoming loose flesh over brittle bones, their eyes as blank as dolls as they stood among the last toys, stiff and still, waiting for death in the great shed both she and her husband had worked hard to forget—was gone, and he shaved each morning before she woke like a young man would, so she never saw the white bristles of his beard unless it was late, late into the night by the firelight in the living room as both of them read their books right before bedtime.

His arms were quite manly. Her waist was just right. These things did make her happy. But there was always the question he wouldn't ask.

She closed her eyes, seeing his arms around her waist. This helped bring to her wrinkled lips the smile she knew she needed to begin.

"The dream?" she said. "It wasn't anything really, dear. I was under our big elm for the very first time. *You* remember that day: I was so giddy and silly. I was as happy as some giggly girl that day in the sun. And when the swarm moved through the branches, I didn't even notice, did I? *You* didn't either. We were so very much in love that day—"

She stopped. It was happening again. His arms were loosening slowly.

"I'm sorry, Sarah," he said. "What was your dream?" His voice was higher and thinner. It had gotten that way over the years somehow, and would never again fill the night, the starry sky over house after house after house. It saddened her a little, but it was all right. His voice had become what a little cottage needed, what the room they stood in together needed, and their bed . . .

"The dream?" she said. "It wasn't anything really, Nick. You remember the day we moved in, how you looked at the chimney and laughed as if you knew I was afraid and needed to laugh, too. Well, in my dream I was climbing the elm. I was climbing it to the roof. When I reached it, I could see rooftops everywhere, though there aren't any here. I was crying. I was crying because *none of them had chimneys*, Nick. They weren't even houses. They were skulls with sockets as black as the darkness every boy and girl fears under the bed at night. . . . Isn't that silly?"

As he pulled back from her—not to be free of her old body, she knew, but of much much more—she turned around slowly and saw how his handsome face was twisted by the question he would not ask.

No matter how many dreams she told him about, no matter how many times she tried to bring the right words into the air around them, he would never ask it.

Should we? Should we have, Sarah?

But that wasn't really it, she realized suddenly. What she needed to hear wasn't the question at all. The years had already answered it. It was his *courage* to ask it that she wanted—the courage that had once filled his belly and laughter as he went out to the stars and did what needed to be done if the faith of a single child in the possibilities of the world were to remain alive. *Courage.* He had lost it as he had lost his flesh—it had become too much for his bones, she realized, uncomfortable for him in his leather chair. He had lost it for *comfort* and this filled her with anger, she saw, one he didn't hear.

His courage. Her anger. That was what their story had become.

She went over to the window and pressed her nose against the cool glass. His face would not be twisted when she turned around, and when asked, he would claim he didn't know what she was talking about, that it was just a dream and made no sense, and wasn't this house, their fireplace, *their* chimney enough at this time in their lives when life should be simple and peaceful?

And he would mean it. He would be *sincere*, out of a determination not to understand, out of wanting only that the bells outside not reach them, even faintly, that the chimney be but a decoration in this little house of their golden years.

When the boy left the great shed in the backyard with its sagging beams and holes in the roof that let the dust and rain in but never enough sunlight to stop the mildewing of the immense canvas bags he slept on, curled each night, vast cobwebs in every dark corner where the short, stocky bones lay, where he had moved them at last so that he wouldn't see them when a shaft of light, like some god's eye, did happen to fall through the roof, he was carrying in his chubby arms as many of the smallest toys as he could—all of them dusty, corroded and colorless. And he had his hammer. He walked out into the sunlight, blinked, and began placing a toy on each flagstone of the path that wound through the garden. When he was finished, he returned to the first flagstone, hammer in hand.

As always, he could see the endless work of the spiders in the garden. They draped everything, the fence and nearby bushes, with their sticky threads, their tiny faces too human to be spiders', and he could never be sure that his eyes and nose weren't just inches away from them, ready to stick to him and blind him with that sudden darkness he couldn't understand, and which he hated. They were like the cobwebs in the shed, yes, like the great gray webbing that covered the piles of bones more and more each night as he slept in another darkness, blind. But these, the ones here, were different—the spider webs of the garden, of the sun and the light he could *see* in, the light he rose eagerly for every morning, hiding in it until the night killed it slowly again.

In what sense the spiders belonged to the old couple in the house, he didn't know. Were they the magic of the old woman? The old man? Both of them? Were they like the strange, wingless insects that swarmed in the garden sometimes, able to fly on four legs somehow, and which he knew for sure were *theirs?* Someone always made sure there were flies and fat moths for the spiders outside, for their human faces, and their broad sprawling traps. Even though the old man and woman never came to the backyard—*wouldn't*, he knew—who else would it have been? Who else—without actually walking to the shed with its bones and dusty toys covering the mildewing and stinking floor in its darkness—could make his own food appear somehow on paper plates each night, so that he would have them in the morning, be able to take them with him as he hurried out into the light? And again—so much food, the chicken and oranges and home-baked cookies or pie on paper plates, too, placed just outside the open door of the dark shed at noon. And again at dusk—dinnertime. It *had* to be the old woman. It just had to be. He could feel it. She did it as she dreamed. She did it without knowing she was doing it. This was how it felt.

Was she the one who also fed the spiders—without knowing she did—without having to enter the garden or the shed where *he* had to sleep each night, while she slept under a comforter on a bed high above the floor? It made him angry to think this. It made him think of the swarm.

When his back was turned, pants down as he wet the ground by the bush or picket fence, he imagined she would appear behind him at any second, surprising him, shaming him. But she never did. And when he made an effort to hear them, stepping up to a wall or window of the little cottage, it wasn't always voices he heard. Sometimes it was the faint echo of bells, the sounds of hooves on wood, a baby's cry, a deep, loving laugh like a father's—someone's. It wasn't real, of course, what he heard. It was a memory, he knew, or a dream, or both—his or someone else's. The old couple were making these things, too—for themselves, like memories they could call back and hold like children, like dreams they could only dream of because they would never come true.

Or were they, he wondered, somehow for *him?* When he thought this instead, his eyes got wet suddenly and made his nose—sensitive to the dust, the smells of the shed, even the sunlight as she stepped into it every morning—start to run.

He went back to his work. His shorts didn't cover his knees and his knees hurt on the stone, but he didn't mind being hurt a little doing the work he knew needed to be done.

The toy on the first stone was a human being. It had a green hat, which had faded. It had eyes and a smile whose color had grayed like death.

He hit it with the hammer. The head rolled away. The legs twitched. Were there bones inside the plastic? he wondered. He hit it again.

The plastic cracked. There were no bones, and this, too, made him mad.

She would find herself hesitating near the living room window where the sunlight—so much—came through like warm velvet to soften her face, relax the wrinkles, the tightness. She would be wearing her most *pastel* nightgown. The first two buttons would be undone for him.

Behind her, in the kitchen, he would still be seated, finishing his breakfast with the occasional sound of silverware on his plate. He would be waiting for her to tell him how happy she was, because if she did, she knew, he would be able to feel it too. *Wasn't that the least she could do?* he was saying—in this little house as they waited peacefully for the final darkness, the one thing no magic could prevent?

She would try her best. It was important, *very* important to him. She would fill her voice with all the joy she could and say:

"Oh, Nick, I'm as happy as any woman—"

And then the spittle, which had gathered inside her bottom lip, would fly out instead of words.

He would wait, and then he would speak himself. His words would be perfect. He had been reading for so many years now.

"I understand your sentiments, Sarah, I do," he would say, to show her how insightful he was, how this was his gift, not unlike love, to her. "There's no need, dear, to pretend that everything is perfect. We knew it would happen some day, didn't we? The regrets. The longings. They're natural, Sarah. As people age, the physiology of their brains changes. Anxiety from decreased physical mobility. Short-term memory loss—a function of anxiety, despite what people in other houses think—leaving them only a vivid past they cannot help but relive again and again. . . . I understand more than you might imagine, Sarah."

Yes, people get older, Nick. But some—like the Little People—die before they have even had a chance to live. Remember?

It would be her turn to speak again, to show him how much they really shared, how terribly close they really were, as any couple their age should be. She would try hard. She would say, "You're so right, Nick. . . . Even the moonlight on the picket fence reminds me of the snow and the time . . ." This would disturb him, she knew, but even then she would hear herself add: ". . . when we brought to the children of this world *less than they really needed.* . . ."

It was cruel, but it was the truth. She could not help it, and he would not answer, would not speak to her for the rest of the day. In the end, she would always regret it.

Sometimes she would wipe the spittle from the windowpane. Sometimes she would let it run down, thinking of it as rain. It didn't matter. That night it would fade from the glass.

That night she awoke again to find herself kicking hard, hanging from the highest shelf in their spacious walk-in closet, which smelled comfortably of its naphthalene. She was, as always, trying to climb up a chimney somewhere, up through it to a freedom only *he* had known in those early years, and which, she understood now, she had always envied.

He was pulling on her nightgown silently, but for all his pulling he was being gentle enough not to tear anything. He never tore her nightgown, no matter how much he wanted to get her down at times like these, to keep what lay so safely (a shadow dappling a leaf) in its corner of memory.

She couldn't see them—it was dark—but her knuckles were pale hooves hooked to the edge of the shelf. Turning to the bedroom lamp's faint glow, she could see how his eyes were closed, as if dreaming the old dream too. When she looked closely, holding her breath to steady her sticky eyes, she could see how shallow his breath was, how close to the final time he was.

He was crouching beside the next toy on its stone—a little car so full of wet earth that something alive, pale and squirming, lived in it. Standing up so that he could get at them, he took one of the three identical matchbooks—the ones that had appeared beside his paper plates three mornings ago—from his back pocket. Then, lit match in hand, he crouched again and tried to light the car with a squirt of the lighter fluid he had found by his lunch plates two weeks ago.

It took two squirts. The flame leaped, crawling across the roof of the car, blistering the paint so that the bright orange of its original color showed for a second, and the thing in the earth squirmed faster and faster.

Two, he said to himself.

On the next one—a duck whose turning wheels had once made a duck sound when they moved and now were too rusted to move at all—he brought the hammer down. The duck—head and wheels—moved at last, flying across the yard into a bush with a great spider's web. There was a cry from the web, and, as he watched, the head and wheels were spun into cocoons. He felt the chill.

Three.

He lit the little sofa from a dollhouse. It smelled terrible.

The plastic squirt gun curled in its flames to become a bubbly green fist.

The little Christmas scene in a bubble—the kind you could make the snow fall in if you shook it—he hit with the hammer, again and again, until all that was left was slivers in a puddle of fluid.

Four, five, six, seven.

His chest had begun to rise and fall. He could hear his heart squishing harder and harder in his chest, but never louder than his *count*, which was not in words now, but colors, in musical notes, in numbers like the strange wingless insects that were searching—in their anger—those who had abandoned them.

He returned to the shed, hesitated before the door, was blinded by the darkness as he stepped in, and with his hands alone forced himself to feel around the immense canvas bags for what he wanted. When he returned to the light, he couldn't see and he stood there for a moment blinking—without a free hand to rub his nose with—and finally went to lay another armload of toys one by one on the stones.

41, 42, 43, 44.

Even as he lit another match or brought the hammer down (*never* losing his count) he was aware of how the backs of his knees hurt, how they had been hurting all day because the legs of his shorts cut into him there, and how it was a burning feeling.

Even his feet hurt, as if the bones had been jammed into little holes in the ground. The soles of his shoes felt like parts of him now, aching against the stone as if he shouldn't be stepping on surfaces as hard as this.

The pain was new, and it made no sense to him. Why his feet? Why his shoes? 52, 53, 54, 55, 56, 57, 58.

When he went back to the shed for the third time, there were no toys among the canvas bags, and he had to grope, continue groping through the bones, holding his delicate nose against what he might smell, what he had smelled in his dreams. Blank eyes. The bones becoming hollow. The skin of their bodies wrinkling like old cloth.

He chose the smallest toys he could find, putting them in three toy trucks and a basket that was rotting. He didn't want to have to return to the shed again.

Some of the toys, he saw in the light outside, had pieces of bone, hair and gristle stuck to them, and, horrified, he set these on fire immediately, his hands shaking. The smell, worse than any he had ever imagined, made him sit back suddenly, closing his eyes and cupping his nose against the stinging.

71, 72, 73, 74, 75.

When his counting stopped, the hammering of his heart was a running man, and when he whispered the number, it was leather slipping from his neck.

106.

It came to him then. He was not accustomed to understandings like this, and when it came, it made his chest, fingers, neck, and back of knees—so close to the last toy he had lit—feel on fire, too.

He didn't look at the house. He didn't listen for a sound that might have been the two of them in the house remembering, or dreaming. It didn't matter anymore. He knew what he had to do. He didn't understand it, but he did know.

The hammer flew straight up. He was nowhere near the flagstones when it came down, striking like a shout

His legs were pumping hard. The insides of his chubby thighs were rubbing together like thick sticks, feeding the fire—the fire he now knew was rage.

Long before he reached the white picket fence that enclosed the garden—the one he had never left in what he could remember of life—he was clawing out with his arms to clear a path through any webs that might be in his way. One in the roses by the fence made it through, catching on his upper lip, making him spit as his head jerked from side to side, as he reached the fence at last, grabbed the top of the pickets, and pulled as hard as he had ever pulled in all those dreams of a screaming wind.

The pickets caught his stomach, hung on to him like an old man's claws, and then, with a rip that tore his T-shirt away, leaving him naked from the belly button up, he tumbled to the other side.

They were in the living room. They always were at this time of day. She was looking a few inches to the right of their brass floor-lamp, at the air—just the air—when she saw it happen. "Oh!" she exclaimed.

He was on the couch. He looked up from his leather-bound book about "Northern European Thought" and shaped his face into another question.

"It's happening at last, dear," she heard herself say. She could hear it in her own voice. *A difference.*

He closed the book, leaving a finger to mark his place. He rose gracefully to his feet. He looked around the room once, pretending he wanted to understand.

He knew about the boy, she told herself. He had dreamed about him, too, as she had. They had both dreamed him, making him what he was, *choosing* him.

She could see her husband in the reflection of the window by the brass floor-lamp. She could see him look at the window, making a show of deciding *it* was the answer, and starting toward her in his smooth, charming stride. When he was at her side, he looked out the window with eyes that meant: *I'm trying, Sarah. I am. . . .*

"No, *you're not,*" she said out loud, hearing what was in it at last. It was *her* courage she could hear.

He looked at her stunned. His long fingers still marking his place in the book, he said quietly, in the only way he knew:

"What do you mean?"

"*He's going. He's finally going, Nick,*" she said. "I'm so happy for him. . . ."

She looked at his face. His eyebrows, those white caterpillars, were shaping that old expression of puzzlement—so sincere, so dramatic—the one they had once laughed at together, because of its silliness.

He looked back at the window, squinting, and as he turned to face her again, he said:

"I don't understand what you mean. . . ." He was not going to finish. He never did. He'd never felt he'd needed to. . . .

"You know what I'm talking about, Nick," she said to him, unable to stop. It was as if she were running, too.

I want you to be stronger, Nick, she was saying—*to be as strong as you were once, so that it can happen, so we can let the shadow from its corner of memory and be free at last.*

He jerked from the words—not the ones she had spoken, but those in the flame of her silence.

He was hearing her at last.

"He's trying to fly, Nick. He's trying *so hard.* . . ."

He could hear courage too, the one they both had needed when they'd needed all the courage and strength they could make, between them, to do what needed to be done in the world. He was listening to her at last, somehow.

. . . to reach, she told him, *the children who dream the Dream of Ice and Death, just as he—and we—have been dreaming it. To put a fire in the chill wind of Forever, which he has known so well in the great dark shed we have worked to forget it. . . .*

He had been moving back toward the stuffed chair, afraid. It was in his old blue eyes, but something else was too. He was sitting, looking at her, and she could tell that his breathing was quicker now. His face, its expression for once sincere, was asking *the question:*

Should we have had one, Sarah? Should we have had a child?

She had to be very careful. Her hand at her forehead to brush away the first whisper of a headache, of the Ice Wind that might take all words, all breath, from her. She said to him, filling the air with words:

"Nicky, when the reins finally slip from our favorite of the eight—and he *will* get them off, I promise you, Nicky—we will be free too. We will be happier than we have ever imagined as we wait for what no magic of any kind can prevent. But we must say the prayer together, Nicky. We must chant it as if the whole world were praying for a single child. Say it with me now. Say it, Nicky: '*Twas the night . . .*'"

He couldn't do it, she saw. He just couldn't bring himself to do it. "*Please,*" she told him in the fire. "*Say it with me: '. . . before Christmas, and all through the house . . .*'"

His face had begun to tremble.

". . . not a creature . . ." he whispered suddenly, as if he did indeed remember. Then he stopped.

She had, she knew, to try the hardest she had ever tried, as if saving all of her strength for this very day, for this look on his face, his trembling.

"*He is afraid, too, Nicky. It's been so long, You know what that is like. You know, Nicky.*" She went on: "' . . . *was stirring . . . Not a creature was stirring.*' But that isn't true, is it? A 'creature' *is* stirring. Our favorite of the eight—what we have made of him because we so loved him for his Light—*is* stirring."

When these words touched him—like snowflakes too new, or too old, to melt—he broke.

He had been staring at their perfect red-brick fireplace and at the leather-bound book in his hand. As if on a signal one he had been waiting for for years. He dropped the books.

He was staring hard into the brick of the fireplace. His hands were curling and uncurling, his tight fists with the blue veins of age raised even bluer, the liver spots on his hands—from a sun reflected on snow and ice—larger and darker now, somehow, the skin of his face like taut parchment. He was an old man now.

Yet he had found it.

What they had both—both of them—been waiting for from him.

When he shouted at last, his voice was hoarse, as if saving these words—their regret and their longing—for this one moment.

"Go," he shouted. "Go, son, go!"

He shouted it in the voice she could remember hearing from the sky, as she waited below, keeping the elves alive with the work they so needed to do, with the love they deserved for it, through the winter wind and eternity's snow, the bellow of his voice as it fell from the stars to one rooftop after another, for the brief moments of magic, then rising again to the stars.

He was standing now. She didn't have to look at him to know it. She was staring a few inches to the right of their brass lamp so that she could watch the boy—the one they had made by the alchemy of dreams.

Her husband's hair, she knew without looking, had turned pale like white wire. The bristles of his beard had begun to grow furiously.

When he raised his fist in his loudest shout yet, she didn't need to hear it at all. She *knew* what it would be, because he understood it all now, but she couldn't afford to listen. Her own legs were *burning,* too. She was running, getting away at last, like the boy, and that was what mattered.

"*Come on, boy!*" the old man shouted somewhere—another house, another time.

The claw, his fist, was falling to his side. His last shout, which she *did* need to hear if she were to stay, to love him until the final dream, was a whisper, a living breath in the cold winds between the stars.

"*Please, God. . . .* Please *let him get through,*" the old man was shouting.

He was running like hell. Voices behind him were shouting things like *Go, boy, go!* and *The toys were never enough, Nicky—never what they really needed* and *Yes, we should have had one* and so many other things that made no sense, that only made him run faster, flesh burning, his chubby hands holding his shorts up and together—the top button gone—his tummy pulled in so hard he could barely breathe, his nose running and red and starting to glow, and his hooves suddenly lighter in what felt like the white-hot hope of a single burning star.

DOODLES

Steve Rasnic Tem

Steve Rasnic Tem grew up in the Appalachian Mountains of Virginia and now lives in Colorado. His novel *Excavations* was published in 1987, but he is better known for his many fantasy and horror stories published in magazines and anthologies in the U.S. and the U.K. He is also a poet, whose work has appeared in our *Year's Best* volumes in the past.

"Doodles" is one man's way of dealing with the unthinkable—or do his actions *cause* the unthinkable? The story was first published in *Sinistre: An Anthology of Rituals*.

—E.D.

"Her drawings know more about the world than she does."

This thing his ex-wife used to say about their daughter eventually led him to take his own absent-minded doodles more seriously. He did them all the time: at work—on the papers due on his boss's desk by the end of the afternoon; at dinner—on napkins, tablecloths, credit card slips; even in his sleep—on the graying walls of his dreams. A nervous habit, or an addiction; he simply could not stop himself. He had to have the pen firmly in his hand, and the pen had to be moving.

His habit underlined, circled, boxed and generally ornamented his days. If he forced himself not to doodle, the days flowed on without form or direction.

"Her drawings are smart drawings."

He had no idea what this really meant, but he agreed completely.

His daughter had drawn pictures of houses mostly: huge, elaborate structures heavy with character. But however wonderful her depictions, she always seemed more careless in her execution than most children. Sometimes she didn't even look down at the page. She just drew, sight unseen. She drew her world, and the houses that were in it, and the creatures who lived in those houses. This ceremony of drawing she performed every day centered her, and seemed to make her happy.

But he scribbled and doodled, late into the night sometimes, and found no peace in it. He wondered if it was because of his age, or because of a long-standing pessimism about all forms of self-help. Whatever the reason, for him it was like worrying an infected wound. And yet he could not stop himself.

*   *   *

"Sometimes there's magic in doing the same thing again and again."

A series of vertical lines running up and down the page. Walls, and borders which were not to be crossed. Some weeks he built these walls before and after everything he wrote: letters, reports, grocery lists. He'd write his name and construct the walls which were intended to hold it in, keep it from expanding so much that it became unrecognizable. Ego expansion could be a problem—it left one open to attack. A few individual walls scattered here and there emulated grass, or the spikes at the bottom of a pit to trap uninvited guests.

Sometimes it was a comfort to go over these vertical lines again and again to make them thicker. The act made his fortifications stronger.

Some days he filled the page with his walls, his borders, his spikes. After hours his wrist would begin to ache, but there was still relief in the repetition.

"You repeat the same old patterns; it's as if you can't help yourself."

Some mornings he would get stuck on a pattern, find himself compelled to repeat it over and over and over again until he broke for lunch. Circles, triangles, squares, the same patterns made by the same muscular movements repeated endlessly. Then after lunch, the pattern broken, variety would suddenly be available to him again. And yet sometimes the pattern had been so worn in to the muscles of his arm, wrist, hand, fingers, that the old pattern would simply reassert itself (phantom circles appearing within a complex network of lines, for example), and there was nothing he could do to stop it.

"There are some things you just have to do, no matter how harmful. It's as if you can't help yourself."

Daggers and other blades were a compulsion at times. As were primitive depictions of murder. They arrived at the most inopportune times: once after his divorce, he was having a romantic dinner with a beautiful young woman, a young woman he someday wished to marry, when she suddenly stopped speaking, stopped smiling, and glared at him with a peculiar expression on her face. He looked down at his place setting then, discovering that he had taken the red ink pen from his vest pocket and used it to sketch the particularly grisly stabbing death of the young woman on his cream-colored linen napkin.

Some days it felt as if his doodles wanted him all to themselves.

"It made no sense. But it was compelling, irresistible, all the same."

He couldn't make heads or tails of some of his more unconscious scribblings. They resembled the webs of hallucinating spiders, he thought, or a cheaply-made house after an explosion had leveled it. After years, however, he came to recognize these works as maps. All he had to do was find the starting point, and his current position relative to it.

"You feel if you do it often enough the very structures of your brain will be altered."

Hours of drawing lines as precisely as possible would sometimes be an aid to linear thinking. Too many nested circles brought a sensation of great fullness, and enormous headaches. Ten thousand sharp edges on a page might lead to a ripping and tearing, and then a brain hemorrhage would begin.

"The more I want not to feel these things, the more I feel them."

Some days he would try *not* to draw certain things. The effort proved to be self-defeating, of course. The more he thought about the image, the stronger the compulsion to bring it to light, capture it in pencil on a napkin, pen on a flap of cereal box. Try *not* drawing a circle. Try *not* drawing a square. Try *not* drawing a small child trapped in a burning window, the window fragmented, blotted out by a furious, pen-wielding hand.

"My father used to say, find one thing you do well, and do it often."

But this was not what his father had imagined, he was sure. If he could be paid for his doodles, of course, he would be quite a wealthy man. But who paid for obsession? Obsession was mostly a matter of self-gratification, a private thing, and powerful in that it belonged to the individual alone. He could take his doodles anywhere, whatever his "regular" job might be. There was power in that.

Drawings of strong, squarish hands that covered page after page after page. Sometimes without thinking he would draw these hands on a business report, and have to do the report all over again before an important presentation.

But no one ever found out. His bosses praised him for his neatness, his calm, his organizational abilities.

"You can live where you dream."

The argument in his head, the on-going argument with his ex-wife, continued as obsessively as his doodling.

Many of his doodles resembled floor plans of unknown structures rendered in a multitude of dimensions and perspectives unavailable to his normal, everyday senses.

They appeared to vibrate on the page—he imagined he could hear the music they made. In dreams, he did hear, and the songs led him off into deeper sleeping.

In daydreams, he would speculate whether it was possible to visit such structures, such estranged, vibratory spaces. He had his doubts—what caused their vibrations would tear a normal, three-dimensional human body apart.

So why did his desire to visit such places still persist? Because he knew he would feel at home there, even if the peculiar geometries destroyed him. What was architecture but an endless and futile quest to recreate the "home" that existed only in the dream of your body, the dream of your cells? Doubly futile since architecture can only create the home from within his body—and the client who must dwell there is immediately trapped within the architect's own body. Primitive peoples had it best: they were their own architects. At least their mistakes in execution in attempting "home" were in service of their own dream, however distorted.

He started renting cheap apartments and trashed-out homes he could redo to his heart's content, destroying if need be. Expensive furnishings were unnecessary—since the attempt at creating home was destined to failure anyway—cardboard and cheap lumber, even papier-mâché would do. It was the *shape* of the space that mattered, the way it fitted around his sleeping form. He made himself cocoons and nests and narrow coffins and sacks that hung from uterine plaster walls. Yet always out of reach, the terror of their vibrations sang across the darkness to him, tearing at his nerves.

"That drawing looks as if it hurts."

Some days there was nothing but claws on the page—hooks and barbed triangles, jagged lines of lightning (*God's claws*, he now realized). And even when they didn't resolutely fill the page, they were a major motif most days (especially in the late afternoon, when his muscles began to stiffen, and the air seemed heated). Sometimes they appeared to move in currents, to form patterns. At times they resembled graphics he'd seen representing electromagnetic currents, or the auras which supposedly radiated from the insane. He knew that visions in ancient times were described in terms of an eagle's talons clawing through the scalp. So it wasn't as if all these invisible razor claws were necessarily a terrible thing. He imagined they must somehow serve to also energize and inspire. On the other hand, perhaps they were the source of migraines in those who relied on them too much.

But whatever the use, they filled the air—we breathed, and drank of their arbitrary movements. Thank god they were invisible, he thought, else we would all be horrified in their presence.

"Sometimes it seems as if everything is falling apart."

There were a number of scribblings which might only be described as representations of "generalized corruption." Lines which broke and ran dribbling down the page, patches of shadowing which bubbled and disintegrated, narrow scratchings chipped and faded away into a dead-skin paleness. It was a game, finding all the ways in which the doodles illustrated death.

Yet even though it might be a game, he thought these doodles were of a particular importance. Corruption itself was a kind of ritual, a kind of obsession, which we ignored at our peril.

"That looks like a naked woman. Is that what you've been thinking about?"

Some of the doodles appeared vaguely pornographic. But a pornography of an elevated sort, as he could detect softnesses here which seemed to go far beyond that of normal flesh, certainly beyond that of any sort of flesh he had ever encountered: the softness of old women losing their hair, of young women in the fullness of life, of his own pale young son, and of his even paler daughter, of the pelts of animals, of silks, of swelling breads.

"You want to leave me, I can tell."

His ex-wife accused him daily of wanting to escape her, until escape her he did. Occasionally a page filled with wings. This happened open during times of great stress. Sometimes he drew them all day, and on surfaces he would never think to scribble on, like walls and floors. Once his ex-wife discovered them drawn on their bedroom wall and he'd been a coward, blamed the doodles on one of the kids and was ashamed of himself for months afterward.

Later he realized he'd blamed *both* of their children. But that was impossible; that was crazy. What had he been thinking of?

It was strange that he never thought consciously of escaping, or felt consciously trapped, for that matter. He felt like a normal human being. But perhaps part of being a normal human being was to be trapped, unable to escape the confines of one's own life and body.

"Sometimes you just talk and talk, but you really have nothing to say."

One day his pen stopped writing, out of ink, then started again in fits and sputters. This disturbed him greatly, because although he imagined he could detect the patterns the pressure of the pen nib had made, he could never be sure he had understood all of it.

And it was important to understand. He didn't know why, but his life depended on it.

"Sometimes you say some pretty hurtful things."

Sometimes the doodles appeared like mutilations of the pure white, expressionless page. They appeared to be angry, even though he didn't think he was an angry man. They appeared to be hateful, even though he could think of no one he hated.

And sometimes they appeared as the worst sorts of obscenity: children being mutilated and destroyed, children burning to death.

"We've lived here so long. Maybe what you need is a change of scenery."

Sometimes what began as a cityscape broke off into other directions which better expressed what the city had become for him. No matter how convoluted the network of lines of this urban representation became, he always seemed able to pick particular houses out of the complexity, important landmarks of his life there.

There was the house where he was born. There was the third floor apartment in which he had first made love to the woman who would become his wife, and then his ex-wife. There was the hospital where his daughter and son had been born.

There was the house on fire, the child burning within, her screams breaking up the lines he frantically drew and redrew, attempting to repair, striving to make them safe and permanent.

"Are you hearing me? Do you see what you're doing to our marriage?"

Ears and eyes appeared frequently, most often together, evidence of a certain paranoia on his part. Everywhere he went, people were watching him, listening to him, and talking among themselves. They'd comment on the look of his face, its shifting expressions of sadness. They'd talk about how he cried, things he'd said when he'd had too much to drink.

Everywhere he went people knew he had lost a child.

"What's that smell? Do you smell something?"

Misshapen noses were less frequent, but were more likely on hot, muggy days in August. Strong smells seemed to increase his need to doodle. Cooking smells, especially. Roasting, in particular.

Sometimes the smells so filled him it seemed as if he were all nose, and yet with no capacity to breathe.

"There are no secret messages here! What are you looking for?"

Sometimes scribbles resembled an exotic handwriting, and he would spend hours trying to decode them. The problems in his marriage had grown quite severe, but when he sought out the spiritualist in order to make contact with his dead daughter, the rift between him and his wife became decidedly more pronounced.

One day he began examining every piece of handwriting that originated from or came into their house. He spent hours, in fact, studying his wife's handwritten grocery lists. He'd become convinced that his daughter was trying to contact him in this manner, embedding her own childish scrawl within the handwriting of others.

He started saving all his own doodles and re-examined them, and found unmistakable proof that, at times, his dead daughter was guiding his hand. Many of the doodles had taken on her whimsical, sensitive nature.

He stopped going to work. He spent all day of every day doodling.

His wife left him after one last appeal to reason. He was barely able to remember their conversation ten minutes after she'd slammed the front door.

"You talk in circles. You make me dizzy."

He never knew quite what to make of spirals. Were they eyes, the insides of wombs, tornadoes as seen from outer space? Their significance was certainly ambiguous, and even when he believed them to be something recognizable and concrete, they maintained a certain abstract quality above and beyond what he could interpret, a spiritual dimension.

He could remember a time when they resembled eyes, and these spiralled eyes were the most threatening thing he could draw. More recently they had become eyes again, but somehow these comforted him. He imagined the blue at their distant bottoms, drawing him into the depths of them, his daughter's endless stare.

"Words, you keep using all these words. When are you going to do something?"

Mouths, he decided these were. They started out as eyes, and then grew teeth. People talked too much, when they should be listening. They talked about how things used to be, when they should be seeing how things really are now.

Eventually the memory of his daughter's endless stare grew teeth, and all the words in the world would not keep that vision away.

After his wife left him, there were no more voices to distract him from his doodling.

Sometimes they were faces turned inside out.

Or the internal organs of dream-selves and friends.

Sometimes they were the face your lover takes when she doesn't believe you can see her.

Some might be the broken bodies of insects, or insects unknown to humankind: the flying brain zipper, the centipede of pain, the butterfly-roach of loss.

He created them at an ever-increasing frequency, drawing them on the bathroom tiles and mirrors using lipsticks his wife had left behind, spray-painting them on the living room and kitchen ceilings, painting them with a broad brush on the outside walls of his house, using the leftover paint in his garage. Neighbors would gather and watch, but out of anger or embarrassment they'd stopped trying to talk to him some time ago.

Once, after a week-long drunk, he'd used his own bodily fluids to smear the doodles across his clean white bedsheets.

He began to write a catalogue of the ones he had neglected—or found impossible—to save, hoping for some new understanding. He wrote captions at the bottoms of the originals, hoping his labels might crystallize and clarify:

> *Topographies of nowhere.*
> *The worms of remembrance.*
> *The absence of love.*

In the masses of doodles he discovered pointilist portraits of children he'd never had, and that made him feel like a traitor to his daughter's memory.

And here were the feathers from birds which were now extinct or which had never existed.

And here were mazes which would forever frustrate him because they had no solutions.

And here were the wriggling walls and strange vegetation which had grown up around him, isolating him from the outside world.

The fire had started in the bedroom. That's what they had said the other time. It had been piled almost to the ceiling with "drawings," someone had called them, although most were no better than hen-scratchings, crudely repeated patterns like those a very young child might make. The drawings had been set on fire, but the rising heat had permitted a few to escape the open window. Several of these were unlike the others, were not crude at all, but were small, obsessive, precisely rendered portraits of a young girl's face, dozens of them covering the pages in somewhat spiral patterns.

All the neighbors said he had been a nervous man, a smoker.

They'd said that the other time as well.

DYING IN BANGKOK

Dan Simmons

Born in Peoria, Illinois, Dan Simmons now lives in Colorado. Since the publication of his first story in *The Twilight Zone* magazine as co-winner of the first *Twilight Zone* magazine short story contest in 1982, his short fiction has appeared in *Playboy, OMNI, Isaac Asimov's Science Fiction Magazine,* and various anthologies. His collection of short fiction, *Prayers to Broken Stones,* won the Bram Stoker Award for Best Collection in 1992, and his story "This Year's Class Picture" from the anthology *Still Dead* won both the Bram Stoker Award and the Theodore Sturgeon Award in 1993. Simmons's first novel, *Song of Kali,* won the World Fantasy Award in 1986; his second novel, *Carrion Comfort,* won the 1990 Bram Stoker Award, and his science fiction novel, *Hyperion,* won the Hugo Award in 1991. His other novels include *Phases of Gravity, The Hollow Man, Summer of Night* and *Children of the Night.* His recently finished comic-horror novel, *Pele's Fire,* will be out shortly.

"Dying in Bangkok" is an excellent example of a successful story that works not because of new ideas but because of the author's treatment of the theme and subject matter. The story was first published under the title "Death in Bangkok" in *Playboy,* an unusual venue in light of the story's view of sexuality. A longer version appears in *LoveDeath,* a collection of five novellas. The version here is the same as that in *Playboy,* with two minor changes. This story is not for the faint of heart.

—E.D.

I fly back to Asia in the late spring of 1992, leaving one City of Angels, which had just exorcised its evil spirits in an orgy of looting and flame, and arriving in another, where the blood demons are gathering on the horizon like monsoon clouds. My home city of Los Angeles had gone up in flames and insane looting the month before; Bangkok—known locally as Krung Thep, the City of Angels— is preparing to slaughter its children on the streets near the Democracy Monument.

All of this is irrelevant to me. I have my own blood score to settle.

The minute I step outside the air-conditioned vaults of Bangkok's Don Muang International Airport, it all comes back to me: the heat, over 105°F, humidity as close to liquid air as atmosphere can get, the stink of carbon monoxide and industrial pollution and the open sewage of 10 million people turning the air into a cocktail thick enough to drink. The smell and the heat and the humidity and the intense tropical sunlight combine to make breathing a physical effort, like trying to inhale oxygen through a blanket moistened with kerosene. And the airport is 25 klicks from the center of town.

I feel myself stir and harden just to be there.

"Dr. Merrick?" says a Thai in chauffeur's livery.

I nod. A yellow Mercedes from the Oriental Hotel is waiting for me. There is no scenic way into Bangkok today unless one were to ride a sampan up-river into the heart of the city. The commute into the old section of Bangkok now is pure capitalist madness: traffic jams, Asian palaces that are really shopping malls, industrial clutter, new elevated expressways, ferro-concrete apartment towers, billboards hawking Japanese electronics, the roar of motorcycles and the constant arc-flash and jackhammer-thud of new construction. As is the case with all of Asia's new megalopolises, Bangkok is tearing itself down and rebuilding itself daily in a frenzy that makes Western cities such as New York look as permanent as the pyramids.

I catch a glimpse of Silom Road, jammed with people but looking empty and lethargic compared with its usual crush of manic crowds. I glance at my watch. It is eight P.M. on a Friday night Los Angeles time; 11 o'clock Saturday morning here in Bangkok. Silom Road is resting, waiting for the evening excitement that emanates from the Patpong entertainment district like the scent of a bitch in heat—an urgent scent like a subtle blend of exotic perfume and the Clorox tang of semen and the coppery taste of blood.

I hurry through the courteous greetings and the bowed *wais* and the gracious registerings of the Oriental Hotel, perhaps the world's finest hotel, wanting only to get to my suite and shower and feign sleep, to lie there and stare at the teak-and-plaster ceiling until the sunlight fades and the night begins. Darkness will bring this particular City of Angels alive, or at least stir the corpse of it into slow, erotic motion.

When it is well and truly dark, I rise, dress in my Bangkok street clothes and go out into the night.

The first time I saw Bangkok had been 22 years earlier, in May 1970. Tres and I had chosen Bangkok as our destination for the seven days of out-of-country R&R we had coming to us. Actually, I don't know many grunts who called it R&R back then. Many called it I&I: intercourse and intoxication. Married officers used their leave to meet wives in Hawaii, but for the rest of us the Army offered a smorgasbord of destinations ranging from Tokyo to Sydney. A lot of us chose Bangkok for four reasons: (1) it was easy to get to and didn't use up a lot of our time in travel, (2) the cheap sex, (3) the cheap sex and (4) the cheap sex.

To tell the truth, Tres had chosen Bangkok for other reasons, and I followed along trusting in his judgment, much the way I did when we were out on a long-range reconnaissance patrol. Tres—Robert William Tindale III—was only about a year older than I was, but he was taller, stronger, smarter and infinitely better educated. I'd dropped out of my Midwestern college in my junior year and rattled around until the draft sucked me in. Tres had graduated from Kenyon College with honors and then enlisted in the infantry rather than go on to graduate school.

His nickname came from the Spanish word for three and was pronounced *tray*. Most of us had been given nicknames in the platoon—mine was Prick because of the heavy PRC-25 radio I'd carried around during my short stint as a radiotelephone operator—but Tres came to us with his nickname in place.

Tres had a deep interest in Asian cultures and was good at languages. He was the only grunt in the company who could speak any real Vietnamese. Most of us thought that *beaucoup* was Vietnamese and felt clever to know *di di mau* and half a dozen other corrupted local phrases. Tres *spoke* Vietnamese, though he kept that fact from reaching any officer other than our own LTC. "I wouldn't let them make me a typist or officer," he used to say to me. "I'll be goddamned if I'll let them turn me into some pissant interrogator."

Tres had never studied the Thai language but he learned quickly.

"Just tell me what the Thai word is for blow job," I'd said to him during the MAC flight from Saigon to Bangkok.

"I don't know," said Tres. "But the phrase for hand job is *shak wao*."

"No shit," I'd said.

"No shit," said Tres. He was reading a book and didn't look up. "It means 'pulling on the kite string.' "

I thought about that image for a minute. The transport was losing altitude, jouncing through clouds toward Bangkok. "I think I'll hold out for a blow job," I said. I was not quite 20 years old and had experienced oral sex only once, with a college girlfriend who had obviously never tried it before, either. But I was full of hormones and macho posturing I'd picked up from the platoon, not to mention the sheer adrenaline rush of being alive after six months in the boonies. "Definitely a blow job," I said.

Tres had grunted and kept reading. It was a dusty book about Thai customs or mythology or religion or something.

I realize now that if I'd known what he was reading about and why he had chosen Bangkok, I probably wouldn't have stepped off the plane.

The floor valet, elevator doorman, concierge and main doormen of the Oriental do not raise eyebrows at my wrinkled chinos and stained photographer's vest. At 350 American dollars a night, their guests can wear whatever they want. The concierge does, however, step out to talk to me before I leave the air-conditioned sanity of the hotel.

"Dr. Merrick," he says softly, "you are aware of the . . . ah . . . tensions that exist in Bangkok at the current time?"

I nod. "The student riots? The military crackdown?"

The concierge smiles and bows slightly, obviously grateful for not having to educate the *farang* in what seems an embarrassing topic to him. "Yes, sir. I mention it only because, while the problems have been concentrated near the university and the Grand Palace, there have been, ah, disturbances on Silom Road."

I nod again. "But there's no curfew yet," I say. "Patpong is still open."

The concierge smiles with no hint of a leer. "Oh, yes, sir. Patpong and the nightclubs are open for business. The city is very much open."

It is not hard to recognize when I get there. The narrow streets connecting

Silom and Suriwong roads are awash with cheap neon signs: MARVELOUS MASSAGE, PUSSY GALORE, BABY A-GO-GO, SUPERGIRL LIVE SEX SHOWS, PUSSY ALIVE! and a score of others. The lanes of Patpong are narrow enough to be pedestrian-only, but the roar of the three-wheeled *tuk-tuks* in the boulevards beyond provides a constant background to the rock-and-roll music that is blaring from speakers and open doors.

Young men or women—sometimes it is hard to tell in androgynous Thailand—begin plucking at my sleeve and gesturing toward doorways the moment I turn onto the lane called Patpong One.

"Mister, best live sex shows, best pussy shows."

"Hey, Mister, this way prettiest girls, best prices."

"Want to see nicest shave pussy? Meet nice girl?"

"You want girls? No? You want boys?"

I stroll on, ignoring the gentle tugs at my sleeve. The last query had come as I entered the lane called Patpong Two. The night zone is divided into three areas: Patpong One serves straights, Patpong Two offers delights to both straights and gays and Patpong Three is all gay. The majority of the action here on Patpong Two is still for heterosexuals, though most of the bars have smiling boys as well as girls.

I pause in front of a bar called Pussy Delite. A little man with one arm and a face turned blue by the flickering neon steps forward and hands me a long plastic card. "Pussy menu?" he says, his voice the epitome of an upscale maître d's.

I take the grubby plastic card and study it: PUSSY BANANAS, PUSSY COCA-COLA, PUSSY CHOPSTICKS, PUSSY RAZOR BLADES, PUSSY SMOKING.

Nodding, I start into the busy nightclub. The one-armed maître d' hurries forward and retrieves his card.

The club is small and smoky, with four bars set in a square around a crude stage. The girl on the stage—she looks no more than 16 or 17—is arched backward so that the top of her head almost touches the rough wood of the stage, her legs and arms supporting her in a crablike backbend. She is naked; her crotch has been shaved. Colored lights shaft down through the smoke and fall on her like soft lasers. The center of the stage is a turntable, and the girl holds the arched position while her body rotates so that everyone can see her exposed genitals. A lighted cigarette has been set between her labia. As the stage revolves toward each section of the bar, smoke puffs from her vulva as if she is exhaling. Occasionally, one of the drunker patrons applauds.

Most of the men in the bar are Thai, but there are plenty of *farang* scattered around: arrogant Germans in khaki with their hair slicked back, beaky Brits paying more attention to their drinks than to the girl on the stage, an occasional frowning Chinese from Hong Kong squinting through glasses and a few fat Americans with untouched drinks and protruding eyes.

I move up to the big bar and take an empty stool. The girl's upside-down face revolves past three feet from me. Her eyes are open but unfocused. Her small breasts seem little more than swellings. I can count her ribs.

A young Thai woman slides close, her left breast touching my bare forearm through her thin cotton tank top. Although she is no older than the girl whose genitals rotate our way, she looks older because of the heavy makeup that glows a necrotic color in the shifting blue light. "My name Nok," she shouts over the rock and roll. "What your name?"

She is so close that I can smell her sweet talcum-and-perspiration scent through the cigarette smoke. Thai are among the cleanest people in the world, bathing several times a day. Ignoring her question, I say, "Nok means bird. Are you a bird, Nok?"

Her eyes widen. "Do you speak Thai?" she asks in Thai.

I show no comprehension. "Are you a bird, Nok?" I ask again.

She sighs and says in English, "Yes, I a thirsty bird. Buy me drink?"

I nod and the bartender is there a fraction of a second later, pouring her the most expensive "whiskey" in the place. It is 98 percent tea, of course.

"You from States?" she asks, a bit of animation coming into her dark eyes. "I like States very much."

I brush her long hair out of her eyes and sip my beer. "If you're a bird," I say, "are you a *khai long*?" The phrase means "little lost chicken" but is often applied to street girls in Bangkok.

Nok pulls her head back and folds her arms as if I have slapped her. She starts to turn away but I grip her thin arm and pull her back against me. "Finish your whiskey," I say.

Nok pouts but sips the tea. We watch her friend on the stage as the girl's hairless vulva rotates our way again. The cigarette has burned down to the exposed labia. Sipping my beer, I marvel—not for the first time—at how human beings can turn the most intimate sights into the most grotesque. At the last second before the cigarette would burn her, the girl reaches down, retrieves it, takes a drag on it with the appropriate lips, tosses it between the stage and the bar and wriggles out of her yoga backbend. Only one or two of the men along the bar applaud. The girl bounces offstage and an older Thai woman, also naked, steps onto the revolving platform, squats and fans four double-edged razor blades for the audience's approval.

I turn back to Nok. "I'm sorry I hurt your feelings," I say. "You are a very pretty bird. Would you like to help me have fun tonight?"

Nok forces a smile. "I love to make you fun tonight." She pretends to frown as if she had just thought of something. "But Mr. Diang"—she nods toward a thin Thai man with dyed red hair who stands in the shadows—"he be very mad at Nok if Nok not work all shift. Him I must pay if I go to make fun."

I nod and take out the thick roll of baht I had changed dollars for at the airport. "I understand," I say, peeling off four 500 baht bills—almost $80. Even the highest-class bar whores in Bangkok used to charge only 200 or 300 baht, but the government ruined that a few years ago by bringing out a 500-baht note. It seemed cheap to ask for change, so now most girls charge 500 for the act, with another 500 to pay their Mr. Diangs.

She glances toward the old man with red hair and he nods ever so slightly. Nok smiles at me. "Yes, I have place for much fun."

I pull the money back. "I thought we might try to find someone to have fun with," I say over the blasting rock and roll. In the corner of my vision I can see the woman onstage inserting the blades.

Nok makes a face. Sharing the evening with other girls will cut down on her profit. "*Sakha bue din*," she says softly. I smile quizzically and ask, "What does that mean?"

"It means you have enough fun just with Nok, who love you very much," she says, smiling again.

Actually, the phrase is short for a northern village saying that goes "Your cock is on the ground, I tread on it like a snake." I smile my appreciation at her kindness.

"This money would be just for you, of course," I say, setting the 2000 baht closer to her hand. "There would be more if we find exactly the right girl."

Smiling more broadly now, Nok squints at me. "You have girl in mind? Someone you know or someone I find? Good friend who also love you much?"

"Someone I know of," I say, taking a breath. "Have you heard of a woman named Mara? Or perhaps her daughter, Tanha?"

Nok freezes and for an instant she *is* a bird—a frightened, captured bird. She tries to pull away but I still hold her arm.

"*Na!*" she cries in a little girl's voice. "*Na, na*—"

"There's more money," I begin, sliding the baht toward her.

"*Na!*" cries Nok, tears in her eyes.

Mr. Diang takes a quick step forward and nods to two huge Thai near the door. The men cut through the crowd toward us like sharks through shallow water.

I let go of Nok's arm and she slips away through the crowd. I hold both hands up, palms out, and the bouncers stop five paces from me. The old man with the red hair tilts his head toward the door and I nod my willingness to go.

There are other places on my list. Someone's love of money will be greater than their fear of Mara. Perhaps.

Twenty-two years earlier, Patpong had existed but American grunts could not afford it. The Thai government and the U.S. Army had cobbled together a red-light district of cheap bars, cheaper hotels and massage parlors on New Petchburi Road, miles from the more businesslike Patpong.

During the first day and night in Bangkok with Tres, I discovered what a no-hands bar was. The food was lousy and the booze was overpriced, but the novelty of having the girls feed us and lift the glasses to our lips was memorable. Between feeding us bites and sips, they cooed and winked and ran long-nailed fingers up the insides of our thighs. It was hard to reconcile all of this with the fact that 24 hours earlier we had been humping our rucks up the red-clay jungle hillsides of the A Shau Valley.

At any rate, we drank and whored our way through the red-light district for 48 hours. Tres and I had taken separate rooms so that we could bring back girls, and this we did. The cost then for an evening of sexual favors was less than what I would have paid for a case of cold beer from the fire-base PX—and that wasn't much. A T-shirt or a pair of jeans given to our little girls would pay for a week's worth of *mia chaos*, or "hired wives." They'd not only screw or give head on command but also wash our clothes and tidy up the hotel rooms while we were out looking for other girls.

You have to remember that this was in 1970. AIDS wasn't even dreamed of then. Oh, the Army had made us take rubbers along and watch half a dozen films warning us about venereal diseases, but the biggest threat to our health was Saigon Rose, a tough strain of syphilis brought into the country by GIs. Still and all, our girls were so young and stupid, I realize now, that they didn't even ask us to wear rubbers. Perhaps they thought that having a child by a *farang* was good luck or would somehow miraculously get them to the States. I don't know. I didn't ask.

But four days into our seven days of R&R, even the attraction of cheap Thai marijuana and cheaper sex was paling a bit. I was doing it because Tres was doing it; following his lead had become a form of survival for me in the boonies.

But Tres wanted something else. And I followed.

"I've found out about something cool," he said early on the evening of our fourth night in the city. "Really cool."

I nodded. Tang, my little *mia chao*, had been pouting that she wanted to go out to dinner, but I'd ignored her and gone down to meet Tres in the bar when he called.

"It's going to take some money," said Tres. "How much do you have?"

I fumbled in my wallet. Tang and I had been smoking some Thai sticks in the room, and things were a bit luminescent and off-center for me. "Couple hundred baht," I said.

Tres shook his head. "This is going to take dollars," he said. "Maybe four or five hundred."

I goggled at him. We hadn't spent a fraction of that during our entire R&R so far. Nothing in Bangkok cost more than a couple of bucks.

"This is special," he said. "Really special. Didn't you tell me that you were bringing along the three hundred bucks your uncle sent you?"

I nodded dumbly. The money was stuffed in a sneaker in the bottom of my duffel upstairs. "I wanted to buy my ma something special," I said. "Silk or a kimono or something. . . ." I trailed off lamely.

Tres smiled. "You'll like this better than a kimono for your mom. Get the money. Hurry."

I hurried. When I got downstairs there was a young Thai man waiting at the door with Tres. "Johnny," Tres said, "this is Maladung. Maladung, this is Johnny Merrick. We call him the Prick in the platoon."

Maladung smirked at me.

Before I could explain that a PRC-25 radio was called a prick-25 and that I'd humped it around for a month and a half before they found a bigger RTO, Maladung had nodded at us and led the way out into the night. We took a *tuk-tuk* down to the river. Technically, the broad river that flowed all the way from the Himalayas to bisect the heart of old Bangkok was called the Chao Phraya, but all I ever heard the locals call it was Mae Nam, or "the River."

We stepped out onto the darkened pier, and Maladung snapped some words at a man who stood on a long, narrow boat that was a mere shadow beneath the pier. The man answered something and Tres said, "Give me a hundred-baht note, Johnny."

Tres paid Maladung, who waved us into the bow of the narrow boat. I know now that these small boats are called "long-tailed taxis" and are for hire by the hundreds. They get their name from the long propeller shaft that has a full-sized automobile engine mounted on it. I noticed that night that the shaft was so well counterbalanced that our driver could lift the prop out of the water with one hand, the heavy engine seemingly weightless in the center.

Bangkok is a city of small canals, or *klongs*. We headed downriver past the lights of the Oriental Hotel, a place Tres and I had heard of but could never dream of affording, and passed under a busy highway bridge. Our long-tailed taxi darted in front of a huge ferry with a roar of its V6 engine, crossed toward the west bank and then turned into a *klong* no wider than one of the narrow *sois* in the Patpong district. The little canal was pitch dark except for the weak glow of lantern light from the tied-up sampans and the overhanging shacks. Our driver had lighted his own red lantern and hung it from a stanchion near the stern, but I had no idea how other boats avoided colliding with us as we roared around blind turns and under low bridges. Sometimes I was sure that the canvas roof of our taxi was going to hit the underside of the sagging bridges, but even as Tres and I ducked we cleared the rotting timbers with inches to spare. The few other water taxis roared past us like noisy wraiths, their wakes slapping across our bow and splashing our knees. I looked at Tres as we passed a dimly lighted sampan, and his eyes were wild. He was grinning broadly.

For half an hour or more we twisted our way through these narrow one-way *klongs*. The stink of sewage was so strong that my eyes watered. Several times I heard voices coming from the lightless and listing sampans that lined the canal like so many waterlogged wrecks.

"People live in those," I whispered to Tres as we passed a blackened mass where tumbledown shacks and half-sunken sampans had narrowed the *klong* to the point that our suicidal driver had been forced to slow the boat to a crawl. Tres did not answer.

Just when I was sure that the driver had become lost in the maze of canals, we came into an open area of water bounded by abandoned warehouses on stilts and the backs of burned-out shacks. The effect was of a large floating courtyard hidden from the city's streets and public canals. Several barges and black sampans were tied up in the center of this watery square, and I could see the dim running lanterns of several other long-tailed taxis that were tied up to the nearest sampan.

The driver cut the engine and we glided to the makeshift dock in a silence so sudden that it made my ears ache.

I had just realized that the dock was only a float made of oil drums and planks lashed to the sampan when two men stepped out through a ragged hole in the canvas side of the boat and stood balancing on the planks, watching us bump to a stop. Even in the dark I could tell that they were built like wrestlers or bouncers. The closer of the two barked something at us in Thai.

Maladung answered and one of them took our bowline while the other stood aside to let us climb onto the small space. I stepped off the taxi first, saw a faint glow of lantern light through the ragged opening and was about to step through when one of the men touched my chest with three fingers that seemed stronger than my entire arm.

"Must pay first," hissed Maladung from his place on the taxi.

Pay for what? I wanted to ask, but Tres leaned close and whispered, "Give me your three hundred bucks, Johnny."

My uncle had sent me the money in crisp fifties. I gave them to Tres, who handed two bills to Maladung and the other four to the closest man on the dock.

The men stepped aside and gestured me toward the opening. I had just bent to fit through the low doorway when I was startled by the sound of our boat's engine roaring to life. I straightened up in time to see the red lantern disappearing down a narrow *klong*.

"Shit," I said. "Now how do we get back?"

Tres's voice was tight with something greater than tension. "We'll worry about that later," he said. "Go on."

I looked at the ragged doorway that seemed to open to a corridor connecting the series of sampans and barges. Strong smells came from it and there was a muted sound like a large animal breathing somewhere at the end of that tunnel.

"Do we really want to do this?" I whispered to Tres. The two Thai men on the dock were as inanimate as those statues of Chinese lion-dogs that guard the entrances to important buildings throughout Asia. "Tres?" I said.

"Yes," he said. "Come on." He pushed past me and squeezed through the opening. Used to following his lead on patrol and night ambush and LRRP, I lowered my head and followed.

I am watching a live sex show at Pussy Galore when four Thai men surround me. The sex show is typical for Bangkok: a young couple screwing on twin Harley-Davidsons hanging from wires above the central stage. The two have been engaged in intercourse for more then ten minutes. Their faces show no feigned passion, but their bodies are expert at revealing their coupling to every corner of the bar. The audience seems to find the primary tension not in the fucking but in the chance that the two might fall off the suspended motorcycles.

I am ignoring the show, interrogating a bar girl named Lah, when the Thai shove in around me. Lah fades into the crowd. It is dark in the bar, but the four men wear sunglasses. I take a sip of flat beer and say nothing as they press closer.

"You are named Merrick?" asks the shortest. His face is ax-blade thin and is pockmarked with acne or smallpox scars.

I nod.

The pockmarked man takes a step closer. "You have been asking about a woman named Mara?"

"Yes."

"Come," he says. I make no resistance, and the five of us move out of the bar in a flying wedge. Outside, a gap opens a bit between the burly men on my left, and I can make a run for it if I choose. I do not so choose. A dark limousine is parked at the head of the lane, and the man on my right opens the rear door. As he does, I see the pearl-handled grip of a revolver tucked into his waistband.

I get in the backseat. The two tallest men sit on either side of me. I watch as the pockmarked man moves to the front passenger seat and the man with the revolver settles himself behind the wheel. The limo moves off through side streets. I know that it is sometime after three A.M., but the *sois* are still strangely empty this close to Patpong. At first I can tell we are moving north, parallel to the river, but then I lose all sense of direction in the maze of narrow side streets. Only the darkened signs in Chinese let me know that we're in the area north of Patpong known as Chinatown.

"Avoid Sanam Luang and Ratchadamnoen Klang," the pockmarked man says to the driver in Thai. "The army is shooting protesters tonight."

I glance to my right and see the orange glow of flames above rooftops. The distant, almost soft rattle and pop of small-arms fire can be heard over the hiss of the car's air conditioner.

We stop in an area of abandoned buildings. There are no streetlights here and only the orange glow of flames reflected from low clouds allows me to see where the street ends in vacant lots and half-demolished warehouses. I can smell the river somewhere out there in the darkness.

The pockmarked man turns and nods. The Thai on my right opens the door and pulls me out by my vest. The driver stays in the car while the other three drag me deep into the shadows near the river.

I start to speak just as the man behind me laces his fingers through my hair and pulls my head sharply back. The third man grabs my arms as the man holding my hair lifts a stiletto blade to my throat. The pockmarked face suddenly looms so close that I can smell fish and beer on the man's breath.

"Why do you ask about a woman named Mara with a daughter named Tanha?" he asks in Thai.

I blink my incomprehension. The blade draws blood just below my Adam's apple. My head is pulled so far back that I find it almost impossible to breathe.

"Why do you ask about a woman named Mara with a daughter named Tanha?" he asks again in English.

My words are little more than a rasping gargle. "I have something for them." I try to free my right hand but the third man restrains my wrist.

"Inside left pocket," I manage.

The pockmarked man hesitates only a second before tearing open my vest and feeling for the hidden pocket there. He brings out 20 bills.

I can smell his breath on my face again as he laughs softly. "Twenty thousand dollars? Mara does not need twenty thousand dollars. There *is* no Mara," he concludes in English. In Thai, he says to the man with the knife, "Kill him."

They have done this before. The first man bends my head farther back, the other man pulls my arms down sharply while the pockmarked man steps back, fastidiously getting out of the way of the arterial spray that is coming. In that second before the knife slashes my throat, I gasp out two words. "Look again."

I feel the tension increase in the knife wielder's hand and arm as the blade cuts deeper, but the pockmarked man holds up one hand in command. The blade has drawn enough blood to soak the collar of my shirt and vest, but it goes no deeper. The short man holds a bill high, squints at it in the dim light and then flicks a cigarette lighter into flame. He mutters under his breath.

"What?" says the third man in Thai.

The pockmarked man answers in the same language. "It is a ten-thousand-dollar bearer's bond. They are all ten-thousand-dollar bonds. Twenty of them."

The other two hiss their breath.

"There is more," I say in Thai. "Much more. But I must see Mara."

We stand there motionless for at least a full minute before the pockmarked man grunts something, the blade is lowered, my hair is released and we walk back to the waiting limousine.

I followed Tres through the tunnel carved through the arched canvas roofs of sampans.

Several Thai men glanced at us as we stepped into the covered barge, and then they looked again, obviously surprised that *farang* were allowed there. But then their attention was drawn back to the makeshift stage in the center of the barge. I stood there blinking, peering through the heavy cloud of cigarette and marijuana smoke. The stage was no more than 6'x4', illuminated only by two hissing lanterns hanging from overhead trusses. It was empty except for two women performing cunnilingus on each other. Crude benches ran four deep around the stage and the 20 or so Thai men there were little more than dark shapes in the haze of smoke.

"What—" I began, but Tres hushed me and led the way to an empty bench to our left. The women on the stage were joined by two thin Thai men, boys, actually, who ignored the females as they caressed each other into an excited state.

I was tired of being hushed. I leaned closer to Tres and said, "Why the hell did we have to pay 300 American dollars for this when we can watch it for a couple of bucks in any bar on New Petchburi Road?"

Tres just shook his head. "This is just the preliminary stuff, Johnny," he whispered. "Warm-up acts. We paid for the main event."

A couple of men in front of us had turned and frowned, as if we were making too much noise in a movie theater. On the stage, the two boys had finished their preparations and had become involved with the young women as well as with each other. The combinations were complicated.

I sat and crossed my legs. We didn't wear underwear in Nam because it caused crotch rot, and like a lot of grunts I'd gotten out of the habit of wearing it even while in civilian clothes on R&R. I wished I'd pulled on some shorts under my light cotton slacks that night. It seemed bad form to have a visible hard-on around all these other men.

The four young people on the stage explored combinations for another ten minutes or so. When they came—almost at once—the women might have faked it, but there was no doubt that the men's orgasms were sincere. One of the Thai girls caught some semen on her breasts, while the other girl spread the second boy's jism on the buttocks of the first boy. The bisexual stuff disturbed me and excited me at the same time. I didn't understand myself well then.

Finished, the four young people simply stood and exited through a tunnel door in the far wall. The patrons did not applaud. The stage was empty for several minutes, but then a short Thai man dressed in a black silk shirt and trousers stepped onto the stage and said something in low, serious tones. I caught the word Mara twice. There was a sudden tension in the room.

"What did he—" I began.

"Shhh," said Tres, his eyes riveted on the stage.

"Fuck that," I said. I'd paid for this crap, I deserved to know what I was getting for my money. "What's a Mara?"

Tres sighed. "Mara is *phanyaa mahn*, Johnny. The prince of demons. He sent his three daughters—Aradi, discontent; Tanha, desire; and Raka, love—to tempt the Buddha. But the Buddha won."

I squinted through smoke at the empty stage and slowly swinging lantern. "So Mara's a man?"

Tres shook his head. "Not when the spirit of the *phanyaa mahn* combines with the naga in a demon-human incarnation," he said.

I stared at Tres. We'd each smoked some good shit since we arrived in Bangkok—the Thai stick was almost free here—but Tres had obviously been doing more than was good for him. He noticed my stare and smiled slightly. "Mara's the part of the world that dies, Johnny . . . the death principle. The thing we fear more than Charlie when we're out on night patrol. Naga is sort of a snake god that's associated with water. The river. It can take or give life. When the spirit of the naga is given to someone possessed by the power of the *phanyaa mahn*—Mara—the demon thing can be male or female. But what we paid to see was a female Mara that's supposed to be *phanyaa mahn naga kio*. That doesn't happen once in ten thousand incarnations."

"What's a *kio*?" I whispered. I had the sinking feeling that I'd blown 300 bucks on nothing.

"A *kio* is a . . . shhh," hissed Tres, pointing to the stage.

A woman came out onto the stage. She was dressed in traditional Thai silk and was carrying a baby. Her face was sharp, almost masculine, and her hair was a nimbus of tangled black. She was older than the sex performers we had seen earlier but still not much more than 20. The baby mewled and tugged at the silk over the woman's small breasts. I realized that the Thai men in the room were bowing slightly from where they sat. Some were making the traditional palms-together *wai* of obeisance. It seemed an odd thing to be doing toward a sex performer. I frowned at Tres but he was *wai*ing, too. I shook my head and looked back at the stage. Most of the men had put out their cigarettes, but there was so much smoke in the barge that it was like peering through a fog.

The woman had gone to her knees on the stage. The baby hung limp in her arms. The man in black silk came onto the stage and said something in low, flat tones.

There was a long silence. Finally, a fat Thai in the front row stood, turned to look once at the crowd and then stepped onto the stage. There was a general expulsion of breath, and I could feel the tension in the room shift focus, if not actually lessen.

"What?" I whispered.

Tres shook his head and pointed. The fat man was handing over a thick roll of baht to the man in black silk.

As if on cue, the two young women we'd seen earlier came back out. They were dressed in some sort of ceremonial garb that I associated with a formal Thai dance I'd seen photos of. Each wore a tall, peaked hat, weird shoulders and a blouse and pants of gold silk. I began to wonder if I'd paid $300 to see four people have sex with their clothes on.

The two boys came onto the stage wearing costumes of their own and carrying an ornate chair. I was afraid we were going to get into more of the gay and lesbian stuff, but the boys merely set the chair down and disappeared. The two girls began to undress the fat man while the woman named Mara stared out at nothing, paying no attention to the man, his attendants or the crowd.

Having undressed the patron in an almost ritualistic manner and folded his clothes away, the girls pushed him back into the chair. I could see sweat beading the man's upper lip and chest. His legs appeared to be shaking slightly. If he had paid for some sort of erotic service, he certainly didn't seem to be in the mood for it. The guy's cock was shriveled to almost nothing and his scrotum looked like it had shrunk to walnut size.

The girls bent over and began to work on him with their hands and mouths. It took a while, but they were very good and within a few minutes the fat man's cock was hard and lifted high enough that the glans almost touched his belly. Meanwhile, Mara was still staring out at nothing, the baby wiggling slightly in her arms. The woman seemed disinterested to the point of catatonia.

My heart began to pound. I was afraid that they were going to do something to the baby, and the thought made me physically sick. If Tres had known that there would be an infant involved—

I glanced at him but he was looking at Mara with an expression of what might have been a mixture of fear and scholarly interest. I shook my head. This was weird shit.

The two girls left. The stage was empty except for the seated fat man with his modest erection and the woman with her child. Slowly Mara turned toward him and a trick of the lantern light made her eyes gleam almost yellow. It suddenly seemed too quiet in the barge, as if everyone had stopped breathing.

Mara stood, took three steps toward the man and then went to her knees again. She was far enough away that she had to bend forward just to set her hand on his thigh. I noticed that her fingernails were very red and very long. The fat man's erection began to visibly flag at that point and I could see his balls rising again as if they wanted to hide in the protection of his body.

Mara seemed to smile at the sight. She leaned forward, still cradling the infant, and opened her mouth.

I expected oral sex then, but her head never came closer than 18 inches to the man's genitals. Instead, her tongue slid out from between sharp and perfectly white teeth until it arched to a point where it could touch her own chin. The fat man's eyes were very wide now, and I could see his arms and belly quaking slightly. His erection had returned.

Mara shifted her head, shook it as if loosening her neck, and her tongue continued to glide out. Six inches of it. Then eight. A foot of fleshy tongue sliding out of her open mouth like a pink adder uncoiling from its dark nest.

When 18 or 20 inches of thick tongue had slid into sight, draped across the fat man's thigh, and begun to wrap itself around his cock, I tried to swallow and found I could not. I tried to close my eyes and found that my eyelids refused to close. Mouth open, breathing harshly, I just watched.

Mara's tongue slid around the head of the man's uncircumcised cock, pulling down the foreskin as it went. The lantern light reflected off the pink moistness of that tongue and glistened where it had lubricated the man's erection.

More tongue uncoiled, the tip of it spiraling down and around like the probing head of a wide-bodied serpent. The fat man closed his eyes just as the long tongue completely encircled his shaft, the narrow tip of that fleshy ribbon swaying and bobbing toward his tightened testicles. Mara's lashes were also lowered, but I could see the glimmer of white and yellow under the heavy eyelids as the man's hips began to move.

The sight of that moist tongue in the yellow lantern light was terrible—nauseating—but it was not the worst. The worst was the glimpse I had caught of the lesions on that tongue: openings, oblong slits, in the fleshy inner part of the tongue as if someone had taken a very sharp scalpel and made a series of bloodless, centimeter-long incisions.

But these were not incisions. Even in the weak light I could see the fleshy openings pulse open and close of their own volition, like the feeding mouths of some hungry anemone surging in a soft tidal current. Then the tongue wrapped more tightly around the man's straining penis, and I could see the almost peristaltic contractions as the ribbon of pinkish flesh pulled and tightened, tightened and pulled. Mara closed her lips, pulled her head back like a fisherman with a hook deeply embedded, and the fat man moaned in ecstasy. He gripped the arms of the chair and pumped his hips more wildly, eyes half open but obviously seeing nothing but the red surge of his own pleasure.

Mara's tongue wrapped in tighter coils and continued to tug and flex. The fat man's face grew redder as he continued to pump his hips. His eyes were still open, but only the whites showed now. The head of his cock, just visible in the lantern light, seemed engorged to the point of bursting. A thick coil of tongue slid across it and around it.

The man went into what I now know are the final stages of ejaculatory response: muscle spasms, loss of voluntary control of facial muscles, respiratory rates exceeding 40 breaths per minute, massive body flush and a frenzied pumping of hips. If someone had taken his pulse, they would have found his heart rate climbing to somewhere between 100 and 175 beats per minute. His systolic pressure would be shooting up by close to 80mm Hg while his diastolic had to be elevated by around 40mm Hg or higher. In those days I just thought of it as coming.

Mara's head lowered as if she were reeling in her extended tongue. Her eyes were open now and very yellow. Eight or more inches of tongue were still wrapped around the man's thrusting cock as Mara lowered her red-lipped mouth to his groin.

The Thai man continued to writhe in the throes of orgasm. There was not a sound from the 20 or so men in the smoke-filled room. The man's groans were the only noise. His orgasm went on and on, far beyond the time it takes for any male to ejaculate. Mara's distended face rose and fell, and each time it rose we could see the tongue wrapped tightly around the man's still-rigid member.

"Jesus Christ," I whispered.

I know now that resolution-phase penile detumescence is rapid and involuntary. Within seconds of expelling seminal fluid, the penis begins a two-stage involution that begins with loss of about 50 percent of the erection in the first 30 seconds. Even when some vasocongestion remains—"keeping a hard-on," I would have called it in my Nam days—it is not, cannot be, a full pre-ejaculatory erection.

This Thai still had a full hard-on. We could see it every time Mara's mouth lifted above her coiled tongue. The Thai seemed to have succumbed to an epileptic fit: His legs and arms thrashed wildly, his eyes had rolled back in his head, his mouth was open and drool ran down his chin and jowls. He kept coming and coming. Minutes passed—five, ten. I rubbed a hand across my face and my palm came away greasy with sweat. Tres was breathing through his mouth and staring with an expression suggesting horror.

Finally, Mara pulled her mouth away. Her tongue unwrapped itself from the Thai's cock and slid back between her lips as if it were on a tension reel. The Thai let out a final groan and slid out of the chair; his erect penis was still thrusting into empty air.

"Christ Almighty," I whispered to myself, relieved that it was over.

It was not over.

Mara's lips looked swollen, her cheeks as puffed out as they had been a second before. I had a momentary image of her mouth and cheeks filled with the huge, coiled tongue and I almost lost my lunch right there in the smoke-filled darkness.

Mara pulled her head back farther and I noticed that her rouged lips seemed to be growing redder, as if she had somehow managed to apply a thick layer of glossy lipstick while performing oral sex. Then her mouth opened a bit more and the red slid down off her lips, dribbled across her chin and spilled onto her gold silk blouse.

Blood. I realized that her cheeks and mouth were filled with blood; her obscene tongue was gorged with blood. She choked it back and something like a smile filled her sharp features.

I fought back the nausea, lowered my head and thought: *It's over now. It's over.*

It was not over.

The baby had been cradled in her left arm during the endless fellatio, hidden from sight by Mara's head and the fat man's thigh. But now the infant was visible as its small arms clawed at Mara's blood-spattered blouse. Even as the woman arched her head farther back, as if sloshing the blood around in her mouth like a fine wine, the baby began pulling itself up her chest with its tiny fists sunken in gold silk, its mewling mouth pursing and opening.

I looked at Tres, found myself unable to speak and looked back at the stage. The Thai boys had carried the still-unconscious fat man off the stage and only Mara and her infant remained in the lantern light. The baby continued climbing until its cheek touched its mother's. I thought of a film I had seen of a tiny kangaroo baby, half-formed and almost embryonic, pulling itself through its mother's fur in the live-or-die trek from the birth canal to the pouch.

The baby began licking its mother's cheek and mouth. I saw how long the baby's tongue was, how it slid like some pink worm across Mara's chin and lips, and I tried to close my eyes or look away. I could not.

Mara seemed to come out of her trance, lifted the baby closer to her face and lowered her mouth to the infant's. I could see the baby girl open her mouth wide, then wider, and I thought of baby birds demanding to be fed.

Mara vomited blood into the baby's open mouth. I could see the infant's cheeks fill and its throat work as it tried to swallow the sudden onslaught of thick liquid. The process was amazingly neat; very little of the heavy blood spilled onto the baby's gold robes or Mara's silk.

Spots danced in my vision and I lowered my head to my hands. The room was suddenly very hot and my vision tunneled to a narrow range. The skin of my forehead felt clammy. Next to me, Tres made a noise but did not look away from the stage.

When I looked up, the baby was almost finished feeding. I could see its long tongue licking at Mara's lips and cheeks for any residue of the regurgitated meal.

Years later I stumbled across a *Scientific American* article titled "Food Sharing in Vampire Bats" dealing with reciprocal altruism in donor bats' regurgitation of blood for roostmates. Vampire bats, it seems, starve to death if they do not get a meal consisting of 20 to 30 milliliters of blood every 60 hours. It turns out that after the proper stimulus—the roostmates' licking under the donor bat's wings and on its lips—the donor regurgitates blood only for those roostmates who would die within 24 hours without a blood meal. This reciprocal-exchange system is survival beneficent, said the article's author, because it allows the recipient bat another night to search for blood, while drawing only 12 hours' worth of blood from the donor bat's reservoir.

But it was that *Scientific American* drawing of the smaller bat's licking its donor's lips, leathery wings entwined, slashlipped mouths moving toward each other in the blood-vomit kiss, that made me vomit into my office wastebasket 20 years after that night in Bangkok.

I remember dragging Tres from that place and have vague memories of pressing a roll of baht into the hands of the driver of a long-tailed taxi on the pier outside. I remember going alone to my room and locking the door. Tang, my *mia chao*, had disappeared, and for that I was grateful. I remember staring at the slowly turning fan in the hour before sunrise and giggling as I worked out a simple translation. Unlike Tres, I had never been good at languages, but this translation was suddenly obvious. *Phanyaa mahn naga kio.* If *phanyaa mahn* was Mara, the prince of demons, and if naga was the serpent-demon, then *kio* could mean only one thing: vampire.

I giggled and waited for the sun to rise so I could sleep.

The city is still burning, and I can hear isolated automatic-weapons fire from the government troops killing students as the four men take me to Mara. The limousine crosses the river, moves south along the bank opposite the Oriental Hotel and stops at an unfinished high rise near a highway bridge. The pockmarked man leads us to an outside construction elevator, throws a switch and we rumble up into the night air. The elevator has no sides, and I see the river and the city across the river with dream-like clarity as we rise 30 stories and more into the thick night air. The river is as empty of traffic as I have ever seen it; only a few ferries fight the dark current downriver. Upriver, toward the Grand Palace and the university, flames light up the night.

We reach one of the top levels and the crude elevator squeals to a stop. A gate slides up and the pockmarked man beckons me out. Somewhere above us a welding torch flashes, strobes and drips sparks. Construction does not stop for sleep in modern Bangkok. The building has no sides, only clear plastic draped from open beams to separate sections of the cement expanse from one another. A hot wind rustles the plastic with a sound not unlike the stirring of leathery wings.

Trouble lights hang from girders and more lights are visible through walls of plastic to our left. The five of us walk toward the light and sound. At the entrance— a sort of tunnel made from rustling plastic sheets—the three bodyguards stay behind while the pockmarked man lifts the plastic, beckons me forward and follows me in.

A dozen or so folding chairs are set up around an open area where an expensive Persian rug has been laid on the dusty cement floor. The lamp overhead is shielded so that the space is more in shadow than direct light. Six men, all Thai and all in sleek tuxedos, sit on the folding chairs, but I have eyes only for the two women sitting across the open space in heavy rattan chairs. The older woman might be my age or a little older; she has aged well. Her hair is still black, but now swept up in a fashionable arc. Her Asian features are unlined, her cheeks and chin still strong, and only a certain corded look in her neck and hands suggests that she is in her 40s. She wears an obviously expensive gown of black and red silk; a gold-and-diamond pendant hangs across her red vest and stands out against the black silk blouse.

The younger woman next to her is infinitely more beautiful. Olive-skinned, dark-eyed, with lustrous hair that has been cut short in the newest Western style, gifted with a long neck and hands that exude grace even in repose, this young woman is beautiful in a way that no actress or model could ever achieve. It is obvious that she is simultaneously aware of and oblivious to her own beauty.

I know that I am looking at Mara and her daughter, Tanha.

The pockmarked man steps closer to them, goes to his knees in the way that the Thai do to show deference to royalty, performs an elaborate *wai* and then offers Mara my roll of 20 bonds without lifting his bowed head. She speaks softly and he answers respectfully.

Mara sets the money aside and looks at me. Her eyes catch the yellow gleam of the shielded lamp above.

The pockmarked man looks up, nods me forward and reaches to pull me to my knees. I genuflect of my own accord before he can grasp my sleeve. I lower my head and keep my eyes on Mara's slippered feet.

In elegant Thai, she says, "You know what you are asking for?"

"Yes," I answer in Thai. My voice is firm.

Mara purses her lips. "If you know about me," she says very softly, "then you must know that I no longer perform this . . . service."

"Yes," I say, head bowed in deference.

She waits in a silence that I realize is a command to speak. "The Reverend Tanha," I say at last.

"Raise your head," Mara says to me. To her daughter she murmurs that I have *jai ron*—the hot heart.

"*Jai bau dee*," says Tanha with a soft smile, suggesting that the *farang*'s mind is not good.

"It would cost three hundred thousand to know my daughter," says Mara. There is no hint of negotiation in her voice; the price is final.

I nod respectfully, reach into the hidden pocket at the back of my vest and remove $100,000 in cash and bearer's bonds.

One of the bodyguards takes the money and Mara nods slightly. "When do you wish this to happen?" she says in liquid tones. Her eyes show neither boredom nor interest.

"Now," I say. "Tonight."

The older woman looks at her daughter. Tanha's nod is almost imperceptible, but there is something in those lustrous brown eyes: hunger, perhaps.

The six men in tuxedos lean forward with bright eyes.

Tres and I met for breakfast in a cheap place near the river the next morning. Our tones were low, embarrassed, almost like when someone from the platoon got blown away and no one wanted to say his name for a while unless it was in the form of a joke. We didn't joke about this.

"Did you see that guy's cock . . . after?" Tres whispered. "It had these . . . lesions. Like marks I saw once when I was a lifeguard on the Cape and this guy swam into a jellyfish."

I sipped cold coffee and concentrated on not shuddering.

Tres took off his glasses and rubbed his eyes. It looked like he hadn't slept, either. "Johnny, you wanted to be a medic. How much blood does the human body have in it?"

"I dunno," I said.

He set his wire-rimmed glasses back in place. "I think it's about five or six liters," he said, "depending upon someone's size."

I nodded, not able to picture a liter. Years later when they began selling soft drinks in liter bottles, I always imagined five or six of them filled with blood equaling what we carry around in our veins every day.

"Imagine an orgasm where you're ejaculating blood," whispered Tres.

I closed my eyes.

Tres touched my wrist. "No, think about it, Johnny. That guy was still alive when they took him out. These guys wouldn't pay big bucks for it if they knew it'd kill them."

Wouldn't they? I thought. It was the first time that I realized that someone might fuck even if it meant certain death. In a way, that revelation in 1970 prepared me for life in the Nineties.

"How much blood could someone lose and still stay alive without a transfusion?" whispered Tres. I knew from his tone that he wasn't expecting an answer from me, just thinking aloud the way he always did when we were planning an ambush site.

I did not know the answer then, but I've had the opportunity to learn it many times since, especially during my residency as an ER intern. A wounded person can lose about a liter of blood volume and recover to make it up themselves. With more than about a sixth of blood volume gone, so is the victim. With transfusions, someone can lose up to 40 percent of his blood volume and hope to recover.

I didn't know any of this then, and I wasn't curious. I was busy trying to imagine ejaculating blood in an orgasm that went on for minutes rather than seconds. This time I did shudder.

Tres waved the waiter over and paid the check. "I've got to get going. I need to get a cab over to Western Union."

"Why?" I said. I was so sleepy that the hot, thick air seemed to slur my words.

"I'm getting some money wired from the States," said Tres.

I sat straight up, no longer sleepy. "Why?"

Tres took off his glasses again to polish them. His pale eyes looked myopic and lost. "I'm going back tonight, Johnny. I don't expect you to come along, but I'm going back."

The women have finished undressing me and the creature named Tanha has come closer to caress me when suddenly everything stops. Mara has given a signal.

"We have forgotten something," Mara says. It is the first time she has spoken English. She makes a graceful but ironic gesture. "The times now demand extra caution. I am sorry we did not ask for it earlier." She glances at her daughter and I can see the mocking half-smile on both of their faces. "I am afraid that we must wait until tomorrow night so that the proper testing can be done," sighs Mara, switching back to Thai. I can tell that the two have played this scene many times before. I can only guess that the real reason is to inflame desire through delay, thus driving up the price.

I also smile. "For the health identity card?" I say. "For one of the clinics to certify that I am free of HIV?"

Tanha is sitting gracefully on the Persian rug near me. Now she shifts in my direction, smiles mockingly and makes a small moue. "It is regrettable," she says, her voice as delicate as a crystal wind chime, "but necessary in these terrible times."

I nod. I have seen the statistics. The AIDS epidemic started late in Thailand, but in 1997—less than five years from now—150,000 Thai will have died from the disease. Three years later, in the year 2000, 5 million out of the 56 million Thai will be carrying the disease and at least a million will be dead. After that, the logarithmic progression is relentless. Thailand—with its lethal combination of ubiquitous prostitutes, promiscuous sexual partners and resistance to condoms—will rival Uganda as a retroviral killing ground.

"You'll send me to one of the local clinics that do a thousand slapdash HIV tests a week," I say calmly, as if I am used to sitting naked between two beautiful, fully dressed women and an audience of strangers in tuxedos.

Mara opens her slender fingers so that the long red nails catch the light. "There are few alternatives," she whispers.

"Perhaps I can provide one," I say and reach for my vest where it has been folded carefully atop my other clothes. I pull out three documents and hand them to Tanha. The girl frowns prettily at them and gives them to her mother. My guess is that the younger woman cannot read English, perhaps not even Thai.

Mara does look over the documents. They are certificates from two major Los Angeles hospitals and a university medical clinic attesting to the fact that my blood has been repeatedly tested and found free of HIV contamination. Each document is signed by several physicians and carries the seal of the institution. The papers on which they are typed are thick, creamy and expensive. Each document is dated within the past week.

Mara looks at me with narrowed eyes. Her smile shows her small, sharp teeth and only the faintest hint of tongue. "How do we know these are valid?"

I shrug. "I am a doctor. I wish to live. It would be easier to bribe a Thai clinician for a health identity card if I wished to deceive. I have no reason to deceive."

Mara glances back at the papers, smiles and hands them to me. "I will think about this," she says.

I lean forward in my chair. "I am also at risk," I say.

Mara arches an elegant eyebrow. "Oh, how can this be?"

"Gingival blood," I say in English. "Bleeding gums. Any open sore in her mouth."

Mara reacts with a small, mocking smile, as if I have made a tiny joke. Tanha turns her exquisite face toward her mother. "What did he say?" she demands in Thai. "This *farang* makes no sense."

Mara ignores her. "You have nothing to worry about," she says to me. She nods to her daughter.

Tanha begins caressing me again.

It was against regulations to take a weapon with us on R&R, but there were no metal detectors in those days, no airport security to speak of. Quite a few of us took knives or handguns with us when we traveled out of country. I'd brought a long-barreled .38 that I had won in a poker game from a black kid named Newport Johnson three days before he stepped on a Bouncing Betty. When Tres left that second night, I got the .38 out of the bottom of my duffel, checked to make sure it was loaded and sat in my locked room wearing nothing but fatigue pants, drinking scotch and listening to the street noises, watching the slow turning of the fan blades above my head.

Tres returned about four A.M. I listened through the wall to his banging and crashing around in his bathroom for a few minutes and then I went back to my bed and closed my eyes. Perhaps now I could sleep. His scream brought me up and out of bed, the .38 in my hand. I tore down the hall in bare feet, banged once on his door, pushed it open and stepped into the room.

Only the bathroom light was on and it cast a thin strip of fluorescent light across the bare floor and tousled bed. There was blood on the floor and a trail of torn linen that was also soaked in blood. It looked as if Tres had tried to tear up sheets to make bandages. I took a step toward the bathroom, heard a moan on the darkness of the bed and swiveled, still holding the .38 at my side.

"Johnny?" His voice was dry, cracked and listless. I stepped closer and turned on a small lamp near his bed.

Tres was naked except for his undershirt. He was sprawled on a blood-soaked mattress, surrounded by blood-soaked strips of dirty linen. His pants lay on the floor nearby. They were black with dried blood. Tres's hands were covering his crotch. His fingernails were rimmed with blood.

"Johnny?" he whispered. "It won't stop."

There's a leech that breeds in the slow-moving waters of Vietnam which specializes in boring up the urethras of men wading in the water. Once firmly lodged in the penis, the leech begins feeding from the inside until it swells to half the size of a man's fist. We'd all heard about the goddamn thing. We all thought about it every time we waded a stream or rice paddy, which was about a dozen times a day.

Tres's cock looked like the leech had been at it. No, it was worse. Besides being swollen and raw-looking, his penis had a series of small lesions spiraling around it as if someone had taken a sewing machine with a large needle and stitched a row of stigmata down his privates. The lesions were bleeding freely.

"I can't get it to stop," whispered Tres. His face was pale and clammy with sweat. I'd seen this look on the faces of wounded guys just before they floated away on the tide of shock.

"Come on," I said, getting an arm around him, "we're going to a hospital."

Tres pulled away and fell back on the pillows. "No, no, no. Just get the bleeding to stop." He pulled something from under a pillow and I realized that he was holding the black-bladed KA-bar knife he used on night patrols. I lifted my .38 and for a second there was silence broken only by the rustle of the fan blades.

Finally, I giggled. This was nuts. Here we were hundreds of miles from Vietnam and the war, me with my sidearm and Tres with his commando knife, ready to do each other in. This was fucking nuts.

I put down the pistol. "I brought some first-aid shit," I said. "I'll get it."

Tres was sitting up now with the bloodied sheet over him. I handed him the bandages and wiped the sweat off his face. "I wonder why it won't stop bleeding," he said.

I shook my head. I didn't know then. I know now.

Vampire bats and some leeches exude the same anticoagulant: hirudin. The bats secrete it in their saliva; the leeches manufacture it in their guts and smear it on the surface of the wound. It keeps the wound from closing and keeps the blood flowing freely as long as the bloodsucker wants to feed. Vampire bats will "nurse" from the neck of a horse or cow for hours, often returning with other bats to continue the meal.

Tres went to sleep after a while and I sat in the sprung chair near the window, watching the door and holding the .38 in my lap. I had thoughts of forcing Maladung to take me to Mara again, and then shooting him and the woman. *And the baby*, I mentally added.

I fell asleep mulling options. When I awoke the room was dark. The fan was still turning in its desultory fashion but the sounds outside the window had shifted to their nighttime volume. The bedsheets were soaked with fresh blood, there was blood on the floor, the bathroom was littered with bloody towels, but Tres was gone.

I ran into the hallway and pounded down the steps to the lobby before realizing what a sight I must be: wild-eyed, barefoot and bare-chested, my rumpled fatigue pants smeared with blood, the long-barreled .38 in my hand. The Thai whores and their pimps in the lobby barely looked my way.

I almost caught up to Tres. I saw him on the same dock we'd departed from two nights earlier. The shadowy figure with him had to be Maladung. They had just stepped down into the long-tailed taxi as I ran onto the dock. The boat pulled away with a roar.

Tres saw me. He stood up and almost pitched out of the accelerating boat. He raised his arm in my direction, fingers splayed, as if reaching for me across 50 feet of open water. I heard him shout at the driver "*Yout! Phuen young mai ma! Yout!*"—which I did not understand then but now translate as "Stop! My friend hasn't come yet! Stop!"

I saw Maladung pull him back into the boat. I held the useless pistol as the taxi bounced across the river, disappeared behind a barge going upriver and then reappeared only as a distant lantern before disappearing down a *klong* on the opposite side of the Chao Phraya.

I knew that I would never see Tres alive again.

Mara lowers her gaze as Tanha brings her mouth to my groin. There is no caress of tongue. Not yet. The younger woman uses her mouth to bring me to full erection.

As much as men talk and write about the joys of oral sex, there is always a slight ambiguity in the male response to the act of fellatio. For some, a mouth is too non-gender-specific to allow the subconscious to relax and enjoy the act. For others, it is the uncontrolled intensity of sensation that causes a flutter of alarm amid the cascade of pleasure. For many, it is just the unbidden thought of sharp teeth. Luckily, the male organ is as simple a stimulus-response mechanism as nature allows. Tanha's mouth is soft and well-educated; my excitement follows its inevitable arc of engorgement.

I close my eyes and try not to think about not thinking about the men in tuxedos behind me. Someone has dimmed the overhead light so that only the flash of sparks dribbling from the welder two floors above lights the scene and the interior of my eyelids with magnesium strobes. Mara whispers something and I feel sudden cold as Tanha's warm mouth pulls away. The shock of cooler air is on me for only a second before a different moisture returns.

I open my eyes just enough to see Tanha's tongue sliding from her mouth, curling around me. The flash from the welding sparks makes the mottled flesh of her tongue look more purple than pink. I catch a glimpse of pulsating slits amid the coated texture there, like tiny feeding orifices. I shut off my thoughts before the grasping mouth-guts of leeches and lampreys come to mind. For years I have trained myself to be equal to this moment.

The sensation is more like a small electric shock than the sting of a jellyfish. I gasp and open my eyes. Tanha is watching me through the curtain of her lashes. The shock comes again, riding down the exquisite penile nerve system straight to the base of my spine and then to the pleasure center of my brain. I close my eyes again and groan. My scrotum contracts with pleasure. The spiral of gentle shocks soars through my body and returns to my penis like a gently moving hand gloved in velvet. My hips begin to move without volition.

My heart is pounding so wildly that the pressure from it seems to replace sound as the only noise in the universe. My skull echoes to the rhythm of my own pulse. The separate, tiny shocks along my groin have grown together to form a perfect spiral of pleasurable sensation. It is as if I am fucking the sun. Even as my hips begin to thrust in earnest and my hands grope for Tanha's head to move that warmth closer, a distant part of my mind observes the classic symptoms of the onset of orgasm and wonders about the rate of tachycardia, myotonia and hyperventilation.

A second later any remaining clinical awareness is washed away in a new and stronger surge of pure pleasure. Tanha's tongue is contracting, tugging from the base of my scrotum to the glans of my penis, tightening as it contracts and relaxes, contracts and relaxes. The shocks have become a single closed circuit of nearly unbearable sensation.

I ejaculate almost without noticing it, so great is the pressure now. From beneath my fluttering eyelids I can see semen dropping like a band of white petals on the hair and shoulders of Tanha. Her tongue does not desist for an instant. Her eyes are as yellow as her mother's now. The orgasm passes without release from the building pressure. My heart strains to pump more blood into my distended organ.

Yes! I will it even as my head arches back, my neck strains and my face distorts. *Yes!* I choose the thing in which I now have no choice.

A second later I come. Blood ejaculates from the tip of my penis and bathes

Tanha's face and breasts. Greedily, she lowers her mouth again, unwilling to spill any of it. My hips pound as I continue to pulse. The moment goes on and on.

Mara leans closer.

It was the Thai police who came for me just after sunrise that next morning 22 years ago. I thought I would be arrested for wandering the hotel halls until the early hours, shouting at no one and brandishing a cocked .38. Instead of arresting me, they brought me to Tres.

The Bangkok morgue was small and insufficiently cooled. The smell reminded me of an orchard where too much fallen fruit had gone bad in the sun. There were no metal cabinets or sliding stretchers as in the American movies. Tres was on a steel slab just like the other corpses in the small room. They had not covered his face. He looked vulnerable without his glasses.

"He's so . . . white," I said to the only policeman who spoke English.

"He was found in the river," said the man in the white jacket and the Sam Browne belt.

"He didn't drown," I said. It was not a question.

The policeman shook his head. "Your friend lost much blood." He tugged his white glove higher, touched Tres's chin and swiveled the corpse's head so that I could see the knife wound that ran from under his left ear to his Adam's apple.

I let out a breath and steadied myself against the steel platform.

"The knife wound did not kill him," said the inspector, tugging off the sheet. Tres's sex organs had been crudely but completely removed. The effect was rather like a Ken doll that someone had spilled fingernail polish on.

The inspector came closer and seized my forearm, whether to steady me or to restrain me from running I do not know. "We think that is—how you say it—a queer thing. A fight between faggots. We have seen this type of injury before. Always it is a type of queer thing. Jealousy."

"A queer thing," I repeated.

The inspector released my arm. "We know that you were not there at the time he was murdered, Private Merrick. The boatmaster at Phulong dock saw you shouting at the boat that carried Corporal Tindale away. The manager at the hotel will testify that you returned only a few minutes later, became drunk and remained visible and audible throughout the night. You could not have been present when the corporal was murdered, but do you have any idea who did this? Your military will demand to know."

I lifted the sheet, draped it across Tres's corpse and then stepped away from the men. "No," I said. "I have no idea whatsoever."

Mara licks the lips of her daughter. Their arms are pulled in to their sides, their hands curled as if palsied. I imagine vampire bats hanging from the cold ceiling of a cave, wings tucked tight, only their lips and their tongues active and engaged.

Tanha arches her head and the heavy red liquid is propelled from her distended lips to the waiting cavity of her mother's mouth. I hear the lapping, gurgling sounds clearly. Tanha's tongue has not relinquished its grip, and I still spasm in her grasp. My heart is straining with the effort. My vision blackens and I can no longer see their feeding and sharing, only hear the thick liquid sounds of it.

My facial muscles are still locked in the myotonic spasm of an involuntary grimace. I would smile if I could.

I found Maladung in the autumn of 1975, not long after I graduated from medical school. The little pimp had retired rich and returned to his northern city of Chiang Mai. I paid off the Thai detective whom I'd hired with the first installment of my inheritance money and spent two days watching Maladung before picking him up. He was married and had two grown sons and a ten-year-old daughter.

He was walking to the small store he ran in the old section of town when I pulled up alongside him in a jeep, showed him the 9mm automatic and told him to get in. I took him into the countryside, to the small house I had rented. I promised him that he would live if he told me everything he knew.

I think he did tell me everything he knew. Mara and her girl child had dropped out of sight and were performing only for the very rich now. Tres had been killed as a simple precaution: He and I had been the first Americans allowed in Mara's presence, and they feared the consequences if word of the performance got back to the platoon. They had planned to murder me that night, but the two men sent to commit the act had seen me drunk and shouting in the upstairs hallway, noted the gun and decided otherwise. By the time others were sent, I had been shipped back to Saigon.

Maladung swore that he had not known about Tres's murder until after it was carried out. He swore it. Maladung had never dreamed that the *phanyaa mahn naga kio* had meant to harm the *farang* beyond the services rendered. I placed the Browning against his forehead and told him to tell me upon pain of death what usually happens to those who received Mara's services.

Maladung was shaking like an old man. "They die," he said in Thai and repeated in English. "First they lose their soul"—*khwan hai* was the phrase he used, "their butterfly spirit flies away"—"and then their *winjan*, life spirit, leaks out. They return and return until they die," he said, voice quavering. "But this they choose."

I lowered the gun and said, "I believe you, Maladung. You didn't know that they'd murder Tres." Then I quickly lifted the Browning and shot him twice in the head.

That same autumn I began the search for Mara.

I open my eyes and the men in tuxedos are gone, Tanha is sitting above me on the chair next to her mother and the two young women are finishing their chore of cleaning and dressing me. I can feel the bandages under the trousers. It feels as if I am wearing diapers. My groin is moist with blood, but I hardly notice the discomfort because of the lingering pulse of pleasure that fills me like the echo of beautiful music.

"Mr. Noi informs me that you said you have more money," Mara says softly.

I nod, too weak to speak. Any thought of attacking the woman is impossible to me now, even if I did not know that her men were waiting just beyond the windfluttered plastic. Mara and Tanha are sources of infinite pleasure. I could never think of hurting them now, of interrupting what is to transpire in the coming nights.

"The limousine will pick you up at midnight tomorrow at your hotel," says Mara. Her fingers move and the four men come in to remove me. I am mildly surprised to find that I cannot walk without assistance.

The streets are empty and tomb-silent. Even the shooting has ended. Orange flames still burn to the north. I close my eyes and savor the fading ecstasy as they drive me back to the Oriental.

I don't think that I knew in Vietnam that I was gay. I disguised the love I felt for Tres as other things: loyalty to a buddy, admiration, even the masculine love that grunts are supposed to feel for one another in combat. But it was love.

I never came out of the closet. Not publicly. While in medical school I learned how to troll the most discreet bars, meet the most discreet men and make the most discreet arrangements for temporary liaisons. Later, as my practice and public persona grew, I learned how to keep my prowlings restricted to rare nights in cities far away from my home in L.A. And I dated women. Those who wondered why I never married had only to look at my busy practice to see that I had no time for a domestic life.

And I continued to hunt Mara and Tanha. Twice a year I flew to Thailand, learning the language and the cities, and twice a year I was told by my paid operatives there that the women had disappeared. Only two years ago, in 1990, did they surface again, driven into accepting expensive performances as their need for money was renewed.

There was nothing I could do then. The more I learned of Mara and Tanha and their habits, the more I was certain I could never get close to them with a weapon. Then, only six months ago, certain results were returned and, after a few hours of almost hysterical anger, I saw that the means had been put into my hands.

I began to make my plans.

"Good morning, Dr. Merrick," says the young Thai valet in the lobby. He politely ignores my bloody collar and disheveled appearance.

I smile and wait for the elevator doors to close before grasping the brass rail and struggling to hold myself upright. I can feel the bandages leaking through my trousers. Only the long photographer's vest hides the blood there.

In my room I bathe, treat the lesions with a special salve I have brought, inject myself with a coagulant, bathe again and pull on fresh pajamas before crawling into bed. It will be light in a few minutes. In 14 hours, darkness will fall again and I will return to Mara and her daughter.

In Chiang Mai, where the whores are cheap and the young men celebrate entry into manhood by buying a fuck, 72 percent of the city's poorest prostitutes tested positive for HIV in 1989.

In the bars and sex clubs along Patpong, condoms are handed out free by a man in a red, blue and gold superhero suit. His name is Captain Condom and he is employed by the Population and Community Development Association. The PDA is the brainchild of Senator Mechai Viravaidaya, an economist and member of the WHO Global Commission on AIDS. Mechai has spent so much of his own time, energy and money promoting condom use that rubbers are called mechais by everyone in Bangkok. Almost no one uses them. The men refuse to and the women do not force the issue.

One out of every 50 people in Thailand makes his or her living selling sex.

I think that the computer projections for the year 2000 are wrong. I think that far more than 5 million Thai will be infected and many more than 1 million will have died. I think that the corpses will fill the *klongs* and lie along the gutters of the *sois*. I think that only the rich and the very, very careful will avoid this plague.

Mara and Tanha were, until recently, very rich. And they have been very careful. Only their need to be very rich again has led them to be careless.

My HIV-negative documents are, of course, falsified. It was not difficult. The lab reports are real; only the dates and name were changed prior to my photocopying them onto official stationery and adding the seals. I serve on the faculty of all three of the institutions whose seals and forms I borrowed.

In the six months since I tested HIV-positive, the plan grew from a scheme to an inevitability.

They are monsters, Mara and her child, but even monsters grow careless. Even monsters can be killed.

There is no fan on the ceiling of my expensive air-conditioned suite at the Oriental Hotel. As the first pale gleamings of the dawn creep across the teak-and-plaster ceiling of my room, I content myself with imagining a fan slowly turning and lull myself to sleep with the image.

I smile when I imagine the coming night's activity and the night that will follow this one. I can see the older woman licking the younger woman's lips, and then opening wide her maw for the cascade of blood. My blood. Death's blood.

Before dropping off to sleep, lulled by the medication I have taken and by the final turn of things, I remember the story Tres told me so many years ago about the temptation of the Buddha by Mara's three daughters: Aradi, discontent; Tanha, desire; and Raka, love. And I know now that in my life I have surrendered to all three of these all-too-human demons, but that the only one worthy of our surrender is Raka. Love.

Trying to sleep now, I summon the image that has sustained me through all these years and through these final months.

I imagine Tres removing his glasses and squinting at me, his face as vulnerable as a boy's, his cheek as soft as only a lover's cheek can be. And he says to me, "I'm going back, Johnny. I'm going back tonight."

And I take his hand in mine. And I say, with the absolute certainty of conviction, "I'm going, too."

Smiling now, having found the place I have sought so long to return to, I release myself to sleep and forgiveness.

PRISONERS OF THE ROYAL WEATHER

Bruce Boston

Bruce Boston's stories and poems have appeared widely in literary and science fiction publications, and have won numerous awards, including the Pushcart Prize for fiction and the Isaac Asimov Readers' Choice Award for poetry. He is the author of nine books of poetry, eight story collections, the fantasy novella *After Magic*, and the recent novel *Stained Glass Rain*.

The language in "Prisoners of the Royal Weather" is sensuous and pungent. Its sharp images communicate with a minimum of words the experience of living in an autocracy. It first appeared in *Weird Tales*.

—E.D.

The royal sun illuminates
the spires and cupolas
of our illustrious city.
It reflects brilliantly
from the whitewashed walls
and coruscates blindingly
on the king's gold armor,
yet never does it shine
upon beggars or thieves.

The royal wind perfumes
the night with the velvet
of cognac and frangipani.
It tousles the tawny locks
of sacrificial virgins
and dares to rumple
the king's jeweled mane,
yet never does it reek
with the stench of corpses.

The royal rain waters
our gardens and limns

the streets with crystal.
It mists like gossamer
in the palace grounds
and washes the stains
from the public square,
yet never does it fall
if the king is on parade.

The royal snow is pure
and refreshingly cool
as our lord staggers
with drunken eyes ablaze
from the smoky inferno
of some ornate dining hall.
It blankets the city
with sovereign silence,
yet never does it chill.

The royal clime envelops
and mandates all of our days.
And four times each year,
often more than that,
the king issues an edict
when the seasons change,
yet never does he forecast
the nature of his tempests
or whom such storms will claim.

THE SNOW QUEEN
Patricia A. McKillip

In the famous Hans Christian Andersen fairy tale, the Snow Queen freezes young Kay's heart and steals him away from his beloved Gerda to a palace of ice. McKillip's Neva is as cold and sharp as ice; she is the kind of Snow Queen any of us might encounter in daily life. This exquisite and sensual story comes from the adult fairy tale anthology *Snow White, Blood Red.*

McKillip hails from Oregon, and currently lives in the Catskill mountains of New York. She is the award-winning author of *The Riddlemaster of Hed, Fools Run, Moonflash, The Sorceress and the Cygnet,* and numerous other works for children and adults.

—T.W.

KAY

They stood together without touching, watching the snow fall. The sudden storm prolonging winter had surprised the city; little moved in the broad streets below them. Ancient filigreed lamps left from another century threw patterned wheels of light into the darkness, illumining the deep white silence crusting the world. Gerda, not hearing the silence, spoke.

"They look like white rose petals endlessly falling."

Kay said nothing. He glanced at his watch, then at the mirror across the room. The torchiéres gilded them: a lovely couple, the mirror said. In the gentle light Gerda's sunny hair looked like polished bronze; his own, shades paler, seemed almost white. Some trick of shadow flattened Gerda's face, erased its familiar hollows. Her petal-filled eyes were summer blue. His own face, with sharp bones at cheek and jaw, dark eyes beneath pale brows, looked, he thought, wild and austere: a monk's face, a wizard's face. He searched for some subtlety in Gerda's, but it would not yield to shadow. She wore a short black dress; on her it seemed incongruous, like black in a flower.

He commented finally, "Every time you speak, flowers fall from your mouth."

She looked at him, startled. Her face regained contours; they were graceful but uncomplex. She said, "What do you mean?" Was he complaining? Was he fanciful? She blinked, trying to see what he meant.

"You talk so much of flowers," he explained patiently. "Do you want a garden? Should we move to the country?"

"No," she said, horrified, then amended: "Only if—Do you want to? If we were in the country, there would be nothing to do but watch the snow fall. There would be no reason to wear this dress. Or these shoes. But do you want—"

"No," he said shortly. His eyes moved away from her; he jangled coins in his pocket. She folded her arms. The dress had short puffed sleeves, like a little girl's dress. Her arms looked chilled, but she made no move away from the cold, white scene beyond the glass. After a moment he mused, "There's a word I've been trying all day to think of. A word in a puzzle. Four letters, the clue is: the first word schoolboys conjugate."

"Schoolboys what?"

"Conjugate. Most likely Latin."

"I don't know any Latin," she said absently.

"I studied some . . . but I can't remember the first word I was taught. How could anyone remember?"

"Did you feed the angelfish?"

"This morning."

"They eat each other if they're not fed."

"Not angelfish."

"Fish do."

"Not all fish are cannibals."

"How do you know not angelfish in particular? We never let them go hungry; how do we really know?"

He glanced at her, surprised. Her hands tightened on her arms; she looked worried again. By fish? he wondered. Or was it a school of fish swimming through deep, busy waters? He touched her arm; it felt cold as marble. She smiled quickly; she loved being touched. The school of fish darted away; the deep waters were empty.

"What word," he wondered, "would you learn first in a language? What word would people need first? Or have needed, in the beginning of the world? Fire, maybe. Food, most likely. Or the name of a weapon?"

"Love," she said, gazing at the snow, and he shook his head impatiently.

"No, no—cold is more imperative than love; hunger overwhelms it. If I were naked in the snow down there, cold would override everything; my first thought would be to warm myself before I died. Even if I saw you walking naked toward me, life would take precedence over love."

"Then cold," she said. Her profile was like marble, flawless, unblinking. "Four letters, the first word in the world."

He wanted suddenly to feel her smooth marble cheek under his lips, kiss it into life. He said instead, "I can't remember the Latin word for cold." She looked at him, smiling again, as if she had felt his impulse in the air between them. His thoughts veered off-balance, tugged toward her fine, flushed skin and delicate bones, something nameless, blind and hungry in him reaching toward another nameless thing. She said,

"There's the cab."

It was a horse-drawn sleigh; the snow was too deep for ordinary means. Had she been smiling, he wondered, because she had seen the cab? He kissed her anyway, lightly on the cheek, before she turned to get her coat, thinking how long he had known her and how little he knew her and how little he knew of how much or little there was in her to know.

GERDA

They arrived at Selene's party fashionably late. She had a vast flat with an old-fashioned ballroom. Half the city was crushed into it, despite the snow. Prisms office dazzled in the chandeliers; not even the hundred candles in them could melt their glittering, frozen jewels. On long tables, swans carved of ice held hothouse berries, caviar, sherbet between their wings. A business acquaintance attached himself to Kay; Gerda, drifting toward champagne, was found by Selene.

"Gerda!" She kissed air enthusiastically around Gerda's face. "How are you, angel? Such a dress. So innocent. How do you get away with it?"

"With what?"

"And such a sense of humor. Have you met Maurice? Gerda, Maurice Crow."

"Call me Bob," said Maurice Crow to Gerda, as Selene flung her fruity voice into the throng and hurried after it.

"Why?"

Maurice Crow chuckled. "Good question." He had a kindly smile, Gerda thought; it gentled his thin, aging, beaky face. "If you were named Maurice, wouldn't you rather be called Bob?"

"I don't think so," Gerda said doubtfully. "I think I would rather be called my name."

"That's because you're beautiful. A beautiful woman makes any name beautiful."

"I don't like my name. It sounds like something to hold stockings up with. Or a five-letter word from a Biblical phrase." She glanced around the room for Kay. He stood in a ring of brightly dressed women; he had just made them laugh. She sighed without realizing it. "And I'm not really beautiful. This is just a disguise."

Maurice Crow peered at her more closely out of his black, shiny eyes. He offered her his arm; after a moment she figured out what to do with it. "You need a glass of champagne." He patted her hand gently. "Come with me."

"You see, I hate parties."

"Ah."

"And Kay loves them."

"And you," he said, threading a sure path among satin and silk and clouds of tulle, "love Kay."

"I have always loved Kay."

"And now you feel he might stop loving you? So you come here to please him."

"How quickly you understand things. But I'm not sure if he is pleased that I came. We used to know each other so well. Now I feel stupid around him, and slow, and plain, even when he tells me I'm not. It used to be different between us."

"When?"

She shrugged. "Before. Before the city began taking little pieces of him away from me. He used to bring me wildflowers he had picked in the park. Now he gives me blood-red roses once a year. Some days his eyes never see me, not even in bed. I see contracts in his eyes, and the names of restaurants, expensive shoes, train schedules. A train schedule is more interesting to him than I am."

"To become interesting, you must be interested."

"In Kay? Or in trains?"

"If," he said, "you can no longer tell the difference, perhaps it is Kay who has grown uninteresting."

"Oh, no," she said quickly. "Never to me." She had flushed. With the quick, warm color in her face and the light spilling from the icy prisms onto her hair, into her eyes, she caused Maurice Crow to hold her glass too long under the champagne fountain. "He is beautiful and brilliant, and we have loved each other since we were children. But it seems that, having grown up, we no longer recognize one another." She took the overflowing glass from Maurice Crow's hand and drained it. Liquid from the dripping glass fell beneath her chaste neckline, rolled down her breast like icy tears. "We are both in disguise."

THE SNOW QUEEN

Neva entered late. She wore white satin that clung to her body like white clings to the calla lily. White peacock feathers sparkling with faux diamonds trailed down her long ivory hair. Her eyes were black as the night sky between the winter constellations. They swept the room, picked out a face here: Gerda's—How sweet, Neva thought, to have kept that expression, like one's first kiss treasured in tissue paper—and there: Kay's. Her eyes were wide, very still. The young man with her said something witty. She did not hear. He tried again, his eyes growing anxious. She watched Kay tell another story; the women around him—doves, warblers, a couple of trumpeting swans—laughed again. He laughed with them, reluctant but irresistibly amused by himself. He lifted champagne to his lips; light leaped from the cut crystal. His pale hair shone like the silk of Neva's dress; his lips were shaped cleanly as the swan's wing. She waited, perfectly still. Lowering his glass, the amused smile tugging again at his lips, he saw her standing in the archway across the room.

To his eye she was alone; the importunate young lapdog beside her did not exist. So his look told her, as she drew at it with the immense and immeasurable pull of a wayward planet wandering too close to someone's cold, bright, inconstant moon. The instant he would have moved, she did, crossing the room to join him before his brilliant, fluttering circle could scatter. Like him, she preferred an audience. She waited in her outer orbit, composed, mysterious, while he told another story. This one had a woman in it—Gerda—and something about angels or fish.

"And then," he said, "we had an argument about the first word in the world."

"Coffee," guessed one woman, and he smiled appreciatively.

"No," suggested another.

"It was for a crossword puzzle. The first word you learn to conjugate in Latin."

"But we always speak French in bed," a woman murmured. "My husband and I."

Kay's eyes slid to Neva. Her expression remained changeless; she offered no word. He said lightly, "No, no, *ma chére*, one conjugates a verb; one has conjugal relations with one's spouse. Or not, as the case may be."

"Do people still?" someone wondered. "How boring."

"To conjugate," Neva said suddenly in her dark, languid voice, "means to inflect a verb in an orderly fashion through all its tenses. As in: *amo, amas, amat.* I love, you love—"

"But that's it!" Kay cried. "The answer to the puzzle. How could I have forgotten?"

"Love?" someone said perplexedly. Neva touched her brow delicately.

"I cannot," she said, "remember the Latin word for dance."

"You do it so well," Kay said a moment later, as they glided onto the floor. So polished it was that the flames from the chandeliers seemed frozen underfoot, as if they danced on stars. "And no one studies Latin anymore."

"I never tire of learning," Neva said. Her gloved hand lay lightly on his shoulder, close to his neck. Even in winter his skin looked warm, burnished by tropical skies, endless sun. She wanted to cover that warmth with her body, draw it into her own white-marble skin. Her eyes flicked constantly around the room over his shoulder, studying women's faces. "Who is Gerda?" she asked, then knew her: the tall, beautiful childlike woman who watched Kay with a hopeless, forlorn expression, as if she had already lost him.

"She is my wife," Kay said, with a studied balance of lightness and indifference in his voice. Neva lifted her hand off his shoulder, settled it again closer to his skin.

"Ah."

"We have known each other all our lives."

"She loves you still."

"How do you know?" he said, surprised. She guided him into a half-turn, so that for a moment he faced his abandon Gerda, with her sad eyes and downturned mouth, standing in her naive black dress, her champagne tilted and nearly spilling, with only a cadaverous, beaky man trying to get her attention. Neva turned him again; he looked at her, blinking, as if he had been lightly, unexpectedly struck. She shifted her hand, crooked her fingers around his bare neck.

"She is very beautiful."

"Yes."

"It is her air of childlike innocence that is so appealing."

"And so exasperating," he exclaimed suddenly, as if, like the Apostle, he had been illumined by lightning and stunned with truth.

"Innocence can be," Neva said.

"Gerda knows so little of life. We have lived for years in this city and still she seems so helpless. Scattered. She doesn't know what she wants from life; she wouldn't know how to take it if she did."

"Some women never learn."

"You have. You are so elegant, so sophisticated. So sure." He paused; she saw the word trembling on his lips. She held his gaze, pulled him deeper, deeper into her winter darkness. "But," he breathed, "you must have men telling you this all the time."

"Only if I want them to. And there are not many I choose to listen to."

"You are so beautiful," he said wildly, as if the word had been tormented out of him.

She smiled, slid her other hand up his arm to link her fingers behind his neck. She whispered, "And so are you."

THE THIEF

Briony watched Gerda walk blindly through the falling snow. It caught on her lashes, melted in the hot, wet tears on her cheeks. Her long coat swung carelessly open to the bitter cold, revealing pearls, gold, a hidden pocket in the lining in which Briony envisioned cash, cards, earrings taken off and forgotten. She gave little thought to Gerda's tears: some party, some man, it was a familiar tale.

She shadowed Gerda, walking silently on the fresh-crushed snow of her foot-prints, which was futile, she realized, since they were nothing more than a wedge of toe and a rapier stab of stiletto heel. Still, in her tumultuous state of mind, the woman probably would not have noticed a traveling circus behind her.

She slid, shadow-like, to Gerda's side.

"Spare change?"

Gerda glanced at her; her eyes flooded again; she shook her head helplessly. "I have nothing."

Briony's knife snicked open, flashing silver in a rectangle of window light. "You have a triple strand of pearls, a sapphire dinner ring, a gold wedding ring, a pair of earrings either diamond or cubic zirconium, on, I would guess, fourteen karat posts."

"I never got my ears pierced," Gerda said wearily. Briony missed a step, caught up with her.

"Everyone has pierced ears!"

"Diamond, and twenty-two karat gold." She pulled at them, and at her rings. "They were all gifts from Kay. You might as well have them. Take my coat, too." She shrugged it off, let it fall. "That was also a gift." She tugged the pearls at her throat; they scattered like luminous, tiny moons around her in the snow. "Oh, sorry."

"What are you doing?" Briony breathed. The woman, wearing nothing more than a short and rather silly dress, turned to the icy darkness beyond the window-light. She had actually taken a step into it when Briony caught her arm. She was cold as an iron statue in winter. "Stop!" Briony hauled her coat out of the snow. "Put this back on. You'll freeze!"

"I don't care. Why should you?"

"Nobody is worth freezing for."

"Kay is."

"Is he?" She flung the coat over Gerda's shoulders, pulled it closed. "God, woman, what Neanderthal age are you from?"

"I love him."

"So?"

"He doesn't love me."

"So?"

"If he doesn't love me, I don't want to live."

Briony stared at her, speechless, having learned from various friends *in extremis* that there was no arguing with such crazed and muddled thinking. Look, she might have said, whirling the woman around to shock her. See that snowdrift beside the wall? Earlier tonight that was an old woman who could have used your coat. Or: Men have notoriously bad taste, why should you let one decide whether you live or die? Piss on him and go find someone else. Or: Love is an obsolete emotion, ranking in usefulness somewhere between earwigs and toe mold.

She lied instead. She said, "I felt like that once."

She caught a flicker of life in the still, remote eyes. "Did you? Did you want to die?"

"Why don't we go for hot chocolate and I'll tell you about it?"

They sat at the counter of an all-night diner, sipping hot chocolate liberally laced with brandy from Briony's flask. Briony had short, dark, curly hair and sparkling sapphire eyes. She wore lace stockings under several skirts, an antique vest of peacock feathers over a shirt of simulated snakeskin, thigh-high boots, and a dark, hooded cape with many hidden pockets. The waitress behind the counter watched her with a sardonic eye and snapped her gum as she poured Briony's chocolate. Drawn to Gerda's beauty and tragic pallor, she kept refilling Gerda's cup. So did Briony. Briony, improvising wildly, invented a rich, beautiful, upper-class young man whose rejection of her plunged her into despair.

"He loved me," she said, "for the longest night the world has ever known. Then he dumped me like soggy cereal. I was just another pretty face and recycled bod to him. Three days after he offered me marriage, children, cars as big as luxury liners, trips to the family graveyard in Europe, he couldn't even remember my name. Susie, he called me. Hello, Susie, how are you, what can I do for you? I was so miserable I wanted to eat mothballs. I wanted to lie on the sidewalk and sunburn myself to death. The worms wouldn't have touched me, I thought. Not even they could be interested."

"What did you do?" Gerda asked. Briony, reveling in despair, lost her thread of invention. The waitress refilled Gerda's cup.

"I knew a guy like that," the waitress said. "I danced on his car in spiked heels. Then I slashed his tires. Then I found out it wasn't his car."

"What did I do?" Briony said. "What did I do?" She paused dramatically. The waitress had stopped chewing her gum, waiting for an answer. "Well—I mean, of course I did what I had to. What else could I do, but what women like me do when men drop-kick their hearts out of the field. Women like me. Of course women like you are different."

"What did you do?" Gerda asked again. Her eyes were wide and very dark; the brandy had flushed her cheeks. Drops of melted snow glittered like jewels in her disheveled hair. Briony gazed at her, musing.

"With money, you'd think you'd have more choices, wouldn't you? But money or love never taught you how to live. You don't know how to care of yourself. So if Kay doesn't love you, you have to wander into the snow and freeze. But women like me, and Brenda here—"

"Jennifer," the waitress muttered.

"Jennifer, here, we're so used to fending for ourselves every day that it gets to be a habit. You're not so used to fending, so you don't have the habit. So what you have to do is start pretending you have something to live for."

Gerda's eyes filled; a tear dropped into her chocolate. "I haven't."

"Of course you haven't, that's what I've been saying. That's why you have to pretend—"

"Why? It's easier just to walk back out into the snow."

"But if you keep pretending and pretending, one day you'll stumble onto something you care enough to live for, and if you turn yourself into an icicle now because of Kay, you won't be able to change your mind later. The only thing you're seeing in the entire world is Kay. Kay is in both your eyes, Kay is your mind. Which means you're only really seeing one tiny flyspeck of the world, one little puzzle piece. You have to learn to see around Kay. It's like staring at one star all the time and never seeing the moon or planets or constellations—"

"I don't know how to pretend," Gerda said softly. "Kay has always been the sky."

Jennifer swiped her cloth at a crumb, looking thoughtful. "What she says," she pointed out, tossing her head at Briony, "you only have to do it one day at a time. Always just today. That's all any of us do."

Gerda took a swallow of chocolate. Jennifer poured her more; Briony added brandy.

"After all," Briony said, "you could have told me to piss off and mind my own business. But you didn't. You put your coat back on and followed me here. So there must have been something—your next breath, a star you glimpsed—you care enough about."

"That's true," Gerda said, surprised. "But I don't remember what."

"Just keep pretending you remember."

KAY

Kay sat at breakfast with Neva, eating clouds and sunlight. Actually, it was hot biscuits and honey that dripped down his hand. Neva, discoursing on the likelihood of life on other planets, leaned across the table now and then, and slipped her tongue between his fingers to catch the honey. Her face and her white negligee, a lacy tumble of roses, would slide like light past his groping fingers; she would be back in her chair, talking, before he could put his biscuit down.

"The likelihood of life on other planets is very, very great," she said. She had a crumb of Kay's breakfast on her cheek. He reached across the table to brush it away; she caught his forefinger in her mouth and sucked at it until he started to melt off the chair onto his knees. She loosed his finger then and asked, "Have you read Piquelle on the subject?"

"What?"

"Piquelle," she said patiently, "on the subject of life on other planets."

He swallowed. "No."

"Have another biscuit, darling. No, don't move, I'll get it."

"It's no—"

"No, I insist you stay where you are. Don't move." She took his plate and stood up. He could see the outline of her pale, slender body under the lace. "Did you say something, Kay?"

"I groaned."

"There are billions of galaxies. And in each galaxy, billions of stars, each of which might well have its courtiers orbiting it." She reached into the dainty cloth in which the biscuits were wrapped. Through the window above the sideboard, snow fell endlessly; her hothouse daffodils shone like artificial light among the bone china, the crystal butter dish, the honey pot, the napkins patterned with an exotic flock of startled birds trying to escape beyond the hems. Kay caught a fold of her negligee between his teeth as she put his biscuit down. She laughed indulgently, pushed against his face and let him trace the circle of her navel through the lace with his tongue. Then she glided out of reach, sat back in her chair.

"Think of it!"

"I am."

"Billions of stars, billions of galaxies! And life around each star, eating, conversing, dreaming, perhaps indulging in startling alien sexual practices—Allow me, darling." She thrust her finger deep into the honey, brought it out trailing a fine strand of gold that beaded into drops on the dark wood. As her finger rolled across his broken biscuit, she bent her head, licked delicately at the trail of honey on the table. Kay, trying to catch her finger in his mouth, knocked over his coffee. It splashed onto her hand.

"Oh, my darling," he exclaimed, horrified. "Did I burn you? Let me see!"

"It's nothing," she said cooly, retrieving her hand and wiping it on her napkin. "I do not burn easily. Where were we?"

"Your finger was in my biscuit," he said huskily.

"The point he makes, of course, is that with so many potential suns and an incredibly vast number of systems perhaps orbiting them, the chances are not remote for life—perhaps sophisticated, intelligent, technologically advanced— life, in essence, as we know it, circling one of those distant stars. Imagine!" she exclaimed, rapt, absently pulling apart a daffodil and dropping pieces of its golden horn down her negligee. The petal pieces seemed to Kay to burn here and there on her body beneath a frail web of white. "On some planet circling some distant, unnamed star, Kay and Neva are seated in a snowbound city, breakfasting and discussing the possibility of life on other planets. Is that not strange and marvelous?"

He cleared his throat. "Do you think you might like me to remove some of those petals for you?"

"What petals?"

"The one, perhaps, caught between your breasts."

She smiled. "Of course, my darling." As he leaped precipitously to his feet, scattering silverware, she added, "oh, darling, hand me the newspaper."

"I beg your pardon?"

"I always do the crossword puzzle after breakfast. Don't you? I like to time myself. Eighteen minutes and thirty-two seconds was my fastest. What was yours?"

She pulled the paper out of his limp hand, and watched, smiling faintly, as he flung himself groaning in despair across the table. His face lay in her biscuit crumbs; the spilled honey began to undulate slowly out of its pot toward his mouth; coffee spread darkly across the wood from beneath his belly. Neva leaned over his prone body, delicately sipped coffee. Then she opened her mouth against his ear and breathed a hot, moist sigh throughout his bones.

"You have broken my coffee pot," she murmured. "You must kneel at my feet while I work this puzzle. You will speculate, as I work, on the strange and wonderful sexual practices of aliens on various planets."

He slid off the table onto his knees in front of her. She propped the folded paper on his head. "Nine fifty-seven and fourteen seconds exactly. Begin, my darling."

"On the planet Debula, where people communicate not by voice but by a complex written arrangement whereby words are linked in seemingly arbitrary fashion by a similar letter in each word, and whose lawyers make vast sums of money interpreting and arguing over the meanings of the linked words, the men, being quite short, are fixated peculiarly on kneecaps. When faced with a pair, they are seized with indescribable longing and behave in frenzied fashion, first uncovering them and gazing raptly at them, then consuming whatever daffodil petal happens to be adhering to them, then moistening them all over her hope of eventually coaxing them apart . . ."

"What is a four-letter synonym for the title of a novel by the Russian author Dostoyevsky?"

"Idiot," he sighed against her knees.

"Ah. Fool. Thank you, my darling. Forgive me if I am somewhat inattentive, but your voice, like the falling snow, is wonderfully calming. I could listen to it all day. I know that, as you roam from planet to planet, you will come across some strange practice that will be irresistible to me, and I will begin to listen to you." She crossed her legs abruptly, banging his nose with her knee. "Please continue with your tale, my darling. You may be as leisurely and detailed as you like. We have all winter."

GERDA

Gerda heaved a fifty-pound sack of potting soil off the stack beside the greenhouse door and dropped it on her workbench. She slit it open with the sharp end of a trowel and begin to scoop soil into three-inch pots sitting on a tray. The phone rang in the shop; she heard Briony say,

"Four dozen roses? Two dozen each of Peach Belle and Firebird, billed to Selene Pray? You would like them delivered this afternoon?"

Gerda began dropping pansy seeds into the pots. Beyond the tinted greenhouse walls it was still snowing: a long winter, they said, the longest on record. Gerda's greenhouse—half a dozen long glass rooms, each temperature controlled for varied environments, lying side by side and connected by glass archways—stood on the roof of one of the highest buildings in the city. Gerda could see across the ghostly white city to the frozen ports where great freighters were locked in the ice. She had sold nearly all of her jewelry to have the nursery built and stocked in such a merciless season, but, once open, her business was brisk. People yearned for color and perfume, for there seemed no color in the world but white and no scent but the pure, blanched, icy air. It was rumored that the climatic change had begun, and the glaciers were beginning to move down from the north. Eventually, they would be seen pushing blindly through the streets, encasing the city in a cocoon of solid ice for a millennium or two. Some people, in anticipation of the future, were making arrangements to have themselves frozen. Others simply ordered flowers to replicate the truant season.

"I'm taking a delivery," Briony said in the doorway. "Jennifer isn't back yet from hers." She had cut her hair and dyed it white. It sprang wildly from her head in petals of various lengths, reminding Gerda of a chrysanthemum. Jennifer loved driving the truck and delivering flowers, but Briony pined in captivity. She compensated for it by wearing rich antique velvets and tapestries and collecting different kinds of switchblades. Gerda had persuaded her to work until spring; by then, she thought, Briony might be coaxed through another season. Meanwhile, spring dallied; Briony drooped.

"All right," Gerda said. "I'll listen for the phone. Look, Briony, the lavender seedlings are coming up."

"Of course they're coming up," Briony said. "Everything you touch grows. If you dropped violets from the rooftop, they would take root in the snow. If you planted a shoe, it would grow into a shoe-tree."

"I want you to sell something for me."

Briony brightened. She kept her old business acquaintances by means of Gerda's jewels, reassuring them that she had only temporarily abandoned crime to help a friend.

"What?"

"A sapphire necklace. I want more stock; I want to grow orchids. Stop by the flat. The necklace is in the safe beneath the still life. Do you know anyone who sells paintings?"

"I'll find someone."

"Good," she said briskly, but she avoided Briony's sharp eyes, for the dismantling of her great love was confined, as yet, only to odds and ends of property. The structure itself was inviolate. She turned away, began to water seedlings. The front bell jangled. She said, "I'll see to it. You wrap the roses."

The man entering the shop made her heart stop. It was Kay. It was not Kay. It might have been Kay once: tall, fair, with the same sweet smile, the same extravagance of spirit.

"I want," he said, "every flower in the shop."

Gerda touched hair out of her eyes, leaving a streak of potting soil on her brow. She smiled suddenly, at a memory, and the stranger's eyes, vague with his own thoughts, saw beneath the potting soil and widened.

"I know," Gerda said. "You are in love."

"I thought I was," he said confusedly.

"You want all the flowers in the world."

"Yes."

He was oddly silent, then; Gerda asked, "Do you want me to help you choose which?"

"I have just chosen." He stepped forward. His eyes were lighter than Kay's, a warm gold-brown. He laughed at himself, still gazing at her. "I mean yes. Of course. You choose. I want to take a woman to dinner tonight, and I want to give her the most beautiful flower in the world and ask her to marry me. What is your favorite flower?"

"Perhaps," Gerda suggested, "you might start with her favorite color, if you are unsure of her favorite flower."

"Well. Right now it appears to be denim."

"Denim. Blue?"

"It's hardly passionate, is it? Neither is the color of potting soil."

"I beg—"

"Gold. The occasion begs for gold."

"Yellow roses?"

"Do you like roses?"

"Of course."

"But yellow for a proposal?"

"Perhaps a winey red. Or a brilliant streaked orange."

"But what is your favorite flower?"

"Fuchsias," Gerda said, smiling. "You can hardly present her with a potted plant."

"And your favorite color?"

"Black."

"Then," he said, "I want a black fuchsia."

Gerda was silent. The stranger stepped close to her, touched her hand. She was on the other side of the counter suddenly, hearing herself babble.

"I carry no black fuchsias. I'm a married woman, I have a husband—"

"Where is your wedding ring?"

"At home. Under my pillow. I sleep with it."

"Instead of your husband?" he said, so shrewdly her breath caught. He smiled. "Have dinner with me."

"But you love someone else!"

"I stopped, the moment I saw you. I had a fever, the fever passed. Your eyes are so clear, like a spring day. Your lips. There must be a rose the color of your lips. Take me and your lips to the roses, let me match them."

"I can't," she said breathlessly. "I love my husband."

"Loving one's spouse is quite old-fashioned. When was the last time he brought you a rose? Or touched your hand, like this? Or your lips. Like. This." He drew back, looked into her eyes again. "What is your name?"

She swallowed. "Why do you look so much like Kay? It's unfair."

"But I'm so much nicer."

"Are you?"

"Much," he said, and slid his hand around her head to spring the clip on the pin that held her hair so that it tumbled down around her face. He drew her close, repeated the word against her lips. "Much."

"Much," she breathed, and they passed the word back and forth a little.

"I'm off," Briony said, coming through the shop with her arms full of roses. Gerda, jumping, caught a glimpse of her blue, merry eyes, before the door slammed. She gathered her hair in her hands, clipped it back.

"No. No, no, no. I'm married to Kay."

"I'll come for you at eight."

"No."

"Oh, and may I take you to a party after dinner?"

"No."

"You might as well get used to me."

"No."

He kissed her. "At eight, then." At the door, he turned. "By the way, do you have a name?"

"No."

"I thought not. My name is Foxx. Two x's. I'll pick you up here, since I'm sure you don't have a home, either." He blew her a kiss. "Au revoir, my last love."

"I won't be here."

"Of course not. Do you like sapphires?"

"I hate them."

"I thought so. They'll have to do until you are free to receive diamonds for your wedding."

"I am married to Kay."

"Sapphires, fuchsias, and denim. You see how much I know about you already. Chocolate?"

"No!"

"Champagne?"

"Go away!"

He smiled his light, brilliant smile. "After tonight, Kay will be only a dream, the way winter snow is a pale dream in spring. Tomorrow, the glaciers will recede, and the hard buds will appear on the trees. Tomorrow, we will smell the earth again, and the roiling, briny sea will crack the ice and the great ships will set sail to foreign countries and so shall you and I, my last love, set sail to distant and marvelous ports of call whose names we will never quite be able to pronounce, though we will remember them vividly all of our lives."

"No," she whispered.

"At eight. I shall bring you a black fuchsia."

SPRING

"Dear Gerda," Selena said. "Darling Foxx. How wonderful of you to come to my party. How original you look, Gerda. You must help me plan my great swan song, the final definitive party ending all seasons. As the ice closes around us and traps us for history like butterflies in amber, the violinists will be lifting their bows, the guests swirling in the arms of their lovers, rebuffed spouses lifting their champagne glasses—it will be a splendid moment in time sealed and unchanged until the anthropologists come and chip us out of the ice. Do you suppose their excavations will be accompanied by the faint pop of champagne bubbles escaping the ice? Ah! There is Pilar O'Malley with her ninth husband. Darling Pilar is looking tired. It must be so exhausting hunting fortunes."

"Tomorrow," said Foxx.

"No," said Gerda. She was wearing her short black dress in hope that Foxx would be discouraged by its primness. Her only jewels were a pair of large blue very faux pearls that Briony had pinched from Woolworth's.

"You came with me tonight. You will come with me tomorrow. You will flee this frozen city, your flower pots, your patched denim—" He guided her toward the champagne, which poured like a waterfall through a cascade of Gerda's roses. "And your defunct marriage, which has about as much life to it as a house empty of everything but memory." He had been speaking so all evening, through champagne and quail, chocolates and port, endlessly patient, endlessly assured.

The black silk fuchsia, a sapphire ring, a pair of satin heels, gloves with diamond cuffs were scattered in the back of his sleigh. Gerda, wearied and confused with too many words, too much champagne, felt as if the world were growing unfamiliar around her. There was no winter in Foxx's words, no Kay, no flower shop. The world was becoming a place of exotic, sunlit ports where she must go as a stranger, and as another stranger's wife. What of Briony, whom she had coaxed out of the streets? What of her lavender seedlings? Who would water her pansies? Who would order potting soil? She saw herself suddenly, standing among Selene's rich, glittering guests and worrying about potting soil. She laughed. The world and winter returned; the inventions of the insubstantial stranger Foxx turned into dreams and air, and she laughed again, knowing that the potting soil would be there tomorrow and the ports would not.

Across the room, Kay saw her laugh.

For a moment he did not recognize her: he had never seen her laugh like that. Then he thought, Gerda. The man beside her had taught her how to laugh.

"My darling," Neva said to him. "Will you get me champagne?" She did not wait for him to reply, but turned her back to him and continued her discussion with a beautiful and eager young man about the eternal truths in alchemy. Kay had no energy even for a disillusioned smile; he might have been made of ice for all the expression his face held. His heart, he felt, had withered into something so tiny that when the anthropologists came to excavate Selene's final party, his shrunken heart would be held a miracle of science, perhaps a foreshadowing of the physical advancement of future *homo*.

He stood beside Gerda to fill the champagne glasses, but he did not look at her or greet her. Not even she could reach him, as far as he had gone into the cold, empty wastes of winter's heart. Gerda, feeling a chill brush her, as of a ghost's presence, turned. For a moment, she did not recognize Kay. She saw only a man grown so pale and weary she thought he must have lost the one thing in the world he had ever loved.

Then she knew what he had lost. She whispered, "Kay."

He looked at her. Her eyes were the color of the summer skies none of them would see again: blue and full of light. He said, "Hello, Gerda. You look well."

"You look so sad." She put her hand to her breast, a gesture he remembered. "You aren't happy."

He shrugged slightly. "We make our lives." His champagne glasses were full, but he lingered a moment in the warmth of her eyes. "You look happy. You look beautiful. Do I know that dress? Is it new?"

She smiled. "No." Foxx was beside her suddenly, his hand on her elbow. "Gerda?"

"It's old," Gerda said, holding Kay's eyes. "I no longer have much use for such clothes. I sold all the jewels you gave me to open a nursery. I grew all the roses you see here, and those tulips and the peonies."

"A nursery? In midwinter? What a brilliant and challenging idea. That explains the dirt under your thumbnail."

"Kay, my darling," said Neva's deep, languid voice behind them, "you forgot my champagne. Ah. It is little Gerda in her sweet frock."

"Yes," Kay said. "She has grown beautiful."

"Have I?"

"Gerda and I," Foxx said, "are leaving the city tomorrow. Perhaps that explains her unusual beauty."

"You are going away with Foxx?" Kay said, recognizing him. "What a peculiar thing to do. You'll fare better with your peonies."

"Congratulations, my sweets, I'm sure you'll both be so happy. Kay, there is someone I want you to—"

"Why are you going with Foxx?" Kay persisted. "He scatters hearts behind him like other people scatter bad checks."

"Don't be bitter, Kay," Foxx said genially. "We all find our last loves, as you have. Gerda, there is someone—"

"Tomorrow," Gerda said calmly, "I am going to make nine arrangements: two funerals, a birthday, three weddings, two hospital and one anniversary. I am also going to find an orchid supplier and do the monthly accounts."

"You're not going with Foxx."

"Of course she is," Foxx said. Gerda took her eyes briefly from Kay to look at him.

"I prefer my plants," she said simply.

An odd sound cut through the noise of the party, as if in the distance something immense had groaned and cracked in two. Kay turned suddenly, pushed the champagne glasses into Neva's hands.

"May I come—" His voice trembled so badly he stopped, began again. "May I come to your shop tomorrow and buy a flower?"

She worked a strand of hair loose from behind her ear and twirled it around one finger, another gesture he remembered. "Perhaps," she said cooly. He saw the tears in her eyes, like the sheen on melting, sunlit ice. He did not know if they were tears of love or pain; perhaps, he thought, he might never know, for she had walked through light and shadow while he had encased himself in ice. "What flower?"

"I read once there is a language of flowers. Given by people to one another, they turn into words like love, anger, forgiveness. I will have to study the language to know what flower I need to ask for."

"Perhaps," she said tremulously, "you should try looking someplace other than language for what you want."

He was silent, looking into her eyes. The icy air outside cracked again, a lightning-whip of sound that split through the entire city. Around them, people held one another and laughed, even those perhaps somewhat disappointed that life had lost the imminence of danger, and that the world would continue its ancient, predictable ways. Neva handed the mute and grumpy Foxx one of the champagne glasses she held. She drained the other and, smiling her faint, private smile, passed on in search of colder climes.

TROLL-BRIDGE
Neil Gaiman

Neil Gaiman is a transplanted Briton who now lives in the American midwest. He is the author of the award-winning *Sandman* series of graphic novels and co-author (with Terry Pratchett) of the novel *Good Omens*. *Angels and Visitations*, a collection of his short prose and poetry, has recently been published in a beautiful hardcover edition.

"Troll-Bridge," a reinterpretation of the fairy tale "The Three Billy Goats Gruff," was originally published in *Snow White, Blood Red*. In Gaiman's version, it's about lost chances.

—E.D.

They pulled up most of the railway tracks in the early sixties, when I was three or four. They slashed the train services to ribbons. This meant that there was nowhere to go but London, and the little town where I lived became the end of the line.

My earliest reliable memory: eighteen months old, my mother away in the hospital having my sister, and my grandmother walking with me down to a bridge and lifting me up to watch the train below, panting and steaming like a black iron dragon.

Over the next few years they lost the last of the steam trains, and with them went the network of railways that joined village to village, town to town. I didn't know that the trains were going. By the time I was seven they were a thing of the past.

We lived in an old house on the outskirts of the town. The fields opposite were empty and fallow. I used to climb the fence and lie in the shade of a small bulrush patch and read; or if I were feeling more adventurous I'd explore the grounds of the empty manor beyond the fields. It had a weed-clogged ornamental pond, with a low wooden bridge over it. I never saw any groundsmen or caretakers in my forays through the gardens and woods, and I never attempted to enter the manor. That would have been courting disaster, and, besides, it was a matter of faith for me that all empty old houses were haunted.

It is not that I was credulous, simply that I believed in all things dark and dangerous. It was part of my young creed that the night was full of ghosts and witches, hungry and flapping and dressed completely in black

The converse held reassuringly true: daylight was safe. Daylight was always safe.

A ritual: on the last day of the summer term, walking home from school, I would remove my shoes and socks and, carrying them in my hands, walk down the stony, flinty lane on pink and tender feet. During the summer holiday I would only put shoes on under duress. I would revel in my freedom from footwear until the school term began once more in September.

When I was seven I discovered the path through the wood. It was summer, hot and bright, and I wandered a long way from home that day.

I was exploring. I went past the manor, its windows boarded up and blind, across the grounds, and through some unfamiliar woods. I scrambled down a steep bank and found myself on a shady path that was new to me and overgrown with trees; the light that penetrated the leaves was stained green and gold, and I thought I was in fairyland.

A stream trickled down the side of the path, teeming with tiny, transparent shrimps. I picked them up and watched them jerk and spin on my fingertips. Then I put them back.

I wandered down the path. It was perfectly straight, and overgrown with short grass. From time to time I would find these really terrific rocks: bubbly, melted things, brown and purple and black. If you held them up to the light you could see every color of the rainbow. I was convinced that they had to be extremely valuable, and stuffed my pockets with them.

I walked and walked down the quiet golden-green corridor, and saw nobody.

I wasn't hungry or thirsty. I just wondered where the path was going. It traveled in a straight line, and was perfectly flat. The path never changed, but the country-side around it did. At first I was walking along the bottom of a ravine, grassy banks climbing steeply on each side of me. Later the path was above everything, and as I walked I could look down at the treetops below me, and the roofs of occasional distant houses. My path was always flat and straight, and I walked along it through valleys and plateaus, valleys and plateaus. And eventually, in one of the valleys, I came to the bridge.

It was built of clean red brick, a huge curving arch over the path. At the side of the bridge were stone steps cut into the embankment and at the top of the steps, a little wooden gate.

I was surprised to see any token of the existence of humanity on my path, which I was by now certain was a natural formation, like a volcano. And, with a sense more of curiosity than anything else (I had, after all, walked hundreds of miles, or so I was convinced, and might be *anywhere*), I climbed the stone steps and went through the gate.

I was nowhere.

The top of the bridge was paved with mud. On each side of it was a meadow. The meadow on my side was a wheat field; the other was just grass. There were caked imprints of huge tractor wheels in the dried mud. I walked across the bridge to be sure: no trip-trap, my bare feet were soundless.

Nothing for miles; just fields and wheat and trees.

I picked a stalk of wheat, and pulled out the sweet grains, peeling them between my fingers, chewing them meditatively.

I realized then that I was getting hungry, and went back down the stairs to the abandoned railway track. It was time to go home. I was not lost; all I needed to do was follow my path home once more.

There was a troll waiting for me, under the bridge.

"I'm a troll," he said. Then he paused and added, more or less as an afterthought, "Fol rol de ol rol."

He was huge: his head brushed the top of the brick arch. He was more or less translucent: I could see the bricks and trees behind him, dimmed but not lost. He was all my nightmares given flesh. He had huge, strong teeth, and rending claws, and strong, hairy hands. His hair was long, like one of my sister's little plastic gonks, and his eyes bulged. He was naked, and his penis hung from the bush of gonk hair between his legs.

"I heard you, Jack," he whispered, in a voice like the wind. "I heard you trip-trapping over my bridge. And now I'm going to eat your life."

I was only seven, but it was daylight, and I do not remember being scared. It is good for children to find themselves facing the elements of a fairy tale—they are well-equipped to deal with these.

"Don't eat me," I said to the troll. I was wearing a striped brown T-shirt and brown corduroy trousers. My hair also was brown, and I was missing a front tooth. I was learning to whistle between my teeth, but wasn't there yet.

"I'm going to eat your life, Jack," said the troll.

I stared the troll in the face. "My big sister is going to be coming down the path soon," I lied, "and she's far tastier than me. Eat her instead."

The troll sniffed the air, and smiled. "You're all alone," he said. "There's nothing else on the path. Nothing at all." Then he leaned down and ran his fingers over me: it felt like butterflies were brushing my face—like the touch of a blind person. Then he snuffled his fingers and shook his huge head. "You don't have a big sister. You've only a younger sister, and she's at her friend's today."

"Can you tell all that from smell?" I asked, amazed.

"Trolls can smell the rainbows, trolls can smell the stars," it whispered, sadly. "Trolls can smell the dreams you dreamed before you were ever born. Come close to me and I'll eat your life."

"I've got precious stones in my pocket," I told the troll. "Take them, not me. Look." I showed him the lava jewel rocks I had found earlier.

"Clinker," said the troll. "The discarded refuse of steam trains. Of no value to me."

He opened his mouth wide. Sharp teeth. Breath that smelled of leaf mould and the undemeaths of things. "Eat. Now."

He became more and more solid to me, more and more real; and the world outside became flatter, began to fade.

"Wait," I dug my feet into the damp earth beneath the bridge, wiggled my toes, held on tightly to the real world. I stared into his big eyes. "You don't want to eat my life. Not yet. I—I'm only seven. I haven't *lived* at all yet. There are books I haven't read yet. I've never been on an aeroplane. I can't whistle yet—not really. Why don't you let me go? When I'm older and bigger and more of a meal, I'll come back to you."

The troll stared at me with eyes like headlamps.

Then it nodded.

"When you come back, then," it said. And it smiled.

I turned around and walked back down the silent, straight path where the railway lines had once been.

After a while I began to run.

I pounded down the track in the green light, puffing and blowing, until I felt a stabbing ache beneath my rib-cage, the pain of a stitch, and, clutching my side, I stumbled home.

The fields started to go, as I grew older. One by one, row by row, houses sprang up with roads named after wildflowers and respectable authors. Our home—an aging, tattered victorian house—was sold, and torn down; new houses covered the garden.

They built houses everywhere.

I once got lost in the new housing estate which covered two meadows I had once known every inch of. I didn't mind too much that the fields were going, though. The old manor house was bought by a multi-national and the grounds became more houses.

It was eight years before I returned to the old railway line, and when I did, I was not alone.

I was fifteen; I'd changed schools twice in that time. Her name was Louise, and she was my first love.

I loved her gray eyes, and her fine, light brown hair, and her gawky way of walking (like a fawn just learning to walk which sounds really dumb, for which I apologize). I saw her chewing gum, when I was thirteen, and I fell for her like a suicide from a bridge.

The main trouble with being in love with Louise was that we were best friends, and we were both going out with other people.

I'd never told her I loved her, or even that I fancied her. We were buddies.

I'd been at her house that evening: we sat in her room and played *Rattus Norvegicus*, the first Stranglers LP. It was the beginning of punk, and everything seemed so exciting: the possibilities, in music as in everything else, were endless. Eventually it was time for me to go home, and she decided to accompany me. We held hands, innocently, just pals, and we strolled the ten-minute walk to my house.

The moon was bright, and the world was visible and colorless, and the night was warm.

We got to my house. Saw the lights inside, and stood in the driveway, and talked about the band I was starting. We didn't go in.

Then it was decided that I'd walk *her* home. So we walked back to her house.

She told me about the battles she was having with her younger sister, who was stealing her makeup and perfume. Louise suspected that her sister was having sex with boys. Louise was a virgin. We both were.

We stood in the road outside her house, under the sodium yellow streetlight, and we stared at each other's black lips and pale yellow faces.

We grinned at each other.

Then we just walked, picking quiet roads and empty paths. In one of the new housing estates a path led us into the woodland, and we followed it.

The path was straight and dark; but the lights of distant houses shone like stars on the ground, and the moon gave us enough light to see. Once we were scared, when something snuffled and snorted in front of us. We pressed close, saw it was a badger, laughed and hugged and kept on walking.

We talked quiet nonsense about what we dreamed and wanted and thought.

And all the time I wanted to kiss her and feel her breasts, and maybe put my hand between her legs.

Finally I saw my chance. There was an old brick bridge over the path, and we stopped beneath it. I pressed up against her. Her mouth opened against mine.

Then she went cold and stiff, and stopped moving.

"Hello," said the troll.

I let go of Louise. It was dark beneath the bridge, but the shape of the troll filled the darkness.

"I froze her," said the troll, "so we can talk. Now: I'm going to eat your life."

My heart pounded, and I could feel myself trembling.

"No."

"You said you'd come back to me. And you have. Did you learn to whistle?"

"Yes."

"That's good. I never could whistle." It sniffed, and nodded. "I am pleased. You have grown in life and experience. More to eat. More for me."

I grabbed Louise, a taut zombie, and pushed her forward. "Don't take me. I don't want to die. Take *her*. I bet she's much tastier than me. And she's two months older than I am. Why don't you take her?"

The troll was silent.

It sniffed Louise from toe to head, snuffling at her feet and crotch and breasts and hair.

Then it looked at me.

"She's an innocent," it said. "You're not. I don't want her. I want you."

I walked to the opening of the bridge and stared up at the stars in the night.

"But there's so much I've never done," I said, partly to myself. "I mean, I've never . . . Well, I've never had sex. And I've never been to America. I haven't . . ." I paused. "I haven't *done* anything. Not yet."

The troll said nothing.

"I could come back to you. When I'm older."

The troll said nothing.

"I *will* come back. Honest I will."

"Come back to me?" said Louise. "Why? Where are you going?"

I turned around. The troll had gone, and the girl I had thought I loved was standing in the shadows beneath the bridge.

"We're going home," I told her. "Come on."

We walked back, and never said anything.

She went out with the drummer in the punk band I started and, much later, married someone else. We met once, on a train, after she was married, and she asked me if I remembered that night.

I said I did.

"I really liked you, that night, Jack," she told me. "I thought you were going to kiss me. I thought you were going to ask me out. I would have said yes. If you had."

"But I didn't."

"No," she said. "You didn't." Her hair was cut very short. It didn't suit her.

I never saw her again. The trim woman with the taut smile was not the girl I had loved, and talking to her made me feel uncomfortable.

* * *

I moved to London, and then, many years later, I moved back again, but the town I returned to was not the town I remembered: there were no fields, no farms, no little flint lanes; and I moved away as soon as I could, to a tiny village, ten miles down the road.

I moved with my family—I was married by now, with a toddler—into an old house that had once, many years before, been a railway station. The tracks had been dug up, and the old couple who lived opposite us used it to grow vegetables.

I was getting older. One day I found a gray hair; on another, I heard a recording of myself talking, and I realized I sounded just like my father.

I was working in London, doing A & R for one of the major record companies. I was commuting into London by train most days, coming back some evenings.

I had to keep a small flat in London; it's hard to commute when the bands you're checking out don't even stagger onto the stage until midnight. It also meant that it was fairly easy to get laid, if I wanted to, which I did.

I thought that Eleanora—that was my wife's name; I should have mentioned that before, I suppose—didn't know about the other women; but I got back from a two-week jaunt to New York one winter's day, and when I arrived at the house it was empty and cold.

She had left a letter, not a note. Fifteen pages, neatly typed, and every word of it was true. Including the PS, which read: *You really don't love me. And you never did.*

I put on a heavy coat, and I left the house and just walked, stunned and slightly numb.

There was no snow on the ground, but there was a hard frost, and the leaves crunched under my feet as I walked. The trees were skeletal black against the harsh gray winter sky.

I walked down the side of the road. Cars passed me, traveling to and from London. Once I tripped on a branch, half hidden in a heap of brown leaves, ripping my trousers, cutting my leg.

I reached the next village. There was a river at right angles to the road and a path I'd never seen before beside it, and I walked down the path and stared at the river, partly frozen. It gurgled and splashed and sang.

The path led off through fields; it was straight and grassy.

I found a rock, half buried, on one side of the path. I picked it up, brushed off the mud. It was a melted lump of purplish stuff, with a strange rainbow sheen to it. I put it into the pocket of my coat and held it in my hand as I walked, its presence warm and reassuring.

The river meandered across the fields, and I walked on in silence.

I had walked for an hour before I saw houses—new and small and square— on the embankment above me.

And then I saw the bridge, and I knew where I was: I was on the old railway path, and I'd been coming down it from the other direction.

There were graffiti painted on the side of the bridge: FUCK and BARRY LOVES SUSAN and the omnipresent NF of the National Front.

I stood beneath the bridge, in the red brick arch, stood among the ice cream wrappers, and the crisp-packets and the single, sad, used condom, and watched my breath steam in the cold afternoon air.

The blood had dried into my trousers.

Cars passed over the bridge above me; I could hear a radio playing loudly in one of them.

"Hello?" I said, quietly, feeling embarrassed, feeling foolish. "Hello?"

There was no answer. The wind rustled the crisp packets and the leaves.

"I came back. I said I would. And I did. Hello?"

Silence.

I began to cry then, stupidly, silently, sobbing under the bridge.

A hand touched my face, and I looked up.

"I didn't think you'd come back," said the troll.

He was my height now, but otherwise unchanged. His long gonk hair was unkempt and had leaves in it, and his eyes were wide and lonely.

I shrugged, then wiped my face with the sleeve of my coat. "I came back."

Three kids passed above us on the bridge, shouting and running.

"I'm a troll," whispered the troll, in a small, scared voice. "Fol rol de ol rol." He was trembling.

I held out my hand, and took his huge, clawed paw in mine. I smiled at him. "It's okay," I told him. "Honestly. It's okay."

The troll nodded.

He pushed me to the ground, onto the leaves and the wrappers and the condom, and lowered himself on top of me. Then he raised his head, and opened his mouth, and ate my life with his strong sharp teeth.

When he was finished, the troll stood up and brushed himself down. He put his hand into the pocket of his coat, and pulled out a bubbly, burnt lump of clinker rock.

He held it out to me.

"This is yours," said the troll.

I looked at him: wearing my life comfortably, easily, as if he'd been wearing it for years. I took the clinker from his hand, and sniffed it. I could smell the train from which it had fallen, so long ago. I gripped it tightly in my hairy hand.

"Thank you," I said.

"Good luck," said the troll.

"Yeah. Well. You too."

The troll grinned with my face.

It turned its back on me and began to walk back the way I had come, toward the village, back to the empty house I had left that morning; and it whistled as it walked.

I've been here ever since. Hiding. Waiting. Part of the bridge.

I watch from the shadows as the people pass: walking their dogs, or talking, or doing the things that people do. Sometimes people pause beneath my bridge, to stand, or piss, or make love. And I watch them, but say nothing; and they never see me.

Fol rol de ol rol.

I'm just going to stay here, in the darkness under the arch. I can hear you all out there, trip-trapping, trip-trapping over my bridge.

Oh yes, I can hear you.

But I'm not coming out.

THE STORYTELLER
Rafik Schami

Once upon a time, Salim the coachman—the most famous storyteller in all Damascus—was mysteriously struck dumb. To break the spell, seven friends gathered for seven nights to present Salim with the gift of seven stories. . . .

This is the premise upon which Syrian author Rafik Schami has constructed an intriguing modern fantasy novel titled *Damascus Nights*, interspersed with stories within stories within stories. One of these stories (related by Fatma, the locksmith's wife) is excerpted here from the thirteenth chapter of Schami's wise and wicked book, translated (from its original 1989 German publication) by Philip Boehm.

Rafik Schami was born in Damascus in 1946 and moved to Germany at age seventeen. He was a baker, a teacher, and a journalist before becoming a successful children's book author and professional storyteller in the Syrian tradition.

—T.W.

Once upon a time there was a young woman whose name was Leila. She herself was neither beautiful nor ugly, but her tongue was blessed.

Leila lost her parents at a young age and from then on lived with her grandparents in a mountain village in the north of Yemen. Even as a little girl Leila loved hearing stories, and whatever she heard once she kept in her heart forever. Nothing in the world could make her forget a story. Well, while the other young women made themselves up every day and sauntered over to the village well, ever on the lookout for men, Leila's only interest was her stories. The strongest man in the village was less attractive to her than a tiny fable, and the most handsome man could not possess her heart even for the length of a brief anecdote. Leila spared no effort to hear a new tale, even if it meant days of travel across dangerous mountains and treacherous steppes.

In any case, the years passed, and Leila became the best-known storyteller far and wide. On those evenings when she told stories, not only did she charm her listeners, she herself was charmed by what she told. She could speak with stars, animals, and plants as if she were the magic fairy of her own stories. People said that her words had so much power that one day she talked to a rotten tree trunk about spring for such a long time that it sent forth new shoots of green. But Leila didn't just tell her stories to people, animals, and plants, she also confided them to the wind and the clouds. One time there was a drought—and believe me, it was merciless. The farmers prayed and prayed, but not Leila. She climbed the highest mountain and waited there until she saw a little cloud moving quickly across the sky. Leila began to tell the cloud a story, and it stopped to listen. Other clouds joined it, and soon the whole sky was overcast. As the story grew more exciting, the clouds grew darker, and when the story reached its most suspenseful moment, Leila broke off, turned to the clouds, and called up: "If you want to hear the rest, you'll have to come down here!" The clouds flashed their lightning and rushed down as a sudden shower, just to be closer to Leila.

Well, there was one summer when it was raining so hard that the people were scared. The earth became sodden, and the swallows hid in their nests on the high cliffs. Late in the afternoon the dogs started howling strangely. When the sun went down, the villagers heard cries for help and shouts of pain coming from a deep grotto not far off. A few of the bravest men and women approached the cave, but they trembled with fear at every cry.

"It must be a monster," said the village elder.

"A monster? Then why is it crying for help?" an old farmer wondered.

"Maybe those are the cries of the people it's eating!" presumed a midwife.

"Or else the monster is trying to lure us in. My father told me that the crocodiles along the Nile hide in the high cattails and cry aloud like a small child until some mother, washing at the river, hears the cries and runs to the place where she thinks a child has fallen into the water. But that's just what the crocodile is waiting for . . ."

"My grandfather told me hyenas sometimes sneeze—" a shoemaker wanted to confirm.

"Crocodiles this and hyenas that," a knight interrupted, "a true Yemenite must always be prepared to sacrifice himself to answer a cry of distress." He took his lance and hurried inside the rocky cave, but the only thing to come back out were more cries for help.

During the day the cave was quiet, but night after night the villagers heard the anguished cries begging for mercy. Grown-ups didn't dare go near the hole, but curiosity drove the children there.

Two children disappeared in the first week, a girl and a boy. The farmers were convinced that the monster had drawn them into his lair and devoured them. More and more children followed. Although none of the farmers had laid eyes on the creature, whenever they talked about the monster they would describe every tooth in its mouth and every spike on its tail. After a month no one dared mention the word *monster*; they just referred to "the thing in the hole."

Whenever anyone mentioned "the thing in the hole," the farmers would call out: "*Auzu billah min al-Shaitan al-Rajim*," to protect themselves from the devil.

One day Leila awoke from a strange dream, put on her clothes, and parted from her grandparents with the words: "I'm going where my dream has called me. In my dream I saw the thirty children who have disappeared. They were laughing at the entrance to the cave. It's time their laughter returned to the village. Please, don't cry, my dreams will never lead me to my ruin."

"*Auzu billah min al-Shaitan al-Rajim!*" the grandparents called out in unison.

"Please," Leila said, "I want to go. Don't worry, my thousands and thousands of stories will protect me." She hurried out, and a flock of children followed her to the entrance of the cave. Leila gave them one last look, waved to them, and walked inside.

"Leila's gone inside the cave! Leila's gone inside the cave!"—the children's cries echoed through the streets. The sad news spread from house to house, and before the sun had set it had reached the farthest corner of the village. When darkness fell, the villagers heard the cries for help, and a few claimed to recognize Leila's voice. Neighbors visited her grandparents and sadly expressed their sympathy, and one or two people whispered furtively that their long-held suspicions had been confirmed, namely that the poor girl had been crazy since birth.

Leila meanwhile saw a small light flickering in the depth of the cave. She walked toward it slowly and wondered at the stone figures crowded around the entrance. No human hand, not even the chisel of time could have sculpted people more true to life than those statues frozen in flight. Not a single buttonhole, not a single hair, not even a single bead of sweat was missing from the stone figures struggling to reach the opening of the cave.

Inside the cave it was so still that Leila could hear her heart beating. After a while she came to a large hall. Here, too, there were stone figures standing all around, facing the hall, frozen in fear. Large beeswax candles were burning everywhere, and in one corner there were more than ten beehives. Across from that was a spring; the water flowed out of one crevice and into another. The bees were buzzing and flying through a hole in the rock out into the open air. Leila saw no trace of a monster. She began to search the cavern for secret entryways—when all of a sudden she stumbled across the horrible creature. May God protect us all from its sight! There it was, lying in a stone trough.

Leila quickly hid herself behind a rock pile. She didn't have to wait long; an hour after sunset the monster awoke. It looked so frightful I'd better not describe it to you; otherwise I would spoil your evening. The monster licked some honey and bewailed its horrible fate.

Leila felt her legs begin to buckle with fear, so she closed her eyes for a minute and borrowed the courage of a wounded mother lion from a story she had kept well preserved inside her memory. This mother-courage could make even the strongest warriors tremble.

Slowly she opened her eyes, and although the walls of the cave shook frightfully with every cry the monster made, Leila's legs were no longer weak. She stood up and with sure steps approached the monster, which looked at her in astonishment, then buried its face in its hands and said, "Go away, or else I will devour you, go!"

"Salaam aleikum! I will gladly listen to your story, but I will not follow your command. I didn't come here to run away!" Leila said and took another step in the direction of the monster.

"Leave, for I am cursed and damned, and whoever touches me will turn into a beast!" the monster begged Leila.

"That's not true, or else I would know a story about it," answered Leila, and she touched the monster's slimy paw that was covered with green scales. "Tell me your story," she pleaded.

"How can I! Every word of my misfortune weighs like a mountain on my breast. Every syllable cuts like a knife. When I want to pronounce it, it rends my throat," the monster groaned and wept.

"Then I'll tell you a story. If it doesn't help you, it may at least relieve your sorrow." Leila then told the monster the story of the seven sisters.

When Leila described what trials and tribulations the first and oldest sister had been forced to undergo before she finally found happiness, the monster calmed down. Instead of crying, it was listening. Shortly before dawn it laid its head in Leila's lap, taking in her every word, just like a child. The monster was so peaceful that Leila thought it was sleeping. She paused, only to catch her breath, but the creature whispered to her, full of concern, "And then what did she do to escape from her prison?" Leila gave a tired smile and went on. Noon came, and night, and still Leila continued her story, and whenever she paused to catch her breath the monster begged her to keep on telling.

Not until the sun stood at its zenith on the second day did the monster fall asleep. Leila lay his head on a stone and walked over to the well. She refreshed herself with the cool water and crept out of the cave unnoticed. Once outside she took off her dress and filled it with pomegranates, figs, grapes, and corn from the nearby fields, then hurried back to the cave. She ate as much as she could, slept just enough to restore her strength, and then waited for the monster to wake up. Then she told him about the sorrows and fortunes of the second sister. Night came and again the new day broke, and the monster listened like a child to the story until it fell asleep. For seven nights Leila held the monster spellbound with her stories. It did not shed another tear.

On the seventh night, the seventh and youngest daughter fell into disgrace with her ruthless father, who was a king, and the stern judge pronounced the royal sentence: the daughter would be beheaded the next day at sunset if no one could be found who would take her place and sacrifice himself. At this point the monster started up, excited.

"But there was no one," Leila spoke on, very moved, "who wanted to give up his life to save the youngest daughter."

"But I want to!" the monster suddenly cried out: "She is innocent. I will gladly give my life so that she may live!"

When the monster spoke these words, its skin split with a resounding clap and a handsome youth stepped out of the shell. He was as beautiful as dew on the petals of a rose. His noble offer to sacrifice himself had proven stronger than the spell that had bound him. "I am Prince Yasid," he said, looking deep into Leila's eyes. "You have freed me from my torment and I shall grant whatever your heart desires."

Suddenly Leila and the prince heard hundreds of children giggling. The boys and girls who had been turned to stone were released from their spell together with the prince and were now laughing at him because he was stark naked. The children who had been frozen in flight were also released. They heard the laughter in the cave and came running in to look. After a while they all went back to the village and reported that a naked youth was living in the cave, and that he was very shy and that he had turned red because he was naked. Leila was well; she was taking a bath in the cool water while the youth was grilling some ears of corn for her over a small fire. The parents of the missing children danced for joy, and the whole village went wild with glee.

"Of all the friends who followed me," the youth told Leila, "these bees are the only ones who stayed. They gave me light and honey. All the others succumbed to fear at the sight of me—except for you—and so they turned to stone. But let me tell you my story from the beginning. You will hardly believe it.

"My father, King Yasid the First, ruled over a happy Yemen for more than twenty years. On the day of my birth, he had a dream . . ." And Prince Yasid told Leila his truly unbelievable story. He went on for three days. In any case, there's not enough time to tell this story to you now, but if I live long enough, I will be happy to tell it to you some other time. As I said, the youth told her his story, and when he had finished, he made his way outside with Leila. People had been waiting anxiously in front of the cave for days, for they had heard whispers and laughter coming from the belly of the grotto, but no one had dared to set foot inside.

Yasid addressed the crowd: "Salaam aleikum, kind grandparents, neighbors, and friends of this storyteller who has freed me from the curse, so that the words from my heart, which have sought the light of the world for so long now, fly to it like butterflies." The farmers shouted with joy.

"I hereby declare," Yasid continued, "as Prince of Sa'na and as the son of King Yasid the First, that I intend to take Leila to be my wife!"

"Your wish is our command," the grandparents stammered in awe.

The villagers cheered the king and his successor, and the grandparents wept tears of joy. But then Leila raised her delicate hand. "No, my prince. You are gracious and kindhearted, but it is my wish to venture forth into the world. Your palace is firmly rooted in the earth and will keep me as painfully chained as the scales that tormented you for all these years. Farewell!"

"But—" the prince began to express his displeasure.

"No but, my prince. You promised to grant me whatever my heart desired—or is your word lightly given and lightly broken?" she said and walked away without haste or hesitation. The people looked at her agape. Now many were absolutely certain that Leila was crazy.

In any case, the prince returned to the capital. He had the treacherous vizier, who had had him changed into a monster, thrown into a dungeon. Out of gratitude he sent seven camels laden with silk, silver, and gold to Leila's grandparents.

But Leila ventured forth into the world. From the mountains of happy Yemen she traveled across the desert to Baghdad. For three years she lived in the city of the Thousand and One Nights until she met a man and fell in love. He was only visiting Baghdad, for he was an engineer on the Hejaz railroad that ran from Jordan to Mecca and Medina. Leila saw this as a gift from heaven. She traveled with her beloved, and whenever she wanted, she would get off the train, to tell stories and to listen to them in the nearby cities, villages, and Bedouin camps until her lover's train returned. Her fairy-tale happiness lasted for years.

She became pregnant, but Leila was like the gazelles that continue leaping about right up to their labor. Her beloved was happy that she was pregnant and even happier that he was promoted. He was named station superintendent, and he joyfully informed Leila that from then on he would no longer have to move around. But she just broke into tears. That same night she fled to Damascus, where she brought a daughter into the world. She named her daughter Fatma. And while a prince, a kingdom, and her beloved all had failed to keep this wonderful storyteller in one place, Leila's love for her daughter bound her to Damascus for eighteen years during which time she earned her living as a midwife. One sad day she came to her daughter. She said she could no longer stay and that for years she had been dreaming of telling stories in faraway cities and villages. Her daughter was dumbfounded. She had only seen the mother in Leila and not the magical storyteller. "You've grown old. Stay here," the daughter begged, "Ali and I will take care of you!"

"Old?" Leila shouted and laughed. "Good storytellers are like good wine—the older the better!" And she left, together with her thousands and thousands of stories.

RICE AND MILK
Rosario Ferré

Rosario Ferré is a Puerto Rican writer whose first book, *Papeles de Pandora*, was praised throughout Latin America. Her other Spanish-language works include collections of stories, essays and poetry. An avid reader of folk and fairy tales, Ferré has also published four books of childrens tales based on stories told to her as a child by her nanny. In her essay "The Writer's Kitchen" she relates how, after the failure of her first writing attempts, she completed her first successful story ("The Youngest Doll") by drawing upon the oral narratives of childhood. The University of Nebraska Press has translated Ferré's work into English in the 1991 collection *The Youngest Doll and Other Stories*.

The following story, "Rice and Milk," is a lyrical and uncompromising modern folk tale, translated from the Spanish by the author. "Arroz con Leche" was first published in *El medio pollito*; it made its first English language appearance in 1993 in the anthology *Pleasure in the Word: Erotic Writing by Latin American Women*, edited by Margarite Fernandez Olmos and Lizabeth Paravisini-Gebert (White Pine Press, Fredonia, NY).

—T.W.

Once upon a time there was a fair-skinned young man named Rice, who for many years had been searching for a bride without any luck. For three days the bride-to-be had to answer all his questions:

> *How can one sew a wave?*
> *How can one shear a mirror with scissors?*

If she could answer them then he would make her his wife and sole heir of his sugar cane plantation.

Rice was not only very fair, he was also very rich. He was the richest young sugar-cane planter in the whole province. When he rode his horse down the streets of the town, the passersby would sing:

> *Rice is looking for a bride*
> *who should be as fair as milk,*

and Rice would answer them:

> *who must knit, who must purl,*
> *gather, stitch and interlace*
> *her needles at a perfect pace.*

One day Rice rode in front of a house where a beautiful girl from out of town was staying for a visit. The girl's name was Milk. She was standing at the window, watering a basil pot, when Rice asked her:

> *Maiden of the basil pot*
> *How many buds in your shrub?*

And the girl answered him:

> *Young man with the dark eyes*
> *How many stars in the sky?*

For the first time in his life, Rice was unable to answer. He looked up at her in surprise, and then rode on down the road. That very afternoon, when he arrived at his house, he sent for the girl to come and visit him.

As soon as Milk heard she was to see Rice that evening, she began to sew a gown made of the finest blue silk, which changed colors as she walked. If she went out on a sunny day, it made her vanish into thin air; if she went walking under the rain, it made her turn all gray.

When the dress was finished, she tried it on. It covered her like a shroud, from shoulder to ankle, so that it was impossible to guess her shape. It had only one small opening, an eyelet through which she would show her hand at the right moment that evening, so that Rice could kiss it.

Rice invited all the important people of the town to meet Milk at a great feast at his house. When they were all seated at the table, he decided to question the girl one more, and he told her:

> *Maiden of iridescent silk*
> *ask for any exotic dish,*
> *a nightingale's heart, a cinnamon star,*
> *a crescent of pink macaroons,*
> *and if it isn't served on the spot*
> *I promise I'll make you my spouse,*
> *and you'll own half my fortune.*

The girl looked at him sadly because she wasn't interested in Rice's money, but only in his love. Suddenly she was afraid, because even though his request seemed harmless enough, it had been made in such angry tones that Milk wondered what he really meant. But she answered bravely:

Young man with the dark eyes,
if you can serve me a slice of baked ice
I'll be your wife.

Rice immediately ordered the cooks to put a slice of ice in the oven, but the minute the fires in the kitchen were lit it melted, and when the servants brought the tray to the table, all the guests could do was ladle water onto their dishes. Then Rice ordered the cooks to build a huge bonfire outside the house, and to put a block of ice ten feet long and ten feet wide on a spigot. They turned and turned the spigot as slowly as possible, but it was no use. The block of ice melted, and the water dripped and put out the fire. That very night Rice announced that Milk had won, and that he would take her to be his bride.

The wedding day came along and Milk walked up the aisle wearing her gown of iridescent silk. When she stood in front of the altar it made her blend with the smoking candles, and when she walked out of the church into the brightly lit street it made her look as if she had vanished into thin air. Rice held her hand tightly, as though afraid to let her go.

That evening Milk locked herself up in the bridal suite in order to make the marriage bed ready. She took off her silk dress and sewed up all its openings tightly. Then she filled it with molasses and layed it out carefully on the bed. She cut several locks from her hair and slipped them under the bedsheet, before hiding behind the drapes. When Rice came into the room he thought Milk was asleep. He sat on the bed, and the first thing he did was look for Milk's hand in order to kiss it. When he couldn't find it he took out a knife hidden under his jacket and without lifting the coverlets, plunged it deep into his bride's body. As the molasses spilled all over the bed and the floor, some drops fell on his lips. Then Rice cried:

Oh Maiden of iridescent silk!
if I had known you were this sweet
I never would have slain you.

The next day, Rice's body was found lying on the bed, with a long knitting needle buried on the left side of his chest. When Milk, now dressed in widow's weeds, went back home to her family, the people of the town sang as she rode by:

Rice at last did find a bride
who was just as fair as Milk,
who could knit, who could purl,
gather, stitch and interlace
her needles in the perfect place.

RIDI BOBO

Robert Devereaux

Robert Devereaux lives in northern Colorado. He has published short stories in a number of anthologies and magazines, including *Metahorror, Splatterpunks II, Pulphouse, Iniquities, Crank!* and *Bizarre Bazaar*. His first novel, *Deadweight*, has just been published and he is reportedly at work on another.

Devereaux has only been publishing for a few years, but his quirky stories have already brought him a strong following. "Ridi Bobo," from *Weird Tales*, enhances his reputation for very odd fiction.

—E.D.

At first little things niggled at Bobo's mind: the forced quality of Kiki's mimed chuckle when he went into his daily pratfall getting out of bed; the great care she began to take painting in the teardrop below her left eye; the way she idly fingered a pink puffball halfway down her shiny green suit. Then more blatant signals: the creases in her crimson frown, a sign, he knew, of real discontent; the bored arcs her floppy shoes described when she walked the ruff-necked piglets; a wistful shake of the head when he brought out their favorite set of shiny steel rings and invited her, with the artful pleas of his expressive white gloves, to juggle with him.

But Bobo knew it was time to seek professional help when he whipped out his rubber chicken and held it aloft in a stranglehold—its eyes **X**'d shut in fake death, its pitiful head lolled against the back of his glove—and all Kiki could offer was a soundless yawn, a fatigued cock of her conical nightcap, and the curve of her back, one lazy hand waving bye-bye before collapsing languidly beside her head on the pillow. No honker would be brought forth that evening from her deep hip pocket, though he could discern its outline there beneath the cloth, a coy mad-dening shape that almost made him hop from toe to toe on his own. But he stopped himself, stared forlornly at the flaccid fowl in his hand, and shoved it back inside his trousers.

He went to check on the twins, their little gloved hands hugging the blankets to their chins, their perfect snowflake-white faces vacant with sleep. People said they looked more like Kiki than him, with their lime-green hair and the markings around their eyes. Beautiful boys, Jojo and Juju. He kissed their warm round red noses and softly closed the door.

In the morning, Bobo, wearing a tangerine apron over his bright blue suit, watched Kiki drive off in their new rattletrap Weezo, thick puffs of exhaust exploding out its tailpipe. Back in the kitchen, he reached for the Buy-Me Pages. Nervously rubbing his pate with his left palm, he slalomed his right index finger down the Snooper listings. Lots of flashy razz-ma-tazz ads, lots of zingers to catch a poor clown's attention. He needed simple. He needed quick. Ah! His finger thocked the entry short and solid as a raindrop on a roof; he noted the address and slammed the book shut.

Bobo hesitated, his fingers on his apron bow. For a moment the energy drained from him and he saw his beloved Kiki as she'd been when he married her, honker out bold as brass, doing toe hops in tandem with him, the shuff-shuff-shuff of her shiny green pants legs, the ecstatic ripples that passed through his rubber chicken as he moved it in and out of her honker and she bulbed honks around it. He longed to mimic sobbing, but the inspiration drained from him. His shoulders rose and fell once only; his sweep of orange hair canted to one side like a smart hat.

Then he whipped the apron off in a tangerine flurry, checked that the boys were okay playing with the piglets in the backyard, and was out the front door, floppy shoes flapping toward downtown.

Momo the Dick had droopy eyes, baggy pants, a shuffle to his walk, and an office filled to brimming with towers of blank paper, precariously tilted—like gaunt placarded and stilted clowns come to dine—over his splintered desk. Momo wore a battered old derby and mock-sighed a lot, like a bloodhound waiting to die.

He'd been decades in the business and had the dust to prove it. As soon as Bobo walked in, the tramp-wise clown seated behind the desk glanced once at him, peeled off his derby, twirled it, and very slowly, very deliberately moved a stiffened fist in and out of it. Then his hand opened—red nails, white fingers thrust out of burst gloves—as if to say, Am I right?

Bobo just hung his head. His clownish hands drooped like weights at the ends of his arms.

The detective set his hat back on, made sympathetic weepy movements—one hand fisted to his eye—and motioned Bobo over. An unoiled drawer squealed open, and out of it came a puff of moths and a bulging old scrapbook. As Momo turned its pages, Bobo saw lots of illicit toe hops, lots of swollen honkers, lots of rubber chickens poking where they had no business poking. There were a whole series of pictures for each case, starting with a photo of his mopey client, progressing to the flagrant delicto evidence, and ending, almost without exception, in one of two shots: a judge with a shock of pink hair and a huge gavel thrusting a paper reading DIVORCE toward the adulterated couple, the third party handcuffed to a Kop with a tall blue hat and a big silver star on his chest; or two corpses, their floppy shoes pointing up like warped surfboards, the triumphant spouse grinning like weak tea and holding up a big pistol with a BANG! flag out its barrel, and Momo, a hand on the spouse's shoulder, looking sad as always and not a little shocked at having closed another case with such finality.

When Bobo broke down and mock-wept, Momo pulled out one end of a checkered hanky and offered it. Bobo cried long and hard, pretending to dampen yard upon yard of the unending cloth. When he was done, Momo reached into his desk drawer, took out a sheet with the word CONTRACT at the top and two X'd lines for signatures, and dipped a goose-quill pen into a large bottle of ink. Bobo made no move to take it but the old detective just kept holding it out, the picture of patience, and drops of black ink fell to the desktop between them.

Momo tracked his client's wife to a seedy Three-Ring Motel off the beaten path. She hadn't been easy to tail. A sudden rain had come up and the pennies that pinged off his windshield had reduced visibility by half, which made the eager Weezo hard to keep up with. But Momo managed it. Finally, with a sharp right and a screech of tires, she turned into the motel parking lot. Momo slowed to a stop, eying her from behind the brim of his sly bowler. She parked, climbed up out of the tiny car like a souffle rising, and rapped on the door of Room Five, halfway down from the office.

She jiggled as she waited. It didn't surprise Momo, who'd seen lots of wives jiggle in his time. This one had a pleasingly sexy jiggle to her, as if she were shaking a cocktail with her whole body. He imagined the bulb of her honker slowly expanding, its bell beginning to flare open in anticipation of her little tryst. Momo felt his bird stir in his pants, but a soothing pat or two to his pocket and a few deep sighs put it back to sleep. There was work afoot. No time nor need for the wild flights of his long-departed youth.

After a quick reconnoiter, Momo went back to the van for his equipment. The wooden tripod lay heavy across his shoulder and the black boxy camera swayed like the head of a willing widow as he walked. The rest—unexposed plates, flash powder, squeezebulb—Momo carried in a carpetbag in his free hand. His down-drawn mouth puffed silently from the exertion, and he cursed the manufacturers for refusing to scale down their product, it made it so hard on him in the inevitable chase.

They had the blinds down but the lights up full. It made sense. Illicit lovers liked to watch themselves act naughty, in Momo's experience, their misdoings fascinated them so. He was in luck. One wayward blind, about chest high, strayed leftward, leaving a rectangle big enough for his lens. Miming stealth, he set up the tripod, put in a plate, and sprinkled huge amounts of glittery black powder along his flashbar. He didn't need the flashbar, he knew that, and it caused all manner of problem for him, but he had his pride in the aesthetics of picture-taking, and he was willing to blow his cover for the sake of that pride. When the flash went off, you knew you'd taken a picture; a quick bulb squeeze in the dark was a cheat and not at all in keeping with his code of ethics.

So the flash flared, and the smoke billowed through the loud report it made, and the peppery sting whipped up into Momo's nostrils on the inhale. Then came the hurried slap of shoes on carpet and a big slatted eyelid opened in the blinds, out of which glared a raging clownface. Momo had time to register that this was one hefty punchinello, with muscle-bound eyes and lime-green hair that hung like a writhe of caterpillars about his face. And he saw the woman, Bobo's wife, honker out, looking like the naughty fornicator she was but with an overlay of uh-oh beginning to sheen her eyes.

The old adrenaline kicked in. The usually poky Momo hugged up his tripod and made a mad dash for the van, his carpetbag shoved under one arm, his free hand pushing the derby down on his head. It was touch and go for a while, but Momo had the escape down to a science, and the beefy clown he now clouded over with a blanket of exhaust—big lumbering palooka caught off-guard in the act of chicken stuffing—proved no match for the wily Momo.

Bobo took the envelope and motioned Momo to come in, but Momo declined with a hopeless shake of the head. He tipped his bowler and went his way, sorrow slumped like a mantle about his shoulders. With calm deliberation Bobo closed the door, thinking of Jojo and Juju fast asleep in their beds. Precious boys, flesh of his flesh, energetic pranksters, they deserved better than this.

He unzippered the envelope and pulled out the photo. Some clown suited in scarlet was engaged in hugger-mugger toe hops with Kiki. His rubber chicken, unsanctified by papa church, was stiff-necked as a rubber chicken can get and stuffed deep inside the bell of Kiki's honker. Bobo leaned back against the door, his shoes levering off the rug like slapsticks. He'd never seen Kiki's pink rubber bulb swell up so grandly. He'd never seen her hand close so tightly around it nor squeeze with such ardency. He'd never *ever* seen the happiness that danced so brightly in her eyes, turning her painted tear to a tear of joy.

He let the photo flutter to the floor. Blessedly it fell facedown. With his right hand he reached deep into his pocket and pulled out his rubber chicken, sad purple-yellow bird, a male's burden in this world. The sight of it brought back memories of their wedding. They'd had it performed by Father Beppo in the center ring of the Church of Saint Canio. It had been a beautiful day, balloons so thick the air felt close under the bigtop. Father Beppo had laid one hand on Bobo's rubber chicken, one on Kiki's honker, inserting hen into honker for the first time as he lifted his long-lashed eyes to the heavens, wrinkle lines appearing on his meringue-white forehead. He'd looked to Kiki, then to Bobo, for their solemn nods toward fidelity.

And now she'd broken that vow, thrown it to the wind, made a mockery of their marriage.

Bobo slid to the floor, put his hands to his face, and wept. Real wet tears this time, and that astonished him, though not enough—no, not nearly enough—to divert his thoughts from Kiki's treachery. His gloves grew soggy with weeping. When the flood subsided, he reached down and turned the photo over once more, scrutinizing the face of his wife's lover. And then the details came together—the ears, the mouth, the chin; oh God no, the hair and the eyes—and he knew Kiki and this bulbous-nosed bastard had been carrying on for a long time, a very long time indeed. Once more he inventoried the photo, frantic with the hope that his fears were playing magic tricks with the truth.

But the bald conclusion held.

At last, mulling things over, growing outwardly calm and composed, Bobo tumbled his eyes down the length of the flamingo-pink carpet, across the spun cotton-candy pattern of the kitchen floor, and up the cabinets to the Jojo- and Juju-proofed top drawer.

Bobo sat at his wife's vanity, his face close to the mirror. Perfume atomizers jutted up like minarets, thin rubber tubing hanging down from them and ending in pretty pink squeezebulbs Bobo did his best to ignore.

He'd strangled the piglets first, squealing the life out of them, his large hands thrust beneath their ruffs. Patty Petunia had pistoned her trotters against his chest more vigorously and for a longer time than had Pepper, to Bobo's surprise; she'd always seemed so much the frailer of the two. When they lay still, he took up his carving knife and sliced open their bellies, fixed on retrieving the archaic instruments of comedy. Just as his tears had shocked him, so too did the deftness of his hands—guided by instinct he'd long supposed atrophied—as they removed the bladders, cleansed them in the water trough, tied them off, inflated them, secured each one to a long thin bendy dowel. He'd left Kiki's dead pets sprawled in the muck of their pen, flies growing ever more interested in them.

Sixty-watt lights puffed out around the perimeter of the mirror like yellow honker bulbs. Bobo opened Kiki's cosmetics box and took out three squat shallow cylinders of color. The paint seemed like miniature seas, choppy and wet, when he unscrewed and removed the lids.

He'd taken a tin of black paint into the boys' room—that and the carving knife. He sat beside Jojo in a sharp jag of moonlight, listening to the card-in-bike-spoke duet of their snores, watching their fat wide lips flutter like stuck bees. Bobo dolloped one white finger with darkness, leaning in to X a cross over Jojo's right eyelid. If only they'd stayed asleep. But they woke. And Bobo could not help seeing them in new light. They sat up in mock-stun, living outcroppings of Kiki's cruelty, and Bobo could not stop himself from finger-scooping thick gobs of paint and smearing their faces entirely in black. But even that was not enough for his distracted mind, which spiraled upward into bloody revenge, even though it meant carving his way through innocence. By the time he plunged the blade into the sapphire silk of his first victim's suit, jagging open downward a bloody furrow, he no longer knew which child he murdered. The other one led him a merry chase through the house, but Bobo scruffed him under the cellar stairs, his shoes windmilling helplessly as Bobo hoisted him up and sank the knife into him just below the second puffball. He'd tucked them snug beneath their covers, Kiki's brood; then he'd tied their rubber chickens together at the neck and nailed them smackdab in the center of the heartshaped headboard.

Bobo dipped a brush into the cobalt blue, outlined a tear under his left eye, filled it in. It wasn't perfect but it would do.

As horsehair taught paint how to cry, he surveyed in his mind's eye the lay of the living room. Everything was in readiness: the bucket of crimson confetti poised above the front door; the exploding cigar he would light and jam into the gape of her mouth; the tangerine apron he'd throw in her face, the same apron that hung loose now about his neck, its strings snipped off and spilling out of its big frilly kangaroo pouch; the Deluxe Husband-Tamer Slapstick he'd paddle her bottom with, as they did the traditional high-stepping divorce chase around the house; and the twin bladders to buffet her about the ears with, just to show her how serious things were with him. But he knew, nearly for a certainty, that none of these would stanch his blood lust, that it would grow with each antic act, not assuaged by any of them, not peaking until he plunged his hand into the elephant's-foot umbrella stand in the hallway and drew forth the carving knife hidden among the parasols—whose handles shot up like cocktail toothpicks out of a ripple of pink chiffon—drew it out and used it to plumb Kiki's unfathomable depths.

Another tear, a twin of the first, he painted under his right eye. He paused to survey his right cheekbone, planning where precisely to paint the third.

Bobo heard, at the front door, the rattle of Kiki's key in the lock.

Momo watched aghast.

He'd brushed off with a dove-white handkerchief his collapsible stool in the bushes, slumped hopelessly into it, given a mock-sigh, and found the bent slat he needed for a splendid view of the front hallway and much of the living room, given the odd neck swivel. On the off-chance that their spat might end in reconciliation, Momo'd also positioned a tall rickety stepladder beside Bobo's bedroom window. It was perilous to climb and a balancing act and a half not to fall off of, but a more leisurely glimpse of Kiki's lovely honker in action was, he decided, well worth the risk.

What he could see of the confrontation pleased him. These were clowns in their prime, and every swoop, every duck, every tumble, tuck, and turn, was carried out with consummate skill. For all the heartache Momo had to deal with, he liked his work. His clients quite often afforded him a front row seat at the grandest entertainments ever staged: spills, chills, and thrills, high passion and low comedy, inflated bozos pin-punctured and deflated ones puffed up with triumph. Momo took deep delight—though his forlorn face cracked nary a smile— in the confetti, the exploding cigar, what he could see and hear of their slapstick chase. Even the bladder-buffeting Bobo visited upon his wife strained upward at the down-droop of Momo's mouth, he took such fond joy in the old ways, wishing with deep soundless sighs that more clowns these days would re-embrace them.

His first thought when the carving knife flashed in Bobo's hand was that it was rubber, or retractable. But there was no drawn-out scene played, no mock-death here; the blow came swift, the blood could not be mistaken for ketchup or karo syrup, and Momo learned more about clown anatomy than he cared to know— the gizmos, the coils, the springs that kept them ticking; the organs, more piglike than clownlike, that bled and squirted; the obscure voids glimmering within, filled with giggle power and something deeper. And above it all, Bobo's plunging arm and Kiki's crimped eyes and open arch of a mouth, wide with pain and drawn down at the corners by the weight of her dying.

Momo drew back from the window, shaking his head. He vanned the stool, he vanned the ladder. There would be no honker action tonight. None, anyway, he cared to witness. He reached deep into the darkness of the van, losing his balance and bellyflopping so that his legs flew up in the night air and his white shanks were exposed from ankle to knee. Righting himself, he sniffed at the red carnation in his lapel, took the inevitable faceful of water, and shouldered the pushbroom he'd retrieved.

The neighborhood was quiet. Rooftops, curved in high hyperbolas, were silvered in moonlight. So too the paved road and the cobbled walkways that led up to the homes on Bobo's side of the street. As Momo made his way without hurry to the front door, his shadow eased back and forth, covering and uncovering the brightly lit house as if it were the dark wing of the Death Clown flapping casually, silently, overhead. He hoped Bobo would not yank open the door, knife still dripping, and fix him in the red swirl of his crazed eyes. Yet maybe that would be for the best. It occurred to Momo that a world which contained horrors like these might happily be left behind. Indeed, from one rare glimpse at rogue-clown behavior in his youth, as well as from gruesome tales mimed by other dicks, Momo thought it likely that Bobo, by now, had had the same idea and had brought his knife-blade home.

This case had turned dark indeed. He'd have lots of shrugging and moping, much groveling and kowtowing to do, before this was over. But that came, Momo knew, with the territory.

Leaning his tired bones into the pushbroom, he swept a swatch of moonlight off the front stoop onto the grass. It was his duty, as a citizen and especially as a practitioner of the law, to call in the Kops. A few more sweeps and the stoop was moonless; the lawn to either side shone with shattered shards of light. He would finish the walkway, then broom away a spill of light from the road in front of Bobo's house, before firing the obligatory flare into the sky.

Time enough then to endure the noises that would tear open the night, the clamorous bell of the mismatch-wheeled, pony-drawn firetruck, the screaming whistles in the bright red mouths of the Kops clinging to the Kop Kar as it raced into the neighborhood, hands to their domed blue hats, the bass drums booming as Bobo's friends and neighbors marched out of their houses, spouses and kids, poodles and ponies and piglets highstepping in perfect columns behind.

For now, it was enough to sweep moonlight from Bobo's cobbled walkway, to darken the wayward clown's doorway, to take in the scent of a fall evening and gaze up wistfully at the aching gaping moon.

PLAYING WITH FIRE

Ellen Kushner

Ellen Kushner is the author of two acclaimed novels, *Thomas the Rhymer* (winner of the World Fantasy Award and the Mythopoeic Award) and *Swordspoint, A Melodrama of Manners*. Formerly a fiction editor in New York City, she currently lives in Boston, Massachusetts, where she hosts and produces programmes of classical and worldbeat music for WGBH Radio.

About the following story, "Playing With Fire," Kushner writes: "The story began as a cynical attempt to do a female version of the male couple in *Swordspoint* (the novel I was mired in at the time) so that I would have something short to sell to the fantasy market. But as the alchemy of gender difference, and my own love of the new characters took over, Crowe and Aelwin acquired their own very separate personae."

The story is reprinted from *The Women's Press Book of New Myth and Magic*, edited by Helen Windrath and published in the U.K.

—T.W.

Nobody went into the Old City without protection. That was only common sense. The place was full of cut-throats and crazies; swordsmen and flimflammers and thieves on the run, as well as certain other types that the young university scholars giggled about in the boldness of their purity. But Aelwin's university career had not been marked by common sense: and now that she was leaving, it was even less so. Besides, there were some things she wanted to find out.

Her black scholar's robe, which she neglected to remove, protected her for a few streets. Then she stepped over a line in the dust drawn by knives she hadn't even noticed—in her black robe at university, she was used to being invisible, anonymous. Things were different here. She was about to lose her life, though not her dignity, when someone took an interest.

"Who's the scholar?" asked a bystander with a sword. The action stopped. She was a young woman, tall and dark and pleasant-faced.

"Scholar!" exclaimed a fighter. "We thought she was a crazy, or a daredevil—walked right into a knife fight!"

Aelwin pressed her lips together. She knew she was doing it, but she couldn't seem to help herself. "You weren't actually fighting," she told them primly, just like one of her professors correcting an inadequate thesis.

One of them brandished a knife under her nose. "Yeah, well we weren't actually playing cards, either! What do you think this is for?"

"Skinning cats," she answered pertly. "Look, you can't expect people to just make way for you if you want to start a fight in the middle of the street. Don't you have—"

The young woman with the sword grabbed her arm and pulled her nearly off balance.

"You can explain it later. To the survivor." The swordswoman surveyed Aelwin from dirty hair to scuffed sandals, not missing the trembling hands clutching the black robe between them. "You are a very strange person. Come have lunch with me."

"So are you. I don't have any money," Aelwin said stiffly.

"I'll take care of it."

"I'm not for sale," the girl said loudly, to anyone who was still listening. "I'm on an important research project. I—"

"You don't know what you're doing. Come and eat; I expect you're hungry. You'll think more clearly when you've had some food. There's a pie shop round the corner."

Aelwin was indeed hungry. She proved to be what the swordswoman's mother had called "a good eater." Not that it showed. She was tall, but she was bony, with knobby wrists. Every joint formed right angles, as if her frame were only meant to hang clothes on rather than to be decorated by them.

"Who are you, anyway?" The scholar spoke around her mouthful of half-chewed pie. "The queen or something? How did you stop those knife people?"

"My name's Isobel Crowe." She took a long pull of cider. "I'm just a swordsman. But that counts for something, around here."

If she expected the scholar to act impressed, Crowe was disappointed.

"Oh, really? Whom do you kill?"

"Whoever they pay me to. When I can get a job. I don't do knifework," Crowe frowned severely. "No stabs in the dark; just duelling. Out in the open."

"Do you have principles?"

"Patrons." Crowe didn't know why Aelwin laughed. "But I'm picky. I like a challenge."

"Killing people's not a challenge?"

"Only in a proper duel, with a good opponent. Otherwise, it's just butchery. You don't fight?"

"Of course not. Putting anything sharp in my hands would be homicide. I don't even sew."

"So you really are a scholar. What do you study?"

"Fish entrails. Menus."

"No, I mean at university."

"I'm not *at* university now, am I?" Aelwin demanded huffily, one hand twisting the sleeve of her scholar's robe. "My name is Aelwin and if you have any other questions you can direct them to the public scandal sheets."

Crowe grinned. "Are you a scandal, Aelwin? Are you a celebrity? I don't read."

"You mean you *can't?*" For a moment, the scholar lost her studied nonchalance.

"Haven't learned; haven't bothered. Plenty of time to learn when I'm old. I'll stop fighting at twenty-five or so."

"Twenty-five's not exactly a crone."

"No, but your edge goes, or your luck, by then. You ever see—" quickly, Crowe amended the question—"I bet you never saw a swordfight."

"How much?"

"How much what?"

"How much do you bet?"

"Well, it was . . . I just . . ."

"Ha," said Aelwin. "You're afraid to lose."

"Actually," Isobel Crowe said slowly, covering her mounting mirth, "I'm afraid to win. You said you didn't have any money."

"I'll owe you," the scholar said doggedly.

"Aelwin . . ." asked Crowe, "have you ever heard of a tavern called the Green Tree?"

"No. I must say, it's not a very original name. There's one on every corner."

"I think you'll like it there," Crowe said, and led the way.

Even in full daylight the Green Tree was dark and smoky. Like birdsong in a murky dawn, the calls of gamblers cut through the cloudy air. You could follow the right sounds to tables where people were challenging each other to a game of dice, or seven-up, or screw-your-partner . . . a game for every temperament, all involving the exchange of money for the illusion of fortune.

Aelwin drew in a long breath, her pleasure unmarred by the coughing it brought on. "This," she said hoarsely, "is something *like!*" Eyes watering, she stared avidly at the scene of debauchery before her.

"What's your game?" asked Isobel.

The terror of the Boar's Head Tavern Ladies' Gambling and Debating Society licked her lips, remembering past triumphs. "Seven-up. But I haven't got any—"

"I'll stake you."

The swordswoman began to flip her coin, but, remembering Aelwin's vaunted athletic prowess, leaned over and handed it to her instead. "You can pay me back when you've won. I'll be at that table there. If you get into any trouble, call me."

Aelwin peered through the murk. "There's nothing *at* that table there. Just drinking. Are you a drunk, or did you promise your dying mother not to touch the cards, or what?"

"No. I just don't enjoy gambling. There's no skill in it. No challenge."

Aelwin shrugged, and shambled off to her destiny.

With the scholar safely pointed at the seven-up table, Isobel Crowe sat herself down for drink and gossip. The Green Tree was a place where jobs turned up, and the truth was, she was getting hungry for one. It had been too long since her last public duel: A nobleman's mistress had hired her in some stupid argument about a rival's false eyelashes. That was the kind of job she got, when she got any. She couldn't turn them down, she needed to eat; but if that was all that anyone ever saw her do, she'd never get the fights she craved. The good ones. With the fighters who counted.

Without being asked, the pot-boy brought her her usual ginger beer, hot enough to burn the mouth but not the judgement. Emma Golightly slid down the bench to Crowe's side, and under cover of a welcoming hug muttered, "Szifre's back. Sitting by the fire. Dirty toad."

He was a sailor, a foreigner with a wicked blade. In his own country, he was said to be in trouble with the law. Whenever Szifre was in town, he made straight for the Green Tree. He'd cut Isobel out of a job once, and was likely to do it again. She'd better keep an eye on him.

Isobel had buried her nose in her tankard when a hand landed heavily on her shoulder. She snorted beer out across the table and spun around.

"Holy *Lucy!*" Aelwin shouted. "What are you trying to do, *kill* me with that thing?"

Crowe palmed the stiletto and slid it back into her sleeve. "Well, yes. If you'd been someone else. You really shouldn't sneak up on me like that."

"So I see," said the scholar drily. "All right. I won't. I just came to tell you, I need some more money. So I can pay you back. Those—*people*—" she jerked her chin at the seven-up table, "they don't exactly play for walnuts. Of course, the bigger the stakes the bigger the win, right? As soon as my luck comes again."

In fact, the pride of the Boar's Head Tavern Ladies' Gambling and Debating Society was in way over her head. But there was no point in backing out now.

Crowe dug out a couple of coins. "Why don't you change games?"

"No, no," Aelwin said distractedly, her eyes already back on the table, glittering with the vision of quick profit. "I'm just getting the hang of this one."

Crowe watched the scrawny black figure weave its way back across the floor, picking between stretched-out legs and clumps of onlookers. Suddenly she saw the unkempt head go down, and then Aelwin rose to her feet, brushing off her sleeves. She seemed to have fallen over the feet of a large man in brightly striped trousers, with heavy black ringlets, who was enthroned on a bench by the fire, his arm around a handsome blond seated on his lap. The blond had been chewing on his ear while the dark man decked him with silk scarves and gold chains. It was Szifre, of course, trying to look innocent. Isobel shifted her weight forward.

"Excuse me," Aelwin said loudly to Szifre. "I hope I didn't hurt your feet."

"My feets is fine, sweetie," Szifre answered. The blond on his lap tittered at this witticism.

"If you moved them," Aelwin said sternly, "they wouldn't be in people's way."

"I no moof them. You find you way." The blond whispered something in his ear, and he laughed.

Aelwin just stood there, glaring in fury as though her eyes could set fire to his beard. Szifre tossed a purple scarf over her head. With great care she pulled it off, blew her nose in it and handed it back. Automatically, he almost took it, before swatting her hand aside in disgust and demanding, "What you want, anyhow?"

"I want you to move those things at the end of your legs that the rest of us in common courtesy have agreed to call feet. Do you understand me, or would you like me to repeat it with shorter words?"

Crowe let out her breath in admiration. The girl was in a kind of verbal berserker rage. Aelwin was very stiff and pale, projecting her words with great clarity. In the tavern, the gaming slid to a halt; the bets now were on the contest that was taking place.

"What you want?" Szifre rumbled. "You want fight?"

"Not particularly," Aelwin rapped out. "I'd like to tear out your liver and roast it over slow coals. And eat it."

"Fight," he concluded. "You got you sword?"

"I don't need one. I'll be happy to strangle you with your own snot-rag—"

"Yes," Isobel Crowe said. "She has a sword."

The blond fell to the floor with a thump as Szifre rose, smiling stickily. "Crowe, my sweetie! Beautiful Crowe. How is it with you?"

Isobel's hand was on her sword. "You want a fight. I'm claiming this one."

"Why you do this thing, beautiful Crowe?"

She shrugged. "You asked for it. Don't back out on me, Szifre."

"Hah!" he roared. "I back out? I roast you coals, you rotten dog-girl, and then I roast you girlfriend's, too!"

Isobel shrugged again, and stepped out into the ring the taverners had cleared for them. Aelwin had scrambled up on to Szifre's bench, and was standing there watching with her back to the wall. Isobel wondered whether she'd had the sense to bet money on the fight.

The crowd grew even quieter when Szifre stepped into the ring. He drew a heavy, wide-bladed sword with a cutting edge—something from Elmat, maybe. She'd heard about them. Her rapier was better for distance, but she'd have to watch the point of impact blade-on-blade, or he might snap her in two. If he had any sense he'd be trying to close on her, to come within her range without letting her under his guard. He had the advantage of height, but she thought she was smarter.

Already it was clear that Szifre was a talker. "Ha-AAH!" he growled, glaring at his opponent. No wonder people hired him; he was as good as a play. Isobel stared back impassively. Let him make the first move. He was bound to: he had the showman's instinct, and would want to establish first control of the bout. But control, she thought, easily deflecting a downward cut with a corkscrew twist that nearly swept open his front, lay not in who made the moves, but who could make the most of them. So she let Szifre show off all his favorite strokes in the first exchange—and all he knew of her so far was that a feint to the left wouldn't fool her, and that she had a trick of disengage that fooled him every time. By the time he'd learned how to react to it, she'd have it changed. Already he was favoring defence on the right side, because he was so sure she would attack there . . .

It was, after all, Aelwin's first duel. The swordswoman couldn't resist showing off for her. Crowe paced Szifre back and forth across the floor, making him fight high, fight low; she even did a little spin. The new sword stretched her in unaccustomed ways. It was like a new dance partner. She went in closer than she should have, just to see what he would do, and nearly had her leg sliced. She spun away, and blocked his upward cut at the last second. That was enough experimenting. The blade darted in her hand now, refusing to let him rest and rethink his attack. His defence was stronger than she'd expected.

Isobel backed off. Now they circled one another, faking starts to entice the other into rashness. All this virtuosity was tiring them both out. Crowe tried the right-hand feint again, but this time Szifre didn't fall for it. She did a little trick with her sword, a tantalizing weave of the tip of total ineffectualness and great aesthetic beauty that maddened slashers like Szifre.

He spat on the floor. "Come on, Crowe," he growled. "Come and kiss it."

To kiss someone else's blade meant you had been killed by it. Alive, you only kissed your own.

She crouched low, where her speed gave her advantage. He aped her posture; they looked like a pair of crabs.

"Get his feet!" someone shouted, amid cackles of laughter.

"SHUT UP, YOU FOOLS!" It was Aelwin's voice, slicing through the tavern air. Szifre's head jerked in the scholar's direction, just for a moment, long enough for him to see Aelwin cast her hand in a throwing motion, long enough for Crowe to see her advantage and take it. She reached through his guard at last, snicked his forearm. Szifre roared in pain and surprise, and came at her, the flat sword spinning like a windmill. She parried the blow, but her wrist stung with the impact. Again his arm rose, streaming now with blood; again she lifted hers, and as the blades struck one another, the whole tavern burst into flame.

Isobel thought, *I'm dead!* and then, as the coiling, heavy smoke entered her lungs, she thought, *No, I'm not.*

"Let's go!" There was a cold hand in hers. It reminded her of her mother's when she had fever. It pulled her along. She had her eyes shut against the smoke, and not to see the flames she knew she must be running through.

"That's better."

Isobel collapsed on the ground, clean air tearing into her lungs, her mouth watering convulsively.

"Just cough, it will clear your lungs out," Aelwin said solicitously. "You must be all worn out. That was a very good fight. At least, I think it was. It looked good, anyhow."

She was perched on the edge of a rain barrel. They were in a side alley, not too far from the Green Tree. Aelwin's face was streaky with soot.

"The fire!" Crowe gasped, stumbling to her feet. "Let's go—whole quarter—easy tinder—"

"Fire? No fire; it was just a lot of smoke. Probably the chimney backed up." As if to belie her words, a trail of smoke wafted down the alleyway. But there were no people, no screaming; no signs of fire in the Old City. "If you're feeling better, I can take you home. You have gotten pretty grimy."

"I'm going to throw up," Isobel said grimly.

"Oh, dear. Here's—have you got a handkerchief?"

Aelwin wet it and put it on the swordswoman's neck. It helped.

Naturally, Isobel thought; *she's the kind of person who never has her own handkerchief.* I'll be lending her mine for the rest of my life.

"I think you'd better go home, now," Aelwin insisted; "if you'll show me where it is."

Isobel Crowe's rooms were not on the ground floor of her lodging house. She preferred to be less accessible. She pulled open her big double doors, and enjoyed Aelwin's gasp of awe.

The house had been someone's mansion, back when the Old City was the only city. Now it was broken up into rented apartments. Isobel lived in the grand ballroom.

She awoke the next morning to the unmistakable, enticing smell of pancakes. Crowe rolled out of the camp bed she slept in in the little chamber off to the side, where ladies had once retired to repair themselves. She had last seen Aelwin winding her way up to the minstrels' gallery.

"I'm a rook," the scholar had said last night over the bottle of wine they'd shared, as she spread the wings of her long black sleeves; "I want my rookery."

"But I'm Crowe!" Isobel objected.

"Don't fence puns with me. You are a knight. I am a rook. Everyone else, of course, is a pawn."

Aelwin had made a small morning fire in the enormous ballroom chimney. Carved cherubs and wyverns looked on with interest as she dropped batter on to an old iron skillet. "My friends and I," she explained, "*survived* on these at school!"

She might not have a handkerchief, Isobel reflected with the philosophical contentment of the well-fed, but she certainly could cook.

They were both still grubby from yesterday's smoke. Carrying water up two flights of stairs was not how Isobel wanted to spend her day. She proposed a trip to the baths.

"That fire," Crowe said as they walked, "there *was* a fire, Aelwin, not just smoke; I saw it when I struck his blade!"

"Hmm," said Aelwin.

"You're awfully calm about it," Crowe accused her. "You were calm yesterday, as well."

"It's my philosophical background," Aelwin explained. "If you read enough, you find there's nothing in the world that hasn't happened before. However strange. Freaks of Nature, they're called. In the year of the Norlan Conquest, when Aelmarl the Gormless finally lost his already shaky throne, there were seen portents of an astonishing nature. Two-headed calves were born, and lightning struck the same house three times."

"What about fire that doesn't burn?"

"Perhaps summer lightning came down the chimney. Perhaps it was a miracle. To save you."

"Save me? From what?"

"From that pig. With the sword."

"Aelwin." Crowe stopped in the middle of the street. "I did not need saving."

"Yes, you did. You'd gotten him bloody, and he was really mad. Also, he was much bigger than you—not to mention his sword."

A sudden wave of sorrow washed over Isobel Crowe. Maybe her friend was right; maybe this was indeed the fight she would have lost, the one that was always coming someday. Without the peculiar smoke, she'd now be laid out flat on a bier, with the shadows and the candles and the chanting . . . she shook her head. It was a bright spring day. The fight had not been determined; she'd had as good a chance at Szifre as he had at her; and she had pinked him first. As for candles and chanting—that was for old dead kings, for someone in a romance.

"Come on." Isobel led the way to the baths. "You really *don't* know anything about fighting, do you?"

First they dipped, and then they went into the steam room. Through the wreaths of mist Isobel saw Emma Golightly, turning gently coral.

"Hello!" said Emma, in the languid way of the truly warm and wet. "It's the hero. Congratulations."

"Is Szifre dead, then?" Isobel eased herself on to a bench.

"No, but he's gone. Shipped out on the *Coriander* first thing this morning, I hear. Can't say I'm sorry."

Isobel waited for her to say something about the fire, but she was disappointed. Finally, she had to ask: "Sweating out the last of the smoke, Emma? What about that fire, then?"

"Ah," Emma said. "That's the real reason he had to go. They're calling it witchcraft. You should have seen yourself, Is! All lined with blue flame—I thought you'd caught on fire, until the smoke started, and then I didn't know what to think!"

"Blue flame?" Isobel looked at Aelwin, who was sitting all hunched up, despite the heat. "You didn't say anything about blue flame."

Aelwin shrugged, ducking her head even deeper between her shoulders. "I must not have been looking."

Isobel shrugged in her turn. Aelwin had been looking, all right. But either Emma was exaggerating, or Aelwin really didn't like thinking about anything she couldn't study in a book.

Crowe lay back, feeling her skin begin to prickle with sweat. She watched dreamily as the steam swirled in the air above her. It was making shapes like summer clouds, right over her head. A flower became a tree became a dragon, growing like a blossom, wings unfurling like rose petals until it filled her eyes, and yet she could see everything on it perfectly, every golden scale rimmed with black, reflecting back at her her own reflection, tiny and pink, her sword upraised—

"*Watch it!*" Emma's voice rang sharply in the tiled steam room.

With effort, Isobel turned her heat-logged head to look at her. Emma said, "You made me jump, poking at me like that. What are you doing, practicing in here?"

Isobel realized that her arm was upraised, extended as if to strike at the ceiling over her head. "Sorry," she said; "I must have been dreaming."

"Melting, more like." Aelwin's skin was as red as a beet. "I'm thirsty. I've been poached. Let's go for another dip."

They ran into Emma again when they were all getting dressed. "I thought you were never coming out of there," Emma said. "Look what I got!"

She pulled a thin book out of her pocket. "More magic: *The Pathways of Love, being a Simple Volume, Easy to Con, wherein Anyone may find the Secrets of True Happiness with Simple Tests of the Lover's Faith and Heart, as whispered at the Death-Bed of Rupert Magus to his Only Loyal Apprentice, Levinson, Doctor of Sorcery, University of Palindrome.*"

It took her a long time to get through the title: Emma's line of work did not call for too much reading. "Sounds pretty good, huh? It's a bunch of magic spells you can do yourself. I tried the first one, 'To Find if Your Lover be True to You,' but it took me so long to get through all the words. I think I got some of it wrong. Anyway, nothing happened."

"Oh, Emma," Crowe said. "You don't believe all that stuff, do you?"

Emma shrugged. "Who cares? It's fun."

"Let Aelwin read it for you. She goes really fast. Here, Aelwin, find us a good one—"

But the scholar was staring down at the proffered book as though it were a dead rat. "The printer ought to have his license revoked. Making money off idiots with this garbage. If people can't manage their own lives by using their brains, they should just kill themselves and spare us the trouble of feeling sorry for them."

Fortunately, Emma was of an easygoing temperament. With anyone else, that speech would have netted Crowe another duel. "Oh, come on, Aelwin." Emma pushed the book into the girl's hands. "It's just a bit of fun."

The snap of Aelwin's wrist sent the book sailing across the room. "Don't give me that! I'm in enough trouble as it is!" Then she noticed the two women staring at her, more shocked than angry. It seemed to occur to her for the first time that she was behaving badly. "Isobel," she said graciously, "Miss Golightly, may I take you out for a drink?"

And that was all the apology they got. She made up for it by being absolutely charming at the tavern they went to, telling them funny stories about a deaf university scholar who'd bought a sailor's talking parrot. For the first time, Isobel noticed the long 'aa's in the scholar's speech; or maybe they were coming out because she was being funny and forgetting to act clever. Her accent, like her name, belonged to the old landed class who had held on to their property after the Norlan Invasion—or later land-owners who liked to pretend they had. Aelwin's quirky, innocent arrogance made her seem both older and younger; when she laughed, she looked about eighteen, not much younger than the swordswoman. Crowe was curious; but in the Old City, people respected each other's privacy.

Isobel paid for the drinks, of course. Aelwin was going to pay it all back when she figured out a way to get some money; but Isobel wasn't really keeping count.

The rest of the day was spent in simple pleasures: eating, drinking and showing Aelwin the vices of the Old City. They went to the market, and bought her a wicked little knife with a bone handle.

Isobel noticed some people staring as she passed, and whispering after. She wished, oh, how she wished that she could even pretend it was about her fighting, that they were saying, "That's Crowe. Remarkable technique. She'll be going far, and soon." But she knew they were only checking to see if she still glowed with blue fire, or had begun to sprout horns from the top of her head! Well, she wasn't a fool. But she made a point of swaggering nevertheless: Any attention was better than none at all.

The only spot of trouble they ran into was with a blind fortune-teller, brought on not so much by Crowe's reputation as by Aelwin's incomparable rudeness. Old Geata, she was called; everyone knew her, and usually it was quicker and easier to pay her the copper she demanded for telling your "lucky fortune" than it was to shake her off. Knowing Aelwin's aversion to non-scholarly superstition,

Isobel tried to steer clear of the old woman; but she seemed to have her blind sights set on Crowe today, and finally cornered them at a fruit stall.

"Ah, you're a lucky lady, a lucky lady," Geata began as usual. "Give me your hand, my darling, let Old Geata tell your lucky fortune." Her withered fingers, with their surprisingly smooth tips, pored over Isobel's palm. "You'll travel far . . . farther, maybe, than you've a mind to. And then—oh, then—" Her blind eyes opened wide: orbs of spilled milk. "Ah, but to see them dancing! Dancing under the stars!" Her hand clasped Crowe's in an iron grip. "To be called through wind and water, and not say them nay—you must call them now, my darling, call them for us all before—"

"What is this claptrap?" Aelwin demanded loudly, on a whinier note than usual. "Doesn't the old bat even know her job? What about your many children, and the tall dark man you're going to marry—not in that order, of course! Honestly, you can't even get a decent fortune for your copper any more."

Geata turned her sightless gaze on the skinny scholar. "You may keep your copper, mistress. For I speak with the true power."

"Oh, come off it." Aelwin was not to be stared down by witchy old ladies. "You've no more true power than a lima bean."

"Do you say so?" The old woman became agitated. "Geata is my name, and that's a good old name that was here before you Norlaners ever came and laid waste to the Power of the land! You thought you burned the last of us on Widmark Field—but the Power lives in me, it does, and you'd do well not to forget it!"

"Do we have to pay her extra for the speech?" Aelwin drawled.

"Come on, Aelwin," Crowe muttered, steering her away, "she's just a poor old lady. Not everyone's had the benefit of your education," she couldn't resist adding. "And she calls everyone she doesn't like a Norlaner."

Talking steadily, she got Aelwin out of there. That night, they got very drunk in Isobel's Grand Ballroom. It may have been a mistake.

Aelwin started off brilliantly, improvising satire on all the Old City characters she'd met, while Isobel rolled helplessly on the floor and begged her to stop. But gradually her talk turned morose.

"People are such fools," she said. "They believe anything they want to. That would be all right, if they didn't insist on *doing* something about it!"

"Like what?" asked Isobel, happily rolling an empty bottle from foot to foot across the floor.

"Like killing people—oh." She looked at the swordswoman. "I beg your pardon."

"Quite all right. But why is that stupid? It seems pretty smart, to me."

"Oh, I didn't mean you. You're an artist, it's not the same. I meant people you don't even *know*, who never did you any harm . . ."

She sounded so mournful Isobel didn't argue. "It's for money," she reassured. "It nearly always is."

"No it *isn't!*" Aelwin rose from the floor with alarming energy, and began pacing and waving her arms. "It's sheer bloody-minded cruelty! It's because they're pigs! Look what they do to thieves like poor Lucas. He'll never get that eye back, not if he devotes himself to good works and knitting socks for the rest of his life! Or traitors—they cut their guts open and let them watch—"

"But they know all that ahead of time." Isobel tried to be the voice of reason. "Thieves and traitors—they know what might happen."

"And the massacre of Widmark Field?" Aelwin said bitterly. "Did they know *that* would happen?"

"You've got Old Geata on the brain. There wasn't any massacre at Widmark— or if there was, it was just part of the war. Why should they round people up and kill them?"

Aelwin brought her face close up to Isobel's. "Because they were *witches!*" she hissed. "They rounded them up from all over the land, the teachers and all of their families, and they slaughtered every one and burnt their bodies and their books and everyone saw the smoke for miles—it's true, I found the records! Well, some of them, anyway; the Norlaners may have destroyed the master lists, but they couldn't keep people from writing about the fire they saw, and the people who disappeared. That old lady was right—we *are* all Norlaners, the blood has intermingled in two hundred years—we *all* set those fires!" she shouted.

Isobel's blood was racing as though she were facing an enemy. She had never seen Aelwin looking so desperate. "Here," she said tentatively, "have some—" But the bottle was empty. "You need some more to drink," she said. "I'll go down to the Cock and Hoop and fetch us a bottle."

"Don't go," Aelwin said, her face drawn. "Let me come with you."

"You're too drunk," said Crowe cheerfully, strapping on her sword. Being able to take action always made her feel better. "You'd break your neck on the stairs. Wait here, I won't be long."

As she shut the door behind her she heard two leathery clunks against the wood: very much the sound Aelwin's sandals would make if she'd thrown them after her.

The night was moonless, but the smoke and dust of the city had cleared enough to uncover a host of stars blazing in the blackness between the rooftops. Whistling tunelessly, Isobel made her way to the Cock and Hoop. She didn't need a light; she knew the streets of the Old City as well as her hand knew the hilt of her sword in the dark.

Just outside the tavern she froze. A shadow by the door had moved slightly. Hand on her hilt, she waited. Then the shadow moved into the light.

It was a child, underfed and ill-clothed like most Old City brats. But when it spoke, its voice was of surprising beauty, liquid and clear. "Crowe," it said. "You are Crowe?"

"I am." She crouched down and it moved back a step, into the shadows.

"I have a message for Isobel Crowe."

It was very likely. Messages were one thing children were good for. "Come inside," Isobel said, "and give it to me. I'll buy you something to eat."

The child shook its head. "Not in there. Come with me."

Isobel laughed mirthlessly. She wasn't falling for that one.

"You are bored, Crowe. They know you are bored. They have a job for you. One you will like. It is . . . a challenge. This is the night. It will not come again."

Maybe she was a little drunk, but the words meant something to her.

"Come with me, Crowe. They know you. They will give you what you ask for . . ."

She thought, not of diamonds and money, but of a stern opponent, bright-bladed and dangerous. With witty eyes and a thin-lipped, silent mouth; sleek and fell, who would know her measure, and not know fear.

"I'll come," she said.

Aelwin waited, but not for very long. She wasn't thinking about the Slaughter of Widmark now. She wasn't thinking about much except for all the reasons she should not have let Crowe go out alone. The thing to do was to hurry and catch up with her. They could meet at the Cock and Hoop, and walk back together. But she couldn't find her sandals.

Finally she discovered them lying against the double doors. She wondered what they were doing there. She pulled them on, and fastened her robe, and clattered down the stairs and out into the night.

Isobel Crowe followed the child out of the Old City. It seemed sure of the way, though it bore no light; and she followed surely in the white gleam of its body. They passed through the artisans' quarter, the echoes of their feet whispering off the bolted shutters. On to broader streets, now, the occasional clip-clop of carriage horses passing by, the drumming hooves of outriders, their torches streaking the road with shadow. Closely packed hosues gave way to gates and green lawns (spreading grey now in the starlit dark): the manors of the rich, where Isobel had been before. Still they walked on.

Isobel drew closer to the child. "Aren't you tired?" she asked. "Do you want a rest?"

"It isn't far," the child answered. "They are waiting."

And she knew that they were. A special summons, just for her, and the night stretching on in endless walking, past the houses and on into the fields with their windmills and empty shacks. And through the fields alongside a silver stream that flowed backwards into the shadows of trees. And then the shadows engulfed her.

"Where are you?" Isobel said. "I can't see!"

"Don't stop now," the liquid voice chimed from between the trees. "Come!"

And, following the voice, Isobel Crowe pushed her way between branches, pulling her feet free of the tangle of root and thorn. Her hands were scratched, and her face was helpless against things she could not see. Blindly, she pushed on; anything was better than being left alone in the dark.

It was dark on the Old City streets. Aelwin couldn't see her feet. She didn't like it. She cut over to Allen's Way, which was broad enough to let some light in between the buildings, although it was the longer route to the tavern. Even so, she nearly tripped over a body lying huddled in the road. The ragged bundle looked up at her, cursing in a muddy voice: "Trying to kill us all . . . I warned 'em, trying to kill me, trying to kill you . . ."

She hurried down the street. Don't run, she told herself, they know you're frightened when you run. It would be better when she found Crowe. Behind her the man had risen to his feet and was screaming, "Kill your feet! Kill your head!" A couple coming from the other way crossed the street to avoid him.

The tavern lights promised warmth and comfort. But as her foot touched the threshold, she stopped. Isobel was not there. Isobel had never gone in at all. She wished she didn't know it quite so strongly; that she could pretend there was a point to going inside where there was light, and people. Shakily, Aelwin turned back into the dark street. Nothing ever came out the way she wanted it.

There was nothing in front of her. In the moment before she opened her eyes, Isobel thought she had fallen off a cliff. But she was in a clearing. There were no trees, no branches; only the flat silver disc of a pool made mirror by starlight. Its reflected glow made it possible to see; but the eerie light did not comfort her.

"Crowe."

She whirled around swiftly, but there was nothing. "Show yourself," she said. The leaves around her rustled. Her ears were straining for a sound she could recognize: a footstep, the sweep of cloth . . . The wind made a noise she couldn't hear through.

"No golden bells, no banners . . ." said the voice, neither male nor female, resonant as thunder, colorless as the wind. "You do not know how to hunt me, street-stalker."

"I was brought here." Her own voice was pitiful; her words meant nothing.

"Come!" She saw a flash of gold, the sun's gold, the midnight trees. Almost she started after it, but her feet were rooted to the ground—by her will, and not by her will: She was afraid to move. She had never known terror like this; not in a fight, not in the city streets.

"We have found a prize for you, Crowe." The voice—if it was the same voice—came now from the other side of the clearing.

"A prize worthy of your mettle. We desire to be hunted. Do not fear us. Come after us."

But they were mocking her. They knew she was afraid. Their voices fed her fear. She didn't want to see them now.

"Oh, Isobel," the wind sighed, "oh, Isobel . . ."

She put her hands over her ears. "Who are you?" she shouted.

"We have forgotten our names," said the voice. "Hunt us, hunt us with banners and bells as you once did. Call out to us, that we may remember. We have been longing for you. We woke in a strange place, where your sword was bright with death. We wanted to follow you, but not in that place. Our place is here, at the center of the moonless night. We came here, and you came after us, my hero."

On the pond, a darkness stirred. Isobel looked behind her and saw empty glade; but across the mirrory water behind her own reflection a man's head and torso were rising. A man's head, with a goat's horns and ears—

Fear was choking her. But the tiny cold portion of her brain that spoke to her when she was in emergency was saying, *Don't run. If you run now, you'll never be able to stop.*

Seeing him in the water was better than not knowing where he was at all; and if he wasn't really there he couldn't really touch her. Another figure now was staining the pond, whiter than the stars' own image. Rippling over the surface of the water across from her, although the glade shone empty. Again that flash of gold; and fire, white fire in the shape of a horse, a terrible glory on the water—

"Maiden," said the golden-horned creature, its thundery voice rich with surprise. "Maiden, let me come to you."

Its reflection burned its way around the edges of the pool. The ache in Isobel's right hand resolved itself into the metal she was clasping: the hilt of her sword. The feel of it made her want to run just a bit less.

"Stand off," she said to the thing that was not there, drawing her blade. She pointed it at the reflection of the golden horn, and then felt it twist in her grasp, as though the sword were trying to escape her. *The weight was wrong—the weight was wrong.* Even the tiny cold portion of her brain was suffused with horror. She was wielding a black and twisting snake, moored to the hilt that was all that was left of her sword. She couldn't throw away her sword—the little grain of thought seemed to have gone mad—*Get rid of it!*—no, not the hilt, she knew that hilt, it fit her hand, it was being twisted out of her hand by the living, flat-headed blade.

And for the first time she heard the laughter of the goat-eyed man.

Another figure appeared now in the water: a woman, her hair long and dark. A light hung about her that was neither sun nor stars. She lifted one arm, its reflection shining over Isobel's head. And the wind, and the terrible laughter, stopped.

"Let the invisible be made visible."

Isobel's sword was still. And so she found the courage to look behind her. The goat-eyed man was goat-hoofed as well. He was smaller than she'd expected, but just as monstrous. And across the glade, the white beast dipped its horn in the water and touched its own image.

"Very good," said the woman sternly. "Now hear me: I raised you by accident, and I'm sorry. I called on power without knowing its source. You are not wanted here. You must go deep into the heart of the forest, and not come near the city, and leave Crowe alone. Your time will come, but it is not here."

"Maiden," the white horse's breath stirred the pond, "will it be soon?"

"It may be soon. I'll do my best. But now is not the time. Now go, and quickly; for the dawn is coming, and the new moon's rising. And may I add," she added shyly, "that you are both very beautiful . . ."

The horse turned a tail of white flame, and the goat-man leapt into the trees. As if only they had been holding back the dawn, now a grey light glimmered, and a few birds began to sing.

"Thank you, Aelwin," Crowe said gruffly.

"I think I had better sit down," Aelwin muttered. "I think I might throw up." Crowe wet her handkerchief and put it on the back of Aelwin's neck.

"It won't be hard to get back," Aelwin said when she could talk again, "just follow the stream to the fields. From there you can see the city."

Isobel thumped her fist on her thigh in disgust. "Of course! I should have—"

"No, you shouldn't!" Aelwin snapped back angrily. "You were facing Powers of the woods at night, on their ground. You were incredibly brave. Nobody else could have done it without panicking—nobody! I don't *ever* want to hear you reproach yourself for *anything* about this night. You were incredible." She twisted her fingers together. "Anyway, it was my fault. I tried to save you from that tavern duel when I didn't know the first thing about it. I let something loose in the city and I didn't even try to find out what it was—inadequate research habits," she muttered. "I thought it would go away because it didn't belong there. I thought it was pestering you because it couldn't get to me. It didn't occur to me that you were one of *them*."

"One of *what?*" Isobel demanded, rankled by Aelwin's tone. "I don't have a horn growing in the middle of my forehead!"

"A hero," Aelwin said glumly. "That's why you followed the sending from the tavern to here. It called to you, and you had to come. They never call to *me*."

"You're too clever for them. They do what you tell them to."

Aelwin was picking blades of grass and tossing them aside, scowling. "I'm a nincompoop. An incompetent. *The Pathways of Love*, that's all I'm good for."

Emma's book! "Did *you* write that?"

"My friend Beata and I did. We needed the money to stay in school," she said defensively. "She was Rupert Magus—I was Levinson. I still get royalties—I'll be able to pay you back soon."

"Aelwin," Crowe said with desperate patience, "let me get this straight. You're some kind of witch—"

"No, no, no!" Aelwin began pacing around the glade. She made a pretty picture with her long strides, her loose hair flying and her exaggerated gestures. "You *haven't* got it straight at all! There *is* magic in the land. The old lady was right. You have to be born here; and you can't practice it anywhere else. That's why magiae were never a valuable export item. Aelmarl and all the old kings thought themselves unconquerable because of it. But the Norlaners figured out a way to take the country, *and* make the magiae helpless just long enough to round them up like any fallen people and kill them. Men, women and children; teachers and students—they weren't taking any chances. I don't know how it was done: treachery, I suspect. Of course they didn't leave any records. If you'd just wiped out an entire population for the purpose of eliminating their knowledge from the earth, you wouldn't want to leave any traces for people to come upon in later years and get interested in."

"But some escaped, right? And you're a descendant—"

Aelwin sneered. "My great-something-grandfather was a Norlan captain. It's a talent that runs in the land, not in particular families. But talent's not enough. There are probably hundreds of potential magiae running around. You have to have training. It's a complicated art. If you'll pardon the obvious parallel: Suppose you'd never seen a sword all your life, or heard of swordplay. It's pretty unlikely you'd just pick up a willow wand and start poking people with it."

"How did you learn, then?" Isobel breathed.

"The same way I learn everything: from the book. Of course the Norlaners took care to find them all and burn them, too. Oh, it was a great time to be alive. Everyone was scared to death: Neighbors were turning each other in for hiding books . . . anyhow, my friend Beata and I were crawling around in a school attic we shouldn't have been in, where students' trunks are stored. We were looking for a box of hers she'd left over the summer. Wedged in between the rafters we found a terribly old trunk, all of wood. It looked as though someone had left it and forgotten it was there. It held what you'd expect: clothes, lamp, toasting fork—and books. First year studies in elementary magic. Also a little hand-written notebook full of love charms, with prolific comments on how well they'd worked. Halmar, his name was; and he never came back for it."

She was standing quite still, now, her face taut with grief.

"Is that what you made the *Pathways* book out of?" Isobel asked, to keep her from crying.

"Yes. We thought, even if they really turned out to work for one person in three hundred, it would only spread general happiness. It couldn't hurt. We thought. That was before we got called up before the Deans. First it was for compromising our academic principles with such nonsense—the *Pathways* book, I mean. No one knew about the real magic books. Then they discovered an old statute in the University code against witchcraft—dating from guess when? Haha, what superstitious fools even those old scholars were; but there it was in the rules, ladies, now pay up or get out." For a moment, Aelwin's face brightened. "The Dean actually tried some of the *Pathways of Love* spells at the trial. Of course they didn't work for her: It's a talent, you know, like being able to sing."

Isobel nodded, remembering Aelwin's tuneless warblings in the bath.

"Beata paid a fine and stayed. She needs her degree—it would kill her parents if she left. And she wants to become a lecturer. In history. She has a whole theory about looking through archives—it was very useful for researching the massacre."

"I thought women weren't allowed to lecture in public."

For the first time, Aelwin smiled. "I'd like to see them try to stop her." She pushed her hair back from her face. "Me, I turned and walked out. I don't need them—and there's nothing I want to study much."

"Except magic."

"I learned all those books could teach me. And you saw how well I did with it in that tavern fire! I'm doomed to be a first-year student for the rest of my life."

"That's not what you said to those . . . powers. You said you would try." Crowe made an intuitive leap. "Where are the other books, Aelwin?"

"North," Aelwin said, her jaw set. "I think they're upcountry, if there are any at all. Hidden in the wilderness, where even the army couldn't go."

"Then we'll go there." She heard herself say it with perfect certainty, and knew as soon as she had that it was right.

Aelwin smiled lazily. "My dear Isobel, do you know what there is upcountry? Pine trees and bears. Snow and more snow. The food is awful, the entertainment worse. You'd be bored out of your mind."

"I think," said Isobel stoutly, trying to match her studied carelessness, "that I need a little training in woodcraft. The city is so dull these days, so . . . unchallenging."

"I think," said Aelwin, "that it will be enough of a challenge to walk all the way back to your place without falling asleep. Do you have some money? I'd like some breakfast, and then I'm going to bed. In my rookery."

"All right," said Crowe. "What kind of bears?"

LATER

Michael Marshall Smith

Michael Marshall Smith was born in Knutsford, Cheshire, England, and grew up in the U.S., South Africa, and Australia. He now lives in London and is a freelance graphic designer as well as a writer. His short fiction has been published in *Dark Voices*, *Best New Horror*, and both *Darkland* anthologies and he has a science fiction story coming up in *OMNI*. His novel *Only Forward* has recently been published in the U.K.

Smith has only been publishing for a few years, yet his writing is polished to perfection. This can be seen in "Later," one of several original stories that appeared in the anthology *The Mammoth Book of Zombies*, edited by Stephen Jones. It is a love story. Smith published two other remarkable stories during 1993 and I recommend them highly—"More Bitter Than Death" in *Dark Voices 5* and "The Owner," from *Touch Wood: Narrow Houses 2*.

—E.D.

I remember standing in the bedroom before we went out, fiddling with my tie and fretting mildly about the time. As yet we had plenty, but that was nothing to be complacent about. The minutes had a way of disappearing when Rachel was getting ready, early starts culminating in a breathless search for a taxi. It was a party we were going to, so it didn't really matter what time we left, but I tend to be a little dull about time. I used to, anyway.

When I had the tie as close to a tidy knot as I was going to be able to get it, I turned away from the mirror, and opened my mouth to call out to Rachel. But then I caught sight of what was on the bed, and closed it again. For a moment I just stood and looked, and then walked over towards the bed.

It wasn't anything very spectacular, just a dress made of sheeny white material. A few years ago, when we started going out together, Rachel used to make a lot of her clothes. She didn't do it because she had to, but because she enjoyed it. She used to trail me endlessly round dress-making shops, browsing patterns and asking my opinion on a million different fabrics, while I half-heartedly protested and moaned.

On impulse I leant down and felt the material, and found I could remember touching it for the first time in the shop on Mill Road, could remember surfacing up through contented boredom to say that yes, I liked this one. On that recommendation she'd bought it, and made this dress, and as a reward for traipsing around after her she'd bought me dinner too. We were poorer then, so the meal was cheap, but there was lots and it was good.

The strange thing was, I didn't even really mind the dress shops. You know how sometimes, when you're just walking around, living your life, you'll see someone on the street and fall hopelessly in love with them? How something in the way they look, the way they are, makes you stop dead in your tracks and stare? How for that instant you're convinced that if you could just meet them, you'd be able to love them forever?

Wild schemes and unlikely meetings pass through your head, and yet as they stand on the other side of the street or the room, talking to someone else, they haven't the faintest idea of what's going through your mind. Something has clicked, but only inside your head. You know you'll never speak to them, that they'll never know what you're feeling, and that they'll never want to. But something about them forces you to keep looking, until you wish they'd leave so you could be free.

The first time I saw Rachel was like that, and now she was in my bath. I didn't call out to hurry her along. I decided it didn't really matter.

A few minutes later a protracted squawking noise announced the letting out of the bath water, and Rachel wafted into the bedroom swaddled in thick towels and glowing high spirits. Suddenly I lost all interest in going to the party, punctually or otherwise. She marched up to me, set her head at a silly angle to kiss me on the lips and jerked my tie vigorously in about three different directions. When I looked in the mirror I saw that somehow, as always, she'd turned it into a perfect knot.

Half an hour later we left the flat, still in plenty of time. If anything, I'd held her up.

"Later," she said, smiling in the way that showed she meant it, "Later, and for a long time, my man."

I remember turning from locking the door to see her standing on the pavement outside the house, looking perfect in her white dress, looking happy and looking at me. As I walked smiling down the steps towards her she skipped backwards into the road, laughing for no reason, laughing because she was with me.

"Come on," she said, holding out her hand like a dancer, and a yellow van came round the corner and smashed into her. She spun backwards as if tugged on a rope, rebounded off a parked car and toppled into the road. As I stood cold on the bottom step she half sat up and looked at me, an expression of wordless surprise on her face, and then she fell back again.

When I reached her blood was already pulsing up into the white of her dress and welling out of her mouth. It ran out over her makeup and I saw she'd been right: she hadn't quite blended the colors above her eyes. I'd told her it didn't matter, that she still looked beautiful. She had.

She tried to move her head again and there was a sticky sound as it almost left the tarmac and then slumped back. Her hair fell back from around her face, but not as it usually did. There was a faint flicker in her eyelids, and then she died.

I knelt there in the road beside her, holding her hand as the blood dried a little. It was as if everything had come to a halt, and hadn't started up again. I heard every word the small crowd muttered, but I didn't know what they were muttering about. All I could think was that there wasn't going to be a later, not to kiss her some more, not for anything. Later was gone.

When I got back from the hospital I phoned her mother. I did it as soon as I got back, though I didn't want to. I didn't want to tell anyone, didn't want to make it official. It was a bad phone call, very, very bad. Then I sat in the flat, looking at the drawers she'd left open, at the towels on the floor, at the party invitation on the dressing table, feeling my stomach crawl. I was back at the flat, as if we'd come back home from the party. I should have been making coffee while Rachel had yet another bath, coffee we'd drink on the sofa in front of the fire. But the fire was off and the bath was empty. So what was I supposed to do?

I sat for an hour, feeling as if somehow I'd slipped too far forward in time and left Rachel behind, as if I could turn and see her desperately running to try to catch me up. When it felt as if my throat was going to burst I called my parents and they came and took me home. My mother gently made me change my clothes, but she didn't wash them. Not until I was asleep, anyway. When I came down and saw them clean I hated her, but I knew she was right and the hate went away. There wouldn't have been much point in just keeping them in a drawer.

The funeral was short. I guess they all are, really, but there's no point in them being any longer. Nothing more would be said. I was a little better by then, and not crying so much, though I did before we went to the church because I couldn't get my tie to sit right.

Rachel was buried near her grandparents, which she would have liked. Her parents gave me her dress afterwards, because I'd asked for it. It had been thoroughly cleaned and large patches had lost their sheen and died, looking as much unlike Rachel's dress as the cloth had on the roll. I'd almost have preferred the bloodstains still to have been there: at least that way I could had believed that the cloth still sparkled beneath them. But they were right in their way, as my mother was. Some people seem to have pragmatic, accepting souls, an ability to deal with death. I don't, I'm afraid. I don't understand it at all.

Afterwards I stood at the graveside for a while, but not for long because I knew that my parents were waiting at the car. As I stood by the mound of earth that lay on top of her I tried to concentrate, to send some final thought to her, some final love, but the world kept pressing in on me through the sound of cars on the road and some bird that was cawing in a tree. I couldn't shut it out. I couldn't believe that I was noticing how cold it was, that somewhere lives were being led and televisions being watched, that the inside of my parents' car would smell the same as it always had. I wanted to feel something, wanted to sense her presence, but I couldn't. All I could feel was the world round me, the same old world. But it wasn't a world that had been there a week ago, and I couldn't understand how it could look so much the same.

It was the same because nothing had changed, and I turned and walked to the car. The wake was worse than the funeral, much worse, and I stood with a sandwich feeling something very cold building up inside. Rachel's oldest friend Lisa held court with her old school friends, swiftly running the range of emotions from stoic resilience to trembling incoherence.

"I've just realized," she sobbed to me, "Rachel's not going to be at my wedding."

"Yes, well she's not going to be at mine either," I said numbly, and immediately hated myself for it. I went and stood by the window, out of harm's way. I couldn't react properly. I knew why everyone was standing here, that in some ways it was like a wedding. Instead of gathering together to bear witness to a bond, they were here to prove she was dead. In the weeks to come they'd know they'd stood together in a room, and would be able to accept she was gone. I couldn't.

I said goodbye to Rachel's parents before I left. We looked at each other oddly, and shook hands, as if we were just strangers again. Then I went back to the flat and changed into some old clothes. My "Someday" clothes, Rachel used to call them, as in "some day you must throw them away." Then I made a cup of tea and stared out of the window for a while. I knew damn well what I was going to do, and it was a relief to give in to it.

That night I went back to the cemetery and I dug her up. What can I say? It was hard work, and it took a lot longer than I expected, but in another way it was surprisingly easy. I mean yes, it was creepy, and yes, I felt like a lunatic, but after the shovel had gone in once the second time seemed less strange. It was like waking up in the mornings after the accident. The first time I clutched at myself and couldn't understand, but after that I knew what to expect. There were no cracks of thunder, there was no web of lightning and I actually felt very calm. There was just me and, beneath the earth, my friend. I just wanted to find her.

When I did I laid her down by the side of the grave and then filled it back up again, being careful to make it look undisturbed. Then I carried her to the car in my arms and brought her home.

The flat seemed very quiet as I sat her on the sofa, and the cushion rustled and creaked as it took her weight again. When she was settled I knelt and looked up at her face. It looked much the same as it always had, though the color of the skin was different, didn't have the glow she always had. That's where life is, you know, not in the heart but in the little things, like the way hair falls around a face. Her nose looked the same and her forehead was smooth. It was the same face, exactly the same.

I knew the dress she was wearing was hiding a lot of things I would rather not see, but I took it off anyway. It was her going away dress, bought by her family specially for the occasion, and it didn't mean anything to me or to her. I knew what the damage would be and what it meant. As it turned out the patchers and menders had done a good job, not glossing because it wouldn't be seen. It wasn't so bad.

When she was sitting up again in her white dress I walked over and turned the light down, and I cried a little then, because she looked so much the same. She could have fallen asleep, warmed by the fire and dozy with wine, as if we'd just come back from the party.

I went and had a bath then. We both used to when we came back in from an evening, to feel clean and fresh for when we slipped between the sheets. It wouldn't be like that this evening, of course, but I had dirt all over me, and I wanted to feel normal. For one night at least I just wanted things to be as they had.

I sat in the bath for a while, knowing she was in the living room, and slowly washed myself clean. I really wasn't thinking much. It felt nice to know that I wouldn't be alone when I walked back in there. That was better than nothing, was part of what had made her alive. I dropped my Someday clothes in the bin and put on the ones from the evening of the accident. They didn't mean as much as her dress, but at least they were from before.

When I returned to the living room her head had lolled slightly, but it would have done if she'd been asleep. I made us both a cup of coffee. The only time she ever took sugar was in this cup, so I put one in. Then I sat down next to her on the sofa and I was glad that the cushions had her dent in them, that as always they drew me slightly towards her, didn't leave me perched there by myself.

The first time I saw Rachel was at a party. I saw her across the room and simply stared at her, but we didn't speak. We didn't meet properly for a month or two, and first kissed a few weeks after that. As I sat there on the sofa next to her body I reached out tentatively and took her hand, as I had done on that night. It was cooler than it should have been, but not too bad because of the fire, and I held it, feeling the lines on her palm, lines I knew better than my own.

I let myself feel calm and I held her hand in the half light, not looking at her, as also on that first night, when I'd been too happy to push my luck. She's letting you hold her hand, I'd thought, don't expect to be able to look at her too. Holding her hand is more than enough: don't look, you'll break the spell. My face creased then, not knowing whether to smile or cry, but it felt alright. It really did.

I sat there for a long time, watching the flames, still not thinking, just holding her hand and letting the minutes run. The longer I sat the more normal it felt, and finally I turned slowly to look at her. She looked tired and asleep, so deeply asleep, but still there with me and still mine.

When her eyelid first moved I thought it was a trick of the light, a flicker cast by the fire. But then it stirred again, and for the smallest of moments I thought I was going to die. The other eyelid moved and the feeling just disappeared, and that made the difference, I think. She had a long way to come, and if I'd felt frightened, or rejected her, I think that would have finished it then. I didn't question it. A few minutes later both her eyes were open, and it wasn't long before she was able to slowly turn her head.

I still go to work, and put in the occasional appearance at social events, but my tie never looks quite as it did. She can't move her fingers precisely enough to help me with that any more. She can't come with me, and nobody can come here, but that doesn't matter. We always spent a lot of time by ourselves. We wanted to.

I have to do a lot of things for her, but I can live with that. Lots of people have accidents, bad ones: if Rachel had survived she could have been disabled or brain-damaged so that her movements were as they are now, so slow and clumsy. I wish she could talk, but there's no air in her lungs, so I'm learning to read her lips. Her mouth moves slowly, but I know she's trying to speak, and I want to hear what she's saying.

But she gets round the flat, and she holds my hand, and she smiles as best she can. If she'd just been injured I would have loved her still. It's not so very different.

DISTANCES
Sherman Alexie

Sherman Alexie is a gifted young writer from Washington state who has gained a considerable reputation with four stunning small press books of poetry and prose: *The Business of Fancydancing, I Would Steal Horses, Old Shirts & New Skins,* and *The First Indian on the Moon.* Happily, his work will now reach an even wider audience with the publication of *The Lone Ranger and Tonto Fistfight in Heaven,* a major story collection which includes the following story, "Distances," as well as "This Is What it Means to Say Phoenix, Arizona" (published in the June 1993 issue of *Esquire* magazine, also highly recommended).

Though Alexie is primarily a realist, drawing on his Native American cultural heritage and background on the Spokane Indian Reservation for inspiration, his work often has a mystical undercurrent which will appeal to readers of fantasy and magical realist fiction. "Distances" is an extraordinary fantasia about the legendary Ghost Dance, and its consequences.

—T.W.

All Indians must dance, everywhere, keep on dancing. Pretty soon in next spring Great Spirit come. He bring back all game of every kind. The game be thick everywhere. All dead Indians come back and live again. Old blind Indian see again and get young and have fine time. When Great Spirit comes this way, then all the Indians go to mountains, high up away from whites. Whites can't hurt Indians then. Then while Indians way up high big flood comes like water and all white people die, get drowned. After that, water go away and then nobody but Indians everywhere and game all kinds thick. Then medicine man tell Indians to send word to all Indians to keep up dancing and the good time will come. Indians who don't dance, who don't believe in this word, will grow little, just about a foot high, and stay that way. Some of them will be turned into wood and burned in fire.

—Wovoka, the Paiute Ghost Dance Messiah

After this happened, after it began, I decided Custer could have, must have, pressed the button, cut down all the trees, opened up holes in the ozone, flooded the earth. Since most of the white men died and most of the Indians lived, I decided only Custer could have done something that backward. Or maybe it was because the Ghost Dance finally worked.

Last night we burned another house. The Tribal Council has ruled that anything to do with the whites has to be destroyed. Sometimes while we are carrying furniture out of a house to be burned, all of us naked, I have to laugh out loud. I wonder if this is how it looked all those years ago when we savage Indians were slaughtering those helpless settlers. We must have been freezing, buried by cold then, too.

I found a little transistor radio in a closet. It's one of those yellow waterproof radios that children always used to have. I know that most of the electrical circuitry was destroyed, all the batteries dead, all the wires shorted, all the dams burst, but I wonder if this radio still works. It was hidden away in a closet under a pile of old quilts, so maybe it was protected. I was too scared to turn it on, though. What would I hear? Farm reports, sports scores, silence?

There's this woman I love, Tremble Dancer, but she's one of the Urbans. Urbans are the city Indians who survived and made their way out to the reservation after it all fell apart. There must have been over a hundred when they first arrived, but most of them have died since. Now there are only a dozen Urbans left, and they're all sick. The really sick ones look like they are five hundred years old. They look like they have lived forever; they look like they'll die soon.

Tremble Dancer isn't sick yet, but she does have burns and scars all over her legs. When she dances around the fire at night, she shakes from the pain. Once when she fell, I caught her and we looked hard at each other. I thought I could see half of her life, something I could remember, something I could never forget.

The Skins, Indians who lived on the reservation when it happened, can never marry Urbans. The Tribal Council made that rule because of the sickness in the Urbans. One of the original Urbans was pregnant when she arrived on the reservation and gave birth to a monster. The Tribal Council doesn't want that to happen again.

Sometimes I ride my clumsy horse out to Noah Chirapkin's tipi. He's the only Skin I know that has traveled off the reservation since it happened.

"There was no sound," he told me once. "I rode for days and days but there were no cars moving, no planes, no bulldozers, no trees. I walked through a city that was empty, walked from one side to the other, and it took me a second. I just blinked my eyes and the city was gone, behind me. I found a single plant, a black flower, in the shadow of Little Falls Dam. It was forty years before I found another one, growing between the walls of an old house on the coast."

Last night I dreamed about television. I woke up crying.

The weather is changed, changing, becoming new. At night it is cold, so cold that fingers can freeze into a face that is touched. During the day, our sun holds us tight against the ground. All the old people die, choosing to drown in their own water rather than die of thirst. All their bodies are evil, the Tribal Council decided. We burn the bodies on the football field, on the fifty-yard line one week, in an end zone the next. I hear rumors that relatives of the dead might be killed and burned, too. The Tribal Council decided it's a white man's disease in their blood. It's a wristwatch that has fallen between their ribs, slowing, stopping. I'm happy my grandparents and parents died before all of this happened. I'm happy I'm an orphan.

Sometimes Tremble Dancer waits for me at the tree, all we have left. We take off our clothes, loincloth, box dress. We climb the branches of the tree and hold each other, watching for the Tribal Council. Sometimes her skin will flake, fall off, float to the ground. Sometimes I taste parts of her breaking off into my mouth. It is the taste of blood, dust, sap, sun.

"My legs are leaving me," Tremble Dancer told me once. "Then it will be my arms, my eyes, my fingers, the small of my back.

"I am jealous of what you have," she told me, pointing at the parts of my body and telling me what they do.

Last night we burned another house. I saw a painting of Jesus Christ lying on the floor.

He's white. Jesus is white.

While the house was burning, I could see flames, colors, every color but white. I don't know what it means, don't understand fire, the burns on Tremble Dancer's legs, the ash left to cool after the house has been reduced.

I want to know why Jesus isn't a flame.

Last night I dreamed about television. I woke up crying.

While I lie in my tipi pretending to be asleep under the half-blankets of dog and cat skin, I hear the horses exploding. I hear the screams of children who are taken.

The Others have come from a thousand years ago, their braids gray and broken with age. They have come with arrow, bow, stone ax, large hands.

"Do you remember me?" they sing above the noise, our noise.

"Do you still fear me?" they shout above the singing, our singing.

I run from my tipi across the ground toward the tree, climb the branches to watch the Others. There is one, taller than the clouds, who doesn't ride a pony, who runs across the dust, faster than my memory.

Sometimes they come back. The Others, carrying salmon, water. Once, they took Noah Chirapkin, tied him down to the ground, poured water down his throat until he drowned.

The tallest Other, the giant, took Tremble Dancer away, brought her back with a big belly. She smelled of salt, old blood. She gave birth, salmon flopped from her, salmon growing larger.

When she died, her hands bled seawater from the palms.

*   *   *

At the Tribal Council meeting last night, Judas WildShoe gave a watch he found to the tribal chairman.

"A white man artifact, a sin," the chairman said, put the watch in his pouch.

I remember watches. They measured time in seconds, minutes, hours. They measured time exactly, coldly. I measure time with my breath, the sound of my hands across my own skin.

I make mistakes.

Last night I held my transistor radio in my hands, gently, as if it were alive. I examined it closely, searching for some flaw, some obvious damage. But there was nothing, no imperfection I could see. If there was something wrong, it was not evident by the smooth, hard plastic of the outside. All the mistakes would be on the inside, where you couldn't see, couldn't reach.

I held that radio and turned it on, turned the volume to maximum, until all I could hear was the in and out, in again, of my breath.

CRASH CART
Nancy Holder

Nancy Holder has published short stories in a wide variety of horror magazines and anthologies, including *Pulphouse*, *Obsessions*, and *Noctulpa*. Her story "Lady Madonna" won the Bram Stoker award in 1992. Her first novel, *Making Love* (written in collaboration with Melanie Tem), appeared in 1993 and more novels are on the way. She lives in San Diego, California.

"Crash Cart," reprinted from *Cemetery Dance* magazine, is a disturbing look at the other side of sexual abuse—the darkly erotic impulses of some abusers. The story steps out of the circle of abused and abuser, however, by including the doctors who must treat these victims, and the strange and chilling effect the experience can have on them.

—E.D.

Alan sat for a long moment with his eyes closed, allowing his fatigue and disappointment to wash through him like a gray haze. Felt himself drifting and sinking; if he didn't move, he would fall asleep. He opened his eyes and picked up his soup spoon, and was shocked at the amount of fresh blood on the sleeve of his scrubs. Perhaps he should have changed into fresh ones.

Then he looked down at his bowl of cream of spinach soup, and winced: It looked just like the stuff that had backed up through the feeding tube in Elle Magnuson's stomach two hours ago as she lay dying. That crap seeping out, then the minor geyser when her son tried to fix it.

Christ, why the hell had her family done that to her in the first place? All the Enfamil had done was feed the tumor, for weeks and days and hours, and the last, awful few seconds. Code Blue, and they had yelled and screamed for him to do something, even though everyone had spoken so rationally about no extraordinary measures when she had been admitted. Her daughter shrieking at him, shouting, crying. Her son, threatening to sue. Par for the course, Anita Guzman had assured him. She'd been a nurse for twenty years, and *hombre*, she had seen it all.

Dispiritedly, he slouched in his chair. He had really liked that old lady. Her death touched him profoundly; his sorrow must show, for no one came to sit with him in the cafeteria. He looked around at the chatting groups of two's and three's. How long before he became the type of doctor for whom nobody's death moved him? Par for the long haul, years and years of feeding tubes and blood. Why had he ever thought he wanted to be a doctor?

Maybe she had been special, and they wouldn't all be this way. Maybe that's why the feeding tube and the shrieking and the threats. It was so hard to let go, of certain people especially.

He pushed the soup away, marveling that he had been stupid enough to order it in the first place. He really had no appetite for anything. Which was bad; he had hours to go until his shift was over. He didn't understand why they worked first-year residents to death like this. He never had a chance to catch up; he always felt he was doing a half-assed job because he was so tired. What if he made a mistake that cost someone their life?

What if he could have done something to save Elle Magnuson? She'd been terminal; he knew that. But still.

Alan unwrapped a packet of crackers and nibbled on one. They would settle his stomach. Maybe. If anything could. Last Tuesday, when he had asked Mrs. Magnuson how she was feeling, she had opened her bone-dry mouth and said, "I sure would love a lobster dinner." And they looked at each other—no more lobster dinners for Elle Magnuson, ever, unless they served them in the afterlife. Jesus, how had she stood it? Spiraling downward so damn fast—her other daughter hadn't made it from Sacramento in time. It had been a blessing, that last, brutal slide, but it didn't seem that way now.

He dropped the cracker onto his food tray and wiped his face with his hands.

"Oh, God, Jonesy! *God!*" It was Anita. She was bug-eyed. She flopped into the chair across from his and picked up his soup spoon. "You're not gonna believe this!"

Before he could say anything, she threw down the spoon and grabbed his forearm. "Bell's wife was brought into the ER."

"What?"

"Yeah. And he comes flying in after the ambulance, just *screaming,* 'I want my wife! Right now!'" She imitated him perfectly except for her accent. "'I want her out of here!'"

Shocked, Alan opened his mouth to speak, but Anita went on. "Then they strip her down, and she's covered with welts, Alan. Cigarette burns. Bell's absolutely ballistic. And the paramedics drag MacDonald—that new ER guy?—over to a corner, and tell him there are whips and chains on their bed and manacles on the wall, and in the corner there's a fucking *crash cart.*" She gripped his arm and leaned forward, her features animated, her eyes flashing. "Do you know what I'm saying?"

He sat there, speechless. Eagerly she bobbed her head. "A crash cart," she said with emphasis. A crash cart, with the paddles that restarted your heart. A crash cart, that brought you back from the dead. In the Chief of Surgery's house.

For his wife.

He reeled. "Holy shit."

Her nails dug into him. "He would torture her so badly she'd go into cardiac arrest. Then he'd bring her back."

"With the crash cart?" His voice rose, cracked. He couldn't believe it. Bell was his mentor; Alan looked up to him like a father. Occasionally they talked about getting together to play chess. This had to be an April Fool's joke. In January.

"Believe it, *mi amor*." Anita bounced in her chair. "He's in custody." Alan stared at her. "I'm telling you the truth!"

"Bullshit," he said savagely.

"Is not! Go see for yourself. His wife's been admitted."

Numb. Scalp to sole. He ran his hand through his hair. A joke, a really stupid joke. Sure. Anita was Guatemalan and she had this very strange sense of humor. Like the time she had stuck that stuffed animal in the microwave. Now that was just sick . . .

"C'mon," she said, grabbing his wrist as she leaped to her feet. "Let's go check her out."

"Anita."

"C'mon. Everyone's going up there."

He'd often wondered what Dr. Bell's wife was like; there were no photos of her in Bell's office. He had imagined her beautiful, talented, supremely happy despite the fact that she and Dr. Bell had no children.

He jerked his hand away. "No," he said hoarsely. "I don't want to see her. And I think it's gross that you—"

"Oh, lighten up. She's unconscious, you know."

"I'm surprised at you." Although in truth he had peeked in on other patients whom doctors and nurses had talked about—the crazies, the unusual diseases, even the pretty women.

"Oh, for heaven's sake!" Anita laughed at him and let go of his arm. "Well, *I'm* going. I have twenty minutes of dinner left. It's room 512, if you're interested. Private. Of course."

"I'm not interested."

"Suit yourself." She grabbed his cracker packet and took the uneaten one, popped it in her mouth. "Eat your soup. You're too skinny."

She flounced away. At the doorway of the cafeteria, she saw more people she knew, and greeted them with a cry. "Guess what!" and they followed her out of the cafeteria.

Alan sat, unable to focus, to think. He couldn't believe it. He just couldn't believe it. Not Bell. Not this. It was a vicious rumor; he knew how fast gossip traveled in the hospital, and how much of it was a load of crap.

His stomach growled. During the long minutes he sat there, the soup developed a film over the surface. A membrane. He stared at it, thought about puncturing it. Making an incision. Making it the way it had been.

With a sigh he covered it with his napkin. Rest in peace, cream of spinach soup.

He jumped out of his chair when St. Pierre, a fellow resident, clapped him on the shoulder and said, "Jesus, Al, you hear about the old man?"

"Yeah." He wiped his face. "Yeah, I did."

Then he went into the men's room, thinking he would vomit. Instead, he cried.

At one in the morning, he went to the fifth floor. The nurses were busy at the station; he wore a doctor's coat and had a doctor's "I belong here" gait, and no one challenged or even noticed him.

The door to 512 was ajar. There was no chart.

A dim light was on, probably from the headboard.

He stood for a moment. Gawking like the other sickos, like someone slowing at an accident. Shit. He turned to go.

Couldn't.

Pushed open the door.

He walked quietly in.

She lay behind an ivory curtain; he saw the outline of her in her bed. The lights were from the headboard and they reflected oddly against the blank white wall, a movie about to begin, a snuff show. He walked past the curtain and looked sharply, quickly to the right, to see her all at once.

Oh, God. Black hair heaped in tangles on the pillow. IV's dangling on either side. An oxygen cannula in her nose. He drew closer. Her small face was mottled with bruises and cuts, but it could have been pretty, with large eyes and long lashes, and a narrow, turned-up nose. He couldn't tell what her mouth was like; it was too swollen.

She stirred. He didn't move. He was a doctor. He had a right to be here. He flushed, embarrassed with himself. All right, call it professional curiosity.

Gawking.

There were stitches along the scalp line. Jesus. He reached toward her but didn't touch her. Stared at the bruises, the long lashes, the poor lips. He saw in his mind Dr. Bell manacling her to the wall, doing . . . doing things . . .

. . . making her heart stop, my God, my God, what a fucking monster . . .

But what about her?

He wouldn't let that thought go farther, wouldn't blame the victim. He'd been commended last month for his handling of the evidence collection for a rape case. Dr. Bell had written a glowing letter: "Dr. Jones has shown a remarkable sensitivity toward his patients."

Dr. Bell. God. *Dr. Bell.*

How could she? How could she let him? Until her heart stopped. Until she was clinically *dead*.

Mrs. Magnuson had clung to life with a ferocity that had proven to be her detriment—cream of spinach—making her linger and suffer, almost literally killing the fabric of her family as they began to unravel under the strain.

He stared at her. And suddenly, he felt a rush of . . .

. . . anger . . .

so fierce he balled his fists. The blood rushed to his face; he clenched his teeth, God, he was so pissed off. He was—

"Jesus." Shocked, he took a step backward.

She stirred again. He thought she might be trying to speak, coming up from whatever she was doped up on.

In the corridor, footfalls squeaked on the waxed linoleum. He felt an automatic flash of anxiety, a little boy sneaking around in places he shouldn't be. Mrs. Magnuson had called him "son" and "honey," and he had liked her very much for it.

The footfalls squeaked on and he shook his head at his reaction. There were few places in the hospital he was actually barred from entering. His mind flashed on Dr. Bell shuffling through the morgue like some demented ghoul; sickened, he shut his eyes and decided to leave.

Instead, he found himself standing closer to her. His hand dangled near all those black curls; and for an instant, he thought hard about picking up some of those curls and pulling—

—hard—

"Jesus." He spoke the word aloud again and wiped his face with his hand. What the hell was wrong with him?

He had a hard-on. He couldn't believe it; he stepped backward and hurried from the room.

Down the corridor, where the physicians' showers were, he washed his face with cold water and dried it with a paper towel. His hands shook. He staggered backward and fell onto a beechwood bench that lined the wall. Across from him, gray lockers with names loomed over him: Jones, Barnette, Zuckerman. Dr. Bell had no locker here; of course he had his own office, his own facilities.

Hurting her.

Jesus. He buried his face in his hands, still shaking. Mrs. Magnuson would be absolutely incapable of believing what he had been thinking while he was in 512.

And what had that been?

He stood and walked out of the room. It was time to go home; he was overtired, overstimulated. Too much coffee, too much work. Losing the old lady. Mrs. Magnuson. She had a name. They all had names. But what was *her* name?

Mrs. Bell. Ms. Bell. What was the difference?

He hurried back down the corridor and back into 512.

She lay behind the curtain; the play of shadow and white somehow frightened him, but her silhouette drew him on. He almost ran to her; he was panting. He had another erection, or perhaps he had never lost the first one. He was propelled toward her, telling himself he didn't want to be here, didn't want, to, didn't. She was unconscious: Sleeping Beauty.

He touched her forearm. There were bruises, cigarette burns. Scars. Didn't her friends wonder? Did she have no friends? Bell was so friendly and outgoing, kind. He would have had lots of parties. He talked about barbecuing. His special sauce for ribs.

His chess proficiency, teasing Alan in a gentle way, telling him how he'd beat him if they ever played.

Beat him.

Alan found a place that had not been harmed and pressed gently. He moved his hand and pressed again.

On top of a bruise.

Pressed a little harder.

His erection throbbed against his scrubs. His balls felt rock-hard; God, he wanted—

—he wanted—

He pressed again, this time on a cigarette burn. Touched his cock. It was so hard. He was short of breath, and he wanted her so badly. He wanted—

He pinched the burn with the tips of his fingers, his short nails. He felt so dizzy he thought he might fall into her bed; he hoped he would. Swimming through something hot and active and moving; with volition and something so powerful, he stretched out his hand and cupped her breast. Squeezed her nipple. Squeezed harder.

She stirred. Her two blackened eyes fluttered open. He did not remove his hand. More blood was rushing to his cock, if that were possible. He was swaying with desire. The room spun. Those black eyes, staring at him, filled with tears as she smiled weakly.

"It's . . . okay," she whispered.

He jerked his hand away and drew it beneath his chin as if it had been severely injured.

"It's okay," she said again.

"I . . . I . . ." He averted his head as bile rose in his throat; he was sick to death; God, what had he been doing?

Her voice came again: "It's okay." Pleading. The hair rose on the back of his neck.

Oh, Christ, she wanted him to hurt her.

He wanted to do it.

As this time the vomit flooded his mouth, he ran from the room.

He didn't take a shower or change his scrubs. In the cold light of his car, he avoided the rearview mirror. He dropped the housekeys twice. His mouth tasted of sickness; he thought of Mrs. Magnuson's cream of spinach soup.

His roommate, Katrina, who was also a doctor but was not his girlfriend, had left on the TV without the sound; a strange habit of hers—she did that when she studied. There was a note that someone had called about the bicycle he wanted to sell. The bicycle. His patient had died and he had molested—

—tortured—

—crash cart—

He opened the fridge and grabbed a beer. Put it back and got Katrina's bottle of vodka out of the freezer. Swigged it. He felt so sick. He felt so disgusting.

There were sounds in her room. Deliberately he reduced his noise level; if she asked him what was wrong, he wouldn't be able to tell her.

Because he didn't know.

An hour later, puking his brains out. Katrina hovering in the background, muttering about God knew what. Praying to the ghost of Mrs. Magnuson, dreaming of Ms. Bell.

Of her versatile heart.

Of the power and the need of that heart.

that so often stopped,

that so often started.

Oh, God.

"What happened tonight?" Katrina was asking, had been asking, over and over and over. "What happened?"

"Lost a patient," he managed between bone-rattling heaves. His knees knocked the tequila bottle and it arced as if they were playing Spin-the-Bottle; they had agreed to be platonic and it had never been a problem. He liked her enormously, respected her.

"Oh, God, Alan. Oh." She stroked his hair. She had a glass of water at the ready; she was solicitous that way. If she'd known what he had done, she would probably move out. At the very least. Maybe she would have him arrested and thrown out of medicine.

"Mrs. Magnuson." He had told Katrina about her.

"Oh, I'm sorry." Soothing, sweet. He could feel himself shriveling inside. He was sick.

He was sick.

"Alan, drink this water." Rubbed his back, rubbed his shoulders.

It's okay.

He sobbed.

A few hours passed; he dozed, then slept. Finally at about seven he woke and realized he hadn't been very drunk; except for a draining sensation of fatigue, he was all right. Katrina left him some toast and a couple of aspirin and a note that said, "I'm really sorry. Hope you feel better."

He showered and changed his clothes, forced down the toast but not the aspirin, had coffee, and drove to the hospital. He had to talk to her, to apologize, to make what couldn't be right, right.

No one paid him much notice when he went into the hospital—a few bobbed heads, a mild expression of surprise that he was back so soon. He pushed the button for the staff elevator; as he waited, a young nurse whose name he couldn't remember joined him. She said, "Did you hear about Dr. Bell?" His terse nod cut off the conversation.

The elevator came. They both went in. He pushed five and stood apart from her, his hands folded. He watched the numbers; at four she left with a little smile. She was very pretty. As pretty as Ms. Bell might be.

The doors opened. Her room was to the left.

He turned right and walked into one of the supply rooms.

Got a hypo.

He put it in his trouser pocket and headed back toward the left. Perspiration beaded his forehead and his hands were wet. He felt cold and tired.

Filled with nervous anticipation.

Sick, Sick. He was almost to her room. He felt the hypo through the paper wrapper. He was going to stick it someplace. Into her shoulder, maybe, or her wrist.

Or her eye.

His erection was enormous; it had never been this big, or hard, or wanting.

God. He sagged against her door. Tears spilled down his face. He held onto the transom and took deep breaths.

He was going to go in there and she would want it.

"No," he murmured, but he was about to explode. "No."

"Hey." He started, whirled around. Anita Guzman stood in the hall. "You okay?"

"Man." He wondered if she could see his erection; as she stood looking at him, it started to go down.

"They're going to fry him," Anita hissed, lowering her voice. "Fucking fry that *chingada* asshole."

"What . . . ?" he asked faintly.

She blinked. "You don't know." She made a helpless shrug. "I had to pull an extra shift. Alan, Bell's wife died last night."

His heart jumped. "No."

She nodded vigorously. "It was her heart. They took her to ICU but—"

"No." He ducked his head inside the room. The ivory curtain was there, the form stretched behind it. He walk-ran toward her, his chest so tight that his breath stopped.

The dark curls, the small face. He whirled around. Anita stood in the doorway. He said. "But she's still here."

"No. I had the room wrong," she whispered, wrinkling her nose in confession. "Mrs. Bell was up on the sixth."

His stomach cramped and the room began to tilt crazily; with a trembling hand, he gripped the edge of the bed. "Then . . . who is this?"

Anita came around the curtain and barely looked at her. "I don't know. But it isn't Bell's wife. This place is full of battered women, you know? Well, I gotta get back." She gave him a wave, which he didn't return.

Not Bell's wife. Not Bell's work.

But partly his.

Dr. Bell, so kind and generous. Dr. Jones, so sensitive.

This place is full . . .

The woman opened her eyes. Her gaze met his, held it, would not let him look away. His penis bobbed inside his underwear.

"It's okay," she murmured. Her broken mouth smiled weakly. "Please. It really is."

SOME STRANGE DESIRE
Ian McDonald

Although born in Manchester, England, Ian McDonald has lived in Belfast, Northern Ireland for most of his life. His first story was published in 1982, and since then his work has appeared in various science fiction magazines and anthologies in Great Britain and the United States. His stories have been collected in *Empire Dreams* and *Speaking in Tongues*. His novels include *Desolation Road*, *Out on Blue Six*, *The Broken Land*, and most recently *Scissors Cut Paper Wrap Stone*. He won the Philip K. Dick Award in 1992 for his novel *King of Morning, Queen of Day*.

McDonald usually writes science fiction or fantastic realism. "Some Strange Desire" is a rare drift into horror for him—it is a chilling story that gives a deft twist to a popular horror archetype. It originally appeared in *OMNI Best Science Fiction Three*.

—E.D.

19 November, 10:30 P.M.

The *hru-tesh* is a beautiful piece of craftsmanship. Mother says he can remember Grandmother taking him, while still very small, to watch Josias Cunningham, Gunsmith by Appointment, of Fleet Street at work on it. In that small shop, in those small hours when the city slept, Josias Cunningham worked away while the spires and domes of Wren's dream of London rose from the ashes of the Great Fire, chasing and filing and boring and inlaying. It was a work of love, I suppose. A masterpiece he could never disclose to another living soul, for it was the work of demons. On the bone-handled stock is a filigreed silver plate on a pivot-pin. Underneath, an inscription: *Diabolus me Fecit*. The Devil Made Me.

He was *ul-goi* of course, Josias Cunningham, Gunsmith by Appointment, of Fleet Street.

After three hundred years, the firing mechanism is still strong and precise. It gives a definite, elegant click as I draw back the bolt and lock it.

Lights are burning in the apartment across the street. The white BMW sits rain-spattered under its private cone of yellow light. Have you ever known anyone who drives a white BMW to do anything or be anyone of any significance? I cannot say that I have, either. I blow on my fingers. I cannot let them become chilled. I cannot let their grip on the *hru-tesh* slacken and weaken. Hurry up and go about your business, *goi*, so I can go about mine and get back into the dry and the warm.

Cold rain finds me in my bolt-hole on the roof, penetrates my quilted jacket like needles. None so cold as the needle I have waiting for you, *goi*. I touch the thermos flask beside me, for luck, for reassurance, for the blessing of the *hahndahvi*.

Come on, *goi*, when are you going to finish what you are doing and go out to collect the day's takings from your boys? Voices are raised in the lighted apartment across the yellow-lit cobbled street. Male voices. I cannot make out the words, only the voices.

Even on my rooftop across the street, the blow is almost palpable. And then the weeping. A door slams. I uncap the thermos, shake a tiny sliver of ice into the breech of the *hru-tesh*. The street door opens. He is dressed in expensive leather sports gear. In the dark I cannot read the labels. He turns to swear one last time at the youth at the top of the stairs.

I let a drop of saliva fall from my tongue onto the needle of ice resting in the chamber. Slide the breech shut. Move from my cover. Take aim, double-handed, over the fire-escape rail.

Coptic crosses and peace medallions catch the yellow street light as he bends to unlock the car door. The silver filigree-work of the *hru-tesh* crafted by the three-hundred-year-dead hand of Josias Cunningham, Gunsmith by Appointment, glitters in that same light. I squeeze the trigger.

There is only the faintest *tok*.

He starts, stands up, clasps hand to neck. Puzzlement on his meatlike face. Puzzlement under that so-cool baseball cap at that ideologically correct angle. And it hits him. He keels straight over against the car. His head rests at a quizzical angle on the rain-wet metal. Complete motor paralysis.

I am already halfway down the fire escape. Flat shoes. No heels. I have it all planned. As I had thought, bundling him into the passenger seat is the hardest part of the operation. I think I may have broken a finger wresting the keys from him. It will be academic, soon enough. As I drive up through Bethnal Green and Hackney to Epping Forest I pass at least twenty other white BMWs. I sample his CD selection, then scan across the AM wavebands until I find some anonymous Benelux station playing hits from the forties. Childhood tunes stay with you all your life. I chat to him as we drive along. It is a rather one-sided conversation. But I do not think he would have been much of a conversationalist anyway. It is really coming down, the wipers are on high speed by the time we arrive at the car park. I shall get very wet. Another crime against you, *goi*.

It is wonderful how much can be expressed by eyes alone. Anger, incomprehension, helplessness. And, as I pull the syringe out of my belt-pouch, *terror*. I tap the cylinder a couple of times. I can tell from his eyes he has never seen so much in one needle before. He may consider himself honored. We have our own discreet sources, but we, like you, pay a price. I squat over him. He will take the image of who I am into the dark with him. Such is my intention.

"Hear these words: you do not touch us, you do not harass us, you do not try to recruit us or bully us into your stable. We are *tesh*, we are older and more powerful than you could possibly imagine. We have been surviving for centuries. Centuries."

He cannot even flinch from the needle.

I find a sheltered spot among the bushes and crushed flat lager cans, away from the steamed-up hatchbacks, and go into *tletchen*. I strip. I dress in the denims and shell-suit top I brought in my backpack. I stuff the rainsoaked clothes in around the *hru-tesh*. I go to the cardphone half a mile down the road and call a minicab to pick me up at the pub nearby and take me back to Shantallow Mews. The driver is pleased at the generosity of the tip. It is easy to be generous with the money of people who have no further use for it.

The *hru-tesh* goes back to its place under the hall floorboards. Rest there for a long time, beautiful device. The unused needles go into the kitchen sink to melt and run and lose themselves in the sewers of London town. The soaked clothes go into the machine, the jacket will need dry cleaning. I make tea for my sister, bring it to him on the Harrods tray with the shelduck on it.

The only light in the room is from the portable television at the foot of the bed. The remote control has slipped from his hand. His fingers rest near the "mute" button. Late-night/early morning horror. Vampires, werewolves, Freddies. A little saliva has leaked from his lips onto the pillow. So peaceful. On the pale blue screen, blood is drunk, limbs dismembered, bodies chain-sawn apart. I want that peace to last a little longer before I wake him. By the light of the screen I move around the room setting the watches and wards, the little shrines and votaries to the Five Lords of the *tesh* that keep spiritual watch around my sister. Père Teakbois the Balancer, Tulashwayo Who Discriminates, Filé Legbé Prince of the Changing Ways, Jean Tombibié with his bulging eyes and hands crossed over replete belly, Saint Semillia of the Mercies: the five *hahndahvi*. I trim wicks, tap ash from long curls of burned incense, pour small libations of beer and urine. I may not believe that *hahndahvi* are the literal embodiments of the character of the universe, I have lived long enough among the *goi* to know the universe is characterless, faceless. But I do believe power resides in symbol and ritual.

He is awake. The brightness in his eyes is only the reflection of the television screen. Awake now, he seems a thing of horror himself. Shrunken, shriveled, transparent skin drawn taut over bird bones, fingers quivering spastically as they grip the edge of the duvet. Trapped in that final *tletchen*, too weak to complete the transformation. His breasts are slack and withered like the dugs of old bitches.

"I've made tea, but it's probably cold now." I pour a cup, milk and sugar it, hold it steady as he lifts it to his lips. The tea is cold, but he seems glad of it.

"You were out." His voice is a grotesque whisper.

"Business." He understands. Our clients, both *ul-goi* and *goi*, are never *business*.

"That pimp?"

"He won't trouble you again. I can promise that."

"This isn't forty years ago. They've got computers, genetic fingerprinting."

"The people in the car park, if any of them even noticed, will tell them it was a woman got out of the car. The taxi driver will swear he drove a man."

"Still . . ."

I take his hand in mine, modulate my pheromone patterns to convey calm, assurance, necessity. It was more than just a pimp harassing us to join his stable, more than him breaking into this apartment, terrorizing my sick sister, overturning the furniture, desecrating the shrines of the *hahndahvi*. It was *security*, *tesh* security, which is more powerful and paranoid than any *goi* conception of the word, for it has its roots in ten thousand years of secrecy.

I offer him a Penguin biscuit. He shakes his head. Too weak. Too tired. I pull the stand from its position behind the headboard close by the side of the mattress. From the fridge in the kitchen I take the next-to-last bag of blood. As I run a line in, he says,

"There was a call for you. I couldn't get to it. Sorry. It's on the answering machine."

I am back in the kitchen, filling a basin with water. I test the temperature with my elbow.

"Vinyl Lionel?"

I fetch the natural sponge I bought from the almost-all-night chemist around the corner, whip the water to froth with Johnson's baby-bath.

"A new one," my sister Cassiopia says.

I pull back the duvet. The smell of the sickroom, the terrible smell of prolonged, engrained sickness, is overpowering. As the blood, my blood that I pumped out of myself into plastic bags yesterday, runs into him, drip by drip, I wash my sister's body. Gently. Lovingly. With the soft natural sponge and the gentle baby-bath; neck and arms and sagging, flat breasts, the small triangle of pubic hair and the tiny, wrinkled penis and testicles, smaller even than a child's, and the shriveled labia.

15–16 November

Only four days. It seems like a small forever, since the afternoon Cassiopia came back from the pitch at Somerville Road with twenty pounds in his pocket.

"He insisted on paying. One of the lace-G-string-and-stocking brigade. Took me back to his place. Why do they always have posters of racing cyclists on their walls?"

Though we do not do it for money—genetic material is the price we ask for our services—cash in hand is never refused. I had taken the twenty down to the off-license for a bottle of Californian Chardonnay and a sweet-and-sour pork while Cassiopia changed for the evening client, an *ul-goi* who liked to tie our wrists to the ceiling hooks while he slipped rubber bands around our breasts, more and more and more of them, tighter and tighter and tighter. Thank God once every six weeks seemed to satisfy him. Vinyl Lionel had Word he was Something in the Foreign Office. Whatever, he had taste in tailoring. We made sure he paid for his game with the rubber bands.

When I returned Cassiopia had *tletched*. He is very beautiful as a woman. When he *tletches*, it is like a flower blossoming. Yet there was a subtle change in the atmosphere, something in his personal aroma that smelled not right.

"It hurts," he said. "Here. Here. Here. And here . . ." He touched breasts, loins, neck and on the final *here*, pressed fingers into belly in the way that says *deep within, everywhere.*

Of course, you never think it can be you. Your lover. Your partner. Your sibling. I gave him two paracetamol and a cup of corner-store Chardonnay to wash them down with.

He scratched all night. I could not sleep for his scratching, scratching, scratching. In the shower he was covered in yellow crusted spots. The sting of hot water made him wince. Even then I pretended not to know. I convinced myself he had picked up some venereal bug from one of the *goi*. Despite the fact that our immune systems make us almost invulnerable to *goi* infections. Such was my self-deception, I even bought some under-the-counter antibiotics from the Almost-All-Night Pharmacy.

You can imagine the smell of sickness. It is not hard, even for your limited senses. Imagine, then, a whole street, a whole town, terminally sick, dying at once. That is what I smelled when I came home after an afternoon with a first-timer who had passed furtive notes—*what are you into . . . I'm into . . . I got a place . . .*—under the partitions of the cubicles in the gents' toilets.

I found him lying on the carpet, hands opening and closing spastically into tight, futile fists. He had failed halfway in *tletchen*, caught between like something half-melted and twisted by flame. I cleaned thin, sour, vomited-up coffee and slimmer's soup from his clothes. Over and over and over and over and over and over, he whispered, *Oh my God oh my God oh my God oh my God.* I got him into bed and a fistful of Valium down him, then sat by his side in the room that was filling with the perfume of poisoned earth, looking at everything and seeing only the shadow my thoughts cast as they circled beneath my skull.

We have a word for it in our language. *Jhash.* There is no direct translation into your languages. But you know it. You know it very well. It haunts your pubs and clubs and Saturday-night scores. It is the unspoken sermon behind every mint-scented condom machine on the toilet wall. Like ours, yours is a little word too. When I was small and ran in gray flannel shorts wild and heedless over the bombsites of Hackney Marshes, my grandmother, who was keeper of the mysteries, taught me that *jhash* was the price Père Teakbois the Balancer with his plumb-bob in his hand demanded of the *tesh* in return for their talents. I think that was the point at which my long, slow slide from faith began: Grandmother had been a gifted spinner of tales and his graphic descriptions of the terrible, enduring agony of *jhash* left me nightmarish and seriously doubting the goodness of a god who would deliberately balance the good gifts he had given us with such dreadfulness.

The bombsites have given way to the towerblocks of the post-war dream and those in turn to the dereliction and disillusionment of monetarist dogma and I no longer need faith for now I have biology. It is not the will of Perè Teakbois, Perè Teakbois himself is no more than the product of ten thousand years of institutionalized paranoia: *jhash* is a catastrophic failure of the endocrinal, hormonal and immune systems brought on by the biological mayhem of *tletchen*.

It can take you down into the dark in a single night. It can endure for weeks. None are immune.

Let me tell you the true test of caring. We may be different species, you and I, but we both understand the cold panic that overcomes us when we first realize that we are going to die. We understand that there is an end, an absolute end when this selfness will stop and never be again. And it terrifies us. Horrifies us. Paralyzes us, in the warmth of our beds, in the dark of the night with our loved ones beside us. The end. No appeal, no repeal, no exceptions.

You are *goi* and I am *tesh* and both love and life are different things between us but this we both understand, that when we contemplate the death of the one we love and it strikes that same paralyzing, cold panic into us as if it were we ourselves, that is caring. That is love. Isn't it?

20 November, 9:15 P.M.

Vinyl Lionel's Law: Everyone is either someone's pimp or someone's prostitute.

By that definition, Vinyl Lionel is our pimp, though he would be quite scandalized to think that the word could be applied to himself.

Vinyl Lionel subscribes to the roller-and-tray school of cosmetics and wears a studded leather collar. Studs, in one form or another, characterize Vinyl Lionel's personal style. Studded wristbands, studded peak to his black leather SS cap, studded motorbike boots pulled up over his zip-up PVC one-piece with studded thighs and shoulders.

I remember PVC from the Swinging Sixties. You sweated like shit in those boots and raincoats. Vinyl Lionel maintains they are trying to remix the Sixties for the Nineties. Vinyl Lionel should know about the Sixties. He has an old-age pensioner's free bus pass, but he won't show it to anyone. If the Nineties are anything like the Sixties, it will be that whatever is happening is always happening somewhere else. My memory of the Swinging Sixties is that they may have been swinging in the next street or the party next door, but never swinging in your street, at your party.

Strangefella's is the kind of place where advertising copywriters and the editors of those instantly disposable street culture magazines like to convince people they party all night when in fact they are at home, in bed, exhausted by their workloads, every night by ten-thirty. If the Nineties are swinging, it is somewhere else than Strangefella's. Vinyl Lionel has a customary pitch as far as the architecture will permit from the AV show and the white boys with the deeply serious haircuts doing things to record decks. He is always pleased to see me. The pleasure is mutual. When he has a couple of gin slings down him he can be a delightfully effervescent conversationalist.

"Darling heart, you're looking especially radiant tonight!" He kisses me, on the cheek, not the mouth-to-mouth soul kiss of *tesh* meeting. He calls for cocktails. "Your mother is well, dismal suburbia notwithstanding?"

I reply that business is booming, and tell him about the pimp.

"I heard about that on *News at Ten*. That was you? A gangland killing, they said, made to look like an overdose." He takes a Turkish from his silver cigarette case, taps it once, twice, three times. "That was bit of a bloody risk, wasn't it, dear heart?"

"He'd broken in. Credit him with some intelligence, he could have worked out something was going on."

"Still, Orion darling, you could have left him to us. It's our job to look after you, and yours to provide us with what we want. You people have a vicious streak a mile wide. One of your less endearing traits. Smoke?" I take the proffered cheroot.

"So, this new client."

Vinyl Lionel examines his chrome-polished nails. "Well, there's not a lot to say about him. Nice enough boy. You wouldn't think to look at him, but then you never do, do you? Fat Willy recruited him, you know, the usual way." He moistens a finger in his Singapore sling, draws a yin-yang symbol on the marble tabletop.

"How much does he know?"

"The bare minimum. He'll talk the leg off you, dear heart. One of those confessional types. Well, fiddle-dee-dee, if that isn't him now . . ." Vinyl Lionel waves flamboyantly, trying to attract the attention of the lost boy by the door, fidgeting and conspicuous in a chain-store gent's-ready-made suit. "Oh God, I told him don't dress up, Strangefella's isn't that kind of place, and what does he do? Well, don't blame me if the gorillas bounce him."

"Nerves, Lionel," I say. "You were as bad the first time."

"Bitch," says Vinyl Lionel. He resents any overt reminder of his fall from youth and beauty while we remain changeless, ageless, ever-young. He beckons the young man between the tables and the smokes and the backbeat and the bass. "I'll bet you fifty he drives a Ford."

One bet I won't be taking, Lionel. A Ford Sierra, metallic gray, F-registration, the odd rust spot. Something to do with metallic finishes, I always think. Garfield crucified upside down on the back window. Open the glove compartment and cassettes fall out. Home bootlegs, all of them, apart from the mandatory copy of *Graceland*. Nothing more recent than three years ago.

He is nervous. I can smell it over his Heathrow Duty-Free aftershave. Nerves, and something I cannot quite place, but seems familiar. I do not much like being driven by someone who is so nervous. Gaily lit buses swing past headed down across the river South London way; girls in smogmasks, denim cut-offs over cycling shorts and ski-goggles weave past on clunking ATBs like the outriders of some totalitarian, body-fascist invasion. I light up a cheroot Vinyl Lionel gave me as a keepsake as we surge and stop, surge and stop along Shaftesbury Avenue. Lionel, the outrageous old *ul-goi*, was right. This one seems to want to talk but is afraid of me. I weave pheromones, draw him into a chemical web of confidence. On New Oxford Street, he opens.

"I cannot believe this is happening," he says. "It's incredible; that something so, so, *huge*, could have been secret for so long."

"It has several thousand years of pedigree as a working relationship," I say. "As long as there have been *tesh*, there have been *ul-goi*. And our mutual need for secrecy from the *goi*."

"Goi?"

"Humans." I wave a lace-gloved hand at the rain-wet people huddling along Holborn. "Those. The ignorant mass."

"And *tesh*?"

I draw a circle on the misted-up quarter-light, bisect it with a curving S-shape. Yin and yang. Male and female in one. From time before time the symbol of the *tesh*.

"And *ul-goi*?"

"Those who can only achieve sexual satisfaction with a *tesh*."

The word seems to release him. He closes his eyes for a reckless moment, sighs. "It's funny. No, it's not funny, it's tragic, it's frightening. It's only recently I've found where it started. When I was a kid I read this comic, the *Eagle* or the *Lion* or the *Victor*. There was one story, one scene, where this skindiver is trying to find out who's been sabotaging North Sea drilling rigs and the bad guys catch him and tie him to the leg of the rig until his air runs out. That was where it started for me, with the guy in the rubber suit tied and helpless, with death inevitable. It was such an anticlimax when he got rescued in the next issue. I used to fantasize about wetsuits. I must have been Jacques Cousteau's number one fan." He laughs. Beneath folding umbrellas, girls in Sixties-revival PVC raincoats and Gerry-Anderson-puppet hairdos dart between the slowly grinding cars, giggling and swearing at the drivers. "You don't know what it is at that age. But it was a major motivation in my childhood: tight clothing. Superheroes, of course, were a real turn-on. I remember one, where the Mighty Thor was being turned into a tree. Jesus! I nearly creamed myself. I was addicted to downhill skiing. If there was ever anything in the Sunday color supplements about downhill skiing, or ballet, I would cut it out, sneak it up to my room and stare at it under the sheets by the light from my electric blanket switch.

"Jane Fonda was, like, the answer to my prayers. I used to borrow my sister's leotard and tights and dress up, just to feel that head-to-toeness. Sometimes . . . sometimes, when the evenings were dark, I'd pass on late-night shopping with the family so I could dress up, nip over the back fence onto our local sports field and walk about. Just walk about. It was good, but it wasn't enough. There was something in there, in my head, that wanted something more but couldn't tell me what it was.

"When I was about seventeen I discovered sex shops. The number of times I would just walk past because I never had the nerve to push that door and go in. Then one day I decided it couldn't be any harder going in than just walking past. It was like Wonderland. I spent the fifty pounds I'd been saving in one pig-out. There was one magazine, *Mr. S.M.* . . . I'd never seen anything like it before, I didn't know people could do that sort of thing to each other. Then, after I'd read them all twenty, fifty, a hundred times, I realized it wasn't doing it anymore. I bought new mags, but they were the same: there were things going on in my head that were far, far more exciting than what was going on in those photographs. In my best fantasies, there were things like no one had ever thought of before."

"This happens," I say. They all think they are the only ones. They start so differently, men and women, back among the sand castles and Dinky toys and Cindy dolls of childhood; they think there cannot be anyone else like them. But already they are being drawn toward us, and each other. They realize that what excites frenzies of passion in others leaves them cold and uncomprehending, and everything falls apart: friends, lovers, jobs, careers, hopes, dreams, everything except the search for that something that will fulfill the fantasy in their heads. Can anyone be as tormented, as depraved, as they? I do not disillusion them: fantasies and confessions, and the small absolutions and justifications I can offer; these are treasures held close to the heart. Tell me your story, then, *ul-goi* boy in your best suit, and I will listen, for, though it is a story I have heard ten thousand times before, it is a story that deserves to be heard. You have had the courage that so many lack, the courage to reach for what you truly want.

For the homosexual, it is the image in the mirror.

For the transvestite, it is the flight from ugliness to imagined true beauty.

For the sado-masochist, it is the two-edged embrace of guilt.

For the bondage enthusiast, it is the relieved plummet from the burden of being adult into the helplessness of childhood.

For the rubber fetishist, it is the return to the total comforting enclosure of the womb.

For the *ul-goi*, it is the frustration of desiring to be what they *are* and what they *are not* simultaneously.

Where have all the fluorescent re-spray Volkswagen Beetles started to come from?

What is he saying now? About some 0898 Sexline he used to dial called "Cycle Club Lust"; how he sat hanging on the line running up obscene bills waiting for the payoff that never came. How Telecom regulations compel them to use words like "penis" and "buttocks" and "breasts." How can you get off on words like that? he says.

And I sense it again. A scent . . . Almost totally masked by my own pheromone patterns; that certain uncertainty. I know it. I know it . . . Tower cranes decked out with aircraft warning lights like Christmas decorations move through the upper air. Towers of London. Close to home now. I show him a place to park the car where it will be fairly safe. In this area, you do not buy car stereos, you merely rent them from the local pub. On the street, with his coat collar turned up against the drizzle, he looks desperately vulnerable and uncertain. The merest waft of pheromones is enough to firm that wavering resolution. Gentle musks carry him through the front door, past the rooms where we cater for the particular tastes of our *goi* clients, up the stairs and along the landing past Cassiopia's room, up another flight of stairs to the room at the top. The room where the *ul-goi* go.

18 November

On the third day of the *jhash*, I went to see Mother, a forty-five-minute train journey past red-brick palazzo-style hypermarkets under Heathrow's sound-footprint.

When the great wave of early-Fifties slum clearance swept the old East End out into the satellite New Towns, it swept Mother and his little empire with it. Three years after the bombing stopped, the Blitz really began, he says. After three hundred years of metropolis, he felt a change of environment would do him good. He is quite the born-again suburbanite; he cannot imagine why we choose to remain in the city. With his two sisters, our aunts, he runs a discreet and lucrative brothel from a detached house on a large estate. The deviations of suburbia differ from, but are no less deviations than, the deviations of the city, and are equally exploitable.

As Mother opened the door to me an elderly man in a saggy black latex suit wandered down from upstairs, saw me, apologized and vanished into the back bedroom.

"It's all right dear, he's part of the family," Mother shouted up. "Really, you know, I should stop charging him. He's been coming twenty years, boy and man. Every Tuesday, same thing. Dresses up in the rubber suit and has your Aunt Ursa sit on his face. Happily married; he's invited us to his silver wedding anniversary party; it's a nice thought but I don't think it's really us, do you?"

To the eye they were three fortysomething slightly-but-not-too-tarty women, the kind you see pushing shopping trolleys around palazzo-style hypermarkets, or in hatchbacks arriving at yoga classes in the local leisure center rather than the kind that congregate at the farthest table in bars to drink vodka and laugh boorishly.

My mother was born the same year that Charles II was restored to the monarchy.

We kissed on the mouth, exchanging chemical identifications, tongue to tongue. I made no attempt to mask my feelings; anxiety has a flavor that cannot be concealed.

"Love, what is it? Is it that pimp again? Is he giving bother?" He sniffed deeply. "No. It's Cassiopia, isn't it? Something's happened to him. The Law? Darling, we've High Court judges in our pockets. No, something else. Worse. Oh no. Oh dear God no."

Chemical communication is surer and less ambiguous than verbal. Within minutes my aunts, smelling the alarm on the air, had cut short their appointments with their clients and congregated in the back room where no non-*tesh* was ever permitted. In the deep wing-chair drawn close to the gas heater sat my grandmother, seven hundred years old and almost totally submerged into the dark, mind wandering interminably and with death the only hope of release from the labyrinth of his vast rememberings. His fingers moved in his lap like the legs of stricken spiders. We spoke in our own language, sharp-edged whispers beneath the eyes of the *hahndahvi* in their five Cardinal Points up on the picture rail.

Jhash. It was made to be whispered, that word.

I suggested medical assistance. There were prominent doctors among the *ul-goi*. Sexual inclinations do not discriminate. What with the advances *goi* medicine had made, and the finest doctors in the country, surely something . . .

"It must be concern for your sister has temporarily clouded your judgment," whispered Aunt Lyra, "otherwise I cannot imagine you could be so stupid as to consider delivering one of us into the hands of the *goi*."

My mother hushed him with a touch to his arm.

"He could have put it a bit more subtly, love, but he's right. It would be no problem to recruit an *ul-goi* doctor, but doctors don't work in isolation. They rely upon a massive edifice of researchers, technicians, laboratories, consultants: how long do you think it would be before some *goi* discovered the truth about Cassiopia?"

"You would let my sister, your daughter die, rather than compromise security?"

"Do not ask me to answer questions like that. Listen up. One of our regulars here is an *ul-goi* lawyer. Just to make conversation I asked him once what our legal position was. This is what he told me: we may think and talk and look like humans, but we are not human. And, as non-humans, we are therefore the same as animals—less than animals; most animals enjoy some protection under the law, but not us. They could do what they liked to us, they could strip us of all our possessions, jail us indefinitely, use us to experiment on, gas us, hunt us down one by one for sport, burn us in the street, and in the eyes of the law it would be no different from killing rats. We are not human, we are not under the protection of the law. To compromise our secrecy is to threaten us all."

"He is dying and I want to know what to do."

"You know what to do." The voice startled me. It was like the voice of an old, corroded mechanism returning to life after long inactivity. "You know what to do," repeated my grandmother, stepping through a moment of lucidity into this last decade of the millennium. "Can I have taught you so badly, or is it you were such poor pupils? Père Teakbois the Balancer demanded *jhash* of us in return for our enormously long lives, but Saint Semillia of the Mercies bargained a ransom price. Blood. The life is in the blood; that life may buy back a life."

Of course I knew the story. I even understood the biological principle behind the spurious theology. A massive blood transfusion might stimulate the disrupted immune system into regenerating itself, in a similar sense to the way our bodies rebuild themselves by using *goi* sex cells as template. I had known the answer to *jhash* for as long as I had known of *jhash* itself: why had I refused to accept it and looked instead for, yes, ludicrous, yes, dangerous alternatives that could not possibly work?

Because Saint Semillia of the Mercies sells his dispensation dear.

Mother had given me a shoeboxful of equipment, most of it obsolete stuff from the last century when the last case of *jhash* had occurred. She did not tell me the outcome. Either way, I was not certain I wanted to know. In the house on Shantallow Mews I ran a line into my arm and watched the *Six O'clock News* while I pumped out two plastic bags. Internecine warfare in the Tory party. Some of the faces I knew, intimately. The blood seemed to revive Cassiopia but I knew it could only be temporary. I could never supply enough: after only two pints I was weak and trembling. All I could do was hold the sickness at bay. I took the icon of Saint Semillia of the Mercies down from the wall, asked it what I should do. His silence told me nothing I did not already know myself. *Out there. They are few, they are not perfect, but they exist, and you must find them.* I *tletched*, dressed in black leotard, black tights, black mini, black heels, wrapped it all under a duster coat and went down to the Cardboard Cities.

What is it your philosophers teach? That we live in the best of all possible worlds? Tell that to the damned souls of the cardboard cities in the tunnels under your railway stations and underpasses. *Tesh* have no such illusions. It has never been a tenet of our faith that the world should be a good place. Merely survivable.

Cloaked in a nimbus of hormonal *awe*, I went down. You would smell the piss and the beer and the smoke and the dampness and something faint and semi-perceived you cannot quite recognize. To me that thing you cannot recognize is what is communicated most strongly to me. It is despair. Derelicts, burned out like the hulls of Falklands' warships, waved hallucinatory greetings to me as I swirled past, coat billowing in the warm wet wind that blew across the wastelands. Eyes moved in cardboard shelters, cardboard coffins, heads turned, angered by the violation of their degradation by one who manifestly did not share it. When it is all you possess, you treasure even degradation. Figures gathered around smudge fires, red-eyed from the smoke, handing round hand-rolled cigarettes. Where someone had scraped enough money for batteries there was dance music from boom boxes. They would not trouble me. My pheromones made me a shadowy, godlike figure moving on the edge of the darkness.

Where should I go? I had asked.

Where no one will be missed, my mother had replied.

I went to the viaduct arches, the motorway flyovers, the shop doorways, the all-nite burger-shops, the parking lots and playgrounds. I went down into the tunnels under the stations. Trains ground overhead, carrying the double-breasted suit men and cellphone women back to suburbs ending in "ing" or "wich," to executive ghettos with names like Elmwood Grove and Manor Grange. The tunnels boomed and rang, drops of condensation fell sparkling in the electric light from stalactites seeping from the expansion joints in the roof. I paused at the junction of two tunnels. Something in the air, a few vagrant lipid molecules carried in the air currents beneath the station.

How will I know them? I had asked.

You will know them, my mother had said.

The trail of pheromones was fickle, more absent that present. It required the utmost exercise of my senses to follow it. It led me down clattering concrete stairways and ramps, under striplights and dead incandescent bulbs, down, under-ground. As I was drawn deeper, I dissolved my aura of *awe* and wove a new spell: *allure*. Certain now. Certain. The lost children in their cribs barely acknowledged my presence, the air smelled of shit and *ganja*.

She had found a sheltered corner under a vent that carried warmth and the smell of frying food from some far distant point of the concourse. An outsize Aran sweater—much grimed and stretched—was pulled down over her hunched-up knees. She had swaddled herself in plastic refuse sacks, pulled flattened cardboard boxes that had held washing machines and CD midi-systems in around her.

I enveloped her in a shroud of pheromones. I tried to imagine what she might see, the tall woman in the long coat, more vision than reality, demon, angel, standing over her like judgment. How could she know it was my pheromones, and not her own free will, that made her suddenly want more than anything, anything she had ever wanted in her life, to bury her face between my nylon-smooth thighs? I knelt down, took her chin in my hand. She looked into my eyes, tried to lick my fingers. Her face was filthy. I bent toward her and she opened her mouth to me. She ran her tongue around the inside of my lips; whimpering, she tried to ram it down my throat.

And I was certain. Truth is in the molecules. I had tasted it.

I extended a hand and she took it with luminous glee. She would have done anything, anything for me, anything, if I would only take her away from these tunnels and the stink of piss and desperation, back to my apartment: I could do whatever I wanted, anything.

The corridors shook to the iron tread of a train.

She loved me. Loved me.

With a cry, I snatched my hand from the touch of her fingers, turned, walked away, coat flapping behind me, heels ringing like shots. Faster. Faster. I broke into a run. Her calls pursued me through the tunnels, *come back come back, I love you, why did you go, I love you. . . .*

I rode the underground into the take-away-curry-and-tins-of-lager hours. *We are not human,* my mother told me from every poster and advertisement, *we cannot afford the luxuries of human morality.* Saint Semillia of the Mercies smiled upon me. I rode the trains until the lights went out, one by one, in the stations behind me, and came home at last to Shantallow Mews.

The house looked and smelled normal. There was nothing to see. From the outside. He had broken in through a rear window and trashed a path through the rooms where we entertained the *goi*. Finding the locked door, he had kicked his way into Cassiopia's room.

The pimp had done a thorough and professional job of terror. Empty glasses and cups of cold tea shattered, a half-completed jigsaw of the Royal Family a thousand die-cut pieces scattered across the floor, magazines torn in two, the radio-cassette smashed in by a heel. Shredded cassette tape hung in swaths from the lights and stirred in the draft from the open door when I stood. The metal stand by the bedside was overturned; the blood, my blood, was splashed and daubed across the walls.

Cassiopia was in the corner by the window, shivering and dangerously pale from shock. Under the duvet he clutched the icons of the five *hahndahvi* and a kitchen knife. Bruises purpled down the side of his face, he flinched from my gentlest touch.

"He said he'd be back," my sister whispered. "He said unless we worked for him, he'd be back again. And again. And again. Until we got wise."

I made him comfortable on the sofa, cleaned the blood from the walls, made good the damage. Then I went to the never-quite-forgotten place under the floorboards and unearthed the *hru-tesh*.

Saint Semillia, the price of your mercies!

20 November, 10:30 P.M.

But for the insistence of my perfumes urging him through the door at the top of the stairs, I think he would run in terror from what he is about to do. Often they do. But they are always drawn back to this door, by the sign of the yin-yang drawn in spilled vodka on a tabletop, by addresses on matchbooks or slipped under toilet partitions. They come back because nothing else can satisfy them.

The *hahndahvi* placed at their five cardinal points about the room fascinate him. He turns the icon of Filé Legbé over and over in his hands.

"This is old," he says.

"Early medieval," I say, offering him a drink from the cocktail bar. He takes a tequila in one nervous swallow. "The *hahndahvi*. The Five Lords of the *tesh*. We have our own private religion; a kind of urban witchcraft, you could call it. Our own gods and demons and magics. They've taken a bit of a theological bashing with the advent of molecular biology, when we realized that we weren't the demonic lovers, the incubi and succubi of medieval legend. Just a variant of humanity. A subspecies. Two chromosomes separate me from you." As I am talking, he is undressing. He looks for a wardrobe where he can hang his smart suit and shirt and jazz-colored silk tie. I slide open one of the mirror-robes at the end of the room. His fastidiousness is cute. I pour him another tequila so that he will not be self-conscious in his nakedness and guide him to the Lloyd-loom chair at the opposite side of the room. As I seat him I smell it again, that uncertain something, masked and musked in a cocktail of his own sweat, aftershave and José Cuervo. Familiar.

He sips his drink, small, tight, fearful sips, as I strip down to my underwear. I slowly peel off panties, stockings, suspenders, kick them away. His penis comes up hard, sudden, taking him by surprise. The glass falls to the floor. The tequila spreads across the carpet. He begins to masturbate slowly, ecstatically. Standing naked before him, I slip into *tletchen*. I feel the familiar warmth behind my eyes as waves of endocrines and hormones surge out through my body. I will them into every part of me, every empty space, every cell, every molecule of me. I am on fire, burning up from inside with chemical fire.

"Do you know anything about mitosis and meiosis?" I ask him as the hormones burn through me, changing me. *Moses supposes mitosis are roses. Moses supposes erroneously.* "The old legend was that incubi and succubi visited humans to steal sexual fluids. Sperm, eggs. It's true, insofar as we need haploid cells to self-impregnate every cell in our bodies and, in a sense, continually give birth to ourselves. That's how we live five, six, seven hundred years, world events permitting. Though, of course, our reproductive rate is very very low." I have found over the years that many of them find the talking as exciting as the physical act. It is the thrill of abandoning themselves to the implacably alien. As I speak my breasts, so full and beautiful, dwindle and contract to flat nipples; the pads of flesh on my hips and ass are redistributed to shoulders and belly; muscles contract my pelvis; my entire body profile changes from wide-hipped narrow-shouldered hourglass femininity to broad-shouldered, flat-chested narrow-waisted triangular masculinity. My genitals swell and contract and jut and fold themselves into new configurations. It excited me enormously, that first time when Mother guided me into *tletchen*, the ebb and swell of my genitals. Now what I sense is an incompleteness, a loss, when I change from female to male. But I can see what a shock of excitement it is to my client.

I come to him, let him savor my new masculinity. He runs his fingers over my flat chest, twists my flat nipples between thumb and finger, caresses my buttocks, thighs, genitals. As he thrills to me, I continue, my voice an octave lower.

"We're essentially an urban phenomenon. We were there in the cities of the Nile and Indus, of Mesopotamia, of Classical Greece and Rome—some lesser members of their respective pantheons are *tesh* in disguise. We need a large population to draw genetic material from without becoming too obvious—in rural communities we have rather too high a profile for our liking. Hence the medieval legends, when the country was almost entirely rural, which died out with urbanization when we could become anonymous in the cities. My particular family came with the Norman invasion; but we're comparative new kids on the block; the branch we bred into one hundred and fifty years back up in Edinburgh has been here since the end of the Ice Age."

There are tears in his eyes. Pressed close within his embrace, I smell it again. Intimate. Familiar.

Too familiar.

I know what it is, and where I have smelled it before. But I am not finished with him yet. I step backward, out of the reach of his imploring fingers and summon up the *tletchen* energy again. Contours, profiles, genders melt and run in the heat of my hormonal fire. My body, my identity, my *tesh*ness, my Orionness dissolve into a multiplicity of possible genders. I blossom out of genderlessness into full hermaphroditism. Male and female, yin and yang in one. He is sobbing now, milking his penis in long, slow, joyous strokes. He is close now to complete sexual satisfaction for the first time in his life. I let him touch me, explore the mystery of my two-in-oneness. He stands, presses his body to mine, shuddering, moaning; long keening, dying moans. Exposed. Truly naked. From every pore of his body, every gland and mucous membrane and erogenous tissue, it pours out. The room whirls with his giddy perfume, the storm of chemicals is overpowering. *Yes! Yes! Yes!*

I look into his eyes.

"Do you know how we get our names?" I tell him. "We have public, *goi*, names, but among ourselves we use our *tesh* names. We are named after whatever constellation is in the ascendant on the night of our birth. My name is Orion. My sister is Cassiopia." I tell him, because I want him to know. I owe him at least a name. I open my mouth to kiss him, he opens to receive me. Thin ropes of drool stretch and break. I taste him. And he is right. It is the work of moment for my saliva glands to work the chemical changes. A drop of toxin falls from my tongue onto his. It runs like chain lighting from neuron to neuron. Even as the thought to react, the awareness that he may have been betrayed, is upon him, it locks him into rigidity.

He is easy to lift. In hermaphrodite gender we have the benefit of the musculature of both sexes, and the hormonal violence of *tletchen* gives us a supernatural strength. I carry him down the stairs and along the little landing into Cassiopia's room. I can feel his heart beating against my shoulder. He fits comfortably into the bedside chair.

Cassiopia is suspended in a fever dream between sleep and waking; muttering, crying out, twitching, eyeballs rolled up in his head, crazy with hallucinations. I fetch the equipment from the Reebok box under the bed, run a line into Cassiopia's right arm, and let the blue, burned poison drip from his arm into a basin on the floor.

Only his eyes can move. He sees the needle I have for him. Have I said elsewhere it is remarkable how much can be expressed by the eyes alone? Say a thing once, and you are sure to have to say it again, soon. He does not flinch as I run a line into his right arm and connect him to Cassiopia. As I pump his blood along the old rubber tubes, I tell him the tale my grandmother told me, of Père Teakbois's bargain and the price of St. Semillia's mercy. At the very end, he deserves to know. And at the very end, I think he does begin to understand. Vinyl Lionel's Law. Everyone is someone's pimp, someone's prostitute. Everyone is user or used. Down in the tunnels, she had loved me. You had desired me. She had not loved me of her own free will. You did. I made her love me. I did not make you desire me. Understand, *goi*, why I could kill the pimp without a moment's moral uncertainty, why now it is your blood pulsing down the rubber tube. We were both the used, she and I. You and he, the users. Believe me, *goi* boy, I bear you no malice. I do what I do because an older, harder mercy demands it.

When the last drop is gone, I close the tubes. Cassiopia has lapsed into a quiet and tranquil sleep. Already the *jhash* pallor is gone from his skin, he is warm to my kiss.

I look at the boy, the rigor of my neurotoxins glazed over now with the serenity of death. When you went to those clubs and bars and made those contacts, did they never tell you the unwritten law of the user?

Every prostitute has his price.

In *tesh*, the words for *love* and *passion* are antonyms. It is not so different, I think, with you.

THE DOG PARK

Dennis Etchison

A resident of Los Angeles, Dennis Etchison has been selling stories since the late 1960s and is now one of the genre's most highly regarded writers of short fiction. His work has won the World Fantasy Award and the British Fantasy Award, and it has been collected in three volumes, *The Dark Country*, *Red Dreams*, and *Blood Kiss*. He has published two novels, *Dark Side* and *Shadowman*, and he is working on a novel called *California Gothic*. Etchison has also written scripts for film and television and is currently developing *American Zombie*, a feature script from a story by himself and Stephen Jones. He has edited several important cross-genre anthologies: three volumes of *Masters of Darkness*, *Cutting Edge*, *Lord John Ten*, and the 1993 World Fantasy Award-winning *Metahorror*.

Etchison's own work is frequently indefinable with regards to genre, but it is usually dark and disturbing. "The Dog Park," from *Dark Voices 5*, shows the influence of living near and doing business in Lala Land.

—E.D.

Madding heard the dogs before he saw them.

They were snarling at each other through the hurricane fence, gums wet and incisors bared, as if about to snap the chain links that held them apart. A barrel-chested boxer reared and slobbered, driving a much smaller Australian kelpie away from the outside of the gate. Spittle flew and the links vibrated and rang.

A few seconds later their owners came running, barking commands and waving leashes like whips.

"Easy, boy," Madding said, reaching one hand out to the seat next to him. Then he remembered that he no longer had a dog of his own. There was nothing to worry about.

He set the brake, rolled the window up all the way, locked the car and walked across the lot to the park.

The boxer was far down the slope by now, pulled along by a man in a flowered shirt and pleated trousers. The Australian sheepdog still trembled by the fence. Its owner, a young woman, jerked a choke chain.

"Greta, sit!"

As Madding neared the gate, the dog growled and tried to stand.

She yanked the chain harder and slapped its hind-quarters back into position.

"Hello, Greta," said Madding, lifting the steel latch. He smiled at the young woman. "You've got a brave little dog there."

"I don't know why she's acting this way," she said, embarrassed.

"Is this her first time?"

"Pardon?"

"At the Dog Park."

"Yes . . ."

"It takes some getting used to," he told her. "All the freedom. They're not sure how to behave."

"Did you have the same trouble?"

"Of course." He savored the memory, and at the same time wanted to put it out of his mind. "Everybody does. It's normal."

"I named her after Garbo—you know, the actress? I don't think she likes crowds." She looked around. "Where's your dog?"

"Down there, I hope." Madding opened the gate and let himself in, then held it wide for her.

She was squinting at him. "Excuse me," she said, "but you work at Tri-Mark, don't you?"

Madding shook his head. "I'm afraid not."

The kelpie dragged her down the slope with such force that she had to dig her feet into the grass to stop. The boxer was nowhere in sight.

"Greta, heel!"

"You can let her go," Madding said as he came down behind her. "The leash law is only till three o'clock."

"What time is it now?"

He checked his watch. "Almost five."

She bent over and unfastened the leash from the ring on the dog's collar. She was wearing white cotton shorts and a plain, loose-fitting top.

"Did I meet you in Joel Silver's office?" she said.

"I don't think so." He smiled again. "Well, you and Greta have fun."

He wandered off, tilting his face back and breathing deeply. The air was moving, scrubbed clean by the trees, rustling the shiny leaves as it circulated above the city, exchanging pollutants for fresh oxygen. It was easier to be on his own, but without a dog to pick the direction he was at loose ends. He felt the loss tugging at him like a cord that had not yet been broken.

The park was only a couple of acres, nestled between the high, winding turns of a mountain road on one side and a densely overgrown canyon on the other. This was the only park where dogs were allowed to run free, at least during certain hours, and in a few short months it had become an unofficial meeting place for people in the entertainment industry. Where once pitches had been delivered in detox clinics and the gourmet aisles of Westside supermarkets, now ambitious hustlers frequented the Dog Park to sharpen their networking skills. Here starlets connected with recently divorced producers, agents jockeyed for favor with young executives on the come, and actors and screenwriters exchanged tips about veterinarians, casting calls and pilots set to go to series in the fall. All it took was a dog, begged, borrowed or stolen, and the kind of desperate gregariousness that causes one to press business cards into the hands of absolute strangers.

He saw dozens of dogs, expensive breeds mingling shamelessly with common mutts, a microcosm of democracy at work. An English setter sniffed an unshorn French poodle, then gave up and joined the pack gathered around a honey-colored cocker spaniel. A pair of Great Dane puppies tumbled over each other golliwog-style, coming to rest at the feet of a tall, humorless German shepherd. An Afghan chased a Russian wolfhound. And there were the masters, posed against tree trunks, lounging at picnic tables, nervously cleaning up after their pets with long-handled scoopers while they waited to see who would enter the park next.

Madding played a game, trying to match up the animals with their owners. A man with a crewcut tossed a Frisbee, banking it against the setting sun like a translucent UFO before a bull terrier snatched it out of the air. Two fluffed Pekingnese waddled across the path in front of Madding, trailing colorful leashes; when they neared the gorge at the edge of the park he started after them reflexively, then stopped as a short, piercing sound turned them and brought them back this way. A bodybuilder in a formfitting T-shirt glowered nearby, a silver whistle showing under his trimmed moustache.

Ahead, a Labrador, a chow and a schnauzer had a silkie cornered by a trash bin. Three people seated on a wooden bench glanced up, laughed, and returned to the curled script they were reading. Madding could not see the title, only that the cover was a bilious yellow-green.

"I know," said the young woman, drawing even with him, as her dog dashed off in an ever-widening circle. "It was at New Line. That was you, wasn't it?"

"I've never been to New Line," said Madding.

"Are you sure? The office on Robertson?"

"I'm sure."

"Oh." She was embarrassed once again, and tried to cover it with a self-conscious cheerfulness, the mark of a private person forced into playing the extrovert in order to survive. "You're not an actor, then?"

"Only a writer," said Madding.

She brightened. "I knew it!"

"Isn't everyone in this town?" he said. "The butcher, the baker, the kid who parks your car . . . My drycleaner says he's writing a script for Tim Burton."

"Really?" she said, quite seriously. "I'm writing a spec script."

Oh no, he thought. He wanted to sink down into the grass and disappear, among the ants and beetles, but the ground was damp from the sprinklers and her dog was circling, hemming him in.

"Sorry," he said.

"That's OK. I have a real job, too. I'm on staff at Fox Network."

"What show?" he asked, to be polite.

"C.H.U.M.P. The first episode is on next week. They've already ordered nine more, in case Don't Worry, Be Happy gets cancelled."

"I've heard of it," he said.

"Have you? What have you heard?"

He racked his brain. "It's a cop series, right?"

"Canine-Human Unit, Metropolitan Police. You know, dogs that ride around in police cars, and the men and women they sacrifice themselves for? It has a lot of human interest, like L.A. Law, only it's told through the dog's eyes."

"Look Who's Barking," he said.

"Sort of." She tilted her head to one side and thought for a moment. "I'm sorry," she said. "That was a joke, wasn't it?"

"Sort of."

"I get it." She went on. "But what I really want to write is Movies-of the-Week. My agent says she'll put my script on Paul Nagle's desk, as soon as I have a first draft."

"What's it about?"

"It's called A *Little-Known Side of Elvis*. That's the working title. My agent says anything about Elvis will sell."

"Which side of Elvis is this one?"

"Well, for example, did you know about his relationship with dogs? Most people don't. *Hound Dog* wasn't just a song."

Her kelpie began to bark. A man with inflatable tennis shoes and a baseball cap worn backwards approached them, a clipboard in his hand.

"Hi!" he said, all teeth. "Would you take a minute to sign our petition?"

"No problem," said the young woman. "What's it for?"

"They're trying to close the park to outsiders, except on weekends."

She took his ballpoint pen and balanced the clipboard on her tanned forearm. "How come?"

"It's the residents. They say we take up too many parking places on Mulholland. They want to keep the canyon for themselves."

"Well," she said, "they better watch out, or we might just start leaving our dogs here. Then they'll multiply and take over!"

She grinned, her capped front teeth shining in the sunlight like two chips of paint from a pearly-white Lexus.

"What residents?" asked Madding.

"The homeowners," said the man in the baseball cap, hooking a thumb over his shoulder.

Madding's eyes followed a line to the cliffs overlooking the park, where the cantilevered back-ends of several designer houses hung suspended above the gorge. The undersides of the decks, weathered and faded, were almost camouflaged by the weeds and chaparral.

"How about you?" The man took back the clipboard and held it out to Madding. "We need all the help we can get."

"I'm not a registered voter," said Madding.

"You're not?"

"I don't live here," he said. "I mean, I did, but I don't now. Not anymore."

"Are you registered?" the man asked her.

"Yes."

"In the business?"

"I work at Fox," she said.

"Oh, yeah? How's the new regime? I hear Lili put all the old-timers out to pasture."

"Not the studio," she said. "The network."

"Really? Do you know Kathryn Baker, by any chance?"

"I've seen her parking space. Why?"

"I used to be her dentist." The man took out his wallet. "Here, let me give you my card."

"That's all right," she said. "I already have someone."

"Well, hold on to it anyway. You never know. Do you have a card?"

She reached into a velcro pouch at her waist and handed him a card with a quill pen embossed on one corner.

The man read it. "C.H.U.M.P.—that's great! Do you have a dental advisor yet?"

"I don't think so."

"Could you find out?"

"I suppose."

He turned to Madding. "Are you an actor?"

"Writer," said Madding. "But not the kind you mean."

The man was puzzled. The young woman looked at him blankly. Madding felt the need to explain himself.

"I had a novel published, and somebody bought an option. I moved down here to write the screenplay."

"Title?" said the man.

"You've probably never heard of it," said Madding. "It was called *And Soon the Night*."

"That's it!" she said. "I just finished reading it—I saw your picture on the back of the book!" She furrowed her brow, a slight dimple appearing on the perfectly smooth skin between her eyes, as she struggled to remember. "Don't tell me. Your name is . . ."

"David Madding," he said, holding out his hand.

"Hi!" she said. "I'm Stacey Chernak."

"Hi, yourself."

"Do you have a card?" the man said to him.

"I'm all out," said Madding. It wasn't exactly a lie. He had never bothered to have any printed.

"What's the start date?"

"There isn't one," said Madding. "They didn't renew the option."

"I see," said the man in the baseball cap, losing interest.

A daisy chain of small dogs ran by, a miniature collie chasing a longhaired daschund chasing a shivering chihuahua. The collie blurred as it went past, its long coat streaking like a flame.

"Well, I gotta get some more signatures before dark. Don't forget to call me," the man said to her. "I can advise on orthodontics, accident reconstruction, anything they want."

"How about animal dentistry?" she said.

"Hey, why not?"

"I'll give them your name."

"Great," he said to her. "Thanks!"

"Do you think that's his collie?" she said when he had gone.

Madding considered. "More likely the Irish setter."

They saw the man lean down to hook his fingers under the collar of a golden retriever. From the back, his baseball cap revealed the emblem of the New York Yankees. Not from around here, Madding thought. But then, who is?

"Close," she said, and laughed.

The man led his dog past a dirt mound, where there was a drinking fountain, and a spigot that ran water into a trough for animals.

"Water," she said. "That's a good idea. Greta!"

The kelpie came bounding over, eager to escape the attentions of a randy pit bull. They led her to the mound. As Greta drank, Madding read the sign over the spigot.

CAUTION!

WATCH OUT FOR MOUNTAIN LIONS

"What do you think that means?" she said. "It isn't true, is it?"

Madding felt a tightness in his chest. "It could be. This is still wild country."

"Greta, stay with me . . ."

"Don't worry. They only come out at night, probably."

"Where's your dog?" she said.

"I wish I knew."

She tilted her head, uncertain whether or not he was making another joke.

"He ran away," Madding told her.

"When?"

"Last month. I used to bring him here all the time. One day he didn't come when I called. It got dark, and they closed the park, but he never came back."

"Oh, I'm so sorry!"

"Yeah, me too."

"What was his name?"

"He didn't have one. I couldn't make up my mind, and then it was too late."

They walked on between the trees. She kept a close eye on Greta. Somewhere music was playing. The honey-colored cocker spaniel led the German shepherd, the Irish setter and a dalmatian to a redwood table. There the cocker's owner, a woman with brassy hair and a sagging green halter, poured white wine into plastic cups for several men.

"I didn't know," said Stacey.

"I missed him at first, but now I figure he's better off. Someplace where he can run free, all the time."

"I'm sorry about your dog," she said. "That's so sad. But what I meant was, I didn't know you were famous."

It was hard to believe that she knew the book. The odds against it were staggering, particularly considering the paltry royalties. He decided not to ask what she thought of it. That would be pressing his luck.

"Who's famous? I sold a novel. Big deal."

"Well, at least you're a real writer. I envy you."

"Why?"

"You have it made."

Sure I do, thought Madding. One decent review in the *Village Voice Literary Supplement*, and some reader at a production company makes an inquiry, and the next thing I know my agent makes a deal with all the money in the world at the top of the ladder. Only the ladder doesn't go far enough. And now I'm back to square one, the option money used up, with a screenplay written on spec that's not worth what it cost me to Xerox it, and I'm six months behind on the next novel. But I've got it made. Just ask the IRS.

The music grew louder as they walked. It seemed to be coming from somewhere overhead. Madding gazed up into the trees, where the late-afternoon rays sparkled through the leaves, gold coins edged in blackness. He thought he heard voices, too, and the clink of glasses. Was there a party? The entire expanse of the park was visible from here, but he could see no evidence of a large group anywhere. The sounds were diffused and unlocalized, as if played back through widely-spaced, out-of-phase speakers.

"Where do you live?" she asked.

"What?"

"You said you don't live here anymore."

"In Calistoga."

"Where's that?"

"Up north."

"Oh."

He began to relax. He was glad to be finished with this town.

"I closed out my lease today," he told her. "Everything's packed. As soon as I hit the road, I'm out of here."

"Why did you come back to the park?"

A good question, he thought. He hadn't planned to stop by. It was a last-minute impulse.

"I'm not sure," he said. No, that wasn't true. He might as well admit it. "It sounds crazy, but I guess I wanted to look for my dog. I thought I'd give it one more chance. It doesn't feel right, leaving him."

"Do you think he's still here?"

He felt a tingling in the pit of his stomach. It was not a good feeling. I shouldn't have come, he thought. Then I wouldn't have had to face it. It's dangerous here, too dangerous for there to be much hope.

"At least I'll know," he said.

He heard a sudden intake of breath and turned to her. There were tears in her eyes, as clear as diamonds.

"It's like the end of your book," she said. "When the little girl is alone, and doesn't know what's going to happen next . . ."

My God, he thought, she did read it. He felt flattered, but kept his ego in check. She's not so tough. She has a heart, after all, under all the bravado. That's worth something—it's worth a lot. I hope she makes it, the Elvis script, whatever she really wants. She deserves it.

She composed herself and looked around, blinking. "What is that?"

"What's what?"

"Don't you hear it?" She raised her chin and moved her head from side to side, eyes closed.

She meant the music, the glasses, the sound of the party that wasn't there.

"I don't know."

Now there was the scraping of steel somewhere behind them, like a rough blade drawn through metal. He stopped and turned around quickly.

A couple of hundred yards away, at the top of the slope, a man in a uniform opened the gate to the park. Beyond the fence, a second man climbed out of an idling car with a red, white and blue shield on the door. He had a heavy chain in one hand.

"Come on," said Madding. "It's time to go."

"It can't be."

"The security guards are here. They close the park at six."

"Already?"

Madding was surprised, too. He wondered how long they had been walking. He saw the man with the crewcut searching for his frisbee in the grass, the bull terrier at his side. The group on the bench and the woman in the halter were collecting their things. The bodybuilder marched his two ribboned Pekingese to the slope. The Beverly Hills dentist whistled and stood waiting for his dog to come to him. Madding snapped to, as if waking up. It really was time.

The sun had dropped behind the hills and the grass under his feet was darkening. The car in the parking lot above continued to idle; the rumbling of the engine reverberated in the natural bowl of the park, as though close enough to bulldoze them out of the way. He heard a rhythm in the throbbing, and realized that it was music, after all.

They had wandered close to the edge, where the park ended and the gorge began. Over the gorge, the deck of one of the cantilevered houses beat like a drum.

"Where's Greta?" she said.

He saw the stark expression, the tendons outlined through the smooth skin of her throat.

"Here, girl! Over here . . . !"

She called out, expecting to see her dog. Then she clapped her hands together. The sound bounced back like the echo of a gunshot from the depths of the canyon. The dog did not come.

In the parking lot, the second security guard let a doberman out of the car. It was a sleek, black streak next to him as he carried the heavy chain to his partner, who was waiting for the park to empty before padlocking the gate.

Madding took her arm. Her skin was covered with gooseflesh. She drew away.

"I can't go," she said. "I have to find Greta."

He scanned the grassy slopes with her, avoiding the gorge until there was nowhere left to look. It was blacker than he remembered. Misshapen bushes and stunted shrubs filled the canyon below, extending all the way down to the formal boundaries of the city. He remembered standing here only a few weeks ago, in exactly the same position. He had told himself then that his dog could not have gone over the edge, but now he saw that there was nowhere else to go.

The breeze became a wind in the canyon and the black liquid eye of a swimming pool winked at him from far down the hillside. Above, the sound of the music stopped abruptly.

"You don't think she went down there, do you?" said Stacey. There was catch in her voice. "The mountain lions . . ."

"They only come out at night."

"But it *is* night!"

They heard a high, broken keening.

"Listen!" she said. "That's Greta!"

"No, it's not. Dogs don't make that sound. It's—" He stopped himself.

"*What?*"

"Coyotes."

He regretted saying it.

Now, without the music, the shuffling of footsteps on the boards was clear and unmistakable. He glanced up. Shadows appeared over the edge of the deck as a line of heads gathered to look down. Ice cubes rattled and someone laughed. Then someone else made a shushing sound and the silhouetted heads bobbed silently, listening and watching.

Can they see us? he wondered.

Madding felt the presence of the doberman behind him, at the top of the slope. How long would it take to close the distance, once the guard set it loose to clear the park? Surely they would call out a warning first. He waited for the voice, as the seconds ticked by on his watch.

"I have to go get her," she said, starting for the gorge.

"No . . ."

"I can't just leave."

"It's not safe," he said.

"But she's down there, I know it! Greta!"

There was a giggling from the deck.

They can hear us, too, he thought. Every sound, every word magnified, like a Greek amphitheater. Or a Roman one.

Rover, Spot, Towser? No, Cubby. That's what I was going to call you, if there had been time. I always liked the name. *Cubby.*

He made a decision.

"Stay here," he said, pushing her aside.

"What are you doing?"

"I'm going over."

"You don't have to. It's my dog . . ."

"Mine, too."

Maybe they're both down there, he thought.

"I'll go with you," she said.

"No."

He stood there, thinking, It all comes down to this. There's no way to avoid it. There never was.

"But you don't know what's there . . . !"

"Go," he said to her, without turning around. "Get out of here while you can. There's still time."

Go home, he thought, wherever that is. You have a life ahead of you. It's not too late, if you go right now, without looking back.

"Wait . . . !"

He disappeared over the edge.

A moment later there was a new sound, something more than the breaking of branches and the thrashing. It was powerful and deep, followed immediately by a high, mournful yipping. Then there was only a silence, and the night.

From above the gorge, a series of quick, hard claps fell like rain.

It was the people on the deck.

They were applauding.

WOODEN DRUTHERS

E. R. Stewart

E. R. Stewart was born on the 146th birthday of Charles Dickens in Altoona, Pennsylvania. He has lived and worked across the U.S. and abroad with his wife, a captain in the U.S. Air Force, and their three children. Stewart has published fiction, nonfiction, illustrations and poetry in *Analog, Asimov's, Aboriginal SF, Thrust SF, MZB's Fantasy Magazine, Cricket for Children, Ladybug for Young Children,* and numerous other magazines and newspapers, as well as several science fiction anthologies.

"Wooden Druthers" is a wonderful, quietly haunting tale that makes deft use of America's own homegrown folklore traditions. It is reprinted from the anthology *The Ultimate Witch.*

—T.W.

He always had the knife. It was one of those penknives, they called them. The blades fold into the handle for safe pocketing. His was so old the main blade was getting skinny from all the stroppings, all the accumulated minutes spent spiraling on the grindstone. The small blade he used for detail work, but the bigger blade could work even hard woods, so both must have been razor sharp and of the hardest stainless steel.

Not that it was an expensive knife; he couldn't even afford shoes, that boy. At age eight, he wandered town barefoot even when there was frost or snow. Many locals had discussed the power of those little feet. They must have some pretty big power to withstand the slush he walked them through, the ice he skated them over, and the drifts he kicked when the real snow came. A tough little kid, all the folk thereabouts agreed.

Where he got the knife is not known. He entered town one cold day, carrying it and whittling on a piece of pine. Town wasn't much back then, both sides of it only a house deep at the time, and the road not even paved with MacAdam then; all the improvements and expansions came much later. Todd Meacham, his lower lip sucked in from sight as he concentrated on peeling off flakes of wood with his knife, probably didn't even notice that town's lack of things, or even it's wealth of poverty and neglect.

No, Tee Em cared little for the things of that town. He noticed the people in it, though.

"Todd," I called. "Tee Em, how about some tag?"

"Looka this." He held up the knife. It had a white pearl handle, with shiny rivets. There were little tiny words down at the base of the main blade, like magic runes to the likes of us, who read only the looks of fury on adult faces, mostly. "Got it this morning."

I reached to take the knife from him, so I could examine it good and proper, but he snatched it back from me before my fingers even got the hint of a touch. Shrugging, I said, "So you want to play some tag?"

"Sure." He dropped the stick he'd been whittling, folded the blade away, and stuck the knife deep into his trouser pocket.

We ran, and I beat Tee Em most times, but he was evasive at close quarters. My feet found most of the rocks and roots to trip over, while his avoided all but the divots, which tended to stiff-leg him to the ground.

Jumping on him after one of these tumbles, I wrestled him, laughing as he struggled to get away from me. We beat each other a few times, pinning and being pinned as if sharing some expensive toy, very careful of each getting his turn in the proper amount.

I was about to try bending his arm around behind his back when he started yelling, "Wait."

Piling off, I stood and said, "What?" I looked around, figuring some adult was heading our way with a war-face on or something.

"My knife," he said. He was on his hands and knees swooshing through the leaves, and I got down to help him find the knife.

That's how I got to be the only other one we know of to touch the thing. My left hand skidded sideways over the hard-packed dirt, under a layer of leaves, and came up against the knife almost right away. Had it wanted me to find it?

The knife was warm, for one thing. And it felt good. I mean it gave pleasure to my hand, like some kind of magnetism that throbbed up my arm and made me smile. It felt too heavy for its size, and there was just the slightest vibration to it, like inside it something was humming a tune from long back, far off.

I brought the knife to me, then dug my right thumbnail into the groove on top of the big blade, to pull it open. That's when Tee Em hit me, all forty-odd pounds of him. He knocked me clean over, and my head was ringing when I came back at him, to hit him, to hurt him back a little, as was only fair. By the time I'd punched his stomach a few times, he had the knife. How he got it I don't know, unless I dropped it.

Maybe the thing flew to him when I let go of it. I just don't know.

"Bob, run," he told me, the look on his face like a crooked mask of fright, with the rest hilarity and high good humor. He dashed off, sprinting out from under the old oak's shade and crossing the village green way ahead of his own shadow, as we used to say about fast-running boys.

I started scrambling to my feet, but before I could push against the ground, a hand clamped on the scruff of my neck and hauled me skyward. I could tell by the feel of the calluses that it was my stepdad, Art. He stank of drinking and sourer things, and I smelled him good and strong then because he shoved his face near mine and yelled, "What do you mean by fighting that retard right here in the middle of town for everybody to see? You shaming me, boy? Is that what? We'll see about shaming."

This for him was a grandiloquent speech, and all the while he was holding me aloft by the neck. You've got to give folks the credit they're due, and his credit was strength. In both smell and muscle, that man was strong.

He proved it further by drop-kicking me just like a football. It wasn't the first time, so I knew how to fall, but there was a lot of forward thrust to it and I kind of rolled too much, and he was on me again before I could scurry to the side. His boots had steel toes. Miner's boots, although he got kicked out of the mines for stealing another man's things, they say. Those boots felt like miner's boots, though, because they felt like they could split the earth itself, if they wanted.

All they did to me was send me flying again. I got to thinking once that I ought to be applying for my junior pilot's license, what with the regular flights I'd been taking since Dad died and Art moved in. Mama'd probably let me, too, for real, but where'd we get the money?

That was always the thing, money. Money made you poor by avoiding you, and it made you mean by letting you down, and it made you hurt by getting adults riled and spit-mad angry. Earning money was one thing we all dwelled on, and I did my share, picking coal by the tracks, selling scuttles of it cheaper than the companies. Between that and running errands for adults too lazy to walk, I got by.

I got by, but Art got my money. And then it was never enough and I would shame him and he'd start to kicking me.

That day, the day I touched the knife, Art kicked me right through town. I guess me shaming him by fighting Tee Em, as he called our roughhousing, wasn't the same as him kicking me with those steel-toed boots of his from one end of town to the other. By the time I got kicked home, I was wearing every kind of mud and dirt there is on that stretch of road, and many samples of shale and red dog, too.

And it was a good thing, or else Mama might have seen the bruises before I got a chance to cool them down at the pump out back. That cold water takes swelling down mighty fast, so it must have Indian magic like the older folk say. All I know is, through it all, the feel of that knife in my hand stayed with me.

Late that night Art finished off another bottle of Wild Turkey and commenced whopping and wailing on Mama, so I got out through my window, the one with cardboard instead of glass. Running through the night helped loosen my stiff muscles.

As always, I ran to Tee Em's. The adults, some of them anyway, call him a retard, but he's not even slow. He's faster in the brains than any adult I know; he's just a different kind of being, like he's blessed or something. I remember Mama, when Dad was around, telling tales of angels sometimes coming down from those icy, glittering stars to bless the lucky few, the ones with grace. Tee Em was like that. He fit into the world like inlaid silver, especially when adults weren't around to spoil his calm.

"You get a beating?" he asked me.

"Nah, just kicked home." I rolled my shoulders and grinned to show him I was fine. "Whatcha got?"

"Just carvin'." He said it like it was nothing, but what he held in his slender, facile fingers looked like a store-bought toy, so real and detailed was it. I looked closer, and he held it up to a moonbeam, and I saw my own face.

"Tee Em, that's me you're carving. Real good, too."

He just nodded and kept working at it.

"Where'd you learn that from?" I couldn't get over how much like me it looked. Like a photograph in wood, kind of, except not flat, but all of me, rounded, three-dimensional. And in it, I wasn't hurting, I could even see that. In his carving, I was okay.

And then he said it the first time, the phrase that still makes me shiver some nights, hell, some days when I think of it. He said, real serious, and not even looking up from his carving, he said, "If I had my druthers every one, I'd have my wooden druthers, too." It sounded like an incantation, or the first couple lines of a poem maybe. It seemed, in the dark and under the moon, like lyrics from a very old song, translated too many times into too many tongues to be traced to ground.

Now, I'd heard that one part—"if I had my druthers"—many times before. It's a common folk saying, nothing special. Sometimes the old ladies of the town said it when they talked about what things would be like if they had a choice of worlds, as they sat quilting or canning currants. "If I had my druthers, no one would be poor," they'd say, or things like that. So I knew it really meant having your "I'd rathers," your preferences. But wooden druthers? That'd be your "wouldn't rathers," I figured.

Who ever heard about having what you wouldn't rather? Or did it maybe mean having your choice of the bad things? Maybe that was it. If you really had your druthers, you'd have your wooden druthers, too.

All this I puzzled out over the years since that night. All I know is what I've come up with on my own, so don't take it to the bank, as they say. In fact, you take anything to a bank, you're a fool. Why give what you earn to other people? Ain't no one going to watch your own things as well or as truly as you yourself. Life's worth more than money, too, keep that in mind. No interest paid is enough to earn back the principle.

Anyway, I watched while he carved me. And a funny thing is, he didn't even look up at me, the way an artist might keep glancing at his subject or model, to get the details right. No, it was more like the details came up out of the wood on their own, with the fast, gentle help of that knife, which shined in the moonglow like a sliver of mountain stream. And the image of me was me, in every detail, but me old, me as an old man. It was eerie, and my skin prickled when I saw the face. The wrinkles were happy ones, earned by smiling more often than crying. My face old looked better to me than my face young, because it seemed like good times knew that face better. The details added up to being happy and living right as the big blade shaped and the little blade detailed.

Those blades made precious few shavings, too, by the way. It was like there was no, or very little, waste. I kind of liked that: it made me feel proud somehow that my image could come out of a common chunk of pine and leave only a small pile of cuttings.

"Done," Tee Em said pretty soon. He folded the knife and slipped it slowly, carefully into his pocket. He looked up at the sky. His face was sad. Looking back down, he started digging a hole with his fingers. He sat with his legs apart, digging a little hole, ignoring me, with that image of me laying there like so much kindling.

"What are you doing?" I asked, having a pretty good idea. And sure enough, he didn't answer me, but buried the little statue of me, and scraped in the shavings, too.

We were sitting in his backyard. The stump for cutting firewood was at his back, the axe embedded with its handle jutting more up than down. I leaned against a stack of logs waiting to be split into cordwood. The ground around that whole area was bare of grass and such, being so often walked on and worked on. That's what made it easy for me to see all the little mounds.

It looked like a miniature graveyard. Tee Em must have had the knife a long time before that day, and he must have been busy most nights, carving and burying.

He looked up, having tamped the new-turned dirt down flat with the heels of both hands. "You're okay now," he told me again, real serious in tone and expression. "I claimed you a time with my wooden druther of ya."

I just nodded. What else could I do?

We went frogging, but didn't catch anything that night. Oh, I caught one frog, but the instant I touched it the darned thing went stiff and died, so we threw it away, figuring it for polluted. It was quiet, so that one frog's splash sounded big enough to drown creation. All the frogs were silent, waiting for summer's end, probably, when they'd bury themselves in cool muck and mud to die for the winter so they could rise again next spring. That was the way of frogs. We knew that much.

I went home nearer dawn than now, approaching the house first with my ears. Everything seemed quiet. I slipped in. Mama was crying, and I peeked around the corner, past my curtain, which is really just an old dress of Mama's hung on cotton rope to screen my bed off from the rest of the room. My gaze found Mama lying on the kitchen floor. On tiptoes I crept to her. Kneeling, I said, "It's okay now, Mama." I touched her hair.

She looked up. "He's gone. Art's gone. He left me."

"Left you bruised and battered," I answered, braver in Art's absence, at least with my mouth.

She only cried, and I thought of Tee Em's carvings. Had his wooden druther of me somehow taken away my biggest hurt?

The very next night I asked if he'd carve one of my mother, and he did. I helped dig the hole, and we buried it together. "Now just wait," Tee Em told me, face watching the ground expectant.

We sat staring, until I started to nod. Tee Em's elbow roused me from sleep a couple times, and the moon got higher, brighter it seemed, and then I saw the wooden druthers rise up and dance, and there were hundreds of them. They weren't just buried in Tee Em's yard, either, but came dancing up the road, clattering together like rhythm sticks surprised to be alive. Each one pushed up from their holes like moles, slowly at first, then quicker, until some fair shot out of the ground. Some flew up around our heads, and one smacked my ear enough to swell it a little.

Tee Em and I laughed and chased them like fireflies, like moths, like clothespins in a twister. We played with them, and had fun, too, until one by one they went back to their proper holes. Then we climbed trees and stole some apples from MacCready's Orchard. They were too sour to eat, but Mama made nice pies from them, and even sold one to Bethy Ann MacCready, her own fine-clothed, greedy self.

We moved out of that place not too long after that, down out of the hills and into the city, where money's braver about getting within arm's length, but Mama and I felt a lot better right from the time I learned about the wooden druthers. I don't rightly know if it was magic or what. I don't know if they mean anything or not, or if it's all in my mind, or if I'll die when I look exactly like that carving of me, but however it works out, I guess it's a fair swap not to know, because I'd rather live my life for a good long while than chase after pain and death every second like a scared animal.

And these days, when chores or debts or burdens come along that I'd rather not face, I tell myself, "Self, I wooden druther do this, but it's better than many another thing that might take its place," and that gets me through, keeps me going. It's also what keeps me checking the used pocketknives in the secondhand shops. You never know.

And one of these days I might just hike back up into those hills, and see if I can't dig myself up some extra comfort. Then again, I might just leave well enough alone, too.

INSCRIPTION
Jane Yolen

Jane Yolen is America's most distinguished writer of original fairy tales, as well as a novelist, editor (with her own imprint for Harcourt Brace & Co.), poet, storyteller, ballad singer, and lecturer. She is the author of more than one hundred books for children, teenagers, and adults, including: *Sister Light, Sister Dark*; *White Jenna*; *Cards of Grief*; *Tales of Wonder*; and *Touch Magic*: essays on fantasy and fairy tales. She has won the World Fantasy Award, the Golden Kite Award, and her picture book *Owl Moon* was honored with the Caldecott Medal. Her most recent works are (for children) *Here Be Dragons*, and (for adults) the extraordinary Nebula award–nominated novel *Briar Rose*.

Yolen and her husband, David Stemple, own homes in both western Massachusetts and in St. Andrews, Scotland. The following adult folk tale takes its inspiration from the inscription carved on a Scottish gravestone. It is told in prose both lovely and stark, like the windswept land it portrays. "Inscription" is reprinted from the anthology *The Ultimate Witch*.

—T.W.

Father, they have burned your body,
Set your ashes in the cairn.
Still I need your advice.
Magnus sues for me in marriage,
Likewise McLeod of the three farms.
Yet would I wait for Iain the traveler,
Counting each step of his journey
Till the sun burns down behind Galan
Three and three hundred times;
Till he has walked to Steornabhagh
And back the long, hard track,
Singing my praises at every shieling
Where the lonely women talk to the east wind
And admire the ring he is bringing
To place on my small white hand.
—Inscription on Callanish Stones, Isle of Lewis

It is a lie, you know, that inscription. From first to last. I did not want my father's advice. I had never taken it when he was alive, no matter how often he offered it. Still I need to confess what's been done.

If I do not die of this thing, I shall tell my son himself when he is old enough to understand. But if I cannot tell him, there will still be this paper to explain it: who his mother was, what she did for want of him, who and what his father was, and how the witch cursed us all.

Magnus Magnusson did ask for me in marriage, but he did not really want me. He did not want me though I was young and slim and fair. His eye was to the young men, but he wanted my father's farm and my father was a dying man, preferring a dram to a bannock.

And McLeod had the richest three farms along the machair, growing more than peat and sand. Still he was ugly and old, older even than my father, and as pickled, though his was of the brine where my father's was the whiskey.

Even Iain the traveler was no great catch, for he had no money at all. But ach—he was a lovely man, with hair the purple brown of heather in the spring or like a bruise beneath the skin. He was worth the loving but not worth the waiting for. Still I did not know it at the time.

I was nursed not by my mother, who died giving birth to me, but by brown-haired Mairi, daughter of Lachlan, who was my father's shepherd. And if she had married my father and given him sons, these troubles would not have come upon me. But perhaps that, too, is a lie. Even as a child I went to trouble as a herring to the water, so Mairi always said. Besides, my father was of that rare breed of man who fancied only the one wife; his love once given was never to be changed or renewed, even to the grave.

So I grew without a brother or sister to play with, a trouble to my dear nurse and a plague to my father, though neither ever complained of it. Indeed, when I stumbled in the bog as the household dug the peat, and was near lost, they dragged me free. When I fell down a hole in the cliff when we went for birds' eggs, they paid a man from St. Kilda's to rescue me with ropes. And when the sea herself pulled me from the sands the day I went romping with the selchies, they got in the big boat that takes four men and a bowman in normal times, and pulled me back from the clutching tide. Oh I was a trouble and a plague.

But never was I so much as when I came of age to wed. That summer, after my blood flowed the first time and Mairi showed me how to keep myself clean— and no easy job of it—handsome Iain came through on his wanderings. He took note of me I am sure, and not just because he told me the summer after. A girl knows when a man has an eye for her: she knows it by the burn of her skin; she knows it by the ache in her bones. He said he saw the promise in me and was waiting a year to collect on it. He had many such collections in mind, but I wasn't to know.

His eyes were as purple brown as his hair, like wild plums. And his skin was dark from wandering. There is not much sun on Leodhas, summer to winter, but if you are constantly out in it, the wind can scour you. Iain the traveler had that color; while others were red as rowan from the wind, he was brown as the roe. It made his teeth the whiter. It made the other men look boiled or flayed and laughable.

No one laughed at Iain. No woman laughed, that is.

So of course I loved him. How could I not? I who had been denied nothing by my father, nothing by my nurse. I loved Iain and wanted him, so I was certain to have him. How was I to know the count of days would be so short.

When he came through the next summer to collect on that promise, I was willing to pay. We met first on the long sea loch where I had gone to gather periwinkles and watch the boys come in from the sea, pulling on the oars of the boat which made their new young muscles ripple.

Iain spoke to all of the women, few of the men, but for me he took out his whistle and played one of the old courting tunes. We had a laugh at that, all of us, though I felt a burn beneath my breastbone, by the heart, and could scarcely breathe.

I pretended he played the tune because I was watching out for the boys. He pretended he was playing it for Jennie Morrison, who was marrying Jamie Matheson before the baby in her belly swelled too big. But I already knew, really, he was playing just for me.

The pipes told me to meet him by the standing stones and so I did. He acted surprised to see me, but I knew he was not. He smoothed my hair and took me in his arms, and called me such sweet names as he kissed me I was sure I would die of it.

"Come tomorrow," he whispered, "when the dark finally winks," by which he meant well past midnight. And though I thought love should shout its name in the daylight as well as whisper at night, I did as he asked.

Sneaking from our house was not easy. Like most island houses, it was small and with only a few rooms, and the door was shared with the byre. But father and nurse and cows were all asleep, and I slipped out, barely stirring the peat smoke as I departed.

Iain was waiting for me by the stones, and he led me down to a place where soft grasses made a mat for my back. And there he taught me the pain of loving as well as the sweetness of it. I did not cry out, though it was not from wanting. But bred on the island means being strong, and I had only lately given over playing shinty with the boys. Still there was blood on my legs and I cleaned myself with grass and hurried back as the sun—what there was of it—was rising, leaving Iain asleep and guarded by the stones.

If Mairi noticed anything, she said nothing. At least not that day. And as I helped her at the quern preparing meal, and gave a hand with the baking as well, all the while suppressing the yawns that threatened to expose me, perhaps she did not know.

When I went back to the stones that night, Iain was waiting for me and this time there was neither blood nor pain, though I still preferred the kisses to what came after.

But I was so tired that I slept beside him all that night, or what was left of it. At dawn we heard the fishermen calling to one another as they passed by our little nest on the way to their boats. They did not see us: Iain knew how to choose his places well. Still I did not rise, for no fisherman dares meet a woman as he goes toward the sea for fear of losing his way in the waves. So I was forced to huddle there in the shelter of Iain's arms till the fishermen—some of them the boys I had lately played shinty with—were gone safely on their way.

This time when I got home Mairi was already up at the quern, her face as black as if it had been rinsed in peat. She did not say a word to me, which was even worse, but by her silence I knew she had said nothing to my father, who slept away in the other room.

That was the last but one I saw of Iain that summer, though I went night after night to look for him at the stones. My eyes were red from weeping silently as I lay in the straw by Mairi's side, and she snoring so loudly, I knew she was not really asleep.

I would have said nothing, but the time came around and my blood did not flow. Mairi knew the count of it since I was so new to womanhood. Perhaps she guessed even before I did, for I saw her looking at me queer. When I felt queasy and was sick behind the house, there was no disguising it.

"Who is it?" she asked. Mairi was never one for talking too much.

"Iain the traveler," I said. "I am dying for love of him."

"You are not dying," she said, "lest your father kill you for this. We will go to Auld Annie who lives down the coast. She practices the black airt and can rid you of the child."

"I do not want to be rid of it," I said. "I want Iain."

"He is walking out with Margaret MacKenzie in her shieling. Or if not her, another."

"Never! He loves me," I said. "He swore it."

"He loves," Mairi said, purposefully coarse to shock me, "the cherry in its blossom but not the tree. And his swearing is done to accomplish what he desires."

She took me by the hand, then, before I could recover my tongue, and we walked half the morning down the strand to Auld Annie's croft, it being ten miles or so by. There was only a soft, fair wind and the walking was not hard, though we had to stop every now and again for me to be quietly sick in the sand.

Auld Annie's cottage was much the smallest and meanest I had seen, still it had a fine garden both in front and again in back in the long rig. Plants grew there in profusion, in lazybeds, and I had no name for many of them.

"She can call fish in by melted lead and water," Mairi said. "She can calm the seas with seven white stones."

I did not look impressed, but it was my stomach once more turning inside me.

"She foretold your own dear mother's death."

I looked askance. "Why didn't I know of this?"

"Your father forbade me ever speak of it."

"And now?"

"Needs does as needs must." She knocked on the door

The door seemed to open of itself because when we got inside, Auld Annie was sitting far from it, in a rocker, a coarse black shawl around her shoulders and a mutch tied under her chin like any proper wife. The croft was lower and darker than ours, but there was a broad mantel over the fire and on it sat two piles of white stones with a human skull, bleached and horrible, staring at the wall between them. On the floor by a long table were three jugs filled with bright red poppies, the only color in the room. From the rafters hung bunches of dried herbs, but they were none of them familiar to me.

Under her breath, Mairi muttered a charm:

> I trample upon the eye
> As tramples the duck upon the lake,
> In the name of the secret Three,
> And Brigid the Bride. . . .

and made a quick sign against the *Droch Shùil*, the evil eye.

"I knew it, I knew ye were coming, Molly," Auld Annie said.

How she knew that—or my name—I could not guess.

"I knew it as I knew when yer mam was going to die." Her voice was low, like a man's.

"We haven't come for prophecy," I said.

"Ye have come about a babe."

My jaw must have gone agape at that for I had told no one but Mairi—and that only hours before. Surely Auld Annie *was* a witch, though if she threw no shadow one could not tell in the dark of her house. Nevertheless I shook my head. "I will keep the babe. All I want is the father to come to me."

"Coming is easy," Auld Annie said in her deep voice. "Staying is hard."

"If you get him to come to me," I answered, suddenly full of myself, "I will get him to stay."

From Mairi there was only a sharp intake of breath in disapproval, but Auld Annie chuckled at my remark, dangerous and low.

"Come then, girl," she said, "and set yer hand to my churn. We have butter to take and spells to make and a man to call to yer breast."

I did not understand entirely, but I followed her to the churn, where she instructed me in what I had to do.

"As ye churn, girl, say this: *Come, butter, come. Come, butter, come.*"

"I know this charm," I said witheringly. "I have since a child."

"Ah—but instead 'a saying 'butter,' ye must say yer man's name. Only—" she raised her hand in warning, "not aloud. And ye must not hesitate even a moment's worth between the words. Not once. Ye must say it over and over till the butter be done. It is not easy, for all it sounds that way."

I wondered—briefly—if all she was needing was a strong young girl to do her chores, but resolved to follow her instructions. It is a dangerous thing to get a witch angry with you. And if she could call Iain to me, so much the better.

So I put my hands upon the churn and did as she bid, over and over and over without a hesitation till my arms ached and my mind was numb and all I could hear was Iain's name in my head, the very sound of it turning my stomach and making me ill. Still I did not stop till the butter had come.

Auld Annie put her hands upon mine, and they were rough and crabbed with time. "Enough!" she said, "or it will come sour as yer belly, and we will have done all for nought."

I bit back the response that it was not *we* but *I* who had done the work and silently put my aching arms down at my sides. Only then did I see that Annie herself had not been idle. On her table lay a weaving of colored threads.

"A framing spell," Mairi whispered by my side. "A *deilbh buidseachd*."

I resisted crossing myself and spoiling the spell and went where Annie led me, to the rocking chair.

"Sit ye by the fire," she said.

No sooner had I sat down, rubbing my aching arms and trying not to jump up and run outside to be sick, when a piece of the peat broke off in the hearth and tumbled out at my feet.

"Good, good," Auld Annie crooned. "Fire bodes marriage. We will have success."

I did not smile. Gritting my teeth, I whispered, "Get on with it."

"Hush," cautioned Mairi, but her arms did not ache as mine did.

Auld Annie hastened back to the churn and, dipping her hand into it, carved out a pat of butter the size of a shinty ball with her nails. Slapping it down on the table by the threads, she said: "Name three colors, girl, and their properties."

"Blue like the sea by Galan's Head," I said.

"Good, good, two more."

"Plum—like his eyes."

"And a third."

I hesitated, thinking. "White," I said at last. "White—like . . . like God's own hair."

Auld Annie made a loud *tch* sound in the back of her throat and Mairi, giving a loud explosive exhalation, threw her apron up over her head.

"Not a proper choice, girl," Auld Annie muttered. "But what's said cannot be unsaid. Done is done."

"Is it spoiled?" I whispered.

"Not spoiled. Changed." She drew the named colors of thread from the frame and laid them, side by side, across the ball of butter. "Come here."

I stood up and went over to her, my arms all a-tingle.

"Set the two threads at a cross for the name of God ye so carelessly invoked, and one beneath for yer true love's name."

I did as she bid, suddenly afraid. What had I called up or called down, so carelessly in this dark house?

Auld Annie wrapped the butter in a piece of yellowed linen, tying the whole up with a black thread, before handing it to me.

"Take this to the place where ye wish to meet him and bury it three feet down, first drawing out the black thread. Cover it over with earth and while doing so recite three times the very words ye said over the churn. He will come that very evening. He will come—but whether he will stay is up to ye, my girl."

I took the sachet in my right hand and dropped it carefully into the pocket of my apron.

"Come now, girl, give me a kiss to seal it."

When I hesitated, Mairi pushed me hard in the small of the back and I stumbled into the old woman's arms. She smelled of peat and whiskey and age, not unlike my father, but there was something more I could put no name to. Her mouth on mine was nothing like Iain's, but was bristly with an old woman's hard whiskers and her lips were cracked. Her sour breath entered mine and I reeled back from her, thankful to be done. As I turned, I glanced at the mantel. To my horror I saw that between the white stones, the skull was now facing me, its empty sockets black as doom.

Mairi opened the cottage door and we stumbled out into the light, blinking like hedgehogs. I started down the path, head down. When I gave a quick look over my shoulder, Mairi was setting something down by Auld Annie's door. It was a payment, I knew, but for what and how much I did not ask, then or ever.

We walked back more slowly than we had come, and I chattered much of the way, as if the charming had been on my tongue to loosen it. I told Mairi about Iain's hair and his eyes and every word he had spoken to me, doling them out a bit at a time because, truth to tell, he had said little. I recounted the kisses and how they made me feel and even—I blush to think of it now—how I preferred them to what came after. Mairi said not a word in return until we came to the place where the path led away to the standing stones.

When I made to turn, she put her hand on my arm. "No, not there," she said. "I told you he has gone up amongst the shielings. If you want him to come to you, I will have your father send you up to the high pasture today."

"He will come wherever I call him," I said smugly, patting the pocket where the butter lay.

"Do not be more brainless than you have been already," Mairi said. "Go where you have the best chance of making him stay."

I saw at last what she meant. At the stones we would have to creep and hide and lie still lest the fishermen spy us. We would have to whisper our love. But up in the high pasture, along the cliffside, in a small croft of our own, I could bind him to me by night and by day, marrying him in the old way. And no one—especially my father—could say no to such a wedding.

So Mairi worked her own magic that day, much more homey than Auld Annie's, with a good hot soup and a hearty dram and a word in the ear of my old father. By the next morning she had me packed off to the shieling, with enough bannocks and barley and flasks of water in my basket to last me a fortnight, driving five of our cows before.

The cows knew the way as well as I, and they took to the climb like weanlings, for the grass in the shieling was sweet and fresh and greener than the overgrazed land below. In another week Mairi and I would have gone up together. But Mairi had my father convinced that I was grown enough to make the trip for the first time alone. Grown enough—if he had but known!

Perhaps it was the sea breeze blowing on my face, or the fact that I knew Iain would be in my arms by dark. Or perhaps it was just that the time for such sickening was past, but I was not ill at all on that long walk, my step as jaunty as the cows'.

It was just coming on late supper when we turned off the path to go up and over the hill to the headland where our little summer croft sits. The cows followed their old paths through the matted bog with a quiet satisfaction, but I leaped carelessly from tussock to tuft behind them.

I walked—or rather danced—to the cliff's edge where the hummocks and bog and gray-splattered stone gave way to the sheer of cliff. Above me the gannets flew high and low, every now and again veering off to plummet into the sea after fish. A solitary seal floated below, near some rocks, looking left, then right, then left again but never once up at me.

With the little hoe I had brought along for the purpose, I dug a hole, fully three feet down, and reverently laid in the butter pat. Pulling the black thread from the sachet, I let the clods of dirt rain back down on it, all the while whispering, "Come, Iain, come. Come, Iain, come." Then loudly I sang out, "Come, Iain, come!" without a hesitation in between. Then I packed the earth down and stood, rubbing the small of my back where Mairi had pushed me into the sealing kiss.

I stared out over the sea, waiting.

He did not come until past dark, which in summer is well into the mid of the night. By then I had cooked myself a thin barley gruel, and made the bed up, stuffing it with soft grasses and airing out the croft.

I heard his whistle first, playing a raucous courting tune, not the one he had played on the beach when first I had noticed him, but "The Cuckoo's Nest," with words that say the one thing, but mean another.

In the dim light it took him a minute to see me standing by the door. Then he smiled that slow, sure smile of his. "Well . . . Molly," he said.

I wondered that he hesitated over my name, almost as if he could not recall it, though it had been but a few short weeks before that he had whispered it over and over into my tumbled hair.

"Well, Iain," I said. "You have come to me."

"I have been called to you," he said airily. "I could not stay away."

And then suddenly I understood that he did not know there was magic about; that these were just words he spoke, part of his lovemaking, that meant as little to him as the kisses themselves, just prelude to his passion.

Well, I had already paid for his pleasure and now he would have to stay for mine. I opened my arms and he walked into them as if he had never been away, his kisses the sweeter now that I knew what he was and how to play his game.

In the morning I woke him with the smell of barley bread. I thought if I could get him to stay a second night, and a third, the charm would have a chance of really working. So I was sweet and pliant and full of an ardor that his kisses certainly aroused, though that which followed seemed to unaccountably dampen it. Still, I could dissemble when I had to, and each time we made love I cried out as if fulfilled. Then while he slept I tiptoed out to the place where I had buried the butter sachet.

"Stay, Iain, stay. Stay, Iain, stay," I recited over the little grave where my hopes lay buried.

For a day and another night it seemed to work. He did stay—and quite happily— often sitting half-dressed in the cot watching me cook or lying naked on the sandy beach, playing his whistle to call the seals to him. They rose up out of the water, gazing long at him, as if they were bewitched.

We made love three and four and five times, day and night, till my thighs ached the way my arms had at the churn, and I felt scrubbed raw from trying to hold on to him.

But on the third day, when he woke, he refused both the barley and my kisses.

"*Enough*, sweet Moll," he said. "I am a traveler, and I must travel." He got dressed slowly, as if almost reluctant to leave but satisfying the form of it. I said nothing till he put his boots on, then could not stop myself.

"On to another shieling, then?"

"Perhaps."

"And what of the babe—here." It was the first time I had mentioned it. From the look on his face, I knew it made no matter to him, and without waiting for an answer, I stalked out of the croft. I went to the headland and stood athwart the place where the butter lay buried.

"Stay, Iain," I whispered. "Stay . . ." but there was neither power nor magic nor desire in my calling.

He came up behind me and put his arms around me, crossing his hands over my belly where the child-to-be lay quiet.

"Marry another," he whispered, nuzzling my ear, "but call him after me."

I turned in his arms and pulled him around to kiss me, my mouth wide open as if to take him in entire. And when the kiss was done, I pulled away and pushed him over the cliff into the sea.

Like most men of Leodhais, he could not swim, but little it would have availed him, for he hit the rocks and then the water, sinking at once. He did not come up again till three seals pushed him ashore onto the beach, where they huddled by his body for a moment as if expecting a tune, then plunged back into the sea when there was none.

I hurried down and cradled his poor broken body in my arms, weeping not for him but for myself and what I had lost, what I had buried up on that cliff, along with the butter, in a boggy little grave. Stripping the ring from his hand, I put it on my own, marrying us in the eyes of the sea. Then I put him on my back and carried him up the cliffside to bury him deep beneath the heather that would soon be the color of his hair, of his eyes.

Two weeks later, when Mairi came, I showed her the ring.

"We were married in God's sight," I said, "with two selchies as bridesmaids and a gannet to cry out the prayers."

"And where is the bridegroom now?" she asked.

"Gone to Steornabhagh," I lied, "to whistle us up money for our very own croft." She was not convinced. She did not say so, but I could read her face.

Of course he never returned and—with Mairi standing up for me—I married old McLeod after burying my father, who had stumbled into a hole one night after too much whiskey, breaking both his leg and his neck.

McLeod was too old for more than a kiss and a cuddle—as Mairi had guessed—and too pigheaded to claim the child wasn't his own. When the babe was born hale and whole, I named him Iain, a common-enough name in these parts, with only his nurse Mairi the wiser. At McLeod's death a year later, I gave our old farm over to her. It was a payment, she knew, but exactly for what she never asked, not then or ever.

Now I lie abed with the pox, weakening each day, and would repent—of the magic and the rest—though not of the loving which gave me my child. Still I would have my Iain know who his mother was and what she did for want of him, who and what his father was, and how the witch cursed us all. I would not have my son unmindful of his inheritance. If ever the wind calls him to travel, if ever a witch should tempt him to magic, or if ever a cold, quiet rage makes him choose murder, he will understand and, I trust, set all those desires behind.

Written this year of our Lord 1539, Tir a' Gheallaidh, Isle of Lewis.

IN CAMERA
Robert Westall

Robert Westall was one of the most acclaimed contemporary writers of children's fiction. His novels include *Break of Dark, Rachel and the Angel, Ghost Abbey,* and *Yaxley's Cat.* His collections *The Call and Other Stories* and *In Camera and Other Stories* were aimed at young adults, but as with his 1989 "adult" collection, *Antique Dust,* they are notable in their appeal to readers of all ages. Since Westall's death in 1993 at the age of 64, production has begun on two major collections of his work. The first of these, *Demons and Shadows: The Ghostly Best Stories of Robert Westall,* appeared in 1993.

"In Camera," from the collection of the same title, is a mystery and a ghost story that demonstrates Westall's deft touch with character and setting.

—E.D.

I first met Phil Marsden when he reported a burglary. The Super sent me. Only routine we thought, but the people who live on Birkbeck Common are rich and can turn nasty if not handled diplomatically.

I rang his chimes and saw him swimming towards me through the pebble glass of his front door. My first thought was that he was quite little.

His first thought . . . he looked crushed as people do when they've just been burgled. Then his little face lit up and he said:

"Helloooooooh!"

As if I was the Easter Bunny and a Christmas hamper all rolled into one. I have that effect on men; it makes life as a policewoman very difficult. I showed him my warrant card to take the smile off his face. He read it with great care, then made the remark I'd learned to dread.

"It's a fair cop!"

I suppose it was funny the first time somebody said it.

"If we can get on, sir?" I said it as severely as I could. I work hard at being severe; even scraping back my hair into the severest bun possible, so tight I give myself a headache. But that only draws attention to my ears, which I have been told are shell-like more often than I care to remember . . .

I sat down briskly with my notebook out. He sat with that stupid look on his face, admiring my legs. But I eventually got out of him that there was no sign of a break-in and that he had a very expensive burglar alarm, which he was sure he'd left switched on that morning, as he never forgot things like that.

"They must've nobbled it."

"That type are very hard to nobble. Have you checked to see if it's still working?"

It was working perfectly; *that* took the look off his face.

"Not nobbled," I said. "Just switched off. By somebody who knew the code. And by the look of your front door, they had a key, too."

"Impossible. I've only got three keys. One with my neighbor and two on my key-ring."

I established that the helpful neighbor was a famous barrister who had no need to resort to part-time burglary to keep the wolf from the door. Then he fetched his key-ring and found one of his keys missing.

"It's somebody you know," I said. He spent the next half hour telling me his friends weren't *like* that. Meanwhile, I found out what was missing. Usual dreary round, hi-fi, video, TV, gold cufflinks. But the thing he was most upset about was three antique cameras, God help us. I didn't know people collected antique cameras; I thought they just threw them away when they stopped working.

"Show me."

He led me to a room quite unlike the others. No designer furniture, just plain shelves filled with old cameras. Things in mahogany and brass, big as briefcases. Tatty little Bakelite Kodaks from the fifties, pre-war things with bellows, Brownie boxes.

The room was also a darkroom, with big black-and-white prints hung up to dry. Off-beat views of the world, taken from funny angles. That was what first intrigued me about him.

"Which cameras have gone?"

He showed me three sad gaps. "Two Leica IIcs and a very old Hasselblad. The only ones worth anything."

That made me prick my shell-like ears. Few burglars are experts on antique cameras.

"Do you show your friends this lot?"

He looked pained. "They're not the sort to be interested."

I betted not; this place was where his funny little heart and soul were; very few of his lovely friends would be shown this.

"But you showed *somebody*? Recently?"

"Only Rodney. Rodney Smith. But he wouldn't . . . I was at school with him."

"Were you and Mr. Smith *alone*?"

"There was his girl friend. Big dishy brunette. Madeleine Something. But she wasn't interested. She was half-pissed. Kept stroking his back and giggling. Wanted bed. Not that Rodney would be my cup of tea . . ."

Well, it transpired that they'd all gone out to the pub before dinner. And Rodney and Madeleine had watched while he banged in the code on the burglar alarm. And Phil had left his keys in the pocket of his raincoat, hanging up in the pub . . .

"But," he kept on saying stupidly, "but . . ."

To cut a long story short, his mate Rodney didn't have any criminal record, beyond drunk-driving. But Madeleine Something had a record as long as your arm, as well as a little friend we knew very well called Spike Malone. And the Met were just about to raid Spike's Mum's tower block flat . . .

Two days later, I laid the cameras at Phil's feet. At least metaphorically, for they were still required as evidence.

"Hey, you're bright, Sergeant," he said. "Sherlock Holmes rides again, eh?"

I could've hit him, except I was on duty. But he got his act together in time and asked me out to dinner. Which I accepted as I like good food but a sergeant's pay doesn't run to it. And we sort of went on from there. Though I never took him seriously, because he was an inch shorter than me. But he was fun. An innocent really. And I had a maternal urge to tidy up his little life for him.

At the first of his parties that I went to, somebody lit up a reefer. I got my coat and left before you could say "New Scotland Yard" and we had the mother and father of a row over the phone afterwards. He promised to get rid of certain people from his life, and he must've done, because I never spotted anything dicey again.

The most interesting friends he had left were John Malpas the painter and his wife Melanie. John wasn't your typical artist. Looked like a worried banker and worked at his paintings like a stevedore, all the hours God sent. He was always so busy talking at table that you had to throw out his glass of wine afterwards. Melanie was painfully thin but very elegant with the most enormous grey eyes. I approved of the fact that unlike most of Phil's friends, they were actually married. Terminally married. They really needed each other, like my Mum and Dad do. So I felt comfortable with them.

That Saturday morning, Phil and I'd been up the Portobello Market and Phil had acquired yet another camera. A 1930s Zeiss Ikon. He had three Zeiss Ikons already, but you know what collectors are. But what had really turned him on was that this Zeiss had a roll of exposed film still inside it. A random slice of somebody else's life, Phil called it, and vanished into his precious darkroom to develop it, leaving me to finish getting dinner ready, because John and Melanie were coming. Ambitious cook, Phil. Always does the main dishes, soaking them overnight in wine or oil, till you can't tell whether you're eating beef or lamb. But he's not keen on doing all the fiddly bits.

He was in the darkroom so long, I had to lay the table as well. And give John and Melanie their first drink and dips. When he finally emerged for dinner, after much screaming and hammering on the darkroom door, he was still in his oldest jeans and a tee-shirt that stank of developer. He was as high as a kite; you would almost have thought he was on a trip. He held a handful of big ten-by-eight enlargements that dripped fixer on the carpet he'd paid thirty-five pounds a yard for.

He shoved one print at John, saying, "What do you make of that?" and then sat with the other prints in his lap, where they made a spreading damp patch on his jeans.

Now John had one little vanity: his powers of observation. He could never see a picture postcard, or a photo on a calendar, or even a half-finished jigsaw, without sitting down to work out what the picture was of, what time of day it had been taken and even what month of the year it was. Shouting, "Don't you *dare* give me a clue!" I think he saw me as a rival. He was always saying that artists had greater powers of observation than any detective.

Determined not to be left out, I took my drink and went to sit beside him. The photograph, needle-sharp, was of a village green, with the parish church in the background.

That would tell him where east lay . . .

"Taken in the evening," he said. "Look at the length of those shadows."

"October," I said. "Leaves still on the trees, but quite a lot fallen."

"Taken after 1937," he said. "There's the last sort of pre-War Austin Seven."

"But before the War," I said, cock-a-hoop. "There's one of those Wall's ice-cream tricycles—you know, 'Stop Me and Buy One.' They never came back, after the War."

"Sergeant, I take my hat off to you!" Then he shot in, "Pantile roofs—that means somewhere near the east coast."

"There's a flint wall—the southern part of the east coast. East Anglia . . ."

"Look at the size of the church. That's Suffolk or I'm a Dutchman."

"There's a white weatherboarded house—you don't get many of those north of Woodbridge." Then I played my trump-card. "A Sunday evening—kids in their Sunday best, people coming out of church, women carrying prayer-books . . ."

"Damn you, Sergeant. This country's turning into a police state." But his eyes were still scanning the photo, looking for the last word.

Phil laughed diabolically, pleased to have set us off against each other. He handed us another photograph.

"Try this, my children!"

It was the photograph of a woman, or perhaps only a girl; holding on to the door of the Austin Seven, looking shyly up into the camera.

"She's not married," I said. "No ring."

"A prim miss—no nail-varnish. Ankle socks."

"But . . . in love, I think. Very much in love. With the man who took the picture."

"You sentimental old sergeant. I didn't know the Met had it in them."

I was silent. Weighing up the girl. She had a shy, self-effacing way of standing. And yet her eyes were huge and glowing, and her lips parted . . . a shy girl made bold by love, I thought. And no engagement ring either. I didn't like to see such vulnerability. Then I told myself not to be an imaginative fool . . . you could read too much into faces.

"Want to know what her fellow looked like?" asked Phil. He passed another photograph. This one was much less professional, with the camera held crookedly, and the man's head hard up against the top edge. He too was leaning against the Austin Seven. It was the kind of photo an inexperienced girl might have taken . . .

"He looks very pleased with himself," said John, rather crossly. Was he a little in love with the girl in the photo? Was he jealous of the man? "And old enough to be her father."

I wasn't so sure about that. The man's hair was cut short at the back and sides, as all men's was in those days. It made his ears stick out and look huge. It also made him look middle-aged, but then that hairstyle in old photographs could make schoolboys look middle-aged.

"Eyes too close together," said John. "I never trust a man whose eyes are too close together." Then he added, "A bit of a puritan, I would say. Look at that mouth, a real thin rat-trap."

Phil gave another of his mock sinister laughs. "Not so sure of that. Look at this one."

It was the girl again. Lying down in what seemed to be a woodland glade. On a tartan rug, with a straggle of items around her: Thermos flask, picnic basket, raincoats. Her clothing was not at all disarranged, except for the skirt which had ridden up over one knee. But her smile, the glow in her eyes, stronger now . . . every hallmark of a girl who has happily made love. A lock of her hair was falling over one eye . . .

"Yes," said John. He wriggled a little, on the sofa next to me. I think he was embarrassed because the same thought had come into his head. A very nice man, John.

"And this," said Phil triumphantly, handing us the last print with a flourish. "Talk about the wreck of the *Hesperus*."

The girl still lay in the forest glade, but she lay full length now, her head resting flat against the ground, her eyes nearly shut, the mouth drooping open in a most unpleasing way . . .

I froze. I had seen such photographs too often to be mistaken. The grace of the long limbs was gone; they were as untidy as a pile of dropped garbage.

"She's dead," I said. "I've seen too many like her. I *know*."

"God, I feel sick," said John. And the next second he was running for the bathroom.

We sat round in a huddled, excited heap.

"Can't *you* do something?" Phil asked me plaintively for the fifth time.

"Not if I value my job," I said, backing off vigorously. "We don't know when that picture was taken or where, or who they were. We only know it was well over fifty years ago. And that last photograph is *not* evidence. It could be a trick of the light, a trick of the camera. Maybe she was just in pain, or feeling sick. We have no evidence it was even taken in England."

"The other photo was—you said it was Suffolk."

"That was the other photograph. They might have taken the camera overseas . . ."

"It looks like an English glade."

"Don't you think they have glades like that in France or Germany? What the hell do you mean, an *English* glade? Are you an expert on English glades or something?" I was starting to get mad.

Poor Phil wilted and looked moodily at his expensive carpet. "We could try and find the place," he said feebly. "That wouldn't do any harm. We could drive over there and make enquiries . . ."

"Have you ever tried making enquiries?" I asked savagely, remembering how many doors I'd knocked on, and my aching feet. "If that girl was alive now, she'd be in her mid-seventies. Most of the people who knew her when she looked like that will be dead long since. Do you see yourself knocking on the door of every old granny in Suffolk saying do you remember this girl?"

"All the same," said John thoughtfully, "I think we ought to try. That girl's face will haunt me. I feel I owe it to her."

I glanced at Melanie, expecting the support of some common sense from the distaff side. But her face, very sad, was watching John's. Again, I felt how close the two of them were.

At last she said, "I think we must. It's so awful to think of him killing her, then photographing her when she was dead . . . as if he wanted to gloat over it. I don't think a man like that should be wandering about loose, however old he is, even if he's eighty. It's like those Nazi war criminals . . . it's never too late to bring them to justice."

"Let's go over and look next weekend," said Phil, a little smile of excitement lighting up his face, so I could have *kicked* him, for his heartlessness.

"A sort of murder holiday weekend," I said bitterly. "Like they lay on at hotels now. Only with an extra luxury, a real corpse."

"C'mon," he said. "I know a super pub we could stay at, at Felsbrough. The cooking is out of this world . . ."

I didn't go for the food. I went to keep him out of trouble.

I didn't see him again until the next weekend, when I'd booked myself three days' leave; I had plenty of rest-days in hand.

He seemed to have regained his high spirits by the time he rang my bell. Regained them indeed, considering he was wearing a ridiculous outfit of white flannels and a pink blazer with white stripes.

"What's this—a fancy-dress ball?" His little face fell, and I felt a bit of a brute.

"Just getting in the spirit of the thing—Albert Campion and all that . . . 1930s."

"I suppose I should give you a clip over the Lugg . . ."

Worse was to follow when I locked my flat and went downstairs. Parked next to my Metro was a huge green object with brass headlights and no roof.

"What's that supposed to be?"

"Bentley four-liter. 1936. Borrowed it off a mate—he owed me a favor."

From the back seat of the monstrosity, John and Melanie waved. They were wearing matching and tasteful tweed suits and deerstalker hats. Melanie's outfit even had a cape. They looked exceedingly chic, and I felt I was joining a circus.

"Where do I put my luggage?" I said tightly. "Where's the boot?"

"Hasn't got much of a boot," said Phil. "I'll strap it on the back with the rest."

God, all that great length, which would be hell to park, and no boot. Even the spare wheel was strapped on the outside. That was the trouble with that monster. It was all outside and no inside. Most of the inside appeared to be occupied by the engine. The accommodation for passengers would've disgraced a First World War fighter plane.

"I hope it doesn't rain."

"There is a hood. But it takes about twenty minutes to put up. My mate *has* done it occasionally. But the weather forecast's good."

Needless to say, they'd found room for a food hamper between John and Melanie. There was the expected clink of champagne bottles, as they shifted uncomfortably in their leather seats.

"Hold on to your hats! We're off!"

I must say Phil seemed to know how to handle it; he was always good at mechanical things. I never actually felt in danger of my life, though the flashy way he showed off his skill at double de-clutching was a little grating after a while. And I suppose there is something in that old saying about the joy of feeling the wind in your hair; fortunately I keep mine in a tight bun, as I said. But what with digging flies out of my eye, and having to scream every remark at the top of my voice over the vroom of the exhausts, and worrying about the straps holding my luggage on the back . . . it didn't improve my temper.

Nonetheless, it didn't stop the conversation.

"We've made a bit of progress since last week," said Phil. "I talked to a feller about that film in the camera. He said it was impossible for a roll of exposed undeveloped negatives to have lasted since the 1930s. Yet they *are* from the 1930s . . ."

"You call that making *progress*?" I snapped (if you can snap while screaming at the top of your voice).

Yet it spooked me, what he said. As a policewoman, I don't go for the inexplicable. I would like a world without the inexplicable. I felt a shiver run down my spine, as if somebody had walked over my grave.

And John and Melanie in the back didn't help any. John had spent the week going over the big prints with a magnifying glass. I began to realize that he had an obsessional personality, and he was obsessed.

"That bloke . . . his hand on the car door . . . he's wearing a wedding ring on the third finger of his left hand. He's got a ring, and she hasn't . . . that's a motive for him doing her in."

"What do you mean, a motive?"

"He might have got her pregnant . . . she might have been threatening to go to his wife and spill the beans. So he had to shut her up, hadn't he?"

"We haven't even proved she's dead yet." The whole thing began to disgust me. John and Melanie were high on what I suppose a bad novelist would call the thrill of the chase.

You don't get the police talking about the thrill of the chase. Or if you do, avoid them, because they're very bad police. If you talk about the thrill of the chase, it means you've decided who's guilty before you can prove it. Oh, you have that temptation inside you all the time, but you sit on it and sit on it and never let it take you over . . .

"I've found something else," said John, not at all abashed. "There's a signpost on the village green in the first print—just in front of the church. You can't read the names on it, even with a magnifying glass. They're out of focus. But you can count the *letters* in the names, as blobs. There are five letters in the top name, and twelve in the bottom name."

"What good is that? Lots of place names have five letters."

"Yes, but not many have twelve, even in East Anglia, which is famous for long names. I've been over the road atlas, and I can only find four. Tattingstone, Wickhambrook and Grundisburgh in Suffolk, and Wethersfield in Essex. It gives us places to start. I suggest we eliminate Wickhambrook first—it's furthest from the sea, and the least likely to have pantiles on the roofs . . ."

"We'll take the M11," said Phil. "Show you what the old girl can do." He put his foot down.

The old girl showed us what she could do. Once, before I put *my* foot down and made Phil take his off, she did well over a hundred. It was very painful. The slipstream came round the tiny windscreen and hit us in the face like a mob throwing half-bricks. And the poor old thing was straining every sprocket; I thought she was going to blow up on us. And then, of course, the modern cars, the Jags and Mercs and big BMWs, began to want to show us what they were made of . . . and since I knew they could do a hundred and thirty without more than a whisper of a whistle . . . We were attracting more male attention than a bitch in heat.

I finally got Phil to cut it to eighty, and that was bad enough. I didn't fancy being pulled up by a jam-butty car for speeding, even as a passenger. They give you such a look . . .

Once we had turned off for Wickhambrook, and I had breath to think, a nasty idea came floating into my mind out of my past. The medieval idea, from Chaucer's day, of the Ship of Fools. Wealthy fools voyaging to their own destruction.

Only we were a Car of Fools.

Of course, Wickhambrook was nothing like the photograph. They hadn't expected it to be. You don't get a signpost saying Wickhambrook in Wickhambrook. You drive round Wickhambrook in ever increasing circles, looking at church towers. A bit like a steeplechase, because the church in our photo certainly had a spectacular steeple. What John referred to as a broach-spire . . .

It was quite fun at first. I had no idea there were so many kinds of church towers. Round ones, ones with octagonal tops, ones with four pinnacles and ones with eight, ones with spectacular gargoyles and even ones with flat plain tops. Needle-spires and broach-spires. I owe all my extensive knowledge of church towers to that weekend.

And just about the time my head began to spin, they got discouraged and had lunch in a sweet meadow in the sunshine. With the champagne, which always improves my temper.

After lunch, we drove on to Tattingstone. After they had despaired of Tattingstone, we went on and despaired of Grundisburgh.

It was when they had reached the point of total despair, when reality was at last breaking in on them, when they were talking about going on to the hotel and the whole thing might have collapsed into a harmless weekend, that I had to go and set them off again.

I don't like being beaten, you see. So I was still keeping my eyes open. And then I saw something. Nothing at all like a steeple, but it was a church just the same. Only this church didn't have a tower at all . . .

I saw a bus outside the church. A luxury touring bus, disgorging a stream of elegant and sprightly pensioners, who were hung about with cameras, binoculars and clipboards. A cultural course on Suffolk churches, in full swing. And I simply got Phil to stop the car, walked over to them, picked out the course leader, who was the only one without camera, binoculars and clipboard, and showed him our photograph.

"Bless me," he said, pushing up his bifocals on to his impressive forehead and squinting at the photo closely. "That's Bendham, before it lost its spire; in the great gale of 1976 . . ."

"But we've *been* to Bendham. It's nothing like. Just a tower peeping above great trees. And no village green."

He twinkled at me. "In the country, trees grow a lot in fifty years. And sadly, developers move in . . ."

I must say, Albert Campion and the two Sherlock Holmeses were not as pleased as I thought they'd be. Downright peevish.

But it *was* Bendham. The post office was still the same.

By then, it was time for a shower before dinner. Their stomachs took over and their brains went dead.

I bought a *Sunday Times* in the hotel next morning, and read right through it while they got on with their tomfoolery. The plan was to seek out old ladies within a ten-mile radius of Bendham.

I had pointed out that the best place to catch old ladies in the countryside on a Sunday morning was coming out of church. After that, the old ladies would sensibly go home, cook their roast lunch and have an afternoon snooze till it was time to go to church for Evensong . . .

They'd agreed with this. But next morning Phil had a hangover, and the breakfast was out of this world, and I couldn't get them moving before eleven. Perhaps it was as well. The vicars might have disapproved of a lunatic dressed as Albert Campion frightening their parishioners in their own churchyard. By the time we reached the first village, however, Matins was over and there wasn't a vicar or an old lady in sight.

What there was was a lot of small boys, born after 1975, drawn by the sight of the car, and even more middle-aged men, born after 1945, on their way to the pub. I suppose that damned car did help in a way . . .

Through them, Phil tracked down some old ladies in their rose-covered lairs, and knocked on their pretty white doors. Most of the old ladies thought he was on a promotion campaign for a new sort of washing powder, and were avid for coupons, free samples and chances to win £100,000 without committing them-selves to buying anything.

But none of them knew the girl in the photograph, though some of them knew an Austin Seven from a Singer Ten.

As I said, I read the *Sunday Times* right down to the Stock Exchange news, and let Phil exhaust himself with his own deadly charm.

Again, it might have trailed off into a normal Sunday, with drinks and crisps in a pub and then a long expensive lunch.

But I had finished the *Sunday Times* and I was getting bored.

"Has it occurred to you," I said to Phil as he leaned exhausted against the bonnet, "that if your girl was murdered when you think, she didn't live around here very long? Whereas your murderer, if, as you think, he got away with it, may have lived round here very much longer?"

"You mean . . . show them *his* photograph?"

"Yes, my sweet love."

He almost vaulted the last old lady's gate, he was so filled with renewed inspira-tion.

And then he came back, looking very solemn and important, and my heart went down into my boots.

"Got 'im," he said. "He was the local doctor. Dr. Hargreaves. Lived in Berpes-ford till he retired in 1967."

"A doctor," said John, suddenly abandoning a lump of the *Sunday Times* he'd pinched off me. "Doctors have more ways of killing people than ordinary folk . . ."

"Doctors," said Melanie dreamily, "like Dr. Crippen and Dr. Buck Ruxton . . ."
She reeled off a list of famous murdering doctors.

God, would you credit it? Bored farce to high drama in ten seconds. The atmosphere grew positively hysterical. I thought it was a good thing we had a police force. If it was left to the general public . . .

"Have you got his old address? Might as well see where he lived . . . and there's a very good pub in this guide, only about three miles from Berpesford," added John.

After an excellent lunch, we found the house. Phil knocked at the front door, asked after the good doctor, and came back looking very disgruntled.

"They haven't a clue where he went. They'd never even *heard* of him. They've only lived there for a year, and they bought the house off some Americans, who bought it off a civil engineer who worked in Ipswich."

"Honestly," said John indignantly. "There's just no continuity in village life any more. Rich outsiders moving in, not caring about the place, not staying five minutes . . . bloody *yuppies*."

They sat for a long time, glaring at the house, as if willing the pillared front door and Virginia creeper to give them a clue. After a while the people inside noticed us, and began glaring back.

"Let's go. Before they call the police," I said.

They pulled up in a lay-by, and sat and talked things over. The best they could come up with was that we should backtrack to all the old ladies we had already spoken to, to ask them if they knew where the good doctor had retired to.

It was not a good idea. It's hard to remember which old lady you've spoken to, in a village where you've only been once. And we'd been to so many villages that I never wanted to see a pretty Suffolk village again, as long as I lived. We slowly foundered in a mass of argument.

"I'm sure it's that street on the left; I remember turning by the pub with the green shutters."

"I don't think it's this village at all; the church was set back among trees and it had a smaller tower."

"That was *Tattersham*, you idiot."

"Fettersham, you mean!"

What old ladies we did find were grumpy at being disturbed again from their naps. They thought the good doctor had retired to Framlingham, Hedingham, Swannington, Walsingham and Clacton respectively. They all said he would be very old by now, well over eighty, and two thought they'd heard he'd died. The only thing they were agreed about was that he had been a wonderful doctor, whom they'd never forget as long as they lived.

Then it began to rain. John and Phil had a marvelous swearing-match over putting up the folding hood, which took much longer than twenty minutes. It reduced the interior of the car to a small dim rabbit-hutch, with yellowing celluloid windows.

Phil said the hood was genuine and authentic.

Melanie said it was leaking in at least three places.

It also obscured Phil's view to the rear, so that he crunched the precious love-object slightly, getting out of a narrow parking space.

He was reduced to a sweating babbling wreck, thinking what the good mate who had loaned him the car would say, and how much the repair would cost him. I gathered he might be drummed out of his city bank, as the mate was considerably senior to him . . .

In the end, they slunk back to the hotel with their tails between their legs, and I went and had a hot shower and changed. I was idly lounging around, waiting for Phil to knock on my door for pre-dinner drinks, when I noticed my room had a telephone.

And of course, a local telephone directory.

And, ever so casually, to satisfy my own curiosity, I picked it up and looked up the name "Hargreaves."

There was only half a column of Hargreaveses; and a Dr. L. Hargreaves sat halfway down it. He lived in Framlingham.

I sat paralyzed.

I was a copper; and coppers become coppers because they believe strongly in law and order, and in making the punishment fit the crime; and as they tell you at training school, a copper is never off-duty.

But this man must be so old, and it was all so long ago, and the only evidence I had was one photographic negative that I'd been told couldn't possibly have survived for fifty years. And I wasn't even on my own patch. I thought of trying to explain it all to some grim, cynical, stolid local Superintendent and I thought he'd give me a pitying look and tell me to run away and play. He'd have a word with my own Super, and I'd be the divisional joke. It's hard enough to get any credence as a woman copper, and this could *destroy* me.

At that point, Phil walked in without knocking. He'd never done that before. I don't know if he was trying to catch me running about stark naked or what.

Instead, his hopeful little eye fell on the open telephone directory. And he got it in one. I mean, he's not stupid, just childish.

"You've *got* him!"

"There is a Dr. Hargreaves in the book," I said coldly.

We had another terrific conference over the crisps and drinks. That awful hunting look had come back into their eyes and I hated them. Talk about blood lust . . . their only problem was whether they should corner their fiend in human form before or after dinner.

I used all the arguments I could: that he was so old, that he might be the son, that he might be a different Dr. Hargreaves altogether. It was no use. They were set on their bit of fun.

"There'd be no harm in ringing him up," said Phil. "Find out if it *is* him."

"No," I said.

"Well if you won't, I will."

That I couldn't allow. He'd go in like a bull in a china shop; he might give the old boy a fatal heart attack.

So I went back up to my room and rang the good doctor's number. They all clustered round to listen.

I knew it was him, the moment he answered. The voice was clear, but faint and a little wavering. His breathing was much louder than his talking. I knew he was not only old, but sick.

"You won't know me, Dr. Hargreaves," I said, "but I've just come across a camera that I think used to belong to you. And there was a roll of film in it. I thought you might like to see the prints we got from it . . ."

After all, what else could I say?

I heard his sharp intake of breath. I was expecting him to put the phone down on me, or at least begin to bluster. But he only said, almost normally:

"The Zeiss Ikon? I've been waiting for you a long, long time, my dear. I began to doubt that you'd ever come."

His voice was calm, resigned. As if he truly had been waiting for me. He was so calm and sure, I grew a little afraid. Then he said:

"Would you like to bring the photographs over? This evening?"

Because I was afraid, because I knew he *was* the one, I said, "I have three friends with me."

"Bring them. They will be quite welcome. Nine o'clock?"

I looked at the avid faces crowding round me, listening to both sides of the conversation. All I could do was say yes.

He gave me directions on how to get there, and rang off.

His garden was an old person's garden, small but as neat as a pin. The knocker was brass, a fox's face, and highly polished. There was a general air of quiet prosperity, and the smell of old age as he opened the door.

It was the man in the photograph all right. Wrinkles gather and gather, but bones don't change. His eyes were still too close together, and his mouth even more like a rat-trap. He had been tall, but now he stooped over two sticks. His hands clenched on the sticks like an old tree's roots clench into the soil.

"Come in, come in." He looked at my friends one by one. Not one of them had the guts to look him in the face. I thought of juries, who will not look at the prisoner in the dock when they have found him guilty.

He asked us to sit down; offered us a drink, which we all declined. I could not tell if his hands were trembling from fear, or whether they always trembled like that.

When he had slowly settled himself and laid one stick carefully on each side of his chair, I gave him the first photograph.

He smiled, remotely. "Bendham. It's changed so much, I wonder you were able to find it. And my old Austin Seven. I had it until 1950. Then I was able to afford something better . . ."

Then I handed him the photo of himself. And he smiled remotely again and said:

"That's still how I imagine myself, in my mind's eye. These days the mirror is always rather a shock. You just can't believe you're getting old, and the older you get, the less you believe it. But there I stand, on the verge of middle age. Still hopeful . . . it's amazing how hopeful middle age can be."

He put it down beside him and gestured for the next print, with what seemed like eagerness. I somehow knew he hadn't forgotten the order in which they'd been taken. He was expecting her . . .

When I handed it to him, he smiled a third time, and this time it was a *real* smile. A smile of joy; a smile so joyful that I gave a little shiver down my spine.

"Peggy," he said. "Peggy. She was so young. Young and hopeful too. And very much in love. Dear Peggy."

I saw Phil's hand grip the arm of the sofa. Melanie kept giving little coughs, as if she was trying to dislodge something in her throat. John's face was white and sweating. I think it was starting to get too real for any of them to cope with. I've long known the feeling, from my job.

I handed him the fourth photograph.

"Bendham Woods," he said. "We had to be so very careful. I was a married man, with three children. And she was one of my patients. I tried to get her to go to another doctor, but she wouldn't. It would have meant her going into Ipswich by bus . . . She was a lovely girl, but unworldly. Never had a job, just looked after her aged parents till they died. They left her comfortably off, but what kind of life was that for a young woman?"

He looked up; looked at me.

"You're very *calm*, my dear! Are you a policewoman?"

I said, "Yes, but not from around here. I'm with the Met."

He said, "I'm glad." I couldn't make out whether he meant he was glad I was a policewoman, or whether he was glad I wasn't from round here.

I handed him the last photograph, and he shook his head sadly and said:

"You spotted she was dead, then?"

"I've seen too many . . ."

"Yes," he said, "yes."

Then he looked at me very straight, with those eyes that were too close together. "What do you want?"

"The truth."

"Yes, I can see that. But what do your *friends* want?"

He surveyed them calmly. None of them would look at him.

"I expect they want me punished," he said. "The world is full of people who want other people punished. I find it a little disgusting. Revenge, I can understand. It's an honest emotion. But people who haven't been harmed themselves, who want people *punished*. What do you think they're up to, eh? I meet people who want the striking miners punished, or unmarried mothers, or drug addicts, or Pakistanis who dare speak up for their beliefs. It's not pretty, my dear. It's not pretty at all."

He let a long and unbearable silence develop, and watched them writhe.

"Such people never seem to think that life itself can be sufficient punishment. Life and the years that pile up. But no, your friends want me *arrested*. Put on trial. In all the papers, so that all the other people who want to punish can read about my punishment, and have their appetite for punishment satisfied. For a little while. Until they find a new victim." Then he added, with another straight look at me, "But I think you only want the truth, my dear. So you shall have it. It's all you will get, I think, because even being arrested would be enough to finish me off. I shouldn't last a week . . . I'm a doctor, and I *know*."

"Are you guilty?" I blurted out. Because the strangest thing was happening. He was separating me from my friends. It was them I saw as monsters now. I was on his side. Had he some strange magic, that still worked, behind those mottled deathly cheeks and weary burnt-out eyes? Was it the strange magic that had lured Peggy to her death?

"I was guilty—of great heartlessness," he said. "And I have been punished for it."

"Heartlessness is not a crime," I said.

"Ah, but it should be. It was right that I was punished." There was no self-pity in his voice, no special pleading. Just . . . I hope when I am old, I can reach that kind of tranquility.

"What happened?"

He shrugged. "We fell in love. With all our hearts. I had thought I knew what love was, with my own wife, for my wife and I were always comfortable together, and I loved her till the day she died. But this . . . It was springtime and . . . I don't think we cared if we died for it. We both knew it couldn't last, somehow. It was as if Peggy gathered all her careful life into a great bundle and threw it to me. My only concern was that my wife should not find out and be hurt. So we were very, very careful. We would meet in a quiet spot, and drive to places where nobody knew either of us. That's how we came to pass through Bendham that day."

"Yes," I said.

"It may sound very strange to you, my dear, but we never made love—not all the way. We were innocents in those days—not at all like now, when people hop into bed the first time they meet. I know I was an experienced married man, but half the time Peggy seemed more like a daughter. I sometimes think we got more out of holding hands than some of them today get from bed."

There was a strangled indecipherable grunt from Phil, and he stirred uneasily.

"What happened?" I asked.

Dr. Hargreaves gave me another of those straight looks from his faded eyes, ghostly eyes, and said:

"She just died, there in the glade, as I was taking her photograph. We had been . . . extraordinarily passionate, for us. She had a weak heart. I saw her die through the camera viewfinder, as I was clicking the release. I ran to her, tried everything. There was nothing I could do. Except leave her where she lay."

"*Leave* her?" All John's suppressed rage boiled out in one terrible shout.

"What else could I do? There was nothing I could do for *her*. She was beyond my aid. And I was a married man and a doctor, with a reputation and a job to lose. My wife would have suffered terribly, if the truth had got out. My children might have starved. Life wasn't a bed of roses in the 1930s, especially for a disgraced and struck-off doctor. I might never have worked again. And I was a *good* doctor."

He put his face quite suddenly into his hands. I thought he had been taken ill, and touched his arm, but he shook me off.

"It was a solitary spot. They didn't find her body for nearly a week . . . the animals had been at her . . . her face and hands."

"We've only got your word you didn't kill her," said John, with a savagery that made me shudder.

"Oh, no," said Dr. Hargreaves, looking up. "There was a post mortem. And an inquest, of course. She died of natural causes. She had an aneurysm. She couldn't have lasted six months more, the coroner said. I have often wondered if she knew that, instinctively, and that was what made her so desperate for love . . . Here's the details."

He handed me a brown newspaper clipping, and the same dark innocent face of Peggy stared out at me. But this was a formal studio photograph; she was wearing a silly little hat. The inquest did record a verdict of death from natural causes. There was a coroner's warning about young girls in poor health going for walks alone in lonely places.

"So you got away with it?" said John savagely.

Dr. Hargreaves eyed him long.

"I suppose you could say that. My name was never connected with hers. My wife never found out; my children got a good start in life, and still think highly of me."

John made a sound of disgust in his throat.

"But I don't think I got away with it," said Dr. Hargreaves. "I was the police surgeon for the area. I was called in to give my professional opinion. I had to help at the post mortem. There was no way I could get out of it."

"Oh, my God," said Melanie. "John, I feel sick."

"I should take your wife home, sir," said Dr. Hargreaves, "while you still have her."

Phil went too. Dr. Hargreaves and I stood up. He looked at me, as if from a great distance, as if from the doors of Death itself.

"You are a good policewoman," he said. "You'll go far. Because you want the truth. God bless you." There were tears in his faded eyes now.

"One last question . . ." I said. Diffidently. Because I didn't want to upset him any more, but I had to know the whole truth.

"Yes, my dear?"

"The camera. How did you come to lose the camera?"

He smiled, a little painfully. "I couldn't bear to touch it again, after what happened. Knowing what film it had inside it. I wanted to have it developed, so I could have a last photograph of her. But I couldn't risk sending it to any chemist for developing, could I? They look at the prints in the darkroom . . . So the camera hung unused in the cupboard in our bedroom for years. It irritated my wife greatly; that I couldn't bring myself to use it. She wanted photographs of the children as they grew up, like any mother, and she couldn't use it herself—she was frightened of it, it wasn't simple like a Brownie box. In the end, in a fit of rage, she sent it to the church jumble-sale. I never knew a moment's peace after that . . . I didn't even dare to try and trace who'd bought it."

"Will you be all right?" I asked.

"Whether I live, or die tonight, I shall be all right now. It's such a relief to tell somebody at last. You were as good as a priest in the confessional, my dear."

I kissed him then; on both withered cheeks. He was so light and frail, it was like kissing a ghost. But a good and faithful ghost.

I have no worries for him. Wherever he has gone.

But I still wonder Who preserved those negatives.

THE WEALTH OF KINGDOMS
(An Inflationary Tale)
Daniel Hood

For a lighter touch, here's an economics lesson from the lands of Mother Goose and fairy stories.

Daniel Hood is the art director for an international financial affairs company. His short fiction has appeared in *Dragon* magazine and his first novel, *Fanuilh*, has just been published.

"The Wealth of Kingdoms (An Inflationary Tale)" comes from the November issue of the new *Science Fiction Age* magazine.

—T. W.

The current local economic and political situation can be traced to the recent destabilizing influx of hard currency, in the form of golden eggs, precipitated by the transfer of assets from the Giant of the Beanstalk to Jack, a poverty-line family agriculturist living in the resource-poor hinterlands in the east of the kingdom.

Jack's rapid ascent from subsistence farming to independent wealth and the concomitant stresses placed on the local economy and later, the entire kingdom's economy, deserve a closer look. Indeed, as we hope to prove in this case study, his ascent lies at the root of many of the troubles our kingdom is experiencing at the moment. We will begin by discussing the microeconomic results and then broaden our discussion to the macroeconomic issues.

JACK'S RISE TO WEALTH AND ITS IMPACT
ON THE LOCAL ECONOMY

The morning after liberating the Golden Goose from the Giant, Jack immediately used his new wealth to hire several local carters to haul away the Giant's corpse. Because he had not yet found a way to break the eggs, he paid the farmers with one apiece, creating a momentary boom for the transport trade in the region and increasing the tax base to the point where local administrators could begin improving roads, bridges and other infrastructures.

In addition, Jack built himself and his mother a new house, a grand estate that sparked a round of conspicuous consumption among the provincial gentry as they tried to keep up with him. He also donated the Beanstalk to the local poor and the struggling farmers, providing a sort of primitive welfare system.

All well and good, it must have seemed at the time, and indeed the media—town criers, wandering bards and the like—applauded the generally positive upward trend, giving Jack much of the credit.

However, after a brief period of relatively high expectations, the provincial economy began to suffer, for the following reasons:

1. Jack's habit of paying for goods and services with whole eggs (he had not yet acquired the necessary technology for breaking them into smaller pieces) caused a rapid inflationary spiral, as people with large, oval hunks of gold began to compete for the few consumer goods available in this primarily agricultural, self-sufficient region.

2. The unrealistic rise in real estate and construction activity, which inevitably slowed after a period of months.

3. An increase in the number of below-poverty-line farmers, as those who could provide neither goods nor services in return for gold were turned off their land, hit by inflation, and forced to join those on the Beanstalk Dole.

4. The depletion of the Beanstalk Dole itself, as more and more people clamored for the rapidly-diminishing trunk. When the Beanstalk was finished, Jack did not realize that a substitute was necessary, and many of those who had been forced to rely on it for food found themselves without. This engendered a rural mob of sorts, a mass of unemployed, jobless wanderers with dangerous expectations of governmental assistance.

5. The strains placed on local government. Noblemen and officials found themselves faced with a growing underclass expecting beanstalk-type largess. At the same time, the rise in tax revenue from Jack's initial infusion of Golden Goose eggs had caused them to invest in long-term infrastructure projects, many of which were financed with equally long-term debt. When the tax revenues leveled off (because Jack had stopped handing out the eggs left and right, as he had at first), the local government was forced into deficit spending.

6. Unrealistic expectations on the part of carters, who began to refuse to transfer goods for any form of payment other than golden eggs. Those farmers who had managed to continue to grow staple food crops found their produce rotting in their barns because wagoners would not carry them. (For more information, see Grimm & Grimm's excellent *Yokes, Yolks and Yokels: The Carter's Guild in the Eastern Provinces.*)

7. Finally, a rash of plagues and diseases that decimated the local population. Environmental studies have revealed that much of this was the result of the Giant's corpse being hauled by the carters into the mountains, which were the source of the area's water. When the corpse rotted, it contaminated the water, which gave rise to devastating diseases.

This last might have had a salutary effect: the decrease in the population of laborers and the rural mob (who were particularly hard hit) might have eventually evened out the inflationary spiral by bringing scant resources and the smaller population into proportion.

However, at this point Jack decided to move to the capital, perhaps because of the growing problems of the countryside (for which he himself was largely responsible), and his actions began to have a much broader effect on the kingdom as a whole.

CRUCIFIED ON AN EGG OF GOLD: JACK IN THE CAPITAL

Jack's entry into the royal city, as initially happened in the countryside, was attended by a honeymoon period. The city was far better able to accommodate the influx of golden eggs, and Jack was also put in touch with the proper smelting technology for breaking his eggs into smaller pieces, facilitating a more reasonable market price.

Indeed, the grace period lasted far longer here, and for almost three years Jack was a force for progress in the national economy. The greater pool of luxury goods at his disposal allowed a natural outlet for his growing income (the goose had, due to the new and scientifically-improved feeds being developed in the capital, nearly doubled production), and the higher taxes imposed by Prince Charming's government siphoned off much of the excess.

Jack's spending encouraged greater trade, and routes were opened or expanded that connected the kingdom with Never-Never Land, Oz and Wonderland. The boost in both exports and imports allowed for higher tax revenues, which the Charming Government used to both improve the infrastructure and deal with many of the problems Jack had caused in the countryside. The Ministers of Straw, Wood and Brick in particular were the main architects of this pump priming (again, for details, see Grimm & Grimm's *Huffing and Puffing and Building Your Economy Up*).

Private sector industry experienced a long-lasting healthy boom as well. In partnership with the venture capitalist Rumpelstiltskin, Jack began the development of the Giant's former kingdom in the clouds. A new Beanstalk was grown and an entire complex of condominiums and amusement parks was erected around the Giant's castle, as well as various public housing projects legislated by the Charming Government. A number of joint ventures were formed, of particular importance those with Mad Hatter, Inc., of Wonderland, for importing tea, and with the Wizard of Oz for importing brains, courage and hearts. (Baum's *Imports and Exports and Tariffs—Oh My!* offers a brief but informative history of the last.)

But the honeymoon was brief. Jack and Rumpelstiltskin's Cloud Kingdom Development Zone began to draw more and more workers from the earth-bound economy. Inflation began to spiral again, and then the Charming Government was rocked by internal dissension. The Three Pigs resigned in disgust and were replaced by the much less effective Three Bears. Various protest groups sprang up, most notably the quasi-socialist Red Seven, former associates of Queen Snow White, who claimed that Jack's Golden Goose was ruining the gold industry by undercutting their prices. Interest groups like the Orphan's Defense Fund, run by social activists Hansel and Gretel, were calling for more governmental funds for the underprivileged and harsher punishments for witches.

Finally, the illusory health of the kingdom's economy was shattered by the Elves' wildcat strike. By walking out on the old Shoemaker, they literally halted the kingdom in its tracks—without shoes, no one could go anywhere. (When told that the peasants had no shoes, King Charming's daughter-in-law Princess Cinderella is reputed to have answered, "Let them wear glass slippers!" Andersen's *Forced to Work All Night: The Unionization of the Shoemaker's Elves* makes the point that Cinderella's comment was typical of the Charming Government's basic failure to understand the situation.)

The unlikely Pinocchio was chosen to replace the disgraced Three Bears. With little credibility and an inability to lie effectively in public, a worse puppet could not have been appointed. He caved in to literally every demand—nationalizing the shoe industry, raising prohibitive tariffs, funding all social programs (whether effective or not) with huge deficits, and raising taxes through the roof.

Wonderland and Oz responded by forming a free trade area that effectively forbade trade with our kingdom, and Never-Never Land's impulsive Minister of Finance Pan enacted an open embargo.

Confidence in the government fell to an all-time low. The Red Seven began a series of terrorist attacks, the Elves took to the streets again, and Jack and Rumpelstiltskin were forced to close off immigration to the Cloud Kingdom.

With the kingdom poised on the brink of disaster, the final straw broke the camel's back. As part of his immense establishment, Jack had hired a cook from England, whose cuisine apparently made up for his stupidity. On Christmas Day, unable to find another goose in the larder, he killed and cooked the golden egg producer, serving it up as the main course at Christmas dinner.

Black Christmas, as it has come to be known, effectively crippled the kingdom. Without the Golden Goose to support the Charming Government's gold standard, kingdom money became worthless, and inflation rose to an unheard-of 200 percent.

Only the immediate declaration of martial law by the Charming Government, now with the shrewd Riding Hood as prime minister, saved the kingdom from potential civil war.

From this point of view, few can doubt that Jack is immediately responsible for most of the ills currently facing the kingdom. Riding Hood's policies—the removal of all subsidies (except those for grandmothers); her vigorous pursuit of harsh punishments for terrorists, monopolists, and wolves; and the reopening of trade with other kingdoms—may enable us to gradually work our way back to economic health.

But recovery is a slow, painful process, with no quick fixes or easy solutions. As Prime Minister Riding Hood herself pointed out (in *What Big Expectations You Have*, a recently released government white paper offering bleak near-term prospects), "If you take short cuts, you usually end up in a wolf's belly."

This is the real world after all—not some fairy tale.

THE CRUCIAN PIT

Nicholas Royle

Nicholas Royle was born in 1963 in South Manchester, England, and now lives in London. Since 1984 he has published stories in *Interzone*, *Dark Voices*, *Obsessions*, *Narrow Houses*, *Little Deaths*, *The Year's Best Horror Stories*, and *Best New Horror*. His first novel, *Counterparts*, was recently published in the United Kingdom.

"The Crucian Pit" is one of three stories in this volume reprinted from Stephen Jones's *The Mammoth Book of Zombies*. As with many of Royle's stories, it begins in seeming normality and descends into darkness. This is Royle's second appearance in our *Year's Best* series; we reprinted "Glory" in our *Sixth Annual Collection*.

—E.D.

It isn't *always* a bad idea to go back. Sometimes you have to.

Nicci and I drove up north on Friday morning in my red Citroen. She'd managed to get someone to cover for her at the bookshop and I'd simply told my art director I needed the day off. As a freelance designer that meant losing a day's pay but I'd been waiting a long time to make this trip, even since before I met Nicci, and I wasn't going to waste half the weekend by driving up on a Saturday. It was bad enough on the Friday morning thanks to two stretches of roadworks between the M25 and Newport Pagnell. By 11:30, however, we were clear and belting up the Ml with the windows down and Chris Rea cranked up to full volume. It was a beautiful day, bright sunshine, no wind—not even the sprawl of the Midlands could spoil it. We invented stories about other drivers. The mid-30s blonde in the BMW was on her way to meet a younger lover in Macclesfield; the rep in the Sierra was working his last day for a pharmaceuticals company and would start a new job as picture researcher for a girlie magazine on Monday. Drivers who'd been pulled over by speed cops we either felt sorry for or laughed at—depending on what car they drove. We were both doing pretty well financially and I'd bought the Citroen almost new as an ex-demonstration model, but we still both felt more of an affinity with the young rocker in his souped-up Singer Vogue than the tosser on the phone in his Porsche.

Nicci's bookshop job was filling in time between college and something more interesting, she said. Acting or music, she was vague about it but she was happy enough. I'd come on since my first job—stuffing envelopes—and prospects were looking good, but I couldn't fully relax at anything until I'd gone back up north and laid certain ghosts to rest. That's why I was getting more and more excited— and nervous—the closer we got. This weekend was important. I wasn't expecting to enjoy every moment but there would be pleasures to be had in touring round the old haunts. We wouldn't be seeing my folks—even though Nicci still hadn't met them—as they had left the area years ago for Scotland and well-earned retirement.

As I began recognizing landmarks I pointed them out to Nicci and she made up little episodes from my childhood to fit around them. "Yes, that's the water tower you walked to from home once in the middle of the night completely naked. You walked all the way because you thought you could hear it singing. The next day you visited your family doctor, Dr. Naik, and he diagnosed tinnitus. Since that day you've been suspicious of water towers." I glanced sideways at her and said, "You're mad, Nicci, completely mad." She threw her head back and laughed, then she said, "This is shit," and ejected the Chris Rea.

"So choose something else," I said, checking my rearview mirror. She went through the tapes on the shelf, picking them up, reading the labels and chucking them over her shoulder into the back as she muttered to herself about how they were all shit and why didn't I have any decent music. It was good fun and I was enjoying it as much as her. She did in fact like most of the tapes but she'd obviously decided only one thing would do. "Ah," she cried in triumph. "This is more like it." And she slid a tape into the machine.

It was Gary Glitter. I looked at her again and laughed. She was right, of course. If I was going back I should have the right soundtrack to go back with. So it was to the accompaniment of "Rock and Roll Part I" that we left the motorway and sailed up the long, straight A road that led back to my childhood. All the place names were practically dripping with nostalgia.

"You loved your childhood, didn't you?" Nicci said. I nodded. But I remembered it with sadness as well as pleasure. Even sitting there in the car with Nicci was tinged with sadness. I was hoping of course, that the weekend would do something about that.

I wasn't planning to go and look for the Crucian Pit until later, perhaps that evening while it was still light. First I just wanted to drive around the city and outskirts looking for anything that would take me back to what it was like then. This kind of stuff, of course, doesn't mean a great deal to someone who wasn't there, but Nicci had insisted she wanted to come.

We drove past the railway depot where I used to go clambering about in old rolling stock and sneaking into the sheds to look at the locomotives. Other kids took down numbers but I just liked being around the place, the smells of diesel and grease, the black-faced engineers working down the inspection pits, the crunch of the chippings between the tracks. Anyone who's ever looked twice at a train will know what I mean. There's romance in railway sheds. We parked for a minute or two and Nicci sat on the bonnet of the car swinging her legs while I went and peered over the fence which I had scaled as a child. I recognized the corner of a shed, the pattern of the tracks going into the sidings. For all I knew they could have been the same old diesels standing idle beside the main line.

We drove on and stopped outside my old school and watched boys playing cricket in front of the pavilion. "A bit posh, isn't it?" Nicci said with a heavy frown. "You weren't by any chance an over-privileged little git, were you?"

I smiled at her and she raised her eyebrows a fraction just like Kathy would have done. Just occasionally she reminded me of Kathy. Who knows, maybe you do spend your whole life looking for one person, someone you were shown a photograph of before you were born, and that's why all your partners look the same. Nicci was funnier than Kathy though and as far as I was concerned they were unalike, apart from the odd expression—the eyebrows, stuff like that.

"I haven't upset you, have I?" she said, worried.

"No, of course not. Sorry, I was miles away. It's seeing the old school. I loved it."

I tried not to mention Kathy. There's nothing worse than going on about your old girlfriend to your current partner. She pretends not to care but she does. Who wouldn't?

I felt Nicci's hand on the back of my neck and turned to smile at her. I *had* to stop thinking about Kathy. She was in the past. They say your first love leaves an indelible impression and they could be right. But this trip was meant to be about forgetting Kathy.

Nicci and I drove away from the school but I was still thinking about her. Ten years ago I didn't drive and if Kathy and I went anywhere out of town we had to use bikes or go by train. We had a few picnics in outlying parks, an unforgettable day in the dunes at Formby, a couple of visits to the Crucian Pit.

I first came into contact with Kathy when we were both about fifteen. Out of the girls who caught my bus to school and sat on the top deck she was the one I fancied the most. I probably fancied them all—even those you could never own up to fancying because they were too fat or had greasy hair—but she was the only one who made my heart beat faster and my mouth go dry. It was largely for her benefit that I ostentatiously folded back the huge pages of the *New Musical Express* each week, thinking it would make me look cool. I made sure the knot of my tie never reached my neck and almost certainly I would have had my blazer collar turned up. For all the trouble I took to look good I didn't have the bottle to speak to her and ask her out, so I wrote a note and left it on her seat one morning. It said something like, "Would you like to go to a gig? I can get tickets."

When she got on, her just-washed fair hair shone in the spring sunlight and she looked as gorgeous as ever. She might have only been fifteen; she was a woman to me, deeply mysterious and alluring, her maroon and blue uniform concealing a body I had wild fantasies about every night. She picked the note up off the seat before she sat down and read it. Instead of looking round immediately she looked out of the window. When she did look round, her eyes giving nothing away, she saw me watching her and that's when our eyes met for the first time. Her friends got on at the next stop and I spent the rest of the journey in an agony of waiting. When they got up in a group to go Kathy avoided looking at me and one of her friends passed me a folded note. The friend even gave me a tiny smile.

It was a very encouraging rejection. Not because she indicated she might ever change her mind but because of the nice tone in which it was written. She hadn't used the opportunity to take the piss, as some girls would have done. She'd been nice about it. Thank you very much, but no thank you. "I think I ought to point out," she wrote "that I am already going out with someone, and have been for the last two months." I pictured him instantly—taller and darker than me with clear skin and a deeper voice. He would live in one of the posh southern suburbs and would be able to afford to take her out anywhere whenever she wanted. He was a total bastard, obviously: didn't have to revise for exams, never suffered from respiratory diseases, probably even smoked joints and tried on Nazi uniforms at home in front of his mirror.

It almost didn't matter that she'd said no because now I had a scrap of paper with her handwriting on. I carried it with me for months, taking it out in school assembly to examine every curve of her signature and feel the underside of the paper where the ballpoint had pressed through, the ballpoint that she'd held in her hand. A kid in my class called Andrew Rosemarine told me there was nothing nobler than unrequited love. I tried hard to believe in this for a few weeks.

I still got the same bus to school and so did Kathy but I made less of an effort. I even started getting *Angling Times* instead of the *NME*. Maybe it was exactly that lack of effort which swung it in the end because when we happened both to be at the same party one Saturday night late in the summer it was Kathy who came out into the garden to look for me and we sort of took it from there. I never asked her about the other boyfriend in case I found out she'd just made him up to have an excuse to turn me down.

Nicci and I stopped for some fish and chips at Jon's Fish Bar. "I know," she said. "You used to nick 50p out of your mum's purse and use 10p of it to get the bus, then you'd spend 40p on a bag of chips which you'd eat walking home. Then you wouldn't want your tea but you wouldn't be able to explain why and you always ended up feeling guilty so it wasn't really worth it."

"Yes," I said, "but you left out the bit about discovering a murdered woman on the way home and not being able to report it because then it would come out about nicking the money to get chips." We were crossing the road and already I could smell the chips. "No. Whenever we went out in the evening and were coming back along this road I'd drop heavy hints about getting some fish and chips, and if my dad was in a good mood we'd stop. He'd park exactly where I've parked in that side street and I'd cross the road to get them just like we're doing now."

It wasn't the same man in Jon's but the chips tasted the same.

We drove further south and soon we were sitting in the car outside the house where I'd been brought up. "It's so upsetting," I said, looking at the huge hole dug in the front garden presumably for foundations to be laid so they could build an extension. I desperately wanted to knock on the door and ask if I could have a look round. But at the same time I knew it wasn't a good idea. Sometimes it is just best to keep things as you remember them.

"Shall we go?" Nicci said, picking up on my mood.

I turned in my seat to look at her and reached out for her hands. I held them tightly. "I mustn't lose you," I said, and thought: like I lost Kathy.

Ten minutes later we were driving south out of town towards the airport. The Crucian Pit was right next to the airport, very close to the main runway. Or it had been in the old days. I didn't know if it would still be there, but I hoped so. It was important I found it.

"When I've had a look at the Crucian Pit we'll find somewhere to stay," I said as I calmly negotiated the double roundabout which I remembered so clearly. Ten years ago and more I'd made this trip on my push-bike, tackle box strapped on the little luggage rack, rod bag slung over my back. By this stage I'd be knackered and longing for the peace of the poolside, the sun beating down on the lily pads, the surprisingly tough little crucian carp throwing themselves at my bread punch.

Getting there had always been a struggle but with paradise at the end of it all.

"Do you want to wait in the car, Nicci?" I asked her. "I won't be long." She looked at me and smiled and nodded.

"Don't be nervous," she said. "I'm sure it'll still be there. I'll wait here for you."

I wanted to tell her I loved her but for some reason felt shy or too much in awe of her. She could tell I wanted to go up there by myself and she didn't mind. Even if she did mind she wasn't going to show it because she knew how important this was to me. Maybe in that moment she seemed too good to be true. I nearly said it but instead left it to my eyes to tell her what I felt.

I walked away from the car, which I'd had to park fifty yards down a narrow track off the main road which itself was too dangerous to park on at that point because of the tunnel—about a hundred yards from the track the main road went into the tunnel under the end of the main runway. I looked back at the car and could see the back of Nicci's head. For some reason I whispered, "I love you."

I crossed the main road and started to climb up the embankment that led to the thick copse that in the old days had concealed the Crucian Pit.

I heard a plane take off but didn't look up. My breathing became quicker and shallower as I climbed and it wasn't just the effort involved. Ten years ago, for a number of reasons, the Crucian Pit had been one of the most important places in my life, probably *the* most important.

I reached the top of the slope and stopped to catch my breath. I looked back down at the road. Cars sped past and were swallowed by the tunnel. I could see the entrance to the little track down which I'd parked the Citroen but the car was out of sight.

One change I had noticed on my way up the embankment was that a mesh fence had been erected along the ridge at head height, replacing an old wooden fence which in my day had been broken in various places. This was a bad sign. I parted the foliage of a young tree to get a look through the fence. My heart sank. The flat land beyond had been cleared. What before had been a virtual forest of entangled vines and brambles and shrubs was now as clear as the runways beyond. I tried to look to the left to see if any vegetation remained but the fence prevented me. I backed away and began picking my way along the top of the slope between trees and overgrown hawthorn hedge. I was oblivious to the sharp little thorns that caught my hands. Already I'd gone beyond the point at which in the past I had climbed through a hole in the wooden fence and started to make my way past a mysterious group of outbuildings to the pit. I was fast losing hope and beginning to curse the authorities for filling in the pit when I noticed a tall hedge on the other side of the fence that met the wire at right angles. I pushed aside branches and tangles of creeper to get a look beyond the fence. There was a small paddock. I didn't remember this, but then I had never needed to come this far along the ridge. On the far side of the paddock was another high hedge. I needed to discover what lay beyond that.

I looked at my watch. I'd been gone ten minutes. I didn't want to leave Nicci waiting too long, but she had seemed to understand what was going on. From beyond the trees I heard the roar of a jet as it accelerated for take-off. I heard it come screaming down the runway and knew exactly when its wheels had left the tarmac. The plane appeared above the trees and I watched it climb with my heart in my mouth.

The fence was high but I was agile and very light. I was over in seconds. The paddock was as quiet as the grave. No planes were taking off or landing. The road seemed to have become distant as well. A light breeze touched my face and whispered through the tops of the trees. A hornet buzzed somewhere behind me and I heard the distinct chirrup of a grasshopper.

I hoped Nicci was all right. The car now seemed a long way away as I approached the hedge on the far side of the paddock. It was thick but I worked my way through it and over a low wire fence. I found a rough path and followed it through a stand of trees until I began to recognize landmarks—a fallen log, a sleek bed of nettles—and I knew I was back on familiar ground.

I smelt the Crucian Pit before it came into view. I felt enormous relief that it was still there. I walked another fifty yards until I could see it before me, not smaller than I remembered it—as I had feared it might be, if I were to find it at all—but slightly bigger if anything. I shivered at the sight of it, feeling a mixture of pleasure and unease. Over on the runway a jet began its take-off run but I looked down at the surface of the pit. There were lily pads still covering the surface at the eastern end. Lose a crucian in them and you wouldn't ever get it out.

I'd fished the pit maybe twenty times in all, in a variety of swims, and it was easily the best stillwater I'd ever visited. If it was stocked with any fish other than crucian carp I'd never caught any. And in all my visits I never saw another angler. I never knew if I was permitted to fish there, though I doubted it because of the difficulty in finding the place, and because there was never anyone else about. The man who had told me about it and given me vague directions—flame-haired Jim, our window cleaner—claimed to have fished there for a couple of seasons and never seen a soul. He stopped going because the cycle ride got too much for him. I was younger and fitter and perhaps fonder of crucians than Jim, who later developed an obsession with specimen mirror and leather carp.

The first day I fished there is as clear in my mind as the last. I broke through the last line of bushes and was profoundly shocked by this sudden expanse of water hidden away in between semi-urban farmland and the airport. Nothing Jim had told me had prepared me for the reality. It was an angler's paradise, nothing less, with its deep green unpolluted water and hosts of lily pads. The bank undulated as it made its way slowly around the water so that there were small promontories and inlets, ideal for getting your bait out among the feeding crucians and steering the exhausted fish into shallow water to land it. There were bulrushes, reeds and weeping willows, and at the far end nearest the airport fences an explosion of yellow gorse.

I completed a circuit of the pit before choosing a swim. Often a previous angler's debris will tell you where there has at least been activity, but there was no sign of anybody having been here at all. Jim, obviously, was not one to give anglers a bad name by leaving old nylon line and maggot dumps lying around. I still didn't know for sure that there were fish to be caught, though I had Jim's word and a growing sense of my own that the pit was teeming with life. I chose a swim where the ground was not too muddy for my basket and I tackled up with nervous fingers. Twice I dropped a size 20 hook in the grass at my feet and had to get down on hands and knees to find it rather than allow it to defile the perfection of the place. I wanted to leave it exactly as I had found it.

I used my favorite float—an orange-tipped quill—with two lead shot pinched on to the line half way up from the hook. I elected to fish without any cocking shot directly under the float, so that if a crucian took the bait on the way down I'd know because the float would continue to lie flat on the surface instead of cocking. This method of presentation had already proved irresistible to crucians and rudd in one of my local ponds that summer. I cast out no more than twenty feet and waited for the float to cock, which it didn't. I imagined the shot caught up with the float and the bread fifty yards away having flown off the hook. But just in case, I struck lightly upwards and to the left and immediately bent into a fighting crucian. The quick, edgy runs and strong tugs would have betrayed the species even without prior knowledge. I landed it in half a minute without a net and admired its beautiful golden flanks.

That was the first of at least twenty-five crucians caught in three hours. I got lightly sunburned. I fished until about eight when the colors in the sky were turning heavier and the landing jets flashed vivid messages across the water. Prior to packing up I pulled my keepnet out of the water and using the pocket camera I always kept in the basket took a perfect little picture before returning my finest catch to the water.

Not all my memories of the Crucian Pit were recorded in this way however. I looked at my watch and thought about Nicci waiting in the car. Would she be getting pissed off? I decided not. She had seemed happy to let me do this on my own. I started to walk around the pit. Much of the vegetation that had graced the shallows was there again ten years later, though the willows and other trees that had stood by the edge of the water were no longer around. I walked past the bulrushes and round the far end by the gorse bushes until I reached the trees on the north side of the pit.

After I'd gone on endlessly about the Crucian Pit to Kathy she had said she wanted to come, so on a scorching afternoon in August I left my tackle at home and took Kathy instead. She fell in love with it at first sight and I swore her to secrecy.

"It can be our secret place," I said. "Whatever happens to us in the future, we can come back here and as good as be with each other." She gave me a sad look. We both knew the summer was drawing to a close and not only were we at the transition between school and university—which had threatened to split us up—but Kathy's father had accepted a twelve-month lecturing post at Phillips Academy, Massachusetts. As far as everyone except Kathy and I were concerned, she was going too, along with the rest of the family. I naturally hoped she would stay.

Kathy herself was still undecided. "I know what I want," she said. "But I know what I should do."

I took her hand and we wandered round to the trees on the north side. There were enough trees to shield us from the runway—though airport ground staff rarely happened to come out this far—and from the farmland on the other side. But in any case, the only people I ever saw while I was at the Crucian Pit were the faces at the windows of planes taking off and landing. Them and Kathy, on the three occasions she came there with me.

We lay down in the long grass using a soft mound as a pillow and I held Kathy by her shoulders and kissed her slowly. She moved like a lizard beneath me and we hugged each other so fiercely a bright pain flared up at the front of my skull. We were both still virgins, but not for very much longer. I whispered my love to her. She responded, "I need you, I need you." We had so far had precious few opportunities to go beyond the limit of our meager experience, taking advantage of evenings when her parents and sister went out, but never quite to the full.

Kathy was wearing a white T-shirt with Peugeot written across the chest and a pair of baggy shorts. As our kissing became more and more urgent I slipped my hand inside her T-shirt and touched her breast, squeezing it and then slipping two fingers inside her bra. With the sun beating down on my back and in the knowledge that we were completely alone I was becoming almost unbearably excited. But still I was nervous and shy. I couldn't bring myself to be adventurous. After a couple of minutes Kathy sat up and peeled her T-shirt over her head and unclipped her bra, pulling it off and dropping it on the grass.

I was shocked by so much bare flesh. We had previously made our limited explorations of each other's bodies in semi-darkness, due partly to shyness and partly to guilt. If we did it in the dark it wasn't so bad. It was that sort of logic.

Shocked but turned on in a way I never had been before I reached out and touched her.

It wasn't awkward and fumbled, nor was it over in seconds and all something of a disappointment. Rocked in the sun's honeyed embrace we pushed out slowly into the furthest reaches of sensation and soared to such heights of emotion as neither of us had imagined to exist. Afterwards we clung to each other and wept. Over on the runway the thrust of jet engines propelled hundreds of helpless passengers time after time into the skies. Gnats danced crazily above our heads as the slowly sinking sun dried the moisture on our bodies. We whispered promises to each other, believing in them with utter conviction. Tiny playful crucians splashed their tails and fins clear of the surface of the pit. If I'd had my fishing basket we would have used my penknife to carve some message into the bark of one of the trees, and we would have taken photographs of each other—one each only. But we sensed it would prove to be an unforgettable afternoon even without photographs. There was a solemnity about us as we got dressed and sat with our arms around each other to watch the sun go down. Then we walked once round the Crucian Pit and regretfully made our way through the bushes and undergrowth to climb back down the embankment and return to a world which would now be transformed.

I was still standing beneath the trees studying the exact spot where we had lain ten years earlier when I heard the faintest of noises behind me and then felt hot breath on my neck. I turned to face Nicci standing right behind me. I was too surprised to speak.

"This was where you made love," she said, laying a light hand to my shoulder and raising her eyebrow a fraction in that way that was not entirely hers.

Head bent again over the soft mound of earth I could only nod silently amid a storm of questions. How did she know that? How had she found me? How had she approached so quietly?

I don't know how many minutes passed but it seemed like there had been an ellipsis in time—almost as if I had blacked out—before I turned round again to find myself alone. "Nicci," I called, my voice tearing through the idyllic scene like a vandal destroying a painting. "Nicci. Where've you gone?" There wasn't a single sign that she'd been there at all, except for a slight chill on the back of my neck. I spun round looking in every direction but couldn't see her. She couldn't have vanished so quickly. Had I imagined her?

Then like a punch in the chest it hit me and I ran, tearing my way through the gorse and trees at the airport end of the pit to get to the thick hedge which led to the paddock. Branches whipped this way and that as I forced my way through. A jet took off from the runway barely a hundred yards away with a great whoosh and its engines screaming. I shuddered with fear.

Imagining her so clearly that I even felt her breath on my neck could only have been a premonition. She was in danger.

I jumped over the low wire fence into the paddock and suddenly everything seemed to slow down. I felt completely exhausted. The long grass drained the energy from my legs and I wanted to lie down. The jet that had just taken off banked steeply so that it seemed to be nosediving towards the paddock. I just wanted to sleep but my legs kept moving. I struggled to reach the fence and somehow found the strength to climb it.

I landed in a crouch and scampered in a crab-like fashion down the embankment, then ran across the main road which was empty, although I had hardly given it a glance. The little track was slippery with gravel underfoot and I was fortunate to stay upright as I sprinted breathlessly to the Citroen. From a distance it looked empty and I prayed it was an optical illusion. When I reached the car and saw that it was no trick I became hysterical—chanting out loud in the thick warm air of the lengthening evening—praying that Nicci had just gone for a walk. I flung open the driver's door and looked at the floor in front of the passenger's seat. Her bag was gone. I looked in the back. The cassettes were still strewn over the back seat where she had tossed them.

My heart beating furiously I looked in the rearview mirror for any lingering shadows but all I saw was my own distraught face, mouth twisted in panic.

Some time later I found myself walking dejectedly back across the road and mounting the embankment. The Crucian Pit was now as still as the paddock had been earlier. No fish jumped and the clouds of gnats had dispersed. I became aware that I was crying. For some perverse reassurance I patted the inside pocket of my jacket. It was still there, the photograph I'd carried for ten years. Over on the runway a jet fired up its engines for maximum thrust then allowed them to die down, presumably in receipt of some instruction from the tower. I sat on the soft mound where Kathy and I had opened ourselves up to each other and contemplated the leathery surface of the pit. The sun had fallen beneath the horizon but the sky was still aglow. As I looked round in case Nicci was about to slip out from behind a tree like some sprite I slipped the photograph from my inside pocket and ran my fingers over its surface. I knew each crease that had appeared in the ten years since I had taken it. I knew every minute detail of the image but I always carried it nevertheless. It was like an act of faith, the patient work of an unquestioning servant. And now the waiting was almost over. It was time to put the past behind me, time to lay all the ghosts to rest. I'd heard their cries in my head every day for ten years.

I continued to fish the Crucian Pit after Kathy and I had christened it. The small carp were still lining up to take my bread punch but as the summer stretched into early September my visits were fruited with the fungus of melancholy. Kathy had bowed to pressure to go with her family to Massachusetts for a year off before she took her place at Southampton. There were tears every time we saw each other after that decision was made. We went for long walks on the Edge and sat on the huge, flat, overhanging rocks for hours dangling our feet into nothingness. I would notice movement out of the corner of my eye and know that Kathy's shoulders were shaking as she sobbed. My own face would crumple like an expiring balloon, but not before I had put my arm around her shoulders and drawn her to me. She would know but not see that I was crying too. We walked by the river south of the Edge, meandering in our conversation too: looking back over the summer and forward to our own personal ambitions. We would keep in touch, we both promised—indeed, Kathy said she would write every day—and, after all, a year was not a long time.

But we both knew that back then it was a very long time.

In an unguarded moment one evening as we sat watching the old men play bowls on the green behind my parents' house Kathy said, "You'll find someone else." I broke down and cried until long after the men had packed up their bowls in their little brown leather cases and shouted their good-byes to each other across the darkening grass. Of course, I didn't want to find anyone else, but the suggestion that I might raised the specter I had not dared to confront: the near certainty that some handsome freshman would sweep Kathy off her feet and she might never come back. I imagined her returning here grey-haired and pudding-shaped to share her early memories with the good grey man that college kid had grown into.

I was crying for more than a lost love though. I was going away too and would have some growing up to do. The summer we'd enjoyed together was the last one in this part of my life. I'd never recapture these scorching afternoons playing the eager, flighty carp as I had. The Crucian Pit was already a memory before the summer was over.

I looked at the photograph in my hand and felt a brief chill invade my chest.

I still don't really know what made me take it; some deep instinct, a need to seize the last guttering of the candle before an indifferent draught snuffed it out. Some compulsion made me delve into the basket for the camera.

It was going to be my last visit to the Crucian Pit in any case. Two weeks into September the carp were neither as hungry nor as lively as they had been. I was trying to concentrate on the fishing but my mind was on other things. Planes took off throughout the afternoon and, whereas normally they hardly impinged on my consciousness, today the constant noise was giving me a headache. I was ready to pack up and go when it happened.

I was watching a plane which had just taken off, at first because its engines sounded different and then because it banked steeply and lost altitude suddenly. The pilot seemed to try to bring the nose around so that he could land again. I heard a bang and saw flames licking out of one of the jet engines at its rear. I stood up though my legs had gone weak and I felt sick. In that moment I was more terrified than I had ever been and I was transfixed. Hundreds of people were about to die and I would be a witness to it and yet could do nothing. I don't know if I imagined it later or if I really could see faces at the porthole windows lining the fuselage. It was only the realization that the crashing plane was heading towards the Crucian Pit that enabled me to move. But before running for my life I thrust my hand into my basket and took out the little camera. I pointed it and took one picture. Then I ran.

I was at the bottom of the embankment when it hit, so thankfully I didn't see the impact. What I did see was an enormous fireball which burst gloriously into flower above the trees and, of course, I felt it. I was thrown to the ground and hit my head, knocking myself out. When I came to there were people around me shouting things, brushing my hair out of my eyes, asking if I could see straight. Apparently I just kept screaming, "Was that the one? Was that the one she was on?" They didn't know what I was talking about. I found out later it was the one she was on. It was no coincidence I was at the Crucian Pit the day she was to fly to Massachusetts. Where else could I go? What else could I do? It was one of those things you don't really have any choice in. It was the obvious place to be. I wouldn't know which plane she would fly out on but I would be right there, as close to her as I could be until the last moment. The idea was it would be better, more appropriate and less painful than saying good-bye in the airport itself.

The plane plummeted into the Crucian Pit and everyone on board, passengers and crew, died on impact, they said. The fire had spread to the cabin before the crash. Because of the fire and the nature of the crash and resulting explosion no actual bodies were recovered. For once the papers were sparing with the detail. The decision was made not to drain the pit and construct some elaborate memorial, but to leave it all pretty much as it was. The accident investigators never arrived at an explanation for the crash, though they did rule out the possibility of a bomb. Pictures of the disaster site appeared in the press but there were no pictures of the plane in the air.

While I'd been sitting on the grassy mound fingering the photograph the sky had slowly got darker. There was still a glimmer however and I pored over the photograph as I had countless times before. I never showed the picture to another living soul; not only was there my private grief but I felt it would be an invasion of some sort into the lives—the lives as they were lived in their very last moments— of all 326 passengers and crew. Time and time again I thought about taking it to a newspaper. As an image it seemed to me to hold great power but I could never work out whether it was potentially a power for good—for healing—or for bad. Would it simply cause fresh hurt to the bereaved? I played safe and kept it to myself. But the pressure told and I knew the day would come when I would have to let go of the past.

The day came. I sat there by the pit as the darkness thickened in the trees like a web. The surface of the water, now black like a pool of engine oil, waited. I took a last look at the photograph—the cigar-like fuselage, the punctuation marks of tiny windows, the terror smeared on faces glimpsed for the last time, the lick of flame—and skimmed it gently on to the water's surface. I watched it drift towards the center of the pit until the water seeped over the image itself—as if tasting it—and swallowed the photograph.

There. I had let go.

In the same way that some mornings I just cannot get out of bed, I found I couldn't leave the waterside. Not so soon after unloading my secret cargo. I sat very still, resting my head in my hands, until I felt part of the landscape. It was by now quite dark. The runway lights were largely obscured by the trees and gorse bushes. I wasn't surprised when I heard the first splash. I supposed this had been at the back of my mind all along and was the real reason why it had taken me ten years to come back.

They say when you take a photograph of someone you steal a small part of their soul.

Now I was giving back what I'd taken.

There was no great frenzy of activity, nothing to match the accident itself, just the sounds of water parting and subsiding, little splashes and trails of drips. I didn't look up but stared at the ground between my feet feeling as if my body and my skull had been completely scoured. I didn't know what I really felt deep down. There was the terror of responsibility but there was also—and I was ashamed and sickened by this—a dull thrill, a terrifying excitement.

I felt something wet brush the back of my neck and rest on my shoulder. I moved my head a fraction and saw a small hand smeared with mud and dripping water on to the front of my jacket. All feeling left me and I rose to my feet. Without focusing on any of the figures in the trees and bushes around me I walked as if in a dream round the edge of the pit towards the thick hedge that led to the paddock. Several times the hand was removed from and replaced on my shoulder.

Passage through the hedge was easy. I scaled the fence with the automatic ease of one who has drunk so much they will attempt—and achieve—any physical act. This was how I was feeling now: dissociated from the world and just passing through it. I clearly recognized the sounds of accompaniment behind me as I descended the embankment. I knew she was there but I couldn't bring myself to turn round and look at her. Crossing the main road I had the impression I was in a corridor which led back to the car. I was beyond fear. I heard water dripping off her body; her shoes made a damp, sucking noise with each small step.

When I reached the car I just opened my door and got in. She did the same. Still I hadn't looked at her. I was sufficiently conscious of what was happening to keep my eyes averted. To that extent, then, I was terrified, but I managed to function. The car started and I backed out of the little track on to the main road. I changed into first gear and started to move forward. Looking up I saw the darkness swarming down the embankment and into the road and I felt a tug of panic. "What about them?" I heard myself say. "I've got to do something."

Kathy spoke for the first time. In a voice dredged up through sediment, slurred and distorted by water and mud in her lungs, she said, "Just drive."

I drove.

THE ECOLOGY OF REPTILES
John Coyne

Here, Coyne again puts his knowledge of and experiences in Africa to good use in this cynical story about the tense relationships among four relief workers—two a married couple, the other two, lovers. Appropriately, it was first published in *Predators*.

—E.D.

From the air it appeared that all the vegetation had been scraped together into a thicket behind the village, stretching a few thousand yards down to the edge of the Baro River at the western edge of Ethiopia. A dozen women of the village were washing clothes among the rocks and children were running along the shore, throwing pebbles at a crocodile that cruised beyond their range.

Four foreign relief workers had camped at the river for the weekend and one of them, an Englishman, Roger Sample, was telling the others about crocodiles, lecturing them in textbook fashion about the ecology of reptiles.

Roger was tall and thin and had deceiving looks. From certain angles, and in certain lights, his profile was strikingly handsome, but full faced, his features were in disproportion. His nose was too small, his lips too thick, and his eyes were set too close together, as if at birth his face had been pinched.

Roger's wife, Hetty, who was from Nice, and who had left the group for a smooth patch of sand, was very unlike her husband. She was small and stout with no startling features, no figure whatsoever. Nevertheless, she was sensuous and in some ways resembled Simone Signoret.

And unlike her husband, people were attracted to her. She had a gracious manner, and went out of her way to make others comfortable.

All of the campers, for one reason or the other, had come on the trip because of her.

It was a trip, however, planned by Mark Mayer, an American CARE employee, and his lover, Paula Lance. Mark had sent out the invitations, had them hand delivered by his houseboy, inviting them to a "Beach Party in the Heart of Africa."

Mark, who had been sitting with Roger in the noonday sun, now stood and walked up the patch of hot sand to join Hetty in the shade of the acacia trees.

The year in Africa had been hard on Mark, leaving him pale and underweight.

Hetty, watching him approach, was swept with a wave of compassion, seeing his gauntness, and wanted to gather him in her arms and hold him close, to comfort him like a child. But instead she looked away, looked out at the muddy Baro River, and let the emotion melt away.

After a moment she realized she had been watching the crocodile, watching it slip and slide in the mucky water, drifting a hundred yards, then with a violent slap turning to go upstream. It was the only crocodile she had ever seen in Africa and she watched it as if it were on film.

"Have you decided?" Mark asked.

"We're breaking up." The hot day flashed before her like photographs.

"Good."

She reached out to touch him and be reassured, but he unexpectedly moved, leaving her to make an empty gesture.

On the very first Saturday afternoon that they had made love Mark had whispered that he loved her. His words had angered her. She had turned away, noticing his new digital Seiko watch and the time, 3:09, then looked across the room and out the window. She could see a bit of the African sky. It was a brilliant March day with a breeze tossing the white curtains cooling the Ras Hotel room. Her husband had flown up to Lalibela that morning to inspect a UNICEF resettlement camp and she was glad he had good weather. She could picture him tramping along in the sun, pushing ahead of all the others, speaking out in Amharic, making his presence known. She had begun to cry.

Paula Lance was also American and a nurse with Catholic Relief. She was assigned to a regional hospital in Debre Marcus, caring for patients suffering from malnutrition. She had never been out of the United States until she flew to Africa, and all of it, the harsh living and primitive conditions, the famine and wholesale poverty, had stunned her so, that even now, eight months after arriving in the country, she was afraid to go anywhere by herself.

She had met Mark Mayer four months after she arrived in Addis Ababa, at the ambassador's July Fourth party. She had been on her way in the hospital's Land Rover, where she knew the driver had a small pistol tucked away under the seat in case they were attacked on the road. She had hoped she was drunk enough to kill herself. Instead, Mark had taken her down in the bushes behind the tennis court and demanded she give him a blow job. He had saved her life, she had told him afterward, making her feel valued.

Now, obediently, she listened to Roger talk about crocodiles and how they were territorial and flesh eaters, though she had stopped paying attention to what he was telling her, and was thinking only that she wouldn't be able to wash her hair in the Baro, not with a twelve-foot crocodile yards from shore. She was also too afraid to ask either of the men why they had chosen such a place for their campsite.

Paula had not been in the country long enough to have the harsh life and the high plateau climate wear her down, and she could obtain enough cosmetics at the American commissary and from the small Italian beauty salons near the Ethiopian Hotel. She really only saw glimpses of the countryside, of the hot desert and the lowlands of the escarpment, when she went off with Mark on weekend trips. She hated to camp. She had only one wish and that was to be out of Africa, away from this place. She knew she would leave Mark if it meant she could go home again to Virginia.

Hetty, squinting into the sun, saw that her husband had been abandoned in the heat. Paula had come up the shore and into the shade and stretched out on her sleeping bag, away from where Mark had fallen asleep beside Hetty. Paula had not said anything to her, Hetty realized, when she came to the shade of the acacia and saw Mark there, beside her.

It was quiet on the bank of the Baro. Hetty panned the shoreline and stopped again to look at Roger. He sat with his back to her, scooping sand with one hand, aimlessly like a bored child. She put her book aside and stood, being careful not to wake Mark.

"The croc is gone?" Hetty asked, walking down to her husband, and shading her eyes to search the surface of the river.

"He's been gone for hours, if it matters to you." Roger kept up with the sand.

"Don't be a sonovabitch, Roger."

"Why the fuck not?"

"You'll get sunstroke staying out in the sun," she advised.

"As if you give a shit."

"You didn't have to come."

"Yes? And let that bloody American bang the both of you all weekend long?"

Hetty's feet turning in the sand crunched in his ears, and then receded. He strained to follow the sound, like listening for an echo, until all he heard was the rush of water, birds shrieking in the trees, and then muffled sounds of the jungle racing to the edge of the bank.

The trees across the narrow stretch of water seemed to teeter against the river. The thick branches pulsed before his eyes like his own heartbeat, palm leaves spread themselves a hundred yards, then shivered, and expanded. In his ears, the sound of the river grew and gushed. He heard Tississat Falls a thousand miles away in the east, and he turned toward the two tents, pockets of darkness in the blaze. He tried to raise his arm in a faulty gesture, then tumbled face forward, teeth biting into the coarse sand. His body twisted on top of him and before he fell, like a crippled bird; his stomach retched an early-morning breakfast of bacon and hard rolls, coffee and melon, onto his face and shirt.

When they reached him sandbugs had already converged on his vomit.

"Put him on the cot and take off his shirt," Hetty ordered. "Get that canteen of water and douse his forehead." She glanced at Mark. A wedge of fear was caught in his eyes and she looked away, ashamed for him.

"We should have warned him about the sun," Paula said.

"He's been in Africa long enough," Hetty answered, peeling off his shirt. "It's his own damn fault." She felt suddenly very tired of having to care for her husband.

Paula, startled by Hetty's anger, went for the canteen. Paula wanted to suggest that they go into the village. The airlines clerk spoke some English, and Mark had told her there was a white missionary at the leprosarium across the Baro, but she was afraid to suggest what to do. She never really knew what to do, not even in the relief hospital in Debre Marcus. She was just thankful people gave her orders, told her what to do for them.

She went into the tent to find her cigarettes and would have liked to hide there a while, but the heavy canvas was airless, and she had to step outside again to breathe.

Her slight body and heavy breasts were hidden in sloppy clothes, a pair of Mark's jeans cut off above her knees, and his old workshirt that she had tied in a knot at the waist because she thought it made her look something like Marilyn Monroe. She loved to wear Mark's clothes. It made her think that she really belonged to him. Her hair had lost most of its color since she had come to Africa, but she was afraid to let any of the hairdressers touch it. Now it had returned to its natural dirty brown, a color she had not seen since she was in junior high. At home in Virginia, she loved to do her hair and put on her makeup in the morning. Now she couldn't bear to look at herself.

Roger had come around. His hand reached for his forehead and he moaned, complaining of a headache. Hetty was kneeling by the cot, mopping his face slowly and efficiently, as if she had always cared for the sick. Paula looked away. She finished one cigarette and lit another from the butt. She was suddenly worried that she hadn't brought enough cigarettes for the weekend. Maybe they'd go home early, now that Roger was sick. That gave her hope, and then she remembered she was told to get the canteen and went rushing to where they had parked the F.A.O. Land Rover, hating Hetty for being so competent. It made her feel small and useless.

"What's eating you?" Hetty asked. She had followed after Mark when he took his cup of tea and walked away from the tents.

"Feeling crowded, that's all."

"You know you have an unique ability to make me feel like shit."

He set the cup on a rock and felt in the pockets of his bush jacket for his cigarettes, letting the remark wither away.

"Can't you be nice? Can't any one of you be nice?" A gush of tears swelled to her throat and she swallowed quickly to keep from crying.

"What do you want, for chrissake?" He turned on her.

"I'd like you to talk to me. Roger gets stupidly sick and you walk off, leaving me to help him. And then Paula. . . !" Hetty could hear her voice whine and it angered her more. It made her feel rotten, depending on others. She prided herself on being resilient, and she spun away from Mark and walked off.

There was always an edge of coolness about Mark, like early-morning frost. It was as though he awoke in a rage, angry with the world.

She hadn't realized this at first. He had been witty and entertaining when they met, and such a change from all the European relief workers. She had lingered over a cappuccino with him, thrilled by the chance meeting at the Ras Makonnon Bar. Then one week later, while she was pulling her VW out onto Menelik Avenue, he had stopped her; he waved from his Land Rover, and pointing toward the Hilton Hotel asked if she had time for a drink.

"Where's my wife?" Roger demanded, sitting up in his cot.

"Would you like some tea?" Paula offered at once, nervous about being alone with him.

"Where is she?" Roger was enjoying the sound of his demands. It made him feel better.

"She's gone for a walk," Mark shouted from the shoreline.

Roger laid back on the cot. He knew Hetty was sleeping with Mark. She had come home after meeting him and insisted that he be invited for dinner, then a week later, Hetty had met Mark again in Addis, and there was more talk about the "witty American." He knew then, and when he pressed her about inviting Mark for dinner, she had made excuses.

"I shouldn't have come along," Paula was saying to Hetty. "It's not my kind of thing, you know." She smiled apologetically. They were sitting together two hundred yards downriver from the campsite.

"Oh, Paula, it's not so . . ."

"I'm uncomfortable, you know, all over. I feel dirty. And my hair!"

"In another hour it will be cooler. We can go swimming. I saw a lagoon earlier . . . just the two of us girls." Hetty smiled, trying to be encouraging. In twenty minutes the sun would be down. There would be no lingering sunset that close to the equator and Paula, she knew, would be happy with a warm fire and something to eat.

"I'm not going swimming! There's a crocodile. I saw it."

"They're territorial; Roger said so. It'll never leave that stretch of the river."

Paula's throat tightened, listening to Hetty's little speech of encouragement. Hetty always had them ready, like mini-sermons, but before she could say more, Paula asked in a rush of words, "Are you sleeping with Mark?"

"Paula! What a thing . . ."

"Everyone says so."

"That doesn't give you . . . Do I pry into your life?"

"Yes, you do!" Paula turned to stare at Hetty. Her eyes were red and puffy from the hot weather and her anger. "You're always interfering," she went on, "telling me what to do."

"Paula, you're upset. I've only tried to be . . ."

"Who asked you?"

Hetty stared back at Paula, then without saying more, she stood. It was time to organize dinner. She forced herself to plan. These people were not dependable. She had to do everything herself, she realized.

Roger, abandoned in the shade, watched his wife prepare dinner. She ran their house in the village that way, relentless in her organizing. It had been a dark, unattractive house when they arrived in Ethiopia, but she had needed only two weeks to make it like their suburban London home. She had it whitewashed, made curtains and pillows herself, put down Dessie rugs, hired the help and trained them. She had planted a flower garden and several yards of vegetables.

Roger had watched with fright and fascination. She had made a portrait of the place for all the Ethiopians to see and marvel at, for the other relief workers to envy. But he hated the house and what she had done with it. It reminded him of London.

After dinner, he would often go back to his office in the resettlement camp where books and papers were left in piles on the floor, in a disarray that Hetty would never allow. He loved his own squalor. It made him feel comfortable.

Hetty insisted Mark get the same room at the Ras Hotel: a corner room with windows that overlooked the garden and interior courtyard. The third-floor room also caught the soft afternoon light and the breeze from Mount Entoto. She would check in early, leaving him drinking in the bar. She wanted to be alone and take a bath, to fill the tub and pour in bubble soap she had purchased in Athens on the way down to Africa. It was French and expensive, even at the duty-free shop, but she loved the scent. She'd slide deep into the water and listen to Addis Ababa outside. She felt as if she were far away from the famine and poverty of Africa. She felt safe, as if she were home again in Nice and listening to the sea.

Hetty showered, washed and set her hair, and then, sitting naked on the bed, did her nails and dried them quickly, wandering about the room barefoot on the hardwood, her arms waving. She combed her hair out next, then stripped the blanket off the bed and slipped between the sheets. Mark would find her sleeping when he came into the room. It was the way she wanted him to find her.

Hetty had stopped sleeping with her husband. One morning she set up a bed in the extra room, and put up curtains and bright furnishings. Nothing was said between them, but both welcomed her decision. They no longer had to worry about each other. When she went off on Saturday morning to the city, he'd bring the maid into his room. They'd get drunk and the girl—giggling and encouraged by Roger—would dress up in Hetty's underwear and prance half-naked about the house.

"Mark, what do you feel about me?" Hetty woke him in the hotel room with her question.

"I'm very fond of you . . . you know that"

"Never mind." She turned away, ashamed of her question, and of his answer, and watched the windows until it was light enough for her to get out of bed and take another bath before Sunday breakfast.

Every week Hetty made out her shopping list and boarded the bus in the dark dawn. Roger would not give her the government Land Rover, saying it might be needed, nor let her drive his VW, so she squeezed onto the local bus with the peasants, their chickens and goats, all bundled and tied up beneath the seats. The bus was full of rancid smells, human and animal odors, and she would always get sick before she reached the city.

Hetty always planned on doing the shopping quickly and returning home that night, telling herself she would not go to the bar and let herself be used by Mark. But she would go anyway, hoping that Mark was not waiting for her.

But he was always waiting, drinking a cup of cappuccino and reading his mail. She was jealous of his mail. Her letters were shared with Roger. Even her mother wrote them both, "Dear Hetty & Roger." Her friends from Paris knew them as a couple. She knew no one alone, except for Mark.

And Mark did not share his mail. It was read and digested in silence, then the thin airmail stationery was folded back into the light blue envelopes and put away. Only then, when he had ordered another cappuccino, would he turn his attention to her.

Tell me why do I make love to you? Why do I strip naked and perfume my breasts, comb my hair, and go to you in those coarse hotel sheets? Why do I let you insult me with your silence? You are not even nice to me. We meet like this in the bar and you treat me with abuse. Why can't you be kind to me? Don't I deserve better?

Late on Sunday afternoons, after he had made love to Hetty, Mark would drive four hours north back into Gojjam Province, and spend the night with Paula in the town of Debre Marcus.

"How's Hetty?" The question was predictable. Mark found himself waiting for it, just to have it out of the way.

"She's fine."

"Are you still sleeping with her?"

"I'm not sleeping with Hetty, now or ever."

"Room 211. Ras Hotel. Everyone knows."

"What the shit do I care?"

"I know you're fucking her."

"And I'm fucking you, too." He sat up, determined to have it over with. "What does it matter?"

"It matters. She's a friend of mine."

"Bullshit! You can't stand Hetty. No one likes her, not even her husband."

"I like her," Paula answered meekly, trying to make an argument. Then she turned away from him. Her body made a shallow mound, like the outline of a grave, in the narrow bed.

"None of your women like Hetty because she has more class and style than the whole lot of you. Goddamn bunch of leeches!" Mark had heard a thousand remarks about Hetty: the other relief workers always watched for her failings. Then he was disgusted at himself for leaving Hetty, for treating her so poorly, for driving out of Addis Ababa and racing up the northern road just so he could sleep with Paula. He got out of Paula's bed and put on his trousers and stepped out into the cold night, needing to get away from the woman. She cried after him, telling him that she was sorry for making such a fool of herself.

"My wife, she thinks a goddamn camping trip is a great way to spend a weekend," Roger complained. He was feeling better. His headache was gone and he had been able to keep down his food. "You know where we are? We're two thousand yards from the Sudan, that's where. There are warring tribes over there. The Nuer cross the Baro and steal cows from the Anuak. They kill strangers; did you know that, Paula? They cut off their tits and balls. How about that?" He grunted and giggled.

"Roger, don't! It only frightens me. Please don't tell me anything about this place."

For a moment he was quiet, and then he asked, "You up for a beer? This village must have one bar. Let's go celebrate."

"What?" she asked, missing the point.

"Us!" he told her, laughing again.

Holding Roger's hand and walking through the woods, Paula got excited. She was not interested in Roger, but she liked the idea of Mark and Hetty turning around on the shore and calling to them through the darkness and finding them gone. It made her feel bitchy and free of Mark.

Roger stopped then in the dark woods and kissed her. It was a sloppy kiss, a fumbling of arms. Paula let him play a moment with her breasts, and hated herself for letting him do it, but she couldn't stop him. She was afraid he'd get mad and leave her there in the middle of the jungle. Mark would not have done this, forced himself on her. He would have waited, gone into the village and drunk beer, let her get an edge on, and then on the way back, he would have taken her down to the Baro, and there on the warm sand, he would have made love to her with the water lapping at their legs.

"What's the matter?" Roger dropped his hands.

"Nothing's the matter. You've startled me, that's all. Let's go get drunk. I feel like getting drunk."

"They must have gone into the village," Mark said, coming down to the river's edge. "Do you want to go too?"

Hetty shook her head. She wanted to be left alone and not to have to contend with him, but he dropped down next to her and put his hand on her thigh.

"Leave me alone, please."

"Aren't you a little bitch tonight?" He stood again and went up the bank to the campsite, and from there through the woods, to the village beyond the thicket, leaving Hetty sobbing to herself.

They would go back late after dinner to the Ras Hotel. A luxurious dinner at the Hilton with cocktails, boeuf bourguignon or galantine of salmon, wine and later liquor. Hetty would get herself drunk so she wouldn't think of all the starving children in the famine camps less than two hundred miles from Addis Ababa.

In their hotel room he would roll dope and they'd smoke a joint, sitting cross-legged on the wide bed. Mark, intent on his task, would speak only occasionally, then just a few mumbled syllables. She would light an incense candle and its fragrance mixed with the grass and took them away from Africa, from the sounds of sporadic gunfire in the streets and from the memory of the famine camps, filled with silent children, too hungry to cry.

Hetty would get off the bed and remove her dress, taking her time, knowing he liked to watch. She moved slowly, barefooted on the hardwood floor. She took off her blouse and felt each of her weighty breasts, the rubbery nipples tensing. She kept moving, unwrapped her skirt and let it slip into a dark corner. Her panties were a patch of white. She stripped them off with a quick tug and turned to let him study her. Her eyes were brown and watery, complacent as a tamed animal.

It was not a compelling body. Her breasts did not soar, her ass was not tucked tight. Yet she knew she was sensual for she had heard the sharp, almost painful intakes of breath men experienced when seeing her naked.

She moved to the edge of the bed and placed both her hands around his head and pulled him forward. Outside their room a noisy couple of foreigners went past, speaking in French, and she felt a shiver of vulnerability at her nakedness. Then she brought Mark's wet lips to her crotch and forgot about everyone else, the couple, her husband, the starving children of Africa.

The next morning they ate breakfast in silence, like airline companions being careful not to touch. They sat at one of the small tables near the open doors. A rose had been picked from the garden and placed in a thin glass vase on their table. Water still clung to the red petals. They could see the garden, lush with vegetation, growing in abundance, and above the trees of the courtyard she saw the windows of their room thrown open, and their bedcovers slung over the ledges of the windows, airing, as if they had been contaminated during the night.

Paula and Roger, in the barren village, were drinking gin in large tumblers without ice. There was no electricity or refrigeration and the bar had no tonic. They sat against the wall at a table made from packing crates, rough hewn and slapped together.

On the table was a blunt candle, waxed to the boards. A half dozen other candles were lit around the small room and on the counter was a kerosene lamp. Its yellowish glow lit up a row of bottles on a shelf behind the counter. The gin they were drinking was homemade and poured into a Gordon bottle. Someone had amended the label to read, "A Type of Gordon's Gin."

Paula had acquired a taste for gin. It was a sharp, cutting alcohol that burned her throat. She could get drunk on it without a next-morning blinding headache and nausea. Instead, she awoke with, at the base of her throat like an irritating itch, the need for another shot, taken neat in her bathroom. The gin purged her and left her trembling.

Then the nag was gone and she recovered, cleared her eyes with drops, brushed her teeth, gargled, combed her thin hair, and with the practice gained from a thousand mornings, pulled her face into order, never once letting her eyes catch her face fully in the mirror.

Now in the comfort of the dark bar she relished the drink, positioned herself for a long night. Roger had quickly finished one glass, banged for another. She nursed hers. She let the alcohol work slowly. It was only the first taste that was truly enjoyable.

Afterward, she just kept drinking, kept pushing herself to catch again those few moments of equanimity.

But the moments always escaped her and she'd become loud and clumsy and then maudlin, weeping herself to sleep toward morning in the little house where she lived alone. She pushed those occurrences from her mind. She had only three more months in Africa. That thought made her feel warm and safe. She sipped the gin to celebrate, watching Roger with a smile. Perhaps she should sleep with him. It didn't seem like a bad idea now, in the candlelight.

Paula had told herself she would not sleep with Mark again, but on Sunday she found herself listening for his Land Rover, and when it roared into the yard announcing his arrival, all her breath escaped, as if he had physically assaulted her.

She sat up quickly and lit a cigarette, listened to his feet grate across the gravel yard and to the door. Mark did not knock. The front door shoved open and he came inside with arrogant self-possession, as if he owned the house, everything in it; owned her. She hated him for that assumption. He stood in the middle of the room and said nothing. He dominated the small house as he shoved his gloves into the pockets of his bush jacket and coldly stared down at her.

He made love to her in the living room, disregarding her protests. His eyes did not flinch from her face, but held her, like a threat.

"My wife is sleeping with Mark," Roger announced.

"He's a son of a bitch," Paula answered.

"I'll get him," Roger nodded knowingly, then sat back against the barroom wall. "And I'll get her."

"How?"

Roger gestured that he had everything under control. He looked pleased, saying, "They're down there right now on the river making love, you can bet your sweet ass on that."

Paula stared into the dim candlelight, too confused by drinking to understand what he was saying.

Roger leaned forward over the crate table and whispered, "Let me tell you something else about the ecology of reptiles."

Hetty could follow them into the village, she knew, but Roger and Mark had taken both flashlights and she was afraid of getting lost in the thicket. She heard noises, rustling in the bush, the crunch of sand on the bank. She peered into the dark, her eyes aching from the smoke of the camp fire.

She had to keep busy to hold off the fear. She would make more coffee and clean up the cups. She took the pot and walked down the bank to the river's edge. Halfway to the water she stumbled in the dark. "Oh, damn," she swore, falling to the warm sand, and thinking she had had too much to drink.

"Crocs sleep on the bank at night, you know that?" Roger said, grinning over the glass of gin. "They come up from the Baro and burrow into the warm sand at the river's edge."

Paula stared at him, trying to catch the drift of his remarks. She was like that. People told her she was a good listener, but she never listened. It was too much work, especially after she'd had a few drinks.

"And you know how they kill you?" he asked.

Paula shook her head.

"They drown the victims. They seize something, someone, in those jaws and pull them into the deep water, drown them. Then in the river itself, on shelves up under the banks, they have secret dry beds. They leave their catch, you see, on the dry shelves and come back later to eat their prey. How about that?"

Paula sat up and tried to clear her mind. Roger was telling her something, but he wouldn't just say it straight out.

"They wanted a little party all by themselves. Well, let them." He sat back, downing the last of his gin.

"Does Hetty know?" Paula asked, beginning to understand him. "I mean, does Hetty know that crocodiles sleep on the bank?" Asking him, she realized that Hetty didn't know anything at all. "Roger!" she said, starting to cry.

"Paula, it's all right; Paula, it is." He reached for her, to pull her into a drunken embrace, but she slipped off the stool and then ran from the dung-hut bar and into the dark night.

She remembered the path, where it went into the thick vegetation, but once in the trees, she did not know what she was doing and she stumbled forward, crying hysterically, but kept running. She would see the camp fire soon. She remembered how it had been blazing when they left the dark shore. She had turned back after Roger's fumbling kiss and wished she were sitting close to the fire, being warmed by the heat. His hands had been cold on her breasts.

She stumbled and fell forward and was caught by Mark.

She screamed then.

"Jesus H. Christ, Paula!"

She kept screaming. She could hear herself screaming and wanted to stop and tell Mark that the crocodile had come ashore and would find Hetty sitting there by the fire, but she couldn't stop screaming. It made her feel immensely better, screaming out in the dark night.

Mark hit her. He slapped her once when she wouldn't stop screaming, then hit her a second time. She fell against him, sobbing and clutching his body.

"What the fuck are you talking about?" He had her by both shoulders and had pulled her face up to his.

In the black night, she could not even see his face.

"The crocodile! Roger says the crocodiles come on shore at night."

"Jesus!" Mark let go of Paula and spinning around, ran back down the sandy path to the shoreline. Paula could hear his soft, sliding footsteps fade away.

"Don't," she whispered, not wanting to be left behind, and she stumbled after him, tried to keep up. She could see only the wavering spot of his flashlight. She kept running, terrified of being alone.

When she came out onto the shore, she realized she had taken the wrong path. There was no camp fire, no parked Land Rover in the grove of acacia trees, no camp fire blazing, signaling her home.

"Mark!" Her panic took the strength out of her voice. "Mark!" she said again, whispering, and then, "Oh, dear mother of God, please help me."

She should never have come to Africa, she thought. It was all a terrible, stupid mistake. What was she doing here, with these people, in this strange place? She started to run again, ran along the shore in what she thought was the right direction, and then through the palm trees, the scrub brush, and the thin thorny acacias, she saw the tiny blaze. It seemed miles ahead of her, flickering like a firefly, but its light melted her fear, and she felt safe. She slowed, exhausted by her effort, and the ground moved under her.

She was hit by the fierce wedge of a crocodile's tail and knocked sideways into the water. The blow killed her outright, and in swift silence a half-dozen crocodiles slipped into the warm river and went after her meat, tearing her limb from limb.

Mark had one flashlight, but he couldn't find Hetty. He reached the Baro's edge and went slowly along the shore. The thin beam was helpless against the enormous black night. It frightened him to see how feebly the flashlight lit the surroundings.

He was hearing every sound in the dark, all of the jungle, and the rushing river. He was hearing as he had never heard in the day. The forest, the river, the whole world of the game park. There were crocodiles here, he knew, and also hippos and lions. Mark had not said anything to the women. They would not have come if they had known the campsite was in the middle of the game reserve.

It was not the wildlife that worried Mark, but the Nuer from the Sudan who he had heard crossed the Baro at nightfall and stole whatever loose cattle they could find, driving them back across the river under the safety of darkness. The missionaries had told him to camp close to the village, warned him about tribal raiding, but he had kept quiet and let Roger pick the site for the campsite, this cluster of acacia close to the water. "We don't want to walk too far for water," Roger had chimed, like a Boy Scout.

"Hetty!" Mark shouted.

Behind him, in the deep night of the woods, something moved.

"Hetty?" he asked again, his voice cracking. He could hear his own fear. He stepped back, away from the trees and underbrush. There was more movement and the swaying of thick palm leaves. Mark stumbled in the sand, but quickly regained his footing, flashed the thin light back and forth, trying to see beyond its pale beam.

"Hetty? Jesus Christ, where are you?" He felt that there were people in the woods: the natives from across the river. He had seen a group of them earlier selling handicrafts. They were tall and slim, with the passive eyes of the dead, like those he had seen in a hundred thousand starving children farther north. They would kill him, he guessed, simply for his flashlight and the dimming batteries. All that they had been waiting for was nightfall.

He felt the wetness of the Baro River. He had stepped backward into the soft sandy shores. The water was warm, and he remembered that the missionaries had told him there was a soda spring nearby where the water bubbled up from the roots of trees. It was something of a tourist attraction, the missionaries had joked.

Now, through the thick growth of trees, he saw more shadows, huge shadows, coming closer, coming down to the water's edge.

"Christ!" he said out loud, realizing it wasn't tribesmen at all, but elephants. They moved slowly like a leather wall, and in the night breeze he smelled their bodies.

He shouted out, trying to frighten away the herd, and a bull elephant roared back in warning.

Mark tripped and fell. He would swim across the river, he thought next. It was, he knew, narrow there at the campsite, and he could spend the night at the missionary complex on the opposite shore. He dove into the mucky water at once and swam for his life.

A crocodile caught him when he was less than twenty yards from the opposite shore. It seized his ankle and pulled him under the tide of water in a swift and sudden plunge. He had no time at all to scream for help.

Roger, coming from the bar, had heard elephants, and circled through the trees to where the Land Rover was parked. He would be safe in the Land Rover, safe until morning, or whenever the elephants finished drinking from the river.

He turned on the flashlight and aimed it at the darkness. The light picked out the water in the thicket. It surprised him, seeing how dark it had become. Earlier, there had been an ocean of stars, but now, after midnight, the sky had closed over. If it rained, they would have a hard time getting the heavy vehicle off the bank, he thought next. There was always something going wrong in Ethiopia. Nothing ever went right. Not the land. Not the people. Not even them, foreigners coming to help. The whole damn country was cursed.

The high-beam lights of the Land Rover popped on and blinded him where he stood on the sand. He raised his arm to cover his eyes.

"Mark! For fuck sake!" He stumbled in the soft earth, trying to see, and then he heard the elephants roar, and he turned toward the herd.

The half-dozen beasts were still at the shore. Several of the bulls had moved onto the shallow reaches of the river. He saw a hippo farther out in the swift river, and a dozen small hartebeests and reed bucks. It looked like a peaceful kingdom, there at the river's edge, all lit by the bright beams of the Land Rover.

He grinned, feeling safe. It was that goddamn Paula getting him so excited. He shouldn't have told her about the crocodiles just to amuse himself with her fear.

Shit, what a stupid American.

The Land Rover moved.

"Mark, for godsake." He tried to walk in the soft sand, but his legs, tired from the hike to the village, and his body, tired from too many days in Africa, too much to drink, wouldn't let him run. He waved his arms, seeing the big machine coming, still coming toward him, down the slight slope, forcing him ahead. "You'll hurt someone, you bloody fool!" He was trying to shout over the roar of the heavy engine, waving at the blinding headlights.

The elephants roared, hearing the beast of machinery behind them, and they spun away from the sound, moving in their slow and graceful dance, swinging their ten tons of weight, their giant and deadly tusks. The reed bucks and hartebeests bolted, and one small roan, stumbling into the Baro, was caught by a submerged crocodile and dragged into the depths of the river.

Caught between the charging elephants, the river, and the Land Rover, Roger raced for the trees, ran to the safety of the dense underbrush, knowing that there would be a low hanging branch that he could grab and swing out of harm's way. He almost made it. The lumbering elephants caught him before he reached the safety of the trees. The heavy club foot of the queen mother kicked him off his feet and a dozen others, all frightened by the beast of the Land Rover, trampled him to death in the soft sand.

Hetty kept driving, following the riverbank for another two hundred yards to where she had earlier found the narrow road into the thick vegetation. She swung right and drove through the village, lit only by candlelights and a few lanterns. She thought a moment of stopping, of telling the locals that there had been an accident at the edge of the Baro River, but she thought better of it and kept driving north out of Illubador Province. In the morning there would be nothing left at the river's edge. The campsite would be stripped by the roaming tribes from the Sudan who, Roger had once told her, crossed the Baro after dark and scavenged the landscape. They would take away all the sleeping bags, tents, and utensils, and in the morning no one would know they had even been there, a camping party from Addis Ababa. As for her husband, lifeless on the soft shore, the crocodiles would have him. It was the way of nature, the only ecology of reptiles.

She kept driving. In eighteen hours she would reach Jimma, and another day's drive would get her to the capital. She would drive for a hundred kilometers and then sleep a few hours to be ready for the long haul in the heat of the next day.

Hetty reached down and rubbed her knees, felt where she had bruised herself tripping over the boulder. It was nothing to complain about. To come away from a camping weekend with only a minor bruise was nothing at all. She thought about the bath that awaited her at the Ras Hotel. The luxury of it, the simple pleasure of the warm water, made her smile as she down-shifted the heavy Land Rover and, picking up speed on the dry road, raced across the lowlands of Africa, raced for the warm water that would clean her body, cleanse her of this night, and of all the reptiles of Africa.

THE LAST CROSSING
Thomas Tessier

Thomas Tessier lives in Connecticut. He is the author of *Rapture, Nightwalker,* and the classic *Finishing Touches.* His latest novel, *The White Gods,* is due soon, along with a new story collection, *The Crossing and Other Tales of Panic.*

Tessier's metier is psychological horror that is absolutely convincing. "The Last Crossing" forays into this realm with the story of a man whose life falls apart, thus freeing him to indulge urges he has never even acknowledged before. The story first appeared in the anthology *Hottest Blood.*

—E.D.

Even when you know it's likely, when you have lived with the fear and uncertainty for weeks, it still comes as a terrible blow to be told that you no longer have a job. Dale Davies had been a trader on Wall Street for more than twenty years. He was a quiet but efficient man. He had risen to a certain level and then held his position. He was never a threat to the ambitions of his more aggressive colleagues. He was not brilliant, but the only people who seriously lost money with Dale were those who would have lost it anyway.

There is a kind of poetry of money, a rhythm to finance that generally follows the heartbeat of society at large. Everyone in business knows that there will be highs and lows, steady periods, slumps, occasional jolts, and shocks. Through it all, the market goes on like life itself.

But this new slide into stagnancy was particularly worrying. It was longer and steeper, and for the first time in memory there was no bottom in sight. Dale sensed early on that it might prove to be a transforming moment, such as happens only once in every two or three generations, when things change fundamentally. If that were the case, he had no doubt that sooner or later he would find himself among those culled from the herd.

He was smack on fifty, a dangerous age: too far from young, too close to old. He believed that his best work was still ahead of him, but Dale knew he was probably wrong. All he wanted to do was carry on where he was for another twelve or fifteen years, to last the course.

He didn't. It was not his fault. Nothing to do with him or his performance.

The firm was downsizing, and Dale was downsized out. The same thing was happening everywhere, a slaughter on the middle ground. The young wouldn't go, because they are young and in touch and cheaper to keep on. The old men on top wouldn't go, because they were, after all, on top. So it was Dale, and others like him, who were thrown onto the street.

He was given his notice on a Friday. He tottered out of the building and hesitated. He should go straight home to New Jersey and break the news to Cynthia, his wife. But he wasn't ready for that yet. Cynthia was a woman with lingering social pretensions. The hard fact of Dale's unemployment would not go down well with her, and sympathy would not be her first response. Joanne, their youngest child, had celebrated her nineteenth birthday last month by moving in with a heavy-metal drummer in Hoboken. Things were tense all around. Dale went into Gallagher's. He needed time to think and calm down. He needed a drink.

Call him old-fashioned, but he believed that the dry martini was a divine creation. It seemed to go from the mouth right into the bloodstream, with welcome effect. But there was still a grim reality to be faced. Good Lord, Dale thought, what is happening? All that wariness and anticipation had failed to weaken the blow. It hurt, worse than he ever expected.

He had grown up reading novels about the exciting, ruthless, high-stakes world of business, and he had longed to be a part of it. He studied through the silly sixties, pursued his dream, and finally achieved it. Twenty years—but where did they go? The world had changed so much, and yet here he was, sitting in a fine old gin mill around the corner from the market, feeling just like a character out of Sloan Wilson or John O'Hara. His life nothing but an empty cellophane wrapper.

There was no future, no job waiting for him elsewhere. Dale was at his peak, but in the marketplace he was finished, or would be by the time this slide ended. A desk in a small brokerage out in the suburbs was the best he could hope for, and in itself that would be a kind of death. His clients wouldn't leave the firm to go with him—not for Dale Davies. He was finished. It was all over but the paperwork.

He hit a few other bars, heading vaguely west, away from the financial district. Too many young Turks gargling happily. They were on the escalator going up, alive with their futures. It was not their fault, Dale told himself. They, too, would eventually take it on the neck. Still, he hated them.

It was dusk when Dale realized that he had wandered all the way to the Hudson. The lights of Jersey City were fuzzed by fog. Over there, in the clean suburbs beyond, was his home: across the river, to hell. Not yet. The night had barely started, and Dale was in the mood to cut loose. Let me get robbed, or beaten. Let me be thrown in the gutter. Let me flirt with some pretty young lady in a dangerous joint. Let there be an operatic moment in my life, and let it be tonight.

The immediate prospects were not encouraging. Dale was in a shabby dockside area full of rotten old offices, warehouses, meat-packing plants, and dubious shops cluttered with second-hand junk. But then he found a place, and almost at once he knew that it was the place he had been looking for all his life. There wasn't any name on the small sign overhead, but the flashing lights promised a BAR and GIRLS, and that was good enough for starters.

He went through a narrow doorway, down a flight of creaking stairs, and paid five dollars to a guy with no neck. Then he was allowed into the main room. He banged his right shoulder against a post thicker than a telephone pole—there were a few of them scattered about the big cellar, he saw, when his eyes adjusted to the gloom. There were faint lights strung along the stone walls, a long bar off to one side, some rickety tables and chairs placed in dark corners. The music was loud but not unbearable.

Dale made his way carefully to the bar. He bought a gin and tonic, asking for extra tonic, as it was a good time to slow down and pace himself for a while if he was going to make a real night of it. There were quite a few customers: men on their own, as he was. And there were a lot of fairly undressed young girls out on the floor: some dancing, some lounging around with disinterest, others working the crowd.

Dale saw stockings with garters, thong bottoms, string tops, gym shorts, hot pants, tiny tennis skirts, halters, T-shirts that were cut off to leave the breasts partly exposed, as well as some skimpy or filmy pieces of lingerie. The girls, who included the odd black and Asian in their number, had good bodies, and some of them were strikingly pretty. The place was kind of a dump but it was definitely no dog pound, Dale thought.

"Mardi Gras?"

She was blonde, with layered curls. She was short and cute, with a thin tube top that barely covered her breasts. Below, she had V-shaped panties that were cut high on each side. Dale found himself thinking of a babysitter they had used for a while, years ago. It wasn't the same girl, of course, but the association was quite pleasant. Lisa, as he recalled.

"What?"

"You want to Mardi Gras?"

"I'm sorry," Dale said. "I don't know what that is."

"Mardi Gras. It's, like, lap-dancing."

"Lap-dancing? What's that?"

"Okay," the girl said, smiling sweetly. "We'll go sit down on one of the couches, where it's nice and private, and you give me five dollars when the next song comes on, and as long as that song is on I'll sit on your lap and wiggle around and rub you up and down and cuddle you. You know? Like that." She tugged down the top of her blouse a little, an artfully nonchalant gesture he appreciated. But still Dale hesitated. "I can tell you one more thing," she went on. "They play long songs here. Not like some places I know, where it's two and a half, three minutes. All the songs on this album are like four, five, six minutes long."

"Really?"

"Sure." The girl moved closer, pressing her soft upper body against his arm and at the same time placing her hand just below the small of his back. "Come on, give it a try anyway. Then if you don't like it, at least you'll know."

"I can touch you?"

"If you're nice about it."

"Okay."

Dale put his hand just below the small of her back, and they made their way across the large room to where there was a battered couch. He noticed that the girl was wearing thick white cotton socks on her feet. That's why she was so short:

The other girls, most of them, were in high heels. He preferred the socks. They were suburban, New Jersey, wholesome, and yet somehow more wicked.

Why didn't Cynthia dress like this? Why didn't she act like this once in a while? Well, nowadays, she would neither look nor sound anywhere near as appealing as this fine young creature. It was a shame; even years ago, when she could have done this sort of thing with great success, Cynthia never had. It had to be his fault, for never telling her, teaching her. He never asked. The two of them had failed each other. Well, she had, anyway. Where was Cynthia's natural lust, her creative sexiness? But where was his, come to that? He had been timid all his life, in the office and at home. In bed. He had taken life as it came to him, which is what Cynthia had done. In some ways, it had never arrived for either of them.

Dale felt so sad that he had a moderate erection even before the girl settled on his lap and began using her body to play with him. He had his feet up and was sitting back against one arm of the couch. She spun around gently, put her face to his belly, and slowly slithered up his chest. Her tube top was pulled down, and her bare breasts—not large but firm, buoyant—brushed across his face, and he kissed them. She took his hair and pressed his face to one breast, then the other. Dale's hands moved down over her back, gliding to her bottom, her taut thighs.

She stood up on the couch, and suddenly she was in his face. He put his mouth against the thin cotton fabric. She turned and deftly bent away from him, her fanny still in his face. He moved his head forward, touching her there. And that was the moment he didn't want to end, not ever. The smell and feel of her sent his mind swirling off in a dozen dizzying spirals. She touched Dale, her hand stroking him lightly, but that wasn't what mattered. It was this closeness—she was a stranger, he didn't even know what her name was—this sudden profound intimacy, much more intimate precisely because it was not the act of sex itself, that made him tremble and ache. In the cellar of this dead factory, warehouse, whatever, to have this contact, this moment.

"I love you," he said faintly.

"The song's over, honey."

But she didn't move. Dale extracted a twenty, put it in her hand. She touched him again. He ran his tongue along the inside edge of her panties. He tasted her. Pushed his tongue into her. Anyone watching? He didn't care. Everything was on the line.

"Oooh . . . honey . . . hey."

He gave her some more bills.

"Oh, God."

"What?" she asked quietly, not moving.

"You have to be home."

"It's okay, I told them I'd be late," she replied after only a brief hesitation. "My folks are asleep by now. Don't worry, I won't wake them when I get in."

"I'll be late getting back."

"You stopped for cigarettes, or milk. Gas."

"I . . . love . . . you."

"Mmmmmh . . ."

Suddenly he splashed her face.

"God . . . help me."

A murmur, but she caught it.

"You don't need any help now, honey."

"Lisa?"

She laughed softly as she moved off him. "Samantha," she corrected. "Sammie. I'm here from four till midnight, every day. You're sweet. You must eat right. I hope you come again."

"Yeah . . ."

"Look for me?"

"Yes, I will."

"If you don't see me, ask."

"Lisa."

Laughter. "Sammie."

"Right. Sammie."

He stumbled around, found his way, lost it, wandered again. The fog was worse now. Rare to see it in Manhattan, and never as thick as this. The streets were choked with mist, the buildings gauzed. It had the effect of dimming all lights, giving them the weak glow of oil or gas lamps. The cars and trucks inching along cautiously seemed like vehicles from another century.

Dale somehow made it down to the pier and got the passenger ferry to Jersey City. As usual, just later and drunker. Though not too much later, and not nearly drunk enough. He had lost the desire to have a roaring great night in the city. The romance in it, spurious at best, had vanished somewhere. Besides, he had to navigate his car home. He could drink more at home. Rip through the night and then pass out. Why the hell not?

The air was damp and raw, but Dale stayed out on deck as the ferry slowly pulled away. Amazing, how little there was to see! The bright lights of the city were feeble specks beneath the fog. Too bad it wasn't daytime, the whole of Manhattan would look like some ghastly cocoon, he thought. It would look like a dead thing, but it would be teeming with tiny insect life.

Dale went inside. There were only a few other passengers on the ferry. Business types going home, sitting apart from anybody else, each in his own bell jar of solitude. A tipsy young couple standing in a corner, bodies tight, a pint in a brown bag passing discreetly back and forth.

Dale sat down opposite a girl who was on her own. He looked across at her just long enough to register that she was a little on the young side, a teenager. Somewhere in that area. She was staring right back at him, so he glanced away. Schoolbooks. It wasn't smart, a youngster out alone at this time of night.

His eyes drifted back to her legs. Pretty. She was wearing a denim jacket and a short skirt. Her legs parted. Bare thighs. Her legs parted a little more. White panties, just a tantalizing glimpse of them. Dale stared for some minutes.

He looked up at her face. Pretty, very pretty, and somehow familiar. She smiled at him, but it was shy, not the bold smile of a blatant come-on. He looked down. Her jacket was open, and her blouse was unbuttoned to the fourth button. Was that really the curve of her breast? She shifted slightly on her seat, as if to help him see that it was, but then she straightened up and the shirt flapped and that exquisite vision was gone. Her legs moved back and forth slightly. Peekaboo.

Dale gazed at her face again. She was still smiling at him, but there was puzzlement in it now, as if she expected him to say or do something and couldn't understand why he didn't. Where had he seen her before? The more it eluded him, the more certain he was that he knew this girl.

"Sammie?" he asked quietly.

She said nothing, but her head tilted a fraction of an inch and her eyes seemed to narrow with interest.

"Lisa?"

The ferry docked with a bump. People were up and moving to the exit. Dale waited until they were all gone, as did the girl. Then he rose from his seat and took one step toward her.

"Do I know you?"

"Do you?"

Dale didn't know what to say. Then she got to her feet and stood in front of him. Waiting, apparently, for him to make some kind of move. She adjusted the schoolbooks in her grip.

"Do you need a ride?" Dale asked. "My car is parked in the lot outside."

"Thanks."

The night was clear, the fog blown away by a sharp wind from the northwest. Dale felt the chill, but it didn't seem to bother the girl. Her long sleek legs flashed as they hurried toward his car, and her blouse hung open in the harsh air. He turned on the heater, watching her intently as he waited for the engine to idle down. She put her books on the floor and sat back, smiling.

"Where do you want to go?"

"Where do you want to take me?"

"Home."

"Sounds good."

"My home," Dale said.

"I know."

It was so outrageous it made perfect sense. Dale could see exactly how it would play out. It was late. Cynthia would be up in bed, sound asleep. Probably snoring. And when she slept, she really slept. Dale would bring the girl in, take her downstairs to the now seldom-used family room, make her a drink, and then see what happened. Later, he would drop her off wherever she had to go. It was like a movie. It was delicious. He accelerated, and soon Jersey City fell behind them.

"I'll make you a drink."

"Thank you," she said enthusiastically.

"How old are you?"

"I'd better not say."

"Well, I bet you've never had a martini."

"No, but I'd love to try one."

"The martini is one of man's greatest achievements."

"Mmmm. Sounds good."

She took his right hand and placed it on her thigh. So warm and soft, yet firm, and gloriously bare. It was such a beautiful feeling that Dale nearly had tears in his eyes. He looked across at her: blouse open, now revealing a lot of breast, those dream legs that seemed so amazingly long, the girlish smile, the finger held to her lips—such a vision. When you find such beauty you can't just walk away from it. Before this night was finished, he would lay his face on her flat belly and cry. With sadness, yes, but also with joy—for being granted this moment at all.

Twenty miles flew by. The house was dark, a very good sign. He pulled right into the open garage, so that no snoopy neighbor would see the girl on the way into the house. She left her books on the floor of the car. They went inside through the breezeway, through the kitchen and downstairs to the family room. He turned on only one small table lamp.

"Ooh, it's nice and warm in here."

"Yes," he said.

The girl threw off her jacket and then flopped onto the sofa like a child. She wiggled and stretched her legs, and her skirt bunched higher. She sat up suddenly, turned, and leaned across to look at the books on the shelf nearby. They were Cynthia's. The collected works of Danielle Steel. But Dale was gazing with awe at the girl's backside, those legs and the way the flimsy panties clung to her heartbreaking fanny.

"Do you want that martini now?"

"Yes, please."

"First take off your blouse."

She smiled. She undid the remaining buttons and slipped out of the blouse. Some cheap gold chains hung between her so-lovely breasts. He went to her and touched one nipple with his cheek in an act of homage. She was still smiling, but with curiosity now, and he knew then that she had never behaved like this before, not with a boyfriend, never. It was new for her, too.

"Come on."

He led her to the bar at the back end of the room and showed her how a martini was made. There had been some noteworthy times in Dale's life, but nothing to compare with this, to have a sweet young thing standing there half-dressed while he fixed a martini. In his own family room!

"Take off your skirt."

She did so. He gave her the drink. While she tasted it, he came closer and ran his hands over her body, dizzy with wonder. She pretended not to notice, concentrating on the martini. Dale was awash with joy. Tomorrow might be the first day of a new era in his life, an Age of Lead, but still he had been given this one final moment of poignant, surpassing beauty.

"How do you like the martini?"

"Wow."

"Good. I'll be right back," he said.

"Okay."

She took her drink to the sofa and stretched out, waving her legs until they found a comfortable position. Dale knelt beside her and put his cheek on her belly. There had never, he thought, been a moment like this in my life.

"I'm going to lick you all over," he said softly.

"Cool."

"In a minute."

Dale went into the unfinished section of the basement, where he kept tools and stored things he didn't really want. He picked up a small hammer, the light little one he used for tapping nails in the walls when he wanted to hang a picture. Then he dashed up the stairs to the kitchen, then the half-flight to the top level, past the empty kids' bedrooms, down the hall to the master suite. The door was ajar. She was snoring. Well, it was more than just snoring. She sounded like a factory in western Massachusetts in some previous era.

One good swing. It made an awful sound. But then there was a tremendous silence. Dale lingered. He became aware of wetness on his cheek. He pulled his shirt off, wiped his face, and tossed the shirt aside. He left the hammer where it was.

Down the hall, down the half-flight, down the regular stairs again—suddenly there was so much motion in his life! Amazing. But when he got to the family room, the girl was gone. He looked around the empty room, catching his breath. Nothing, no one. He ran to the car, but the schoolbooks were gone as well.

Dale sat down on the sofa in the family room. He should be angry with himself, with fate and all of its indignities. But it was no use. A great lassitude came over him, and it was all Dale could do to finish the martini.

SMALL ADJUSTMENTS
Caila Rossi

Caila Rossi is the author of many stories which have appeared in literary magazines, such as *Shenandoah, Quarterly West, California Quarterly,* and others.

"Small Adjustments" is both comical and harsh, both tender and brutal, using fantasy to explore the relationship between a man and a woman: between the one who loves and the one who is loved. It comes from the Spring/Summer 1993 issue of *TriQuarterly* literary journal.

—T.W.

It was the heady aroma of Her, the scent she left on her pillow and sheets, the fragrance he buried himself in when he made her bed. And it was her voice above his head, saying, "He has eyes just like my late husband's."

This must be heaven.

"I think he's got some wolf in him. What do you think?"

"Could be," said a voice in overalls. "He's got the long neck and square muzzle. His legs are a bit short, though. Looks like there's some dachshund in there, too."

Laughter.

Samuel's heart grew light and large as she came near the wire mesh. He felt her soft and loving eyes on him. She breathed into his face. "Will you look at that tail go!" she said.

He turned sharply to look behind him and saw, curving towards his head, a long, horizontal back covered with wiry, muddy-colored hair. At its end was a feathery tail that thumped, though he'd hardly been aware of it, against a black Labrador-mix on his left.

"He thinks he's a puppy. Don't you, pooch? Don't you?"

"Don't," said the attendant, opening the cage. But it was too late. Before Samuel could be separated from the whining crowd, Hazel had reached in to scratch his head.

He felt closer to her now than he had been in years. Eyes wide, he nudged her hand with his nose. He could smell every hidden fold of her skin, from her fingertips to the crevices between her toes. He smelled the wax in her ears, the sweat at the roots of her hair.

Hazel led him through the parking lot holding one end of a long leash. "Come, King," she said.

Feeling breathless, Samuel let his legs carry him, afraid he'd topple over if he thought too much about how they moved, towards each other, then away. He looked straight ahead at tires, wheel hubs and the knees of other pedestrians. He wished he were taller.

When she opened the door he instinctively slid behind the wheel.

"You're going to drive, are you?"

How long it had been since she had spoken to him like that, gently mocking, affectionate. He smiled. Of course he wouldn't, couldn't drive. One fatal mishap behind the wheel was enough. He lumbered over the front seat.

He had not felt so lighthearted in ages, not since their first years together, not since their honeymoon, perhaps, in Lake George. Hazel had worn an array of swimsuits but never gone near the water because she couldn't swim. Nor, it turned out later, could she cook or iron, and she stayed away from mechanical things like washing machines. He had taught her to drive—not easy, especially on the car, which needed a new transmission before it was six months old. She cried when it was towed to the junkyard ten years later. Samuel, though moved by her attachment to an inanimate object, knew by then that she would never cry such tears for him. Even after thirty-five years of marriage, there remained something left undone, a small adjustment needed, an "if only" to be fulfilled before she could love him as much as she had loved her Studebaker.

In response to murmured condolences, Hazel replied, "I'm fine." Stroking him with one hand, she added, "I always wanted a dog."

Now that he was helpless as a baby she was more pleased with him than ever before.

"You'd hardly know Samuel was gone," her friends whispered when she was out of the room.

"You hardly ever knew he was here!"

Their laughter, cast up from the dark side of their hearts, sounded hideous to him.

"Did he ever take off those rubber gloves?"

"Only to tie his apron!"

How glad he was not to be human anymore. Now Hazel fed him meaty bones. She brushed him, lavished tenderness on him, even followed him on the street with a wad of paper towels in hand. All this attention made him lighthearted. Even his body felt light. His bare feet were soft but tough. The nails were long and clicked on hard surfaces as though he were wearing taps. He would run if he could see better, but what from?

Noise, maybe. It came at him from all directions. She was oblivious, serene, enjoyed the peace of the deaf. He wanted to warn her at every frightening sound, but a dog had to play his cards right. He calmed himself, found he could distinguish a threat by its smell: sounds without smells could be ignored. Smells, though, could not. Even harmless smells: milk, the scent of warmth, smoke, cooking meat and he would remember walking upright, using his hands, the fit of shoes, weight of clothes, their comfort, discomfort, speaking, doing. Nostalgia was never so painful as this fitful longing to be a different species altogether.

But let him stay here, for a while, at least. Let him lie close to her as she slept, across her feet at the bottom of the bed, by her side on the floor, closer than he had been in his room across the hall. Let him feel secure in her affections, safer than he had ever felt.

Now every day was Sunday, slightly convalescent, reluctant to get started, one long morning that suddenly turned into night and then Monday. On a morning full of church bells, a real Sunday, Edna Clay was the only visitor. She sat in a chair across from Hazel who sprawled on the sofa, Bloody Mary in hand. Edna's cup clicked against her dentures as she drank her coffee. She pretended to like Samuel for Hazel's sake, but her feet and hands were hesitant. Perfume and sweat mixed, disagreeably, with the synthetic fabric of her dress.

"Didn't they have any puppies in the pound?" she asked.

"I didn't want a puppy peeing on my carpet," said Hazel. "Besides, they would have destroyed King that afternoon. I had to save him."

"Breaks your heart, doesn't it?" said Edna. "I once got a cat from the Bide-A-Wee. 'Baby,' I called her. She shredded my upholstery, so I had her declawed. Then she started biting, so I had to have her teeth pulled. The poor thing was so miserable after that she had to be put to sleep."

Samuel sighed: he knew what it was to be at a woman's mercy, yet there was no place he would rather be. Sprawling at what felt a safe distance on the floor, he nevertheless attracted Hazel's attention. She gestured to him. Her hand smelled fresh, of lemon and water. He closed his eyes and sniffed the air.

"King!" she insisted. "Come!"

He ambled over.

"Does he know any tricks?" said Edna.

They gave him simple commands: Roll over, Sit, Beg, Fetch the cocktail stick.

"It's almost like having Samuel back," said Edna.

"It's better." Hazel scratched him intently behind his right ear. Then, placing her hands on either side of his face, she looked into his eyes. "A dog is much easier to love," she said. "Even to kiss." And she planted one right on his mouth.

"Euw!" said Edna.

Winged insects whirred about the room, stirring the heat around them in soft waves. He moved his nose up and down the smooth flesh of Hazel's inner arm. She smelled of talc and vodka and he could even smell the blood flowing through veins close to her pale skin. Downstairs, the washing machine clicked into a new cycle. Hazel was doing her own laundry.

He had been circling the globe, seen the sun set and rise in quick succession numerous times. He had gained and lost days, gained and lost. He had been suspended in time, so it felt, and now he had a serious case of jet lag.

"Pretty girl. Pretty pretty girl."

Worse, though he hated to dwell on it, but he felt pilloried, tarred and feathered, otherwise naked, his hair completely gone. His bones were light but compacted, his equilibrium undone.

"Do you think she's a little too green?" Hazel asked.

"She's fine," said the vet, "for a bird her age."

"How old do you think she is?"

"Difficult to say. I suppose we could count the rings on her tail."

"Let's!" she said.

The veterinarian laughed and Samuel felt safe, for the moment, perched on his hand. Despite her ignorance, maybe because of it, Hazel still looked young. Her straight brown hair was graying, but worn in the same shag style as on their wedding day. She was beautiful.

"What happened to that funny-looking dog you adopted?"

"It was terrible," she said. "He bit a friend of mine."

"No kidding?"

"My first date in ten years and we ended up in the emergency room."

Ten years? thought Samuel. Surely that much time hadn't passed since his accident.

"You put the dog to sleep?"

"It was terrible," she said, unable to confess.

She must have dated other men while they were still married. A sad surprise—he had never thought her fickle. Flighty, yes, but loyal. Now he remembered being locked up again, waiting for Hazel to retrieve him, being led into an antiseptic room much like this one, the injection, the horrible "sleep." Though death, in retrospect, was sweet oblivion: it was life that took getting used to. To think, just when they had finally achieved a perfect rapport, she'd had him put to sleep at his first jealous outburst. No wonder, when he saw her gazing at him again through the wires of a cage, his first impulse was to flee for a long, happy life. Which was when he discovered he had wings, and that they were clipped, useless.

"Hmm," said the vet, "cataracts. She's not young. Any idea what happened to her last owners?"

"Redecorating, I think."

Hazel called him Sheila, a name he had suggested himself, inexplicably. Words and commands jumped out of his mouth at strange moments. He felt shallow. His soul was restless, too big for this body. He dreamed of flight.

Hazel dreamed of flying, too. She told Betty Burkle about her dream as they sorted through his clothes one afternoon. Samuel watched and listened quietly from a perch near her bedroom window. "I've had dreams like that," said Betty. "Makes you wish you could, doesn't it?"

Not Hazel. "It was a nightmare!" she said. "I kept getting tangled in the telephone wires. Have you noticed how low they hang these days?"

Shorts and shirts fluttered past him and sank to the floor. Samuel had discovered he could fly short distances, but the frantic flapping made Hazel screech in fright. She poked food and fingers at him in an effort to get close, not understanding that he needed a shoulder, a firm hand beneath his feet. If he tried, however gently, to nudge her fingers away with his beak, or raised his wings to retreat, she got indignant.

Samuel knew his days were numbered. Soon she would realize she didn't want a parrot, after all.

"Ink stains everywhere," said Betty, holding up a striped shirt. "Have you thought of getting help?"

"You mean live-in?"

"No." Betty paused, frowning. "I was thinking psychological."

"Oh, Sam took care of that years ago."

Had he? It seemed only he had changed, and that change remained his singular option. He should have taken better advantage of his time with the therapist. Now there was no one to talk to and the changes were out of control.

"How do you feel?" she had asked him. Young, dark-haired, wearing dark wool, she had leaned forward on her desk, holding her own pale hands. Outside there had been other people waiting, sad, distraught, angry people. Samuel had felt nothing in common with them.

He had never recognized his own unhappiness. Even there, in the therapist's office, thoughts of Hazel made him smile: Hazel dancing through the streets after seeing the movie *Isadora*; Hazel explaining to a friend that the way to stay thin was not to eat anything too bulky—a chocolate bar was less fattening than a head of lettuce because it took up less room in one's stomach. Then he had seen Hazel perhaps at that moment, scowling, struggling with bags from the supermarket, needing his help, needing him there, but needing him here, too. Hazel unhappy.

"I love my wife."

"Yes?" The young woman leaned closer. "And how does that make you feel?"

"She's not very well. Menopause, I think."

"How does it feel to love your wife?" the therapist asked again.

She doesn't know, he'd thought. She's collecting information for emotions she has never experienced. He had tried to help her. "It's like a tide," he said. "You're a swimmer and you hope the tide will bring you to shore, but instead it pulls you farther away. So you grow fins and gills to survive and you keep hoping. And sometimes the tide does seem to bring you closer to land."

"How does it feel to be a fish?" she'd asked.

What prescience! He squawked miserably. If only he had taken her seriously. At the time, all that concerned him was what he might be doing wrong at home. "I should be more sympathetic to her," he had said. "I should anticipate her needs instead of waiting for her to tell me what they are."

The therapist had looked disappointed; he had ignored her question. But he had come for Hazel's sake, not hers. "Yes. That's it. I'm sure that's what I have to do."

"Now that you've solved your wife's problems," said the young woman, "how do *you* feel?"

"Much better, thank you." And he had never gone back.

"He's very loud, isn't he?" said Betty. She and Hazel stared at him. His outburst had amused them, briefly, but now Betty continued stuffing a pair of his shorts into a plastic garbage bag. "So what did the telephone company say?"

Hazel sighed. "I should never have mentioned my dream. They must think I'm some sort of kook."

"A good-looking kook," Betty assured her. Hazel had begun wearing makeup every day. She had had her hair permed, painted her nails. She was becoming more like Betty Burkle, who had been married four times, widowed the last two, who boasted of dating men half her age. A couple of men already hung about, sometimes spending the night with Hazel.

"I'm not getting married again," she insisted, "if that's what you're saying. Once was enough."

"Once was never enough." Betty forced his robe into the overstuffed bag, secured it tightly and threw it against the wall. "There!" she said. "That's the last of it. Why didn't you divorce Sam if you weren't happy?"

"On what grounds? Besides, he needed me. He loved me. Whatever that means."

"Don't you know?"

"Do you?" Hazel's voice rose plaintively.

Betty Burkle got to her feet. She put her arms around her friend's shoulders.

Pained to see Hazel so unhappy, Samuel broke the silence with a "RRRinggg," surprising himself. "Good morning!" he said brightly, though it was afternoon. "Oh George!" He couldn't help himself.

Hazel's laugh enveloped him.

She had many friends. The phone rang often. Hearing her laugh into the silent space of the house, Samuel felt intensely lonely. Perhaps he always had. He had always known she didn't love him, but he had never stopped hoping she would. And that was how it felt to be a man and a bird, and how it would probably feel to be a fish.

But now he discovered he could laugh. It was Hazel's laugh, and though it lacked human conviction, she didn't seem to notice. Thinking it a perfect echo, she would laugh, and he would laugh: they laughed together, filling the house with laughter. At these times she seemed happy enough with him.

"I think you'd like some sunshine, wouldn't you?" she said one day, smiling at him through the bars of his cage. He edged away, leery of new ideas.

Hazel was determined. "We're moving outside," she said, lifting the cage with both hands. "It's a beautiful day and I want to work in the garden."

His head rang as she knocked the cage against the doorframe.

The yard was large, with a flower garden along the back and side fences. Hazel had wanted lupines, hollyhocks, foxglove, an English garden. It had taken him years to get it right.

"How's this?" she said, placing him on the edge of the fountain in the middle of the yard. She surveyed the overgrown garden. Samuel was sure she would give up immediately and carry him back inside, but instead she leaned toward him. "Enough air?" she said. And for some reason, or lack of it, she widened a couple of bars before wandering off in search of the garden tools.

She's getting old, he thought sadly, staring at the gap in the cage. Briefly, he considered escape, but decided against it. However painful life was with her, he knew that without her he would not exist at all.

A stealthy movement through the grass reminded him of the neighbor's cats, forever stalking the fountain, waiting for some hapless bird to take a dip. Few birds did anymore, but the cats hung out anyway, sunning and sparring in the grass. When the ginger cat landed on the rim of the fountain, Samuel laughed for the first time as a bird with his own laugh. A hysterical laugh. His last laugh.

Like a leg with a sock pushing and pulling along it, he worked his way through Hazel's garden. He had shoveled, hoed and raked this garden, but never had he known it so intimately. His mouth was filled with it. Only when water clogged his pores did he surface into light and shadow, into the arena of flowers, grass, the cacophony of machines and insects, night creatures whining in their sleep, perhaps remembering past lives.

Life was all reflex now, leaving him free to dwell in the senses. In memory he inhaled her scent, felt her touch, her warm breath in his face, the pressure of her hand behind his ears, against his wings, her responsiveness to his moods, even if she sometimes guessed wrong. How sensitive her fingers were, how loving her arms, how generous she was. Surely she was wrong to say she didn't know what love was.

"I'm so glad the rain stopped," she said. "We can try out my new chairs."

"It's a shame Samuel never had a chance to sit here," said Betty. A metal chair scraped pleasantly against the wood deck he'd had built one autumn, before the weather changed. "He might have made sure the carpenters finished it right."

"It slopes, doesn't it?" said Edna.

"They didn't put a low rail around the edge," said Betty, "or boxes for plants. A deck should have flowers, don't you think?"

"Oh yes. I love flowers."

"I told Sam I wanted a hot tub, just like in the ashram. But then he had the accident."

"Too bad," said Edna.

"And there's no shade," Hazel continued. "You'll see when the sun gets hot."

"These decks always look unfinished to me," said Edna. "Not like a nice porch."

"He did plant a pretty garden," said Betty.

"Yes. And left me to take care of it."

Samuel inched his way along the cement walk feeling for a dry spot. Calm industry prevailed around him. All was bliss. What luxury, this pleasant exhaustion, what quietude in restricted movement. He felt safe, at a safe distance, anyway, from Hazel. Anonymity was a small price to pay for helping her garden grow. She might complain, but he knew she was pleased, especially to think she had done it all herself.

"Why don't you get a new pet?" Betty asked.

Hazel sighed. "I do miss the exercise, but I'm no good with animals."

"Gardening is good exercise," said Edna.

"Would you like to see my columbines?" Hazel rose from her chair. Her heels sounded friendly on the hollow platform, less so on the cement walk. "Be careful of the puddles," she said. "Watch where you step."

Breathing distantly, his long arms bent sometimes at surprising angles, Samuel reach toward what he had once thought of as heaven. Hazel had grown old as he had just grown. For the first time in years, he feared he would outlive her. She might not even survive his next thought, which took seasons to complete. And the seasons were so endless now. He felt a perpetual boy, slowly growing in place. Worms crawled around his many roots, squirrels and birds flitted in and out of his leafy arms, and below him Hazel lay in her recliner, frail, with fleeting moments of pleasantness.

"Where'd that tree come from, anyway?" she asked her nurse one afternoon. Age had not helped her memory. "It blocks the sky."

Samuel felt a tremor. His leaves fluttered in the still air.

"It's been there for years," said the nurse, who had started off as a daily companion and now lived in. "You must have planted it yourself."

"Why would I do a thing like that? Call the tree surgeon. It should be half that size."

"You can't do that," the nurse objected. "It'll die."

"I'm sick of all this life and death stuff," Hazel said. "I've had enough!"

He was a punctuation mark in a curl of smoke: Why? But Samuel could not answer himself—he was not that sort of question. Dispersing in the wind, he was blown out over the ocean and ended up in the hands of a young Frenchwoman. She shaped him in a soft oval and packed him in a garden of perfumes, rose, lemon, vanilla. His own scent was written over him in clear letters: VERVEINE. A strong, sweet, grassy smell; he might have luxuriated in it had he not known where he was headed.

The nurse unwrapped him. And he felt the light. It was her touch, too, those responsive hands. That was what he had needed all along. Of course. He had his answer now. It was his own fault. Had he pursued someone worthy of his love, he might have found, while still a man, the happiness he had wanted. And yet, and yet, turning over and over in Hazel's long fingers, across her palm, he regretted nothing. Would he not have lived his lives all over again for the privilege of being with her, catching her affection where it fell, breathing the air she exhaled, laughing with her, making her laugh; but especially for these last moments, fading together, chased by her grasping fingers across the sink, taken into her bath, cuddled in a soft pink washcloth against her bosom where for days he dissolved into her skin, leaving behind, at last, his pleasing scent?

PRECIOUS

Roberta Lannes

Roberta Lannes lives in Los Angeles, where she works as a teacher, freelance designer, and graphic artist. Her first published story, "Goodbye, Dark Love," appeared in Dennis Etchison's 1986 anthology *Cutting Edge*. Since then she has had stories in such magazines and anthologies as *Iniquities, Fantasy Tales, Lord John Ten, Splatterpunks, Alien Sex, Pulphouse,* and *Still Dead*. She is working on a novel entitled *The Hallowed Bed*.

Some readers may find "Precious" hard to take. It's about a doctor with a peculiar obsession and it's the gynecological equivalent of Christopher Fowler's dental nightmare "On Edge," which we reprinted in last year's volume. "Precious" first appeared in *Dark Voices 5*.

—E.D.

There are parts of a woman, Harris Stone thought, that are like vegetables gone rotten, not worth saving. Disgusting. He cast a cold eye upon the beautiful patient who waited primly in the chair opposite his office desk. He knew that in this one, there were places rife with mould, dark and grimly furred, pocked with nodes of fungal proliferation. He would draw a laser over them. Erase the mistakes nature cursed her with.

A woman's parts could indeed become perfect. He believed this or he wouldn't have became an Ob-Gyn. Once, just once, he saw the perfectly formed part of a virginal female. In medical school. A cadaver. She was seventeen. Not an attractive girl in death. But her parts were without comparison. Almost too painful to dissect, he considered removing the entire area and saving it in a jar of formaldehyde, but there would have been repercussions. He had his future to protect. But that perfection remained a paradigm in his memory.

Natalie crossed her slender legs, her manicured nails clicked on one another like ruby castanets. She felt scared. Donald wanted a child. Soon. If she couldn't have Dr. Stone finally and completely remove the venereal warts on her cervix, her child would have to be born by Caesarean section to protect it. That was unacceptable. She couldn't ruin her body. There was her movie career to consider.

Dr. Stone settled into his creaky leather swivel chair and steepled his fingers over her chart. His dark graying hair formed a handsome widow's peak over pale blue eyes. She noticed how hairy his fingers were. She thought of them inside of her and her stomach lurched.

"I see Dr. Bernstein sent you here. A stubborn case of warts. What can I do for you?" He raised his eyebrows and pulled his mouth into a chalky grin.

"If you read my chart, you'd know," she snapped, then recovered. "I'm sorry."

"Tell me what the problem is, in your own words." His grin faded.

Natalie folded her hands. "I want to have a baby, but I don't want to conceive until I'm free of the warts. They pose a threat to the child."

"There's no danger if you have a caesarean. And the scar I leave is almost undetectable."

"I'm glad to hear that, but you see I'm an actress. My body is exposed sometimes . . . it's just, I don't know, vanity. And box office." She smiled, a bit embarrassed.

"I see on your chart that Dr. Bernstein has removed cervical warts twice before and that they've recurred. Has your husband been checked out?"

"Dr. Stone, my husband did not give me the warts. The story behind them is ancient history. A poor choice in men, made when I was doing theater in the West End . . ." She looked into her lap.

"Well, perhaps Dr. Bernstein never explained how you could give them to your husband, then . . ."

"You don't understand. My husband's never had them. They're my problem."

"Look, I'm not Dr. Bernstein. I don't have a celebrity clientele who can't afford to hear the truth and pay dearly for the right to be lied to. I can remove the warts. Maybe they won't return during your pregnancy. But, as long as your husband has had contact with these warts, he carries the virus. If you want to believe he isn't reinfecting you, that's your choice. I can only do what I can do." He grimaced slightly as he tried to regain his composure.

Natalie felt stunned. The thoughts of Donald, his errant sexuality, the sicknesses that she inherited with his every dalliance, sought illumination, but once more she forced them into darkness. She nodded numbly.

"All right. Let's get on with it, then." They both stood, stiff, the moment awkward.

Stone's shiny faced nurse, Marci, led Natalie away to an examination room.

Harris sat down, overwhelmed. Natalie Bright was absolutely the most beautiful woman he had ever been so close to before. Her skin was flawless, her features classically proportioned. He recalled seeing the beads of perspiration on the cleft of her buttocks in *The Last Train*; sweat just sitting there like dew on a rose petal, until the hand of some young actor swept over the flesh with all the grace of a windshield wiper. She was lovely in person in a way he could never have imagined.

He thought of George Bernstein, with his movie star clientele—one beauty after another. But they were all fantasy queens, full of plastic parts and tucked-back droops, who would rather hear they were "ripe" than harboring trichomoniasis. So many of them seeking to retain the illusion of a pristine female condition. George Bernstein sent the needy ones to Harris, the women whose lives depended on unflinching reality and real care. He often sent them too late. Or like Natalie, when he found it easier to have Harris dole out the truth. Beauties with so much ugliness inside.

Harris reread George's chart on Natalie. His eyes kept catching on the doctor's unnecessarily graphic descriptions, growing gradually aroused.

Strawberry-pink vulva. Beet-colored knob of clitoris. Velvety corrugated vaginal walls. Lubrication like fine oil of pearl.

That George Bernstein. He really loved women. Even the parts of them that went bad, gruesome with fetid and foul ailments. All women were flowers to George. Harris shivered at the thought. Flowers were precious. Nature's perfection. Women were flawed and certain to wither and decompose through half their lives, while flowers only went that way in death. He thought of his grandmother, teaching him of a woman's parts from when he was eight or nine. Showing him the ruins of what a woman becomes before he could discover beauty in his own naïve explorations.

George's descriptions were of quintessential things. Things that brought Harris to the point of erection.

Could Natalie be as he said?

The "ready" light winked by his door. Harris trembled, feeling suddenly virginal.

Natalie sat nude except for the pale green paper vest that hung from her shoulders like a sandwich board over her breasts. The vest grazed a paper blanket Marci had drawn over her hips.

Stone bothered her. He was abrupt and ill-mannered. But, she didn't have to invite him over for lunch. He would fix her up so that she could get pregnant soon. Yeah. And the sooner the better. After this last miscarriage, Donald had begun to stray. He seemed to need a child as if it were some kind of a testament to his virility. That frightened her.

Dr. Stone entered with a glassy, vacant look on his face. Marci stood by cheerily. As she aligned herself for the exam, Natalie noticed Stone staring at her crotch the way she noticed tourists admiring Michelangelo's David. She was oddly disturbed and warmed at once. His face grew youthful, full of awe. She held a smirk in check.

The examination was the usual uncomfortable poking and probing invasion that led to the snapping off of latex gloves and the dispensing voice, void of balm.

He jotted notes on her chart as he described four warts, advised early surgery, asked her to make an appointment, thanked her and left, avoiding eye contact. She blinked at Marci, who shrugged.

Soon. It would be done soon.

Every word was right, thought Harris Stone. Bernstein had described a perfection of form that probably no one but Natalie's wandering husband and her physician knew of. But no one appreciated it like Harris. The folds in her vagina were like sculptural silk bathed in liquid pearls, a soft downy halo of cinnamon-colored pubic hair so unlike the usual bristle and wire, the labia so symmetrical, cloaked in equally perfect lips of flesh, like pale hands praying, and a scent much like the breeze over a window sill on which sat a freshly baked peach pie. He played the scenario over and over behind heavy eyelids, his face flushing, his groin tingling.

After so little beauty, he'd found something so precious he couldn't think of it without also considering its rarity. His ex-wives, girlfriends, had come close. Only close. Natalie Bright was a singular wonder. Yes, he'd take the mephitic part from deep inside her to create the finite. Then he would go to any lengths to preserve it.

Donald sat across the glass-topped dining table from Natalie as she poked a fork into a log-jam of baby corn. He held a cordless phone between his ear and shoulder, shovelling food into his mouth as he barked at someone. She watched him.

He'd been selfish when she told him about the surgery.

"Nat, then we won't be able to have functional sex for at least two weeks . . ."

She'd lowered her head to hide the rage she felt. She guessed he thought her penitent as he petted her arm and said, "Oh, sugar, I'm just scared you will go through all this pain and suffering to have our baby and you'll lose it again."

She recalled the night of tears, how Donald had wept in her arms. She had been more touched by his sorrow than by her own loss. Her tears came later.

Another call came through on his call-waiting. She knew. His tone changed. She recognized the timbre, the monosyllabic cooing. Her stomach clenched as she rose, grasped her glass of wine and went to her den.

Standing amidst the hundreds of first editions lining the walls, Natalie breathed in the scents of fading ink, yellowing paper, oxidizing gilt and worn leather. The smell, the cool dim room, usually calmed her. Instead she went cement-hard inside. Cold. Grey. Walled in. Her arms went about her as she repelled the desire for vengeance that rocked her like a minor earthquake.

Harris wiped his eyes with his sleeve as he held a beaker up in the light of his lab. The consumptive-grey strands of tissue wriggled like the fine feathers of an ostrich boa. They were parasitic worms brought back from Peru by his friend Eduardo Barraza. They would die soon without a host.

On the counter in identical beakers, were two other worm-like creatures. One, he'd found himself in Venezuela, a carnivorous caterpillar, deep yellow-orange with red and black markings. Its blind eyes, the stark white of a bleached sheet, rolled from side to side. The other was the result of his own venture into genetic engineering; a two inch long, potato bug-ugly thing with a snakebody writhing, a tail-end jabbing at the glass with a dark pin-sharp hook-seeking root. Large black bead eyes rotated, taking in all sights until faced with the light. Then it curled its head protectively under its body.

Harris took the caterpillar from the beaker with stainless steel tongs and set it in a dish lined with epithelial cells. Its tiny needle teeth grasped and tore hungrily at the viscera. Like a piranha, the caterpillar had its fill quickly, and soon curled up laze and fat in a curve of the dish.

The other creature jumped at the metal tongs as Harris reached for it. It attacked anything it perceived as a threat. He grabbed it behind its head and lifted it into a dish of endometrial tissue. Like a sand crab sucked from its home by a curious child and dropped back on the beach to burrow deep away, the creature made it way out of sight. Sanctuary.

Harris watched and waited. No movement. No disturbance in the tissue. He still was uncertain about just how much and what kind of tissue it ate to live.

He thought of Natalie Bright. So precious. Once he removed the blight caused by her husband, he would make certain she would not be tainted again. He closed his eyes and imagined her sweetly hooded clitoris arching itself against his wet finger. Her vulva parting with the insistence of his tongue. He grasped the counter as he pressed himself against it.

He glanced down at the dish of tissue. Monday. Natalie.

Natalie held Donald's hand loosely as they sat in the waiting room. She felt calm, ready, detached. She'd wanted to be put out for the procedure. Dr. Stone had given her a Valium just to ease her initial tension. Now she floated in a surreal clarity devoid of concern.

"This is it, baby." Donald kissed her temple. She blinked.

"We're going to have a gorgeous son and your body will stay just as luscious as it is today." He kissed her jaw. She twitched under her eye.

Stone came in. Natalie noticed his face fall momentarily as he saw Donald.

"My husband, Donald Forrester." Dr. Stone shook his hand.

"Take good care of my wife. She's the most important person in my life." Natalie rolled her eyes. She caught Dr. Stone wincing.

"We intend to do our best." He smiled warmly at Natalie as he turned to go.

Blissfully uncaring, she leaned back and shut her eyes.

"She's really beautiful, isn't she?" Harris brushed his scrub nurse aside to stand between Natalie Bright's long soft legs. Her ankles hung in padded slings so that the legs made a deep pale "V."

"She's lovely." The scrub nurse grinned at the well-known face.

Harris tersely addressed his surgical crew. After they set up, he would be doing the procedure alone. The women looked at each other and shrugged.

His nurse-practitioner checked Natalie's vital signs, then all of the nurses left. He waited a few moments, then began stroking Natalie's labia with his bare fingers. He parted the flesh, exposing her clitoris. With some gentle nudging, it became erect.

In his peripheral vision, Harris saw the beaker and tools that sat on the table beside him. He could hear his paper slipper-covered feet shuffling beneath him, then silence. His fingers probed and prodded Natalie's flesh with adolescent inquisitiveness. Lust surged in him as he remembered it had in his youth. It grew into a wanting so large and engulfing it nearly suffocated him.

His mouth went to the engorged flesh, tasting, ferreting out the folds and curves he'd only sought with his fingers before. She was sweet, warm, everything he'd ever imagined perfection to taste and feel like.

His grandmother had told him lies about what other women would feel like. Taste, the taste of her flesh had been like licking a wound, coppery and sharp, and she felt like a cat's tongue. It was all he'd known during the years most boys were feeling up their first girl. It colored his choices. He'd spent his life in search of something so alien, so distant and distinct from the familiar blemished flesh he'd known then, until now.

He pulled down the surgical jams and took his rigid cock in hand. He knew what he wanted to do was unethical. He also knew it would be something he would never know again in his life if he didn't have it now. And so he pressed his sheathed cock into her. Into perfection. Moving his hips in long rehearsed rhythms, he clutched her breasts. Too soon, he felt himself falling. Falling.

He fell against her, his chest heaving, heart hammering. Slowly, he regained his composure, cleaned himself and Natalie up, and began the job he'd been called in to do.

He deftly lasered off the warts, deposited the offensive tissue into a specimen jar and proceeded to cauterize the site of the surgery.

"Done. Now for the keeper of perfection."

The creature's hooked tail thrashed the air, its eyes, unprotected from the brilliant operating room lights, couldn't seek asylum under its body as Harris held it in a hemostat. He pressed it to the cervix. With one disengaging twist of his fingers, Harris pulled the hemostat away, leaving the creature there. It coiled itself at the cervical opening, its eyes adjusting, its head poked at the tiny opening, then writhed inside. Home.

Harris put his gloved hands together and stared at his work. At perfection. And he wept.

Natalie saw Donald's face as she swam back from oblivion. She felt wonderful. Warm and groggy. He embraced her.

"I love you, Nat. You're my brave girl."

She fell back to sleep and dreamed again and again over the next forty-eight hours of dragons and knights and being saved.

Harris called Natalie three days after surgery. She said she had some cramping, but expected her period soon. He told her she might not get her period, but not to worry. Surgery is a trauma and the body reacts in many strange ways. He thought of the creature that now lived inside of her, and wondered if it could live on the endometrial tissue that was shed during menses. Had she felt the thing rooted there within her?

He rolled over in bed, thinking of her spread out before him, opening herself to him, willingly, holding him inside of her, receiving him, his essence. For that moment, she owned him, body and soul. As his grandmother had sought to do.

It occurred to him suddenly, that he had found a place far away from the hold his grandmother had had on him all of his life, and there was a key—Natalie Bright, in all her perfection. No longer did the thought of his grandmother shrivel him up like an October leaf. Natalie had saved him. As he had saved her.

In front of the mirror, Natalie admired her body. She ran her hand over her lower belly, her fingers splayed into the hair there. She smiled. She felt strong, healthy, sure. It would be all right now.

The "ready" light winked by his door. Harris gathered himself up to do another exam. Mrs. Shrader. Marci stood waiting at the door to the examining room, concern marked her face.

As he stood between Mrs. Shrader's legs, Marci took his elbow. It was happening again. He saw the crenelated, sagging flesh of Mrs. Shrader's thighs, the labia like the garroted innards of a fish drooping from a hook, smelling the putrid, yeasty scent, and knowing that deep inside her was a void he'd made, now filled with intestine and a stretched out bladder, he grew sickly faint. Disgusted was too pale a word. *Repulsed.*

He strained to remain expressionless, but Mrs. Shrader's shrill voice broke his consciousness.

"Are you all right, Dr. Stone?"

He nodded. "Working too hard."

He somehow worked his fingers into her. He closed his eyes.

"My husband just loves the way I feel now, if you know what I mean . . ."

Harris withdrew his fingers. The squishing sound, the cheesy odor, the ugly reality crashed in on his senses. His gorge rose. He turned quickly to the sink, ripped off his gloves, washed and mumbled to Marci before hurrying from the room.

He retched into his private toilet. How was he going to go on today? How was he about to keep a practice at all if he found looking at women's parts *this* horrendous? They were all like that for him now. He washed his face, closing his eyes to see Natalie's precious mons, her labia peeking out. It was the only thought that eased the revulsion. Erased it. In a few days she would be in for a check-up. He dried his face and looked at himself in the mirror, trembling. She owned him. It was what he wanted?

Natalie found a note in Donald's pants pocket. In his secretary's hand it read, "Call Kami. The doctor said *YES*." Her mind reeled. Had Donald gotten someone else pregnant? Or had he contracted the warts and given them to someone else? No matter what she wanted to believe, the cheating wasn't over.

She packed a bag and ran off to their other house in Palm Springs. Away from him. The truth.

Harris sat at his desk watching the dark "ready" light as if he were a ship seeking harbor. When it was lit, it would be for Natalie. He willed it to go on. Nothing. Now. OK, *now*. He felt stupid and awkward and giddy.

Marci knocked, then stuck her head in.

"Bright is a no-show. I've got Kosicki in two."

"Did she call in?"

"Nope. Can I tell Miss Kosicki you'll be in?"

He shook his head. No more. Not even one more. Marci disappeared. His fists fell into his lap. When he closed his eyes, all he could see was a field of animal traps, all sprung, the maws full of blood and flesh contorted, bones distorted, faces set in masks of pain. In every one, he could see his grandmother. Even near death, she had sent everyone out, including her own daughter, just to get Harris into her bed one last time—an opportunity for him to show her how much he loved her. He'd been afraid, too afraid to say no, and so he crawled in, the scent of death already seeping into the sheets. He prayed she would die before he had to do the things to her parts, her awful ugly parts. But she lived until morning, leaving Harris all of her estate, and the legacy of vision he now struggled to kill.

"Oh, Natalie," he whispered. "Don't abandon me now."

*   *   *

Donald wasn't contrite, as Natalie had expected. He told her a too-perfect story, but true, he said. Kami had gone through breast enhancement surgery and didn't know if she could be back on the set of the soap opera Donald directed that Monday. The message just confirmed that she could make it. He gave Natalie Kami's phone number to verify his story. She took it.

Guilt didn't stop her from watching the show to see who Kami was, but it did stop her from calling. She came home the next day.

Harris jerked awake with the phone's trill. It was Marci. Did he want to cancel his patients again today? Natalie Bright had called. She could be in around four. He would rally, Harris told Marci. He'd be in by ten.

Natalie knew it wouldn't be a good idea to make love before the doctor saw her, but Donald was so insistent. He would wear a rubber for infection's sake. Anything. He loved her, dammit, and he wanted to prove it to her. She balked. It stoked his lust. He would be gentle.

His kisses were deep, meaningful, wet. He let his tongue reacquaint itself with every crevice of her body. When he slipped inside her, she was deliciously shivering under his weight.

His thrusts were short and easy. She watched his face grow beatific.

"Ow!" Donald pulled out and held the end of his erection. "What the hell . . . ? Something bit me." He crawled over to the bedside lamp and flicked it on. "Look!"

Natalie lay there, frozen. She could see blood on the end of the rubber. "Maybe it caught on some stitches."

"I . . . don't know." He shook his head.

"Come here and let me kiss it." She tried to smile.

He lay back and let her minister to him.

She admitted she'd let Donald make love to her too soon. Harris was stern in his reprimand. She promised she wouldn't do it again. He assured her that it was in her best interests not to.

As he inserted the speculum to check on the healing, he could see the creature's head at the mouth of the cervix.

"Do you feel anything?" He wanted to kiss the delicate flesh of her mons.

"A little cramping. Nothing bad."

Its black eyes scanned the vagina, ready to attack, its teeth bared. He released the speculum, and as he pulled it out, the creature disappeared.

"Give yourself a couple of weeks. You look fine. I suggest you come in then before resuming intercourse and I'll see how you've healed up."

She smiled. "I didn't like you much when I first met you, but I have this feeling . . . I don't know . . . like you really want to take care of me. That's so rare in doctors these days."

Harris caught Marci's grin and blushed. He wanted to tell Natalie all of it.

That night he kicked himself for not having taken more time, touched her more, joked around. It was too late anyway. He'd done what he could for her,

and he'd known all along she wasn't his. She'd been a gift to save him from the
past and it was up to him to use what she'd given him. Not to use her.

He fell asleep to the memory of his operating room ecstasy.

Three weeks after the surgery, Donald took Natalie to stay at the New Otani Hotel
for their first efforts at "babymaking." She glowed with anticipation. They had
honeymooned in the same room.

After a bath together, a massage together, and lots of saki, they were locked in
each other's embrace when the phone rang. Donald lurched for it.

"Donald!" Natalie barked.

Before he hung up, his silence told her someone was downstairs. Someone
blonde, young, and probably obsessed with him. Someone he had stashed in the
hotel, or had followed him, certain she could lure him away.

"I've got an emergency. I'm going downstairs. I'll be back in fifteen minutes.
I promise!" He dressed in a hurry.

Natalie let the door settle in its jamb before she dressed and followed him. The
elevator opened on the lobby and Natalie saw the young and blonde Kami of
Donald's *Restless Love* fame, recent breast enhancement recipient, and now the
object of Donald's attention. He handed Kami some money, kissed her long and
hard, then hurried her out to a taxi.

Natalie fled back to the room, out of her clothes, her heart turning black as
she waited to do the acting role of her life.

Harris sat alone at the bar waiting for George. Their bi-monthly drink meetings
were the only times Harris got away from his lab and out socially anymore. An
attractive brunette sat across from him, her fingers caressing her glass in a suggestive
gesture. Her eyes told him how hungry she was. She uncrossed her legs, leaving
them apart long enough before recrossing them for him to see that she was without
panties. He envisioned cankers, sores oozing in engorged labial tissue, a stench
of purulence, pus the colors of pale butter and pea soup, and dark scaly scabbing
there. He closed his eyes, feeling faint, until Bernstein's voice burrowed into his
reverie.

"Hey, Harris, you falling asleep on me?"

"George, how's it going?" Harris stood and shook his friend's hand.

"Well, I can't complain. I have lots of business and the most gorgeous wife
plastic surgery can manufacture. You?"

"Work, work, work. Not much of a life, huh?"

"As long as there are women and sex, there will be work."

Harris cut through the small talk. "How did you come to send Natalie Bright
to me?"

George chuckled. "Same old thing. Patient doesn't want to live in the real
world, but I couldn't do any more of my magic on her. It's always time to send
to Harris Stone when I run out of fairy dust." He saw Harris grow serious. "How'd
it go?"

"Took out the defect. She's still denying her husband's part in the recurrence
of the virus. It is a possibility, and of course the rumor mill on that guy has
it . . ."

"No shit, the guy's trash. Hell, love is blind, ain't it?"

Harris stared into his empty glass. "I'd rather believe it comes when you truly open your eyes and see."

"Dream on, Harris. Dream on."

It seemed to take forever to get back in the mood. Natalie burned with anger, ached with hurt. Donald was distracted, but determined, feral.

He plunged into her. She felt a sharp pain, as if something had pinched her inside. The pain stopped and there was only Donald, ramming into her, deeply. She thought about faking her orgasm, the imagined shriek in her head was echoed aloud in the room,

Donald was up on his knees between her legs, his penis deep inside her, his face contorted, the cries coming from his mouth. He appeared to be struggling to pull away, scrambling like a spinning tire in mud. He arched his back and howled, then fell back on to the bed, released.

She looked over at him, hating him. His hands flapped uselessly over his groin like two flesh butterflies, his mouth working wordlessly. There, where his erection had been was a gnawed stump of gristle, blood everywhere. Natalie turned away and vomited.

His beeper howled into the silence as Harris wended his way up the hillside, into the driveway of his home. He picked up his car phone. The service said it was Ms. Bright, hysterical. She was at his clinic waiting for him.

He pulled into the clinic parking lot with the squeal of tires. He was barely out of his car when she leaped at him. Weeping.

"There's something wrong. Inside." Her fingers combed the front of his sport coat. Her face was streaked with tears.

"Let's go inside." He hurried her to the door.

Once they were in his office, he sat her down. She was shaking. She seemed so small, fragile. He wanted to hold her.

"Tell me what happened. Are you hurt?"

"Oh, God. No. There's something wrong. Terribly wrong. Inside." Every breath was another sob.

"I need to know what happened." He tried to appear calm. His heart thrummed at the back of his throat.

"There was . . . so much blood!" Natalie caught herself. "We were making love. All of a sudden, Donald started to scream. He fell away from me. I could see it. Blood everywhere. And it was gone. Like it was eaten away. Inside of me." And she wept again.

"We'd better take a look. Come. Follow me." He took her hand and led her to an examination room.

Natalie whimpered behind him. "Please. Take care of me."

Harris's heart was pounding. He hated what he'd done to her, too late. As she sat down on the table, he removed his coat and rolled up his sleeves.

"I'm going to put you out. Take everything off and pull one of these over you." He handed her a paper blanket. "You're going to be perfectly fine. I promise you."

After the injection, Natalie's whimper faded into a low moan, then she was quiet.

Her legs fell apart as he set her feet in the stirrups. There was dried blood on her thighs. He stared at her.

"Precious. You'll never know what you have given me. I hope you can forgive me for this. I meant only to protect you."

He worked the metal clamp into her, light finding her cervix. The creature pushed its head and bloated body partway into the canal. Harris looked into its eyes. It waited. Watched.

He blinked. In that instant, he felt the hot sting and force of a blow to his eye. He reached for the creature. Its hooked tail ripped at his hands, his face. He fell against the wall, then to the floor, the thing chewing, blood blinding him. He called out.

"Natalie! Please. Natalie!" He tasted blood.

He tried to sit up, get a hold of the thing, but he couldn't. It slipped away, thrashed about, crawling over to his other eye. Gnawing, rending, working its way in. Deeper. Burrowing. Home.

SUSAN

Harlan Ellison

Harlan Ellison, who resides in Los Angeles, is one of the most lauded fantasists of contemporary America and a consummate artist of the short story form. He has published nearly sixty books of fiction and essays (including the influential media critiques *The Glass Teat* and *The Other Glass Teat*), more than thirteen hundred stories, and is the editor of the landmark *Dangerous Visions* anthology. He has won the World Fantasy Award, the British Fantasy Award, the Mystery Writers of America Edgar Award, the P.E.N. award for journalism, and more Hugo and Nebula Awards than any other writer. His short fiction has been included in *Best American Short Stories*, as well as in our *Sixth Annual Collection*.

Because Ellison is best known for iconoclastic fiction so sharp it draws blood, the following story may come as a surprise to some readers. It is a gentle, subtle magical tale that speaks straight from the heart. "Susan" is reprinted from the December issue of *Fantasy & Science Fiction*, and is dedicated to Ellison's wife Susan. (Ellison's long novella "Mefisto in Onyx," from the October issue of *OMNI* magazine, is also recommended as one of the best of the year.)

—T.W.

As she had done every night since they had met, she went in bare feet and a cantaloupe-meat-colored nightshift to the shore of the sea of mist, the verge of the ocean of smothering vapor, the edge of the bewildering haze he called the Brim of Obscurity.

Though they spent all of their daytime together, at night he chose to sleep alone in a lumpy, Volkswagen-shaped bed at the southernmost boundary of the absolutely lovely forest in which their home had been constructed. There at the border between the verdant woods and the Brim of Obscurity that stretched on forever, a sea of fog that roiled and swirled itself into small, murmuring vortexes from which depths one could occasionally hear something like a human voice pleading for absolution (or at least a backscratcher to relieve this awful itch!), he had made his bed and there, with the night-light from his old nursery, and his old vacuum-tube radio that played nothing but big band dance music from the 1920s, and a few favorite books, and a little fresh fruit he had picked on his way from the house to his resting-place, he slept peacefully every night. Except for the nightmares, of course.

And as she had done every night for the eight years since they had met, she went barefooted and charmed, down to the edge of the sea of fog to kiss him goodnight. That was their rite.

Before he had even proposed marriage, he explained to her the nature of the problem. Well, the curse, really. Not so much a *problem*; because a problem was easy to reconcile; just trim a little nub off here; just smooth that plane over there; just let this bit dangle here and it will all meet in the center; no, it wasn't barely remotely something that could be called a "problem." It was a curse, and he was open about it from the first.

"My nightmares come to life," he had said.

Which remark thereupon initiated quite a long and detailed conversation between them. It went through all the usual stages of good-natured chiding, disbelief, ridicule, short-lived anger at the possibility he was making fun of her, toying with her, on into another kind of disbelief, argument with recourse to logic and Occam's Razor, grudging acceptance, a brief lapse into incredulity, a return to the barest belief, and finally, with trust, utter acceptance that he was telling her nothing less than the truth. Remarkably (to say the least) his nightmares assumed corporeal shape and stalked the night as he slept, dreaming them up. It wouldn't have been so bad except:

"My nightmares killed and ate my first four wives," he had said. He'd saved that part for the last.

But she married him, nonetheless. And they were extremely happy. It was a terrific liaison for both of them. But just to be on the safe side, because he loved her very much, he took to sleeping in the lumpy Volkswagen bed at the edge of the forest.

And every morning—because he was compelled to rise when the sunlight struck his face, out there in the open—he would trek back to their fine home in the middle of the forest, and he would make her morning tea, and heat and butter a muffin, or possibly pour her a bowl of banana nut crunch cereal (or sometimes a nice bowl of oatmeal with cinnamon or brown sugar sprinkled across the surface), and carry it in to her as she sat up in bed reading or watching the Home Shopping Channel. And for eight years she had been absolutely safe from the nightmares that ripped and rent and savaged everything in sight.

He slept at the Brim of Obscurity, and he was a danger to no one but himself. And whatever means he used to protect *himself* from those darktime sojourners, well, it was an armory kept most secret.

That was how they lived, for eight years. And every night she would go barefoot, in her shift, and she would follow the twenty-seven plugged-together extension cords—each one thirty feet long—that led from the house to his night-light; and she would come to him and kiss him goodnight. And they would tell each other how happy they were together, how much every moment together meant to them, and they would kiss goodnight once more, and she would go back to the house. He would lie reading for a time, then go to sleep. And in the night, there at the shore of fog, at the edge of the awful sea of mist, the nightmares would come and scream and tear at themselves. But they never got anywhere near Susan, who was safely in her home.

So as she had done every night since they had met, she followed the extension cords down through the sweet-smelling, wind-cooled hedges and among the whispering, mighty trees to his bed. The light was on; an apple ready to be nibbled sat atop a stack of books awaiting his attention; the intaglio of a tesseract (or possibly a dove on the wing) lay in the center of a perfectly circular depression in his pillow where he had rested his head. But the bed was empty.

She went looking for him, and after a time she found him sitting on the shore of fog, looking out over the Brim of Obscurity. But she heard him crying long before she saw him. The sound of his deep, heartfelt sobbing led her to him.

And she knelt beside him, and he put his arms around her, and she said, "I see now that I've made you unhappy. I don't know how, but I can see that I've come into your life and made it unpleasant. I'm sorry, I'm truly sorry."

But he shook his head, and continued to shake it, to say no . . . no, that isn't it . . . you don't understand.

"I'm so sorry . . ." she kept saying, because she didn't understand what it meant, his shaking his head like that.

Until, finally, he was able to stop crying long enough to say, "No, that isn't it. You don't understand."

"Then what *are* you crying about?"

He wasn't able to tell her for a while, because just trying to get the words out started him up all over again. But after a while, still holding her, there at the Brim of Obscurity (which, in an earlier time, had been known as the Rim of Oblivion), he said softly, "I'm crying for the loss of all the years I spent without you, the years before I met you, all the lost years of my life; and I'm crying that there are less years in front of me than all those lost years behind me."

And out in the roiling ocean of misty darkness, they could both hear the sound of roving, demented nightmares whose voices were now, they understood, less filled with rage than with despair.

FREUD AT THIRTY PACES

Sara Paretsky

Sara Paretsky is the acclaimed bestselling author of the V.I. Warshawski mysteries. Her work is informed by a keen ear for dialogue and a sly sense of irony, yet retains a strong humanity. Vic, as only her friends may call her, works Chicago, where Paretsky lives.

"Freud at Thirty Paces" is a hilarious account of two men at war with each other whose weapons are theory, Freud, and their own enlarged egos. The story comes from the pages of *1st Culprit: A Crime Writers' Association Annual*, edited by Liza Cody and Michael Z. Lewin.

—T. W.

I

Dr. Ulrich von Hutten saw patients in the back drawing-room of his Fifth Avenue house. Minor reconstruction of the ground floor had created a private hallway through which patients bypassed the front drawing-room and the stairway to the upper floors. In the back, a door led from the consulting room to a sidewalk connecting the house to 74th Street. A hedge separated this walk from the minuscule garden where Mrs. von Hutten raised begonias and herbs.

This engineering separated the Von Hutten family from his patients. Indeed, some were never sure if the doctor was married. Others suspected the presence of a child (children?) from the faint sounds of piano practice seeping into the private hallway, or the rising smell of *sauce madère* on afternoons when the doctor was entertaining for dinner.

If they were punctual, patients never met one another, either—they left through a different door than the one they entered by. Von Hutten saw no need for a waiting room. He provided a small armchair outside the consulting room where the over-anxious could sit, waiting for the soft yellow light that showed the doctor was ready.

The meter began running precisely at the start of one analytical session and stopped exactly forty-five minutes later. Dr. von Hutten pressed a floor button which simultaneously unlocked the entrance, turned on the yellow light, and started the meter. The unpunctual patient, racing from a hairdresser at 60th and Madison, or a meeting in Wall Street, would find the doctor sitting expressionlessly

in a leather armchair behind the shabby couch inherited from the great Dr. L——
in Berlin.

The flustered patient dropped parcels, coat, briefcase on a side table and scrambled on to the couch. Dr. von Hutten remained ostentatiously silent. The only
noise was the faint humming of the meter against the far wall. After forty-five
minutes, the meter shut off, the street door automatically unlocked, and Dr. von
Hutten uttered his first words of the session: "Our time is up. I will see you
tomorrow at two." Or Friday at nine-thirty, or whenever.

Dr. von Hutten belonged to that strict class of analysts who believe they must
say as little as possible to the patient. The patient should know nothing about the
doctor—all transference should operate in one direction only. The doctor felt
strongly about this. In addition to articles for the professional journals, he had
written several impassioned columns for the *New York Times,* deploring the tendency of modern analysts to talk, to tell their patients of their love for Mozart,
their hatred of begonias.

Dr. von Hutten would not attack a fellow analyst in the popular press. Still,
most of the New York psychoanalytic world knew that his remarks were not
general. The specific object of his rage had an office across Central Park from
him.

At 62nd and Central Park West, Dr. Jacob Pfefferkorn saw patients in an untidy
room whose curtained windows overlooked the park. A small room across the
hall had been turned into a waiting area, where novels and magazines were
jumbled in a stack on a side table.

The Pfefferkorn family correctly never went into the waiting room nor spoke
to any patients. Still, the latter would often see Mrs. Pfefferkorn sweep by with
one or more of her noisy children *en route* to the ballet lessons, riding lessons,
music lessons, or private school whose fees were covered by the massive bills
generated by the meter ticking away on the analyst's wall.

In addition to these signs of life, the patients learned some things about Dr.
Pfefferkorn himself. For example, he loved Mozart and hated begonias. Whether
this knowledge helped or hindered their therapies, no one could judge—except,
perhaps Dr. von Hutten. Other analysts wondered whether Pfefferkorn's well-
known prejudices had inspired Mrs. von Hutten to raise begonias at the Fifth
Avenue house.

Besides their disagreement over silence in the consulting room, the doctors
had a second rivalry. Both enjoyed doing literary psychoanalysis—analyzing the
personalities of writers based on their work. Dr. Freud set the example. His
brilliant deduction that Moses was an Egyptian, rather than a Hebrew, was based
chiefly on biblical texts, with little corroborative historical evidence.

His disciples were inspired to undertake similar researches. Some studied figures
like Virginia Woolf or Henry James, who left a large body of letters explaining
their work. Others preferred to look at writers like Augustine, who left no external
evidence other than his writings. With very little historical research, these literary
analysts were able to perform astounding analytical *tours de force,* uncovering
Oedipal relations, impotence, and other previously unknown traits of the fifth-
century saint.

Dr. Pfefferkorn had previously analyzed Thomas à Kempis, Cardinal Newman
and Emily Dickinson. Von Hutten's greatest prior efforts were devoted to the

anonymous author of *The Cloud of Unknowing*. The two pointedly ignored each other's researches. Unfortunately, in 1980 both settled on the same writer as the passionate object of their research.

Saint Juliet of Cardiff (?1149–1203) had written numerous mystical works in a crabbed combination of Latin and Welsh. Little enough is known of the saint's life. She was canonized in 1560, in the great rash of pork-barrel canonizations following the Council of Trent, for miracles performed in connection with women hemorrhaging after childbirth.

Juliet's work in modem translation runs to some three volumes of meditations, ecstasies and prayers. From this effusion, the doctors were able to glean much about her life.

Dr. Pfefferkorn recognized from her writings that Juliet had been a mistress of Henry II, taking the veil only after Eleanor of Aquitaine intervened in one of her rare wifely moods. Juliet's mother had died in the saint's infancy. Her doting father, a man of substance, had her educated in a way open to few twelfth-century men and almost no women. He introduced her to court life. Dr. Pfefferkorn speculated on an incestuous love between father and daughter, but felt the texts were ambiguous there. Juliet joined the Convent of St. Anne of Cardiff late in life. Her ecstasies were primarily eulogies of her liaison with Henry, disguised in theological language.

To Dr. von Hutten, Juliet's work proved incontrovertibly that she had died a virgin. Dedicated to the Convent of Our Lady of the Sacred Heart of Cardiff at birth, she came from an impoverished family which could not provide a dowry. Juliet therefore performed manual labor for the convent, learning writing from cleaning the heavy bible chained to the altar in the convent chapel. Since she spoke no Latin, her own writing combined her native Welsh with what Latin she picked up from her secretive reading. Her ecstatic outpourings came from her sublimated, unrecognized sexuality. The fact that Welsh women believed she could stop post-partem bleeding was a folk testimony to her virginal state.

The bi-monthly *Psychoanalytical Review of Literature* published Dr. Pfefferkom and Dr. von Hutten's articles side by side in their winter issue, and battle was fairly joined.

A mutual friend had warned Dr. von Hutten that Dr. Pfefferkom had picked St. Juliet as the subject of his research, but Dr. von Hutten was staggered at the level of Pfefferkom's stupidity. How could the man not recognize such a clear case of frigidity? How could he frivolously write of liaisons between a king and a commoner of demonstrably menial state?

Von Hutten fumed. With difficulty he listened to fears of impotence, fears of rejection, fears of frigidity from his own patients. He counted the minutes until the meter shut off for the day and he could settle down to attack Dr. Pfefferkorn as he deserved. A man who told his patients he hated begonias was capable of anything, but this time he had *gone too far*. His letter to the editor covered the major defects in both Pfefferkorn's research and his medical practice.

Across the park on 62nd Street, Dr. Pfefferkorn was equally enraged. Von Hutten's rigid attitudes—stemming doubtless from too early toilet-training and his morbid fears of castration—had led him into an utterly imbecilic account of Juliet's life. No man who had worked through his own neuroses could doubt that this was a woman whose physical life had been superbly fulfilled.

At the end of the workday, Pfefferkom turned off the meter, told his wife to bring him sauerbraten and potatoes in his study, and settled down to a scathing attack on Von Hutten. His letter encompassed the doctor's inadequate analysis, his inability to separate his own fantasies from what he read, and then a line-by-line textual refutation of Von Hutten's major points.

Both letters appeared in the February issue of the *Psychoanalytical Review of Literature*. If Von Hutten was pleased at the accusations of impotence and projection, he gave no sign of it to his wife, who had also read the criticism.

As for Pfefferkom, the charge that his analytical methods were as slovenly as his appearance provoked him to widen the circle of argument. He called on Walter Lederhosen, Professor of Middle English History at Columbia, and on Mark Antwerp at New York University.

As it turned out, neither was familiar with St. Juliet. Neither could read the medieval Welsh-Latin in which she wrote. They both composed long treatises on twelfth-century England. Antwerp sidestepped the Juliet virginity issue. However, he proved that Henry was in Cardiff several times during what could be thought of as the relevant period. He also had a lot to say on Henry's love life and the strained relations between him and Eleanor.

Lederhosen concentrated on twelfth-century politics, especially Henry II's infrequent appearances in his English possessions, which did not please Pfefferkom at all—how could he have inflamed the passions of the saint if he wasn't around to meet her? So he discarded the Columbia professor's remarks and produced a small pamphlet which contained the original articles, the rebutting letters, and Professor Antwerp's lengthy essay.

Pfefferkorn concluded the pamphlet with a summary in which he tied Antwerp's arguments back to his own. The whole thing was published in a little booklet entitled *The Mirror of the Eye*, and distributed at the summer meetings of the International Convention of Psychoanalysts. In the introduction, Pfefferkorn explained how in their writings psychoanalysts mirrored the distortions with which their own eyes presented the world to them. He then detailed his own diagnosis of Von Hutten's various psychosexual maladies and how Von Hutten had projected these on to the writings of St. Juliet of Cardiff.

Von Hutten was speechless when he saw the pamphlet. He left the meeting a day early and flew back to Manhattan, where he consulted an old colleague now teaching history at Yale. Like Lederhosen and Antwerp, Rudolph Narr had not read Juliet's works. However, he discoursed most learnedly for forty pages on analytical techniques applied to history, with a major subsection on frigidity and sublimation in the Middle Ages.

The essay delighted Von Hutten. He published it in a booklet called *The Mirror of the Hand*, along with his original essay from the *Psychoanalytical Review of Literature*. In a pithy introduction, he exposed Pfefferkorn's fraudulent analytical methods. Because Pfefferkorn's own internal neurotic problems were unresolved, he was unable to withdraw himself from center stage in interacting with his patients. His needy ego took over from his patients: he projected his own desires and uncertainties on to what went on in the consulting room. Pfefferkorn's literary researches mirrored his intrusion into the patient's landscape—his hand, so to speak, covered the canvas.

The publication of *The Mirror of the Hand* coincided with the December meetings of the New York Psychoanalytical Association. While Pfefferkorn was furious—and made no secret of it—the other analysts were delighted. What a welcome change from the usual round of "Undifferentiated Narcissism in Post-Adolescence Transference Neuroses" and other learned talks.

Partisans for both men sprang up among the New York analysts. Pfefferkorn's most vocal supporter was Everard Dirigible. Carlos McGillicutty soon led the Von Hutten group.

Dirigible scored a great coup early in the battle: He found a scholar at the University of Chicago who actually could read St. Juliet's work in the original. Bernard Maledict leapt happily into the fray. Unacquainted with both the techniques and the language of psychoanalysis, he nonetheless had a great deal to say about Juliet's sexuality.

Maledict rejected Von Hutten's work: Juliet's writings could not possibly support a charge of frigidity. He was less clear in discussing an affair with Henry II—or any affairs with anyone. Instead, he described sexuality in the Middle Ages, explaining that the reasons for going into conventual life were often economic and had nothing to do with sexuality at all. In addition, virginity was not valued as highly in that era as it is today and while celibacy was expected in convents, no one was too shocked at lapses.

After Maledict's work appeared simultaneously in the *Psychoanalytical Review of Literature* and the *Journal of Medieval History*, Von Hutten and McGillicutty were almost foaming with rage. McGillicutty saw his duty clear: He unearthed a second St. Juliet scholar at University College, Oxford. Robert Pferdlieber had devoted his life to translating and analyzing *The Veil Before the Temple,* Juliet's major opus. He welcomed a chance to present his views to a wider audience. Without commenting precisely on the original Pfefferkorn-Von Hutten debate, he roundly condemned all of Maledict's research. Von Hutten saw to it that his article—with an appropriate commentary—appeared in all the important European psychoanalytic publications, as well as those in America.

By now Pfefferkorn's energies were so consumed with this debate that he refused all new patients: he needed every hour he could grab to fight Von Hutten. He spent long evenings in the Freud archives, seeking evidence from the Master that his analytical techniques were correct.

Mrs. Pfefferkorn became concerned: the eldest Pfefferkorn offspring was in his first year of Harvard Medical School; the youngest had embarked on some costly orthodonture; and in between lay three others with expensive needs. What did Pfefferkorn propose—that Ermine give up her horse? that Jodhpur sell his Ferrari? For those were the sacrifices she foresaw if the doctor's practice shrank. The rivalry with Von Hutten she dismissed with a contemptuous wave of the hand—could he not be adult enough to take a little criticism in his stride?

Across the park, Von Hutten had better self-control, at least on the surface. He continued his usual sixty analytical sessions a week. But his attention in the examining room began to wander. When you are not speaking yourself, it is hard to feel engaged in a dialogue: He found himself listening to Mrs. J——'s sexual fantasies when he thought he was hearing about Mr. P——'s hatred of his mother.

For years Von Hutten had prided himself on his perfect control and involvement in the consulting room. He could only blame Pfefferkorn for his failure to maintain his own rigid standards. His fury with Pfefferkorn turned into a hatred which absorbed most of his waking moments and quite a few of his sleeping ones as well. He was analyst enough to know that a dream of his father lunging at him with a baseball bat was a long-forgotten memory stirred to life by Pfefferkorn's abuse, but the knowledge did not ease his rage.

By lunch Von Hutten realized that the fantasy of murdering Pfefferkorn which had absorbed all his morning sessions was only a fantasy and would not solve his problem. But his rage at the other analyst increased: Pfefferkorn had caused him to contemplate his murder all morning, instead of the more important needs of patients. Usually a self-contained man who asked no one for help, Von Hutten poured his anguish out to his wife.

Mrs. von Hutten raised perfectly manicured eyebrows as she served him a piece of poached salmon and some green salad. "I don't think his murder would help matters, Ulrich," she pronounced majestically. "You would still feel that he had defeated you."

"I know it!" Von Hutten almost screamed, pounding the table with his fist. "And root out all those damned begonias after lunch. I never want to see another one of them."

Mrs. von Hutten ignored this with the same authority that she had ignored all her husband's greater and lesser pleas over the years. After lunch, however, she turned her own considerable intellect to the Von Hutten-Pfefferkorn debate. She pulled his Pfefferkorn files from the file cabinets in his study. By now, correspondence and articles filled a drawer and a half.

At five o'clock, she called down to the maid on the house phone that she would not be in for dinner: would Birgitta please inform the doctor. She took the remaining files to her dressing-room, locked the door, and continued reading until close to the following dawn.

Mrs. von Hutten was one of those rigidly self-controlled people who set mental clocks for themselves and get up accordingly. She lay down for six hours' sleep and rose again at ten. Despite a heavy downpour, she walked across the park to 62nd Street, her pace brisk but not hurried. By noon she was back at the Fifth Avenue house, calmly serving her husband a small slice of chicken breast and some steamed vegetables.

II

When the meter shut off for the day, Dr. von Hutten dictated a few case notes. He stood frowning at the back window, staring at the drenched begonias with unseeing eyes for long minutes, until a firm knock roused him. Doubtless some patient had forgotten an umbrella, although he saw nothing on the side table. He went slowly to the door.

"You!" he hissed.

Dr. Pfefferkorn shook his umbrella out on the mat and shed his bulky trench coat. "Yes, Von Hutten. My wife persuaded me I ought to see you in person. Get this matter cleared up. We've become the laughing-stock of the New York analytical profession."

"You may have," Von Hutten said coldly. "Your ideas are ridiculous and insupportable. I, however, notice no one laughing at me."

"That, my dear Von Hutten, is because you are so self-centered that you notice nothing anyone else says." Seeing that his host made no motion to invite him in, Pfefferkorn pushed past him and sat in an armchair facing the analyst's chair. "So this is where it all takes place. Sterile atmosphere suitable for the sterile, outmoded ideas you profess."

Von Hutten nearly ground his teeth. "I have no need to see your consulting room—I am sure it is as sloppy as your thinking. As sloppy as your alleged research into Juliet of Cardiff."

Pfefferkorn frowned. Mrs. Pfefferkorn had persuaded him to make this trek, persuaded him against his better judgment, and now see what came of it: nothing but insults.

"Look, Von Hutten. Everyone knows your ideas on Juliet of Cardiff are as out of date as your so-called analytical methods. But let's agree to disagree. We can't keep escalating this scholarly battle. It takes too much time from my—our—practices."

Von Hutten almost choked. "That you dare call yourself an analyst is an insult to the memory of Freud. Agree to disagree! With you! I will not so demean the analytical profession."

"Demean!" roared Pfefferkorn, springing to his feet. "You should be decertified by the New York State Medical Society. Decertified? What am I saying! You should be certified as a lunatic and locked up where you can no longer hurt the innocent and vulnerable."

Von Hutten jumped at him, grabbing his shoulders. "You will eat those words, you miserable scum."

Dr. Pfefferkorn, equally enraged and seventy-five pounds heavier, wrenched Von Hutten's hands away and shoved him to the floor. "You're welcome to try to make me do it, *Doctor* von Hutten. When and where you please, with weapons of your choosing. You'll live to regret this moment."

He picked up his dripping trench coat and strode from the room, slamming the door behind him.

III

The morning of the duel was clear and sunny. At five-thirty, Dr. von Hutten slid out of the Fifth Avenue house. A note to his wife lay on his study table, explaining everything in case he did not return home. He did not really expect to lose: he had practiced all weekend and felt totally confident.

His second, McGillicutty, was waiting for him at the 72nd Street entrance to Central Park, carrying the weapons.

"Feeling fit, Doctor?" McGillicutty asked respectfully.

"Never better. We'll make short work of this charlatan."

"Good. I've ordered breakfast at the Pierre for seven-thirty: We'll have a little champagne to celebrate."

When they got to the trees behind the zoo, they found Pfefferkorn and Dirigible already waiting. Pfefferkorn was eating a ham sandwich and drinking from a thermos of coffee, arguing points with his mouth full. Disgusting, Von Hutten thought. It really was time to end the man's career.

The weapons were so heavy that the seconds violated the code of honor by each bringing the opponent's to the site. As soon as Dirigible saw McGillicutty, he excused himself to the wildly gesticulating Pfefferkorn and beckoned the other second to join him a little way away.

"You have brought all twenty-four volumes of the Standard Edition?"

McGillicutty nodded. He was as aware as Dirigible of the solemnity of the moment. They solemnly laid out two sets of the *Complete Works of Sigmund Freud* on the grass in front of them and counted each volume, fanning the pages to see if any were missing. This task completed, they returned again to the principals and called them together.

"Gentlemen—Doctors," Dirigible cleared his throat nervously. "The code of honor demands that we try one last time to reconcile you without a mortal blow being struck. Will you consider—for the sake of your wives, your patients, the honor of the entire psychoanalytical profession—will you bury your differences?"

Von Hutten said coldly, "I came to see that this charlatan, this impostor, is unfrocked as he deserves."

Pfefferkorn snorted, "I would as soon touch an embalmed halibut as shake this man's hand. Sooner—the halibut would have more life to it."

McGillicutty, too, tried a plea, with equally poor results. At last he said, "Gentlemen: if it must be, let us begin. You understand the rules. Each of you may fire one shot. If the other does not fall, you may fire again."

Dirigible and McGillicutty stood back to back. Each stepped forward fifteen paces. Von Hutten and Pfefferkorn came to stand beside their seconds, who then moved to the center of the field.

Dr. Dirigible held up a white handkerchief. As it fluttered to the ground, Dr. Pfefferkorn bellowed, "You have a castration complex, Von Hutten, which interferes with your establishing any meaningful counter-transference!"

Von Hutten flinched but did not fall. "You suffer from undifferentiated narcissism which leads to regression complexes and inability to distinguish between patients and your external speaking object."

Without waiting for a nod from the seconds, Pfefferkorn shouted furiously, "You are impotent both physically and psychologically. Your criticisms stem from your own inadequacies. They would be laughable if they didn't harm so many patients!"

A policeman patrolling the park strolled over, attracted by the shouting. He stood puzzled, not knowing whether to interfere.

"What's going on?" he finally asked the seconds.

"A duel," McGillicutty said briefly. "Freud at thirty paces."

The policeman frowned uncertainly, not sure whether he was being laughed at. "Who are these guys, anyway?"

"Psychoanalysts," Dirigible replied, keeping his eyes on the action on the field. "They're trying to resolve some underlying theoretical differences."

"Oh, analysts," the policeman nodded. "You gotta expect strange behavior from them." He nodded again to himself several times to confirm this diagnosis and wandered off towards the reservoir to see if anyone had fallen in during the night.

Meanwhile, on the field of battle, argument was becoming more personal and less analytical. Dirigible and McGillicutty both tried to interrupt.

"Gentlemen, please. You're straying far from Freud." Each went to reason with his own principal, but neither was willing to listen. Pfefferkorn, in fact, knocked Dirigible to the ground in his fury at being interrupted.

"And your mother! Oedipal fantasies about her? No wonder you're such a cold bastard. Imagine being in bed with that woman—enough to traumatize any child."

"And you!" screamed Von Hutten. "You never broke the tie with Mummy. You keep trying to recreate that experience with your patients—be Mummy for me—support me—love me!"

At this taunting, Pfefferkorn picked up *The Interpretation of Dreams* from the stack next to him and charged across the open space to Von Hutten. He flung the volume at his opponent. The book caught Von Hutten underneath the left eye. Blood poured down his face on to his immaculate shirt front. He ignored it. Snatching *The Psychopathology of Everyday Life* from the ground, he smashed it into Pfefferkorn's nose.

Pfefferkorn, too, began to bleed. *Jokes and their Relation to the Unconscious* lay close at hand, it landed on his opponent's left shoulder. Von Hutten was more successful with *Moses and Monotheism*—the book glanced off Pferrerkorn's ear.

In vain McGillicutty and Dirigible tried to separate the men. This failing, they quickly snatched all copies of Freud's works out of the way. The analysts promptly went for each other's throats.

"Blackguard! Impostor!" Von Hutten panted, trying to bite Pfefferkorn's ear.

"Charlatan! Imbecile!" hissed Pfefferkorn, sticking his knee in Von Hutten's stomach.

Pfefferkorn was by far the larger man, but Von Hutten's rage gave him superhuman strength. Neither could get close enough to the other to make a telling blow.

McGillicutty and Dirigible wrung their hands, anguished. How could they stop these giants of the New York Psychoanalytical Association from making fools of themselves? Worse, what if one of them really got in a solid blow and injured the other seriously? What if Pfefferkorn, already overheated and sweating, had a heart attack?

They debated nervously about whether to try to find the policeman again and get him to break up the fight. But what if he arrested the doctors? What harm would that publicity do the analytical world? As they talked agitatedly, Mrs. von Hutten swept into the park. She quickly located her husband and walked up to the seconds, her golden hair shining magnificently in the morning sunlight.

"Why have you allowed this farce to continue so long?"

"Mrs. von Hutten!" McGillicutty gasped. "I—this is no sight for you. What are you doing here?"

"My husband left a note for me in his study. When he failed to show up for breakfast I naturally looked for him there and found his message. A duel in Central Park! I can't believe four adult men—so-called adults—could carry on in such a fashion."

She moved to the heaving contestants, "Ulrich! Dr. Pfefferkorn! Please stop this at once. You are making a ridiculous spectacle."

Her voice was low-pitched but penetrating. The two analysts pulled apart at once. Dr. von Hutten tried to straighten his tie.

"Vera! What are you doing here?"

"More to the point, Ulrich, what are you doing here? What is the purpose of this duel with Dr. Pfefferkorn? When Mrs. Pfefferkorn and I spoke three weeks ago, it was in the hope that you two would resolve your problems, not that you would carry on like beasts in a side-show."

"This—this man calls himself an analyst," Von Hutten hissed through clenched teeth. "But he makes a mockery of the teachings of Freud. There is no talking to him."

Dr. Pfefferkorn had moved to one side to clean off the blood caked around his nose and mouth. At that, he turned back. "Your husband is a menace to the population of New York with his undifferentiated castration complex and fears of impotency."

Mrs. von Hutten raised a gloved hand. "Please do not repeat your arguments: I have read the Juliet of Cardiff file and I am well aware of the names you have been calling each other for the past two years. I should point out—and Mrs. Pfefferkorn is in total agreement with me—that you are jeopardizing your practices by your obsession with this Juliet of Cardiff. Put her aside. Do no more literary criticism. For neither of you is skilled at it."

Both men gasped. Dr. Pfefferkorn saw his wife walking towards them through the park. He waited for her to come up, then exclaimed, "Not understand literary criticism! Cordelia—don't tell me you have been discussing this serious intellectual matter with Mrs. von Hutten here. Really, you should have better things to do with your time."

"I do," Mrs. Pfefferkorn said drily. "It was most annoying to have to spend that time looking at Juliet of Cardiff. But Vera and I have examined both your files on the subject. We have also looked at the saint's writings. And we discovered that neither of you—nor your learned colleagues in Chicago and Oxford—know what you're talking about. Please go back to analysis—about which you both know something, even if it is something different—and leave St. Juliet to the experts."

Von Hutten found his voice first. "You don't know what you're talking about. My analysis conclusively proves—"

"Yes, dear," Mrs. von Hutten cut him off indulgently. "You had some preconceptions, and you found answers to those in your analysis of *The Veil Before the Temple*. Dr. Pfefferkorn, you did the same thing."

"Yes, Jacob," Mrs. Pfefferkorn said. "Vera and I have discovered that St. Juliet never existed. The writings which are imputed to her are the composite literature of the Convent of the Blessed Virgin in Cardiff for a period of about a hundred years, beginning in 1203, long after Henry II died."

The duelists were momentarily silent. Then Dr. von Hutten said aloofly, "Are you certain?"

"Positive," his wife answered briskly. "There are significant textual indicators for this, not just stylistic ones. You may have noted that the latter sections of the books are written entirely in Latin, the earlier in Welsh-Latin. The last parts were written in peacetime by women who had the leisure to learn scholarly Latin—the first were composed during the great upheaval surrounding John and the barons. There are numerous other pointers, of course—we can go over them when we get home if you'd like."

"No, thank you," Von Hutten responded coldly. "I don't imagine I'll have the time."

He and Pfefferkorn glowered at their wives. "Improperly sublimated penis envy," Von Hutten muttered.

"Separation from fathers never fully established; no proper internal integration," Pfefferkorn added sullenly.

They looked at each other. Von Hutten said, "How truly Freud spoke: Women will never understand themselves, for they themselves are the problem." Ignoring his swollen left eye, bloody shirt and torn jacket, he flicked back his cuff to look at his watch. "Vera, will you please call my morning patients and reschedule their appointments? I'm going to breakfast at the Pierre. Coming, Pfefferkorn?"

The women watched their husbands stride from the park together, the seconds trailing behind them carrying Freud's works.

Mrs. Pfefferkorn relaxed. "An impressive performance, Vera. But what if—?"

"What if they ask for a point-by-point critique of St Juliet's writings to see how we know they were composed by a group? They won't: They're too embarrassed . . . speaking of breakfast, I haven't had any. Champagne at the Plaza?"

IF ANGELS ATE APPLES
Geoffrey A. Landis

Geoffrey Landis, winner of the Nebula Award for Best Science Fiction, is the author of a number of fine SF and fantasy stories. He formerly lived in Cambridge, Massachusetts where he was a member of the group who put together the collective *Future Boston* anthology about a Boston submerged by flood water and alien tourists. He now lives in Brook Park, Ohio.

His charming poem, "If Angels Ate Apples" comes from the June issue of *Asimov's Science Fiction*.

—T.W.

If angels ate apples, potatoes and pears
they'd grow to be chubby and cheerful as bears
nibbling knishes and other such things,
tickling your face with the tips of their wings

If seraphim shouted and whistled at girls,
drank drafts from thimbles, all friends with the world
drained the best ale and chased it with rye,
then fluttered in circles while trying to fly

Angels on tables! (Watch out for your glass!)
Slipping on puddles, right plop on their ass!
Laughing at music that only they hear,
then tweaking the barmaids a pinch on the rear.

Fuzzy fat angels, that's something to see,
as they dance to the jukebox at quarter to three,
and ace out the pinball, a marvelous feat,
the lights and bells flashing (though sometimes they cheat).

If angels made merry, would that be so odd?
Must they always be solemn, to stay friends with God?
It's a pity that Heaven is so far away
angels hardly ever come down and just play.

EXOGAMY
John Crowley

John Crowley is one of the finest writers of our time, an absolute master of the literary fantasy form, for which he has twice won the World Fantasy Award. He is the author of several unusual and highly recommended novels, including *Engine Summer*, *Little, Big*, and *Ægypt*, as well as two excellent collections of short fiction, *Novelty* and *Antiquities*. His most recent novel, *Love and Sleep*, has just been published. Crowley lives with his wife and daughters in the Berkshire Hills of western Massachusetts.

"Exogamy" is a luminous, thought-provoking little fable that was one of four "short short" stories commissioned for the anthology OMNI *Best Science Fiction Three*, edited by Ellen Datlow. It was also included in *Antiquities*, a beautiful small press collection of seven stories published by Incunabula (Seattle, Washington).

—T.W.

In desperation and black hope he had selected himself for the mission, and now he was to die for his impetuosity, drowned in an amber vinegar sea too thin to swim in. This didn't matter in any large sense; his comrades had seen him off, and would not see him return—the very essence of a hero. In a moment his death wouldn't matter even to himself. Meanwhile he kept flailing helplessly, ashamed of his willingness to struggle.

His head broke the surface into the white air. It had done so now three times; it would not do so again. But a small cloud just then covered him, and something was in the air above his head. Before he sank away out of reach for good, something took hold of him, a flying something, a machine or something with sharp pincers or takers-hold, what would he call them, *claws*.

He was lifted out of the waters or fluid or sea. Not his fault the coordinates were off, placing him in liquid and not on dry land instead, these purplish sands; only off by a matter of meters. Far enough to drown or nearly drown him though: he lay for a long time prostrate on the sand where he had been dropped, uncertain which.

He pondered then—when he could ponder again—just what had seized him, borne him up (just barely out of the heaving sea, and laboring mightily at that) and got him to shore. He hadn't yet raised his head to see if whatever it was had stayed with him, or had gone away; and now he thought maybe it would be best to just lie still and be presumed dead. But he looked up.

She squatted a ways up the beach, not watching him, seeming herself to be absorbed in recovering from effort; her wide bony breast heaved. The great wings now folded, like black plush. Talons (that was the word, he felt them again and began to shudder), the talons spread to support her in the soft sand. When she stepped, waddled, toward him, seeing he was alive, he crawled away across the sand, trying to get to his feet and unable, until he fell flat again and knew nothing.

Night came.

She (she, it was the breasts prominent on the breastplate muscle, the big delicate face and vast tangled never-dressed hair that made him suppose it) was upon him when he awoke. He had curled himself into a fetal ball, and she had been sheltering him from the nightwinds, pressing her long belly against him as she might (probably did) against an egg of her own. It was dangerously cold. She smelled like a mildewed sofa.

For three days they stayed together there on the horrid shingle. In the day she shaded him from the sun with her pinions and at night drew him close to her odorous person, her rough flesh. Sometimes she flew away heavily (her wings seeming unable to bear up for more than a few meters, and then the clumsy business of taking off again) and returned with some gobbet of scavenge to feed him. Once, a human leg that he rejected. She seemed unoffended, seemed not to mind if he ate or not; seemed when she stared at him hourlong with her onyx unhuman eyes to be waiting for his own demise. But then why coddle him so, if coddling was what this was?

He tried (dizzy with catastrophe maybe, or sunstroke) to explain himself to her, unable to suppose she couldn't hear. He had (he said) failed in his quest. He had set out from his sad homeland to find love, a bride, a prize, and bring it back. They had all seen him off, every one of them wishing in his heart that he too had the daring to follow the dream. Love. A woman: a bride of love: a mother of men. Where, in this emptiness?

She listened, cooing now and then (a strange liquid sound, he came to listen for it, it seemed like understanding; he hoped he would hear it last thing before he died, poisoned by her food and this sea of piss). On the third day, he seemed more likely to live. A kind of willingness broke inside him with the dawn. Maybe he could go on. And as though sensing this she ascended with flopping wingbeats into the sun, and sailed to a rocky promontory a kilometer off. There she waited for him.

Nothing but aridity, as far as his own sight reached. But he believed—it made him laugh aloud to find he believed it—that she knew what he hoped, and intended to help him.

But oh God what a dreadful crossing, what sufferings to endure. There was the loneliness of the desert, nearly killing him, and the worse loneliness of having such a companion as this to help him. It was she who sought out the path. It was he who found the waterhole. She sickened, and for the length of a moon he nursed her, he could not have lived now without her, none of these other vermin— mice, snakes—were worth talking to; he fed them to her, and ate what she left. She flew again. They were getting someplace. Then, one bright night of giddy certainty (Was he mad? What possessed him?) he took hold of her in the cave where they hid, and, cooing wordlessly as she did, he trod her like a cock.

Then at the summit of the worst sierra, down the last rubbled pass, there was green land. He could see a haze of evaporating water softening the air, maybe towers in the valley.

Down there (she said, somehow, by signs and gestures and his own words in her coos, she made it anyway clear) there is a realm over which a queen rules. No one has yet won her, though she has looked far for one who could.

He rubbed his hands together. His heart was full. Only the brave (he said) deserve the fair.

He left her there, at the frontier (he guessed) of her native wild. He strode down the pass, looking back now and then, ashamed a little of abandoning her but hoping she understood. Once when he looked back she was gone. Flown.

It was a nice country. Pleasant populace was easily won over by good manners and an honest heart. That's the castle, there, that white building under the feet of whose towers you see a strip of sunset sky. That one. Good luck.

Token resistance at the gates, but he gave better than he got. She would be found, of course, in the topmost chamber, surmounting these endless stairs, past these iron-bound henchmen. (Why always, always so hard? He thought of the boys back home, who had passed on all this.) He reached and broached the last door; he stepped out onto the topmost parapet. It was littered with bones, fetid with pale guano. A vast shabby nest of sticks and nameless stuff.

She alighted just then, in her gracious-clumsy way, and folded up.

Did you guess? she asked.

No, he had not; his heart was black with horror and understanding; he should have guessed, of course, but hadn't. He felt the talons of her attention close upon him, inescapable; he turned away with a cry and stared down the great height of the tower. Should he jump?

If you do, I will fall after you (she said) and catch you up, and bring you back.

He turned to her to say his heart could never be hers. She was, simply and absolutely, not his type.

You could go on, she said softly.

He looked away again, not down this time but out, toward the far lands beyond the fields and farms. He could go on.

What's over there? he asked. Beyond those yellow mountains? What makes that plume of smoke?

I've never gone there. Never that far. We could, she said.

Well hell, he said. For sure I can't go back. Not with—not now.

Come on, she said, and pulled herself to the battlements with grasping talons; she squatted there, lowering herself for him to mount. It could be worse, he thought, and tiptoed through the midden to her; but before he took his seat upon her, he thought with sudden awful grief: *She'll die without me.*

He meant the one he had for so long loved, since boyhood, she for whose sake he had first set out, whoever she was; his type, the key that fit this empty inward keyhole, the bride at the end of this quest, still waiting. And he about to head off in another direction entirely.

You want to drive? she said.

The farms and fields, the malls and highways, mountains and cities, no end in sight that way.

You drive, he said.

THE PRINCESS WHO KICKED BUTT

Will Shetterly

Minneapolis author Will Shetterly has written six fantasy novels for children and adults, including *Elsewhere, Nevernever*, and the forthcoming *Dogland*. He has also written short fiction, comic books and (with his wife, writer Emma Bull) has edited the anthology series *Liavek*. In addition, Shetterly is the publisher of Steeldragon Press, which issues limited edition books, comics, and music CDs.

"The Princess Who Kicked Butt" is a deliciously fractured fairy tale (reminiscent of the television cartoon series of that name), one of several entertaining stories published in the children's anthology *A Wizard's Dozen*, edited by Michael Stearns. Readers of all ages will enjoy this wry collection, as well as the following wicked tale about a wonderfully resourceful princess who lived, of course, Once Upon a Time. . . .

—T. W.

Once upon a time, not so very long ago, there was a land ruled with the very best intentions, if not the very best results, by the King Who Saw Both Sides of Every Question and the Queen Who Cared for Everyone. When their first child was born, the Fairy Who Was Good with Names arrived at the castle in a cloud of smoke and said, "Your daughter shall be known as the Princess Who Kicked Butt."

Before anyone could say another word, the fairy sneezed twice and disappeared. A page ran to open a window, and when the smoke had cleared, the king said, "What did the fairy say?"

The queen frowned. "She said our daughter shall be called, ah, the Princess Who Read Books. I think."

"Hmm," said the king. "I'd rather hoped for the Princess Who Slew Dragons. But reading books is a sign of wisdom, isn't it? It's a fine title."

"I think she'll be happy with it," said the Queen.

So the Princess Who Kicked Butt was surrounded with books from her earliest days. She seemed happy to spend her time reading, when she wasn't riding or dancing or swimming or running around the kingdom talking with everyone about what they were doing and why they were doing it and how they might do it better.

The king and the queen were delighted with their daughter, and only once did they express any doubt about her title.

The king said, "Have you noticed that she doesn't read very often?"

The queen shrugged. "The fairy didn't call her the Princess Who Read All the Time."

"That's true," said the king. And then he said, "Have you noticed that she reads fairy tales and adventure novels and almost nothing else?"

The queen shrugged again. "The fairy didn't call her the Princess Who Read Schoolbooks."

"That's true," said the king. "And if history remembers her as the Princess Who Read Silly Stories When She Had Nothing Better to Do, well, what does that matter if she's happy?"

One day when the princess was older than a girl but younger than a woman, a page hurried into the throne room where the King Who Saw Both Sides of Every Question and the Queen Who Cared for Everyone were playing cards while they waited for some royal duties to do. The princess sat on a nearby windowseat, reading *The Count of Monte Cristo*.

"Your Majesties!" the page cried. "The Evil Enchanter of the Eastern Marshes demands to be admitted into your presence!"

"Well, then!" the king said. "Admit him immediately, lest he be angered by the delay."

"At once," said the page, and he turned on his heel to bring in the enchanter.

"Or perhaps," said the king (and the page turned back to face the king and queen so quickly that he almost fell over), "we should make the enchanter wait a few minutes, lest he think he can easily sway us to his whims."

"As you wish," said the page.

"Wait, wait," said the king. "Go at once to admit the enchanter. Not because we fear him, but because we would not have him think us rude."

"I go," said the page, turning to do so.

"But," said the king (and here the page did trip on the carpet as he turned, though he sprang quickly back to his feet), "if the enchanter is demanding to be admitted, that's rather rude, isn't it?"

The queen said, "For an evil enchanter, being rude might be the very best manners." Then she asked the page, "Have you had enough to eat? If you're dizzy from hunger, we should give you a raise."

"Thank you, Your Majesty," said the page. "But I had a raise just last week, and I ate an excellent lunch."

The queen nodded. "Be sure you have milk with every meal. Milk builds strong bones."

"I don't think there's anything wrong with his bones, Mama," said the princess, who secretly liked the page.

The king smiled. "If the enchanter's being polite, we should be polite too, and if he's being rude, we'll look better by answering rudeness with civility. Don't dawdle, page. Admit him at once."

"At once," said the page, sprinting for the throne-room doors.

"Unless—" began the king. But the page slipped through the doors and closed them firmly behind him. The king barely had time to sigh before the doors opened again and the page returned. "Your Majesties, I give you the Evil Enchanter of the Eastern Marshes!"

The king smiled at the Evil Enchanter. "Welcome to our castle. Unless you'd rather not be."

"Oh, I'd rather be," said the Evil Enchanter. "Indeed, I feel most welcome to your lands, your people, and your treasure."

"Oh, good," said the king.

"I don't think so, dear," said the queen.

"What?" said the king, staring at the Evil Enchanter. "Do you mean that you feel welcome to keep my lands, people, and treasure?"

"I do," said the Evil Enchanter. "And I shall. My immediate marriage to your daughter followed by Your Majesties' abdication of the throne in my favor would be the simplest solution. Oh, and triple the taxes on the people. That would make a fine wedding present."

"Yes, I suppose so," said the king.

"Dear!" said the queen.

"—if I intended to permit that," said the king.

"I won't marry him," said the princess, thinking it best to let her father know her position on the matter as soon as possible.

"Of course not," said the king. "Arrest that man!"

The page looked around to see if there were any palace guards in the room. Since there were none, he said, "Sir? I'm afraid you're under arrest. Please step—"

The Evil Enchanter made a careless gesture. The page said, "I'm sorry to say I cannot arrest this man, Your Majesty. I cannot move my legs."

The king said, "Give my page the use of his legs! Immediately!"

"Certainly," said the Evil Enchanter. "When the princess consents to marry me."

Before the princess could speak, the queen turned to her. "Oh, my poor darling, how cruel of this enchanter! People will suffer, no matter how you choose!"

"It's kind of you to notice," said the Evil Enchanter.

"You're right, my dear," the king told the queen. "We shall decide, not she." He nodded at the princess. "And I say you shall marry this evil enchanter, lest he be provoked to further mischief."

"What?" said the princess, the Evil Enchanter, and the page simultaneously.

"But," said the king (and in different ways, the princess, the Evil Enchanter, and the page relaxed), "if we permit this, the enchanter's next demand will surely be even more unforgivable. Therefore, I say you shall not marry him."

"That's your last word?" said the Evil Enchanter.

"It is," said the king.

"Very well." The Evil Enchanter waved his arms once in a broad pass, and he, the king, and the queen disappeared in a cloud of smoke, just as the king said, "Unless—"

The princess and the page stared at the places where the three people had been. The page carefully lifted each of his feet, just to be sure that he could, then ran to open a window. When he quit coughing, he said, "What shall we do, Your Highness?"

"Why, I'll rescue them, of course," said the princess.

"I'll accompany you!" said the page.

The princess said, "Don't be silly. Someone has to run the country while I'm gone." Before the page could reply, the princess strode from the throne room into the inner waiting room, and then into the outer waiting room, and then into the long hall, and then into the entryway, and then into the courtyard, and finally into the royal stables.

The royal hostler bowed as she said, "I need a horse."

"Of course." He gestured toward a lean midnight-black mare. "This is Arrives Yesterday, the fastest horse in the land."

"Won't do," said the princess.

"Of course not," said the royal hostler, stepping to the next stall, which held a broad-shouldered golden stallion. "This is Carries All, the sturdiest horse in the land."

"Won't do," said the Princess. She stepped to the next stall, which held a wiry horse with black-and-white splotches on its gray hide. "And this?"

The hostler swallowed and said, "This is Hates Everything, the angriest horse in the land."

"Perfect," said the princess. And before the hostler could say another word, she saddled Hates Everything and rode out from the palace.

The moment they passed through the palace gates, Hates Everything tried every trick that every horse has ever tried to escape from its rider, and then Hates Everything invented seventeen new tricks, each cleverer than the one before. But the princess held onto Hates Everything's back when he bucked, and she lifted her right leg out of the way when Hates Everything scraped his right side against the wall of the palace, and she lifted her left leg out of the way when Hates Everything scraped his left side against a tree. She ducked when Hates Everything ran under a low branch. She jumped off when Hates Everything flipped head over heels onto his back, and then she jumped right back into the saddle when he stood up again. Finally Hates Everything stood perfectly still in the middle of the road, snorting steam and glaring angrily from side to side.

Two palace guards stood by the gate, watching helplessly. One whispered to the other, "Did the fairy really call her the Princess Who Read Books?"

"Maybe she read a book about riding," said the other guard.

"You're just wasting time," the princess told Hates Everything. "You're not going to get rid of me."

Hates Everything jumped straight up in the air, did a triple somersault, and landed on his feet with the princess still on his back. "You see?" said the princess. "When you carry me to the palace of the Evil Enchanter of the Eastern Marshes, I will set you free."

Hates Everything turned his head to look back at her.

The princess said, "Don't you hate wasting time?"

Hates Everything raced eastward toward the marshes and the palace of the Evil Enchanter.

When they came to a raging river where the bridge had been swept away, Hates Everything halted and reared up on his hind legs. The princess clung to his back and whispered, "Don't you hate being stuck on this side?" Hates Everything plunged into the fierce currents and swam, carrying the princess across the water.

When they came to a landslide that blocked the road, Hates Everything halted and reared up on his hind legs. The princess studied the mountain of rocks and boulders before them. Then she whispered, "Don't you hate stopping when you're almost at your destination?" Hates Everything charged forward, bounding from boulder to boulder, carrying the princess up and over the landslide.

When they came to a pack of gray wolves that growled as they paced back and forth across the road, Hates Everything reared up on his hind legs and turned to gallop away. The princess whispered, "Don't you hate people who get in your way?" Hates Everything bolted forward, and the leader of the wolves had to jump aside lest he be trampled by Hates Everything's hooves.

They came at last to the Evil Enchanter's castle in the Eastern Marshes. A goblin the color of granite stood in front of the Evil Enchanter's gates. He called, "Have you come to marry my master?"

"No," said the princess.

"Then I cannot let you pass," said the goblin. A long sword appeared in his hands.

"Your fly's open," said the princess.

"Oh!" said the goblin, dropping the sword and turning away to button up its trousers. Then it turned back. "Wait a minute! I'm a goblin! I don't wear clothes!"

But the princess and Hates Everything had already ridden past the goblin and into the Evil Enchanter's courtyard. "Mama! Papa!" called the princess. "I've come to rescue you!"

The Evil Enchanter appeared in a cloud of smoke. He waved his arms to fan away the fumes, and when he quit coughing, he said, "You've come to rescue no one. Now that you're here, you shall marry me." He waved his arms once, and a priest appeared in a cloud of smoke. After everyone quit coughing, he turned to the priest and said, "Marry me!"

The priest said, "But I don't know you."

"No, no, no!" said the Evil Enchanter. "Marry me to the princess!"

"Oh," said the priest. "That's different."

The princess whispered to Hates Everything, "When we've defeated the enchanter, you'll be free. Don't you hate—"

But Hates Everything had already lunged forward and begun to chase the Evil Enchanter around the courtyard.

"Wait! Stop!" cried the Evil Enchanter. "I can't make a spell if I can't stop to think!"

"That's the idea," said the princess.

"Stop this crazy horse, please!"

"Then free my parents and quit trying to marry me and promise not to bother anyone ever again."

"What!" said the Evil Enchanter in outrage, and then "Ow!" said the Evil Enchanter in pain as Hates Everything nipped his buttocks. "It's a deal!"

"On your word of honor as an evil enchanter!"

"Yes! Yes!"

"Very well." The princess leaped down from the saddle. "Hates Everything, you're free to go."

Hates Everything seemed as if he hated having to stop chasing the Evil Enchanter (and he probably did), but he came to the princess and looked at her as if maybe he didn't hate her as much as he hated everything else. The princess removed his saddle and gave him a hug, and he let her do that, even though he clearly hated it. Then he charged away from the enchanter's palace as if he didn't hate anything at all.

The Evil Enchanter said, "You didn't really beat me. The horse beat me."

The princess yelled, "Goblin!"

The goblin ran into the courtyard. "Hey, it's you! Couldn't you tell that I wasn't wearing any clothes? So how could my fly be open, huh?"

Instead of answering that, the princess said, "I'll double your salary if you'll cut off the enchanter's head."

"Good deal!" said the goblin, and his long sword appeared in his hands.

"Wait!" said the Evil Enchanter. "Okay, okay. You beat me fair and square."

"Don't cut off his head," said the princess.

"Darn," said the goblin.

"You can still come and work at our palace," said the princess.

"Good deal," said the goblin.

The Formerly Evil Enchanter waved his arms, and the king, the queen, the goblin, the enchanter, the priest, and the princess all appeared in the throne room where the page was assembling the country's generals to go rescue their missing royal family. The page ran to open a window, and when everyone had stopped coughing, the princess said, "Papa? See how well the page managed things while we were gone? Don't you think you should make him a prince and engage him to your daughter?"

"I hadn't—" said the king, but the queen nudged him with her elbow, and he said, "Oh, right. That's exactly what I was planning to do. If that's all right with you, young man."

The page smiled shyly at the princess, then said, "Yes, Your Majesty, that's very much all right with me."

The Formerly Evil Enchanter said, "What about me?"

The king said, "You can't be engaged to my daughter, too."

The princess said, "That's not what he meant. He meant it gets awfully lonely on the Eastern Marshes." She cupped her hands and yelled, "Fairy Who's Good with Names! Am I really the Princess Who Read Books?"

The Fairy Who Was Good with Names appeared in a cloud of smoke. When everyone had quit coughing, the fairy said, "Indeed not! You're the Princess Who Kicked Butt."

"That's more like it," said the princess.

"Oh, my," said the queen.

"Hey," said the Formerly Evil Enchanter to the Fairy Who Was Good with Names. "Nice smoke!"

And then the priest, who still didn't know what was going on but who knew a good opportunity when it presented itself, gave everyone a business card that said, in large print, MARRIAGES ARE OUR FAVORITE BUSINESS.

And they all lived happily ever after.

THE APPRENTICE

Miriam Grace Monfredo

Miriam Grace Monfredo lives in Rochester, New York. She is the author of two historical mystery novels, *Seneca Falls Inheritance* and *North Star Conspiracy*, and in "The Apprentice" she uses storytelling and fantasy as a means to delve into a little girl's unconscious and solve a mystery. "The Apprentice" was first published in *Ellery Queen's Mystery Magazine*.

—E.D.

The child huddled on narrow concrete steps that led from the basement of an Eighth Street brownstone. Above her the sidewalk shimmered with heat. Although Kelsey didn't think anyone could see her, she wriggled down one more step— but now she couldn't see anyone coming. Sweat made her T-shirt stick to her skin; she stretched out the neckband to blow on her bare chest. It had been cooler in the brownstone. But she couldn't go back inside yet. She laid her cheek against the cold iron railing. And wished she would stop crying.

When she inched up one step for a quick look, a man with a beard was rounding the street corner. Kelsey stiffened and ducked, and her stomach fluttered like a snared bird. She ground her fists into her eyes, pushing hard against the tears. But then she thought of something: that might be the *sorcerer* coming.

Cautiously poking her head up between the black bars of the railing, Kelsey peered through it. The bearded man walked toward the brownstone across the street, and now that she could see him clearly, Kelsey grinned. Yes, it was the sorcerer. She pushed red wisps of hair away from her eyes so she could watch him.

He didn't look much like a sorcerer. But she decided she might not know exactly how real sorcerers did look. She had seen drawings of wizards with tall pointed hats and purple cloaks covered with curved moons and stars. They always had long gray beards. *He* had a short black beard and wore a brown raincoat. Mostly he looked to her like a regular person. Of course, the wizard of Oz looked like a regular person, too—but he wasn't a very good wizard.

She felt better now. Summer dampness had turned to drizzle, and the headlights of cars were round yellow eyes staring at her through the grayness. Kelsey crouched in the stairwell, listening to tires slicking over wet pavement. Exhaust and gasoline mixed with the thick, rich smells of stores and restaurants and the hot-dog stand around the corner.

She waited while the sorcerer went into his brownstone. Then she scampered up the basement steps and ran across the street. She rang his doorbell with the secret signal—two long and one short—he had taught her to use. When he opened the door, he had already taken off his raincoat and was pulling a black sweater over his head. His face looked sharp and pale between the sweater and his black hair. Kelsey thought his nose was like the curved beak of a bird. He drew her inside, closed the door, and locked it.

"Does anyone know you're here?" he said, looking down at Kelsey with dark, careful eyes.

"No," she said. "I didn't tell anyone."

He nodded and walked toward a kitchen—at least Kelsey thought it must be a kitchen because it had a microwave. She followed him, smelling orange and cinnamon tea in the mugs he put on the desk top.

He pulled a chocolate bar, lumpy with nuts, from his pocket and held it out to her. Kelsey took the bar, broke it in half, and handed his piece back to him, then slid onto a chair and watched him pour boiling water from the microwave into the mugs. He set one down on the desk in front of her.

She let the chocolate melt in her mouth, but she didn't want the tea. It took too long to cool. "Can we do it?" she asked him.

"Right this minute?" he said, his black eyebrows lifting like wings. Then, "Where are your father and mother?"

"They've gone. Took my Aunt Lucy and Uncle John, and my Grandmother and Grandfather Crane home. They won't be back for a while. Please, can we do it now?" she said, slipping off the chair to stand close in front of him.

"Go over there," he said, pointing to a black sofa. He switched on the lamp that cast a circle of yellow light.

The great river rocked in the cradle of its banks, as slowly it moved south to the sea. Willows poured green-leafed falls into the river, and the summer sky overhead was so blue . . .

"Blue as yer eyes, Miss Kelsey," called Huck.

Kelsey heard him just as her head broke the surface of the water. Huck sat cross-legged on a raft of rough logs. Standing beside him; a tall black man poled past the shallows. Kelsey drifted beside the raft and listened while Huck told about when he and Jim set off downstream, running away, both of them, from their own particular slavery.

Huck puffed little clouds from his corncob pipe. He told her about the lickin's, and the time he'd had to set up all night with a gun on his lap, 'cause he was scared his pap was gonna kill him with a knife.

Kelsey liked most of Huck's story, but not the parts about lickin's and knives.

"Why do children get lickin's?" asked Kelsey.

"Appears like you don't know a whole lot, do you, girl?" said Huck. "Well, big people lick li'l kids—'cause they's kids, I'd reckon."

"Is that fair?"

"It ain't a case of fair, Miss Kelsey. It's a case of size. A case of size fer sure! Hey, ain't *you* ever bin licked?"

Kelsey felt her stomach flutter. "Are you and Jim going to ride on this river forever?" she asked.

Huck nodded. "Reckon it sure beats gettin' civilized. But you sure you ain't been licked?"

"I need to go now," Kelsey said.

"Okay. Jim," he said to the silent man with the pole, "Jim, we got to pull into shore."

Kelsey felt the water suddenly swell, lifting her toward the sky.

"Hey there," yelled Huck, "don't go flyin' off. Grab hold of the raft now, y'hear?"

Kelsey looked down and saw the sorcerer sitting under a willow in an arc of sunlight.

The autumn afternoon without wind was like magic, Kelsey decided; the trees let go and their leaves fell down straight and soft as golden snow. By the next day they would cover the sidewalk like an enchanted carpet.

Her stomach had stopped hurting, but her face felt cold. She pulled her sweatshirt down, then yanked the hood up over her head. While she waited, she sniffed at the sharp fall air—like the red spaniel that lived down the street.

The sorcerer walked toward her through the leaf snow, his head and shoulders flecked with gold stars. Kelsey remembered when she had first found out for certain about him.

"Why is this spiky tree growing here inside your house?"

"It is a hawthorn tree," he had said, as though that explained everything.

And it did. When Kelsey found *hawthorn tree* in her father's encyclopedia, the entry ended with: *It is still believed by some that ancient sorcerers stood under hawthorn trees to cast their spells.*

Well, of course.

Now, while he brushed the leaves from his coat, Kelsey told him about the funeral. Her Aunt Lucy had died. Kelsey had had to sit quietly in the church pew between her father and mother; the funeral service went on forever and ever.

After forever, all the relatives gathered at her Grandmother and Grandfather Crane's house to eat and cry. Kelsey saw her Uncle John, his eyes red and swollen, holding the hand of her cousin Melissa. Now Melissa had no mother. Kelsey wondered what it would be like not to have a mother—what a horrible girl she must be to wonder that! No wonder her stomach hurt.

Kelsey had gone to stand beside the front door. She had wanted to go home.

While she told him this, the sorcerer had been silent, watching her with his careful eyes. Now he asked her, "Does your stomach still hurt?"

She realized she'd been rubbing herself. "No!" she said quickly. "No."

The sorcerer kept watching her as he said, "Shall we do it again?"

Kelsey nodded. "But not the river this time. I don't want to hear about children getting lickin's. It's not right, is it?"

The sorcerer leaned down until his face was close to hers. "What do *you* think?"

"I think it's not right," Kelsey said. She remembered the enchanted leaves on the sidewalk. "This time, can we go on a flying carpet?"

The sorcerer led her toward the sofa in front of the bookcase; a beam of light appeared over his fringed rug—just before it soared into the air.

Sunbeams slanted through the pink marble arches of the palace courtyard. Under every arch was a fountain. The water leapt in the sun and fell with a tinkling sound on fronds of huge-leafed palms. The air smelled of sugared dates and spices.

All the other children clustered together on marble steps, but Kelsey floated just above a silk cushion. She reached down to finger its long tassels. On other cushions sat Ali Baba and Sinbad, Aladdin, and Princess Buddir al-Buddoor.

Under a purple-fringed canopy, Scheherazade knelt on a pink cloud and told wondrous tales, weaving threads of the stories together like the strands of silk running through Kelsey's hands.

Scheherazade told of Ali Baba and the cavern of forty thieves; of Aladdin and his powerful genie with a voice like thunder; of Sinbad enslaved by corsairs, almost eaten by a one-eyed giant, and carried through the air by an enormous bird.

When she ended the story of Sinbad's adventures, Scheherazade said in a flutelike voice, "And so Sinbad escaped the most terrible circumstances by his quick wit and his courage."

Sinbad jumped up and bowed low. Kelsey thought his billowing pants looked like the legs of the elephants he had ridden. How could he be so brave? He was so small.

Kelsey drifted on the magic carpet up through the long, misty corridor. The sorcerer, from far away, said to her, "What did you think about Aladdin's uncle, the evil magician, who beat the boy and buried him alive under a great stone?"

"The genie in the lamp saved Aladdin," said Kelsey. "Do you think I could find a genie?"

"That is not an answer to the question I asked," said the sorcerer, his voice now so close Kelsey wanted to cover her ears.

"Well, *my* uncle isn't an evil magician," she said, after she'd thought hard about his question. "My Uncle John is Melissa's father. And he's a nice man."

The sorcerer looked at her intently. "Are you sure about that?" he said softly.

Kelsey concentrated on the snowflakes hitting the windowpane, trying not to hear the baby wailing in the bedroom. It wasn't that she disliked the new baby. But there wasn't much to like. At least, not yet.

Her mother was tired. But as long as Kelsey could remember, her mother had been tired. She almost always stayed in her bedroom, sipping from a flower-shaped glass.

The worst thing about the baby arriving was all the people who arrived with it. Kelsey was glad to see her Granny Stuart from Rhode Island, who was her father's mother, and a widow. But the cousins and aunts and Uncle John, and her Grandmother and Grandfather Crane who lived across town—it seemed there was always someone who shouldn't be there in the brownstone every day.

There was no place to hide. But sometimes, she would sneak out and run across the street to the sorcerer's house. If only she wasn't so small. She wished the sorcerer would turn her into a ferocious red lion. But probably he wouldn't. He thought she should be a girl.

One silent white afternoon she ran out of the brownstone, pulling on her jacket and mittens. She crossed the street and waited on the sidewalk, watching birds swooping over snow-shrouded trees and crying into the wind.

She saw the birds' beaks open and close against the sky, but there was no sound. Why couldn't she hear the birds? Maybe it was true: maybe if she told something bad, she would never hear anything again.

Then the sorcerer came down the brownstone steps, and they walked together into the park and sat on a stone bench. He handed Kelsey a chocolate bar. She inched closer to him and heard the pigeons murmuring at their feet.

Startled birds scattered as the horse's hoofs click-clacked over the cobblestoned London street. Kelsey hovered just above a young man driving a carriage, who pointed out bleak factories looming into the sky. Smoke and soot hung in the air. The smell from the gutters along the street made Kelsey's eyes water.

She heard a high-pitched whining sound. It became one great keening voice, and scores of children tumbled out of the factories' doors as though they had been spewed from dark open mouths.

Kelsey stared at their rags, their thin, hungry look. They blended somehow into the street so that it seemed the very cobblestones were moving.

"What were they doing in those places?" she asked the young man.

"Working," said Oliver. His face was tight and closed as he motioned the coachman to stop the carriage.

Kelsey watched the children run off down the dozens of narrow alleyways growing like twisted arms from the trunk of the main thoroughfare. "Who takes care of them—where are their mothers and fathers?" she asked. "Where do they live?"

"For some, the streets are their families. They sleep in the alleys, the thieves' kitchens, and the night shelters."

"You don't," said Kelsey.

"I used to," Oliver said harshly, twisting on the seat to watch a man emerging from the shadows of a building. "Fagin," he muttered.

Kelsey saw a shriveled old man running bony white fingers through his matted hair. He grinned hideously, and his long fingers never stopped moving, turning and twisting around one another.

"Who *is* he?" she whispered to Oliver.

"Watch," he said.

Several children ran up to the man, gave him something, then darted away into the shadows like small brown birds. One boy, shaking his head, stretched out an open hand, then drew it back.

Fagin hit him. Hard. The boy doubled over and rolled groaning into the filthy gutter.

Kelsey tried to fly away, but she couldn't. And she couldn't stop looking at the man's long white hands, constantly moving, never still. . . . Her Grandfather Crane always had dirty fingernails. Kelsey hated that.

"No, please." She was trying not to cry. "I want to go away from here. Please." Her eyes cast frantically over the dark street.

The sorcerer appeared at the corner, holding the horse's reins.

Kelsey was quiet as she rode up through the foggy cobblestoned corridor. Back in the sorcerer's house, she said, "That boy . . . I think that man hurt him. And the boy didn't even do anything bad—did he?"

The sorcerer looked his careful look and shook his head.

Kelsey said, "It's a very lucky thing that Oliver grew up."

"But sometimes," said the sorcerer, "if a child does not know she is being hurt, she might never grow up."

Kelsey walked slowly, head down, sneakers scuffing the new spring grass growing in the sidewalk cracks. Her report card was stuffed in her jeans' pocket. The teacher hadn't said anything, just handed her the envelope with a frown. When Kelsey opened it in the girls' room stall, she felt a kind of disappointment, as though she had lost something important that she thought was hers. She threw up in the toilet, but she didn't feel better afterwards.

She stopped walking to hitch up her jeans and pull her belt a notch tighter. She had to go home. Granny Stuart was visiting again from Rhode Island, but she would be disappointed with Kelsey, too.

Kelsey stood just outside the door of her mother's bedroom. Did they know she was still there? She probably shouldn't listen.

"Adrienne, something's *wrong* with that girl!" It was Granny Stuart's voice.

"What do you mean—wrong, Mother Stuart?" asked Kelsey's mother.

"I've told you before, she's not the same grandchild I knew a year ago, when you lived in Providence."

"Well, now, Mother Stuart, you don't see her all the time. Just on your visits. So, of course she looks different to you. For one thing she's older. . . ."

There was a long silence, so Kelsey squatted in front of the door to look through the keyhole.

Her grandmother was just staring at her mother. "*Older* has nothing to do with her thinness, her withdrawn look, that tenseness," Granny Stuart said. "The child I knew in Providence was outgoing. Friendly. And bright. Look at this report card. Her grades are below average. Something's very wrong with her, Adrienne!"

Kelsey pulled away from the keyhole. She shouldn't listen—they were talking about someone else. Some other girl.

But she could hear her mother's voice scale upward. "So why don't you talk to her father. He's what's wrong. Your son, Mother Stuart, is never home. He stays at the university almost every night. I feel so alone. Talk to *him* about what's wrong . . ."

Her voice trailed off in a whisper. Kelsey couldn't hear any more. But she was scared for the girl Granny Stuart had been talking about. What if the girl couldn't tell what was wrong? What if she didn't know?

Beneath a ray of sunshine streaming into his hole, the White Rabbit rolled off the edge of the chessboard. He scurried to safety just before the scepter crashed down.

"Off with your head," screamed the Red Queen.

"Off with *yours*," Kelsey said, glaring at the creature. Then she drew back, suddenly frightened. What had she said? She bit her lip and whirled around to look for the sorcerer. He floated up through the hole, but she had glimpsed his face.

Why was his mouth twitching?

* * *

A week before, Granny Stuart had had to go home. Kelsey cried, and wanted to go with her to Rhode Island, and even though Granny Stuart said, "Yes," her father had said, "No—why would Kelsey want to leave her family?"

And now it was the Fourth of July. Her Grandmother and Grandfather Crane always had a picnic on the Fourth. This year's had begun in the early afternoon and Kelsey, in the crush of people, had lost her mother and father. Now she ran out of the house to look for them. When she found her father, he was standing with her Uncle John and others who had gathered in the backyard.

"Can we go now?" Kelsey asked him. "Can we go home, please?" She felt frightened and confused, and her stomach ached. She thought she might throw up.

Kelsey heard her father's voice from so far away she had to strain to hear him answer, "We have to stay for the fireworks. But why do you want to leave? Do you feel all right, Kelsey?"

She thought her father looked at her anxiously. But she knew that he wouldn't take her home. "I'm okay," she said.

"You seem flushed. It's hot out here. Why don't we go in the house where it's cooler." Her father reached out his hand toward her.

"No!" She backed away from him.

He looked surprised, then angry. "Kelsey, what's the matter with you? You act like you're afraid of me."

Kelsey shook her head, the confusion closing around her like a giant hand. She wanted to say—something. But she didn't know what to say.

Her father turned to answer something Uncle John asked him. Kelsey waited as long as she could, then slipped away from him into the shadow of trees surrounding the house.

She looked back. No one was watching. She reached the front sidewalk and started running.

"I want to do it right now," she told him, pressing her stomach—she could feel it trying to climb into her throat. Probably from running up the steps.

"Where are your mother and father?" asked the sorcerer.

"At the picnic."

"How did you get back here alone?"

"I walked to the subway."

"You must never, *never* do that again. It's not safe for you."

"Who cares? No one . . . no one cares about me. But I'm not bad—am I?"

He shook his head, while his dark eyes studied her; they had an expression Kelsey had never seen before. "Where was the picnic?" he said softly.

"You know where it was." Did he know? *Did he know?*

"Yes. I know."

She hugged herself, shivering in the July heat. "I want us to do it. Right now."

"Yes," he said. "I think this is the time."

They watched the little girl in a red hooded cape pick wildflowers in the deep green woods.

"How old is she?" Kelsey asked the sorcerer.

"She could be any age," he answered as they followed the little girl through the trees.

"Where is she going?" Kelsey said.

"To her grandparents' house."

Kelsey felt the flutter, as if a soft-winged bird had flown inside her, hovered a moment, and then flown on.

Outside the woods the sun shone brightly, but inside the trees grew so thick, so tall, that the light was dim and silvery. Suddenly they came to a circle of sunlight over a grassy clearing. A tiny house stood in the clearing. Carrying her flowers, the little girl ahead of them climbed the steps and went inside.

The sorcerer motioned to Kelsey. "Follow her. Go and see what is inside."

Kelsey hung back, shaking her head. The soft-winged bird had returned and stayed.

"Go inside," said the sorcerer. "Look for the girl in her grandmother's bedroom."

He gave her a nod, but Kelsey hesitated. Again the sorcerer nodded, and touched her shoulder. Kelsey bit her lip and looked up at him. When he nodded again, she slowly climbed the steps and entered the house.

It seemed very quiet inside. The front room was bare, as was the long hall beyond. Kelsey heard a murmur of voices and followed the sound down the hall. She came to a small room and stopped just inside the door.

The little girl stood talking to her grandmother, who was sitting in a large bed. The grandmother's head was turned away and covered by a white ruffled cap, so Kelsey couldn't see her face.

The little girl talked softly; Kelsey could hardly hear her until she said, "But, what big hands you have, Grandmother."

The bird inside Kelsey began to beat its wings faster. The grandmother climbed out of bed, the large figure covered by a long nightgown. A deep voice said, "My hands are big to hold you better."

The hands reached toward the little girl and pushed back the red hood. They unbuttoned the cape, and it dropped to the floor.

Kelsey felt strong wings beating inside her. "No," she whispered to the little girl. "No. Run away." But she couldn't run.

The big hands held the child's shoulders; then they began to move. The child whimpered and tried to pull away, but the hands gripped her tightly. The grandmother's white ruffled cap fell back from her face.

A face with a gray beard.

Kelsey felt the scream in her stomach fly to her throat, but the room remained silent. She squeezed her eyes closed. And felt the big hands move again. Now Kelsey could hear the scream; she stumbled out of the room and ran, while the sound of fear raced ahead of her down the endless hall.

The door . . . where was the door? The door was gone!

Crying, she beat on the walls with her fists, the hurt and shame as thick as the walls. "Let me go. Let me go or . . . or I'll tell. *I'll tell.*"

The walls disappeared.

The house around her vanished.

The man with black hair and the nose of a bird sat in his circle of light. Kelsey jumped off the sofa and ran to him.

"Who has been hurting you?" he said. "Tell me."

"It was . . . I can't tell," she cried.

His arms went around her, holding her cries. He wiped her eyes with the tissue from a box on his desk, then said with great care, "Evil things have been done to you. You have to tell."

Kelsey struggled against the tears. "I don't know if I can—he told me not to."

"He won't hurt you anymore," the sorcerer said, "if you can tell me, Kelsey. *Tell me.*"

"It wasn't . . . wasn't Grandmother in the bed."

"Who else would be in Grandmother's bed?"

"You *know.*" She hit his chest with her fists. "You know it was Grandfather Crane!"

"Yes, now I know," he said. "And you have to tell."

"I just told you."

He shook his head. "You must tell your Grandmother Stuart in Rhode Island. She will help you—she promised me she would."

Kelsey pulled away and looked up at him. "Then you're not a sorcerer—at least not all the time—are you?"

She thought she'd said something he didn't like; his mouth twitched, but then it curved upward. Kelsey had never before seen him smile.

He put the volume of fairy tales back in the bookcase and, while he telephoned, Kelsey stood close beside him. She heard Granny Stuart say, "Hello?"

"Mrs. Stuart? This is Dr. Sorensen. We have the answer to what you and I . . ." He stopped when Kelsey held out her hand. "Do you want to tell her, Kelsey?" he asked.

Kelsey nodded slowly and reached for the phone.

ALVYTA (A LITHUANIAN FAIRY TALE)

O.V. de L. Milosz

Born in Czarist Russia, O.V. de L. Milosz (1877–1939) was Lithuanian by both ancestry and citizenship, but spent much of his adult life in France. As a French language writer, he is well known for his poetry, autobiographical prose, and writings of mystical philosophy. In 1985, his writings were collected and translated in *The Noble Traveller*, with an introduction by poet Czeslaw Milosz.

"Alvyta" is one of two unusual fairy tales beautifully translated from the French by the late Edouard Roditi and published in *Conjunctions 18*, a literary journal edited by Bradford Morrow. (This story is published with gratitude to Nevenah Smith for all her literary detective work in the long, transatlantic search to track down the story's copyright holder and obtain the right to reprint it.)

—T.W.

Once upon a time, there lived a King who had three daughters. The youngest was five years old but could already dream only of alarums, trumpets and drums, and so she had already been commissioned as a colonel of a regiment of Grenadiers of the Palace Guard. The next youngest was seven years old and wore spectacles, recited sonnets all day long by heart, and her favorite pastime was to ride horseback on the knees of one of the gentlemen of the Academy of Letters. As for the eldest of the three, her name was Alvyta and she had already learned in the twelve years of her life enough about the vanities of this world to have made up her mind, very wisely, to cultivate her own garden, where she enjoyed the company of the rarest and most beautiful blossoms from all possible climates.

The father of these three young ladies was very fond of the people he ruled, and he supervised in person the government of all his provinces, so that his appearances at Court, which he hated, were indeed rare and brief. But he never returned to his castle and Court without bringing back to Alvyta, his favorite among these three daughters, the sweet-smelling tribute that all the gardeners of his Kingdom always handed to him for their dear Princess, whose passion for flowers was well known to all of them.

One day, as the King was returning from such a journey of inspection and happened to be passing through some woods, he suddenly noticed that the usual precious tribute of flowers offered by the gardeners for Alvyta had somehow disappeared from his baggage train. Searching everywhere in the hope of finding something to replace it, the King spied, at the top of a bushy young pine tree, a magnificent blossom that was quite dazzlingly white.

"Look here, Sirs," the King exclaimed in surprise as he turned towards the gentlemen following him, "have I lost my wits, or have our evergreen conifers suddenly decided to compete with magnolia trees?"

A young page boy then clambered up the trunk of the tree and, in a jiffy, was seen to stretch out an arm toward the lovely tulip, but to withdraw it at once in haste without having plucked the bloom, after which he slithered down the treetrunk and, quite shamefaced, declared to the King:

"Sire, close to the flower, there lurks in that tree a White Wolf watching over it, and it nearly frightened the life out of me because it has only one head, whereas all our masters teach us that such watchdogs as Cerberus generally have two or three heads. 'Friend,' it also said to me in the purest Lithuanian, 'if the King, your Lord and Master, wishes to possess my little ward, he must begin by promising to grant me the first living being that comes forth to meet him now on his return to the Palace.'"

The King was much intrigued by all this and in no way averse to agreeing to the proposed deal. The first person who usually came forth to greet him on his return from such inspection tours as the present one was his Chief Chamberlain, an insufferable old aristocrat, extremely punctilious about formalities and Court etiquette and protocol, though at the same time hesitant and confused about such matters and always obsequious toward his superiors but contemptuous of all his inferiors. The mere idea of being rid of him for good by handing him over to the White Wolf was greeted by the King and his whole retinue with all possible expressions of delight, and the young page was instructed to climb up the tree again and bring to the White Wolf His Majesty's agreement to the proposed deal.

Let us refrain from criticizing here the behavior of all these august personages whose malice, in any case, could barely have serious consequences, since the White Wolf is known to feed exclusively on dewdrops and marjoram and to tease a human prey only as a pastime in occasional moments of boredom.

Bearing the noble blossom in his hand, the King thus came very soon within sight of his Palace. Glad to be bringing so rare a gift, he hastened ahead through the copse that gave onto the lawn of the park when, to his utter horror, he perceived, at the bend of the path ahead of him, instead of the old Chief Chamberlain, his dear daughter Alvyta. Seeing from the top of a tower her father approach, she had rushed ahead to greet him.

"Unfortunate child," the King began to exclaim, but the rest of his lament was hushed in the curly blond tresses that were pressed against his cheek, while the resinous tulip provoked the girl's cries of delighted admiration and of endearment lavished on her father. The mere sight of those white petals crowned by a fine golden pistil seemed to cast a supernatural spell on her. Her eyes glistened with an unaccustomed fire, and an amorous tremor hovered on her lips and soon spread throughout her whole body. In vain the King and her fat old governess, who had hastened to the scene on hearing such outcries with her bonnet all askew on her head, now tried to calm Alvyta and make her understand what dangers threatened her. The White Wolf? Well, what of it? Seeing her now burst out laughing at the mere mention of the Beast, one might have bet that her fondest wish was to see it appear there and then.

When this guardian of the enchanted flower presented itself, a few days later, at the gate of the royal gardens to demand its due, it saw the King come toward it, leading by the hand a young girl who was magnificently dressed and adorned and as lovely as the light of day. Yet the White Wolf felt in its heart none of the expected tremors of joy, and even found it hard not to lose countenance when it witnessed the parting of the King and the girl, all of which appeared to be somewhat affected. Considering, however, that the whole matter, when all was said and done, appeared to be fair exchange and no robbery, the Wolf led the girl away; but it kept on muttering, as they went, as if to convince itself of its good luck: "Yes, she's pretty, she's young, and she'll look good in my pine tree."

Toward noon, after a fairly long walk, our travelers paused in a lovely clearing. When she saw the tall and luscious grass that was billowing there in the breeze, the Princess, who had kept her reserve until now, suddenly appeared to be ill at ease and exclaimed: "Lawks! Ain't these fine grasses, well, look at 'em, all luscious and well nourished and watered, but there ain't a single nanny goat here, not a single little lamb to feed and fatten itself 'ere."

The White Wolf could scarcely believe its ears as it heard such rustic exclamations, and uttered with such a rustic accent. Being a high-born lord, it stared at the girl, its mouth agape and its eyes popping out of its head: "What next, Madam!" it protested. "Is an immoderate taste for pastorals making you forget all that you owe to your own royal birth as well as to the rank of your humble servant?"

At the very mention of pastorals, the poor girl lowered her head, blushed and promptly burst into tears. "Good Sir," she sobbed, "I'm only too much aware of my own faults and shortcomings and truly deserve a good spanking, but it's the King, not I, who cooked up this whole business with my parents. No, I wasn't born anywhere near the steps of a royal throne, but my job has long been to herd my father's flock of sheep to pasture. To sum it all up, I'm only a poor little shepherdess, but I am nonetheless at your service."

The White Wolf had a tender heart and did his best to dispel the poor child's fears. Once she had wept to her heart's content, he said to her very gently: "You're but the unfortunate victim of the intrigues of the great, so let us now go back to the King, my royal kinsman." And, in order to soften the taunt that such a return might imply, he added, with a courteous bow: "Now His Majesty will surely send you back to your dear herd of bleating subjects."

The scene that then occurred between the monarch and the guardian of the magic flower was anything but friendly. To meet the White Wolf's insistent demands, the poor King amply implored all the inhabitants of Heaven to come to his aid, including Saint Wolfgang. Then he suddenly tugged nervously at his beard and rushed to the servants' quarters of his Palace, where there happened to live a girl who looked as if she might well be Alvyta's twin sister. Without further delay, this girl was hastily dolled up to look like a real Princess.

"My dear kinsman," the King now declared as he returned with this girl from the servants' quarters, "may I introduce you to Her Highness Madam First-born, my eldest daughter. The little shepherdess that I offered you earlier was just a trick to test your wisdom, since blue blood will always reveal itself, sooner or later. I'm well pleased with your flair in these matters, and hereby dub you a Knight. May you now bring happiness to the Duchess of Wolves and Countess of Pine Trees."

The wolf and the child set out on their way to the woods. The newly fledged Knight was not insensitive to the charms of his companion, though these seemed to correspond even less than those of the shepherdess to all hopes that the fragrance of the miraculous flower had aroused in him. After thus traveling several hours, our friends halted to rest a while in a great garden. All around them, the lovely flowers supplied a worthy subject for conversation, but the girl considered them without any real interest, though she appeared to know all their names, species and varieties, all of which, of course, surprised somewhat her new suitor, who pointed out to her a shrub that struck him as having a particularly odd appearance.

"Oh," she remarked condescendingly, as if shocked by his ignorance. "It's only a kind of cashew tree, in fact one of those anacardiacea with a trifoliate leafstalk. They come originally from the island of Gilolo in the Moluccas, though I've forgotten this one's full name according to the categories of Linnaeus. But my father is the King's gardener, and he . . ."

She blushed and hurriedly swallowed the rest of her sentence, but somewhat belatedly, having already let the cat, so to speak, out of the bag. After this, the Wolf simply told her to mount on its back, then sped posthaste all the way back to the King's Palace.

The King was an experienced politician and now knew at a glance that the hour had struck when, willy-nilly, he could no longer avoid keeping his word, which he did, in spite of his regrets, promptly enough. But when Alvyta at last saw the White Wolf, she lapsed into a deep reverie which her father mistook for sorrow, though Madam First-born's feelings were really of an entirely different nature. The countless joys that she owed to her passion for flowers since her earliest childhood seemed to her suddenly to melt into a single ravishing delight, a mysteriously angelic bliss. As for the Wolf, he needed no time to perceive that she was young and lovely, nor to picture her already enthroned in his pine tree. At his first glance, he recognized in her the form, now live and visible, of the fragrance of his beloved blossom, which had originally come to him from the Empyrean.

The two newfound but eternal friends rushed off breathlessly, without a word of leave-taking, to fill together their common destiny. Only from time to time, as they went, did the Wolf's lovely eyes rest on Alvyta's features, and she could then read in his glance these words: "Do you remember? Do you remember?" To which her own eyes replied with the same idea: "Need I remind you? Need I remind you?"

At the foot of the flower-bearing pine tree, which the young Princess, for unknown reasons of her own, now insisted on calling an apple tree, another White Wolf was awaiting them, not quite as snow-white as its lord and master but as full of grace and dignity. When it saw the young couple approach, it blew as loud as it could in a conch-shell, and all the wolves, bears, boars, elands and smaller creatures that the woods harbored, even the humble meadow mouse and the dragonfly that lives only one day, all these denizens of the innocent Garden of Eden, of the saintly virgin forest gathered together, whether on earth, through the waters or in the air, to greet the Queen of Primeval Nature who had at long last returned to reign over them.

Alvyta greeted them all to her right and her left, gaily waving her scarf at them. In the wayward May breeze, the population of flowers also bowed down before its Sovereign, then rose and bowed again. From the topmost crest of the pine tree, a cheeky squirrel shook onto the girl's shoulders a shower of tiny apples as it cried in a thin treble: "Here's some of the fruit of your apple tree, you unorthodox botanist!"

Indignant at such a display, a cat set about sharpening its claws on the bark of the tree, and this was enough to put a stop to the whole demonstration. On a sign from the Wolf that was acting as herald, all these creatures were suddenly silent and, from among the birds, a blackbird that thought it was white but was only pearly gray came forth and, after bowing low before Alvyta, burst into a nuptial epithalamium that was as young as life and as old as the world. As it developed its motet, the singer puffed up its breast until it seemed likely to burst, while its head was raised to the sky and seemed more and more enraptured. Suddenly, toward the end of its song and after a longish pause, the little singer turned its head backwards toward its shoulder and, casting a piercing and puckish glance over its whole audience, began to quiver with joy as it let out so droll and unexpected a whistle that the Princess, in spite of all her recent emotions, had to stuff her handkerchief into her mouth in order to refrain from laughing out loud.

At that very moment, she heard behind her so frank and fresh a laugh that she thought it came from a child. Turning around in her surprise, she beheld, instead of the White Wolf, her new master, a young Prince of truly celestial beauty, who was no longer laughing, but was smiling at her and waiting with open arms to embrace her. With a great cry repeated by her whole audience, and by all the echoes of the Immortal Garden, she threw herself into his arms and thus fulfilled, at long last, the beautiful prophecy that had foretold the Reconciliation of Beasts and Man.

THE PIG MAN

Augustine Bruins Funnell

"The Pig Man" is a disturbing story about a strange hired hand who does his job and fits into the family he works for just a little too well.

Augustine Funnell has had works of SF and fantasy published, both novels and short fiction. This superlatively subtle and disturbing grotesquery was first published in *Cemetery Dance*. Funnell lives in St. Johns, New Brunswick, Canada.

—E.D.

The memory remains, like a scar on the soul.

I was nine that spring, yearning for summer vacation so I could run free through the fields and hills surrounding the farm, or spend lazy August afternoons reading comics with Gene. Vacation loomed like a reward, and the closer the middle of June came, the more I looked forward to it.

I came home from school the last Friday in May, and found that my father had hired someone to help with the chores and the haying. He was introduced to me as Mr. Spafford, but the minute I saw him he received the sort of name only a child could give: the pig man. He had a prominent nose, protruding and blunt at the end, with squinting eyes set close to either side; the way his chin rose made his mouth seem to start just beneath the nose. The thick jowls of his cheeks were covered with coarse beard stubble, and only added to the porcine image. First sight of him made me nervous, but when he spoke in a gentle voice and held out a thick hand as if I were already grown-up, my uncertainty softened.

At supper he told us interesting little stories, not a one of which I could remember afterward. But it didn't matter; I liked the sound of his voice and the way he strung words together. When he complimented my mother on the meal and made appreciative noises over the dessert—lemon meringue pie—it was like watching the glow of firelight off my grandfather's silver watchchain: smooth and warm. But he still resembled a pig to me, and even though I respectfully called him "Mr. Spafford" whenever I addressed him, I was thinking "Mr. Pig Man" every time.

After supper my father and our new hired hand went to the barn to finish the chores, and I busied myself helping my mother clear the table.

"So what do you think of Mr. Spafford?" my mother asked.

"He looks like a pig," I said, snickering.

Her look was disapproving, but a smile crinkled the corners of her mouth. "He does, a little," she agreed, "but we don't judge people by their looks, Artie. We judge them by what they say and do."

I couldn't find anything to argue with in that. "He talks nice," I said, and her smile told me I'd atoned for my uncomplimentary remark. "And he sure liked your pie." Her smile widened, and when I left to start my homework she was humming contentedly.

About half an hour before I went to bed the pig man knocked softly on my door and came into my room for a few minutes. We talked about how I was doing in school, what I wanted to be when I grew up, and half a dozen other things. His voice was hypnotic, and twice when he asked me things about my mother I didn't catch the questions the first time, and he had to repeat them. When he left he said we could go into town someday and see a movie if my parents didn't object, and the wink he gave me suggested it was all but settled.

It wasn't until after he'd gone that I realized he smelled funny. Not anything disagreeable, but unusual. As unusual and unexpected as the smooth silver voice flowing out of that ugly face. But it didn't matter; I liked him.

"Worth every penny," I heard my father tell my mother a week later while he washed up for supper. Through the window I could see the pig man just leaving the barn and latching the door behind him. He stood for a moment, peering at the western sky while my father continued, "As a matter of fact, if he gets a better offer I'll match it."

My mother smiled, nodding.

"Damn good man," my father finished, and took his place at the table.

When the pig man came in to clean up he winked at me, and told my mother the smell of supper was even better than the last smell of supper. She beamed and made an embarrassed noise, then began humming to herself as she brought food to the table.

After supper my father went back to the barn, and the pig man came upstairs with me to offer five minutes of help with my arithmetic. When he went downstairs I heard muted conversation between him and my mother, then my mother's tinkling laughter just before he went out to the barn.

"Damn good man," I whispered, echoing my father with a delicious twinge of excitement at the feel of the curseword rolling off my tongue. I hurried through my homework, then raced outside to the barn to help. I watched surreptitiously as the pig man fed the pigs, amused in my childish way at the resemblance between human and animal. What made the similarity even more amusing was the way the animals responded to him. They were much less zealous in their gluttonous pursuit of room at the trough, managing an almost patient half-scramble. Even our gravid brood sow sequestered by herself in a corner pen, always belligerent and as willing to chomp fingers and legs as corn or barley or oats, approached her trough with restraint remarkable for a pig, and ate quietly. The cows didn't kick at him when he milked them, even when he performed the job on the side opposite to which they were accustomed. The cats curled around his legs, purring expectantly every time he emptied milk from its pail into the larger can, and although he didn't overdo it, he seldom disappointed them.

Of all the farm animals, only Buster, our mongrel-collie dog, didn't take a shine to the pig man. He didn't growl or bark or threaten, but whenever the pig man got near, old Buster—half-blind and not long for the world—would get laboriously to his feet and pad away into the shadows. If the pig man's chores took him there, Buster would again struggle to his feet and pad away. I figured the dog only wanted a quiet corner all to himself. He was old and dying, after all, and I didn't begrudge him the solitude.

Summer vacation. I had my chores, of course, but I also had plenty of free time to wander through the hills behind our house, playing at the dozens of roles my child's imagination created, not one of them having anything to do with Grade Five. I also had Gene's place to bike to, a couple of miles up the road, and his hills to wander through. We seemed to spend every other day together, either playing or reading comics, or, sometimes, making up our own comics. They were good days, and I thought the warmth and freedom and contentment of summer would last forever.

I was wrong.

It was a Saturday, and for a change, Gene was to bike to my place, bringing with him a stack of new comics I hadn't seen yet, which we planned to carry into the attic to read and copy in the dim light there. I met him halfway and we biked back together, chattering about all the important stuff boys chatter about, and when we went through the kitchen I had my first intimation that there were things beyond the world of boyhood, things which couldn't be put behind me with the arrival of the newest *X-Men* or *Avengers* comic.

My mother sat alone in the kitchen, early afternoon sunlight streaming through the windows and bathing her like one of the saints I'd seen in our family Bible. When she looked at our entrance it was as if she'd just awakened from a deep sleep, and she looked at us for a full ten seconds before the film over her eyes finally lifted and she recognized us. She spoke, but the words were dreamy and disconnected, and I couldn't be sure of what she'd said. I knew something was wrong, and a cool tingle danced along my spine. When she hugged herself as if for warmth, the tingle got very cold indeed.

Gene didn't notice, or if he did he must have thought she'd been asleep. But she was *my* mother, and I saw in her eyes something I couldn't explain, didn't understand, and which frightened me terribly. Why? Because the person looking out of those eyes *wasn't* my mother at all; it was someone else with her face and her body wearing her clothes, but it wasn't her.

Then, abruptly, it *was* her again, and she smiled and got up and hugged me and asked if we were going into the attic to read comics. We told her we were, and she smiled again and told us to have fun. Then, humming, she busied herself at the sink.

When we climbed the stairs I should have noticed the scent, but my mind was still trying to deal with the unexplainable feelings I'd had in the kitchen. So I missed it. But Gene didn't.

"What's that smell?" he asked me.

It took no more than that to focus my attention on the scent, and I recognized it at once: the scent of the pig man. Not the barn smell or the hayfield smell, but his own unique human smell, the one I'd noticed that first time he came to my room. It still wasn't disagreeable, just stronger. And as we walked past my parents' bedroom toward the second flight of stairs I realized it was coming from inside. Closed doors were not inviolate in our family in those years, so I pushed it open and stood staring dumbly at the room. Sunlight splashed across the floorboards and the unmade bed, and my mother's bottles of perfume and such rested on the bureau as sedately as ever. But the scent of the pig man, like something between peppermint and brandy (I realize now) was overpowering. Fainter at other times, it had been indescribable to me, but here in such concentration it was unmistakable.

The sound of my mother's arrival sent slivers of guilt through me, and when I turned to face her I caught fear dancing through her eyes. For what seemed forever but couldn't have been more than a couple of seconds we stared at each other, mother and child sharing something that one understood all too well, and the other not at all.

I was saved by Gene's, "Boy, that's a nice smell. What is it?"

My mother smiled at him. "Probably just my perfume," she said. "You boys scoot now; I've got housework to do."

And that gave substance to the unease I'd felt since we entered the kitchen, because I couldn't remember my parents' bed ever going unmade. My mother made it as soon as she got up, often as soon as she donned her housecoat. Yet here it was afternoon, and she was just making the bed. But I was a child, nine years old, and I didn't understand. I knew there was something unusual about the situation, but that was all. In the attic the scent of the pig man reached us only faintly, and after a while I was able to forget it entirely. But later, when I heard the clank and rattle of my father's truck returning from town where he'd gone earlier in the day, I couldn't suppress my fear and guilt. When I peered through the dusty window as he got out of the vehicle, alone, and traipsed toward the house I was afraid, and I didn't know why.

At four o'clock, Gene had to start home, and I rode with him halfway. On the ride back I pedaled slowly, stopping several times to listen to the birds, check out water gurgling slowly through a culvert, or peer through the trees to see squirrels and chipmunks. Anything to keep from getting home too soon.

Suppertime found me without an appetite, which worried my mother, but I stayed in my room anyway, and when she left to serve my father and the pig man their suppers I crept slowly down the hallway to my parents' bedroom. I opened the door softly and entered, and was not at all surprised to find the window open and the curtains blowing gently in the breeze. The scent of the pig man was still there, faint to be sure, but definitely still there. It didn't smell anything at all like my mother's perfume.

When I crept back to my room I felt as guilty as I had earlier, but I hadn't matured any that afternoon: I was still only nine years old, and I didn't understand.

After supper my mother came to check on me, but I couldn't meet her eyes. I heard something in her voice I'd never heard before, but I kept my attention riveted to the Sgt. Fury and His Howling Commandoes comic I was pretending to read, and I answered her questions with grunts and monosyllables. She was a different woman now, and I was afraid.

Later, the pig man came, but there was nothing different about him at all. He smiled and joked that he sure appreciated my not feeling well enough to eat, because that extra piece of chocolate cake sure had been good. Then he produced a piece of it from behind his back and set it on my study table. The scent of brandy and peppermint was faint, but it seemed overpowering to me at that moment.

I wanted him to go, but he sat on the bed and took my shoulders in his hands. When that voice of liquid silver told me to look into his eyes I was powerless to resist, but I felt no fear, no menace. As he kept talking I felt far away, different, no longer Artie hiding in his room because he was afraid and guilty without knowing why, but another kid somewhere else, content with the world and his place in it. It felt strange, but good, too. Very, very good. It made me feel important and happy, for no reason I could get clear in my mind, and when he left, it took me a long time to readjust to the bed and table and walls and posters. For a little while, there, everything had been perfect.

The week before school started, the sow produced a litter of pigs, and I went to the barn a dozen times a day to check on them and watch them and listen to their squeals. They were so much cuter than the adult versions that I asked my father if I could have one for a pet. He explained that pigs weren't the same as dogs, and no matter how much attention and affection I gave one, it wouldn't grow up to be like Buster. Since Buster was only slightly more pet-like than the average fence post these days, I took precious little consolation from that, and I sulked for two days.

Until the pig man woke me one morning as the sun cracked the eastern horizon, and thrust into my arms a soft, hyperactive ball of fur that seemed intent on licking the skin off my face. Later that day Buster died, but I didn't care: he'd been my father's dog anyway, and I had one of my own now.

Exactly when my father began to suspect, I don't know. It simply dawned on me one day that the lines in his forehead had deepened, and the tightness around his eyes was so severe that he seemed to regard the world through a perpetual squint. After I noticed that I discovered he and the pig man no longer spoke, that amusing stories at the supper table were nonexistent, and my parents seemed to argue an awful lot. While these arguments exacted a terrible toll on my father, they seemed to affect my mother hardly at all. She still hummed as she worked, told me stories, cooked fabulous meals, and smiled when the pig man paid her a compliment. Which was often.

In the barn I felt the strong tension between the men, but most of it seemed to originate with my father. The pig man remained oblivious to Father's hardened expression and surly attitude, and after a while I began to ignore it myself . . . because the pig man touched me often, clamped his thick hands around my shoulders and stared into my eyes and let me feel better and happier than I was. I began to wonder why my father didn't avail himself of this magical feeling; still nine, I didn't understand the intensity of that other magical feeling, the one that brings men and women together, and far too often drives them apart.

My father began to drink that winter. The pup and I found him at suppertime one evening in January, sitting on a bale of hay and staring at the concrete floor of the barn, a bottle of some foul-smelling liquid warmed by his huge hands. When he saw me two distinct emotions flickered through his eyes: hurt and resentment. They scared me, but fortunately they disappeared almost at once.

"C'mere," he said with a jerk of his head, and although I didn't want to go, I went. He moved over and I sat beside him, noticing the smell of days-old sweat and too-long uncleaned barn clothes.

"It's suppertime," I told him.

He nodded, but said, "I ain't eatin'. Ain't goin' in." The words were slurred. He took a long drink, and wiped the back of a dirty hand across his mouth, then fixed me with a narrow gaze. "Bet you can't wait to get back in there, eh?"

I was beginning to get scared. I shrugged. My pup got bored with the conversation and padded toward one of the stalls to investigate the actions of a couple of the cats. When I called him back he bounced across the straw-strewn concrete and wagged his tail furiously until I picked him up and cradled him in my arms. He was getting close to being too big for that sort of treatment, but at that moment I felt a lot more secure with him in my lap . . . after all, the pig man had given him to me, and the pig man could make me feel perfect.

"I would'a got you a goddamn dog," my father said, and his eyes narrowed even further. When he looked from it to me all the resentment was gone, but the hurt that had overcome it was complete. "And we could'a got a kid to adopt too . . . Christ knows there's enough of 'em nobody wants." He took another drink. "Whaddaya think it'll be Artie? Boy or a girl?"

I didn't know what he was talking about, and the longer I thought, the more curious it became. At that instant I didn't want to ever grow up; the world of adults was a place far too mysterious for the likes of me. I couldn't think of anything to say, so I shrugged.

"A pig, maybe," my father said. "A horny old boar. Or twins. A horny old boar and a horny old sow." He took another drink, then looked again at the pup, squirming to be free of my grasp. "I would'a got you a goddamn dog," he said softly.

To his eternal credit he reached over then and patted my dog, then rested his hand on my head and stroked my hair. To my eternal damnation, I flinched. Drunk as he was, he caught it, and there flashed through his eyes something I hope I never see again.

Fathers are bulwarks; they stand invincible against the vagaries of the world, and they absorb the best shots fate can deliver. They do not cry. It cost him, but my father maintained the fiction. At least long enough to tell me, "You better get inside; you'll miss your supper."

Relieved and glad to be away from him, I left at once. The dog and I raced along the path through the snow, and when we got to the house I found my cooling supper on the table in an empty kitchen. The scent of peppermint and brandy was strong.

It was late that evening that my mother, her eyes alive and her face aglow, told me I would have a sibling.

Whether he was determined not to be driven off his own farm, or there was a streak of emotional masochism in him, my father did not leave. Nor, curiously, did he fire the pig man. Perhaps he knew the pig man wouldn't go. Or if he did, my mother would go with him. It was the natural course of events as I passed my tenth birthday, and no cause for wonderment at all. The strain between the various elements of adulthood on the farm *was* a cause for wonderment, though, and not just mine. Gene wondered aloud one cold Saturday afternoon why my father slept out in the barn and why he never spoke, and I began to feel the first touches of humiliation visited upon those related to people who do not measure up to the norm. "Man, he's weird," Gene told me when I explained that my father simply preferred to sleep in the barn, and he looked at me as if I too might soon begin acting oddly. But I didn't take the opportunity to tell him about the pig man. We'd been pals for a couple of years, ever since his family had moved into the old MacDonald house up the road, and we had shared everything. But not the pig man and his magical ability; I kept that to myself, held it tight to my heart like a special possession.

We'd never had many visitors anyway, but when word got around that the hired hand was sleeping in the house and the husband was bunking out in the barn, the trickle dried completely. Sometimes at school I was the butt of jokes from the other kids, but it was usually the older ones who initiated the teasing, and I could ignore them because more often than not I didn't understand what they were talking about. I understood the derision though, and when the kids my own age picked it up there was more than one bloodied nose. Unfortunately, the other one was usually mine. Gene did a precarious balancing act between support and laughter, depending upon which of his other friends was teasing me at the time. It was good to know there were some kids he liked less than me, but disappointing to realize I wasn't at the top of his list in the same way he was at the top of mine.

To this day I don't know how my father managed to get through the winter months of that new year. He refused to enter the house if either my mother or the pig man were inside, but once they left he would go in, eat, and sometimes wander through the rooms like a lost child. Gene and I came upon him once as we descended the stairs from the attic, and the look he turned on me made me want to cry. He was standing in the doorway of the bedroom he'd shared with my mother, but he seemed unable to step inside. Perhaps the scent of the pig man, mildly all-pervasive now, kept him out.

Sometimes when he returned to the barn he'd take a loaf of bread and a jar of cheese spread or peanut butter, and occasionally when I played there or helped with the chores I'd find him sitting in the corner where he slept on pallets softened with straw, eating quietly and carefully. He hadn't shaved since I'd found him drinking that night the previous August, and crumbs would lodge in his thick beard, making him look slovenly and mean.

For all that the situation took out of him, it could not rip loose his love of the land and the farm he'd built on it. He worked tirelessly, mending fences, repairing the barn, measuring feed to the animals as diligently as he always had, and all without ever a glance or word to the pig man. Those jobs which required two men were performed by two men, one sullenly oblivious to the other, the second whistling and occasionally asking questions which went unanswered, or making conversation which went unheeded. It always made me uneasy, but the pig man could remedy that simply by taking my shoulders in his big hands and talking to me and staring into my eyes for a mere two minutes. I'd go away happy, another boy in another world, and the peculiarities of life at the farm would seem as natural as dirt, unchanged and eternal.

The horror came at the end of April. My mother's belly had swollen monstrously, and I was hard-pressed not to think of her as resembling the fat-bellied brood sow in the barn, also gravid once more. Had she not seemed happy and excited I would have been afraid for her. But these were adult mysteries, and I trusted her ability to cope with them.

We were sitting at the supper table, my mother, the pig man and I, when a sudden pain shot through my mother's eyes. She gasped, dropped her fork, and activity blossomed around me. The pig man helped her to her feet, told me to stay where I was and finish supper, then gently guided my mother out of the kitchen and through the living room. I heard their steps on the stairs, and a muffled reassurance from the pig man every time my mother gasped.

My nervous excitement wouldn't let me eat. I paced through the kitchen with the still-unnamed dog following mindlessly, then stole quietly into the living room; but waiting at the bottom of the stairs only heightened my excitement, and almost without realizing what I was doing I began climbing the stairs, slowly, softly. As if he understood, the dog made no noise behind me.

At the landing I had to stop to breathe; all the way up I'd held my breath, and my lungs were ready to explode. In the stillness of the hallway the exhalation seemed inordinately loud, but it was drowned almost immediately by a cry of pain from my mother.

The scent of peppermint and brandy was strong and getting stronger as I crept down the darkened hallway toward the bedroom, but I barely noticed it. A sliver of light showed under the door, and when I stepped into it I was so scared I thought I'd drop dead on the spot.

My mother wasn't making any noises now, but the pig man was speaking softly to her, words I couldn't decipher. His liquid silver voice went on and on for a long time, and when I could take it no longer I turned the doorknob and opened the door a crack.

My mother rested on the bed, her eyes closed and a soft smile playing about her lips. More than ever she resembled one of those martyred saints in the Bible, even with the sheen of perspiration across her forehead and trickling down her cheeks. Her dress was bunched up around her thighs, the almost obscene mound of flesh just above it rising and falling gently with each measured breath. The pig man sat on the edge of the bed with his back three-quarters to me, still speaking softly. His hands were on my mother's shoulders, kneading gently in rhythm to the cadence of his voice. The scent of peppermint and brandy was overpowering, but I forced myself to stand there, my heart thudding like a hammer on stone. When the pig man's hands gradually began to move from my mother's shoulders to her collarbones, then down further toward her breasts, I turned like the child I was to flee the dark mysteries of the adult world.

Half an hour later the pig man found me in the kitchen, toying with what remained of my supper while the dog waited patiently for such scraps as I deigned to give. He smiled at me in such a way that I knew he knew I'd disobeyed and gone upstairs, but also in such a way that I knew he wasn't going to punish me. He pulled his chair across the floor and placed it beside mine, and I knew what was coming.

He said nothing at first as his hands clamped around my shoulders very close to the throat, then he began speaking in that unique way, and in seconds Artie disappeared from the face of the planet, replaced by another boy who understood everything and was happy and content and liked and loved.

When it was over and he told me, "Your mother's fine, Artie; she's going to have a baby soon," I thought it the most natural news in the world, and could not conceive of any objection anyone anywhere might have.

"Will you be okay down here?"

I nodded, because I was absolutely certain I would be, that I would live a thousand years and never know anxiety or fear or loneliness, but if I did I could handle them all perfectly.

"Good." He clapped me gently on the shoulder. "I'm going back upstairs now, but I'll call you later. Okay?"

I nodded and smiled, and when he patted the dog and scratched its ears it seemed to me the dog nodded and smiled too. He left, but the scent of peppermint and brandy remained, a reassuring fragrance in that house of uncertainties.

Exactly when I heard the first of my mother's cries I'm not sure, but it must have been a couple of hours at least. I hadn't moved from the chair, my contemplations of the universe and my place in it so thoroughly absorbing that little but her cries *could* have intruded. The euphoria dissipated a little more when my mother cried again, a piteous sound that made me squirm. Her outbursts continued for a while, then there was complete silence and I waited desperately for the pig man to call me.

He didn't. Instead, I heard a sharp slap and a sudden high pitched wail, and even I knew what had happened. I hopped out of the chair, certain I could go up now without waiting for a summons, too excited to wait in any event.

I hadn't even gotten to the living room doorway when the kitchen door burst open and my father, ragged and dirty and wild-eyed, charged through like some huge, mad dog. His glazed eyes riveted me to the floor almost in mid-step, and when he took his first rapid stride toward me I thought he was going to kill me. But he brushed past without a word, the breeze of his passing foul with days-unwashed perspiration and the myriad smells of the barn. It was then that I noticed the axe he was carrying, newly-honed and glittering in the warm kitchen light.

Rabid, he charged through the living room and up the stairs. I knew something horrible was about to happen, but my rising excitement and morbid fascination at the expected violence would not let me stay downstairs. My father in miniature, I charged up the stairs too, the dog yipping with excitement.

My father was just disappearing through the bedroom doorway when I reached the landing. He roared something I couldn't decipher, and I heard the liquid voice of the pig man, containing urgency for the first time I could remember, reply . . . but that was lost when my mother screamed.

By the time I reached the doorway my father had axed the pig man at least once, and was making sure of his handiwork with a second or third blow. A serenity far inside me evaporated with the sickening sound of the blade demolishing flesh and bone, and I turned from the carnage with a hopelessly lost feeling inside.

When the sounds of savagery stopped I turned back, but I didn't focus on the grisly remains of the pig man. I watched my father instead as he dropped the axe and advanced on the bed, infinite hurt and sorrow and rage virtually pouring out of him. My mother's eyes were wide with shock, and she barely resisted as my father ripped from her arms the blanket containing the newborn infant. Then reality registered, and she struggled to regain the baby.

Too late. My father shoved her, hard, and after her ordeal she crumpled like a rag. A corner of the blanket fell away, and I stared open-mouthed at a tiny pink version of the pig man, identical except for beard stubble.

When my mother made no further move to interfere, my father turned to look at the child in his arms. He saw its features, and a strangled gasp of horror and revulsion bubbled through his lips. I think that until that moment he'd harbored the desperate, secret hope that it might after all be his. The hard lines in his face deepened. He forced himself to stare at it long and hard, and for one terrible instant I thought he would dash it to the floor.

"Pig!" he hissed. "It's a goddamn pig." He moved quickly then, was by me and out of the room before I could say anything. I started after him, then stopped when my mother's sobbing finally cut through the lingering internal echoes of the axe striking the pig man. But there was nothing I could do for her, and my morbid fascination with the final product of my father's humiliation forced me from the room and after him.

Even in the darkened hallway I could see the bloody footprints, and at a breathless clip I followed them to the landing and down the stairs, then through the living room and into the kitchen where, finally, they disappeared. But the kitchen door was open, and coatless I rushed into the April night, the dog bounding excitedly behind. My father was almost to the barn, already bathed in light streaming through its dusty windows. I yelled at him, but if he heard he paid no heed. I sped over the path, reaching the barn just a handful of seconds after he disappeared. I darted through the door, but he was already where he wanted to be, and there was no power on this tortured earth that could have stopped him.

He hurled the blanketed bundle into the brood sow's pen, and when I heard the beast's grunts and squeals as it scurried toward the squalling infant I turned and bolted back toward the house. Halfway there I threw up, and a few seconds later I passed out.

My mother was never the same after that, and perhaps it was just as well. She spent a week in the hospital and I stayed at Gene's, but when she came back she looked at me without recognition, and often I'd find her wandering about the yard, sniffing, looking under the steps, searching the bushes, all the while humming softly to herself.

My father spent a couple of weeks in jail awaiting trial, but obviously crazy, they locked him up somewhere far away, and no one would ever take me to see him. By the time I was old enough to go myself he was a long time dead and buried.

My mother's brother quit his job in the city and came to look after the farm and us. He brought with him his wife and three children, and after a while I was able to sleep at night without dreaming of Father charging through the house with an axe in his hands, then charging back out with a blanket. But now thirty-four, I still can't sleep without that other dream snaking its way into my mind, night after night after night. No matter how hard I try I can't forget the sight of the brood sow a month later as she nursed her litter of seven squalling piglets, each with its hairy pink body and the pig man's features, all smelling of peppermint and brandy.

The memory remains, like a scar on the soul.

TATTOO

A. R. Morlan

A. R. Morlan has had short stories in the magazines *Night Cry, The Twilight Zone, Weird Tales, The Horror Show, Cold Shocks, Obsessions, The Ultimate Zombie, Women of the West, The Year's Best Fantasy and Horror,* and a host of other magazines and anthologies. Her two novels, *The Amulet* and *Dark Journey,* were published in 1991.

"Tattoo," from *Sinistre: An Anthology of Rituals,* is a powerful and moving statement about empowerment, written in a hard-boiled style.

—E.D.

"Like your 'mum," the girl in the plastic raincoat said, shifting her glass of cola around on the sticky bar surface until the rounded nubs of dying ice cubes sang a soft, desultory melody. Reflexively, I rubbed my right forearm, where the two-dimensional chrysanthemum bloomed soft red, and nodded *Thanks.*

It was *that* kind of night in the grimy Village bar: when the jukebox is stuck on "Walk on the Wild Side," the flames gutter low and smokey in squat pebbled glass globes, and the neon bar signs flicker and sizzle. And it was hot, hot enough for the thin girl sitting beside me to sip cola with dying ice not three minutes after the bartender had set the glass in front of her. But yet—

The raincoat she was wearing was translucent green and covered a snug, long-sleeved sweater and skin-tight jeans. There were tiny patches of condensation inside the plastic coat, like when you put a hot roast beef sub into a sandwich bag. Wondering what her temperature was, I longed to take her pulse, listen to her heartbeat and tell her—

What? I thought, stubbing out my cigarette in a hobnail ashtray. *That she shouldn't go trying to smother herself in Saran Wrap? That you're a doctor, the voice of authority? Not smoking two packs a day, you aren't.*

The girl shifted beside me, the rounded ice cubes piling against her lips as she tilted her glass high, draining it. In the brief silences between the notes of the jukebox and the hum of the neon, I heard the cubes striking her teeth. For no good reason, I shivered.

"You have to keep that out of the sun, y'know," the steaming girl said, placing her empty glass on the formica bar top, neatly covering an old burn scar in the artificial wood grain surface.

"Keep what out?" I asked around the cigarette I'd just placed in my mouth. There was no one else sitting at my end of the bar, save for the girl. Her raincoat crinkled damply as she replied, "Your tattoo. They fade. In the sun. Unless you're careful." She paused to push a strand of limp light brown hair out of her eyes; each strand of hair looked thick, coated with sweat. Then:

"I mean, after all the trouble, y'know, to get it—"

I was tempted to either get up and leave or tell her off, but like I said before, it was *that* kind of night: brownout season, when the sidewalks resemble blackhead-pitted skin, and the air is so grimy you can almost feel it blackening up your nostrils. And down in the subways, all you see are hands, palms up, intruding on your space, and those defensive eyes—

Hell, maybe she doesn't want to go home either.

Putting my lighter back in my shirt pocket, I said, "Doesn't matter much if it fades or not. I just got it to cover something up. Looks better than what was under it."

The girl started nodding, her bangs slithering across her colorless brow, as if she agreed that my tattoo was, indeed, an improvement over the vaguely oval scar which had once graced my arm—even though she couldn't have known about it.

For a moment, everything swam around me, good old *déjà vu*. I felt a need to right the situation, to loop back and give the woman (her coat was now completely steamed over inside; I could barely make out the brown dots on her sweater) a reason for nodding at me.

I took a sip of my beer, another puff, and began, "It was a bite. Human. Good thing it happened in ER, one of the nurses swabbed it out before infection set in, gave me a tetanus. Happened when I was a resident in Manhattan, five, six years back. Some guy I was treating in the same ER suggested it. I was setting his leg—he'd been in a car accident, bad fender-bender—and he's looking *me* over noticing *my* arm and said, 'Somebody was mad at *you*, eh, Doc?'—"

"But they weren't, were they?" The girl crossed her legs, thin calves ending in hightops over scrunched cotton socks.

Again, my head swam. Behind the bar, the "d" on a Bud sign fizzled into a glassy colorlessness, and all the lights went slightly darker: brownout coming.

"No . . . the person who bit me wasn't mad at me. I was mad at *her* for a minute there, but. . . ."

How could I tell her about the woman in the ER, the harsh billion-watt lights bouncing off her bruises, her welted flesh? Rape is never pretty, and gang bangs are ugly. Cops found her, running naked down West 57th, away from the wacko section where women shouldn't linger come sundown. Some creeps had dragged her into an alley, a bunch of them. Cops caught most of the punks, not quite enough to account for all the different semen, but enough of them to satisfy the brass downtown.

But it didn't do squat for the woman: no sound left, just this tiny wheeze that's even worse than a wall-shaking howl. And she wouldn't let us look her over, she kept trying to cover herself with arms so thin they barely hid her wounded nipples, her damp mons. And before the shot I gave her could work, she leaned over and bit me. Had to grab her by the hair to make her let go of my arm, shake her head like a bird-eating cat. Cops took pictures of her: every time the bulb flashed, it was like her wounds rose off her skin for a second, hovering there before settling back down to hurt her again. And you could see the hurt there; every cut, welt and bruise spoke to me, and the throbbing bite on my arm answered them.

I made myself stare at the flickering Bud sign; my cigarette ashed almost to the filter before I went on, "I don't even think she knew she'd done it . . . maybe she thought I was one of the cruds who did it. Attacked her. Things like that happen in ERs more than you realize. Too much hurt has to spill over somewhere. Whitecoats make easy targets. Anyhow, the bite scarred up, was easy to see what happened to me. Rough types, they got to thinking it was an invite to abuse me some more. Easy mark. I could've had the thing removed, but I couldn't see losing skin like that. And even then, the new scar would've reminded me of the old, like it was never gone at all.

"But this—" I twisted my arm, watched the flat flower glisten in the murky bar light (the girl stared at it, mesmerized) "—it hides the whole scar. Guy who did it suggested a 'mum, said the petals followed the same configuration of the scar, the teeth, you know. And he said even if the tattoo did fade, the scar would still look like some of the petals." I ran my finger over the flower; lubricated with sweat, the outlines of the scar were easy to feel, impossible to see. But I always knew they were there, those two almost-connected half-moon ridges on my flesh.

"—a good job," the girl was saying; somehow, she'd asked for and gotten a fresh glass of cola, without my noticing. The fresh but sweating cubes tinkled brashly as she slid the glass around on the bar top, before asking, "But does it . . . uhm, does it make you feel *strong*? Inside, y'know, like the bite really *isn't* there?"

"I'm sorry, I don't follow—"

The green raincoat crinkled as she shifted on her stool to completely face me, her knees almost touching my jeans-covered hip. Brushing her pale, stubby fingers (her nails were short, with no white tips remaining) through her hair, she said softly, urgently, "Does it give you *strength*? So no one thinks you're an easy mark anymore, in the ER? Or anywhere? Do people . . . *fear* it?"

I ground my butt into a mash of filter before replying carefully, mindful of her abrupt intensity, "The little kids who come in are fascinated by it. Some guys have asked me where I had it done. Only complaint I ever got was from an old woman—and she had a head and feet on her fox stole, so I didn't take her *too* seriously—"

The girl smiled, slightly, perfunctorily, before going on, "Yeah . . . I suppose a flower wouldn't do that to people. . . . But they must think you're strong, right, to go through with it?"

"Well . . . yes, the children I see sometimes ask if it hurts, but that's about it. I guess that's what you mean, isn't it?"

The girl nodded vigorously, her right hand wrapped around the weeping glass of cola. Suddenly the gritty sidewalks and the panhandlers in the subway didn't look so bad, nor did the air seem too coarse. Sliding some bills across the bar, toward the distant bartender, I shifted in my seat saying, "It's been nice, Miss, but I have to be—"

"I'm sorry, y'know?" the girl said quickly, before turning to stare at the sputtering sign, where the "B" was on the verge of winking out.

My head wasn't swimming then, it pounded in time with the blood-roar in my ears.

I'm sorry, y'know?

With her face turned to the bar, and her eyes focused away from me, I finally recognized the girl. From the ER. Clothing made a big difference; when someone is nude, your eyes instinctively go to the parts you can't see otherwise, the parts you shouldn't really stare at, but do anyhow. And being a doctor, I was supposed to look there. Her face wasn't a primary concern, until her teeth were sunk in my skin.

Were *still* sunk in my skin . . .

"I don't know how many of them there were . . . just a blur of dicks and faces, crowding in on me . . . *looking*. That was the worst, y'know? Their bodies wouldn't remember me, but their eyes would. I was so . . . *exposed*. Like I was transparent, and they could see *all* of me. What I was, *inside*. What made me *me*. Nothing hidden, nothing I could hold dear to *me*, nothing I could *choose* to reveal anymore. Everything was naked about me. And for a long, long time there weren't enough clothes in the *world* I could wear. All at once. It was like the clothes weren't enough to cover me, make me not *naked* anymore." She made the word "naked" sound hideous, filthy.

"You went to get help," I asked rhetorically, my voice not rising at all at the end of my sentence; and I was mildly surprised when she nodded, took a gulp of cola, and replied, "Oh yes, I did get help . . . it took a long time, but . . . I think it's okay now. At least . . . I . . . at least—" she chewed flaky skin off her bottom lip, then went on quickly, her voice a gentle, yet triumphant whisper, "—at least I don't have to worry about being *naked* again. That's why I asked you, but maybe it isn't the same for you—"

"What '*isn't the same*'?" I fumbled another cigarette out of my pack, and patted my chest, feeling for my lighter, all the while not taking my eyes off the girl, as she casually, innocently loosened her raincoat undoing the belt just enough to let the top gape. With her dark sweater coming down to her wrists and up to her neck, the gesture was somehow *uns*exual, *un*provocative. I smelled a strong tang of sweat, and in the dim glow of the globe candles near her elbow, I finally saw—

That she was naked . . . naked, but *covered*. Completely.

The tattoo ran from just below the hollow of her throat down to her raincoat-belted waist, then down, down, into a mass of darkness, until her indigo blue legs met with her crumpled cotton socks. The pattern of the tattoo was dense, fabric-complete, and when I leaned a couple of inches closer, I saw why her "sweater" bore a pattern of brown dots. Two of the dots were her nipples. And when she pushed up her plastic sleeves, I realized that she'd removed the hair from her forearms, had most likely removed the hair elsewhere on her body— permanently, no doubt. There were even pocket lines and seams on her lower limbs. I could just make them out under the green folds of her raincoat. One look, even two, and you'd see clothes, clothes so sexless you wouldn't bother to look a third time.

And she acted as if she were covered with them, layer on top of layer, never to be naked again. And she wouldn't be, never, *never* again. Not if she took care of them, kept them from the sun.

I hadn't had my scar removed because I couldn't get rid of the memory of it, the ugly sights and sounds of that evening in the ER. I'd covered it, made it something pretty, something whimsical for a doctor, something to charm frightened young patients. But I still had the scar. I wasn't strong enough to make it go away.

But she'd made herself strong . . . made herself *clothed*, forever. Never to be truly naked again—it was a heady thought, a powerful concept.

Does it give you strength? So no one thinks you're an easy mark anymore. . . . Do people . . . fear it?

I wanted to tell her that it was a toss-up: yes for the strength, but no for the fear—unless a person was easily frightened by an ultimate show of discipline, of wanting to be whole again in such a desperate way, such a beautiful way. Never again would a bruise ruin her, show her to be weak. Never again would she be quite so *exposed*.

I wanted to tell her how beautiful she was, comment on how strong she must have been, to endure her nakedness for one last time, while the person who did her tattoo worked . . . and *worked* on her (it took a "long time," she'd said—but how long, how very *long*?). But she got up before I could speak, placed some money on the bar, and was gone, out the door and onto the dark, sour-smelling streets.

As I was watching her, the lights went dim, dimmer, then remained brownish-yellow. Through the distant window, I saw the whole city darken, guttering like a dying candle. But I didn't watch where she went. She was clothed, and she was strong. I went back to my beer.

It was that kind of night, y'know?

LADY OF THE SKULLS
Patricia A. McKillip

Patricia A. McKillip is a peerless modern fantasy writer. Her work is complex, lyrical and enchanting: including the groundbreaking *Forgotten Beasts of Eld*, the sensual *Stepping from the Shadows*, her new contemporary fantasy *Something Rich and Strange*, and many other novels for both children and adults.

For years this author rarely wrote short fiction; a McKillip short story was a rare event. Recently, however, this has begun to change. A sudden windfall of short fiction publications has appeared, crossing the spectrum from traditional mythic fantasy tales to magic realism and straight realism (such as the excellent "Xmas Cruise" in *Christmas Forever*). All have one thing in common: that distinctive McKillip magic with words.

Thus we have included two of Patricia McKillip's stories in this volume of the year's best: "The Snow Queen," published elsewhere in this volume, and the following poetic and poignant tale. "Lady of the Skulls" is reprinted from Stephen Donaldson's anthology *Strange Dreams*. (I also recommend seeking out "The Stranger" in *Temporary Walls*, edited by Greg Ketter and Robert T. Garcia.)

—T.W.

The Lady saw them ride across the plain: a company of six. Putting down her watering can, which was the bronze helm of some unfortunate knight, she leaned over the parapet, chin on her hand. They were all armed, their war-horses caparisoned; they glittered under the noon sun with silver-edged shields, jeweled bridles and sword hilts. What, she wondered as always in simple astonishment, did they imagine they had come to fight? She picked up the helm, poured water into a skull containing a miniature rose bush. The water came from within the tower, the only source on the entire barren, sun-cracked plain. The knights would ride around the tower under the hot sun for hours, looking for entry. At sunset, she would greet them, carrying water.

She sighed noiselessly, troweling around the little rose bush with a dragon's claw. If they were too blind to find the tower door, why did they think they could see clearly within it? They, she thought in sudden impatience. They, they, they . . . they fed the plain with their bleached bones; they never learned. . . .

A carrion-bird circled above her, counting heads. She scowled at it; it cried back at her, mocking. *You,* its black eye said, *never die. But you bring the dead to me.*

"They never listen to me," she said, looking over the plain again, her eyes prickling dryly. In the distance, lightning cracked apart the sky; purple clouds rumbled. But there was no rain in them, never any rain; the sky was as tearless as she. She moved from skull to skull along the parapet wall, watering things she had grown stubbornly from seeds that blew from distant, placid gardens in peaceful kingdoms. Some were grasses, weeds, or wildflowers. She did not care; she watered anything that grew.

The men below began their circling. Their mounts kicked up dust, snorting; she heard cursing, bewildered questions, then silence as they paused to rest. Sometimes they called her, pleading. But she could do nothing for them. They churned around the tower, bright, powerful, richly armed. She read the devices on their shields: three of Grenelief, one of Stoney Head, one of Dulcis Isle, one of Carnelaine. After a time, one man dropped out of the circle, stood back. His shield was simple: a red rose on white. Carnelaine, she thought, looking down at him, and then realized he was looking up at her.

He would see a puff of airy sleeve, a red geranium in an upside-down skull. Lady of the Skulls, they called her, clamoring to enter. Sometimes they were more courteous, sometimes less. She watered, waiting for this one to call her. He did not; he guided his horse into the tower's shadow and dismounted. He took his helm off, sat down to wait, burrowing idly in the ground and flicking stones as he watched her sleeve sometimes, and sometimes the distant storm.

Drawn to his calm, the others joined him finally, flinging off pieces of armor. They cursed the hard ground and sat, their voices drifting up to her in the windless air as she continued her watering.

Like others before them, they spoke of what the most precious thing of the legendary treasure might be, besides elusive. They had made a pact, she gathered: If one obtained the treasure, he would divide it among those left living. She raised a brow. The one of Dulcis Isle, a dark-haired man wearing red jewels in his ears, said,

"Anything of the dragon for me. They say it was a dragon's hoard, once. They say that dragon bones are worm-holed with magic, and if you move one bone the rest will follow. The bones will bring the treasure with them."

"I heard," said the man from Stoney Head, "there is a well and a fountain rising from it, and when the drops of the fountain touch ground they turn to diamonds."

"Don't talk of water," one of the three thick-necked, nut-haired men of Grenelief pleaded. "I drank all mine."

"All we must do is find the door. There's water within."

"What are you going to do?" the man of Carnelaine asked. "Hoist the water on your shoulder and carry it out?"

The straw-haired man from Stoney Head tugged at his long moustaches. He had a plain, blunt, energetic voice devoid of any humor. "I'll carry it out in my mouth. When I come back alive for the rest of it, there'll be plenty to carry it in. Skulls, if nothing else. I heard there's a sorceress' cauldron, looks like a rusty old pot—"

"May be that," another of Grenelief said.

"May be, but I'm going for the water. What else could be most precious in this heat-blasted place?"

"That's a point," the man of Dulcis Isle said. Then: "But no, it's dragon-bone for me."

"More to the point," the third of Grenelief said, aggrieved, "how do we get in the cursed place?"

"There's a lady up there watering plants," the man of Carnelaine said, and there were all their faces staring upward; she could have tossed jewels into their open mouths. "She knows we're here."

"It's the Lady," they murmured, hushed.

"Lady of the Skulls."

"Does she have hair, I wonder."

"She's old as the tower. She must be a skull."

"She's beautiful," the man of Stoney Head said shortly. "They always are, the ones who lure, the ones who guard, the ones who give death."

"Is it her tower?" the one of Carnelaine asked. "Or is she trapped?"

"What's the difference? When the spell is gone, so will she be. She's nothing real, just a piece of the tower's magic."

They shifted themselves as the tower shadow shifted. The Lady took a sip of water out of the helm, then dipped her hand in it and ran it over her face. She wanted to lean over the edge and shout at them all: Go home, you silly, brainless fools. If you know so much, what are you doing here sitting on bare ground in front of a tower without a door waiting for a woman to kill you? They moved to one side of the tower, she to the other, as the sun climbed down the sky. She watched the sun set. Still the men refused to leave, though they had not a stick of wood to burn against the dark. She sighed her noiseless sigh and went down to greet them.

The fountain sparkled in the midst of a treasure she had long ceased to notice. She stepped around gold armor, black, gold-rimmed dragon bones, the white bones of princes. She took the plain silver goblet beside the rim of the well, and dipped it into the water, feeling the cooling mist from the little fountain. The man of Dulcis Isle was right about the dragon bones. The doorway was the dragon's open yawning maw, and it was invisible by day.

The last ray of sunlight touched the bone, limned a black, toothed opening that welcomed the men. Mute, they entered, and she spoke.

"You may drink the water, you may wander throughout the tower. If you make no choice, you may leave freely. Having left, you may never return. If you choose, you must make your choice by sunset tomorrow. If you choose the most precious thing in the tower, you may keep all that you see. If you choose wrongly, you will die before you leave the plain."

Their mouths were open again, their eyes stunned at what hung like vines from the old dragon's bones, what lay heaped upon the floor. Flicking, flicking, their eyes came across her finally, as she stood patiently holding the cup. Their eyes stopped at her: a tall, broad-shouldered, barefoot woman in a coarse white linen smock, her red hair bundled untidily on top of her head, her long skirt still splashed with the wine she had spilled in the tavern so long ago. In the torchlight it looked like blood.

They chose to sleep, as they always did, tired by the long journey, dazed by too much rich, vague color in the shadows. She sat on the steps and watched them for a little. One cried in his sleep. She went to the top of the tower after a while, where she could watch the stars. Under the moon, the flowers turned odd, secret colors, as if their true colors blossomed in another land's daylight, and they had left their pale shadows behind by night. She fell asleep naming the moon's colors.

In the morning, she went down to see who had had sense enough to leave.

They were all still there, searching, picking, discarding among the treasures on the floor, scattered along the spiraling stairs. Shafts of light from the narrow windows sparked fiery colors that constantly caught their eyes, made them drop what they had, reach out again. Seeing her, the one from Dulcis Isle said, trembling, his eyes stuffed with riches, "May we ask questions? What is this?"

"Don't ask her, Marlebane," the one from Stoney Head said brusquely. "She'll lie. They all do."

She stared at him. "I will only lie to you," she promised. She took the small treasure from the hand of the man from Dulcis Isle. "This is an acorn made of gold. If you swallow it, you will speak all the languages of humans and animals."

"And this?" one of Grenelief said eagerly, pushing next to her, holding something of silver and smoke.

"That is a bracelet made of a dragon's nostril bone. The jewel in it is its petrified eye. It watches for danger when you wear it."

The man of Carnelaine was playing a flute made from a wizard's thigh bone. His eyes, the odd gray-green of the dragon's eye, looked dream-drugged with the music. The man of Stoney Head shook him roughly.

"Is that your choice, Ran?"

"No." He lowered the flute, smiling. "No, Corbeil."

"Then drop it before it seizes hold of you and you choose it. Have you seen yet what you might take?"

"No. Have you changed your mind?"

"No." He looked at the fountain, but, prudent, did not speak.

"Bram, look at this," said one brother of Grenelief to another. "Look!"

"I am looking, Yew."

"Look at it! Look at it, Ustor! Have you ever seen such a thing? Feel it! And watch: It vanishes, in light."

He held a sword; its hilt was solid emerald, its blade like water falling in clear light over stone. The Lady left them, went back up the stairs, her bare feet sending gold coins and jewels spinning down through the cross-hatched shafts of light. She stared at the place on the horizon where the flat dusty gold of the plain met the parched dusty sky. Go, she thought dully. Leave all this and go back to the places where things grow. Go, she willed them, go, go, go, with the beat of her heart's blood. But no one came out the door beneath her. Someone, instead, came up the stairs.

"I have a question," said Ran of Carnelaine.

"Ask."

"What is your name?"

She had all but forgotten; it came to her again, after a beat of surprise. "Amaranth." He was holding a black rose in one hand, a silver lily in the other. If he chose one, the thorns would kill him; the other, flashing its pure light, would sear through his eyes into his brain.

"Amaranth. Another flower."

"So it is," she said indifferently. He laid the magic flowers on the parapet, picked a dying geranium leaf, smelled the miniature rose. "It has no smell," she said. He picked another dead leaf. He seemed always on the verge of smiling; it made him look sometimes wise and sometimes foolish. He drank out of the bronze watering helm; it was the color of his hair.

"This water is too cool and sweet to come out of such a barren plain," he commented. He seated himself on the wall, watching her. "Corbeil says you are not real. You look real enough to me." She was silent, picking dead clover out of the clover pot. "Tell me where you came from."

She shrugged. "A tavern."

"And how did you come here?"

She gazed at him. "How did you come here, Ran of Carnelaine?"

He did smile then, wryly. "Carnelaine is poor; I came to replenish its coffers."

"There must be less chancy ways."

"Maybe I wanted to see the most precious thing there is to be found. Will the plain bloom again, if it is found? Will you have a garden instead of skull-pots?"

"Maybe," she said levelly. "Or maybe I will disappear. Die when the magic dies. If you choose wisely, you'll have answers to your questions."

He shrugged. "Maybe I will not choose. There are too many precious things."

She glanced at him. He was trifling, wanting hints from her, answers couched in riddles. Shall I take rose or lily? Or wizard's thigh bone? Tell me. Sword or water or dragon's eye? Some had questioned her so before.

She said simply, "I cannot tell you what to take. I do not know myself. As far as I have seen, everything kills." It was as close as she could come, as plain as she could make it: Leave. But he said only, his smile gone, "Is that why you never left?" She stared at him again. "Walked out the door, crossed the plain on some dead king's horse and left?"

She said, "I cannot." She moved away from him, tending some wildflower she called wind-bells, for she imagined their music as the night air tumbled down from the mountains to race across the plain. After awhile, she heard his steps again, going down.

A voice summoned her: "Lady of the Skulls!" It was the man of Stoney Head. She went down, blinking in the thick, dusty light. He stood stiffly, his face hard. They all stood still, watching.

"I will leave now," he said. "I may take anything?"

"Anything," she said, making her heart stone against him, a ghost's heart, so that she would not pity him. He went to the fountain, took a mouthful of water. He looked at her, and she moved to show him the hidden lines of the dragon's mouth. He vanished through the stones.

They heard him scream a moment later. The three of Grenelief stared toward the sound. They each wore pieces of a suit of armor that made the wearer invisible: one lacked an arm, another a thigh, the other his hands. Subtly their expressions changed, from shock and terror into something more complex. Five, she saw them thinking. Only five ways to divide it now.

"Anyone else?" she asked coldly. The man of Dulcis Isle slumped down onto the stairs, swallowing. He stared at her, his face gold-green in the light. He swallowed again. Then he shouted at her.

She had heard every name they could think of to shout before she had ever come to the tower. She walked up the stairs past him; he did not have the courage to touch her. She went to stand among her plants. Corbeil of Stoney Head lay where he had fallen, a little brown patch of wet earth beside his open mouth. As she looked, the sun dried it, and the first of the carrion-birds landed.

She threw bones at the bird, cursing, though it looked unlikely that anyone would be left to take his body back. She hit the bird a couple of times, then another came. Then someone took the bone out of her hand, drew her back from the wall.

"He's dead," Ran said simply. "It doesn't matter to him whether you throw bones at the birds or at him."

"I have to watch," she said shortly. She added, her eyes on the jagged line the parapet made against the sky, like blunt worn dragon's teeth, "You keep coming, and dying. Why do you all keep coming? Is treasure worth being breakfast for the carrion crows?"

"It's worth many different things. To the brothers of Grenelief it means adventure, challenge, adulation if they succeed. To Corbeil it was something to be won, something he would have that no one else could get. He would have sat on top of the pile, and let men look up to him, hating and envying."

"He was a cold man. Cold men feed on a cold fire. Still," she added, sighing, "I would have preferred to see him leave on his feet. What does the treasure mean to you?"

"Money." He smiled his vague smile. "It's not in me to lose my life over money. I'd sooner walk empty-handed out the door. But there's something else."

"What?"

"The riddle itself. That draws us all, at heart. What is the most precious thing? To see it, to hold it, above all to recognize it and choose it—that's what keeps us coming and traps you here." She stared at him, saw, in his eyes, the wonder that he felt might be worth his life.

She turned away; her back to him, she watered bleeding heart and columbine, stonily ignoring what the crows were doing below. "If you find the thing itself," she asked dryly, "what will you have left to wonder about?"

"There's always life."

"Not if you are killed by wonder."

He laughed softly, an unexpected sound, she thought, in that place. "Wouldn't you ride across the plain, if you heard tales of this tower, to try to find the most precious thing in it?"

"Nothing's precious to me," she said, heaving a cauldron of dandelions into shadow. "Not down there, anyway. If I took one thing away with me, it would not be sword or gold or dragon bone. It would be whatever is alive."

He touched the tiny rose. "You mean, like this? Corbeil would never have died for this."

"He died for a mouthful of water."

"He thought it was a mouthful of jewels." He sat beside the rose, his back to the air, watching her pull pots into shade against the noon light. "Which makes him twice a fool, I suppose. Three times a fool: for being wrong, for being deluded, and for dying. What a terrible place this is. It strips you of all delusions and then it strips your bones."

"It is terrible," she said somberly. "Yet those who leave without choosing never seem to get the story straight. They must always talk of the treasure they didn't take, not of the bones they didn't leave."

"It's true. Always, they take wonder with them out of this tower and they pass it on to every passing fool." He was silent a little, still watching her. "Amaranth," he said slowly. "That's the flower in poetry that never dies. It's apt."

"Yes."

"And there is another kind of Amaranth, that's fiery and beautiful and it dies. . . ." Her hands stilled, her eyes widened, but she did not speak. He leaned against the hot, crumbling stones, his dragon's eyes following her like a sunflower following the sun. "What were you," he asked, "when you were the Amaranth that could die?"

"I was one of those faceless women who brought you wine in a tavern. Those you shout at, and jest about, and maybe give a coin to and maybe not, depending how we smile."

He was silent, so silent she thought he had gone, but when she turned, he was still there; only his smile had gone. "Then I've seen you," he said softly, "many times, in many places. But never in a place like this."

"The man from Stoney Head expected someone else, too."

"He expected a dream."

"He saw what he expected: Lady of the Skulls." She pulled wild mint into a shady spot under some worn tapestry. "And so he found her. That's all I am now. You were better off when all I served was wine."

"You didn't build this tower."

"How do you know? Maybe I got tired of the laughter and the coins and I made a place for myself where I could offer coins and give nothing."

"Who built this tower?"

She was silent, crumbling a mint leaf between her fingers. "I did," she said at last. "The Amaranth who never dies."

"Did you?" He was oddly pale; his eyes glittered in the light as if at the shadow of danger. "You grow roses out of thin air in this blistered plain; you try to beat back death for us with our own bones. You curse our stupidity and our fate, not us. Who built this tower for you?" She turned her face away, mute. He said softly, "The other Amaranth, the one that dies, is also called Love-lies-bleeding."

"It was the last man," she said abruptly, her voice husky, shaken with sudden pain, "who offered me a coin for love. I was so tired of being touched and then forgotten, of hearing my name spoken and then not, as if I were only real when I was looked at, and just something to forget after that, like you never remember the flowers you toss away. So I said to him: no, and no, and no. And then I saw his eyes. They were like amber with thorns of dark in them: sorcerer's eyes. He said, 'Tell me your name.' And I said, 'Amaranth,' and he laughed and laughed and I could only stand there, with the wine I had brought him overturned on my tray, spilling down my skirt. He said, 'Then you shall make a tower of your name, for the tower is already built in your heart.'"

"Love-lies-bleeding," he whispered.

"He recognized that Amaranth."

"Of course he did. It was what died in his own heart."

She turned then, wordless, to look at him. He was smiling again, though his face was still blanched under the hard, pounding light, and the sweat shone in his hair. She said, "How do you know him?"

"Because I have seen this tower before and I have seen in it the woman we all expected, the only woman some men ever know. . . . And every time we come expecting her, the woman who lures us with what's most precious to us and kills us with it, we build the tower around her again and again and again. . . ."

She gazed at him. A tear slid down her cheek, and then another. "I thought it was my tower," she whispered. "The Amaranth that never dies but only lives forever to watch men die."

"It's all of us," he sighed. In the distance, thunder rumbled. "We all build towers, then dare each other to enter. . . ." He picked up the little rose in its skull pot and stood abruptly; she followed him to the stairs.

"Where are you going with my rose?"

"Out."

She followed him down, protesting. "But it's mine!"

"You said we could choose anything."

"It's just a worthless thing I grew, it's nothing of the tower's treasure. If you must take after all, choose something worth your life!"

He glanced back at her, as they rounded the tower stairs to the bottom. His face was bone-white, but he could still smile. "I will give you back your rose," he said, "if you will let me take the Amaranth."

"But I am the only Amaranth."

He strode past his startled companions, whose hands were heaped with *this, no this,* and *maybe this.* As if the dragon's magical eye had opened in his own eye, he led her himself into the dragon's mouth.

TO SCALE
Nancy Kress

Nancy Kress was born in Buffalo, New York, and now lives in upstate Brockport. Her books include the novels *The Prince of Morning Bells, The Golden Grove, The White Pipes, An Alien Light, Brain Rose,* and *Beggars in Spain* (expanded from her Nebula Award-winning novella of the same name) and the collections *Trinity and Other Stories* and *The Aliens of Earth. Beggars and Choosers,* a sequel to *Beggars in Spain,* is due out shortly. Nancy Kress won a Nebula Award in 1985 for her short story "Out of All Them Bright Stars."

"To Scale" is a dark coming-of-age story in which a young man must decide how to use the power he finds within. It first appeared in the anthology *Xanadu.*

—E.D.

When you get home on Saturday night, your father is drunk again. He's a polite drunk; nothing in the living room is broken. There's only the spreading stain of his last whiskey on the worn carpet beside the overturned glass. You gaze down at the small, wispy man lying there unconscious, the hems of his polyester suit pants twisted up over white sweat socks to reveal the skinny, hairy ankles underneath. One shoe off, one shoe on, diddle-diddle-dumpling my dad John. Everyone says you are the spitting image of him at your age—everybody, that is, who ever notices either of you. Usually you try to avoid mirrors. You are seventeen.

After you get him into bed—he's very light—you scrub hard at the whiskey spill on the roses-on-black carpet. It was your mother's. The smell disappears, replaced by pine-scented ammonia like hospitalized trees, but the petals of one rose stay discolored no matter what you do. Finally you give up and turn out the living room lamp.

It's 11:00 P.M. Not very late; you didn't stay long in town. Just went to the hardware store, had a hamburger, drove around awhile in the battered pickup, watching couples whose names you know from school walking and laughing on the summer streets. Then home again, because where else was there to go?

There isn't anywhere else now, either. But you're restless. You can't sleep this early. You go through the kitchen out onto the porch, banging the screen door behind you.

A little wind murmurs in the trees. You put your hands on the splintery porch railing and lean out into the night. It smells of wild thyme, hemlock, mysteries. But through the open bedroom window comes the sound of your father's snoring, arrhythmic and faltering. You go down the steps and start across the weedy lawn.

Here, the stars are magnificent: sharp and clean in a moonless sky. You tip your head back to study them as you walk. Halfway to the road, a huge black shape hurls out of the darkness straight at your throat.

You scream and throw up one arm. The shape hits and you both go down. You scream again, a high-pitched shriek that echoes off something, and try to roll away from the beast's jaws. Someone shouts, "King! King! Here, boy! Yo!"

The dog hesitates, then opens its mouth and snarls at you. From over your own upflung arm you see its eyes glow. Starlight reflects off its teeth. Frantically you keep rolling, but then the dog turns and trots across the road, where the voice is still yelling, "Yo! King, yo!"

Shakily you get to your feet. Mr. Dazuki strolls up, flicking cigarette ashes. "He get you?"

Your jeans are torn at the knee. Your arm is bloody, but that's from scraping the ground. "No," you say. And then, "Yes!"

"He break the skin?"

"No."

"Then you're all right," Dazuki says casually, and turns to leave. On the other side of the road he half turns. You can hear his grin in the darkness. "Don't be such a wimp, boy. Dogs're only afraid of you if you're afraid of them."

You are shaking too bad to risk an answer. You force yourself to walk slowly. Back inside your house, you lock the door and then stand for a long time against the refrigerator, your cheek pressed to its smooth coolness.

When your breathing has slowed, you go through the basement door down to the cellar.

Forty years ago the cellar had been subdivided into a maze of small rooms. Some have concrete or plywood walls; a few are walled in hard, bare dirt. You go past the discarded furniture, the broken washer/dryer set, the chamber with the sad piles of frayed rope and rusted fishing poles and paint cans whose contents have congealed into lumps of Slate Blue or Western Sky. Nobody but you ever goes down here.

At the far end of the house, in a cool windowless room that once was your mother's fruit cellar, you turn on bright 200-watt bulbs wired into overhead sockets. The room springs into light. It is about twelve feet square, but less than half of the floor space is left. The rest is occupied by the dollhouse.

It started with the fruit shelves. After your mother died, you ate one jar of her preserves every day, until they were all gone. Strawberry jam, apple butter, peach jelly, stewed rhubarb. Sometimes you got queasy from so much sweetness. Your stomach felt like a hard taut drum, and that made you a little less empty. But then the fruit ran out. The shelves were bare.

You covered them with her collection of miniature glass animals: swans and rabbits and horses of cheap colored glass, bought at state fairs or school carnivals. They looked awful on the bare, splintery shelves, so you brought in weeds and rocks and made a miniature forest. On the central shelf you put some dollhouse furniture you'd found in a box at the back of her closet. It looked old. You wanted to make it look better, so you found a scrap of carpet for a miniature rug. You found a doll's tea set at the Wal-Mart. You built a little table.

When the fruit shelves were full, you had no more reason to stay down here.

You built another row of shelves in front of the first. You've always been good with your hands, even at twelve. The shelves had a professional look. Making tiny furniture for each shelf wasn't hard. The scale was easy to work with, easier than real furniture would have been. You found you could make it look exactly how you saw it in your mind.

When you were fourteen, you read about a craft fair in the next town. You took your father's truck and drove there, even though fourteen is too young to drive legally in this state. Already your father didn't notice.

Miniature dishes for sale. Pillows, mailboxes, tea towels, cat bowls, weather vanes, scythes, doorknobs, toothpaste tubes, televisions, Tiffany glass, carpenter's chests. You couldn't believe it. You had seven dollars in your jeans. You bought a package of Fimo dough, a pamphlet on electrifying dollhouses, and a set of three tiny blue canning jars filled with miniature jelly.

By now the dollhouse is eleven or twelve layers deep. You built each one out in front of the next, with no way through except unseen doorways seven inches high. Official miniature scale is one inch to one foot. Each layer reaches to the ceiling and has twelve floors, with several rooms on each floor. Some rooms are furnished with cheap plastic dollhouse furniture you found in bulk at a factory closeout, dozens of pieces to the two-dollar pound. Some are furnished with simple, straight-lined beds and tables of balsa which you can turn out three to the afternoon. Some are elaborate period rooms over which you worked for months, with furnishings as authentic as you could devise or could buy mail-order. You work twenty hours a week at Corey Lumber for twice minimum wage, forty hours a week in the summer; Mr. Corey feels sorry for you. Your father never asks what you do with your money.

Somewhere in the impenetrable maze of tiny rooms is a Georgian drawing room with silver chandelier and grand piano from Think Small. Somewhere is a Shaker dining room with spare, clean lines in satiny cherry. Somewhere is a Tidewater Virginia bedroom, copied from a picture in *Nutshell News*, with blue velvet hangings, inlaid table, and blue delftware on the polished highboy. You will never see these rooms again; they've been covered over by newer layers. You don't have to see them again. You know they're there, hidden and unreachable. Untouched. Safe.

You pick up a piece of 32-gauge, two-conductor stranded wire and a 25-watt pencil-tip soldering iron from your workbench. You are wiring a room for a pair of matching coach lights. They go well with a six-inch teak table you found cheap at a garage sale. Some kid had thoughtlessly carved HD across its top, but you can sand and restain that. The three matching side chairs are also restorable. You have learned to reupholster seats one and a quarter inches wide.

School lets out in mid-June. You work full-time at the lumberyard. Your father gets up after you've left the house for his drive into the city, where he works as a data-entry clerk. You get home before he does, fix something to eat, leave his food in a covered dish in the oven, and go to the basement. By the time you come up, he is sitting in the living room, lights off in the summer dusk, drinking. His speech is very careful.

"Hello, son."

"Hi, Dad."

"How was work?"

"Good," you say, on your way out.

"Going out?"

"Gotta meet some friends," you say, which is a laugh. But he nods eagerly, pleased you have such a social life. When you come home at ten or eleven, he's passed out.

This is the only way, you think, that either of you can bear it. Any of it. Most of the time, you don't think about it.

In July a girl comes into the lumberyard—not a woman looking for newel posts or bathroom tiles, but a girl your own age, with high teased bangs and long earrings and Lycra shorts. This is so rare in the lumberyard that you stare at her. She catches you.

"What're you staring at?"

"Nothing," you say. You feel yourself blush.

"Yeah? You saying I'm nothing?"

"No, I . . . no, you . . ." You wait to see if more words will emerge, but no more do. Now she stares at you, challenging and sulky. You remember that you don't like this kind of girl. She is the kind who combs her hair all class period, gives teachers the finger, sneers at you if you answer in history, the only class you like. You start to turn away, but she speaks to you again.

"You got a car? Want to drive me home after this dump closes?"

You hear yourself say, "Sure."

It turns out she is Mr. Corey's niece, sent to live with him for the summer. She works the register afternoons. You suspect she's been sent away from her own town because her family can't cope with her, and that Mr. Corey's taken her in out of the same sympathy that made him pay you more than he had to. You've never known how to think about that extra money, and you don t know how to think about Sally Corey, either. You still don't like her. But she tosses her head at the register and rolls her eyes at customers behind their backs and sticks out her ass when she dances in place between sales, and you feel a warm sweet hardness when you look at her. By the end of the week you have driven her to a roadside bar where neither of you got served, out to the lake, and to a drive-through ice cream place.

"Hey, let me see where you live," she says, for the third or fourth time. "What are you, too poor or something?"

"No," you say. At that moment, as in several others, you hate her. But she turns on the pickup's front seat and looks at you sideways over the lipstick she's smearing on her mouth, and maybe it's not hatred after all.

"Then what?" she demands. "What is it with you? You a fag?"

"No!"

"Then take me home with you. You said no one's there but your old man."

"He'll hear us."

"Not if he's *asleep*," she says with exaggerated patience. "We'll go downcellar or something. Don't you have a cellar?"

"No."

"Well, then, the backyard." She lays a hand on your thigh, very high, and something explodes inside your chest. You start the truck. Sally grins.

At home, your father's silhouette is visible through the living room window. The television is on; sharp barks of canned laughter drift into the night like gunfire. You lead Sally in through the kitchen door, finger on your lips, and down the basement stairs. You lock the basement door behind you with a wooden bar you installed yourself.

In the first of the tiny cellar rooms, across from the broken Westinghouse washer, is an old sofa. You and Sally fall on it as if gravity had just been invented.

She tastes of wild thyme, strawberries, mystery. After several minutes of kissing and wild grabbing, she pushes you away and unbuttons her blouse. You think you might faint. Her breasts are big, creamy-looking, with wide dark nipples. You touch them just as she reaches for the zipper on your jeans. You forget to listen for footsteps above. You forget everything.

But later, afterwards, something is wrong. She rolls lazily to her feet and looks down at you, splayed across the couch, gloriously empty.

"That's it?" she says. "*That?*"

You are apparently supposed to do something more. Shame grips you as you realize this. You can't think of anything more, can't imagine what else is supposed to happen. Her glare says this stupidity is your fault. You stare at her dumbly.

"What about *me*?" she demands. "Huh?"

What about her? She was there, wasn't she? Does that mean she didn't like it? That you—oh, God—did it wrong somehow? How? Can she tell you were a virgin? You go on lying across the sofa, a broken spring pressing into the small of your back, helpless as an overturned beetle.

"*Christ*," Sally says contemptuously. She drags her blouse across her chest and flounces off. You expect her to climb the steps, but instead she moves into the next room, idly flicking light switches and peering around.

In a second you are on your feet. But you're dizzy from getting up too fast, and your fallen jeans hobble your ankles. By the time you catch her, she has reached the fruit cellar and switched on the light.

"Jesus, Mary, and Joseph!" She stares at the looming density of the dollhouse. Only one shelf of the current outermost layer is still empty. "*You* do this?"

You can't answer. Sally fingers a miniature plastic chair, a stuffed cat, a tiny rolling pin from Thumbelina's. She walks to your workbench. You have been antiquing a premade Chippendale sofa: darkening the fabric with tea, wearing out the armrests with fine steel wool. Vaseline, you have discovered, makes wonderful grease stains on the sofa back.

Sally starts to laugh. She turns to you, holding the Chippendale, her face twisted under her smeared makeup. "Doll furniture! He plays with little dollies! So *that's* why your prick is so itty-bitty!"

You close your eyes. Her laughter goes on and on. You can't move. This is the end of your life. You will never be able to move again. It's all arrived here together, in this moment, under the 200-watt bulbs, in the sound of this girl's ugly laughter. The kids at school who don't know you're alive (but they will now, when Sally meets them and spreads this around), your father's distaste for you because you're not good enough, the wussy way you're terrified of King's teeth, the endless days where the only words anyone ever says to you are "Twenty-pound bag of peat moss." Or "Hello, son." And the two are the same words.

A howl escapes your lips. You don't know it's going to happen until it does, and at the sound of it your eyes fly open. Something has left you, gone out on the howl—you can feel it by its absence. Something palpable as the hiss of escaping gas under boiler pressure. You can feel it go.

Sally is gone.

At first you think she's gone back upstairs . But the wooden bar at the top of the steps is still in place. You grope your way back downstairs and stare at the dollhouse.

The plastic chair is tipped over, and the tiny rug askew, as if Sally had just dumped them contemptuously back into their miniature room. You look closer. There are tiny scuff marks on the floor beneath the far doorway, the one leading into the dollhouse's inner regions.

The next morning Mr. Corey meets you at the lumberyard gate. "Billy, what time did you bring Sally home last night?"

You are amazed how easily you lie. "About nine-thirty. She wanted me to drop her off at the corner, so I did."

Mr. Corey doesn't seem surprised by this. "Do you know who she was meeting there?"

"No," you say.

The corners of his mouth droop. "Well, she'll be home when she's ready, I guess. It's not as if it's the first time." After a moment he adds hopelessly, "I knew you'd be too good for her."

You have nothing to say to this.

When you get home from work there is blood on the porch steps. Heart hammering, you start through the kitchen towards the cellar stairs, but your father calls to you from the living room.

"It's okay, son. Just a flesh wound."

He is sitting in the rocker, his hand wrapped in a white pillowcase gone gray from washing. The whiskey bottle is a new one, its paper seal lying on the table beside his glass. The glass is unbroken. Your father's face looks pale and unhealthy. "I didn't see the dog in time."

"King? King attacked you?" A part of your mind realizes that these are the first nonstandard sentences the two of you have exchanged in weeks.

"Is that the dog's name?" your father says blearily.

"Did he break the skin?"

He nods. You feel rage just begin to simmer, somewhere below your diaphragm. It feels good. "Then we can sue the bastard! I'll call the police!"

"Oh, no," your father says. He fumbles for his glass. "Oh, no, son . . . that's not necessary. No." He looks at you then, for the first time, a look of dumb beseeching undercut by stubbornness. He sips his whiskey.

"You won't sue," you say slowly. "Because then you'd have to go to court, have to stay sober—"

Your father looks frightened. Not the terror with which he must have met King's attack, but a muzzy, weary fear. That you will finish your sentence. That you will say something irrevocable. That you, his son, will actually talk to him.

You fall silent.

He says, "Going out, son?"

You say, your voice thick, "Gotta see some friends."

On the porch, you start for the truck. Something growls from the hedge. King barks and breaks cover, rushing at you. You jump back inside and slam the door. After a minute, when you can, you pound your fists against the refrigerator, which rattles and groans.

Your father, who must surely hear you, is silent in the living room.

You go down the cellar stairs. You don't even turn on any lights. In front of the dollhouse, you close your eyes and howl.

The suffocating anger leaves you, steam from a kettle. Coolness comes, a satiny enameled coolness like perfect lacquer.

From somewhere deep inside the dollhouse comes a faint, high-pitched bark.

You turn on the overhead bulbs and peer inside as far as you can. It appears that three layers in, a wing chair might be overturned, but it's hard to be sure. Two layers in, a hunting print from Mini Splendored Thing is askew on a wall.

At the foot of the cellar stairs you notice something white. It's Sally's cotton panties, kicked into a corner. You don't remember the kicking. The panties aren't what you expect from hasty scans of *Playboy* at the Convenient Mart, not black lace or red satin or anything. They're white cotton, printed with small blue flowers. The label says "Lollipops." You dangle them from your fingers for a long time.

You go back to the dollhouse. You think about King hurtling himself out of the darkness, the gleam of his teeth by starlight. Those teeth closing on your father's hand. The speck of blood already soaked through the gray pillowcase.

You close your eyes and concentrate as hard as you can. Afterwards, you peer into the mass of the dollhouse, trying to gaze through tiny doorways, past Federal highboys and plastic refrigerators. You see nothing. There is no sound. Eventually, you give it up.

You feel like a wimp.

The next day Sally is back at the cash register. She wears no makeup, and her hair is wrapped tightly in a French braid. When you catch her eye, she shudders and looks wildly away.

"Where's my dog?" Dazuki demands. "I know you did something to my dog!"

"I never touched your dog," you say truthfully.

"You got him in there and I'm coming in to get him!"

"Get a search warrant," you hear yourself say.

Dazuki glares at you. To your complete amazement, he turns away. "You damn well bet I will!" But even to your ears this sounds like bravado. Dazuki believes you. He doesn't think you'd imprison his dog, whether from cowardice or honesty or ineptitude. There will be no warrant.

You glance at the living room window, which was wide open. Your father must have heard how you told off Dazuki. Both you and the asshole were shouting. He must have heard. You go into the house.

Your father has passed out in his rocking chair.

Two days later, an upholstered Queen Anne chair on the fourth shelf of the first layer has been chewed. The bite marks look somehow desperate. But each one is only three twenty-fourths of an inch deep, to official scale. They are mere pinpricks, nothing anyone could actually fear.

The first day of school comes. By the end of third period, American Government, it is clear to you that Sally Corey has said something. When you walk into a room, certain girls snicker behind their hands. Certain boys make obscene gestures over their crotches. Very small obscene gestures.

You spend fourth period hiding out in the men's room. While you are there, hands bracing the stall closed while delinquent cigarette smoke comes and goes with the bang of the lavatory door, something happens to you. Fifth period you walk into Spanish III, coolly note the first boy to mock you, and listen for his name at roll call. Ben Robinson. You turn in your seat, look him straight in the eye long enough for him to start to wonder, then turn away. The rest of the period you conjugate Spanish verbs so the teacher can find out what useful information everybody already knows.

At home, in front of the dollhouse, you close your eyes. Ben Robinson. Ben Robinson. You howl.

There is a scuffling noise deep in the dollhouse.

For an hour you work at your bench. The Chippendale sofa is finished; you are building a miniature American Flyer sled of basswood. It will have a Barn Red finish and a rope of crochet cotton. You think of this sled, which you have never owned, as the heart of rural childhood.

After an hour, you close your eyes again and concentrate on Ben Robinson. When you're done, you inspect the dollhouse. The second-layer furniture that has been knocked over ever since the night with Sally Corey is now standing upright. On the bottom shelf of the first layer, which is coincidentally where you plan to put the American Flyer, you find very small, dry pellets. When you carefully lift them to your nose on the blade of an X-acto knife, they smell like dog turds.

The second weekend in September there is a miniature show in the Dome Arena in the city. The pickup truck has something wrong with the motor. You take the bus, and spend time talking with craftsmen. To your own ears your voice sounds rusty; sometimes days go by without your speaking two sentences to the same person. At school you talk to no one. No one meets your eyes, although sometimes you hear people whispering behind you as you walk away from your locker or the water fountain. You never turn around.

But here you are happy. An artisan describes to you the lost-wax method of casting silver. A miniature-shop owner discusses the uses of Fimo. You study room boxes from the eighteenth century and dollhouses extravagantly fitted for the twenty-first. You buy some miniature crown molding, wallpaper squares in a William Morris design, a kit to build a bay window, and a bronze bust of Beethoven seven eighths of an inch high.

At home, the fruit cellar is not completely dark. Tiny lights gleam deep inside the dollhouse, too deep for you to see more than their reflected glow through doorways and windows. You stand very still. Only the outer two layers of the pile have any electrified rooms. Only in the last year have you learned how to wire miniature lamps and fake fireplaces.

While you're standing there, the small lights go out.

You start skipping school one or two days a week. You aren't learning anything there anyway. What does it matter if the tangent of the sine doesn't equal the tangent of the cosine, or the verb *estar* doesn't apply to permanent states of being? You are tired of dealing in negatives. You can't imagine any permanent states of being.

"Going out, son?" he asks. His hand trembles.

"No," you say. "Leave me alone!"

Sometimes there are lights on deep in the dollhouse, sometimes not. Occasionally furniture has been moved from one room to another. The first time this happens, you move the wicker chair back from the Federal dining room to the Victorian sun porch, where it belongs. The next day it is back in the Federal dining room, pulled up to the table, which is set with tiny ceramic dishes. On some of the dishes are crumbs. You leave the wicker chair alone.

At the end of September you find a tiny shriveled corpse on the third shelf of the bottom floor, in a compartment fitted like a garden. It's King. The dried corpse has little smell. You cover it with a sheet of moss and carve a tombstone from a half-bar of hand soap your mother once brought from a hotel in New York.

Once or twice, sitting late at your workbench, you catch the faint sound of music, tinny and thin, from an old-fashioned Victrola.

"Listen," Mr. Corey says, "this can't go on."

You wipe your hands on your apron, which says COREY LUMBER in stitched blue lettering. In your opinion, the stitching is a very poor job. You're thinking of reinforcing it at home. "What can't go on?"

He looks you straight in the eye, a big man with shoulders like hams, fat veined through the muscle. "You. You talk short and mean to customers. Yesterday you told old Mrs. Dallway her windows weren't worth repairing, and your voice said she wasn't worth it, neither. You never used to talk to people like that."

You say, "I keep the stock better than it's ever been before."

"Yeah, and that's another thing. It's too good. Too neat."

You just look at him. He rubs a hand through his hair in frustration.

"That's not what I mean. Not too neat. Just too . . . it doesn't have to be that exact. Paint cans lined up on the shelf with a ruler. The same number of screwdrivers in each bin. You fuss over it like an old hen. All the small crappy details. And then you're rude to customers."

You turn slowly, very slowly, away.

"Just forget the small stuff and concentrate on the service that people deserve, all right?" Mr. Corey's tone is pleading now. He always liked you. You don't care.

"Yeah," you say. "What they deserve. I will."

"Good kid," Mr. Corey says, in tones that convince neither of you.

Dazuki has a new dog, a pit bull. It's chained in his front yard just short of the road. You stand by your mailbox and watch it stretch its chain, leaping and snarling. You go downcellar and give the dog two hours in the dollhouse, while you work on a nanny-bench kit from Little House on the Table. Banging and yelping, very faint, come from deep in the dollhouse. Once there is a grinding sound, like a dentist's drill. Glass breaks. For the last twenty minutes, you add Dazuki himself.

When you go back outside, about 7:30 P.M., the pit bull is lying across its chain. Its neck is bloody; one ear is torn. It catches sight of you and cowers. You go back inside.

The nanny bench turns out perfectly.

On Saturday afternoon Mr. Corey fires you. "Not for good, Billy," he says, and somehow he is the supplicant, pleading with you. "Just take a few weeks off to think about things. We're slow now anyway. In a few weeks you come back all rested, snap bang up to snuff again. Like you were."

"Sure," you say. The syllable tastes hot, like coals. You take off your apron— you reinforced the stitching last night—and hand it to him. You seem to be seeing him from the small end of a telescope. He is tiny, distant, with few details.

"Billy . . ." he says, but you don't wait.

The house is silent. In the mailbox is the new catalogue from Wee Three. Holding it, you go in through the kitchen, down the stairs, and jab the light switch in the fruit cellar. Nothing happens.

You reach to the ceiling, remove one of the bulbs, and shake it. It doesn't rattle. The disc-belt sander on your workbench won't turn on. But inside the dollhouse are the reflections of lights. In the windowless dark of the fruit cellar they gleam like swamp gas.

Upstairs, the refrigerator doesn't hum. The kitchen lights won't turn on. In the living room your father lies in a pool of his own vomit on your mother's rug.

You yank open the drawer in the scarred rolltop where bills are kept. It's all there: Three monthly warnings from the electric company, followed by two announcements of service cutoff. Threatening letters from collection agencies. Politer ones from the bank that holds the mortgage. Your father's pay stubs. The last one is dated four months ago.

Your father is shrinking. He looks like Corey did: a speck viewed from the wrong end of a telescope. The speck dances randomly, a miniature turd in Brownian movement on the end of an X-acto blade. You realize you are shaking. You kick him, and he grows again in size, until he and his pool of vomit fill the living room and you have to get out.

You go downcellar.

More lights gleam inside the dollhouse, some of them a lurid red. The dentist-drill grinding is back. There are other noises, fitful and rasping but faint. Small. Very small.

You close your eyes and the howl builds, against your father, against Corey, against the world. It builds and builds.

Before the howl can escape, your mind is flooded with objects, all miniaturized, all familiar, whirling in the fireball path of some tiny meltdown. Your work apron is here—COREY LUMBER—and your mother's rug, with all its stains. Sally's Lollipop panties and the rolltop desk. The set of baseball cards you had when you were ten, and the set of Wedgwood china inexplicably left to you in your grandmother's will. Your mother's hairbrush, the old cookie jar with the faded green giraffes, even the pickup truck, littered with McDonald's wrappers. Everything rushes at you: small, petty, and in shreds. The rug has been chewed. The desk legs, broken off, lie among shredded books. Splinters that were once nursery toys catch at the inside of your eyelids. Shards of Wedgwood are razor-sharp. Everything whirls together in a space of your soul that is shrinking still more, contracting like a postnova star, collapsing in on itself to the howl of a frightened dog.

Your yell comes out. "Noooooooooo . . ."

You open your eyes. The fruit cellar is completely dark.

You grope your way upstairs, outside, gulping huge draughts of air. It is later than it could possibly be. Orion hangs over the eastern horizon. It is past midnight.

You lean against the mailbox for support, and look up at the vast immensities of the stars.

In a few more minutes you will go back inside. You'll clean up your father and get him to bed. You'll start to sort through the bills and notices and make a list of phone numbers to call. In the morning you'll call Mr. Corey, set up an appointment to talk to him. You'll use ammonia on the rug.

And then you'll bring the dollhouse upstairs, layer by layer, piece by piece. Even though there's no place to put it all. Even though the miniatures that you made won't look nearly as realistic by sunlight, and some of the tiny pieces will surely end up lost among the large-scale furniture in the rest of the house.

ROAR AT THE HEART OF THE WORLD

Danith McPherson

Danith McPherson currently lives on the shore of a lake in Minnesota. She has had short fiction published in various anthologies and magazines. She's also published poetry and longer fiction.

"Roar at the Heart of the World" is a powerful, magical story set in the heart of Africa. It is both modern and mythic, evoking a land that does not exist—but *should*. One may note the influence of Elspeth Huxley's *Flame Trees of Thika*, which inspired McPherson to write of Africa.

The story is reprinted from volume 4 of the *Full Spectrum* anthology series.

—T.W.

I remember the day the world changed. Not by a date or a time or by any number. I remember it by the low voices of men in dusty boots who hunched over the table on our veranda and drank gin and tonic. I remember it by the dry wind through the weaving grass and the red-maned lion's roar. I remember because that day Africa changed. And Africa was my world.

"One man dead and a war begins." Young Mr. Finch tapped the side of his glass but ignored its contents. "South Africa seems so far away, and yet—If only they hadn't killed him."

"They were looking for an excuse," Mr. Kreshenko said, his Romanian inflection rumbled deep from a round chest. "Any would do, but they got about the best possible. The real reasons are more complex—economics, dignity, power, ego. So it has always been. This is only the lit match tossed onto the pile of straw."

Poor Mr. Finch. Thin and pale, he seemed unsuited to the wilderness of the Kenyan highlands, newly reopened to foreign ownership a century after the remnants of the first settlers were expelled. "The blaze is out of control," he muttered. "What will we do when it reaches us?"

From my child-sized chair at my child-sized table set a short distance from the adults' furnishings I searched the horizon for the glow of flames. I sniffed the air for smoke. I listened to the animals for panic. A fire is a frightening thing in a land that gives water more by whim than by season. Beyond the veranda the night was black and still. I heard my dog Orion patroling the stable. In their boxes the horses dreamed of familiar things. In the hills a leopard circled its prey without a sound. They did not know of a fire. Not then.

I bent over my paper and finished covering the flaming yellow with black. Africa was like the drawing I made. A layer of colored patches—red, blue, green, every pigment in the crayon box—then a dark layer covering it like the night. The wax sticks grew soft in the hot day. I kept them in a cool place and took them out after sunset. In the brittle light from the battery-powered torch I scratched off a design of hills and wattle trees, antelope and grasses. The colors beneath the black appeared in sudden vividness.

"Hah!" Mr. Haugen gave a single sharp laugh. "We'll be murdered in our beds by the natives, that's what."

I fussed with my crayons while I pulled the meaning from his thick German accent. The Romanian spoke like the ocean; I floated on the rolling rhythm. But the German ground out his words, and I had to pick through the rubble.

"Hush, you'll frighten the child." Finch touched me with a concerned look, quick as a feather.

"Frighten Lizzy?" my father said. He leaned against a post that supported the slanting roof of the veranda and swirled the liquid in his glass. "Lizzy stalks wild boar with the Nandi hunters. A little war won't frighten her."

No. I was not afraid. I was not afraid of the faraway fire. I was not afraid of a war, barely knew what one was. There was history, of course, but Father had little interest in the past and I had less, having less past to be interested in. He told me nothing of wars, except that there had been some. I was too young to read the thick books wrapped in tooled leather. When I did read, it was about horses.

Togom told me about the many battles between the Nandi and the Masai. But that was different. They were both warrior tribes; it was their heritage to fight. Tribe against tribe. Not Black against White as in the war my father and his friends whispered about.

I preferred the stories of great hunts. A hunter armed with spear and shield against a lion was braver than human against human—be it with spears or guns. There was little challenge in an opponent who had the same kind of strength, the same weapons, the same thoughts as you, whether or not the skin was the same color.

But a lion thinks differently from a human and a leopard thinks differently from a lion. Each animal is a separate challenge: That is the essence of the hunt.

"They can't force us out," my father said. "It's only an excuse to take back the land now that we've paid for it and spent four years proving we're not crazy, that it can produce."

"It isn't just the Kenyan government," Finch said. "England and all the other countries have told their citizens to leave. Burton," he said to my father, "you received your notice officially signed by His Royal Majesty the same time I did."

"And what would I do back in Germany?" Haugen asked the insects buzzing around the spots of light hanging from the bare rafters. "Can't raise coffee there. My older brother inherited the family vineyard. That's why I came here in the first place. Invested my meager inheritance in the land. Now they want me to leave. Burton, not to minimize your situation, but at least you can train horses anywhere, even back in England. You still have connections there."

My father's chin was set with a determination I knew well. "And what about the mill? I have contracts to deliver flour."

"There may not be anyone to deliver the flour to," the German said.

"Well," Finch said with forced vigor, "Diana and I haven't been here that long. We still have investments in London and a little money. Of course this isn't the way I planned. . ." He let it trail off. Nothing seemed to turn out as he planned. "You're staying then, Burton?"

I pretended absorption in my artwork. As if there was any doubt, I thought. "Yes."

"Suspected you'd feel that way." Finch stared at the table cut from the cedar forest a short distance behind the house. "Burton, Diana and I talked it over. This war is going to be tough, no other way about it. And—I hope you won't think me critical—Elizabeth is beyond the age when most girls begin formal schooling. And you know that we adore her. We practically think of her as our own, especially since the baby—Diana and I would like to take her back to England with us, just until things are settled here or until you decide to come home. It makes perfect sense, really.

"Damn it," he said with more weariness than strength. "I'm trying to make it sound so noble, as if we'd be doing you a favor. Truth is, it would break Diana's heart to be separated from Lizzy. Mine too, I'm afraid."

My father showed no surprise. Since my mother died when I was two years old, people who wanted to take me away from him had lined up like mismatched beads on a string. Each argued that it was for my own good. I should have been too young, yet I remember every one.

A particularly ugly bead—one of my mother's aunts, I think, in a wide hat covered with impossibly large net flowers—proclaimed that with her social contacts and careful guidance I would "get on in the world very nicely" and probably "marry above my station." But her real thoughts were simple and close to the surface. She wanted a little princess buried in taffeta flounces to show off to her friends. As always, Father politely declined the offer.

No previous bead was as honest as Finch, few were as nice. Still, I was surprised when my father said, "I'll think about it."

What was there to think about? Of England I remembered only starched dresses, tight shoes, overly perfumed relatives in stuffy rooms, and boredom.

I belonged to Africa. Finch and his equally porcelain wife could no more uproot me, transplant me into British soil, and expect me to thrive than they could a bamboo tree. And yet I heard my father say, "I'll think about it."

The guests left. Kreshenko and Finch lived the farthest away on farms with a common border, their houses still kilometers apart. Haugen was our closest neighbor, but he lived on the other side of the wide Rongai Valley, quite a distance by road, a bit less cross-country. The headlights of their tough, battered vehicles caught the eyes of animals along the edge of the ruts that served as a road.

Do not move, I told them. The noisy motor-beasts will soon rumble past and be gone.

"If war was an animal, I would hunt it and kill it," I told Sayid that night when he tucked me into bed. The Somali served as housekeeper and nanny. He was one of the colors of Africa that I tried to capture in my drawings. Unknown to outsiders. Unseen unless you scratched the continent's surface. His face was grim in the pale glow from the lamp on the narrow table beside my bed.

"It would not let you, Lizzy. It is not a natural beast."

I leaned over the edge of my little cot and gave Orion's brown-and-white coat a pat good night. A fusion of hard muscle and simple mind, he stood waist-high to my child body. My father made him for me, so he was of no discernible breed. He sauntered to the end of the bed, respectfully avoiding Sayid, who was a Muslim and could not touch or be touched by a dog, and curled up on his rug. I didn't think of him as big, for as the years passed he seemed to shrink. But I suppose that my own growth caused it to seem so and that he was larger than most dogs.

Sayid pressed the button that turned off the light. He stepped out of the room, leaving a trail of spice and soft rustles. As every night since we have lived in this little house, he left the door tilted open the width of his hard, narrow body, so I would not be alone, so he could slip in if I cried out in my sleep. To my knowledge, I never did.

For a moment I listened to the animals—Orion at the foot of the bed, the horses in their boxes, the large cats prowling, the slim eland sleeping yet watchful for the cats. I never heard the smaller animals—the chickens in our coop, my pair of chameleons in their cage. Either the smaller animals spoke in voices too soft for my sense or their tiny brains made no noise.

Only rarely did I hear humans. Perhaps their thoughts were too deep within them and too complex. I especially never heard my father. Perhaps he could protect himself from my intrusion. Usually I had other ways of knowing his thoughts.

Because of the company, I had been allowed to stay up past my bedtime. Drowsiness crept in and enveloped me sooner than I expected, so I had no time to consider the adults' concerns about this faraway war. As was my habit every night, I consciously stopped listening. Otherwise the animals kept me awake with their triumphs of life and screams of death. I was instantly asleep.

In the morning before a proper dawn had the chance to announce the day I took my knife and spear and slipped out of the house with Orion at my side. The cool air bit my legs below the khaki shorts, nipped my arms exposed by the brief sleeves of my blouse. Soon my father would be up to begin the daily work with the racehorses. I wanted to be gone so he could not turn me back to my neglected lessons in grammar and arithmetic. Like the horses, I, too, had daily work.

In all other things my father allowed me the freedom of a sprite, an independence that shocked the other farmers and gave Sayid nervous fits. But my studies were carefully monitored, and I received scoldings for hunting when my lessons had shown no progress. I was a child and endured them with a penitent bow, but without remorse or the resolve never to do it again.

The banks of solar panels sat expectantly beside the mill, tilted toward the point of sunrise, ready to power the machinery. Shiny solar flats, similar to the others but portable, leaned against the building. Each morning Kitau, one of the Kikuyu workers, set them up as needed to recharge the batteries for the lamp in my room and the torches that we relied on at night for the veranda and the stable.

Wheat stalks swayed in the field, each slim plant reaching above my head. Beside the golden spears, Father's prized patch of genetically enhanced maize rustled with health. Less tall than the wheat, its thick shafts supported a heavy crop that my father was already using as a wonderful excuse to plan a party for harvest. Farther up in the hills there was a cluster of coffee trees, the traditional crop of the area left over from the first wave of European settlers long ago. My father's nature rebelled at tradition, but I think their untended survival intrigued him. He fussed over the plot as if it were nature's equivalent of his maize.

I traveled over the hill and into the valley. Three hundred meters below, smoke from the Nandi village drifted up in thin lines that converged into one, then faded. I descended through the half light at the edge of day. The mongrel dogs yapped at my approach. They were ill-mannered and barked at everything. Orion refused to answer their coarseness with anything but silence. They shared an inherited memory; but because of his mixed genes, Orion felt no kinship with them.

Togom and Ruta ducked out of their huts and greeted me. They each wore a *shuka*. The single piece of cloth wrapped under one arm, sloped across the chest and back, and was knotted at the opposite shoulder.

Togom gave Orion a pat. The motion seemed a wasteful use of the strength stored in his lean muscles, but the fluid body, like shadowed water, craved movement. "How are the animals this morning?" he asked me in Swahili.

I wasn't fluent in Nandi, but Swahili was accepted as a common language. The Kavirondo and Kikuyu workers on the farm used it. I spoke it better than I did English, which appalled the fragile Mrs. Finch. I could substitute a few Nandi, Kikuyu, even Masai words if they fit my purpose. "Nervous," I said. Did I describe them or myself? Although it dominated my thoughts, I didn't say that my father might send me away.

Togom, the village's *ol-oiboni*, spiritual leader, nodded. "The sun quivers, afraid to come out." His soul grew from this land. He didn't need me to tell him how the animals felt, so I knew it was a lesson. He recognized my distraction. He wished me to stay alert, to push deeper into my sensitivity.

Ruta shook his head. His shoulders were wide for a Nandi's, and he carried more weight on his round chest than Togom. But he was just as quick with a spear. "*Mbaisa sana*," terribly bad, he said. "This is not good for hunting."

"Ahh, but we have Elisbet to tell them not to be so, to say they die honorable deaths on murani spears," Togom said.

I knew the other message in his words. I am *ol-oiboni*, he said, I can do much but this I cannot do: I cannot make the animals hear me. Only you can do this, Elisbet.

Togom motioned. A girl no older than my eight years dressed in a skirt of skins that brushed her ankles brought three gourds of blood and curdled milk.

In the village there is no division between life and ceremony, living and religion. Solemnly we observed the pre-hunt ritual. We each took a gourd and drank in turn, chanting praise to the blood of the bull. Togom first as leader. Then Ruta. Then me, Orion respectfully sitting at my feet.

The girl watched me because it was not allowed for her eyes to touch the men. Nandi women do not hunt. I'm sure she wondered how I dared to stand beside the strong warriors and drink warm bull's blood, how I dared to lift a spear against a boar. I had no answers for her unasked questions. Only that it seemed natural to hunt and that I wasn't afraid with Togom and Ruta and Orion.

Togom and Ruta hefted their spears and shields. Morning blossomed across the flat sky. In this part of Africa, so near the equator, the sky is very close to the earth. I imagined that when I grew as tall as a muran, I would be able to stand on Mount Kenya and stretch my fingertips to touch the blue.

We crossed a pasture crowded with indulged cattle. The uncircumcised boys who tended them watched covertly as we passed. When we cleared the worst of the slippery dung, we ran in single file. The floor of the long, winding valley is clogged with foliage and impassable from one end to the other. Togom led us up over the lip, then along the perimeter of the Mau Forest. We descended back into the Rongai as the sun rose. I listened.

Impala, eland, kongoni—all to the sides of us, all scattered. And below us—

"Boar," I said, trying not to let my excitement rattle my voice, trying to be a calm hunter. "But it is too quiet between here and there."

We reached the jumble of rocks where water trickled through the scarlet dust, turning it to sucking clay. In the heat, mist rose from the puddle that formed.

Mist. The Masai word is *E-rukenya*. Kenya.

The meager watering hole was always populated with sleek impala, eland, zebras. I saw nothing except the indentations of hooves and paws in the clay. I heard nothing.

Togom and Ruta froze, experience guiding them. In imitation, I stood still. Orion moved in front of me. He sniffed the ground, the air. His thoughts danced bright and expectant.

"*Simba*," I whispered. "Orion tells me this."

"Ahh," Ruta whispered back, "the one with the red mane who will not talk to you."

"It must be," I said.

"But you can talk to it," Togom said. "Say that today we do not hunt lion. Say that we hunt boar."

In my mind I repeated Togom's message to the invisible animal. I sent the thought across the crimsons and coppers of the clearing, into the tawny grass and skeletal brush that clawed the stones, not knowing if I was heard.

From the deep, cool shadow of an overhanging rock drifted a huge golden cat, a muted color of Africa silently revealed. It shook the cinnamon halo surrounding its head and flicked its cinnamon-tipped tail with impatience. The steady eyes evaluated Togom. Then Ruta. Then Orion. I cried to the dog to hold. The lion's stare was a challenge. Orion's every muscle tightened to spring. He was furious with me for the restraint.

The lion's eyes slid to me. The stare burned and chilled. "I know you," the eyes said, although I heard nothing.

The lion's eyes returned to Togom—muran, leader of murani, *ol-oiboni*. This beast had no time for lesser beings such as Ruta, Orion, and me.

Togom raised his shield and held his spear ready, but already he battled the lion with a returned stare. "He is furious with us for disturbing him," he said calmly, almost mockingly to shame the lion. I knew the cat did not speak to him. Togom read the animal's stance and breathing and eyes. Face to face with an adversary, he did not need my assistance. He understood the lion's thoughts because they were both warriors, both proud.

A lion saunters with a lazy economy, but it charges with speed and conviction.

If the red-maned beast attacked, it would seriously rip apart or kill at least one of us. But it could not win. Together the two murani would bring it down. And in my youth I imagined that I could play a role in this, too. Certainly Orion, who saw all encounters with cats as great sport, would do his share. Still, the cold of one of us dead or nearly dead—

I repeated the message because it was all I could do. I was certain it heard, but I feared it did not listen.

The lion claimed a step of ground toward us. I held my spear ready. Now I saw wet patches on the lion's paws. Blood. It had a fresh kill nearby, one worth protecting if only to protect its honor.

I squinted against the sunlight to peer into the shadow behind the lion. A slain boar, the hide shredded by a dozen slashes, stained the crimson soil darker.

We will kill our own boar, I told the lion with false bravado. We are hunters, not hyenas who take from others.

I saw no change in the lion, but Togom quietly said, "Let us leave this place."

We moved away from the water hole. Ruta and I did not ask Togom how he knew that the lion had decided not to attack. The beast watched our cautious retreat, then went back to its kill.

Orion was especially valiant in our quest for a boar, putting all of his frustration over the lost cat into it. Ruta brought down a large one with his spear and Orion ripped out its throat, suffering a wound in the flank from one of the curved tusks. The dog's tough hide held scars from worse encounters, still I worried about the bleeding and possible infection.

We returned to the village with fresh meat, avoiding the water hole on the way. Dusk gently moved through the valley. One of Togom's wives met us and hurried us into his hut. The wise men of Togom's age group who served as a village council sat cramped and cross-legged around a freshly lit fire.

Room was made for Togom, Ruta, and me. The warm, moist smell of unbathed humans who had labored through a hot afternoon was stronger than the smoky odor.

I held a strange position in village life and politics. I am White, child, female. According to Nandi laws, these should have excluded me from the circle. Yet there seemed to be a rule that said uniqueness exempts one from the rules. I was accepted because of my differences. So, as I had done before, I sat with the old men.

"While you were hunting, ol-oiboni, a magistrate came from Nairobi," one of them explained intensely. "With him were two askari who did not look like askari. They were natives, true, but they behaved like mongrel dogs, not like police officers. Our young men must go into the militia, the magistrate said. He strutted through the village as if he had a right to be here and bothered the young men, even the uncircumcised boys, for their names and the names of their brothers. He will be back, he said, with many more askari to take the young men away, even if they do not want to go."

"I will go to this war," said the youngest of the old men—for sometimes in the village old had nothing to do with years—still full of uncooled fire. "I will show the bravery of the Nandi murani." He shook a fist as if it held a spear.

"Aiyee," Togom said, "this is not a war of spears. This is a war of weapons falling from the sky. It is no place for a true warrior. There is honor in a spear, in staring into the eyes of your enemy, in judging his character and acknowledging his bravery. There is no honor in bombs."

"What do you know of bombs?" he challenged.

Togom's face took on the glow of the new fire. His eyes transformed from the hard black of the warrior into the soft brown of the seer. He looked through the flames, through the earth to the world's core. "A great bomb has already fallen. Hate explodes from its depths. We feel the heat. Soon we will know the burning."

The old men made it law: No Nandi will fight in this war.

It was almost too dark to find my way home when the meeting ended. Togom walked with Orion and me up the valley slope to the top of the hill closest to our farm. I would have to hurry, and there was still my father's wrath to face.

Togom put a hand on my shoulder as he often did when he had something important to say, as if the weight of his hand paralleled the weight of his words. A rim of soft brown still circled his black eyes. He moved dreamily, and I wondered if the vision he had had in the hut moved with him at the edge of his sight.

He blinked several times before focusing on my face. "Elisbet, you must call to the animals. Tell them, do not go south, do not go west, do not go north. You must say, come to this valley. Kill only for food, not for territory. And do not kill until your hunger is very strong. The Nandi promise to do the same. Tell them, come close and be ready."

"Ready for what?" I asked, afraid he would tell me. My small, tired body trembled at the unknown image that circled his vision.

"Tell them."

Togom turned and walked unsteadily back toward the village. Limping from his wound, Orion did his best to guide me home in the closing darkness.

There is a human thing called a war that brings many dangers, I sent into the night to the animals. You must come to Njoro, to Rongai, because the *ol-oiboni* says it should be so. He sees many things that you and I cannot see. He knows many things that you and I cannot know. He thinks many things that you and I cannot imagine. Come close so you will be ready.

That night in my little bed the village drums woke me. I was too exhausted from the day's hunt to decipher their meaning. Just as quickly the rhythm lulled me to sleep.

The next morning I sneaked out of my room and headed for the village to find out about the drums. I made Orion stay at the farm to give his injury time to heal. He scowled at me in his wide-jowled way but obeyed. The pain meant nothing to him, he told me.

I am not going hunting, I assured him. My knife and spear are only for protection.

He remembered charging the boar, Ruta's spear sticking from its back like a narrow third tusk. He remembered clamping his teeth into the boar's throat and shaking his head until the flesh tore and warm blood sprayed across his face. He did not remember the tusk ripping a gash across his flank. I am a better weapon than a knife and spear, he told me through his memories.

With longing, he remembered the lion at the water hole, an opportunity missed because I held him back. You owe me a cat, he said.

Another time, dog, I told him with affection.

I took my usual path to the valley, reached the crest of the hill, and looked down, eager to see the comforting domed roofs of the huts around the circular clearing, the wisps of smoke.

I saw nothing but the valley floor thick with foliage. My breathing came so fast I could scarcely draw oxygen from it and I thought I might faint. Tears blurred my sight. How could they leave? I thought, when I really meant *How could they leave without me?* How could they move a village and close plants over the spot where it had been so there was no sign it ever existed?

They couldn't, my mind shouted in disbelief. They couldn't leave without me—

They couldn't. Of course. So simple.

I hefted my spear and boldly walked into the valley as I always did, straight through the thick growth that should have swallowed me but didn't. As I descended, the surroundings blurred. I stepped, uncertain if my foot would find the earth. It settled on cleared ground despite what my eyes told me. I stepped again. Again.

The grass and leaves reformed into familiar patterns and opened a trail at my feet. Before me a village snapped into existence with the sudden sound of barking dogs and the smell of cooked boar from yesterday's hunt.

Ruta greeted me with a wide grin and twinkling eyes, as if this was a joke meant just for me. "You have found us then, Elisbet. Our little trick did not fool you." Yet obviously he knew that it had, at least for a little while, and he took some delight in that.

I tried to laugh through the rags of my fear. "So this is what you did with the drums making such noise all night so no one could sleep. You have made yourselves invisible."

He proudly pointed out the boundary of the illusion. "It is a small thing for an *ol-oiboni* as skilled as Togom," he said.

I followed the ripple that circled the village like a great ring of heat. It was not a small thing. Not a small thing at all.

Four days later open trucks rumbled along the road from Nairobi. I was at the edge of the farm exercising Valiant Lady, a golden beauty with more loyalty than legs. Her tendons were weak, and she required easy handling. She had been custom-designed, the fertilized egg smuggled into Africa, then implanted into our roan mare. Father forbade me to go hunting until my lessons were satisfactory, and he punished my disobedience by placing this wonderful creature in my care.

He said nothing of Finch's offer to take me to England; but nightly during supper while we discussed each horse's progress and possible training strategies, I knew he thought about it. Thought about sending me away. Away from him. Away from Africa.

The noisy trucks were empty, which meant they expected to pick up something to haul back to the capital. I followed the caravan, staying to high ground. The vehicles bumped onto the cart trail that twisted into the Rongai, then stopped where Togom's illusion dissolved the road and barricaded the narrow entrance with phantom bamboo trees and thick vines.

A Black man dressed in blazing white shirt and shorts got out of the cab of the lead truck. He might as well have had MAGISTRATE stamped on him in bright letters. He fumbled with a map. The driver got out, pulling something with him. A large rifle, the kind for firing many bullets very quickly. Not a rifle to be used against animals but one to be used against humans. The man slung a strap over his shoulder to support the heavy gun. He strolled to the magistrate's side with an ease that said he was used to the extra weight and hardly knew how to walk without the additional appendage at his side.

I suspected that the men packed into the cabs of the other trucks also had such rifles and such walks.

The two studied the map for a long time. They poked fingers at it, gestured in confusion to the road and the hills. The gunman strolled a little way into the bush, then returned, rubbing his temple as if it ached.

They came to take the young Nandi men, to train them as soldiers to fight in the war that had begun in the far south and moved closer each day.

I watched them and knew that the war was already here.

The magistrate shouted orders. He and the gunman got back into the truck. Vegetation pushed as close to the trail as it dared, sometimes snaking over it with great bravado. There was no clearing large enough for a truck to turn around in. The entire caravan crawled backward along the cart trail like a segmented worm. The string of dust-caked vehicles had to back up all the way to the Nairobi road. And it would return to the capital empty.

I laughed, urging Valiant toward the farm. She shook her pure white mane and flicked her snowy tail, ready to do anything I asked.

Two days later in the grey morning, Kitau stumbled onto the veranda, panting like an ill-used steeplechaser. He and some of the other workers took turns going to Nairobi, so we had daily bulletins about the war.

Father and I were just about to go to the stables. Father, broad and beefy, supported the wiry Kitau and placed him in a chair. The young man's appearance with the sunrise spoke more eloquently of horror than his words ever could.

"*Bwana* and *Memsahib* Kreshenko," Kitau puffed out between gulps of air, "murdered." He glanced at me, then quickly returned his water-smoothed-stone eyes to my father. "And their little ones with them."

I was only eight, but I knew both masks death wore, the natural and the tragic. I felt more rage at the injustice of murder than sorrow at the loss of the Kreshenkos.

Violence had moved north blindly. The animals' increasing distress had become an expanding roar in my head. Cats. Monkeys. Elephants. Rhinos. Zebras. They rushed like a stampeding zoo before the advancing guns and bombs. Some had been caught in bursts of fighting that flared like spontaneous combustion.

Humans have gone mad, they told one another. Humans have gone mad.

Father put his hands on his hips. He shifted his mouth as if he chewed a piece of tough meat. "Who did it? Their servants?"

"No, no," Kitau protested. "You must not think such a thing. For the servants are dead beside their master and mistress. Much was burned. It is the police who believe that this and other things were done to hide the identity of the murderers. In front of their clerk the police say it was activists from South Africa who wish once again to form the Mau, so they can drive out all Whites. They say they know this from other police. *Bwana* Kreshenko and his family are not the only Whites to be killed. The police say this in front of their clerk and their clerk says this to me."

"You ran all night?" It seemed unfair that the thoroughbreds in our stable rested comfortably while Kitau traveled from Nairobi to Njoro on foot. Father wanted the workers to take the horses, but they were experienced runners, not riders. They had more stamina, were more surefooted in the uncertain terrain, and needed less rest than the products of royal bloodlines who still slumbered in their boxes.

Kitau nodded.

"That's dangerous."

The Kikuyu silently told my father that it was necessary, and my father silently thanked him.

"The Haugens?"

"Gone quickly more than a day ago. The servants bring many boxes to the city to send after them."

"Any news of Finch and his wife?" my father asked carefully, as if he suddenly had difficulty speaking.

"Safe. In Nairobi. That is the other message I bring. They leave tomorrow for England and say they would be most pleased to take little Elizabeth with them."

My world stopped. I closed my eyes, afraid to blink, afraid any movement would start time again and I would be on my way to Nairobi with a suitcase, wearing the dress from last Christmas that was too small for me but was the only one I owned.

My father looked at his boots. His shoulders lifted with the intake of a great breath, then sagged with decision. "No." A long word that hung in the growing heat. "Lizzy belongs here. I'll send word to the Finches. Kitau, get some food and rest. I'll have guards posted around the farm."

My world had movement and meaning again. I ran into my father's arms; they were suddenly low enough to catch me up and swing me to his chest. We held one another and let the horses wait.

That night snarls and screams woke me to the dark. At the foot of my bed raged a battle of teeth and claw. Orion and the red-maned lion.

I heard the lion carry the dog from the room in triumph. Heard Orion struggle and snap in the grasp of its jaws, taking away any dignity the lion had hoped for.

Sayid appeared with an electric torch, Father with the rifle that lately was never far from his hand. Together we followed a broken line of shiny blood while I followed Orion's anger.

I knew the dog twisted in the lion's jaws and was released. I knew he rolled, then gained his feet and faced the glittering eyes. To Orion's credit, he didn't challenge the lion's right to sneak into the house if it could, nor to enter my bedroom if it went undetected, nor to grab a sleeping dog and make off if nothing stopped it.

With bleeding pride Orion stared at the lion. He had not smelled the lion, not wakened to the soft padding of its paws as it entered the house or the little bedroom. He was humiliated by being snatched up in his sleep, then dropped in the dust. He barked fiercely, demanding a rematch.

We reached the animals, a composite of light and shadow in the beams of our torches. I ordered Orion into silence and was surprised when he obeyed.

The red-maned lion stood calmly. Scarlet dripped from the wounds Orion had managed to inflict.

My father pressed his torch into my hand. Slowly he raised the rifle to his shoulder.

Why did you do this? I asked. No reply.

"It's not going to charge," I whispered. Togom's training told me, not anything I heard.

Before I finished the words, the cat melted into the night.

The next morning I forced a sulking Orion to stay at the farm while I disobeyed my father and went to the village. The dog's neck was torn open in many places from the lion's teeth, but most of the wounds were not deep.

I had seen what a lion could do, what the red-maned lion had done when its purpose was death. It had not dragged off Orion in order to slay him. It had not taken him because he was a fierce dog who killed cats for the challenge. That was Orion's right as a hunter. The lion had another purpose. I was a child and wished I had Togom's wisdom so I could understand.

"The lion would not tell me why," I complained to Togom after telling of the attack. The *ol-oiboni* and I shared a breakfast of fruit and flatbread baked from flour Father had sent some time ago as a present.

Togom sat cross-legged and rocked slightly in thought. "Perhaps the lion is saying, 'I do not like what is happening. I do not like what these human animals do.'"

"Then why didn't it just tell me instead of hurting poor Orion?"

"Perhaps the message was not for you." He rocked and pursed his lips. His hard eyes grew soft at the edges. "I will think of this, Elisbet. I will think like a lion, then the meaning will come to my mind."

I didn't go hunting that day. I followed my own trail back to the farm to nurse Orion.

A battered blue truck sat in the bare space before the house. It was an ancient, wasteful vehicle without a fluid unit to store energy when it idled or went downhill. The official seal on the door was unreadable through the thick coating of reddish dust, but it must belong to a Nairobi magistrate. No other official would come to Njoro.

A Black man, tall and thin as most natives with the sculptured features of the Kamba tribe, stalked from the house, a piece of paper clenched in his hand. He folded himself into the truck, and it took him away with much chugging and complaining.

My father stepped onto the veranda. His boots made solid clomps on the cedar boards. He put his hands on his hips and watched the dust plume grow thin.

I came up beside him. Although he didn't look at me, he knew I was there. I slipped my hand through the triangle his arm made and placed my small fingers on the back of his hand.

"They can't order me off my own land," he said softly. The more angry my father was, the lower he spoke. The quiet of his words made me shiver. "I chose this country and earned my keep. I've no intention of leaving."

Sayid was at his other elbow. "What will we do, *Bwana* Burton?"

My father, Sayid, and myself. Whenever I think of the old Africa, my memories are always of the three of us and the house as it used to be. I can close my eyes now and feel as I did at that moment, with my hand touching my father's and the fragrance of curry that lived in Sayid's flowing clothes. This is the last of those memories.

"Pack my bag," my father told Sayid. "I'm going to Nairobi to straighten this out."

I didn't expect Father to come home that night. When he didn't return the second night, I could do little except sit on the veranda and watch the road until long after sunset.

Sayid tucked me into bed. Orion, much recovered and burning with the desire to kill a cat, took his usual place on the rug. The guards Father posted patroled the immediate grounds of the house and stable. The red-maned lion roared just before I fell asleep.

Sayid woke me by the light of a small torch. I reached for the lamp switch, but he grabbed my hand. "There are headlights on the road," he said. "They do not belong to your father's truck." I couldn't tell if his hand shook or if it was mine wrapped in his that quivered.

My knife and spear lay in the rippled folds of my covers, placed there by Sayid.

"Go to the village," he said. "Not to worry. They are only government officials come to make you leave. I will tell them *Bwana* Burton went to Nairobi two days ago and has not returned, for that is the truth. And if they know that a daughter lives here also, I will say that little Elizabeth went to England with *Bwana* and *Memsahib* Finch. If they search your room, I will say you took little because these things are not what young girls wear in England, and these things are not what young girls play with in England."

His quick cadence told me it was a well-rehearsed speech, something he and Father prepared before Father left.

In a sharp flash I heard the approaching intruders. Their thoughts were simple and loud. They had not come from the government at Nairobi to enforce an evacuation of the White farmers. They came only to destroy.

I gripped Sayid's sleeve with my free hand. "Order the horses released, and the chickens. Send everyone away. You must go too."

Sayid looked deeply at me. In the torch's glow his face was round shadows and curved dark skin. He seemed relieved that I knew what he tried to hide from me, that we parted without a lie between us, even one meant in kindness. I hugged him completely and forever.

I dressed quickly and took up my weapons. Then I opened the door to my chameleon cage and left, warning Orion to be quiet. I went as far from the farm as the dog could lead me in the dark. I heard the confusion of the horses as they were turned out into the night. "There is danger here," I told them and the other animals. "I flee from it myself. Move quietly, now, away from this place."

I stopped to wait for the full moon to rise, so I could find my way to the village by its light. From my hiding place I watched the farm.

Four Jeeps roared like blind elephants into the yard and abruptly halted. The headlights turned movement into a grotesque dance. The shadows of men jumped from the Jeeps. They fired guns into the air, large guns, the kind carried by the man with the magistrate. I buried my face in Orion's scarred coat and held him fiercely to me.

A growing brightness came too soon and harsh to be the gentle moon. The stable glowed, then exploded in heat. Flames waved like wheat stalks. The house burned with the reflection; the reflection became flames. Timbers crackled, cracked, and fell. I heard rifle shots but could not guess what they meant.

From an adjoining hill the roar of the red-maned lion shook the earth. I watched until the slanted roof over the veranda crumbled to meet the cedar boards. "*Kwaheri*," I told Njoro. Farewell.

The moonlight was soft. I blinked until the images of flames dissolved, then crossed over the hill into the valley. I passed through the blurry illusion that surrounded the village, barely aware of the distortion.

In the center of the circle formed by the huts stood Togom. Moonlight spread from him and filled the village. Beside him stood a man and a woman I did not know. The man seemed older than Togom, wrinkled like a dried creek bed, hair grayed to a cloud of white. The woman was smooth-skinned. At the focal point of what must be a ceremony, she was composed beyond her youth.

The villagers sat in the worn dirt, forming a thick moat of dark water around the island of soft light occupied by Togom and his companions. But there were far more people than this village usually held, and there were many faces I did not recognize.

Togom held out his hands to me across the moonlight and gestured. Waves passed through the water and a path opened. I walked through to the center, Orion at my heels. The dog held his head high, aware that there was honor in this. I took my clues from him and from the young woman beside Togom. I would not let the sorrow of Njoro that cried out for comfort mar my behavior.

"*Koaribu*," come you are welcome, Togom said. "We have been waiting for you, Elisbet. Maina," he gestured to the old man, "has brought his people. And Jebbta," he moved a hand toward the young woman, "has brought her father's people that we might unite the power of the Nandi against this war that has no honor."

I entered the island of light and stood with the straight posture of a muran.

Togom spoke to the valley. "In the timeless past the Nandi walked Africa, moving as the hunt and grazing land for our cattle took us. But the government of Whites and the government of Blacks who had given up their tribes told us we must live on only one part of the land, that only certain places in Africa were ours and only the game on that land was ours, and that we must live by these laws."

The *ol-oiboni* gave a little smile. "To their eyes, we obeyed; but we are Nandi and will not be ruled by others." The smile dissolved into pain. "Now they invade the little plots of land they said were ours, with their bombs and their guns and their war. We must protect ourselves from their foolishness until Africa is again ours to walk as we will.

"Elisbet, call the animals into the Rongai. Say they must come over the top of the hills and onto the slopes that bend to the valley." Togom's eyes had grown soft, as if he dreamed. "Tell them that this is Africa now. Life and death hold equal honor here."

I listened. Panic echoed from the farm and from other places I could not identify.

Come, I called into the moonlight. It is not a child who calls to you but the noble Nandi. We invite you to this valley, to the land we have shared with you since before time. And we will hunt. And you will hunt. Here, all will be as it was.

Silence. Silence. Silence. My heart stopped beating.

The red-maned lion roared, accepting the bargain.

Leopards snarled, elephants trumpeted, zebras neighed. I covered my ears against the answers but I could not keep them out of my head. Nor did I want to.

Up in the hills the jungle rustled slightly with eland and impala as if no more than a breeze stirred. Under my feet the ground quivered. In my mind I heard animals crest the hill, heard the horses from the farm, heard the ones already in the valley adjust to make room.

They took positions watching the village. And waited.

I nodded to Togom, but he already knew.

Togom spoke to the humans and the animals. "What we do has not been done since before the birth of my father and his father and his father and more fathers before that. One *ol-oiboni* cannot accomplish it alone. This is why *ol-oiboni* Maina and his people have come. This is why Jebbta and her people have come. Jebbta's father is dead, killed by a bomb dropped from the sky. It is a bad way for a Nandi muran to die, and it is bad for an *ol-oiboni* to die so young without another ready. Jebbta takes his place tonight. Although female and not formally trained, she knows her father's work and she will do well."

The three formed a circle, arms outstretched, palms upward, fingertips touching. The moon floated above as if its light fell only on the Rongai.

The drums began a slow rhythm. The assembly seemed gently pulled to its feet. Ruta came forward and took my hand. He led me into the gathering of villagers and those newly arrived. With the others I swayed and danced to the drums.

Orion sat and watched the three immobile *ol-oiboni*, as if it were his duty to witness for his kind. But I knew what the dog did not. The red-maned lion stood in a moon-cast shadow on the nearest slope, *ol-oiboni* for the animals.

The moon slid behind a hill. The drums stopped in the darkness. Togom broke the circle and smiled tiredly, sadly at Maina and Jebbta. "The valley is sealed. The outside cannot see us, can no longer touch us. So it will be until the time arrives for us to take back what was once ours."

Togom carried me into his hut because I was too tired to make my own way. I dreamed of hot flames and cool moonlight and quivering earth.

In the morning the village was busy accommodating its new residents and setting up a system for handling the limited resources.

"Elisbet," Togom said, "you must help the animals establish territories that will keep them from arguing with one another. Their numbers must be balanced so every kind will survive."

I called Valiant Lady and the other horses to the village. They were beautiful and strong and very fast, but they didn't know how to protect themselves against cats and boars. I loved them so and was glad to stroke Valiant's silky coat.

Their lives were now changed as much as mine. They would be useful. There were many places they could not go because of the dense growth, but also many in the valley and up the steep hills where they could carry a rider. I didn't think beyond that. Not then. I didn't consider that their descendants would be useful to my descendants. But I think in such terms now.

I ride a three-year-old stallion, one of Valiant's line, to the crest of the hill nearest where the farm used to be. The same hill I scrambled over in the moonlight with Orion nine years ago when I was eight. The dog slowed with age, and on one of his cat hunts he lost the battle. I have no interest in another dog.

I was such a small child, my father would be surprised to see how tall I have become. I am as long-legged and straight and graceful as any Nandi.

I stretch out a hand and touch the smooth, hard nothingness of the elongated bubble that separates the winding valley from the charred wasteland beyond. I stroke the ancient protection that Togom called up, as I call animals, from the depth of the Nandi heritage. It is not magic. It is something more solidly rooted in the earth and the rightness of things and the place where life began and will not let go.

I close my eyes and concentrate as hard as I can. I listen beyond the barrier, hoping.

Nothing.

I turn and gaze across the valley thick with green, noisy with life. A patch of moisture at the top of the otherwise invisible dome forms a cloud that will become rain.

Very close I feel the presence of the red-maned lion, although he doesn't speak to me. Old enough to be immortal, he often stalks the perimeter, as I do, to assure himself that it still stands and that all is well.

Some day the descendants of the three *ol-oiboni* will open the bubble; and the Nandi will reclaim the wounded world, heal it with their own health. By then I will be dead for centuries.

No matter. Although at times I dream of more, of what used to be and what could have been, this is enough. This valley is my world.

This is my Africa.

Honorable Mentions 1993

Aiken, Joan, "Birthday Gifts," *A Fit of Shivers* (Delacorte–YA).

——, "Cousin Alice," Ibid.

——, "Earrings," Ibid.

——, "The Cockatrice Boys," *Christmas Forever* (Tor).

——, "The Rose Garden Dream," *A Fit of Shivers*.

——, "The Shrieking Door," Ibid.

——, "Watkyn, Comma," Ibid.

——, "An L-Shaped Grave," Ibid.

Alexie, Sherman, "This Is What It Means to Say Phoenix, Arizona," *Esquire*, June.

Allyn, Doug, "Dancing on the Center Line," *Ellery Queen's Mystery Magazine*, November.

——, "Pageant," *EQMM*, mid-December.

Ames, John Edward & Bergman, Susan, "Dance Colina," *New Orleans Stories*, winter.

Anthony, Patricia, "Dear Froggy," *Aboriginal SF*, spring.

——, "Guardian of Fireflies," *Asimov's Science Fiction*, April.

——, "Gingerbread Man," *Aboriginal SF*, fall.

Ardai, Charles, "Nobody Wins," *Alfred Hitchcock Mystery Magazine*, mid-December.

——, "The Rememberer," *AHMM*, February.

Baker, Nancy, "Consent," *Deathport* (Pocket).

Baker, Scott, "Virus Dreams," (novella) *OMNI Best Science Fiction Three* (OMNI Books).

Bannon, Fergus, "Burning Bright," *Interzone* 71, May.

Barker, Clive, "Pidgin and Theresa," *The Time Out Book of London Short Stories* (Penguin–U.K.).

Barker, Nicola, "A Necessary Truth," *Love Your Enemies* (Faber & Faber).

——, "Country Matters," Ibid.

——, "Food With Feeling," Ibid.

——, "John's Box," Ibid.

——, "Layla's Nose Job," Ibid.

——, "Symbiosis: Class Cestoda," Ibid.

——, "The Butcher's Apprentice," Ibid.

Barrett, Jr., Neal, "Cush," *Asimov's*, November.

——, "Hard Time," *Ten Tales* (James Cahill).

Beatty, Terry & Lee, Wendi, "Special Effects," *Frankenstein: The Monster Wakes* (DAW).

Beckert, Christine, "Maintenance," *Tales of the Unanticipated* 12.

Bedford, Jean, "Finding Fire," *Crosstown Traffic* (Five Islands).

Belcampo, "Funeral Rites," *The Dedalus Book of Dutch Fantasy* (Dedalus).

Bendel, Stephanie, "Kay," *AHMM*, June.

Benesch, Amy, "The Honeymooner," *Space & Time* 82.

Bennett, Ronan, "The Crime & Suicide of Harry D'Souza," *The Time Out Book of London Short Stories*.

Bergin, John, "There Is No Dog," *Underground* 1 (Dark Horse).

Billson, Anne, "Sunshine," *The Time Out Book of London Short Stories*.

Bishop, Michael, "Beginnings," *Christmas Forever*.

Block, Lawrence, "Someday I'll Plant More Walnut Trees," *Some Days You Get the Bear* (Morrow).

——, "Keller's Therapy," *Playboy*, May.

——, "The Merciful Angel of Death," *The New Mystery* (Dutton).

——, "The Tulsa Experience," *Some Days You Get the Bear*.

——, "How Would You Like It?" *Monsters in Our Midst* (Tor).

Bogart, Brett, "Wolfword," *Grue* 15.

Bohem, Lelise, "Fohn," *Strange Days*, spring.

Boston, Bruce, "Curse of the Merman's Wife," (poem) *Midnight Zoo* vol. 1, issue 2.

Boucher, Brad, "In the House of Sin," *Bizarre Sex and Other Crimes of Passion II*.

Bowers, William, "The Diabolist," *Deathrealm* 20.

Bowes, Richard, "A Beggar at the Bridge," *The Magazine of Fantasy & Science Fiction*, December.

——, "The Judges of the Secret Court," *Tomorrow* 3, June.

Boyczuk, Robert, "Falling," *On Spec*, spring.

Bradfield, Scott, "Calendars of the Heart," *Bad Sex* (Serpent's Tail).

——, "The Last Man That Time," *Greetings From Earth* (Picador).

Brantingham, Juleen, "Little Men," *The Silver Web* 10.

Braunbeck, Gary A., "Haceldama," *Cemetery Dance*, fall.

——, "Rag Dolls," *After Hours* 20.

——, "The Guilting of Rowen Byrne," *Not One of Us* 10.

Brooke, Keith, "Witness," *Interzone* 70, April.

Brown, Molly, "Choosing the Incubus," *Bad Sex*.

Brown, Sherrie, "Stolen Sisters," *Heliocentric Net*, autumn.

Brown, Simon, "Brother Stripes," *Aurealis* 11.

Brust, Steven K. Z., "Attention Shoppers," (poem) *Xanadu* (Tor).

Bryant, Taerie, "The Bearing Tree," *Prisoners of the Night* 7.

Buchanan, Ginjer, "Catachresis," *More Whatdunits* (DAW).

Burford, Steve, "Dead Weight," *Strange Days*, summer.

Burleson, Donald R., "The Pedicab," *100 Ghastly Little Ghost Stories* (B&N).

——, "Mikey Joe," *Lemon Drops and Other Horror* (Hobgoblin Press).

Burn, Gordon, "Memorials," *The Time Out Book of London Short Stories*.

Burns, Cliff, "RSVP," *The Silver Web* 10.

Burris, Michael, "Dietperfect," *The Scream Factory* 11.

Cacek, P. D., "In the Meantime," *Bizarre Bazaar* 1993.

Cadger, Rick, "The Brothers," *Sugar Sleep* (Barrington).

Cadnum, Michael, "Letter to a Ghost," (poem) *Poetry Northwest/The Cities We Never See*.

Cady, Jack, "The Night We Buried Road Dog," (novella) *F&SF*, January.

Campbell, Ramsey, "For You to Judge," *Monsters in Our Midst*.

Campbell, Terry, "Lycanthrophobia," *Redcat Magazine*, fall.

Camperus, Louis, "Bluebeard's Daughter," *The Dedalus Book of Dutch Fantasy*.

Campo, Susan, "A Stay-in Story," *Malingering*.

Cantrell, Lisa W., "Taking Care of Georgie," *Monsters in Our Midst*.

Carrabis, Joseph David, "Them Dore Girls," *Haunts* 26.

Carter, John, "Your Card's Marked," *Dementia 13* 12.

Casper, Susan, "Betrayal," *Dinosaur Fantastic* (DAW).

Castle, Mort, "Hansel, Gretel, the Witch: Notes to the Artist," *Dead of Night* 7.

Castro, Adam-Troy, "Playing With Dogs," *Pulphouse* 15.

——, "Scars: A Romance in Seven Act," *Bizarre Bazaar* 1993.

——, "The House of Nails," *Air Fish*.

——, "The Miracle Drug" (novella) *Lost in Booth Nine* (Silver Salamander).

——, "The Pussy Expert," *Lost in Booth Nine*.

——, "The Telltale Head," *Deathport*.

Cave, Hugh B., "Another Kind of Enchanted Cottage," *Journeys to the Twilight Zone* (DAW).

Charnock, Graham, "On the Shores of a Fractal Sea," *New Worlds* 3 (Gollancz).
Chesbro, George C., "Tomb," *AHMM*, October.
Chetwynd-Hayes, R., "The Switch-Back," *Weird Tales*, spring.
Chizmar, Richard T., "Heroes," *Predators* (Roc).
Christie, Mike, "Replay," *Tomorrow*, January.
Citro, Joseph A., "Kirby," *After the Darkness* (Maclay).
Clark, Simon, "Salt Snake," *Peeping Tom* 12.
Clegg, Douglas, "The Hurting Season," *Deathrealm* 19.
——, "Damned, If You Do," *Cemetery Dance*, spring.
Cohen, Lisa R., "Rainbone," *F&SF*, April.
Collier, Catrin, "Poppies at the Well," *Cold Cuts: Tales of Terror* (Alun Books–U.K.).
Collins, Nancy A., "The Killer," *Thrillers*.
——, "Freakbabies," (revised) Ibid.
——, "Seven Devils," Ibid.
Congreve, Bill, "Red Ambrosia," *Terror Australis* (Coronet Books).
——, "I Am My Father's Daughter," *Crosstown Traffic*.
Constantine, Storm, "The Green Calling," *Interzone* 73, July.
Corwin, Steve, "Hot Oil," *AHMM*, February.
Costello, Matthew, "Abuse," *Hottest Blood* (Pocket).
——, "Thank You for Your Patience," *Deathport*.
——, "The Man Who Knew Things," *Thunder's Shadow*.
Couperus, Louis, "Bluebeard's Daughter," *The Dedalus Book of Dutch Fantasy*.
Coville, Bruce, "With His Head Tucked Underneath His Arm," *A Wizard's Dozen* (Harcourt Brace & Co.).
Cox, Deidre, "Vein," *Not One of Us* 10.
Crawford, Dan, "Only Nights," *AHMM*, June.
——, "The Scholar and the Rose," *AHMM*, September.
Cross, Ronald Anthony, "Puss In Boots," *SF Age*, January.
Crowther, Peter, "Dumb Animals," *Danger in DC: Cat Crimes in the Nation's Capital*, (Donald I. Fine).
——, "Head Acres," *Interzone* 72, June.
——, "Fallen Angel," *Frankenstein: The Monster Wakes*.
——, "Rustle," *Cemetery Dance*, fall.
Csernica, Lillian, "Saving Grace," *Space & Time* 82.
——, "Masquerade," *Midnight Zoo*, vol. 3, issue 6.
D'Ammassa, Don, "Passing Death," *Deathrealm* 18.
——, "Cleansing Agent," *Deathport*.
——, "Friday Nights at Home," *Sinistre: An Anthology of Rituals*.
Daniel, Tony, "God's Foot," *Asimov's*, May.
Daniels, Les, "The Man in the Mirror," *Deathport*.
Dann, Jack, "Vapors," *Amazing*, June.
——, "The Extra," *Journeys to the Twilight Zone*.
Day, Holly, "Liberation," (poem) *The Tome*, winter 1992/93.
De Lint, Charles, "Coyote Stories," chapbook (Triskell Press).
——, "Fairy Dust," *A Wizard's Dozen*.
——, "Pal o' Mine," *Christmas Forever*.
——, "Small Deaths," *Dreams Underfoot* (Tor).
Dean, Pamela, "Owlswater," *Xanadu*.
DeAndrea, William L., "A Friend of Mine," *Frankenstein: The Monster Wakes*.
Dedman, Stephen, "Heir of the Wolf," *Terror Australis*.
Dee, Ron, "The Turning," chapbook (Simulacrum Press/Ozark Triangle Press).
DeLynn, Jane, "Faithfully Yours," *Infidelity* (Chatto & Windus).

Del-Pizzo, Jane, "A Hazy Shade of Winter," *Cold Cuts: Tales of Terror*.

Devereaux, Robert, "Clap if You Believe," *Crank!* 1.

DeWinter, Corinne, "Absinthe Room," (poem) *Dreams & Nightmares* 41.

Donaldson, Stephen R., "The Woman Who Loved Pigs," (novella) *Full Spectrum 4* (Bantam).

Doolittle, Sean, "All Their Own," *Palace Corbie*, Autumnal.

——, "David," *Deathrealm* 19.

Dorr, James, "The Swineherd's Tale," *Pulphouse: The Hardback Magazine 12: The Last Issue*.

Doyle, Debra & MacDonald, James D., "The Queen's Mirror," *A Wizard's Dozen*.

Dozois, Gardner, "Passage," *Xanadu*.

Drennan, Tom, "The Children China Made," *Writers of the Future IX* (Bridge).

Dumars, Denise, "The Mirror," *Deathrealm* 20.

——, "Event," *Pangaea* (Wordcraft of Oregon).

——, "The Original," *Ibid*.

Dunn, Dawn, "The Lonely Heart," *Bizarre Sex and Other Crimes of Passion II*.

Dyer, Lawrence, "The Four-Thousand-Year-Old Boy," *Interzone* 73, July.

Effinger, George Alec, "Beast," *Confederacy of the Dead* (Roc).

Eikamp, Rhonda, "The Thief of the Earth," *The Barrelhouse*, spring.

Ellison, Harlan, "Mefisto in Onyx," (novella) *OMNI*, October/Mark V. Ziesing.

Engstrom, Elizabeth, "The Fog Knew Her Name," *In the Fog* (Tor).

Eskridge, Kelley, "Somewhere Down the Diamondback Road," *Pulphouse* 15.

Evans, Christopher, "The Hiss of Life," *Cold Cuts: Tales of Terror*.

Ferret, Tim, "Through the Wire," *Avant-Pop* (Black Ice Books).

Fisher, David Lincoln, "I Hear Always the Dogs on the Hospital Roof," (poem) *Xenophilia* 6.

Flinn, Maggie, "A Present for Hanna," *Christmas Forever*.

Ford, John M., "Dateline: Colonus," *Temporary Walls* (Dream Haven Books).

Foster, Alan Dean, "Laying Veneer," *Journeys to the Twilight Zone*.

Fowler, Christopher, "Chang-Siu and the Blade of Grass," *Sharper Knives* (Warner–U.K.).

——, "Mother of the City," *The Time Out Book of London Short Stories*.

——, "Outside the Wood," *Sharper Knives*.

——, "Persia," *Ibid*.

——, "Revelation's Child," *Ibid*.

——, "Norman Wisdom and the Angel of Death," *Ibid*.

——, "Last Call For Passenger Paul," *Ibid*.

Fox, Daniel, "How She Dances," *Dark Voices 5* (Pan).

Frahm, Leanne, "Catalyst," *Terror Australis*.

Frank, Diane, "The Seduction of Bathsheeba," (poem) *The Urbanite* 3.

Frazier, Robert, "Night Vision," *F&SF*, July.

Friesner, Esther M., "Puss," *Snow White, Blood Red* (AvoNova/Morrow).

——, "Three Queens," *Asimov's*, January.

Frost, Gregory, "Some Things Are Better Left," *Asimov's*, February.

——, "The Root of the Matter," *Snow White, Blood Red*.

Furie, Ruthe, "Before My Eyes," *EQMM*, August.

Fyfield, Frances, "Cold and Deep," *Malice Domestic 2* (Pocket).

Gaiman, Neil, "Mouse," *Touch Wood: Narrow Houses 2* (Little, Brown–U.K.).

——, "Pansy Smith and Violet Jones," *The Flash Girls: The Return of Pansy Smith and Violet Jones*.

Gilbert, Michael, "Judith," *EQMM*, April.

Goldman, Ken, "A Head Full of Pigs," *UnReality* 3.

Goldstein, Lisa, "Breadcrumbs and Stones," *Snow White, Blood Red.*
——, "Infinite Riches," *Asimov's*, April.
Good, Julie R., "The Hawk's Road," *Bizarre Bazaar* 1993.
Good, Tina, "Lorelei," *Sword & Sorceress* X (DAW).
Gordon, Jimm, "Skinned," *Weird Tales*, spring.
Gorman, Ed, "Mother Darkness," *After the Darkness.*
——, "The Face," *F&SF*, April/*Confederacy of the Dead.*
——, "Anna and the Snake People," *Malice Domestic 2.*
Gorog, Judith, "Damascus," *Please Do Not Touch* (Scholastic).
——, "My Elder Sister," Ibid.
——, "The Coffeepot," Ibid.
——, "The Phantom Touring Car," Ibid.
——, "The Rented House," Ibid.
——, "Variations on a Theme: The Grateful Dead," *Don't Give Up the Ghost.*
Grabinski, Stefan, "A Tale of the Gravedigger," translated by Miroslaw Lipinski, *The Dark Domain* (Dedalus/Hippocrene).
——, "The Grey Room," translated by Miroslaw Lipinski, *100 Ghastly Little Ghost Stories.*
Graham, David, "Third Wheel," *After Hours* 18.
Grant, Charles L., "Name That Tune," *Monsters in Our Midst.*
——, "Sons," *Confederacy of the Dead.*
——, "Josie, In the Fog," *In the Fog.*
Greenland, Colin, "The Girl Who Changed Everything," *The Weerde Book 2: The Book of the Ancients* (Roc–U.K.).
Greenwood, Kerry, "I Am Dying, Egypt, Dying," *Crosstown Traffic.*
Griffith, Nicola, "Touching Fire," *Interzone* 70, April.
Grimaldi, Laura, "Fathers and Daughters," *The New Mystery.*
Hahn, Mary Downing, "The Last House on Crescent Road," *Don't Give Up the Ghost.*
Haldeman, Joe, "Feedback," *Playboy*, March.
Hall, Roberta, "I Like the Dark," *AHMM*, September.
Hand, Elizabeth, "Justice," *F&SF*, July.
Hansen, Joyce, "Sweet Hour of Prayer," *Don't Give Up the Ghost.*
Hansen, Sharon A., "Chameleon," *Terror Australis.*
Hargreaves, Stella, "Steps," *Touch Wood: Narrow Houses 2.*
Harper, Rory, "Do Me Good," *Pulphouse 12: The Last Issue.*
Harrington, Joyce, "Cop Groupie," *EQMM*, July.
Harrison, M. John & Ings, Simon, "The Dead," *The Sun Rises Red/Interzone* 67, January.
Hart, Frank, "Possession," *Palace Corbie*, Vernal.
Hartnett, John, "Blacken," *Tales of the Unanticipated* 12.
Hautala, Rick, "Cousin's Curse," *Dark Seductions* (Zebra).
Heeresma, Marcus, "Dumping Ground," *The Dedalus Book of Dutch Fantasy.*
Hendershot, Cynthia, "Basement," *City of Mazes: And Other Tales of Obsession.*
——, "Blackness," Ibid.
——, "Feet," Ibid.
——, "Killer," Ibid.
——, "Left Hand," Ibid.
——, "Photograph," Ibid.
——, "Red Light Story," Ibid.
——, "Silence," Ibid.
——, "Twenty Shores," *Asylum Annual.*
——, "Seven Days," *City of Mazes.*
Henry, Sharon, "Voodoo Silences," *Mondo Barbie* (St. Martin's).

Hester, Phillip, "Pooch," *Underground* 1.

Higgins, Graham, "Sounds and Sweet Airs," *The Weerde Book* 2.

Hightower, Lynn S., "Point Man," *F&SF*, September.

Higson, Charles, "The Red Line," *The Time Out Book of London Short Stories*.

Hill, Reginald, "Stonestar," *1st Culprit* (Chatto & Windus/St. Martin's).

Hillerman, Tony, "First Lead Gasser," *EQMM*, April.

Hirsch, Connie, "Prayers and the Material Girl," *Sinistre*.

Hodge, Brian, "Sacrament," *Deathport*.

——, "A Loaf of Bread, A Jug of Wine," *Frankenstein: The Monster Wakes*.

Hoffman, Nina Kiriki, "God Rest Ye Merry, Gentle Ghosts," *F&SF*, January.

——, "The Pulse of the Machine," *Weird Tales*, spring.

——, "Valentines," Ibid.

——, "Ceciley in the Supermarket," Ibid.

Hogan, Linda, "The Grandmother Songs," (poem) *The Book of Medicines* (Coffee House Press).

Holder, Nancy, "In Search of Anton La Vey," *The Ultimate Witch* (Dell).

——, "O Love, Thy Kiss," (novella) *In the Fog*.

——, "Strawman," *Confederacy of the Dead*.

——, "The Beard," *After the Darkness*.

——, "Tire Fire," *Deathport*.

——, "I Hear the Mermaids Singing," *Hottest Blood*.

Holdstock, Robert, "Having His Leg Pulled," *Dark Voices 5*.

Holliday, Liz, "Cover Story," *The Weerde Book* 2.

Holt, Esther J., "Cemetery Flowers," *AHMM*, April.

Hood, Robert, "Mamandis Dreaming," *Eidolon* 12.

Houarner, Gerard Daniel, "Hidden Agendas," *Sinistre*.

Howard, Clark, "The Long Drop," *EQMM*, February.

Howe, Harrison, "The Screech," *Haunts* 25.

Huff, Brian, "Hanging Out on the Back Stairs," *Grue* 15.

Husted, Marilyn, "Rachel, Come Out," *Magic Realism*, spring.

Ibeji, Michael, "Deep in the Native Land," *The Weerde Book* 2.

Indiana, Gary, "Land's End," *Infidelity*.

Ings, Simon, "The Black Lotus," *OMNI Best Science Fiction Three*.

Jeapes, Ben, "Getting Rid of Teddy," *Interzone* 76, October.

Jillet, Neil, "Aurora Australis," *AHMM*, April.

Johnson, Kij, "Last Dance at Dante's," *Tales of the Unanticipated* 11.

——, "Fox Magic," *Asimov's*, December.

Johnston, Jim, "How it Analysed Her Tears," *Grotesque* 3.

Joyce, Graham, "The Apprentice," *Interzone* 77, November.

——, "The Ventriloguial Art," *Dark Voices 5*.

——, "Gap-sickness," *New Worlds 3*.

Julian, Astrid, "Irene's Song," *Interzone* 69, March.

Kapalka, Jason, "Godeaters," *On Spec*, spring.

Kaveney, Roz, "Ignorance of Perfect Reason," (novella) *The Weerde Book* 2.

Ketchum, Jack, "The Holding Cell," *Bizarre Bazaar* 1993.

Kilpatrick, Nancy, "The Power of One," *Sinistre*.

——, "I Am No Longer," *Deathport*.

——, "Mother Mountain Waits," *Crossroads*, October.

Kilworth, Garry, "Oracle Bones," *Touch Wood: Narrow Houses 2*.

——, "Punctuated Evolution," *Crank!* 1.

Kinder, R. M., "Jeremy," *EQMM*, March.

King, Tappan, " 'Come Hither'," *A Wizard's Dozen*.

Kirk, Kevin, "Pest," *Prisoners of the Night* 7.

Klein, T. E. D., "One Size Eats All," *Outside/Kids*, summer.

Koja, Kathe, "I Shall Do Thee Mischief in the Wood," *Snow White, Blood Red*.

Koja, Kathe & Malzberg, Barry, "The High Ground," *Temporary Walls*.

——, "The Timbrel Sound of Darkness," *Christmas Ghosts* (DAW).

Kopaska-Merkel, David, "On Becoming a Fish," (poem) *Air Fish*.

Kress, Nancy, "Dancing on Air," (novella) *Asimov's*, July.

——, "Grant Us this Day," *Asimov's*, September.

Laidlaw, Marc, "The Diane Arbus Suicide Portfolio," *OMNI*, May.

——, "Terror's Biggest Fan," *F&SF*, May.

Lane, Joel, "And Some Are Missing," *The Sun Rises Red*.

——, "Wave Scars," *Sugar Sleep*.

——, "Among the Leaves," *Peeping Tom* 12.

——, "Other Than the Fair," *Maelstrom* 6.

——, "The Public Domain," *Dementia 13* 12.

Langford, David, "The Lions in the Desert," *The Weerde Book* 2.

Laughlin, William, "Commuter," *Sinistre*.

Laymon, Richard, "A Good, Secret Place," *A Good, Secret Place* (Deadline).

——, "Joyce," Ibid.

——, "Slit," *Predators*.

——, "Stickman," *A Good, Secret Place*.

——, "The Mask," Ibid.

Lee, Tanith, "The Witch of the Moon," *The Ultimate Witch* (Dell).

——, "Winter Flowers," *Asimov's*, June.

——, "Antonius Bequeathed," *Weird Tales*, spring.

——, "Unnalash," *Xanadu*.

Leech, Ben, "The Dying Game," *Peeping Tom* 10.

Lepovsky, Lisa, "Our Lady of Guadalupe," (poem) *The Barrelhouse*, winter 1992.

Leslie, Mark, "Phantom Mitch," *Wicked Mystic* 22, October.

Levesque, Richard L. & Boucher, Brad J., "Coldest Touch," *Palace Corbie*, Vernal.

Lewis, D. F., "The Horn of Europe," *The Silver Web* 10.

——, "The Night of the Lovelies," *Deathrealm* 20.

——, "The Walking Mat," *Sugar Sleep*.

Lewis, Paul, "The Ten O'Clock Horses," *Touch Wood: Narrow Houses* 2.

Lilly, Rebecca, "Guesthouse," (poem) *Magic Realism*, summer.

Limón, Martin, "Lady of the Snow," *AHMM*, June.

——, "Nightmare Range," *Pulphouse* 15.

Little, Bentley, "Deadipus Rex," *Palace Corbie*, Autumnal.

——, "Llama," *Hottest Blood*.

Lock, Bob, "The Leaves in the Stone," *Cold Cuts: Tales of Terror*.

Lockley, Steve, "Funny Weather," *Touch Wood: Narrow Houses* 2.

——, "Touching," *Cold Cuts: Tales of Terror*.

Lodi, Edward, "In Their Agonie, They Byte," *Terminal Fright* 1.

Logan, David, "Thirteen and Deadly," *Black Tears* 2.

Lynch, H. Andrew & Sallee, Wayne Allen, "The Givers of Pain and Rapture," *Bizarre Bazaar* 1993.

Mallory, Michael, "Black Saturday," *Midnight Zoo* vol. 2, issue 6.

Malzberg, Barry N., "Andante Lugubre," *SF Age*, May.

——, "The Lady Louisiana Toy," *More Whatdunits*.

Malzberg, Barry N. & Dann, Jack, "Art Appreciation," *OMNI*, September.

Mapes, Diane, "Globsters," *Asimov's*, May.
Marshall, Don, "Never Bite the Hand That...," *AHMM*, mid-December.
Martel, J. R., "Saints," *On Spec*, winter 1992–93.
Massie, Elizabeth, "Damaged Goods," *Hottest Blood*.
Masterton, Graham, "Sex Object," Ibid.
——, "Making Belinda," *After the Darkness*.
Matozza, Francis J., "The Revision," *Weirdbook Encore* 13.
Márquez, Gabriel García, "The Ghosts of August," *Strange Pilgrims* (Knopf).
——, "Tramontana," Ibid.
——, "I Only Came to Use the Phone," Ibid.
——, "I Sell My Dreams," Ibid.
McBride, D. R., "Derrotados," *Sinistre*.
McConnell, Frank, "They Won't Get Hodge," *EQMM*, January.
McDowell, Ian, "Some Old Lover's Ghost," *Asimov's*, December.
McElroy, Wendy, "Good Fences and Good Neighbors," *Heliocentric Net*, autumn.
McGarry, Terry, "Cadenza," *Christmas Ghosts*.
McKenna, Bridget, "Probability Factor," *Pulphouse 12: The Last Issue*.
——, "The Good Pup," *F&SF*, March.
McKillip, Patricia A., "Ash, Wood, Fire," *The Women's Press Book of New Myth & Magic* (The Women's Press).
Mecklem, Todd, "Sweet Strawberry," *Skinned Alive* 5.
Meehan, Bart, "Canals," *Aurealis* 11.
Meikle, William, "The Colour From the Deep," *Threads* 1.
——, "Crossroads," *Grotesque* 2.
——, "The Last Days of Summer," *Fiction Furnace* 3.
Melville, James, "Programmed for Murder," *1st Culprit*.
Metzger, Thom, "Down Bound Train," *Air Fish*.
Moody, Susan, "Oh, Who Hath Done This Deed?" *1st Culprit*.
Mooney, Brian, "The Lady of Dubhan Alla," *Dark Voices* 5.
Moore, Robert C., "D.E.R.O.S.," *Unreality* 5.
Moore, Shelley, "Stigmata," *Not One of Us* 11.
Moral, Anthony Gael, "Fetish of the Coil," *Haunts* 25.
Morlan, A. R., "Locher (Holes)," *Erotic Horror* (Heyne Verlag).
——, "The Toddler Pit," *The Ultimate Zombie* (Dell).
Morressy, John, "A Boy and His Wolf: Three Versions of a Fable," *Xanadu*.
Morrison, Grant, "The Room Where Love Lives," *Hottest Blood*.
Mullins, Kevin, "The Night Before," *Peeping Tom* 11.
Murakami, Haruki, "The Little Green Monster," *The Elephant Vanishes* (Knopf).
Murphy, Jim, "Footprints in the Snow," *Night Terrors* (Scholastic).
Murphy, Pat, "An American Childhood," (novella) *Asimov's*, April.
Myman, Francesca, "Night, Who Creeps Through Keyholes," *Sword & Sorceress X*.
Nasir, Jamil, "The Dakna," *Asimov's*, September.
——, "Sleepers Awake," *Asimov's*, July.
Navarro, Yvonne, "For Love of Mother," *Touch Wood: Narrow Houses* 2.
Newman, Kim, "Ratting," *Constable New Crimes 2* (Constable–U.K.).
——, "The Big Fish," *Interzone* 76, October.
——, "Where the Bodies Are Buried," *Dark Voices* 5.
Nicholson, Geoff, "The Guitar and Other Animals," *Best English Short Stories* V (Norton).
Nicoll, Gregory, "Terrible Swift Saw," *Confederacy of the Dead*.
——, "The Ripper's Tune," *Kinesis* 7, March.
——, "55-Gallon Drums Along the Mohawk," *Deathport*.

Nielsen Hayden, Patrick, "Return," *Xanadu*.

Nunez, Sigrid, "The Loneliest Feeling in the World," *Glimmer Train* 5, summer.

Oates, Joyce Carol, "Thanksgiving," *OMNI*, November.

Ordover, John, "All Flesh Is Clay," *Weird Tales*, summer.

Orem, William, "Thing," *After Hours* 19.

Orlock, Carol, "Out of Sight, Into Mind," *The Hedge and the Ribbon*.

Osier, Jeffrey, "Algae Angels," *Driftglider and Other Stories* (Montilla).

——, "Father's Workshop," *Not One of Us* 11.

Owens, Barbara, "All in the Eyes," *EQMM*, October.

O'Driscoll, M. M., "Seamless Dreams," *Cold Cuts: Tales of Terror*.

O'Driscoll, Mike & Kenworthy, Chris, "The City Calls Her Home," *The Sun Rises Red*.

O'Keefe, Claudia, "On the Lake of Last Wishes," *Shudder Again* (Roc).

Palwick, Susan, "Force of Habit," *Ghosttide*.

Partridge, Norman, "The Man with the Barbed-Wire Fists," *Frankenstein: The Monster Wakes*.

——, "Velvet Fangs," *Haunts* 25.

Pastor, Ben, "Kiria Andreou," *The Barrelhouse*, spring.

Pastor, Verbena, "The Meeting," *Thin Ice* XIV.

Patterson, Kathleen J., "The Mould-Kissers," *Weirdbook* 28.

Patterson, Margot, "Hero's Journey," *Asylum Annual*.

Perry, Clark, "Buzzkiller," *Deathport*.

Phalen, David, "A Child's Handful of the Moon," *Writers of the Future IX*.

Plumbridge, Martin, "The Exhibit," *Chills* 7.

Potok, Chaim, "The Seven of the Address," *Winter's Tales*, New Series 8 (Constable-St. Martin's).

Ptacek, Kathryn, "The Home," *In the Fog*.

——, "Bruja," *Deathport*.

——, "Neighbors," *Ghosttide*.

Ragan, Jacie, "Cult of Rain," (poem) *Skeletal Remains* 2.

Rainey, Stephen Mark, "Deliverer in Darkness," *Bizarre Bazaar* 1993.

——, "Portals," *Best of the Midwest's SF/Fantasy/Horror*.

——, "The Scorching," *Thin Ice* XIII.

——, "Canvas Haunts," *Sinistre*.

——, "Charon's Wings," *Fugue Devil and other Weird Horrors* (Montilla).

——, "Fugue Devil," Ibid.

Ramseyer, William L., "Nuts," *Jellyfish Mask* (Buy Yourself Press).

——, "Train Station," Ibid.

——, "Hole in the Darkness," Ibid.

Ransom, Daniel & Miller, Rex, "Valentine," *Predators*.

Redd, David, "The Old Man of Munington," *Asimov's*, mid-December.

Reed, Robert, "The Toad of Heaven," *Asimov's*, June.

——, "On the Brink of that Bright New World," *Asimov's*, January.

Relling, Jr., William, "The Ghost and the Soldier," *Touch Wood: Narrow Houses* 2.

Rendell, Ruth, "The Man Who Was the God of Love," *EQMM*, March.

Resnick, Mike, "The Pale Thin God," *Xanadu*.

Reynolds, Barry, "Auto Da Fe," *Tomorrow* 3, April.

Reynolds, III, James D., "That Is What I Think," *Sinistre*.

Richerson, Carrie, "By the Waters of Lethe We Sat Down and Wept," *Amazing*, July.

Riley, David, "Out of Corruption," (novella) *The Mammoth Book of Zombies* (Carroll & Graf).

Rimmer, John M., "Winning the War," *Paper Clips*, July.

Robinson, Frank M., "The Greatest Dying," *Dinosaur Fantastic.*
Rogers, Lenora K., "Dolly," *Palace Corbie*, Vernal.
Rollinson, Andrew, "What in Me Is Dark, Illumine," *Sugar Sleep.*
Rosen, Barbara, "Wolfie," *Thin Ice* XIII.
Ross, Patricia, "Sacred Wheel," *Deathport.*
Royle, Nicholas, "The Mainstream," *The Sun Rises Red.*
——, "The Nightingale," *Sugar Sleep.*
——, "Red Christmas," *Peeping Tom* 12.
——, "Shades of Monk," *Sunk Island Review*, issue 7.
——, "The Editor," *Dark Voices 5.*
——, "The Goalkeeper's Fear of the Crowd," *Chills* 7.
——, "Ronald Dale and the Art of the Short Story," *Black Tears* 2.
Ruckley, Brian, "Farm Animal," *Interzone* 74, August.
Rusch, Kristine Kathryn, "Strays," *Danger in DC.*
Russell, John, "A Case of Mutiny," *Weirdbook Encores* 14.
Rysdyk, Leonard, "A Sound, Like Angels Singing," *Snow White, Blood Red.*
Sallee, Wayne Allen, "Don's Last Minute," *Palace Corbie*, Autumnal.
——, "The American Dream Meets the Couch Potato," *Grue* 15.
——, "Family Fiction," *Bizarre Sex and Other Crimes of Passion II.*
——, "How the Zombies Down Division Street," *The Scream Factory*, zombie issue.
Sallee, Wayne Allen & Partridge, Norman, "Those Kids Again," *Cemetery Dance*, winter.
Salmonson, Jessica Amanda, "The Toad Witch," *Asimov's*, June.
Sampson, Robert, "Dead Gods," *Asimov's*, July.
Saplak, Charles M., "Cemetery Seven," *Terminal Fright* 1.
——, "Lady's Portrait, Executed in Archaic Colors," *Writers of the Future IX.*
Savage, Ron, "Piano Pony," *F&SF*, December.
Sawyer, Robert J., "Just Like Old Times," *On Spec*, summer/*Dinosaur Fantastic.*
Schaeffer, Dirk L., "Three Moral Tales," *On Spec*, spring.
Schimel, Lawrence, "In Sheep's Clothing," *Sword & Sorceress X.*
Schow, David J., "Penetration," *Ghosttide.*
——, "Where the Heart Was," *Hottest Blood.*
Schwarz, Mauricio-José, "Soul Sculpture," *EQMM*, October.
Schweitzer, Darrell, "Angry Man," *Pulphouse 12: The Last Issue.*
——, "The Liar's Mouth," *Cemetery Dance*, spring.
Segriff, Larry, "A Debt Repaid," *Frankenstein: The Monster Wakes.*
Self, Will, "The Indian Mutiny," *Winter's Tales New Series Eight.*
Sellers, Peter, "Whistling Past the Graveyard," *EQMM*, May.
Semionov, Julian, "The Summer of '37," *The New Mystery.*
Shepard, Jim, "Nosferatu," *TriQuarterly* 87.
Shepherd, Annis, "I Am the Camera, Mr. Joans!" *Tomorrow* 6, December.
Shiner, Lewis, "Voodoo Child," *Asimov's*, July.
Shirley, John, "The Rubber Smile," *Predators.*
Siebelink, Jan, "Affection," *The Dedalus Book of Dutch Fantasy.*
Silva, David B., "A Time to Every Purpose," *Amazing*, August.
——, "Because I Could," *Pulphouse 12: The Last Issue.*
——, "Fade In/Fade Out," *Eulogy Magazine* vol. 2, issue 1.
Simmons, Dan, "The Great Lover," (novella) *LoveDeath* (Warner).
Simon, Kelly, "Objects in Mirror," *EQMM*, June.
Sims, Denise, "Many Voices," *Xenos*, June.
Smith, D. Lynn, "The White Geese," *Mythic Circle* 16.
Smith, Michael Marshall, "More Bitter Than Death," *Dark Voices.*

——, "The Owner," *Touch Wood: Narrow Houses 2*.

Smith, Sarah, "When the Red Storm Comes," *Shudder Again*.

Smith, Sherwood, "Faith," *A Wizard's Dozen*.

Smyth, Peter C., "Strange Tan," *Strange Days*, spring.

Soares, John, "Black Widow Spider," (poem) *Midnight Zoo* vol. 3, issue 1.

Solomon, Barbara, "The Bertlemunster Effect," *UnReality 2*.

Somtow, S. P., "Though I Walk Through the Valley," *The Ultimate Zombie*.

——, "Fish Are Jumpin', and the Cotton Is High," *Monsters in Our Midst*.

Soto, Gary, "The Sounds of the House," *Don't Give Up the Ghost*.

Soukup, Martha, "The Story So Far," *Full Spectrum 4*.

Spencer, William, "Striptease," *Interzone* 72, June.

Spencer, William Browning, "Your Faithful Servant," *Air Fish*.

——, "Daughter Doom," *The Return of Count Electric* (Permanent Press).

——, "Irrational Fears," *Ghosttide*.

——, "Best Man," *The Return of Count Electric*.

Springer, Nancy, "Hubris," (poem) *Stardust Songs*.

Stableford, Brian, "Riding the Tiger," *Interzone* 68, February.

Stafford, William, "It Comes Lightly Out of the Sea," (poem) *Xanadu*.

Stone, Jr., Del, "Companions," *Crossroads*, spring.

Swanwick, Michael, "Picasso Deconstructed: Eleven Still-Lifes," *Asimov's*, May.

——, "Cold Iron," *Asimov's*, November.

Taylor, Lucy, "Blood Secrets," *Bizarre Bazaar* 1993.

——, "Extinction," *Pulphouse* 15.

——, "The Family Underwater," *Close to the Bone* (Silver Salamander).

——, "A Safe Place to Die," *Palace Corbie*, Autumnal.

——, "Animal Souls," *Close to the Bone*.

——, "Close to the Bone," Ibid.

——, "Going North," (chapbook) (Rubén Sosa Villegas Publication).

——, "Spellbound," *Crossroads*, April.

Tem, Melanie, "Jenny," *Asimov's*, mid-December.

Tem, Steve Rasnic, "Ice House Pond," (novella) *In the Fog*.

——, "Little Poucet," *Snow White, Blood Red*.

——, "Passing Through," *Deathport*.

——, "The Child Killer," *Monsters in Our Midst*.

——, "Brooms Welcome the Dust," *The Ultimate Witch*.

——, "Stones," *Constable New Crimes 2*.

Tem, Steve Rasnic & Tem, Melanie, "Safe at Home," *Hottest Blood*.

Tessier, Thomas, "In the Desert of Deserts," *After the Darkness*.

——, "Mr. God," *Cemetery Dance*, fall.

Thomas, Jeffrey, "Stench," *UnReality 3*.

——, "Mandril," *Doppelganger* 15.

Thomas, Scott, "Photos of a Leg," *Deathrealm* 19.

——, "The Wreck at Wickhampton," *Dead of Night* 8.

Thomese, P. F., "Leviathan," *The Dedalus Book of Dutch Fantasy*.

Thorpe, Adam, "Nothing But Bonfires," *The Time Out Book of London Short Stories*.

Tiedemann, Mark W., "The Playground Door," *F&SF*, May.

Tilton, Lois, "The Princess Who Danced Until Daybreak," *SF Age*, May.

Tolnay, Tom, "The Fine Line," *EQMM*, December.

Traub, Tom, "This House," *The Silver Web* 9.

Travis, Tia, "Date With the Hangman's Daughter," *Chills* 7.

Treat, Lawrence, "Tableau," *EQMM*, April.

Trotter, William R., "The Siren of Swanquarter," *Deathrealm* 20.
Tuttle, Lisa, "Lucy Maria," *Xanadu*.
——, "Turning Thirty," *The Time Out Book of London Short Stories*.
Updike, John, "The Black Room," *The New Yorker*, September 6.
Utley, Steven, "The Country Doctor," *Asimov's*, October.
Vachss, Andrew, "A Flash of White," chapbook (Crossroads).
——, "Bum's Rush," *Underground* 1.
——, "Cain," *The New Mystery*.
——, "Drive By," chapbook (Crossroads).
——, "Head Case," *Hard Looks* 8 (Dark Horse).
van der Heijden, A. F. Th., "Pompeii Funebri," *The Dedalus Book of Dutch Fantasy*.
van Deyssel, Lodewijk, "Curious Things on the Plain," Ibid.
Van Pelt, James, "Plant Life," *Aberrations* 9.
van Schendel, Arthur, "The White Woman," Ibid.
van Dullemen, Inez, "After the Hurricane," Ibid.
VanderMeer, Jeff, "Excerpts From the Diary of an Artiste," *The Tome*, winter 92/93.
——, "The Emperor's Reply," *Magic Realism*, summer.
Vardeman, Robert E., "A Gentle Breeze Blowing," *Monsters in Our Midst*.
Vukcevich, Ray, "There Is Danger," *Pulphouse* 16.
Wade, Susan, "Like a Red, Red Rose," *Snow White, Blood Red*.
Wagner, Karl Edward, "Little Lessons in Gardening," *Touch Wood: Narrow Houses* 2.
Walker, Sage, "Roadkill," *Asimov's*, April.
Walsh, Jackie, "Playland," *EQMM*, July.
Watkins, Graham, "Wooden Cows," *Sinistre*.
Watson, Ian, "King Weasel," *Weird Tales*, summer.
Watts, Nigel, "The Gift," *The Time Out Book of London Short Stories*.
Watt-Evans, Lawrence, "Larger Than Life," *The Ultimate Zombie*.
Webb, Don, "Seven-Four Planting," *New Farmer's Almanac* chapbook (Chris Drumm).
Webb, Wendy, "A Dress for Tea," *Confederacy of the Dead*.
——, "Soul Catcher," *Deathport*.
Wein, Elizabeth E., "Fire," *Writers of the Future IX*.
Wellen, Edward, "Mind Slash Matter," (novella) *Predators*.
Wells, Heather G., "Marlene's Secret," *After Hours* 20.
Wells, J. A., "A Day in the Lake, With Aces," *UnReality* 5.
Wentworth, K. D., "Along the Old Rose Trail," *Tomorrow* 6, December.
Westall, Robert, "Charlie Ferber," *In Camera and Other Stories* (Scholastic).
——, "Henry Marlborough," Ibid.
——, "Blind Bill," Ibid.
Wheeler, Wendy, "Little Red," *Snow White, Blood Red*.
Wiater, Stanley & Wilson, Gahan, "Mysteries of the World: A Dark Fable," *Touch Wood: Narrow Houses* 2.
Wilber, Rick, "With Twoclicks Watching," *Asimov's*, January.
Wilhelm, Kate, "Reforming Ellie," *EQMM*, December.
Williams, Conrad, "The Bone Garden," *Northern Stories* 4.
Williams, Sean, "White Christmas," *Eidolon* 11.
Williams, Sidney G. & Sallee, Wayne Allen, "Skull Rainbow," *Constable New Crimes* 2.
Williams, Walter Jon, "Wall, Stone, Craft," *F&SF*, Oct./Nov.
Williamson, Chet, "The Moment the Face Falls," *Monsters in Our Midst*.
——, "Dusty Death," *Thrillers*.
——, "Perfect Days," *After the Darkness*.
——, "Scalps," *Deathport*.

——, "Watching the Burning," *Thrillers.*

Williamson, J. N., "Frankenstein Seen in the Ice of Extinction," *Frankenstein: The Monster Wakes.*

——, "Reality Function," *Monsters in Our Midst.*

——, "Just One More Thing People Can Do," *Dark Seductions.*

Williamson, Neil, "Angelique's Lament," *Territories,* summer.

Willis, Connie, "Death on the Nile," *Asimov's,* March.

Wiloch, Thomas & winter-damon, t., "The Key," (poem) *Dreams & Nightmares* 41.

Wilson, Gahan, "The Frog Prince," *Snow White, Blood Red.*

——, "The Marble Boy," *After the Darkness.*

——, "It Twineth Round Thee in Thy Joy," *OMNI Best Science Fiction Three.*

winter-damon, t., "Beyond Judgement, Beyond Thought or Supposition," *Nova* 5.

——, "Touch Wood," (poem) *Touch Wood: Narrow Houses* 2.

Wisman, Ken, "Canon in D," *Pulphouse 12: The Last Issue.*

——, "Captain Seofin," *Weird Family Tales* (Earth Prime Productions).

——, "The Carousel Horse," *Midnight Zoo* vol. 2, issue 6.

Wolfe, Gene, "And When They Appear," *Christmas Forever.*

Wolkers, Jan, "Feathered Friends," *The Dedalus Book of Dutch Fantasy.*

Wolverton, Dave, "My Favorite Christmas," *Christmas Forever.*

Wrede, Patricia C., "The Sixty-two Curses of Caliph Arenschadd," *A Wizard's Dozen.*

Yarbro, Chelsea Quinn, "Whiteface," *In the Fog.*

——, "Echoes," *Deathport.*

Yolen, Jane, "Harlyn's Fairy," *A Wizard's Dozen.*

——, "The Ring at Yarrow," *Xanadu.*

——, "The Snatchers," *F&SF,* Oct./Nov.

Zelazny, Roger, "The Salesman's Tale," *Ten Tales.*

The People Behind the Book

Horror Editor ELLEN DATLOW has been fiction editor of *OMNI* magazine for over a decade. She has edited a number of outstanding anthologies, including *Blood Is Not Enough, A Whisper of Blood, Alien Sex, The OMNI Books of Science Fiction,* and (with Terri Windling) *Snow White, Rose Red* and *Black Thorn, White Rose.* Her latest anthology, *Little Deaths,* has just been published by Millennium (U.K.) and will be published later in the U.S. by Dell/Abyss. She lives in New York City.

Fantasy Editor TERRI WINDLING, five-time winner of the World Fantasy Award, developed the innovative Ace Fantasy line in the 1980's. She currently is a consulting editor for Tor Books' fantasy line, and runs The Endicott Studio, a transatlantic company specializing in book publishing projects and art for exhibition. She created and packages the ongoing *Adult Fairy Tales* series of novels (Tor), the *Borderland* "punk urban fantasy" series for teenagers (Tor & HBJ), and co-created the *Brian Froud's Faerielands* series (Bantam). She has published over a dozen fine anthologies, has novels forthcoming this year from both Tor and Bantam Books, and a TV film in development at Columbia Pictures for NBC. She lives in Devon, England and Tucson, Arizona.

Packager JAMES FRENKEL & ASSOCIATES is JAMES FRENKEL and NEVENAH SMITH. James Frenkel edited Dell's SF line in the 1970s, was the publisher of Bluejay Books and was Consulting Editor for the Collier-Nucleus SF/Fantasy reprint series. A Consulting Editor for Tor Books since 1986, he edits and packages a variety of science fiction, fantasy, horror and mystery books from his base in Madison, Wisconsin. Nevenah Smith is an award-winning glass artist, published poet, and book designer. Her editorial career began in 1992.

Comics Critics EMMA BULL and WILL SHETTERLY are the publishers of SteelDragon Press, and the co-editors of the *Liavek* series. Bull is the author of the acclaimed urban fantasy *War for the Oaks*; her fourth novel, *Finder,* was published this year by Tor Books. Shetterly is a popular fantasy author, and has recently written two *Borderlands* novels, *Elsewhere* and *Nevernever.* They live, along with several cats, in Minneapolis, Minnesota.

Media Critic EDWARD BRYANT is a major author of horror and science fiction, having won Hugo awards for his work. He reviews books for a number of major newspapers and magazines, and is also a radio personality. He lives with his rubber sharks in the Port of Denver, Colorado.

Artist THOMAS CANTY is one of the most distinguished artists working in fantasy. He has won World Fantasy awards for his distinctive book jacket and cover illustrations, and is a noted book designer working in diverse fields of book publishing; he has active projects with a number of publishers, including some with various small presses. He also created children's picturebook series for St. Martin's Press and Ariel Books. He lives in Massachusetts.